The Tides of Avarice

A SAGARIA LEGEND

© John Dahlgren 2011

First published in 2011
by Editions Didier Millet Pte Ltd
121 Telok Ayer Street #03-01
Singapore 068590

www.edmbooks.com.sg

Illustrations by Laura Diehl

ISBN: 978-981-4260-53-4

Printed and bound in Singapore.

The Tides of Avarice

A SAGARIA LEGEND

John Dahlgren

www.tidesofavarice.com

edm EDITIONS DIDIER MILLET

To William and my godson Axel

CONTENTS

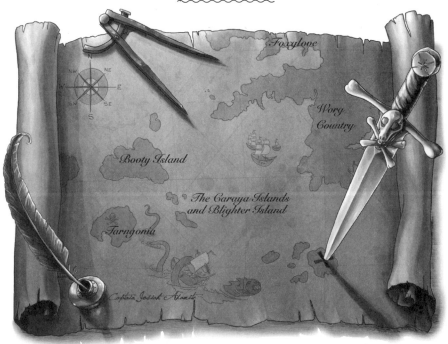

TWO PARTS OF A MAP, THREE ENDINGS

The first thing you notice is the smell. It hangs like an almost visible miasma in the sluggish air of Darkwater – or, at least it does here, in the meanest, rottenest and generally most lethal part of Darkwater, the only town on Booty Island and, in its turn, the meanest, rottenest and generally most lethal part of the Toxic Archipelago. Darkwater is probably the only town in the whole wide world of Sagaria where murder isn't a criminal offense: in the local terminology it's called "justifiable homicide." The men here will slit your throat for free and send a selection of your bodily organs to your loved ones for no more than the cost of the postage stamp.

The women are worse.

And as for the kids? Don't even ask.

The smell that hangs around the tavern called The Moldy Claw, here in the dankest, dismalest, most corpse-littered part of Darkwater, is made up of varying parts of stale ale, rigor mortis, unwashed undergarments, rotting teeth, dead fish, deader rats, salty dogs, stagnant pools of various excretions and, not least, the outhouse behind The Moldy Claw, a structure of awesome venerability and the source of a stench so profound that, on those rare occasions when sunlight manages to penetrate the oily clouds above Darkwater, the outhouse's very brickwork seems to shimmer yellowly. No one in a generation has dared – not even the cutthroats who frequent The Moldy Claw, who've been known to face down sea monsters and sorcerers – make use of the outhouse of their own volition. Or, if they have, none have returned to tell the tale. Skullface Jack Moriarty, the cruelest pirate who ever sailed the seas of Sagaria, used to have his worst enemies thrown in through its age-smirched doorway, and some say that, on those cold nights when the stars seem to be made of crystal, you can still hear their screams.

Tonight, for once, no one had smashed the streetlight that stands on the corner outside The Moldy Claw. Through a layer of dead insects trapped inside the glass, it cast its pale illumination over a plain of broken barrels and bottles, making them appear to smolder with a sickly yellow glow – a glow the same color as the smell, in fact.

Inside the tavern, if you'd been foolhardy enough to go there, the noise would have hit you like a punch on the nose – that is, if the *real* punch on the nose hadn't reached you first. Most of the clientele who could still stand up were gathered in the far corner eagerly cheering on either Thick-Skulled Skully or Stoneface Muldoon, who were displaying all the tactical intricacies and strategic subtleties possible within a head-banging contest. Spectators and contestants alike were pouring rum down their throats at frequent intervals and by the flagonful, almost as if it were water – although it wasn't, in fact, quite as brown as the local water. Some had profitable looting to celebrate. Others were merely drowning their sorrows. All had reached the state where you couldn't tell the difference.

At this time of night, only the lowliest and foulest of pirates roamed the streets. Anyone else who had any common sense, or at least a trace of survival instinct, stayed well clear of the harbor area or, preferably, the entire town.

Best of all was to avoid Booty Island altogether.

No one in their right mind would stand in the dock area, just on the edge of the nervous pool of light The Moldy Claw's streetlamp cast, trying to tempt the rare passerby with bits of assorted booty, and yet two individuals were doing exactly this. They weren't exactly planning to *sell* the stuff, you understand. They just wanted to lure people with trinkets of silver and precious stones, then slit their throats, take all their money, grab their rings and other jewelry, and throw their corpses into the deep, dark, obliterating waters of the harbor. Then they'd offer the newly acquired gewgaws to the next person, and so on. It was what folk with a firmer grip on the technicalities of commerce might have called stock rotation.

The taller of the two was dressed in a long coat whose high collar reached all the way up to the greasy bandanna wrapped around what was presumably a forehead. All you could see of him was the occasional flash of an earring, or the glint of jingling jewelry as he proffered it to any late-arriving cutthroat who was headed for the tavern. The other peddler, slightly shorter, preferred a shorter coat so that people could better see the cutlass hanging at his side and the dirk stuck in his belt. It wasn't hard to guess that he, though the smaller, was the Muscle to his companion's Brains.

"Brains" being a strictly relative term, of course.

"Heard that *he's* back on the island, eh?" said Brains.

"Aye, that he is," replied Muscle, batting his arms together as if to keep out the chill of the night, even though the air of Darkwater was always too laden with fermenting chemicals to cool down much.

"Arrived this morning, so I heard. Came here on the lookout for something. Something or some*one*. The good news is he ain't killed no one yet. They say he has to kill a man every day or he can't digest his supper right."

"The day ain't over yet," observed Brains. "Not quite."

"So?"

"So that means it's *bad* news he ain't killed nobody yet."

"Why's that?"

"He's only got about twenty minutes left. Gotta be killing someone real soon."

Muscle grunted in gloomy acquiescence.

There was silence between them for a few moments, a silence broken only by the din of revelry and screaming from within The Moldy Claw.

Then Muscle added, "You heard what happened to Longnose Dobby?"

"No. Not old Dobby? What'd he do?"

"He was in one o' they taverns on Blighter Island," said Muscle, clearly ready to settle into a long narrative. "The Voodooer, it was, or maybe The Zombie Parrot. Dobby was just sitting there minding his own business, tossing back a few noggins of the dark stuff, when along *he* comes and asks him if he'd like a game o' shrunkhead pool."

"No!"

Shrunkhead pool was a game rather like billiards except that, instead of using billiard balls, you played with those little wizened shrunken heads people brought back from their holidays in exotic lands. It was, accordingly, a game of considerably greater skill than ordinary pool or billiards, in that the heads rarely traveled in a straight line, tending to be bounced off their trajectory by things like their ears.

"Shrunkhead pool it was," Muscle confirmed. "Worst of it all was that Dobby didn't know who *he* was. Thought it was just the tavern drunk."

"One of the tavern drunks," Brains corrected.

"That too," agreed Muscle.

"So Dobby didn't know to let him win?"

"Beat him three games in a row. They bet twenty doubloons a game, and you can buy a lot with sixty doubloons. Dobby thought he was going to get hisself a nice little house in the country, settle down and start breeding himself a few grandchildren."

A frown slowly twisted Brains's face. "Wouldn't he have to have some children first?"

"Why?"

"Before he had grandchildren, I mean. It's the orthodox way of going about it."

Muscle considered this, then dismissed it with a shrug of his shoulders. "Doesn't matter nohow, anyway."

Brains shuddered. "He didn't get his sixty doubloons?"

"Not just that."

Brains shuddered again. "So Dobby'll not be having any children, I s'pose. Who bought the postage stamp?"

"Not that!" snapped Muscle. "It's just that … just that … well, Longnose Dobby's had to get hisself a new nickname, is all."

"Well, shiver me timbers."

"And," said Muscle, "that was one of his good days. If *he* had been in a bad temper, now …"

He let the word peter away into a fog of nightmarish images.

There was another silence, this one longer than the first. Through the open window of The Moldy Claw came the distinctive soggy *crrrrrack* of a skull splitting.

"You heard tell about the enchantment?"

Muscle snorted. "Enchantment my, ah, foot. Reckon he's just as vuln'able as all the rest of us."

Brains looked doubtful. "'Blade cannot cut him,'" he recited, "'nor rope hang him. Bullet cannot hole him, nor water drown him.'"

"Where'd you hear that?"

"Everybody knows it. You can hear it sung in any tavern, aboard any ship."

"I ain't never heard it."

"You just has."

"Oh."

"And it's true," said Brains, rubbing in his advantage. "Two times has he been sent to the gallows, and two times he's walked away again."

"Pull the other one. It's wooden."

"'S a fact. Twice over he's been invited to dance with ol' Jack Ketch, and each time the rope's broke and he's managed to escape. Four times he's been stabbed in the gizzard, and just laughed it off. And no one knows how often he's had to walk the plank . . ."

This time the two men shuddered in unison.

"It's said," whispered Brains, "that the Devil hisself walks close behind him, guarding his back."

"Nah."

"'S what they say."

Even though both Brains and Muscle were cutthroats of many years' standing, and had seen and done things that would give most ordinary people nightmares for the rest of their lives, mention of the Devil was, to them, something infinitely more bloodcurdling. It was as if further words were frozen solid in their throats.

Muscle resumed batting his arms together.

Brains looked out into the darkness of the street in hope of spying a potential customer. There wasn't one, of course. As we've already said, nobody in their right minds would be out this late in this part of town unless they were going to The Moldy Claw, and everybody who was going to The Moldy Claw tonight was either in there already or by now too drunk to reach it.

Still, there was this feeling someone else might be around.

After a while, Brains forgot about it.

"Here," he said more quietly, quickly looking up and down the street and then beckoning Muscle to come closer. "Here, I got something to show you."

Once the eyepatched man was beside him, Brains took another precautionary glance in all directions before pulling from a hidden pocket of his coat a roughly triangular, much-creased sheet of paper. He straightened out the wrinkles and then held the paper up so that it better caught the feeble light.

"See?"

Muscle stared at the paper. "That's writing," he said, squinting. "I think."

"It's a treasure map," said Brains smugly. "Leastwise, it's part of a treasure map. And it's me ticket to a lifetime of luxury and wealth. I kin shake the mud of Darkwater off of me heels, settle meself somewhere in the country with a few bevies of buxom babes, maybe open meself a nice little pub . . ."

"Nah," said Muscle. "You? The scourge o' the Sev—" He cut the sentence short, realizing, although he did not know the word, that he'd been about to plunge headlong into the quicksand of hyperbole. "Or at least a lake or two, anyway," he compromised hurriedly.

"Just like Dobby's dream," said Brains, nodding. "Only, for me, it's gonna come true."

"There ain't no buried treasures left," said Muscle. "They've all been unburied. How much d'you pay for that thing, anyway? You been had, I tell you."

"No," said Brains, looking quite obnoxiously confident. "This map's a genuine 'un, and so's the treasure it'll lead to. See here? See the signature at the bottom?"

Muscle peered closer. "Blimey!"

"Yes. It's him."

"But the legend says—"

"The legends all say he took it with him when he went to Davy Jones's Locker," said Brains, completing the sentence, "but he obviously didn't. He was a cunning one, he was, was Cap'n Adamite. But so am I. All I needa do is find the other two parts of this here map and Cap'n Adamite's treasure will be mine. And that's where you come into the pitcha, my fine friend."

"Me?"

"None other. I could do with help hunting down the other pieces of the map, and, like they always says, three eyes is better than one. How 'bout it? Cap'n Adamite's treasure – leastwise, the treasure of the Zindars, the map to find wot he discovered – is big enough for both o' us. Fifty-fifty, we could split it."

Muscle narrowed his eye, considering.

"Whassat?" he said suddenly, jerking his head toward the harborside.

"What's what?"

"That sound. Din't you hear it?"

"No."

"There 'tis again."

"'S just the seaweed slapping 'gainst the mooring poles."

"No," said Muscle. "'S a different sound."

He began to creep in the direction of the water, and Brains, the torn portion of map drooping between his fingers, followed him willy-nilly. Soon they were both standing on the very edge of the rotting dock, the tips of their toes seeming to be peeking down into the lifeless black water.

"I can't hear nuffink," said Brains, his voice no more than a whisper.

High above them, the clouds shifted and momentarily permitted a ray of light from a single bright star to pierce through to ground level, where, unnoticed by Brains, it glinted for an instant off the blade that suddenly materialized in Muscle's hand. As his mother had always said fondly to him before he'd sold her to a slaver from far Bojingle, "Just 'cause your head is filled with solid muscle, darlin', don't mean you can't have brains too."

"Lemme have another look at that map," said Muscle.

Stupidly, Brains handed the scrap over.

The blade seemed to hiss as it darted through the air. It certainly squelched a bit as it sank to the hilt in Brains' flesh.

Aside from that, there was no sound, not even the slap of seaweed, as Muscle adroitly caught the slumping body of his erstwhile friend and lowered it to the slimy wooden dock. It took him scarcely a moment to rummage through the numerous pockets of the dead man's coat and transfer their contents to his own. Then he rolled the corpse over once, twice, and watched as it vanished with a gentle sound of squeezed jello into the black depths.

He tucked the map for safekeeping behind his eyepatch, then rubbed his hands together in satisfaction at a job well done. The future beckoned brightly. No quiet country pub for him, although the bevies of buxom babes bit had been a good idea, one that he noted for future reference, and . . .

"The ocean tells no tales," said a soft, sinister voice behind him.

Muscle almost jumped out of his shoes. "Whassat?"

There was no reply.

"Who goes there? Show your face, or by Davy Jones I'll . . ."

Muscle wasn't certain exactly what it was he *could* do, but he hoped the dangling sentence sounded sufficiently threatening. Maybe there hadn't really been a voice at all; maybe it had been just a trick of his ears.

"Only a local resident out for an evening stroll," claimed the voice improbably.

Straining his single eye to penetrate the darkness, Muscle watched as a small, slight figure, moving with the predatory silence of a weasel, slipped out from behind a stack of disintegrating crates.

"Good evening," said the stranger. "Beautiful night, isn't it?"

Muscle struggled for words. This was no local out for a postprandial constitutional. All the locals who thought it was a bright idea to go out for postprandial constitutionals around here had been murdered long ago by opportunists like Muscle. He knew exactly who this was. His heart sank into his boots and, albeit rebelliously, stayed there.

This was – could be none other than – *him*.

"C-can't c-complain," Muscle finally managed to stammer.

"Oh, good. Then you won't be complaining about handing it over. Hm?"

"Handing what over?"

"You know perfectly well what I mean."

Muscle gave a laugh, a sort of oh-*that*-silly-old-thing laugh intended to display sophisticated nonchalance. Instead, it sounded as if he'd just swallowed some bilgewater and it had gone down the wrong way.

"You stowed it away behind your eyepatch," explained the stranger, as if Muscle might have carelessly forgotten.

"'S my 'nheritance."

The stranger looked startled. It was not an expression that fitted easily on his countenance. You could sense that he wasn't startled very often.

"Your *what*?" he said.

"'Nheritance. Was given to me by my ol' buddy just before he passed away. His last wish was that I should have it. Leastwise, his second-last wish. His *very* last wish was to be buried at sea." Muscle gestured with his thumb toward the harbor. "Wot I just done."

The stranger snickered incredulously. "I really do think you should give me that map, inheritance or not."

Muscle had been threatened during his lifetime more often than anyone could have counted, and by people who were more powerful and more terrifying than anyone could have described, and always he'd stood up courageously against such threats, even though, here and there, they'd cost him an eye, a leg, and numerous scars and amputations that fortunately were hidden by his clothing. If the stranger had threatened him, Muscle would undoubtedly have resigned himself to losing an ear or a few fingers, perhaps, but he'd have been defiant. Yet the quiet, insinuating *suggestion* the stranger had offered . . .

Muscle's nerve broke.

"Here, you have it." Now that he'd made the decision, he could hardly get the crumpled paper out from behind his eyepatch fast enough, out of his hands, out of his possession. "Take it. Take it."

"I shall indeed," said the stranger, doing so. "My considerable thanks to you."

"'S all right." Muscle resisted the urge to touch his forelock. "Any time."

The stranger turned as if to leave, then turned back. "Oh, just one more thing."

"Whassat?"

"I'm sure you'll understand."

And Muscle *did* understand. This was going to go way beyond the loss of a couple of fingers.

"I didn't get a chance to have a proper look at it," he babbled, "and even if I had I wouldn't tell nobody, honest!"

"Safety first, I'm afraid," said the stranger. "No hard feelings, eh?"

There was the vicious *whoooosh* a diving hawk makes, followed an instant later by the noise a sack of potatoes makes when you drop it onto soggy, rotting planks – assuming the sack of potatoes has a wooden leg, that is.

The only public clock in Darkwater, the one on the tower of Darkwater Jail, began to strike midnight. The clock was the most unreliable timekeeper in the whole of the Toxic Archipelago, perhaps even the whole of Sagaria, so it was not uncommon for midnight to start chiming long after daybreak, but tonight, for once, the clock was more or less on the mark.

The little stranger murmured, "Moments to spare," as he rolled Muscle's body over the edge of the dock, just as Muscle had rolled Brains's body over not long before. There was a very similar sucking splash. The stranger liked to keep up his steady average of a murder a day, so Muscle had died just in the nick of time.

"One more port of call," said the stranger to the unhearing night as he ducked away once more behind the crates, "and then I should be almost done . . ."

✦ ✦ ✦ ✦ ✦

It was one of those exquisite days when all of Sagaria seems tranquil and at peace. A grassy hillock dappled by sunlight, in the midst of a vast meadow where blades of grass and golden buttercups sway majestically in the symphonic whispers of the wind. The soothing, barely audible buzz of small insects going about their rituals. Birdsong in the air. High in the sky, one or two fluffy clouds chasing each other.

Bliss.

And then . . .

A mighty explosion ripped the air.

Daffodils and grass flattened for tens of yards around the little hill.

Insects plummeted to the ground, struck stone-dead midflight.

Billows of noxious green-brown gas spread across the meadow.

The little fluffy clouds fled for the safety of the horizon, where their mommies might be waiting to comfort them.

Birdsong came to an abrupt, strangulated halt.

Death stalked.

"That's better," said Growgarth, shifting his rear to make himself more comfortable. The worg sat on a shattered rock atop the meadow's central hillock. He grinned, displaying a mouthful of pointy teeth. A *lot* of pointy teeth. A look of sheer content spread itself across his broad, warty face. He was very proud of those warts, which had won the admiration of lady worgs for many miles around. Lady worgs were disturbingly difficult to tell apart from male ones, but still their praise counted for something.

Growgarth glanced down at his hand, which looked like a clenched boxing glove, only wartier. A lot wartier. The fist held the splintered remains of the spruce branch with which he'd been about to scratch his behind. He threw the wreckage aside. This was the life.

Worgs aren't pretty – at least, not to human eyes. If you said they looked like trolls, you'd soon start hearing from trolls' lawyers. Worgs are a lot uglier than trolls. And nastier, definitely nastier. People who've seen a worg before they've had their supper end up not eating it. They may never sleep a whole night through again, and if they do, they may wish they hadn't.

Out of the pocket of his filthy loincloth Growgarth pulled a dead rat. Half a dead rat, to be precise. He'd eaten the other half a few weeks ago and then decided the rest needed to be kept a while longer until it reached the appropriately delicious state of decay.

He held the mangled corpse to his nose (don't even ask about his nose) and took a deep breath.

Just right.

Into his mouth the half-rat went, the last bit to go being the tail, which wriggled like a withered worm before vanishing between his warty lips.

Growgarth shut his eyes the better to enjoy the flavor.

A voice spoke behind him. "I'm here."

The worg's eyes sprang open in astonishment. How could anyone have approached the hillock on which he sat without him having noticed? It would have been difficult enough before, when the ground was carpeted in long grass and tall flowers, but now that it had been seared to a flat, smoking waste? No way.

Yet, somehow, his visitor had achieved the impossible.

This visitor often did. Growgarth knew him from the days of yore.

"Oh hello dhere," said the worg, affecting nonchalance. He didn't turn round to look at the newcomer, partly in hopes of impressing him, partly because in his surprise he had a rat bone stuck between his front teeth, but mostly because he didn't want to see the newcomer's eyes. Growgarth was maybe four times as tall and four times beefier – and many, many times wartier – than the man behind him, but looking into those dead, distant eyes always shrank him. Even Growgarth was glad he hadn't gazed upon what those eyes must have gazed upon during their owner's long and ruthless life.

"I bin expectin' you," the worg continued, lying through his teeth – and, as noted, he had plenty of those to lie through. "I bin sayin' to meself, 'Wunner what's bin happnin' to me ol' pal Ter—'"

"*Don't*," hissed the voice, "say my name."

Growgarth gulped at the threat that lurked behind the newcomer's words, but he tried to keep his own voice as casual as before. "Oh, calm down, willya? Ain't nobuddy here but us."

"That's what you think. You didn't see *me* coming, did you, you great oaf? Don't bother lying to me. So how're you so sure there aren't others hiding out there?"

Because you'd have seen them if there were, Growgarth wanted to say, but he kept his silence.

"We don't know who might be watching," the visitor went on. It was odd to hear the worry in his voice. Growgarth had never known him to sound anything but icily confident before. "I don't like meeting you in person like this. There could always be somebody spying on us – somebody, or some*thing.*"

Growgarth looked around him. "Yeah. Right."

For a few moments silence hung between them, except for a strange sound not dissimilar to distant thunder. The half-rat was sitting less easily in Growgarth's stomach than he'd expected.

"You have it for me?" said the other at last.

"I promised, di'n' I?" The worg made no movement.

Over his shoulder something flew, something that landed on the blackened ground in front of him with a muffled chink. A leather purse.

"Your payment," whispered the seemingly disembodied voice.

Without quite knowing how he'd got there, Growgarth was on his knees on the ground, ripping open the purse with his clawed fingers, spilling the gold coins out. Counting them was beyond him, but there seemed to be the right number: lots.

For long seconds he slavered eagerly, drooling on the little heap of treasure.

"Ahem," said his black-clad visitor.

Growgarth looked up at him for the first time. The worg's vision was colored red with avarice. He could hardly see the visitor's eyes through the crimson haze.

"My purchase," the visitor explained.

"Oh. Ah. Yah. The fing."

Once more the worg dug in his loincloth pocket and his hand emerged clutching a crumpled sheet of brownish paper. There was a smear of very old rat blood on it, but this didn't seem to concern the stranger in black, who seized the paper from Growgarth's warty grasp. He scanned it for a brief moment, then tucked it away somewhere in his long cloak.

"Pleasure doin' bizniss wit' you, I's sure," said Growgarth, hoping the other would take this as his cue to leave. "Any time dere's sumpin' else you wanna buy . . ."

The visitor clapped his forepaws, like a small boy whose birthday party is just about to begin. "Business is over," he said brightly. "Now the socialization can begin!"

"Soshio . . . ?"

"The socialization."

"Oh, yeah. Dat."

"The fun."

"You got sumpin' to eat?"

"The bonding, my good fellow. The companionable sharing of the fruits of the day. Soon it'll be time for sunset, and it looks like it'll be a pretty one, no? What do you say we watch it together, side-by-side, discussing matters of little consequence, just getting to know each other better?"

Growgarth did not know very many things, but one of them was that he was sure that under no circumstances did he want to get to know his visitor any better.

"Duh," he said expressively.

"Good, then that's settled." The visitor moved as if to join him on the rock, then paused, pointing.

"Oh, look, you've dropped a couple."

"Wha?"

"A couple of the coins."

Growgarth's eyes searched. There was a definite shortage of hiding places left on the hillock. "Can't see 'em."

"But I can. Just there."

Still Growgarth could see no glint of gold. On the other hand, as one of the few wise sages of worg mythology so prophetically remarked, gold is *gold*. Growgarth got down on his knees again and started beating the ground with the flats of his hands, hoping to find the errant coins by touch if he couldn't do so by sight.

There was a click behind him. Then another.

Suddenly Growgarth felt like you do when the fuse has burned the whole way down but your firecracker hasn't gone off. You know it's idiotic to pick the firecracker up, because it'll probably, with your lousy luck, explode in your hand, but you go ahead and do it anyway because there's nothing more frustrating than a dud firecracker. His movements becoming slower and less certain, he kept patting the ground in front of him.

There's a counting song that's popular among worg children. It's a very short song, for obvious reasons. It started running through Growgarth's head.

One's for my gulp as I bite off your head . . .

But there had been *two* clicks, not one.

Two's for barrels on shotgun – it shoots you, you're . . .

He couldn't remember the end of the line. *But there's a lot o truth in dem ol' countin' songs,* he thought.

Then the word came to him.

Ah.

Before the echoes of the two loud *bangs* had fully died down, the visitor in the long black cloak, his gun safely stowed away once more among its folds, was leaning over the lifeless worg to retrieve his coinage.

"Sorry about this, old chap, but you'll understand I have a business to run. Bottom line and all that."

Unlike Growgarth, the visitor was extremely good at counting. Once he'd satisfied himself that all the coins were present and accounted for, he carefully retied the drawstring on the leather purse. It too vanished into the folds of his cloak, where it sat alongside the scrap of brown paper he'd so desperately needed to possess.

Standing on top of the huge corpse, the killer looked sharply all around him. There was no sign of life anywhere in the blasted meadow.

He whistled quietly to himself as he trotted down the side of the hillock and began making his way with deceptive speed toward the distant, dark line of trees.

"As for the last piece," the stranger murmured to himself. "I think it's time I visited an old friend . . ."

UNSUITABLE QUESTIONS

nock, knock.

Sylvester Lemmington didn't bother answering. He recognized the knock and knew who the visitor was: his boss, Celadon, the Chief Archivist and Librarian. When Celadon knocked on a door, he entered. There was no point telling him to do so because he was going to anyway. At least, that was what Sylvester had decided not long after he'd got the job as Junior Archivist and Translator of Ancient Tongues, and he'd never seen any reason to change his attitude since.

He welcomed the interruption. He'd been working long and hard on his translation of *The Great Exodus: The Third Attempt*, and his eyes were tired and beginning to show a tendency to cross – a tendency which is very disturbing if you're a lemming. He could do with the break. He set down his goose-quill pen in its holder, being careful not to drip any ink, and removed the reading glasses from his whiskery nose.

"Good evening, Sylvester," said Celadon, pushing the door open with his frail shoulder. Grayed and bent, the Chief Archivist always looked as if the slightest puff of wind could blow him away like thistledown. He was dressed as usual in a plain, ratty muslin robe that matched the color of his fur and beard. His arms were full of yellowing scrolls that seemed to be of similar vintage to his robe. He peered around through thick spectacles for somewhere to put the scrolls down. Sylvester put his arms defensively out in front of him, shielding his desk, which was already quite full enough.

"I hope I'm not distracting you from your work," Celadon continued, a trace of waspishness entering his voice. He hefted the scrolls as if to communicate that Sylvester was being exceptionally selfish and inconsiderate.

Sylvester didn't care. He knew that if Celadon put those scrolls down he'd forget them when he left, and then tomorrow Sylvester would have to waste time making sure the old lemming got them back.

"I've nearly finished the translation of *The Great Exodus*," he said truthfully. "And," he added, not so truthfully, making a show of scrutinizing the parchment in front of him, "I'm not sure this ink's quite dry yet."

"Hmmf," said Celadon skeptically, but then his face brightened and his whiskers began trembling with delight. "That's excellent news that the translation's almost done, young fellow. I knew I'd entrusted the task to the right person. You've worked very quickly and diligently on this. I shall make sure your superiors are informed."

"Thank you, sir," said Sylvester politely. "But, er, you *are* my superior."

"Oh, quite right, quite right. Thank you for reminding me. This is the most important piece of work you've done for us, Sylvester. There are so few scholars nowadays who've taken the trouble to learn the ancient tongues our forefathers used, and you must surely be the youngest – the last of the line perhaps, although I do hope not. Why don't you marry and have a few children you can teach the old languages to, eh, my lad?"

Sylvester blushed under his fur. "I haven't yet met the right girl." This was another lie. He had met the right girl – or, at least, so he thought most of the time. The trouble was that she didn't always seem entirely convinced he was the right guy.

Yet.

"You'll be Chief Archivist yourself one of these days," said Celadon, risking dropping the scrolls to wag a finger at him. "You tell any girl that, and she'll leap gratefully into your arms, mark my words."

Sylvester tried not to roll his eyes. Sure. Chief Archivist. Try boasting about that to the average young lemming of the female persuasion and she'd be fast asleep before you'd finished saying the word "archivist." What the girls today wanted in their males were brawny muscles, fearlessness, and preferably a strong dose of stupidity. The role of bookish lemmings like himself was to watch from the sidelines as the girls swooned over these paragons of virility.

"I can see you don't believe me," said Celadon, reading his expression well, "but one day you will. If nothing else, you'll be able to tell the world that you're the translator of one of the most important historic documents of all, *The Great Exodus*."

"*Third Attempt*," added Sylvester automatically.

"Indeed. *The Great Exodus: The Third Attempt*. Now everyone will be able to read it and find out for themselves what our roots are."

"True," said Sylvester, looking down at his own neat script on the parchment. He wasn't going to be the one to tell the Chief Archivist that there was barely a lemming left who *cared* about their people's roots.

"You don't know where you're heading if you don't know where you've come from," said Celadon.

"If you say so, sir."

"And this invaluable document tells us so much about where we've come from."

"Um," said Sylvester, but Celadon didn't notice.

"You see," the old lemming carried on, getting into the spirit of his own oratory, "we lemmings of Foxglove may well be the last lemmings of all, but we're a proud species, dear boy, and we're destined for greatness." He began to make a sweeping gesture with his arm to the sleepy town of Foxglove beyond the window, then realized he was about to drop the scrolls. Clutching them hurriedly, he instead nodded his head toward the outside world. "The great spirit Lhaeminguas himself said we are destined for all-encompassing glory, when he wrote in . . . in . . . a very long time ago, anyway."

"In the year 362," said Sylvester quietly.

"I was just about to say that. 362. You have a remarkable memory, young Sylvester. Nothing escapes you, eh?"

Sylvester bowed his head modestly. "Thank you, sir. I know how lucky I was to be born with a memory as retentive as mine. Not everyone's so fortunate."

"It's a rare and wonderful gift."

"But a *gift*," Sylvester stressed, under his breath. It wasn't something he'd gone out and earned. All very well to be born clever. If he wanted to attract the approval of Viola, he'd have to do something a bit more exciting with his cleverness than translate a dusty old document she was never going to read anyway.

Aloud he said, "One thing's been troubling me, sir."

"Yes?"

"*The Great Exodus* doesn't really tell us very much about where we've come from – it doesn't tell us anything about that at all, in fact. What it *does* tell us is that in the old days a whole lot of lemmings went away, and they never came back. Where do you think they all went to, sir?"

Celadon whuffed and tut-tutted, and once again looked as if he were desperate to find somewhere he could put the scrolls down.

"You know, boy," he said when at last he had his words under control, "that's most assuredly not the kind of question it's proper to ask. You know the old saying, 'Ours not to reason why, ours not to search and spy or try to pry, ours not to—' Oh my. Where was I?"

"Telling me not to be curious about our roots, sir."

"Was I? Oh, yes. What I was *trying* to tell you, Sylvester, is that you and I are in a way merely the humble servants of those great lemming forefathers of ours who ventured forth into the world to seek their fortunes. They were great travelers and explorers and it is our duty, here in this library of lemming lore and

24   THE TIDES OF AVARICE

history, to honor their valor and their deeds."

"But what *were* their deeds, sir? So far as we know, they set off for the edge of the Mighty Enormous Cliff. That's what *The Great Exodus* tells us, listing hundreds and thousands of the names of those who went, and so do other ancient documents we store here. They set off for the edge of the Mighty Enormous Cliff and they never came back. They just disappeared, exactly like those of their forebears who left in the First Attempt and the Second – and, for that matter, later, in the Fourth, and Fifth and Five Hundred and Fifty-Fifth. They all just . . . go. We don't know what happened to them. From what we can tell, they just go straight over the edge of the cliff, and then . . ."

"Don't disturb yourself so, my boy," said Celadon soothingly, finally dropping his scrolls on the floor and coming round behind Sylvester's desk to put his arm across the younger lemming's shoulder. "I'm sure those great ones have found what they were looking for, out there in the wide world. So wondrous were the, er, wonders, that those brave lemmings never thought to come back here to stuffy little Foxglove to—"

"But—"

"I told you, Sylvester. Don't agitate yourself. Agitation is not a frame of mind fitting for an archivist. When you get to be my age you'll learn that—"

"But I'm not agitated. I'm just curious."

"You're upset."

"Not even that. I just want to know—"

"Why don't you take the rest of the afternoon off, my boy?" said Celadon, patting Sylvester's shoulder paternally. "You're obviously greatly disturbed by these thoughts of yours, however much you might think otherwise, and you could do with some rest and relaxation to calm those jangling nerves of yours. Go for a walk. Get a bit of fresh air. Then ask that fine mother of yours, matron Hortensia, to fix you up a big, hot supper so you forget your doubts."

Sylvester had the feeling this wasn't exactly how the spirit of intellectual inquiry was supposed to be handled, but on the other paw the prospect of stopping work for the day was an appealing one. At most he had three or four hours left to do of the translation, and if he carried on with it now he'd undoubtedly push to finish tonight. By the time he was done he'd be too exhausted to stand up straight. Much better to leave the rest of the task until the morning.

"Perhaps that'd be the wisest thing to do," he murmured, beginning to gather his things.

"Yes, it is," said Celadon. "Do me a favor and pick up those scrolls, will you?"

⚜ ⚜ ⚜ ⚜ ⚜

For a long time after Sylvester had gone, Celadon remained in the younger lemming's room, staring sightlessly out the window and over the rooftops of Foxglove as the sun slowly lowered behind them.

Poor Sylvester, he thought. *Assailed by the same doubts that assail us all at some time or another during our lives before wisdom catches up with us and we learn to rely on the tradition that makes our people strong. Sylvester's probably not the only one of the younger folk to be troubled like this, just the only one with the courage to speak up and ask me about it. I can remember when I was his age – it seems like such a terribly long time ago now – and all I could think about was: Where did they all go? Why did none of them ever come back? All those expeditions our people have mounted, all those waves of settlers leaving Foxglove with their promises to return for the rest of us once they've found greener lands to settle. Not so much as a scut of a tail have we seen of them again. It's enough to make anyone wonder, it is, but the only thing that lies down that road is frustration and misery . . .*

In the distance, mothers were yelling to their small children to come in from playing, right now this minute, because your supper's on the table and you make sure your grubby paws are properly washed before you sit down or it'll be straight back to the bathroom until I'm satisfied, do you hear? In the distance, two farmers were leaning against their hoes, discussing the day's work they'd done and how tomorrow would hold another one very like it. The stallholders in the marketplace were covering their wares with weighted cloths to protect them from the elements overnight.

Celadon was only dimly aware of any of this.

I suppose none of us ever do stop wondering about it, not really. Especially not poor Sylvester. He lost his father to one of the exoduses when he was just a baby. I wonder if he remembers Jasper at all? I wonder if Hortensia's decided yet if she should regard herself as a widow, and stop numbly waiting for Jasper to return? She's a fine figure of a female, Hortensia is, and if I were just a few years younger I'd . . .

The Chief Archivist shook his head crossly. He'd been thinking about all the things he could do if only he were a few years younger for so many years now that he was beginning to sound senile, even to his own ears.

It's the eternal question, though, isn't it? The question that guides our people every step of the way along our path through history.

What's happened to all those lemmings who've ventured over the edge of the Mighty Enormous Cliff?

What have they found on the far side?

♦ ♦ ♦ ♦

Although the marketplace was closing down for the day, the square was still fairly crowded. Seekers after last-minute bargains mingled with traders who were trying to shut up shop. Sylvester decided he didn't want to face the bustle, and turned his steps instead towards one of his favorite spots, the peaceful graveyard behind the temple that overlooked Foxglove. It was on the far side of the little settlement from the library where Sylvester worked. It took him a while to get there, and as he walked he thought through that curious little scene he'd experienced with Celadon. The question he'd asked had made the older lemming assume Sylvester was going through emotional turmoil. Why? To Sylvester the matter was one of profound puzzlement, and he was determined to weasel out the answer somehow. What could be of more importance to the last survivors of the proud lemming people? There was nothing emotionally *disturbing* in the mystery, yet clearly Celadon thought there was.

Maybe the old bozo's right in a way, thought Sylvester as at last he entered the graveyard. High, slender birch trees were like cathedral pillars on either side of the long path down which he walked, but they weren't what he'd come here to see. His destination was at the far end of the path.

Soon he was in front of the tall white monument. As always, he fussily pushed away some of the longer grass that had grown up around its base since last he'd been here. Then he settled back on his haunches to read for the thousandth time the letters carved high on the stone:

In Memory of Those Brave Lemmings
Who Ventured Forth in the Great Exodus
Towards Fortune & Glory,
In Search of the Land of Destiny
Across the Great Wet Without End.
They Fulfilled Their Duty with Courage & Honor.

Sylvester's gaze drifted down the two columns of a long list of carved names until he found the one he was looking for, near the bottom of the right column:

Jasper Lemmington

"Dad," he whispered.

Sylvester reached out a paw and gently touched the stone. During his countless visits since infancy, first with his mother and then later alone, he'd worn the edges of the letters smooth. It was becoming harder to read his father's name but Sylvester didn't need to see the words to read them. They were engraved on his heart.

"I hope you found what you were looking for in the Land of Destiny," he said to his father. He had the sense that, somewhere, Dad could hear him.

The young lemming stayed like that a long while before letting out a heavy breath and turning away from the monument. There was an old stone bench by the cemetery wall, and he sat himself down on it, squirming in an attempt to make himself comfortable. Benches were human inventions. Lemmings had copied them and tried to adapt the design so that it suited the lemming form, but with limited success.

Two or three sparrows alighted on the grassy ground in front of him and strutted up and down, obviously hinting at him that any tidbits he might chance to have about his person would be most welcome. He fumbled in his pockets and at last found the remains of an oat biscuit his mother had thrust at him a few mornings earlier, as he'd been leaving for work at the library. "Don't you go getting so engrossed in your work that you starve yourself to death, dearie." He'd meant to ditch it as soon as he was out of her sight, the way he ordinarily did with the snacks she forced on him, but this time he'd forgotten. Well, his forgetfulness was the sparrows' gain.

Or not. You never could tell, his mother's cooking being what it was.

He crumbled the cookie, not that it needed much more crumbling, and scattered the pieces.

"Thank you, kind sir," said one of the sparrows, its beak already full.

"You're welcome," said Sylvester.

He closed his eyes wearily.

When he opened them again a few moments later he found himself surrounded by half a hundred birds – blackbirds, pigeons, more sparrows – all looking at him with a certain pointed interest.

He laughed, rose from the bench, and made a performance of turning his pockets inside-out to show he didn't have any more food.

Huffily, the birds swarmed off toward the marketplace in hopes of richer pickings there among the debris left on the ground at the end of the day.

It was about time Sylvester himself went home.

As he was emerging from the graveyard, he saw Viola coming towards him, and his heart picked up a beat. She was with her younger brother, Bullrich, but that couldn't be helped.

Ah, Viola, thought Sylvester with a mixture of infatuation and bewilderment. It was the way she always affected him. She'd been his best friend ever since childhood, and nine times out of ten Sylvester was convinced the friendship had blossomed into something more than that. The tenth time, though, always found him backing away from the something more. She was lively, "full of vinegar," as

Celadon had said a little testily the day she'd come bursting into the library to drag Sylvester off to join in the celebrations of her having won a canoe race. And that was the problem, the difference between them. It made Sylvester wonder if the whole notion of them being made for each other was madness. Viola liked doing things like compete in canoe races, clamber around the mountainsides or search along the river bank for treasurable flotsam and jetsam. Sylvester preferred to spend his waking hours with his nose tucked into a book, or perhaps discussing philosophy with Celadon. They were chalk and cheese. Yet, he couldn't deny that Viola was the most important person in his little world. The fact that she was the prettiest lemming in Foxglove certainly also helped.

Watching her approach now, he felt a sudden wash of emotion swell his chest. *What if I could be a hero? What if I could go off and have adventures and face perils? Me. Sylvester Lemmington. What if I could stop being such a dull old stick and . . . ?*

Then the thought faded.

It's something to dream about, anyway . . .

Viola had noticed him. "Hi there, Sylvester!"

He raised a paw in greeting.

She and Bullrich had been out mushrooming. Viola was carrying a basket of inky caps. Her little brother was trailing along behind her, staggering under the weight of the biggest parasol mushroom Sylvester had ever seen.

"What do you think of this, eh?" said Viola, nodding towards the giant fungus.

"It's amazing," said Sylvester, honestly.

She wrinkled her nose. "We found all these inky caps sheltering under the big one at the edge of Mugwort Forest. Took us nearly an hour to gather everything up. Bullrich practically wore his teeth flat gnawing through the parasol's stalk." She laughed. "Well, not quite. I had to threaten him with a dozen different forms of gruesome death to stop him from eating half of it before we got it home. Didn't I, Bullrich?"

"Yes, sis," said her brother resentfully, looking up at Sylvester as if to say that it was the duty of two males to bond together against the common threat.

"Now you're going to trot along home with all our mushrooms, aren't you, dear brother, while I spend some quality time with my friend, Sylvester?"

Bullrich's eyes brightened with interest. "Whatcha going to do?"

"Never you mind."

"Mom'll ask me."

"Mom won't. She wouldn't be so stupid."

"We're going to race to the top of Greenbriar Hill," said Sylvester hastily. He hardly ever blushed, but this was the second time this afternoon.

"Can I join in? Can I? Can I? Can I?"

"No," said Viola firmly.

"Why not? Oh, *why* not?"

"Because you're a pain in the bottom is why not. Now go on home with those mushrooms or I'll tell Dad why the level of his acorn whiskey keeps going down faster than he thinks it should."

"Aw, siiiiiiis."

"And don't drop any."

"Huh. As if I—"

"No snacking on them, either."

"You're no fun."

"You're a brat."

"Sisters! They're, they're, they're *poison*."

"Shut up."

"*You* shut up."

"Toad!"

"Bumface!"

"Go look in a mirror!"

"You snore!"

"Don't. You little—"

Eventually Viola and Sylvester managed to divest themselves of Bullrich. Moving slowly now he was burdened with the full basket as well as the gigantic parasol, the smaller lemming tottered off down the hill away from them, leaving a trail of surprisingly inventive curses in his wake.

"He's lucky your mom and dad aren't here to hear him," observed Sylvester.

"That was a good idea of yours," said Viola, ignoring what he'd just said.

"Idea?"

"Racing up Greenbriar Hill."

"It was only a . . . a . . ."

"Lie?"

"A *pretext*. That's what it was. A pretext. A way of getting Bullrich off our backs for a while."

"It was still a good idea. I had to be slow and patient while we were gathering mushrooms, and then I couldn't walk too quickly as we were coming home from the woods in case I left my little brat brother behind. I'm in the mood for a run."

"Well, I'm not."

"Oh, come on, Sylvester. It'll be fun."

"For you."

"For you, too, if you catch me." She batted her eyelashes.

This was, Sylvester reflected, definitely one of those nine times out of ten. He'd never have admitted it to anyone, but the occasional kisses he and Viola shared were an exquisite bliss unlike anything else he knew.

"We could just walk up there," he said, but in his heart he knew the argument was lost.

"Good. I knew you'd be keen to race me. Ready?"

"I suppose so."

"Right. One. Two. Two and a half, and . . ."

She grabbed the reading glasses from his nose and was away like the wind.

"Oi!" he shouted after her, and then, laughing, he was running too.

By the time they reached the base of the little hill, no more than a quarter of a mile away, Sylvester was definitely gaining. This was not usual. Viola was as fit as any lemming he knew while he himself, well, what could you expect with such a sedentary lifestyle? But today he was catching her up. Either he was in better condition than he'd thought or . . .

She glanced over her shoulder at him, making a face of mock terror.

. . . or she was letting him catch her. No question which of the two it was.

Climbing the hill was more of a difficulty. Not only was the slope steep, but in among the loose grass were countless little viny weeds that seemed intent upon tripping up unwary lemmings. Viola was accustomed to dashing about in the countryside and managed to keep her balance, although she had a few close calls, but Sylvester went flat on his face more than once.

Even so, by the time they neared the summit he was only a few paces behind her, and the sound of her labored breathing told him it was no longer entirely the case that she was running slowly for him. Mind you, his own breathing had gone beyond the labored stage to the point where he could hardly suck in air at all.

Snatching an extra spurt of energy from somewhere, he threw himself forward and grabbed her around the waist.

She let out a whoop of surprise, and then the two of them were rolling together through the lush grass of the hilltop, trying to giggle but too breathless to do much more than squeak.

"I won," Viola gasped as they lay on their backs looking up at the darkening blue of the sky.

"You cheated," Sylvester protested.

"Who said there were any rules?"

It was a good question. Sylvester chose not to answer it. He was too busy trying to get his vision back under control so that the sky would stop looking like it was made of quivering gelatin.

Viola rolled toward him and planted a wet kiss on his furry cheek. "Come on. Let's go watch the sunset from the top of the cliff," she said.

"I'm not sure I can walk."

"Then hobble."

Between the summit of Greenbriar Hill and the Mighty Enormous Cliff there was a saddle of land. The two young lemmings ambled easily along it, pausing every now and then to exchange a kiss or two. There was no one else around at that time of day – at least, Sylvester thought so until one of a flock of swallows flying overhead yelled, "Get a room!" at them.

The sun was halfway below the horizon when they reached the edge of the cliff. Far, far below them, waves broke ferociously against the rocks, the sound seeming thin and high at this distance. All the way to where the great yellow orb of the sun was sinking stretched the Great Wet Without End.

"It's beautiful, isn't it?" said Viola dreamily, her shoulder leaning against Sylvester's.

"I suppose so. I've never liked it, though."

"The Great Wet Without End? Whyever not?"

"I don't know why not. Well, maybe I do . . ."

"The Land of Destiny lies on its far side, after all."

"Does it have a far side? Isn't it without end, just like its name says?"

"That's only a name." She was obviously trying to jolly him. He was in no mood to be jollied. His high spirits of a few moments ago had troughed precipitously.

"All I know about the Great Wet Without End," said Sylvester, "is that it takes people you care about away from you, and it never gives them back."

"Never?"

"Never."

He said the word with finality, silencing anything she might have been about to say. It was difficult for her to always remember the kind of pain her friend must have been going through daily since his father had departed on the Exodus.

For several minutes they just sat there, companionably yet wrapped in the blanket of Sylvester's misery, while more and more of the sun disappeared from view.

"You don't know that, Sylvester," Viola said at last. "You don't know they'll never come back. Perhaps they're having a wonderful time in the Land of Destiny and'll soon remember to come home to fetch the rest of us. I'm sure that's it. Your dad'll be back someday soon."

"I hope you're right," Sylvester said. "I wish I could believe it."

"Besides," Viola continued as if he hadn't spoken, "how could something as beautiful as the Great Wet be dangerous?"

Easily enough, thought Sylvester, but he didn't say it. Instead he said, "Wouldn't it be great to be able to fly? Like those seagulls over there? We could whoosh all the way across to the Land of Destiny and be back home in time for supper!"

Viola giggled. It seemed Sylvester's mood was lightening again. "Hey, mom. What's for eats? Oh, by the way, I've brought a few thousand hungry lemmings back with me from the Land of . . ." She broke off. "What's that?"

"What?"

"Over there. Oh, it's gone now."

"What was it?"

"Probably nothing. I thought . . . just for a moment I thought I saw something. A little black speck near the edge of the sun, as if there was something floating on the Great Wet. But then I blinked and it was gone." She gave a snort of laughter that didn't contain much humor. "Maybe it was all the lost lemmings swimming home from the Land of Destiny."

"Maybe it was just a bit of grit in your eye," said Sylvester sourly, keeping out of his voice the momentary surge of excitement her words had caused him. "I saw nothing."

"Just a trick of the light, I guess," said Viola, picking herself up and turning to look back in the direction of Foxglove. "Time we were on our way."

Sylvester glanced at the sunset. As he did so, the last thin fiery line of the sun winked out on the horizon. "Past time."

"But we'll meet again later tonight," she said.

"We will?"

"Yes. It's your forfeit for having lost the race."

"But I didn't lose the—"

"Shush. We're going midnight fishing."

"We are?"

"The river's full of bleaks – bubbling over with them, I'm told – so it's our duty to go and help ourselves to a few as a contribution to feeding our families."

"It is?"

"It is. I'm very strong on duty, I am."

"First I ever—"

"Of course, if you'd prefer a girl to go on her own in the cold and lonely dark and maybe fall in and drown, or get attacked by murderers or—"

"I'll go with you," he said hurriedly, running after her. "Where d'you want to meet?"

"At the stroke of midnight." Her words came floating back to him. "By the knoll with the rotting dinghy."

He knew where she meant.

"Okay." This time she was running as fast as she could, which was a lot faster than Sylvester was able to. She was receding from him rapidly.

"Be there!" she commanded.

Sylvester gave up the chase.

A RUSTLE IN THE REEDS

When Sylvester opened the door to the little house he shared with his mother he was greeted by the smells of home: warm lemming and hot supper. The odor did as much as Viola's kisses had to ease the tension that had been building up within him all day. This was the familiar; this was the world he had grown accustomed to. He closed his eyes for a moment, breathing deeply.

His mother's temper, however, was not so calming.

"You're late."

"I, ah, Mom, I . . ."

"Where've you been?"

"Out on the cliff."

"With Viola?"

"Yes."

"Well, you got one thing right anyway. Come in, wash those filthy paws of yours, and sit down at the table for your meal. It's probably not burnt."

Sylvester did as he was told, and quickly. His mother, Hortensia, didn't fall prey to foul moods very often, but when she did, like now, it was only a fool who risked getting on her wrong side. He wondered what had happened to upset her. Perhaps she too had been thinking about his father again, about how Jasper left on that day so many years ago and, despite all his promises, never came back. Hortensia could have taken advantage of the law in Foxglove that, once people had been missing for seven years, they could be declared legally dead. She would have been given the status of Jasper's widow, not his wife. If she'd wanted, she could have remarried and Sylvester knew for a fact she'd had a few offers. There had been a few inquiries as to whether she might be interested in setting up home with another, but she'd chosen not to, believing that Jasper must still be alive out there somewhere, must still be depending upon her . . .

She slapped a bowl of something brown, steaming and unidentifiable down on the table in front of him.

"Eat."

He did, even though the food scalded the roof of his mouth. It was a little burnt, as she'd indicated it might be, but that wasn't its real problem. Its real problem was that his mother had been the one to cook it. Hortensia was still a comely female, hence the tentative offers of marriage. If her suitors had ever been unlucky enough to sample her cooking they might have thought twice.

"Anything happen today, Mom?" he said after a while.

Sitting opposite him and eating her own supper, though rather more slowly, she made no reply for a few moments, long enough for Sylvester to assume she really was in a bad mood this time and was going to ignore him.

Then at last she did answer. "This and that."

"A good this and that, or a bad this and that?"

"Promise me one thing, Sylvester." She raised her gaze from her bowl and stared straight at him. He noticed for the first time the tears in her eyes. "Promise me that, whatever happens, you'll never turn out to be like that fat, stupid, pompous, filthy-minded, self-serving boor."

It wasn't the first time they'd had a conversation like this, and probably wouldn't be the last. Hortensia couldn't bring herself even to say the person's name, but Sylvester knew who she meant. There were several lemmings in Foxglove who could be accurately described as fat, stupid, pompous, filthy-minded, self-serving and boorish, but there was only one who regularly drew the venom of his mother, and with such intensity.

Hairbell.

Hairbell had been Foxglove's mayor for the last three years, and he reveled in the power and what he envisioned as the glory. No one in Foxglove could understand how he'd come to be elected to the position, because it was impossible to find anybody who'd admit to voting for him, but elected he'd seemingly been. Hairbell had the appearance and general physical characteristics of a fat, juicy slug, Sylvester always felt. Being not especially handsome himself, except in his mother's eyes, he might have had sympathies were it not for the fact that Hairbell's personality matched his outward appearance. Foxglove's mayor was slimy, slithery poison. Like almost everybody else in the town, Sylvester avoided him as much as he possibly could.

As did his mother, normally. She was a kind soul, and for a long time had done her best to be friendly to the mayor to make up for the obvious loathing the general public felt for him, but then had come the day, a few months ago, when he'd proposed marriage to her. In this case, "proposed marriage" was a euphemism for what Sylvester understood to have been an unusually frank and physical proposition. Hortensia's knuckles had been in bandages for a week; Hairbell's jaw still didn't seem to fit properly into the rest of his face.

"What about him, Mom?"

"He's going to announce another Exodus. Next week, or the week after, he'll be making the proclamation, but I heard about it tonight from Cissy Fairbeetle, who had it direct from the lips of Dimity Scoby, whose brother used to work for—"

"Maybe it's just one of those crazy rumors, Mom?"

She shook her head sadly, letting her gaze fall once more to the half-finished bowl of food in front of her. Impulsively she pushed the plate away. "I don't think so."

"What makes you say that?"

"Something the oaf said when . . ."

"When what?"

"When he . . ."

"When he asked you to marry him?"

Sylvester's mother flushed, and he could see why so many of the males around Foxglove were so keen on her. One of the other junior archivists at the library had once let slip to Sylvester, after they'd both had a bit too much birthday beer, that Hortensia was regarded by everyone there as the hottest mom in town.

"When I'd told him I wouldn't," she said quietly. Sylvester guessed there was a long story behind those words, a story he was probably never going to hear, at least certainly not tonight. "He was yelling at me, threatening all kinds of things. One of the things he threatened was . . ."

She gripped the edge of the table tightly with both front paws. Her mouth was moving but no words were coming out.

Sylvester, food forgotten, leaned across the table towards her intently. Mom was a very private person. She kept far too many things to herself. He sensed this was one of those rare occasions when she would open up to him a little, raise the curtain.

"What did he threaten, Mom?"

"He'd got it into his head," and Sylvester had to strain to hear her now, "that the only reason I was saying no to him was because of you."

"That's idiotic! You know I'd never stand between you and happiness, Mom."

Even as Sylvester said the words he knew his feelings were a lot more complicated than that. If Mom took another lemming for her husband, it wouldn't be just her who'd be having to say that Dad was lost forever, that he was dead. Sylvester himself would have to make that admission too. If he had to he would – he was sure he'd be able to – but it'd be like swallowing a whole bucket of sharp stones.

"Of course it was stupid," Mom was saying, "but that's what he thought. I told him over and over that Jasper's still alive and I'm still Jasper's wife, that even if I wanted to I couldn't marry someone else, but he just wasn't listening. You know how dimwitted and stubborn males can be."

Sylvester let that one slide.

"Then he said . . . he said . . ."

She put her face in her paws.

"What did the scoundrel say?"

Her voice squeaked out in dribs and drabs between her claws. "He said there was a way of getting rid of you. As Mayor of Foxglove, it's Hairbell's role to administrate the lottery for those who go on the Exodus. He said it'd be easy enough for him to arrange things such that your name appeared on the next list."

"But there's not another Exodus due for . . . for . . ."

Sylvester's words ground to a halt as the implications sank in. One of Hairbell's other duties was to schedule when the Exodus should be. If he called one a few years early there'd be a lot of grumbling but no one would seriously dispute the decision, or Hairbell's right to make it.

"You think he's really going to do it?"

Dropping her paws into her lap, Hortensia nodded mutely.

"Well, if he tries it, I just won't go."

Despite his defiant words, Sylvester felt a rising pulse of excitement. If he went on an Exodus maybe he could find his father, somewhere in the Land of Destiny.

But he didn't say any of that. Not with the way he knew his mother felt about losing someone else she loved. Besides, this talk about Hairbell announcing another Exodus was probably all just gossip anyway.

As he rose from the table his mother put her paw on his arm. "Don't do anything foolish, darling."

He smiled down at her. "Don't worry, Mom. I won't. Let's get the dishes done. You look like you could do with an early night."

◆ ◆ ◆ ◆ ◆

Much later, after Sylvester had told Viola about his conversation with his mother, they sat in silence on the riverbank, rods in their paws, their feet in the cool water. There was a bright, high moon tonight, and in its silver light they could see the smooth dark surface of the water. The river seemed curiously life-like at night, snaking its way toward the Great Wet Without End like a scaly dragon that had feasted too enthusiastically on the knights and maidens it had encountered during the day.

"You know the thing that's oddest of all?" said Viola, breaking the stillness at last.

"What?"

"I thought it was *me* that old scumbag had his eyes on."

"You?"

"Yes. He's certainly had his paws on me often enough, but always with a good excuse. 'Just let me assist you up the steps, Miss Pickleberry, in case you trip and hurt yourself.' 'What a pretty dress! Can the fabric really be as smooth and silky as it looks?' You know the kind of thing. He's even been to see my father to ask if Dad has any definite marital plans for me yet."

"He did?"

"Believe me, he did. The worst of it is Dad didn't just sock him one right in the eye. 'S far as Dad's concerned, wedding me off to the Mayor of Foxglove could make for the perfect union. 'My daughter, the Mayor's wife.' Ugh!"

"You're not serious?"

"About the 'ugh'? I assure you, I've never been so serious about simulated vomiting in all my life. I could probably do the real thing, if you'd like me to try."

"No, er, not that. Serious about your dad, I mean."

"Yes. That's what he thought. He was going around with his head in the clouds, imagining everyone being all respectful to him for once, until Mom had a word with him."

"What happened then?"

"He didn't speak very much for the next week or two. Just went pale every time she opened the knife drawer in the kitchen."

Sylvester chuckled.

"It didn't matter, anyway."

"Well, it could have ma—"

"No, it couldn't. Dad's not the one who's going to decide who I marry. Nor will Mom. I'm going to do the choosing myself."

"Good."

"I don't care if he *does* disinherit me."

Sylvester thought worriedly about the diminutive size of a Junior Archivist's salary, even a Junior Archivist who was also a fully qualified Translator of Ancient Tongues – but he was getting way ahead of himself. What in the world gave him the idea the prettiest girl in Foxglove might choose to marry *him*? Oh, he was all right for occasional kissing and cuddling, that was what old friends were for, after all, but marriage was serious business and—

"I suppose I'll probably end up marrying you," said Viola ruminatively.

"Huh?"

"Well, you're handy and you're, what's the word I'm looking for? Steadfast. That's it. Steadfast. Loyal to a fault, and steadfast."

Sylvester wasn't sure he liked this character description.

Viola carried on. "You've got a nice respectable job, which is something any sensible girl ought to be thinking about, and . . ."

Dropping her fishing rod into the river, she collapsed in a fit of giggles.

"Oh, Sylvester, you should see the look on your face."

Splashing his paw in the water to retrieve her rod, he said nothing. She must know how he felt about her. How cruel of her to tease his affections so heartlessly.

"If I thought for one moment," she said, helping him resume his position on the riverbank, "that I was good enough for you and that you'd want to marry an airhead like me, I'd be tripping over myself to grab you before you escaped."

"You're not an airhead," was all Sylvester could think of to say, confused by the sudden turnabout in his assumptions.

"Tell that to the air in my head," she replied cheerfully, casting her line. "I'm as pretty as they make 'em, I'll not put on false modesty about that, but I'm flighty and shallow, and people get bored of me quick when they stop noticing my prettiness. It's a fact of life. I've learned to live with it. It doesn't bother me."

"Oh, Viola."

"Lovely night, isn't it? In the unlikely event that I catch any fish, I'm going to smoke 'em."

"I don't think that about you at all."

She turned her face instantly towards him, the moonlight picking out the exquisite line of her mouth and making her alert little eyes glitter. "You don't?"

"No, of course I don't."

"You're just saying that."

"I'm not. Well, I am saying it, of course, but I'm not just saying it. I really mean it. You're . . ." he was lost for words again. "You're *everything*."

"Charmer."

"Yeah right, Sylvester Lemmington, the charmer. I can just see them putting that on my tombstone: 'Lovingly Remembered For His Ability to Charm the Pants Off—' oops, er, I didn't mean it like that."

She fluttered her eyelashes in the way that always drove him crazy. "Doesn't sound such a bad idea to me."

Sylvester didn't know where to look, so he looked out over the smoothly rolling sheet that was the river's surface.

Then he heard something in the stillness that had fallen between them.

"What's that?"

"I heard it too," she said. "On the other side of the—"

"Like someone—"

"—gasping and gulping for breath—"

"—when they've been kicked in the stomach."

"What a violent thing to say, Sylvester."

"Well, ah, I've seen it happen on the sports field and . . ."

"But never done it?"

"Of course not! What kind of a lemming do you think I am?"

"Why're we talking about *you*? Perhaps there's someone in trouble over there."

They both stopped talking and, as if in response, the sound of someone gasping for breath was joined by another strange noise, like something struggling and squelching about in the mud. They could just make out, on the far side of the river, a place where the tops of the rushes were twisting and thrashing.

Then a figure burst into clear view on the opposite bank.

A tall, slinky ferret.

As a rule, lemmings steered as far clear of ferrets as possible. The skilled predators had an agreement with their more placid allies that there was to be no snacking, but every now and then the ferrets forgot. This particular ferret, though, didn't look as if he'd present any danger. Clutching his shoulder as if to staunch the flow of blood, he was barely able to stand on his own two feet.

"What's he doing so far from home?" Viola whispered.

"Help!" called the ferret weakly.

Although ferrets occasionally wandered far afield on quests of one inscrutable nature or another, for the most part they dwelled in their own settlement on the far side of Mugwort Forest. But Mugwort Forest was behind Sylvester and Viola, on the same side of the river as they were sitting. The wounded ferret was coming from the direction of the Great Wet Without End. Injured as he was, he must be trying to make his way home – perhaps to die. Except, of course, nobody could remember anyone ever coming home from the Great Wet Without End.

The ferret wobbled a couple of times on the edge of the water and then, with a despairing cry, fell in. He managed to push himself to his knees in the shallows, and started floundering towards them, but his energies shortly gave out and once more he was submerged. He was in more danger than he knew. The river bottom dropped off sharply, the shallows by the shore giving way abruptly to treacherous depths.

"Come on!" cried Viola, throwing her rod to one side.

Before Sylvester could move a muscle, she had hurled herself into the black water and was swimming strongly toward the commotion that marked where the ferret was struggling.

Sylvester dithered for just a few seconds longer. Ferrets were notoriously good swimmers – far better than lemmings, in fact. They were certainly whole orders of magnitude better than Sylvester. There was every chance this particular ferret, though wounded, didn't need help from anybody, least of all a pair of lemmings.

He stopped his thoughts, aghast at himself. What was he thinking?

Ferret or no ferret, Viola could be in danger!

He plunged headfirst into the cold river, and was immediately forced downstream by its slow but relentless current. He came to the surface gasping, and for a moment was completely disoriented, the water streaming in his eyes. Then the sounds of splashing penetrated his blind funk, and turning his head he could see that Viola had already reached the struggling stranger. She was looking back at Sylvester, clearly wanting his help.

"I'm coming," he cried, though most of what came out of his mouth was water he'd been in the process of swallowing.

Swimming did not come naturally to Sylvester. Like most lemmings he was not frightened of the water, he was just slow at moving through it. The uncoordinated movements of his limbs as he pulled himself along could not have been more different from the sleek efficiency with which Viola swam.

It seemed to take him forever to reach her, but at last he was treading water beside her.

"Where's the ferret?"

She nodded grimly downward. "I've got his leg. At least, I think it's his leg. Every time I try to grab any other part of him he just slithers out of my grip."

Sylvester groped underwater and got hold of what seemed to be some kind of leathery garment. A jerkin? The whole thing had happened so fast and he'd been so startled that he couldn't remember what the ferret had been wearing.

Hoping for the best, he hauled with all his might.

He was in luck. It was indeed the ferret's jerkin he'd managed to snag. The back of the injured creature rose above the surface.

Letting go of the ferret's leg, Viola took a couple of strokes and fished beneath the water. Soon she had the ferret's head out of the water.

"I can't keep this up for long!" she panted. "Try to roll him over."

Sylvester gave a heave on the leather jerkin, and obediently the ferret's body turned. The only trouble was that the turning had the effect of submerging Sylvester himself. He didn't want to lose his handhold, but it was either let go or drown.

He came up sputtering. Now that the ferret was on his back, it was easier for

Viola to keep the stranger's nose and mouth out of the water, but the current was doing its best to tear the slippery body from her.

Flailing blindly, Sylvester got a foreleg around the ferret's waist. With his other three limbs he strove to keep himself afloat.

"My hero," cried Viola tersely. "Let's get him to shore."

During the ordeal the current had been pulling them along, and they were now perhaps fifty or sixty yards downstream from where, just a couple of minutes ago, they'd been placidly fishing and canoodling. Luckily, they'd also drifted quite a lot closer to the bank.

A floating log appeared out of the night, coming at them. Sylvester thought it was going to brain him, but at the last moment an eddy made it swerve to one side and instead he was able to snatch a protruding branch as it swept past.

"Hold on!" he shouted at Viola.

He sensed rather than saw her nodding her agreement before a gush of water, created by the slowly turning log, splashed him in the face.

Now that he had the log to hold on to he didn't think they would drown immediately, a fear that had loomed very large in his mind ever since he'd dived into the water. Nonetheless, they had to get to the bank or they ran the very real risk of being carried out into the infinite expanse of the Great Wet. He kicked with his hindlegs, hoping against hope to be able to influence the log's movement in the direction of the shore, but his efforts didn't seem to be making any difference.

Then there was a thump beside him.

Holding the ferret's head above the water by one of the creature's ears, Viola had thrown her free arm over the log. She must have deduced what Sylvester was trying to do. Now she could add the force of her limbs to his, and she was a far more powerful swimmer than he was.

The log lurched in the water, as if protesting the sudden addition of extra force, but began cruising in fits and starts towards the near bank.

"We're getting there!" yelled Sylvester elatedly. "We're going to make it."

Afterward, he was never able to remember how they negotiated the final few yards and got themselves and the ferret up onto the bank. His next clear memory was of himself and Viola standing over a form that was terrifyingly, chillingly, dishearteningly still.

Viola was the first to voice the near-certainty both of them felt.

"Do you think he's dead?"

Sylvester thought he probably was, but didn't say so. He crouched alongside the ferret and put one furry ear against the cold, wet chest.

He heard a faint but steady pounding.

"He's alive!" cried Sylvester. "We've done it, Viola. We've saved him!"

He wanted to dance and sing with her in celebration, but his legs felt like lead. She was grinning like a mad thing, and he found he was doing the same himself.

"You stay here with him," she said. "I'll run and fetch Doc Nettletree."

Sylvester knew better than to argue. She was the faster runner. As well as the better swimmer. Her legs probably weren't four great, heavy weights that would simply slow her down.

No, that wasn't right. You couldn't run slower with heavy legs than without any legs at all. What he meant was . . .

By the time he'd got the thought sorted out in his mind, Viola was gone.

Sylvester sat up and looked around him. He was alone except for the limp, ominously silent ferret lying on the ground beside him. There was nothing to hear except the sound of the great river. That and an occasional whisper as a stray breeze pushed its way through the tall reeds. The moon had dipped behind a cloud, so that the only sign of its presence was what looked like a pale ghost, flapping robes and all, in the sky. By way of compensation, there were about a hundred million stars.

He shuddered. He was freezing cold and soaking and he had rarely in his life felt so exposed and lonely.

To take his mind off his situation, he began counting the stars. After about the tenth time that he'd lost count, the moon sailed clear of the obscuring cloud, dimming everything else in the sky, and he gave up. He turned instead to look at the ferret beside him.

Because of the general lemming distrust of ferrets, Sylvester had seen only two or three of them before in his life. Usually, when there was a ferret around, sensible lemmings were too busy pointing the wrong end of themselves in that direction to do much observing. Even so, this specimen seemed very oddly garbed. In the moonlight it was impossible to distinguish the colors of his different garments, but the oddly puffy shirt he was wearing looked to be white. The jerkin he wore over that (the jerkin that had probably saved his life, because it had given Sylvester something strong to cling on to) was presumably leather-colored. Even darker in the pale light were the ferret's trousers; they bulged as if he might be storing supplies in there, and they reached only as far as his knees, where they were tied tight to the short fur by some kind of cord. There was another cord around his neck, and as soon as Sylvester noticed this he reached out to loosen it; he found it was attached to a weird three-cornered hat that had been hidden, crushed, under the ferret's head.

"A wonder you didn't strangle yourself," he said almost chidingly to the motionless creature.

In its right forepaw the ferret was tightly clutching something that looked like a piece of crumpled paper; Sylvester chose not to investigate further for the moment. What held his attention the most was a strange mark on the ferret's left shoulder. Probing gingerly in the near-darkness, Sylvester soon discovered this was a hole with dirty smudges all around it. He gasped as he realized the hole went not just through the jerkin but also through the shirt and the flesh of the ferret.

Sylvester gulped uneasily. *I am not, not, not going to be sick.*

"What could have done this?" he asked the moonlight.

He decided not to lever the ferret off the ground to check that indeed the hole went all the way through. That was Doctor Nettletree's job, surely, not his.

I am really not going to be sick.

I am not even going to think about being sick.

Well, okay, maybe I'll think about it, but not much. Just enough so that I won't actually be *it. A fine sight it'd be for Viola when she gets back if she discovered me covered from head to foot in—*

An iron band sprang into being around Sylvester's throat.

"Who're ye, matey?" said a hoarse, threatening voice.

Sylvester tried to get out at least a croak.

"Answer me quick, or I'll have yer liver on a stick."

Sylvester thrashed his arms about to indicate his predicament. The one saving grace of it, a distant part of his mind coolly thought, was that, with his throat blocked off like this, even if he wanted to be sick the puke would just have to stay inside him.

His message seemed to have reached his captor, because the grip on his neck eased.

"Tell me now."

"S-Sylvester L-Lemmington. J-Junior Archivist and T-Translator of Ancient T-Tongues."

"Oh really? And what's a harchivizzer when it's at home?"

"Archiv-vist. Not a . . . what you said." *This isn't the time to be correcting his grammar, you oaf!*

"Ye one o' those mental defectors?"

Sylvester tried to draw himself up proudly, but when he did that the ferret tightened his stranglehold. "N-No. I told you. I'm an archivist. P-Please don't h-hurt me."

The ferret drew his face even closer, so Sylvester could feel the harsh rush of hot, foul breath on his cheek.

"He mustn't find me at any cost," the ferret muttered to himself.

"Who?"

Instead of answering, the ferret said, "He'll kill me if ever he finds me, he will. It's been many a year since he's had to take more than the one try at killin' someone, and his passion'll be high to make sure he finishes the job he started. So hide me, ye great lump. Hide me somewhere I can never be found."

Back in the river seems a good option, thought Sylvester, who was becoming rapidly fed up with being threatened by someone whose life he'd just saved.

"Not until the doctor's had a look at you."

"Doctor? *Doctor*? Yer fetchin' a sawbones, are ye? It'll be the death o' me, I tell ye. Before I let a sawbones touch me I'll—"

"Oh, shut up!" snapped Sylvester. "Doc Nettletree's jolly good. Hardly any of his patients die. You're damn lucky you've got a medic as good as he is coming to look at you." He warmed to his theme. "You're damn lucky to be alive at all, in fact. Viola and me, we could just have left you to drown. I'm beginning to wish we'd done exactly that, now, instead of risking our lives to save some ungrateful piece of scum."

I shouldn't have said all that, should I?

"Er," he added, and waited for death.

It didn't come.

Instead the ferret let go of his throat and slapped him on the back. "I likes the spunk o' ye, young Master Lemmingtree."

"Lemming*ton*."

"Lemming*ton* then. I likes ye, lad. Likes ye mighty fine. For a landlubber, anyhow. A right good thankee to ye as well for savin' the life o' old Keelhaul Levantes from the briny deep, or at least from that snot rag river back there." The ferret jerked his head toward the water, then winced. "Think I'll be just a-lyin' down again, if ye'd forgive me."

"Be my guest," said Sylvester politely, still amazed to be alive.

With a groan the ferret collapsed on his back again.

Sylvester wished Viola would hurry up. Where was she? Maybe she was having difficulty getting Doc Nettletree to wake up.

He looked at the stars again but, even with the moon having cut down so savagely on the number he could see, there still seemed uncountably many of them. But he couldn't just sit here next to . . . what had the ferret said his name was? Keelhaul Levantes. Funny sort of name, but each to his own. He couldn't just sit on the riverbank ignoring Keelhaul Levantes, could he?

"Where did you say you were from?" he asked by way of starting a conversation.

"I didn't." Now the pain was more obvious in the ferret's voice.

"Oh. Thought you had."

"No I didn't."

"I just—well, where *are* you from?"

"From the far side o' the sea."

"The sea?"

"That's right. The ocean, near enough. It's as big as most oceans are, anyhow. Seems that way when yer sailin' it on a little boat with nary enough water and yer lifeblood leakin' out yer shoulder."

The young lemming was incredulous. "You mean the Great Wet Without End?"

Levantes considered. "'At's as good a name as any for it, young Sylvester Lemming*ton*. The Great Wet Without End. Except it does have an end, me hearty, because that's where I's just come from, see?"

Sylvester could feel his heart beginning to pound faster and faster. "You mean there *is* a land beyond the Great Wet?"

"Ain't that what I's just been tellin' ye?"

"Yes, but . . ."

For a moment, Sylvester's thoughts blotted out whatever the ferret was saying. This meant his father really *could* be alive somewhere – in the Land of Destiny – and could come back to Foxglove one day. Even if Sylvester couldn't remember much about his dad, for Hortensia the return of Jasper would be the restitution of her life. Should Sylvester tell her, once he got home, what he'd learned? Or might that just risk cruelly raising her hopes and expectations too high?

After a few seconds, he became aware once more that Keelhaul Levantes was speaking.

". . . so I went on the run, and I been that way for months now. Got meself a little sailin' boat, just room enough for me 'n' me supplies, then headed north, where I thought I'd be safe as toast. Then one day, with land in sight ahead, there was that accursed ship o' his behind me, far in the distance but gettin' closer 'n' closer, 'til at last he was able to come for me, the blackguard. Near as bootlicks got me too, but Keelhaul Levantes, he's tougher than he looks, likes an old fightin' gamecock. The bullet missed me heart, which was where it'd been aimed, and left me with still enough strength to make landfall."

His words were interrupted by a bout of coughing. Sylvester saw a dark stain spreading on the ferret's chin, and after a moment realized to his horror that it was blood.

"Stay quiet, my friend," he urged. "The doc'll be here soon and I'm sure he'll be able to fix you up."

"Not in time, I fear," gasped the ferret, slumping back. "Not in time."

Sylvester put his arm around the other's shoulders. "Just a few minutes longer, I'm sure. I can't think why they're not here already."

"Old Keelhaul Levantes has gone past the reach o' any sawbones, I's thinkin'."

"Don't think like that!"

"Just the way it is."

"But . . ."

The ferret's eyes, which had been glazing over, suddenly gained a renewed focus. "I wish this could o' been otherwise, but ye got a face looks as I can trust it, young Sylvester Lemming*ton*."

"Over there, look! See those bobbing lights? They're lanterns, that's what they are. Doc Nettletree! Viola! They're here." At last, someone who could take over responsibility from Sylvester for what he was now convinced was a dying ferret.

"Heed me, ye blitherin' idiot!" hissed Levantes, but Sylvester ignored him.

"Ahoy there!" cried Sylvester, starting to struggle to his feet so he could better attract the attention of his friends.

Then that clamp of steel was around his throat again. The ferret was using the last of his strength to pin Sylvester where he sat.

"If ye utters one more word before I lets ye, I'll have yer gullet on the ground in front o' ye."

Sylvester froze.

"'At's better. Now listen, 'cause we don't have long. *I* don't have long."

The lemming nodded frantically.

"Take this," wheezed the ferret, stuffing something into Sylvester's pocket. "It's yers now. Good riddance to it, is what I says, because all it's brung me is misery and now me death, yet it'll give ye great good fortune if yer cards all play theyselves right."

Sylvester gulped. He swore silently to himself that at the very first opportunity he'd ditch the whatever-it-was Levantes had forced on him. To good fortune he wasn't averse, but misery and death seemed a rather high price to pay.

"Strange things'll start happenin' to ye from now on," Levantes was warning him, but the ferret's voice was growing fainter, as was his grip around Sylvester's neck. Clearly this last major effort had drained him.

"Strange, strange things . . ."

He flopped back suddenly onto the wet grass, his eyes rolling upward in their sockets.

"Levantes," croaked Sylvester. "Levantes."

"Well, and what do we have here?" came a professionally jolly voice behind him, drowning any response the ferret might have made.

Sylvester looked up. Doctor Nettletree, the elderly physician, was still in his pajamas. The lantern he was holding head-high seemed to be in danger of igniting his ornately tasseled nightcap. The doctor looked tubby at the best of times; the pajamas did not flatter his figure.

"Take this," said Nettletree, pushing the lantern at Sylvester. "Get out of my way and let me see him. Hold the light still, boy, can't you?"

Without any conscious awareness of having moved, Sylvester found he'd been efficiently displaced by the physician, who was now alternately listening to Levantes's chest and pummelling it with his plump fists.

"This doesn't look good," muttered Doc Nettletree. Louder, he called, "Pico, Newter, here with the stretcher!"

His two young assistants emerged in the lantern's glow, as did Viola, who moved nervously to Sylvester's side and took his arm. Together they watched in silence as Pico and Newter, under Nettletree's supervision, gingerly lifted the ferret onto the stretcher, maneuvered their burden onto their backs, and trotted away into the darkness towards Foxglove and Doc Nettletree's clinic.

Just before they left, the ferret found one last bout of strength. He opened eyes that were filled with death and turned them towards Sylvester.

"Remember, don't trust *anyone*." The words were so quiet and hoarse as to be almost indistinguishable from the wind moving through the riverside trees. "Beware of . . . appearances. *He* will seem yer . . . best friend. And *he* will come."

His head fell back onto the stretcher. His arm dangled limply.

"What was all that about?" said Viola as they stared after Doc Nettletree, who was scuttling in the stretcher party's wake.

"I'm not really sure," Sylvester said slowly. He seemed to be in some kind of trance.

"Are you all right?"

"I guess so." He twitched his head as if to shake away cobwebs. "A bit shaken. You were a while fetching the doc."

"He was fast asleep. His wife had a devil of a job wakening him."

"I thought it must be something like that. Let's follow them to the clinic to see if the ferret pulls through."

She looked down at her soggy clothes, then at his. "We ought to get into something dry and warm. I'm freezing."

"Okay, let's get you home then. I'll go to Doc Nettletree's after."

More than once, as they walked back to Foxglove, Sylvester started to tell her about the strange conversation he'd had with Keelhaul Levantes. Each time the words seem to die in his throat. So much had happened in such a short space of time, more than had happened in all the rest of his life, it seemed. He needed to get it sorted out in his own head before talking about it with someone else, even Viola, or perhaps *especially* Viola. Seemingly unaware of the dark, confused thoughts racing through his mind, she spent the trip prattling away about such inconsequentialities he wondered if she might be trying consciously to forget all that had occurred.

But there was another reason Sylvester was eager to get Viola to the safety of her home.

Soon after Doc Nettletree and his two nurses had left them alone on the riverbank, the sense had begun creeping through Sylvester that there was someone watching them from the darkness, and that sense had grown until he could no longer ignore it.

Although he could see and hear nothing, he was certain that someone was following them.

♦ ♦ ♦ ♦

"Sylvester," said a voice.

Sylvester stirred. He was flying smoothly and aerobatically in great, long loops from one little white cloud to the next as he made his slow descent toward the welcoming surface of his friend, the Great Wet Without End. Viola was to his left, flying as gracefully as he. Between them, they had solved the mystery of the Mighty Enormous Cliff, and he was proud in the knowledge they'd done this – even though he couldn't remember what the solution actually was.

Now this damned intrusive voice was disrupting his bliss. "Sylvester."

"Push off."

"Sylvester, wake up. It's me, Doctor Nettletree."

The bright light wasn't the sky, he realized. It was the inside of Doc Nettletree's little clinic in the center of Foxglove. He must have stretched himself out along a row of three or four of the hard upright chairs in the waiting room and, despite the discomfort, dozed off.

"Whaaa—?"

"It's about your friend."

"He's not my friend." *Except maybe he is. Those warnings he gave me; that was the act of a friend.* "What about him?"

Doctor Nettletree lowered his gaze. "I'm sorry to tell you this, but . . ." the portly lemming took a deep breath and looked Sylvester in the eye, "he didn't make it."

"Died?"

"Yes. I did everything I could, but . . ." The doctor shrugged.

"Did he die of that hole in his shoulder?"

"Yes. If it'd been treated right away, he'd have nothing left but a scar to show for it by now. He must have suffered it days ago, perhaps a week or more, and the wound had festered. He had the black rot, and it was reaching out to touch his heart."

Sylvester shuddered. Just hearing Doc Nettletree talking about it was making him feel sick.

"What punched the hole in him?"

"This," said Doc Nettletree, fishing in a pocket of his coat and producing a small black metal object. He put it into Sylvester's outstretched paw.

This was inside Levantes, inside the body of a living person, thought Sylvester, feeling sick all over again. Even so, he couldn't help but stare at the thing. It was roughly a sphere, but looked as if it had gotten a bit squashed at some stage.

"What is it?"

"It's made of lead," said the doctor. "That's about all we know. How did it get into his shoulder? Don't ask me, I haven't the faintest idea."

"Can I keep this?"

"If you want to, but why in the world would you?"

"Because at least I know where it came from. Knowing that much, maybe one day I'll be able to find out the rest about him and who killed him."

"How and where?"

"He told me himself, while the two of us were by the river waiting for you to arrive. He said he'd come from the far side of the Great Wet Without End, and he'd been injured while sailing the sea."

Doctor Nettletree smiled sympathetically. "You've had a lot of stress, young fellow, and very little sleep. The shock of a wild rescue, your vigil beside a dying creature – no wonder your memory's getting a little jumbled. It won't last and if it does, come back here in a couple of days' time and I'll give you a tonic that'll soon have you sorted out."

"But there's nothing wrong with my—"

"Oh, and I'll give you a note to give to Master Celadon. You must be exhausted. Go in to work at the Library in the afternoon if you feel up to it, but as your physician I insist you spend the morning at home. You're something of a hero, young Sylvester, and even if I didn't think the relaxation was required medically, I'd still think you deserve a morning in bed!"

Patting his stomach, he beamed at Sylvester.

Perhaps it's as well that he doesn't believe me, thought the younger lemming. *If he did, then I might have to tell him all the other things Keelhaul Levantes told me, and I'm not sure I want to do that. I'm not sure it'd be wise. Until I know a little more, I should keep it to myself, and maybe Viola. She deserves to know.*

"I s'pose I am a little tired after all," he muttered.

"Good night, Doctor Nettletree," said Sylvester as he rose from his uncomfortable bed and made his way to the door. "Thanks for everything you've done, and tried to do. It's just a shame death took him."

"You win some, you lose some," said the physician, spreading his paws. "It's that horrible fact every doctor has to face."

You win some, you lose some, thought Sylvester as he made his way home through the night. *Keelhaul Levantes lost one and it was one too many. Why do I get the impression that from here on I'd better win everything there is to win, or I'll go the same way as Levantes?*

MR. FOURFEATHERS

ews spread swiftly around the town about the mysterious visitor and his equally mysterious demise. In bars and eateries, huddles of people formed and dissolved as everyone wanted to exchange news and views about what had transpired. Of course, there wasn't any real news to share beyond the bare bones of what had happened, but that didn't stop anyone. The tale was embellished and further embellished, until a newcomer might have guessed that an army of ferocious weasels had arisen from the west and marched upon the land of the lemmings, only to be beaten back by a citizen militia led by the doughty Doctor Nettletree.

Luckily for Sylvester, no one could believe that somebody as unassuming as himself could have played any significant role in the proceedings, or even know very much about them, and so he was largely left alone by the gossip-mongers.

Naturally, it didn't suit Mayor Hairbell that the rumors should have placed Nettletree at the vanguard of the resistance rather than himself, and so he hastily convened a public meeting in the Town Hall to explain his side of the story. Sylvester went along because Viola had told him she was going to be there.

Just about everybody else in town was there, too. Looking around while they waited for Hairbell to appear on the dais at one end of the chamber, Sylvester became increasingly concerned by the uncertain faces he saw. If ever an army of weasels or any other form of life did attack, here was not a community geared to defy it. The lemmings seemed to have lost something, and for a while Sylvester couldn't put a mental finger on what it might be.

Then he had it.

What the lemmings had lost was their sense of identity. Once upon a time they'd had a strong feeling of community, of the ties that bound them together as citizens of the last great lemming stronghold in Sagaria. But things had changed since Hairbell had come to power as their mayor. Now the attitude seemed to be "every lemming for himself and the devil take the hindmost." Oh, to be sure, this mentality hadn't infected everyone. There were lemmings like Sylvester and Mom and Viola and old Doc Nettletree and even older Celadon who still abided by the old ways, but it had influenced enough people so that lemming society as a whole was weakened. The people of Foxglove could find themselves enfeebled and directionless should they encounter any serious adversary, or any powerfully threatening circumstance.

Sylvester shivered.

These were gloomy thoughts to be having when you were holding the paw of the girl you thought you might just possibly, however unlikely it seemed to be on the face of it, be in love with.

As if hearing his thoughts, Viola turned towards him, a quizzical look on her face. "Are you all—?" she began, then her voice was drowned out by the ballyhoo of Mayor Hairbell appearing on the stage.

Once the audience had quieted a bit, the portly mayor started to address them. He spoke for a long time about his own magnificent achievements as their mayor, and confessed humbly to being perhaps the greatest leader the lemmings of Sagaria had been lucky enough to know.

"The secret of a safe and happy Foxglove," he cried at one point, punching the air with a furry forepaw, "is a strong Foxglove. Foxglove *is* strong, thanks to my vision, and I intend to keep it that way."

There were a few weak cheers, evidently enough of them to convince Hairbell the audience was as enthusiastic as he was, because, licking his lips, he launched into yet another fervent paean of his mayoralty.

Sylvester tuned in and out of the oration. Looking around him, he could see most of the citizens were doing much the same.

He squeezed Viola's paw tighter, and was rewarded by her squeezing back.

"So," said Mayor Hairbell after the minutes had dragged on, "the purpose of this meeting is to reassure you all that you have nothing to worry about. Despite rumors to the contrary spread by our enemies, there *was* no army from beyond the Great Wet – just a single, solitary, criminal ferret, and even he came from nowhere more exotic than Ferretville. He was a con artist, my friends, a scumbag of the worst sort. The authorities in his hometown were close to arresting him, so he fled and arrived here in Foxglove, ready to play the same tricks all over again. But he had the, ah, misfortune to suffer a fatal accident here, no doubt after overindulgence in our excellent apple wine" – there was some tittering among the audience – "and even the best efforts of our revered Doctor Nettletree weren't enough to save him. Not that he merited saving, anyway. We're better off without him."

To one side of the stage stood a lemming of such antiquity and venerability as to make Sylvester's boss, Celadon, look like a street urchin: High Priest Spurge. Spurge nodded his sage agreement with this last comment of Hairbell's.

Funny, thought Sylvester, *how it's always those who tell you, "you're better off without so-and-so" that are usually the ones you're* actually *better off without. Only it's so infernally hard to get rid of them.*

"So go to your homes now," concluded Hairbell, "secure in the knowledge that my staff and I, not to mention our High Priest" – he cast a glance in the direction of Spurge – "have ascertained that everything is in safe paws and, er, that's that."

"What did you think of it all?" murmured Sylvester to Viola as they jostled with the throng of lemmings leaving Town Hall.

"Absolute twaddle," she replied cheerfully.

⚘ ⚘ ⚘ ⚘ ⚘

By the weekend, everyone seemed to have forgotten about the dramatic events – everyone except Sylvester, Viola and, Sylvester assumed, Doctor Nettletree. It was as if the people of Foxglove had decided that, if they told themselves there'd never been an intruder, reality would adjust itself until this became the truth.

Sylvester arrived early at the temple for the weekly act of worship and, as always, found himself a seat at the back where he could easily vanish into the shadow of a pillar. Mom, whom he'd, as always, walked here with, sniffed at him as she went up the aisle and very pointedly selected a chair right in the middle of the front row. She knew precisely why he'd chosen such an obscure place to be during the service or, at least, she thought she did. It had been quite a few years since Sylvester had stopped thinking it was hilariously funny to poke out his tongue at High Priest Spurge during the sermon.

Today, Sylvester was in a sour mood. He watched with even more distaste than usual the various slow rites of the ceremony. His thoughts became especially acidic when High Priest Spurge – a lemming who'd taken the art of looking unctuous to a whole new pinnacle – trod solemnly to the front of the altar, from where he usually delivered his sermons. As always, his text concerned the great spirit Lhaeminguas and the glory of being chosen to go on the Exodus.

Sylvester could barely contain his anger as he listened. Ever since childhood he'd known this was all – what was Viola's word? – twaddle. But now he really knew. He had *proof* and the authorities in Foxglove chose to sweep this proof under the carpet because it clashed inconveniently with the myths and legends they preferred to believe.

Or did they truly believe in the myths? Maybe they just used the myths as a way of keeping everyone in line. This was a notion that hadn't occurred to Sylvester before, and he tucked it away at the back of his mind for deeper contemplation later. For the moment he had enough to occupy him just keeping his wrath in check – and it was important that he did so, for Mayor Hairbell had a nasty habit of planting agents in the congregation who were alert for any signs of dissidence.

But the agents couldn't read his thoughts.

He hoped.

The Great Wet Without End does have an end. Levantes told me that, and he should have known because he'd just come from the far side of it. It's just a . . . just a very large lake is all it really is. So Lhaeminguas was talking through a hole in his hat about this. So, if he could talk through a hole in his hat about one thing – one such important thing, how many other holes in his hat was he talking through?

High Priest Spurge's droning eventually came to an end, and everyone shifted in their seats in relief. Just the concluding hymn and the responsorial benediction to go, and then the devout assembly could flee the temple and start tucking into a hefty lunch and copious amounts of apple wine.

The hymn was, Sylvester knew, one of Viola's favorites, and he imagined he could single out her voice among the hundreds of the congregation.

As the last note tapered off, High Priest Spurge advanced until he was almost nose to nose with the lemmings in the front row. Rearing up on his hind legs, he raised his forepaws high to either side of him. As he spoke each line, the congregration responded as one, obediently echoing his pronouncements.

We are mindless lemmings.
Like all those of virtue,
we have forsworn independent thought,
and have devoted our lives to the following glorious leaders,
as the spirits have commanded,
We thank the Great Lemming Spirit Lhaeminguas,
for having given us leaders so noble and honorable,
as High Priest Spurge and Mayor Hairbell,
who labor for us, and for our children, and for all here in Foxglove.
It is thanks to them and to the Great Lemming Spirit Lhaeminguas that we are such a prosperous and proud community, and so shall remain for ever and ever.
It is our duty,
never to question why,
never to search and spy,
never to try to pry,
or we shall incur the everlasting damnation of the spirits.
For so it is written.
Amen.

High Priest Spurge bowed his head, as if in humility, and this gave the signal to everyone else there that they could finally begin to head for the doors. Sylvester hung back a bit, appalled, as he was after every temple service, by what he had just witnessed. Although he'd mouthed the responses – for fear that one of Hairbell's agents might notice if his lips were still – he'd been unable to bring himself to actually speak any of them. Whether or not there were any great lemming spirits in the sky was something Sylvester didn't think he knew enough about to judge, although he thought it exceptionally unlikely. Even if there were, surely that had absolutely nothing to do with the nauseating adulation Spurge demanded the congregation express toward those spirits, toward the town's sleazy little mayor and even towards the High Priest himself. Yet, no one else in the temple seemed aware of this at all.

Maybe, like me, a lot of them were just mouthing the words, Sylvester told himself, but he didn't believe it.

He hadn't even been mouthing the real responses. Face lit by radiant piety, he'd been saying things like, *Spurge hasn't changed his underwear since this time last year.*

A childish game, only one rung up the ladder from sticking his tongue out at the High Priest from behind a pillar, but it gave Sylvester much satisfaction.

He'd hoped for a word with Viola, but she was swept off by her family. Sylvester's mother would spend the rest of the day here in the temple conducting her own private prayers for the husband she had lost. Sylvester was on his own for the afternoon.

Mom had left food out for him at home, but he wasn't really hungry. He decided to go for a long stroll in hopes the fresh air would blow his mind clear of the gloom that always filled it after he'd attended temple.

It was the perfect day for a stroll: blue sky with streaks of puffy white clouds. On an ordinary day, it would quickly have cheered him – especially once he'd cleared the edge of town and was walking between fields, with the sunshine on his face and the smell of lilac in his nose, but today was different.

What finally distracted his mind from its blank dejection was the discovery by the side of the road of a pair of quill feathers that he could see would make perfect pens. The library was always on the lookout for new quills.

Celadon will be pleased with me, Sylvester thought smugly as he tucked the feathers into his vest pocket.

A few paces further along the road he found another pair, and he added them to his pocket. The four formed a little fence along the top of his pocket that he imagined looked quite decorative.

As he was straightening up for the second time, a movement on the road ahead of him caught his eye.

Lemmings don't have the most acute vision. Sylvester had to squint against the sunlight as he struggled to make out what had attracted his attention.

Yes, there it was. Someone was coming toward him along the dusty road. Sylvester wasn't frightened, even after his experiences the other night down by the river. The world was, he knew, a dangerous place, but all the really dangerous bits seemed to be a long way from Foxglove. Round here the worst that was likely to happen to a young lemming was getting stung by a wasp or scalded by a kettle.

Even so, Sylvester was puzzled by the distant figure. This was someone far larger than a lemming but, even as the shape became more distinct as the figure came closer, Sylvester couldn't identify what type of animal it was. It looked like a fox, he decided, but foxes were reddish-brown and white, while this newcomer's furry coat was varying shades of gray.

Whatever the creature was, it was limping.

Sylvester walked forward more slowly than before, becoming a little nervous for the first time. He drew his breath, ready to call out a greeting to the oncoming stranger, but the stranger beat him to it.

"Ahoy there!"

The voice had a foxy rasp. This must be a fox after all, just an unusually colored one. Maybe he came from another part of Sagaria where foxes were gray rather than red.

"Me?" said Sylvester, glancing back over his shoulder and then pointing at his chest.

"Aye, aye, guv'ner," the fox answered. "I mean, 'Yes, sir.' There ain't no one else on this road but thee and me. And I'm not so sure about thee."

He laughed at his own weak joke.

"Have you hurt yourself?" said Sylvester, speeding up his stride toward the stranger.

"Hurt? Me?" said the fox. "Oh, the limp, you mean. It's nothing, not really. I just stuck me foot in a pothole and got me ankle twisted for me pains. 'For me pains,' get it?" Again, that high snickering laugh. "But it'll be fine in a couple of days once I give it some good resting, it will."

"Are you sure?"

"Sure I'm sure."

The fox was wearing simple farm clothes that were far too large for him, as if he'd borrowed them in an emergency from a much bigger friend. He'd had to jam his ears into his broad-rimmed straw hat to stop it from sliding around. His furry paws were studded with spiny burdocks. His slanted green eyes held a sadness that belied the forced cheeriness of his speech; those eyes seemed to have seen far too many things they'd rather not have seen.

Now that Sylvester was next to the fox he could smell the musty, moldy odor coming off the larger animal. Or maybe it was just the fox's clothes that smelled that way?

"Where am I, kind sir?" said the fox.

Sylvester gave a wan chuckle. "You're in the right place, if names are anything to go by," he said. "This is Foxglove."

"Ah, Foxglove. That's the home of the lemmings," said the fox, nodding his head wisely. "If I do not be mistaken, young fellow, you're a lemming yourself. And a fine specimen of the lemming stock, if it not be too forward of me to be making mention of that fact."

Despite himself, Sylvester felt his chest beginning to swell with pride. It had been a long time since anyone had called him a fine specimen of lemminghood. In fact, it might not ever have happened before.

"The home of the lemmings," he replied. "Indeed it is. Where are you heading, sir?"

"To the nearest town in this area."

"Well, you just reached it."

"I'd been a-guessing that, me friend. It's lucky for me that it should be so fine a burg as Foxglove, ain't it?"

Something bristled at the back of Sylvester's neck, as if in warning, but he ignored it.

"I'm sure the folk of Foxglove will be glad to welcome you, stranger," he said dutifully, "although" – he cast a doubtful eye over the fox's form – "I'm not sure we have any beds big enough for you to rest in." *Or doors big enough for you to get through,* he added silently. *But that's a problem you can face when you come to it.*

"I'm perfectly accustomed to resting myself on the good, soft ground," said the fox.

He suddenly lurched and grabbed Sylvester's shoulder.

"*Ouch!* Beggin' your pardon, young fellow, but it's this—" a long string of adjectives followed "—leg of mine. Musta hurt me dratted ankle worse'n I be having thought."

Sylvester felt his knees beginning to buckle under the larger animal's weight. "Sorry to hear that," he puffed.

"Still, it be only a trifle," said the fox, relaxing his grip a little. "Just a little bit o' a twisted ankle that be hardly being any tr—ouch! Ouch! Owowowouch!— any trouble at all. I didn't mean to be a-botherin' you with me trivial ailments, young Master Lemming. This sheer, stark, nerve-strangling agony is the merest bagatelle, I do be assuring you."

Again, Sylvester sensed that funny prickling of suspicion at the back of his neck. Again, he ignored it.

"Would you like to see a doctor?"

"Oh, I do be a-sure that's not being necessary. It's just a little—aargh! Ooya! Yikes!— twinge or two it be a-giving me, that's all."

"It sounds a lot worse than that."

"Well, maybe. This doctor of yourn, is he being a good one?"

"Doctor Nettletree is the finest doctor in the whole of Foxglove." *In fact, he's the* only *doctor in the whole of Foxglove, but there's no need to cloud the issue by telling this fellow that.*

"Then I s'pose I'll be a-takin' your advice, young Master Lemming," said the fox, still leaning heavily on Sylvester's shoulder. "Might I be imposing on your kindness enough to ask you to take me his way?"

"It'd be no trouble at all," lied Sylvester gallantly. "I was just out for a walk. I was planning to go by Doc Nettletree's cottage anyway."

The fox grinned, showing a lot of teeth. "Then you're a good person, you are."

They began making slow progress back towards Foxglove. The stranger's limp seemed to be getting worse. Sylvester did his best not to pant too loudly from the effort.

"What's your name?" he said as the main gate of the town came into view.

The fox hesitated a moment before answering. "Fourfeathers it is they call me, young fellow. Robin Fourfeathers, and yourself?"

"Sylvester Lemmington."

"A fine name, if ever I heard one."

"What brings you to these parts?"

"I'm looking for a friend of mine, the very best friend a fellow did ever have. We were sailing on the silvery sea when a wave came along and tipped our boat right over, it did. We swam our own two different ways to the shore, and I ain't not been able to catch up with him since. My bet is he's a-lookin' for me as hard as I be a-lookin' for him, and that's why we ain't found each other yet. Leastwise, that's the way it seems to me. Say, could you have been a-seein' of him?"

Immediately Sylvester thought of Levantes, but surely that couldn't be. He'd never heard of a fox and a ferret being friends. Usually the two species were at each other's throats.

"What does he look like?" said Sylvester, stalling for time to think this through.

"He's a ferret," said Fourfeathers, audibly wincing for the umpteenth time as he put his weight on his ankle. "Name of Levantes. Not perhaps the most prepossessing of fellows, he ain't, but—*yaarrooo!*"

The fox toppled sideways and fell into the ditch at the side of the road, clutching his leg and howling.

Sylvester had been just about to say that, yes, he'd met the fox's friend and to break the sorry news, but all thought of this fled from his mind as he gazed down at the writhing, squirming Fourfeathers.

"I could run and fetch Doc Nettletree," he said hesitantly.

The fox opened his eyes a slit. The green was blurred by tears of pain.

"I'll be able to walk again in just a moment, young Master Sylvester," he grunted. "This has happened before. It doesn't last long, I know."

It doesn't sound like any sprained ankle I've ever come across, thought Sylvester. *It's something different, something different . . . and worse.*

"How did you *truly* hurt your leg, Mr. Fourfeathers?" he said once the fox's breathing seemed to have become a little easier. "That isn't just an ankle you twisted when you put it in a rut in the road, is it?"

The fox's mouth made a jagged little line. "Not exactly, no. Here, help me be getting back to my feet again."

"What really happened?" said Sylvester a moment later, breathing heavily from the exertion of getting Fourfeathers back on to the road again.

"How far do we be from this doctor friend of yours?"

"Far enough for you to answer my question."

"Persistent little bugger, ain't thee?" The fox breathed out heavily through his nostrils, turning things over in his mind. "Well, all right then, I'll tell. I be being a mite reluctant about it because, well, of me innate modesty."

"Modesty?" Sylvester tried to keep the incredulity out of his voice.

"Yes. Many people do describe it as a-bein' my most endearing trait. Anyway, young Sylvester, I would ask you, once I be having told to you my story, just to carry on treating me the way you already are – not as anyone special. Not as a hero."

"I think I can guarantee that."

The fox seemed faintly miffed by the promptness of Sylvester's reply, but carried on nevertheless. "It cannot have been many miles from here—"

"Why're you lowering your voice like that?"

"To be creating a little atmosphere, youth."

"Oh."

"It cannot have been many miles from here that, ahead of me on the road, I espied . . . a cart."

Sylvester waited. This seemed a bit of an anticlimax.

The fox, once he'd allowed time for his first, portentous sentence to sink in, continued. "A cart was not being the whole of it. There were also, standing by the side of the road, a mother mole and her diminutive offspring."

"A mole? We don't often see them around here."

"Pray, do not be interrupting. There was being the mother mole, like *so*, and beside her the infant mole, just *so*." Fourfeathers tried to show the relative positioning with his front paws but, discovering that he'd have to unhook his arm from Sylvester's shoulder, abandoned the idea. "*Here*" – he bobbed his nose to indicate proximity – "you be having meself, Robin Fourfeathers, walking along in all innocence, minding me own business, in the direction of the molish duo, and *there*" – he squinted his eyes to give the impression of distance – "you be having the aforementioned cart speeding, *hurtling* even, toward the mole mother and the mole offspring, and not to mention, *moi*."

"'Moi'?"

"'Me,' lad. It be a manner of speaking."

"Ah."

"Now, you be a-knowin' about molish eyesight?"

"Yes."

"The lack thereof, I mean."

"Yes," said Sylvester. He wished Fourfeathers would get on with it. He wished Doctor Nettletree's cottage were a bit closer than it was. He wished quite a lot of things.

"I had a chilling premonition about what was going to happen."

"Yes?" said Sylvester, a bit of testiness creeping into his voice.

The fox seemed to notice this. His eyes narrowed. "Are you yessing me?"

"I don't know what that means."

The fox gave him a thoughtful sidelong look as they passed through the main gate of Foxglove. Sylvester noticed, although at that moment he did not register, that the sidelong glance just happened to turn Fourfeathers's face away from the lemming guard who was standing there, a ceremonial pitchfork firmly gripped in front of him. Sylvester gave the guard a wave of his free paw, and received a nod of admission in return. If the guard saw anything unusual about the sight of an obviously injured fox limping into the town he gave no sign of it.

"One thing I not be a-likin' of," explained Fourfeathers, seeming to relax a little, "and that be impertinence to strangers."

"I can assure you, my dear fellow, that I wasn't—"

"Least said, soonest mended."

"Good."

"Now, where was I?"

"You were having a premonition."

"Was I? Oh, yes. Premonitizing, I was. I thought to meself, I thought, *that pair of moles, they might well step out right a-front of that speeding cart*. So I sped me own step, I did."

"You did?"

"I just said so, didn't I? Anyway, the skies darkened. Clouds roiled. The birds hushed. The trees stilled. The air seemed to turn to ice."

"And?"

"Sure thing, the little mole, without looking one way or t'other – not that it'd a done him any good even if he had, moles being as blind as bats is – without looking one way or t'other he, or she, lets go of its mother's paw and runs straight out into the middle of the road, letting out a lightsome little cackle of sheer happiness at the joys of the world, as moles is prone to do."

Most of the moles Sylvester had encountered had such a gloomily suicidal bent as to make lemmings seem like laughing jackasses, but he decided to let it pass. Any more interruptions from him and Fourfeathers's story wouldn't be done by the time they got to Doc Nettletree's – not that Sylvester hadn't guessed the end of it anyway.

Or thought he had.

"I burst into a trot," continued Fourfeathers. "And from a trot into a run, then from a run into a veritable flat-out sprint. Me lungs fair a-burstin' out of me ears, I reached that young, rapscallion mole just in time to whip him out of the path of the trundlin' cart wheels and threw meself clear, with the little one over me shoulder. The spinning wheels missed me by no more'n the thickness of a claw, they did, and I was being fair a-winded as I landed on me tum on the 'ard, 'ard mud of the roadway edge.

"But at least the younker was safe. That was what I was being a-thinkin' as I sat up and dusted meself down as best I was able. It was all worth it, these little sufferings of mine."

The fox nodded to himself in a self-satisfied way. Sylvester didn't begrudge him the smugness. Fourfeathers really had been the hero he so obviously wanted Sylvester to say he was.

There was something missing from the story, Sylvester realized.

"Was it when you threw yourself clear of the wheels that you twisted your ankle?" he said.

If gray foxes could blush, Fourfeathers would have done so.

"Ah, not quite. No, not quite."

"Then what did happen?"

"Like I've been of a-tellin' thee, moles ain't no great shakes in the seeing department."

"They're almost blind," agreed Sylvester, "although they can see real well underground, they tell us."

"And this mother mole was no exception to the rule. All she could make out through the dim, fuzzy mists of her vision was that her spotty, little brat, wot had been right next to her but a moment before, was now bruised and battered on the far side of the road. What the great racket of creaking wheels and galloping hooves and cursing coachmen had been all about, she had no strong-founded opinion, having noticed nuttin of the cart going by. All she could be a-thinkin' of was that some great gallumpher – meaning me in case you's not been paying proper attention – had grabbed her horrible little progeny."

Fourfeathers took a deep breath, as if forcing himself to remember something he'd tried to banish into the black vaults of oblivion at the back of his mind.

"She advanced upon me, she did," he said. "Wrathfully."

"On the warpath, was she?" prompted Sylvester.

"On more than just the one warpath. She had a whole spaghetti junction of them." The fox's lips had gone white and his eyes rolled in their sockets. "She thought I was attackin' of her firstborn, she did, and there ain't no fury like a mother mole's when she be havin' her dander up."

"Yes, but your *leg*. How did you hurt it?"

"I'm getting there. Patience, youth."

"Ah, sorry, Mr. Fourfeathers."

"Picture the scene. Me a-lyin' there in the dust. The little mole a-bawlin' his guts out, and of course not a-tellin' his mommy that he was the one had been a blithering banana running out in the way of the cart like that. And Mamma Mole vengeful as a scorpion whose toe you trod on. She, she . . ."

It seemed Fourfeathers was at a loss for words to describe the full ghastliness of what happened to him next.

Sylvester glanced ahead of them down the quiet lane to which he'd been guiding their footsteps. Doctor Nettletree's snug little house was not far now.

"Tell me," he said. "You'll feel better once you've gotten it off your chest."

Fourfeathers heaved yet another enormous sigh. "I wouldn't be a-tellin' of just anyone, young fellow-me-lad," he replied. "But you've already earned yourself a place in me heart, you have, and I reckon I can trust thee. So, the next thing was—say, you won't be a-spreadin' of this all over town, will you?"

Sylvester assured him that it would be the strictest of secrets between them, and that he hoped the Great Lemming Spirit Lhaeminguas would strike him dead where he stood should he ever breathe a word of it to any other living soul (all the while resolving to tell Viola the best and juiciest details at the first possible opportunity).

"Well, what happened next," said Fourfeathers heavily, "was that Mamma Mole picked up me very own leg and started a-beatin' me over the head with it."

"She *what?*"

The fox nodded confirmation. "I ain't never seen it done afore," he added dolefully. "And I hopes, as sure as I be a-limpin' here, that I don't ever see it again. But that's exactly what she did."

Sylvester did his best not to giggle at the images cavorting across his mental gaze.

"That sounds, well, dreadful."

"It was, and the worst of it was, as I discovered when she'd swept off with her brat under her arm, the inconsiderate besom had sprained me ankle where she'd been a-grippin' it with what to belabor me, see?"

"I think I've got a frog in my throat."

"That all you can be a-sayin', young Master Sylvester, to this tale of tragedy?"

"Something in my eye too."

"Perhaps that be tears of sympathy?"

"Perhaps. Oh, look, we're at Doc Nettletree's house. Let's hope he's in."

❖ ❖ ❖ ❖

"Doctor Nettletree, I've got another patient for you," said Sylvester, pushing the door open.

"Well, you'll just have to wait," said Nurse O'Reilly, looking up from her magazine. "Doctor's doing surgery, and there's a queue."

She gestured around the waiting room where, sure enough, two or three other lemmings waited. There was old Mrs. Beesworth, holding the most enormous goiter in her paws in front of her. Billy Swampers had something in his paws too but it was less savory than any goiter: a brown paper bag that he seemed just to have finished using. Mrs. Perkins was there with an unidentifiable junior Perkins who'd managed to get his head stuck inside an item of porcelain usually found under people's beds. An item not normally mentioned in polite conversation.

"Oh," said Sylvester. "But this is an emergency, you see, and—"

"It's emergency surgery that Doctor's *in*," said Nurse O'Reilly harshly. "So don't give me none of your lip, Sylvester Lemmington, or I'll be telling your mother."

"Oh."

"And she'll give you what for, I can bet."

Sylvester distinctly heard her add, under her breath, "Little pipsqueak."

Doctor Nettletree had two nurses, a friendly one ("Too friendly, if you ask me," Sylvester's mother had once said darkly, but then had clammed up completely when Sylvester had tried to get her to explain what she meant), Nurse Gillespie, and a bullying martinet, Nurse O'Reilly. It was just Sylvester's rotten luck that today was a day when Nurse O'Reilly was on duty.

Still . . .

He gestured behind him, and Fourfeathers obediently filled the doorway. More than filled it.

The fox stooped to put his head through the doorway. He gave Nurse O'Reilly a gallant, brave but desperately suffering grin that had a remarkable number of teeth in it.

"But some emergencies," said the nurse, trying desperately to retain her cool as she floundered toward the door to Doctor Nettletree's consulting room, "are more urgent than others."

Mrs. Beesworth stared at Sylvester as if she'd like to strangle him with her goiter. She'd obviously been waiting quite a while. For a moment Sylvester felt guilty, but only for a moment. If Fourfeathers had been just another lemming, or at least lemming-sized, Sylvester would have been happy for the pair of them to sit in the waiting room for as long as need be, but the fox was far too big for that to be a sensible option. Doc Nettletree was going to have to tend to him outside.

The unidentifiable junior Perkins made an equally unidentifiable echoing sound from within the porcelain container. Sylvester guessed it was probably a protest, but chose not to inquire.

"Great Spirit above," exclaimed Doctor Nettletree, emerging from his consulting room with Nurse O'Reilly fluttering behind him. "A fox. I'll be damned and double-damned!"

"Doctor!" cried Mrs. Perkins, gesturing toward the anonymous occupant of the chamber utensil beside her . "There are children present!"

"Yes. Of course, m'dear. Terribly sorry, I'm sure. Probably scarred the innocent little mite for life."

"I think," said Sylvester tentatively, "it might be best, Doctor, if you examined my friend in the open air?"

Doctor Nettletree rubbed his chin. "You may be right. Nurse O'Reilly? Fetch me my—oh, where has the dratted woman gone?"

"She's fainted," said Mrs. Perkins.

"Fainted?"

"She took another look at the monster and went over like a ninepin."

How typical of bullies, thought Sylvester. *All bluster and bravado when there's no danger to them and other people are taking the risks, but as soon as there's the slightest chance that they themselves might have to—*

His thoughts were cut short by Doctor Nettletree. "Remind me to fire her one day. Well, Sylvester Lemmington, if I haven't got one of my regular nurses to assist me, I suppose you'd better do your best to fit the bill."

Sylvester felt his head begin to swim. Visions of cutting open raw flesh and handling squishy intestines swarmed through his mind. For a moment he wished he could join Nurse O'Reilly stretched out on the floor.

"There'll be none of that, lad," said the doctor, as if he realised what Sylvester was imagining. "You say he's got a gammy leg, that's all?"

"That be being the extent of my suffering, yessir," confirmed Fourfeathers. He tried to demonstrate his limp while still standing in the same place.

"Then with luck there shouldn't be any dicing and slicing involved at all," said Doctor Nettletree. "Unless we have to amputate, of course. I say, are you all right, young Sylvester? You're looking a bit green."

"I'm fine," lied Sylvester.

"Then let's get to it, shall we?"

There was a neatly trimmed patch of lawn at the back of Doctor Nettletree's cottage, and that seemed the best place for him to conduct his examination of the injured fox. With his arms around the shoulders of Sylvester and Doctor Nettletree, Fourfeathers limped valiantly around the side of the building. Once they reached the lawn, he let go of his supporters and sprawled on his back on the grass.

"Do thy worst, sawbones."

"Right then," said Doctor Nettletree, putting down the bulging, clanking leather bag he'd brought with him. "Let's take a look, shall we? How did you do this to yourself?"

Sylvester answered for the fox. "He was quite a hero, actually. He saved a mole-child from being run over by a cart, but managed to get hurt himself."

"Really?" murmured Doctor Nettletree, kneeling down beside the flank of the much larger creature. Fourfeathers's stomach rose and fell rapidly as he breathed. Clearly the fox, for all his earlier bravado, was terrified of doctors. "Where did this happen?"

"A few miles out of town," said Sylvester.

"And he limped the rest of the way?"

"Until I met him, yes. I was able to help him after that."

"He was lucky."

Sylvester responded with a blush.

"Well," continued Doctor Nettletree, kneading the fox's outthrown leg as he spoke, "I don't think he has too much to worry about. I can't find any damage to the tendons or the bone. There's just a little strain to the muscle down here," he prodded a finger firmly into Fourfeathers's ankle, and the fox let out a high yip of pain which Doctor Nettletree ignored, "and it's making it difficult for him to walk. Other than that he's got a clean bill of health, at least so far as his leg's concerned. A few days' rest should see him right as rain again."

"Pleased to hear thee a-sayin' that, Docko," said Fourfeathers, still lying on his back and staring at the blue sky far above.

Doctor Nettletree winced. "Please don't call me Docko."

"'Pologies, I'm sure."

"Accepted."

"It's good I'll not be out of sorts for too long, because I'm a fox of many concerns, see, and there's pressing matters that insist I not be a-stayin' here in your lovely burg of Foxglove for too long."

"What does bring you here, Mister . . .?"

"Fivefeathers. Robin Fivefeathers."

"Huh?" said Sylvester.

The gray fox darted him a startled look. "Math was never me strong point," he muttered. "Fourfeathers, I mean to say," he told the doctor. "Like I told young Master Lemmington here, I be a-comin' to try to find my good friend, Levantes, a prince among ferrets, what I lost when—"

"I've seen Levantes," said Doctor Nettletree somberly.

"You have?" Robin Fourfeathers propped himself up on his elbows.

"Yes, and so has young Sylvester here."

Fourfeathers swiveled his head to stare accusingly at Sylvester. "Why didn't you be a-tellin' of—"

"I started to, but then—"

"Then what?"

"You fell in a ditch."

"Fell in a—oh." The fox began to laugh. "You're right. I did, didden I?" He reached over to slap Sylvester dizzyingly on the back. "My mistake, forgive the impatience. I been a-lookin' for that ba—for my old pal, Levantes, for many a long day, and it be natural that—"

"Quite," said Doctor Nettletree. "You fail to understand one thing, however, my good man."

"And that a-bein'?"

Doc Nettletree said it flat out. "He's dead."

"*Dead?*"

"As a doorn—er, I'm afraid so."

For the first time since Sylvester had met him, the fox seemed genuinely agitated. Not even the obvious pain he'd been in when he'd tumbled into the ditch had thrown him as off-kilter as this. Doctor Nettletree's announcement apparently came as a complete shock to him.

"When?"

Doctor Nettletree waved his hand vaguely. "Two, three nights ago, here in this clinic. He'd been very badly wounded, and—"

"No chance you could be wrong?"

"No. Not unless he was lying to us about who he was. He was a ferret, and he told us his name was Levantes. Of course, there could be two ferrets cal—"

Fourfeathers dismissed the suggestion with a snort and an angry gesture. He was sitting up fully now, which meant he was about as tall as Doctor Nettletree. "And he was really, *really* dead?"

"Absolutely. No chance of a miracle recovery, or whatever you might be thinking of."

"Doctor Nettletree's an excellent doctor," put in Sylvester. "He wouldn't be wrong about something like this."

The fox's eyes narrowed. "Wounded, you say?"

Between them Sylvester and Doctor Nettletree told him the story of how the ferret had been brought to shore and had later expired.

Fourfeathers turned his gaze inquisitorially toward the young lemming. "He tell you anything he shouldn't have?"

"I don't know what you mean by 'shouldn't have.'"

"Secrets."

"We didn't have very long to speak at all."

"Long enough."

That prickle of suspicion at the back of Sylvester's neck started up again. How could he tell how much of what Levantes had told him was supposed to be kept a secret from anyone who came inquiring afterward? The answer was that he couldn't, but he could err on the side of caution when it came to recounting the conversation he'd had with the dying stranger.

"He told me that the Great Wet Without End doesn't go on forever, the way we lemmings have always thought it did, but that there's a far shore, and it was there that he'd come from. He may have told me other things but if he did I've long forgotten them." Sylvester shook his head, pretending to be rueful. "And that's if I was able to hear anything at all. I couldn't think of anything other than the news about the Great Wet. It's the biggest news to reach Foxglove since . . . since . . ." He looked around him for inspiration. "Since I don't know when!"

The fox gave a bitter chuckle. "All right, all right, I believe you." He shook his big gray head. "'Sides, me old pal, Levantes, be having been too cautious a fellow to go a-blabbin' his heart out to any Tom, Dick or Sylvester he chanced across, I'll be a-warrantin'."

He glanced up at Doctor Nettletree, who was showing all the signs of anxiousness to get back to his other patients.

"Would you do me a favor, Docko—er, Doc I mean, a-beggin' your parding. Would you let me see the body of me ol' sea buddy, Levantes, so that that I might be a-biddin' him a tearful farewell one last, tragic time?"

"I don't see why not. He's still in the cool-room at the side of the cottage waiting for someone to bury him."

"And who would that someone be?"

"The town authorities, of course," replied Doctor Nettletree, drawing himself up. "We're not one of those barbaric communities who throw the cost of burial onto the grieving survivors at a time when they can least afford it. But Mayor Hairbell has been so busy of late that he's not yet found the time to drop by and sign the necessary documentation."

"Then let me see him," said the fox.

Using Sylvester's arm for leverage, Fourfeathers managed to get himself to his feet. Once again, squinting up at the fox's face against the brightness of the sky, Sylvester was reminded of how much larger the newcomer was than any lemming.

How much larger, and how much better equipped for a fight.

Sylvester decided not to enter Doctor Nettletree's little morgue alongside the doctor and Fourfeathers. Levantes hadn't exactly been a friend, and they hadn't really talked together long enough for Sylvester to even count him as an acquaintance. Nevertheless, the prospect of seeing the ferret laid out cold and dead made something go *kerflop* in Sylvester's stomach. Instead, he leaned against the fence at the bottom of Doctor Nettletree's front garden and watched as a pair of bright yellow butterflies danced their courtship dance. Sylvester wondered if he ought to learn to dance like that for Viola.

A cry of distress from the cool-room made him turn to look.

"Oh, cruel, cruel world!" cried the fox.

Moments later, Fourfeathers burst into the open weeping histrionically, and threw himself down on the little patch of grass at the center of the doctor's front garden. It was only just big enough to hold his outstretched form. As he pummeled his fists in woe he was crushing Doctor Nettletree's prize petunias flat.

More slowly, Doctor Nettletree followed him out through the door, looking worried. He pulled Sylvester aside, not that there was much aside to be pulled to with the garden almost filled by the sprawled and writhing fox.

"Sylvester," muttered the doctor, "something funny happened in there."

"Funny?"

"Funny as in peculiar. Not enough for me to call the constables or anything like that, but . . . Look, Sylvester, just how well do you know this friend of yours?"

"I told you, Doctor Nettletree. I just met him on the road an hour ago, maybe less."

"So he could be anyone?"

"All I know about him is what he's told me."

"He could be lying?"

Sylvester remembered the occasional little tickle of suspicion that had disturbed the hairs at the back of his neck.

"I suppose so," he said reluctantly. He didn't like thinking ill of people. Yet it was true, for all he actually knew, Robin Fourfeathers could be the vilest cutthroat in the whole of Sagaria.

Doctor Nettletree let a few meaningful seconds pass.

"Keep a very careful eye on him, if you'd be so good," he said at last.

"Why do you say that?"

The doctor gestured behind him toward the cool-room. "When I first showed him the body of the ferret he was like any other grieving friend, but *more so*, if you know what I mean. There were too many tears, I thought. Still, who am I to be a judge of these things? Some people are just more demonstrative than others, you know. I simply thought the fox was what we call in the medical biz a, ahem, 'weeper.' I pretended to look out the window and let him get on with it.

"When I turned around to see how he was getting on he was, well, he was running his paws up and down the body like he was searching for something. Checking the pockets, the whole routine. He was still sobbing loudly like a bereaved friend, mind you, but it was as if his arms belonged to a different person than the rest of him. I 'stinctly heard him muttering, 'Where is it? Where in tarnation *is* the thing?' So then I said to him, 'Mr. Fourfeathers, are you all right?' And he stepped back from the remains of his supposed friend, looking quite calm, and said he was all right. Then he burst into buckets again and came running out here."

"Making a stage entrance," said Sylvester. "For my benefit."

"That was what it looked like to me, yes," said Doctor Nettletree. "Someone overacting their role."

"Thanks for telling me this."

"The least I could do. As I say, keep a wary eye on him, will you?"

"I'll do my best."

"There should be a spare room for him at the Snowbanks Inn where he can get a couple of days' bed rest. Then, with luck, he'll be on his way and leaving Foxglove far behind him. I'll be a happier lemming when that happens. If he doesn't have any money for the room, tell that old crook Artie Snowbanks I'll settle his bill so long as he doesn't try to gouge me like he did the last time."

Sylvester couldn't imagine delivering this message to Mr. Snowbanks word for word, but he promised to convey its meaning.

"And drop in to see him from time to time, Sylvester," continued the doctor. "I'll do the same. All in the guise of being solicitous about his good health, of course."

"But really to make sure he's up to no mischief," murmured Sylvester, looking askance at the prone form of the stranger. Not for the first time he wished he'd decided to do something else after temple other than go for a stroll. Then Robin Fourfeathers would have been someone else's problem.

"You take my point exactly," said Doctor Nettletree. "Why are people always so insistent that the young are irremediably stupid?"

Because they're stupid themselves, thought Sylvester, but said nothing.

Doctor Nettletree crouched beside Fourfeathers and jabbed his shoulder. "Are you all right?"

The gray fox dredged up one last long, low, racking moan and then pulled himself up on all fours. The expression of tormented grief seemed to drain from his face as he did so.

"I'll survive," he admitted.

"Glad to hear it," said Doctor Nettletree, unimpressed. "Your young friend Sylvester here is going to escort you to the Snowbanks Inn in town, where I want you to spend the next two days in bed. That should be enough time to allow that leg of yours to heal. Before you go, I'll have Nurse O'Reilly, assuming the damned silly woman has recovered from that swoon of hers, prepare a tincture for you which I want you to apply three times a day after meals. There'll be instructions on the bottle. Perhaps you would like a sedative in case you have difficulty sleeping, what with all the memories you'll be having of your deceased friend."

Behind Fourfeathers's back, Doctor Nettletree gave Sylvester a wink, the meaning of which the young lemming for a moment couldn't decipher. Then he guessed it. The sedative wasn't to prevent against bad dreams or sleeplessness. It was to knock the stranger out at night so that Sylvester and Doctor Nettletree could rest secure in their own beds, knowing the fox wasn't out and about and up to mischief.

"That be being very kind of you, Mister Doctor Nettletree," said the fox unctuously as he stood up to his full height.

A few minutes later Sylvester and Fourfeathers were back on the road.

"I'm so sorry about your friend, Mr. Fourfeathers," said Sylvester to fill up a silence that had been growing between them as they walked. The fox's leg seemed to have improved remarkably already, thanks to Doctor Nettletree's ministrations. He was able to walk largely unaided, a great blessing so far as Sylvester was concerned. His shoulders still ached from the burden they'd been forced to bear earlier.

"Alas, poor Levantes," said Fourfeathers.

"I didn't know him well, but—"

"Did any of us?" interrupted Fourfeathers dolefully.

"Did any of us what?"

"Know him well."

"I assumed *you* did."

"I'd have said so before today, him having been me billy-cuddy shipmate and closest pal for many a long year, but now . . . now I'm forced to be asking of meself if perhaps all I saw was the face he was a-bein' prepared of to show the world. If mebbe he . . ."

Sylvester tuned it out. Back at Doctor Nettletree's house he'd begun to suspect that all of Fourfeathers's ostentatious sorrowing was just a sham, and he was becoming more and more convinced of it with every pace they took. He'd rather spend the time thinking about Viola, so that was exactly what he did.

He waited until he sensed the fox's stream of words had run dry before yanking himself back to the real world. Viola blew him a last kiss saucily over her shoulder before, with a wink of her eye, she evaporated like steam.

"I knew him only for a short while . . ." Sylvester began.

"Yes, and I been a-meanin' to ask thee about that, my little sporran of a lemming. Like I said back at the sawbones', did me dear, dear, *dear* old chum, Levantes, tell you any secrets before death snuffed out the candle of his soul for the very final time?"

"Secrets?"

"Yes. Con-fid-ensh-ial-it-i-ays."

Caution, Sylvester reminded himself. *You already know this fellow's not as straightforward as he seems. Levantes was very emphatic that you should be careful to whom you blabbed.*

"What sort of secrets would they be?" he said innocently. "Stuff about the loves of his life, you mean?"

The fox growled, but the expression of anger that crossed his face was gone almost before it had arrived. "No, lad. It be more to being do with an object he mighta had with him."

"An object? What sort of object?"

"You be better off not a-knowin'." Fourfeathers put a big arm around Sylvester's shoulders again. "Suffice it to be saying that, when a great wave threw me dear boon companion, Levantes, off the little ship we were both a-sailin' in, he was a-holdin' in his darling little paw something that was mighty important to yours truly, swelp me . . . swelp me, Lhaeminguas. It's something I'd been a-searchin' for for many a long year, and a-somethin' I'd be almighty glad to be having back." He lowered his brows and looked around him as if the cottages they were passing might be full of spies. "'Less, of course," he added, "it's gone to the bottom of the deep, blue briny."

Sylvester became uncomfortably aware that in the nethermost depths of his right-hand jacket pocket there was a crumpled piece of parchment. The ferret, Keelhaul Levantes, had stuffed it in there that night down at the river, but with all that had happened immediately afterward Sylvester had forgotten its existence until now. What on Sagaria could it be? The almost uncontrollable urge came over him to drag the scrap of paper out right in front of the gray fox to find out.

"Levantes didn't tell me anything about that," he said, hoping that for once it wouldn't be obvious he was lying.

"You didn't see him be a-hidin' anything?" The fox's tone was becoming inquisitorial, and at the same time losing some of its accent. "Perhaps digging a hole and stuffing a-somethin' into it?"

"No, I don't remember anything like that at all." It was a relief to be telling the truth again. Sylvester didn't like lying. It wasn't just that he was lousy at it. It was that it went against the grain, however honorable the motive for the deception.

The fox stopped dead in his tracks, and automatically Sylvester stopped along with him. For a long moment Fourfeathers held Sylvester's gaze. At last, he appeared satisfied by whatever he thought he could read behind the lemming's eyes, and resumed walking. His limp, Sylvester noticed, was almost gone now.

"I wish I could tell where this . . . this *thing* is." The fox seemed to be talking as much to himself as to Sylvester. "There's another after it, you see. Someone who'd kill to get it – kill without nary a second thought. A terrible fellow he is. It's of crucial significance that he not be a-gettin' his greedy paws on it. You understand me, young Master Lemmington?"

Sylvester shivered. "I think I do, yes."

"Well, don't just think it, make sure. You been good to me, and I'd not like to see any harm befalling you. And if perchance you haps to remember a-somethin' after all that dear Levantes might have been concealing, don't trust *anyone* with the news – not no one but me, and even when I'm no longer here in Foxglove, not no one at all. You be a-hearing that?"

"I be a-hearing that," Sylvester confirmed, feeling a sense of *déjà vu*.

The fox grinned suddenly. "You be a-mocking of me, young shaver."

Sylvester put his forepaws up in front of him. "No, not at all. I assure you. It's just that your way of speaking, it's, well, it's a bit infectious, that's all."

"Nivver thee mind." Fourfeathers gave a barking laugh. His tone changed yet again as he continued to speak, becoming both superficially lighthearted and yet confiding, like Sylvester's mother when she was pretending she didn't *really* want to know how things were going between Sylvester and Viola.

"Do you have a special friend?" the fox asked.

Sylvester was flustered by the abrupt change in subject. "I, ah . . ."

"I suppose you still be being of an age when you live with your parents, is that not so?"

"Well, ah, yes. Not with parents, though. Just with my mother."

Sylvester told the story of how his father had gone away on an Exodus to the Great Wet Without End and had never been seen again.

As Sylvester spoke, a tear trickled down the fox's cheek and he sniffled loudly, "Ah, that be being sad, so sad."

It was obvious, even to Sylvester, that the display was false but nonetheless, without really intending to, Sylvester told the fox about his mother. About how she was widely regarded as the prettiest widow in the town and how it was a nuisance for her that Mayor Hairbell seemed to have set his sights on her. Yet there were other times when it seemed as if the mayor was simply putting on a show of yearning after the pretty widow, when his fancy turned instead in the direction of someone far younger than himself.

"Viola, you say?" interrupted the fox.

Again, Sylvester was flustered. "Yes, that's right. Viola Pickleberry."

"I can tell by the way you've just tripped over your two hind legs, Master Lemmington, that you don't approve of this potential match?"

"Indeed I don't." Sylvester's cheeks were hot.

The fox gave a soft, sympathetic chuckle. "Partic'larly because this Viola Pickleberry – well, you be a-havin' got your own heart set on her, am I right?"

Sylvester stared angrily at the ground in front of him. He hadn't actually tripped over his own hind—oops, he'd just gone and done it again.

"She and I are very good friends."

"An item, the pair of you?"

"An, er, item. Yes."

"Little loveybirds?"

"We're almost at the inn."

"You'd trust this Viola Pickleberry with your life, wouldn't you?"

"Of course, I would!"

"I can tell you're a remarkable judge of character, young fellow," said the fox, beginning to sound more earnest again. "It's a trait'll stand you in good stead later on in life. Even so" – Fourfeathers tapped the side of his own nose – "take a warning from me. However much you trust your darlin' Viola, don't trust even *her* with anything you be a-rememberin' about your time on the riverbank with me pal, Levantes."

Sylvester swallowed. The idea of not trusting Viola with even one of his deepest secrets . . . Well, okay, he hadn't as yet mentioned to her the little cache of racily illustrated scrolls he'd discovered on a secluded shelf at the Library, but—

"Not even her," the fox repeated, underscoring his point by patting Sylvester's shoulder firmly with each syllable. "You'd be a-puttin' her in danger if she knew. Him who's also looking for that object of mine – he'd have nary a second thought about torturing the truth out of her if he thought she possessed it!"

But then, thought Sylvester perplexedly, *it's surely better if she* does *know, because she can tell him all about it at once, before he's properly got started with the torturing. If she doesn't know, the torture could go on forever, until she's, until she's—*

The fox's voice intruded into his misery. "Be a-believin' of me, Master Sylvester Lemmington. I do be a-knowin' what I be a-talkin' about."

Then they were at the Snowbanks Inn.

🌢 🌢 🌢 🌢 🌢

Fourfeathers was welcomed by the innkeeper, the fussy, gossiping Artie Snowbanks. "Oh, my, my, my, what a rare delight to have a fox amongst us! It doesn't happen very often, let me tell you, but we have different suites always made up and ready for whichever kind of creature should happen by. There is a badger and a mole room in the basement and then for foxes, a room (I'm sure you'll find it nice and comfy) on the ground floor, while upstairs—oh, and Mr. Fourfeathers, we have a visiting coach party of duckling majorettes and I must ask you on your honor not to pester them. And . . ."

Sylvester left him with a promise to return later in the evening, perhaps accompanied by Viola.

Remembering Doctor Nettletree's charge, Sylvester would certainly be back after he'd had his supper and told his mother what was going on, but he'd most definitely not be bringing Viola. He had the sense that Fourfeathers spelled danger to anyone who came into contact with him.

As he walked home, Sylvester had that creepy feeling once more that someone – someone who always kept just out of sight, but whose presence could be detected as the faintest of blurs at the very corner of Sylvester's eye – someone was watching him.

He quickened his pace.

FUGITIVE CARTOGRAPHY

By the time Sylvester get home that night he was feeling distinctly ... muzzy. Luckily, Mom had gone to bed some while earlier, so she couldn't witness him fumbling three times before he could find the knob on the cottage's front door to open it. Fourfeathers had proved to be excellent company for the evening, regaling the regulars of the Snowbanks Inn with a seemingly endless string of anecdotes and jokes, most of them satisfactorily off-color, and also a seemingly endless supply of drinks. It had crossed Sylvester's mind more than once that people who were as generous as this usually didn't plan on settling their bills, but he'd shoved that thought aside. It was something for Snowbanks to deal with, not him – Snowbanks and possibly, he thought with a twinge of guilt, Doc Nettletree.

Dropping as few crocks and utensils in the kitchen as possible, Sylvester made himself drink several cupfuls of water before stumbling upstairs to his bedroom. Jumbled head or no jumbled head, he was determined that, before he stretched himself out on his bed and tried to stop the world spinning, he was going to take a quick look at that document Levantes had stuffed into his pocket.

Lighting a candle took an inordinate amount of time because of the danger of setting the entire cottage on fire, but the moonlight streaming in through his bedroom window was a help.

At last, sitting on the end of his bed, Sylvester pushed his spectacles firmly onto his nose and dug to the very bottom of his coat pocket, where he found the squashed paper.

Immediately, he could see it was incomplete. The edges were torn, and the sheet of paper, once he'd roughly flattened it out, had the shape of an irregular triangle. The portion he had was covered in numbers, incomprehensible symbols, and what looked like random squiggles. Holding it as steadily as possible under the circumstances, Sylvester peered at it in the silvery gleam of the moon and the flickering candlelight. In the bottom left-hand corner was a cluster of dozens of irregular shapes, one of the larger of which had a big, bold "X" marked next to it.

In the bottom left-hand corner there was an untidy signature. It took Sylvester several minutes to decipher the tangled handwriting:

Captain Josiah Adamite

"What in the world is this all about?" he said, not realizing until he heard the words that he'd spoken them out loud. He glanced nervously over his shoulder at his bedroom door, as if someone might be listening there, but the house was silent except for the distant, soft sound of his mother's snoring.

Levantes was willing to die for this, Sylvester thought. *And he may not have been the only one who's lost his life over it. It's obviously of the greatest possible importance, and yet I haven't the first idea what it could possibly be.*

There was no sense in continuing to tussle with the problem, not with his mind refusing to focus. Even had it not been for the numerous tankards of apple wine he'd drained (and he had a vague memory of there having been a few shots of artichoke brandy mixed in there somewhere as well) he was exhausted. It was long after his normal bedtime, and the sooner he got some shuteye the better.

Before he could allow himself to sleep, however, he had to hide the document somewhere safe. Somewhere where his mother wouldn't chance across it while she pottered around the house. Somewhere a burglar wouldn't think to look if Fourfeathers was right and that dreaded *other* person he'd warned about came to Foxglove in search of the paper.

Sylvester tried to place himself in the mind of a burglar, and found he couldn't do it. Lemmings weren't very possessive people. In Foxglove, if you wanted something that belonged to somebody else, the best way of getting it was usually just to ask them if you could have it. They'd tell you yes or no. It never occurred to anyone to argue with the decision. Theft was almost unknown among the lemmings, not because they were particularly virtuous, but simply because it was, for the most part, quite unnecessary.

In the end, he stuffed the crumpled document in the very bottom of his dirty socks and underwear basket. Any burglar would likely asphyxiate if he tried to burrow down that far. The Lemmingtons did their wash on a Tuesday, and today was still only Sunday – or (Sylvester glanced out through the window at the starry sky) make that more like Monday. Surely by Tuesday Sylvester would be able to think of a better, more permanent hiding place.

It was only as he stood up from the dirty-clothes basket, having come quite close to asphyxiation himself, that he realized he'd seen something odd when he glanced out at the sky.

Something that didn't quite jibe with the customarily placid nighttime Foxglove scene.

He was woozily prepared to write it off as just another side-effect of the apple wine, but some deeper instinct drew him back to the window.

Leaning on the sill, he surveyed the sleeping town. He might be the very last person in all of Foxglove to be falling into bed tonight.

There's nothing unusual out there. You were just seeing things.

Pink elephants, anyone?

Just as he turned gratefully away, he saw it again.

One of the stars was winking.

Except that it *wasn't* a star. You couldn't see any stars in that direction because the bulk of the temple blotted them out.

As Sylvester watched, the "star" winked back out of existence but then, a moment later, it blazed back into being again.

Stars didn't do that.

Even with a head in which a brass band was playing raucous dance music to the rhythm of apple wine, Sylvester knew that.

Wink! The "star" was gone again.

Someone on the temple roof was flashing a lamp.

But why would they do that?

Three times in quick succession the light blinked on and off, then there were two slower appearances, and then there was nothing but unbroken darkness until Sylvester shook himself out of the stupor he'd fallen into and pushed himself away from the window.

As he pulled the bedcovers up to his ears, he didn't know which he found more puzzling, the mysterious document Levantes had forced on him with its funny little squiggly lines and its arcane symbols, or the flashing light he'd seen on the gloomy temple roof. In fact, there may have even been more than one light now that he thought about it. Maybe it was just the candle flame burning an after-image onto his eyes or the apple wine playing tricks with his mind, but he thought he perhaps saw a fainter light floating somewhere far away out in the midst of the Great Wet. No, the light on the temple had been real enough, but not the other. No one would be adrift on the Great Wet.

Yet. Levantes had said he'd sailed there, and so did Fourfeathers.

Two mysteries to solve.

Both intractable.

Before he had the chance to choose between them, Sylvester fell asleep.

✧ ✧ ✧ ✧ ✧

When Sylvester woke up the following morning, all he could see out of his bedroom window was a gray blur.

That accursed apple wine, he thought, angry with himself for being inveigled by Fourfeathers into drinking so much of it, but then he realized his eyes were, surprisingly, functioning normally. It was the day that was out of focus. A carpet of heavy-looking clouds filled the sky, and from them fell a slow, steady, depressing drizzle of rain.

Sylvester stretched his limbs, then froze when he had the disconcerting sensation that if he stretched any further one of them might fall off.

The apple wine was exacting its toll after all.

Breakfast was a painful experience, as was the walk to the Library. In order to distract his own attention from how the world seemed to be *pulsing* at him in a red and angry way, he tried to think of other things.

Anything complicated was out of the question but—*oh, what are these sticking out the top of my pocket?*

He'd completely forgotten until now about the four quills he'd picked up not long before meeting Robin Fourf—

Robin *Fourfeathers!*

He recalled that the gray fox had hesitated just a moment before telling Sylvester his name.

The rascal must have seen the tops of the quills poking out of Sylvester's pocket, added the first bird's name that popped into his head, and . . .

Sylvester stopped in the middle of the road and swore.

Of course. Robin Fourfeathers. How could he have been so stupid?

At any other time, Sylvester would have known what to do – run to Doctor Nettletree, perhaps, to tell the physician what he'd just learned, or sprint instead to the Snowbanks Inn to confront the impostor – but the apple wine was making his thoughts sluggish.

Best to get to the Library as quickly as he could in his dilapidated state, then decide on the right course of action when he was feeling a bit readier to cope with the world. The fox couldn't do anything too disastrous that might endanger the good citizens of Foxglove in the next hour or two, could he?

Could he?

✧ ✧ ✧ ✧ ✧

Unfortunately, old Celadon was in the mood for conversation.

"I hope all the strange events of the past few days haven't upset you, young Sylvester."

Why do people call me "young" the whole time? Sylvester's mind painfully blasted at him. *Too loud, too loud! If only I could find a mental volume control.*

He mumbled something in response to the older lemming, hoping Celadon would go away and leave him alone to his misery.

No such luck.

"You remember what I told you the other day, Sylvester, about the dangers of unsound thinking?"

Sylvester nodded, then regretted the gesture. "You can be reassured. I'm no longer thinking unsoundly."

"I'm glad to hear it." The Archivist rested his paw on the edge of Sylvester's desk and gave a creaking sigh. "It must have been tempting for you to revert to unsound ways after the shock of that poor ferret dying and then the appearance of the fox."

"The two incidents didn't affect me like that at all."

"Good."

"Really."

"I believe you."

"Good."

Celadon seemed to be settling in for a nice, long heart-to-heart with his younger colleague.

"These things, young Sylvester, are sent to try us. They happen every now and then, even in the best-regulated communities, like Foxglove here, but fortunately they don't happen very often, if you know what I mean. And when they do" – the elderly lemming shrugged – "when they do, the only way to deal with them is just to see them out. Yes, the best we humble archivists can do under the circumstances is muddle on through and—"

Sylvester's patience evaporated.

"Muddle on through and *what?*" he cried.

Celadon took a nervous couple of paces backward. "Ah . . ."

"And *what?*" repeated Sylvester, hardly recognizing the sound of his own voice. "I sit here day after day translating scriptures by ancestors of ours who were either batty or senile or too self-righteous to see one single hairsbreadth beyond the ends of their whiskered noses. In order to give themselves some purpose in life, to make themselves seem important, they wrote down these" – with a dash of his paw he sent a pile of untranslated scrolls to all corners of the room – "these *myths.*"

He picked up a parchment at random and flourished it like a weapon. Celadon backed farther away. A look of consternation crossed the older lemming's face as he realized Sylvester was between himself and the door.

"Look at this nonsense," cried Sylvester, rising to his hind legs. "Some daft old dodderer tells us, like all the other daft old dodderers before him, that the Great Spirit Lhaeminguas Suicidalius ordains that at regular intervals swarms of lemmings should hurl themselves off the Mighty Enormous Cliff. After which Lhaeminguas himself will guide them to the mystical far shore of the Great Wet Without End – and only he has the ability to do this. It's *not true*, I tell you!"

"Perhaps I should call Doctor Nettletree," attempted the archivist, but Sylvester didn't hear him.

"I *know* it isn't true! To ask me to pretend otherwise is to ask me to live a lie. I've met not one but *two* people who've come here from the far side of the Great Wet. They did it without the aid of the Great Spirit Lhaeminguas, or any other spirit for that matter, great or small!"

"And look what happened to them, eh, boy?" Celadon protested. "One of them ended up dead and the other one found himself in the Snowbanks Inn, which is almost as—"

"To everyone else in the world, what we call the Great Wet Without End is just an ocean, a sea, and it's not without end at all. There's land on the other side of it, and you can get from there to here, or even from here to there, riding in something they call a boat or a ship. It's nothing magical, nothing miraculous, although from what I can gather it can sometimes be dangerous. To the rest of the world it's just a perfectly normal way of getting around. You want to go from A to B and there's an ocean in the way? Well, you just hop on a boat or a ship and you float across it."

"Perhaps this could be true but—"

"Of course it's true," Sylvester interrupted. "And I've spent all morning wondering if I'm not the first lemming to have discovered it's true – wondering if there've been lots of others before me. But instead of anyone admitting it, we've all got to pretend that this . . . venerable *hocus pocus*," he threw the scroll he'd been brandishing down on his desk and it bounced off onto the floor to join the others, "this holier-than-thou fable is somehow truer than the truth!"

Celadon made the mistake of trying to argue the point. "Well, in a way it is, dear boy. In a very deep and spiritual way it's true, you must see that."

"I do see, and that's the trouble. I see that for centuries lemmings have been deceiving each new generation with fairy tales about where we came from and how we should be, when the truth's been right there in front of us! Oh, sure, we don't know *everything*. We don't know the whole of the truth, and perhaps we never will. But we know enough of it to know that all the philosophical ramblings and supernatural speculations in these treasured old manuscripts are nonsense."

"They offer answers to the things we don't know."

"No, they don't. They don't offer any answers at all. All they do is make things up. Just because we don't know an answer doesn't mean we should believe the first fantasy some madman comes up with, does it?"

This time it was Celadon's turn to gesture at the jumble of scrolls on the floor. "If you don't know the truth about something, how can you be so positive the answers given by the prophets are wrong? Can you disprove them? If you're so clever, young Sylvester, what answers do you have that you can put in their place?"

"I don't have to make up explanations for things that aren't known. That's the whole point, don't you see? I can just say they're unknown and then do my best to find out the truth about them. I don't know what the moon's made out of, and perhaps no lemming ever will. Yet one of these wise old sages writes (with not the slightest sign of a smile on his face, let alone the fits of hysterical laughter any normal person would show) that the moon's made of ripe, green cheese! How does he know? He's never *been* there. Nobody's ever been there. He can't have met someone who'd been there and told him all about it. Maybe in the wider world there are scholars who've spent their lives studying the moon, and they can make a guess as to what it might be made of, but our wise lemming didn't bother to go and consult them before putting quill to parchment. No, he just had a bad dream one night. Perhaps he'd been eating too much of that ripe, green cheese. Then, the following morning he wrote down his fantasies about the moon as if they were genuine facts whispered directly into his hairy little ear by Lhaeminguas himself."

"How do you know they weren't?"

"Because there's not the slightest scrap of evidence that Lhaeminguas exists. He's just one of those answers people have made up to fill in the gaps of things they don't know."

Celadon gasped and groped around him for support. "You young *blasphemer*."

"Yes, I'm young. What of it?"

"Countless older and wiser heads than yours have thought about these things for years and years and they have found out the facts."

"Have what? Gone along with the fantasy because it suits them to do so?"

"They've seen the *truth*," said the older man hotly. "They've heard the holy voice of Lhaeminguas."

"They've heard their own voices, more like."

"How can you say that? Were you there?" Celadon looked triumphantly at him.

"No, of course I wasn't there. What a stupid question."

I'm crossing far too many bridges and burning them behind me, thought Sylvester in a brief moment of calmness. Then his raging thoughts picked him up again and carried him along with them.

"Then how," Celadon was saying, "can you prove they weren't indeed listening to Lhaeminguas?"

"Haven't you been listening? I can't prove the moon's not made of green cheese either, but that doesn't mean it is. There's a billion other things the moon could be made of, almost all of them more probable than ripe, green cheese. The burden of proof isn't on me to show it isn't; I'm quite happy to say I don't know what the moon's made of, and won't until someone goes there and digs up a chunk. The person who's got the proving to do is the one who makes the ridiculous claim!"

"What's that got to do with hearing the blessed voice of the Great Spirit Lhaeminguas?"

"If people start hearing voices, the simplest and most probable explanation is that the voice they hear is in their own mind. Isn't that the truth?"

Too late, Celadon saw where this was leading. "Well, in a way, I suppose that's—"

One of the Library's youngest apprentices, having heard the voices and wondering what could be going on, popped her nose round the door inquisitively. As one, Sylvester and Celadon turned toward her with glares of such torrid ferocity that she fled with a squeak.

"You do it. I do it," said Sylvester, dropping his voice to a more normal level. "We argue things out with our own inner voice. Should I do this, should I do that? Sometimes our inner voice tells us very firmly it's right we should do one thing rather than another. At times like this, we call it the voice of our conscience but we know full well the whole time that the voice we're hearing doesn't belong to someone else: a ghost or a spirit or a demon. It's our mind that's speaking to us, nothing stranger than that."

"But that's *different*."

"What do we call someone who thinks his inner voices are coming from somewhere else?"

"We, er, we . . ."

"Or, who's so filled with his own self-importance that he believes the musings of his inner voice should be imposed upon everyone else, that it should have the force of law?"

Celadon's eyes twitched this way and that as if looking for an escape route. "Well, naturally we'd say he was, well, not to put too fine a point upon it, we'd say he was . . . but that's different, I tell you."

"No, it's not different at all!"

"But—"

"We'd say he'd lost his mind, wouldn't we?"

"Are you saying the prophets were mad?"

"Why shouldn't I be?"

"Because they—"

"Not *all* of them. Some of them were just woefully ill-informed, and were doing their best to make sense of a mysterious world. How were they to know their dreams weren't communications from a spirit world? But some of the prophets, yes. If they were alive today we'd all agree they were as mad as hatters and needed some of Doc Nettletree's strongest sedatives. All of us are mad if we listen to the ravings of crackpots and insist they're the truth without questioning them."

The words hung in the air between the two archivists.

"If you said these words in the town square you'd be jailed," said Celadon very quietly. "If you were lucky. More likely the good citizens of Foxglove would rise up and tear you limb from limb before anyone had a chance to jail you."

"That doesn't make it the truth." Sylvester looked down at the mess he'd made. Somehow, just at this moment, he didn't want to meet Celadon's gaze full on.

The older lemming took a cautious step toward him and patted him lightly on the chest. "You're right, it doesn't, but we have to live in the world as it is, not as we'd like it to be."

"I know. Forgive me. I just—"

"There's nothing to forgive. Once upon a time I'd have been saying those exact same words alongside you. When I was young."

"You would?"

Celadon chose to misunderstand. "Improbable as it might seem to you, Sylvester, I was young once as well."

"That wasn't what I—"

"Younger than you can imagine. Younger than almost any other lemming I can think of has ever been."

Despite himself, Sylvester smiled.

"When I was about the same age you are now, I questioned the scriptures too, just like you've begun to do."

"But you learned better?"

"Yes and no. I learned better than to do so out loud. In my heart of hearts, I still question them every day – and I'll be doing so even more after today."

"Why even more?"

"Because of what you've been saying."

"Me?"

"You've summed up all the reasons for disbelieving the ancient prophets far better than I ever managed to."

Then you didn't manage very well, thought Sylvester. *I was so angry and hung over I was just saying the first things that came into my head.*

"That's kind of you to say so, Celadon."

"Not kind at all." The Archivist chuckled. "It's *you* who're owed the debt of gratitude. Despite what you may have thought, your words were filling me with great joy. I've obviously trained you well. The time will come, Sylvester, when every lemming in all of broad Sagaria will speak as you have today, but that time is not yet, and I'm afraid it will not be in our lifetimes or our children's lifetimes ,or even the lifetimes of our children's children's children."

"Why shouldn't it be?"

"Because people would rather believe something that seems simple, even if it's rubbish."

Sylvester stood silent for a moment, thinking through the implications of Celadon's bald statement.

"But it *isn't* simple," he said at last. "Adding the notion of Lhaeminguas and all the other invisible spirits to the mix just makes things more complicated. Pretending the Great Wet doesn't have a far side isn't simple at all, because then you have to explain how it could possibly not have another side."

"No you don't. Have to explain it, I mean. Most people don't really want explanations. What they want is not to have to think about things. If someone gives them something they don't have to think about and calls it an explanation, they grab it with all four paws and their teeth as well. It really doesn't matter if the 'explanation' doesn't explain anything at all. It really doesn't matter if the 'explanation' is obvious nonsense. People will accept it as the truth – in fact, they'll start fights to insist it's the truth – because doing that is a whole lot easier than having to think."

"But thinking is fun," Sylvester said.

"You think so. Even I think so, though you might not believe it of this old stuffed shirt, but the vast majority of lemmings don't like it. Either they're too lazy or they're frightened of it, or both. And they hate anyone who reminds them of the fact. Which is why, even though I'm proud of you for what you've said this morning, you must be careful never to breathe a word of it outside these walls . . . and think twice before doing so even here in the Library. Be careful who you trust."

Be careful who I trust? Everybody's telling me that at the moment, thought Sylvester.

Out loud he said, "But what could anyone possibly do to me?"

"I've already told you, you could be jailed or lynched. Or there's another way you could be gotten out of the picture."

Celadon's voice dropped during the last few words, so that Sylvester had to lean toward him to hear what he was saying.

"You could be named to go on the Exodus."

"Huh?"

"In fact, you already have been. However—"

"I have?" This meant that at last he could have the opportunity to go searching for his lost father. "How do you know?"

"Because I've seen the list Mayor Hairbell posted on the temple wall."

"He has?" Sylvester looked around the room to check in case there was anything he needed to take with him or if he could just dash to the temple the way he was to see his name there for himself.

Celadon put a hand on his arm.

"I erased it," the old lemming said.

"You did *what*?"

"I made sure no one was looking, then I pulled up a corner of my shirt and dampened the cloth with spit and wiped your name off the list."

"But that's ... that's ..."

Sylvester didn't need to tell Celadon what it was. Everyone knew that tampering with the written proclamations posted at the temple was a serious crime. The punishment was excommunication from Foxglove, and hence from lemming society as a whole.

"I know," said the Archivist. "But it was worth the risk."

Once again Sylvester felt fury rising within him. His big opportunity – dashed before he'd even known it existed. What right did this elderly bookworm have to interfere with something as important as the Exodus. *Sylvester's* Exodus?

"Because if you go on the Exodus," Celadon continued, "you never come back. I told you, the authorities have a subtler way of making sure malcontents disappear from the scene and stay disappeared. It's called the Exodus."

The implications of what Celadon was telling him began to sink in. "You mean—?"

"Keep your voice down. I'm a criminal, remember? I don't want you shouting the details of my crime to all and sundry."

"I'm sorry."

"We're all told to believe, and most of us do, that the leap over the Mighty Enormous Cliff gives the lucky leaper a moment of true transcendence, an entry into another and completely wonderful realm, a realm of the spirit wherein – well, you know the rest of it. My own belief, although I keep the silence of the grave about it, is that the lucky leapers plummet like stones into the Great Wet – and that's if they're lucky, because drowning can take time and be painful – they smash on to the rocks of the shore. That's why they never come back."

"But that's just their physical bodies they're losing," said Sylvester. "Once they've made the leap of faith, they get new ones."

He didn't believe his own words, even as he said them. He was just repeating the teachings he'd heard so often at the temple. It was difficult to shake off the indoctrinations of his youth.

"That's not what you really think, is it?" said Celadon reprovingly, looking disappointed.

"No, of course it isn't. The words just came out like . . . but, you see, I've been waiting so long for this moment, for the chance to follow after Dad and this may be my greatest chance of finding out where he is or what happened to him."

"I remember your father well."

It was as if a bucket of cold water had been thrown over Sylvester. "You do?"

"Yes. Jasper Lemmington was a friend of mine. Not a close friend, but a friend nevertheless. What drew us together were the doubts we shared about the holy writings; sometimes we'd sit up until dawn talking about them, analyzing them. What made us different, on the other hand, was that Jasper believed in voicing his skepticism out loud, however hard your lovely young mother tried to hush him, whereas I tended to keep mine hidden away. He hadn't been very long asking his inconvenient questions when, by an astonishing coincidence, his name appeared on the list for the next Exodus. Your mother and I guessed what had happened, and did our best to persuade him to slope off in the dead of night to hide himself in the forest – anything to avoid the Exodus, but Jasper was adamant. Even though he must have been as aware as we were of what was going on, he was determined to take the leap from the Mighty Enormous Cliff in the hope of finding out if there was any truth at all lying out there."

"They killed him," said Sylvester heavily. "By sending him on the Exodus, they killed him."

Celadon turned the pads of his forepaws upwards. "Who's to say? Perhaps he's still alive."

"You don't think so, do you?"

"No." The older lemming bowed his head. "No, Sylvester. I'm sorry, I don't."

There was a long silence. Sylvester stared at his clenched paws, resting on the desk, through a red haze of angry tears.

Eventually he was able to force out some words. "Who was involved?"

"It was a long time ago."

"I don't care how long ago it was. I just want to know."

Celadon sighed. "The High Priest at the time was our present Sardonicus Spurge, although he obviously looked younger and was actually more carefree then. The Mayor was our very own Broncolard Hairbell whose appearance actually hasn't changed much. I've always been convinced that it was those two who were behind the conspiracy to get rid of your father. Anyone else involved was just a catspaw."

"Who were the others?"

The Archivist spread his arms. "I honestly don't know. That's the truth, Sylvester. I'm not trying to shield anyone, not at this late stage in the game. There must have been minions, I'm sure, but I don't know who any of them were. I'd tell you if I did."

"I believe you. You're a good friend to me, Celadon. Better than I sometimes realize, I think."

"It's the least I could do for your father."

Sylvester chose not to think about that.

He clenched his paws again and pushed himself to his feet, walking across to the window. Not far below, beyond the edge of the Library's peaceful grounds, he could see the bustle of Foxglove. Everyone was walking around on their errands without any knowledge that the world they lived in was based on a lie. They had no awareness that the people who controlled it were prepared to kill, without a moment's pause for regret, in order to maintain the illusion. There was some kind of commotion going on in the far distance, but he couldn't make out what it was.

"This can't be allowed to go on forever," he hissed quietly. "They can't be allowed to get away with it."

"Those are dangerous things to say, Sylvester," came the Archivist's voice from behind him. "Dangerous even to think."

"It's a danger I'm prepared to accept."

"Spoken like your father's son," said Celadon. "Which means, Sylvester, that it was a damn stupid thing to say. There's nothing to be gained from rebellion against the authorities. Go along with their fairy tales, boy. Pretend you believe in the scriptures, just like you're supposed to do. Acceptance – that's the name of the game, the key to survival."

Sylvester banged his own forehead with the side of a fist. "That may very well be true, old friend, but it's a charade I can no longer play a part in."

There was a long, sad sigh from the Archivist. "I should never have allowed this conversation to develop. I should have stamped down hard the moment I heard you begin to utter a word of heresy."

"Would you have been able to live with yourself if you'd done that?"

"Most certainly. It's a compromise I've been making for decades. Besides, it's not all bad. Some of the use of language in the scriptures is magnificent. It's glorious."

Sylvester began to snigger derisively. "You can't mean what you've just said."

"I do. I wish I didn't, but I do."

"Beyond these walls no one knows yet. Well, perhaps some of them are just beginning to."

"Knows what? Don't speak in riddles, Sylvester."

"The arrival of the strangers; it's changed everything, *everything*. And it seems I'm the only person who's aware of it."

Celadon's voice grew stiff. "You're one of the most gifted translators the Library has had the privilege of employing, Sylvester, but that doesn't mean you're some kind of immortal genius who's able to understand the world better than anyone else. You're still just a youngster, with the cocksureness that drives youngsters to make stupid mistakes their elders would never make."

Sylvester turned back to look at him.

"I know all of that," he said. "I realize perfectly well that I'm too young to have acquired much wisdom, that there are a million things I don't know yet, that I'm a bit of a dimwit if you take the quill pen out of my hand and the parchment away from in front of my nose. But I say it again. The arrival in Foxglove of the ferret, Levantes, and now the gray fox who calls himself Robin Fourfeathers has changed everything. Our people can't look back and pretend none of it happened. Can't you feel, beneath your feet, the shockwaves beginning to spread out? If it doesn't come from these two rogues, soon there'll be others coming to our town and spreading the word about the truth of the world. The day's very soon coming when the lies we've been living by will be exposed in the glare of the sunlight for all to see."

"But that day is not here yet," hissed Celadon. "And until it dawns, Sylvester, you'd be wise to keep your lips tightly shut."

"In case they do to me what they did to my father?"

"Yes, exactly. Think of how your mother would suffer if, having lost Jasper to the Mighty Enormous Cliff, she were to lose her only son as well."

Sylvester didn't like to admit it, but Celadon had a point. Hortensia would be devastated if anything happened to the apple of her eye.

Nevertheless, he hardened his resolve. Progress was a structure built of sacrifices. Only the most cowardly would expect the sacrifices always to be made by other people.

He changed the subject.

"What does happen to the lemmings who go over the Mighty Enormous Cliff?" he said.

"I wish I knew."

Just then, through the open window behind Sylvester, there came a long, piercing shriek of terror.

"What's going on?" cried Celadon, pushing Sylvester aside to look through the opening.

"I don't know," he replied, but in his head, for no immediately apparent reason, there came the sound of Levantes's voice as the wounded ferret lay dying in Sylvester's arms: "Beware of . . . beware of appearances. *He* will seem yer . . . best friend. And *he* will come."

Levantes had never said who *he* was, but now Sylvester could make a pretty shrewd guess.

He was the fox who went by the name of Robin Fourfeathers.

And *he* was already here!

CAPTAIN TERRIGAN RUSTBANE, AT YOUR SERVICE

Sylvester barged past Celadon, making the old lemming stagger. "Sound the alarm!" Sylvester yelled. "It's started."

He didn't wait to see whether the Archivist obeyed or not. Instead, he charged for the door. He was aware of shocked faces staring at him as he sprinted through the Library, not caring who or what he shoved aside in his dash.

The scream heard by him and Celadon hadn't reached the inner areas of the Library, but Sylvester had heard it clearly enough to recognize the voice.

Viola!

What a fool he'd been.

Last night, already aware that the gray fox was someone not to be trusted a millimeter, he'd nonetheless been jollied into admitting that Viola Pickleberry was someone special to him. The most important person in the world, to be precise. He'd admitted that the two of them were an item.

No wonder the gray fox had wanted to worm this information out of him. The only individual in the whole of Foxglove who had spent any time with Levantes was Sylvester. Levantes had died knowing something that Fourfeathers desperately, desperately wanted to learn. There was a chance, a very good chance, that Levantes had communicated something to the young lemming but, if so, the young lemming wasn't prepared to admit it. What better way to change his mind about that, to put persuasive pressure on him, than to seize the person he loved beyond even his own life?

It was so obvious, with the benefit of hindsight.

Hadn't Levantes warned Sylvester about exactly this sort of thing?

Later, thought Sylvester as he sprinted down the Library steps and along the path towards the gate. *Later I can beat up on myself for being the idiot I am. First I've got to get Viola out of the jam my stupidity's got her into.*

If I can . . .

It seemed to take him hours, and yet just the merest of moments, to reach the town square.

When he did, he skidded to a halt, aghast at what he saw.

The normally orderly lines of market stalls around the sides of the square were in disarray. Several of them had been thrown over, their wares strewn across the ground. Most of the traders had fled.

No wonder.

The area had been taken over by scores of the most disgusting looking creatures Sylvester had ever seen. There were rats, bobcats, weasels, ferrets, skunks, raccoons, possums and groundhogs, and those were only the ones he could identify. It seemed there was not one of them that hadn't been maimed in one way or another. There were wooden legs, eyepatches, hooks for paws. Amongst them, teeth bared in a hideously threatening grin, was a mongoose with only a knot of tormented flesh where his right ear should have been.

All of the invaders were heavily armed with swords, daggers, cudgels, maces – weapons he recognized only from the illustrations in old scrolls, and some he didn't recognize at all. He could even see a couple of crossbows.

No wonder the vendors had scattered.

Wait . . . not all of the vendors.

Viola's mother sold pies here on Mondays, and today was a Monday.

Some Mondays Viola helped, and today was evidently one of those Mondays.

There was a large, grease-stained rat leaning weakly against a wall, who could attest to the fact that Viola had been helping her mother today. He was still spitting out pieces of his teeth while trying to get his jawbone to fit back into its sockets.

The cause of his misery, standing just a few paces away and threatening another even larger rat with what appeared to be a rolling pin, was Viola's mother.

"I'm warning you, buster. You lay one of your filthy paws on a pie you haven't paid for and—"

"Mrs. Pickleberry!" howled Sylvester.

Viola's mother shot a glare in his direction. The rat she'd been intimidating grabbed the chance to sneak away.

"What do you want, boy?"

"Viola, where is she?"

"How the devil do you expect me to know?"

"I heard her scream."

Mrs. Pickleberry turned back to where the rat had been and discovered it wasn't there any longer. She took two determined strides and grabbed by the scruff of his neck a mangy ocelot who'd been planning to feast on the pastries that bedecked the stall next to Mrs. Pickleberry's. She whirled the ocelot around and threw him face-first into the nearest wall. There was a sickening *crump* before, almost to Sylvester's relief, the ocelot started to wail in agony.

At least she hasn't killed him.

"How the blazes do you expect anybody to tell one scream from another in the middle of all this?" bellowed Mrs. Pickleberry at Sylvester. "Grab yourself a cudgel and start smashing yourself a few skulls."

She was a tough lady, was Mrs. Pickleberry.

Any other time, Sylvester would have done exactly as she ordered him to. But he hadn't been imagining things when, from the Library window, he'd identified the scream as Viola's.

He paused then.

Viola had been known to scream just for the heck of it, high spirits, *joie de vivre*, call it what you will.

Sylvester's mouth set in renewed determination.

No, Viola hadn't been screaming just for fun when this cutthroat army invaded Foxglove. She'd been terrified; he'd heard the terror in her voice.

"*Where is she?*" he thundered.

Mrs. Pickleberry froze as if he'd administered a physical blow. When she looked at him again there was a new expression on her face, one of dread.

She dropped the weasel she'd just picked up and came storming across to Sylvester.

"Stupid ol' besom," snarled a raccoon she'd shouldered aside. She paid him no attention as he wheeled toward her, his pikestaff held high above him, ready to strike her a killing blow. "How'd ye like me to slit yer gizzard and feed ye to the sharks?"

Mrs. Pickleberry seemed to pay him no attention at all. She didn't break stride. The rolling pin in her hand suddenly became a blur.

There was a soggy *sppllattt* that Sylvester hoped wouldn't haunt his dreams for the rest of his life. The raccoon vanished head-first through a shop window. His dilapidated boots remained upright in the roadway.

Sylvester gulped.

No wonder Mr. Pickleberry was always so very, very polite and deferential toward his wife.

And everyone said Viola took after her mother.

"Leave her alone," he cried at the miscreants in a general sort of a way, feeling it was his masculine duty to do so. He wished his voice hadn't sounded so shrill and squeaky just then – a lot shriller and squeakier, in fact, than Mrs. Pickleberry's.

There was a tap on his shoulder.

He turned and found himself looking at a mass of scar tissue, on each side of which was an ear. He recognized it as a face, but with some difficulty.

"Oh, wot 'as we 'ere?" came a sarcastic voice out of a toothless mouth. "We 'as a 'ero 'amster, that's wot we 'as. And 'e wants to rescue the lady 'amster, like wot 'ero 'amsters do in books. But Jolly Jack Cutlass 'ere 'as different ideas about that." The creature drew an immensely long, curved, blood-encrusted sword from its scabbard and swung it back, preparatory to a lethal swing. "Such as, 'ow do 'ero 'amsters do any rescuing when they is in two 'alves? Lessee now. They could—*aaargh!*"

There was another of those terrifying blurs and Sylvester's assailant dropped, amid a spray of blood, like a stone to the ground.

For a moment, Sylvester thought the swordsman must be dead, but then the creature started pawing its way through the dust in a very slow attempt to escape.

"You want to know where Viola is?" came Mrs. Pickleberry's harsh voice in Sylvester's ear.

"Yes. I heard her scream and I simply can't find her."

"Last I knew, she'd gone off with some of her fancy friends to have a preprandial cocktail in the Snowbanks." Mrs. Pickleberry jerked a claw back over her shoulder toward the tavern. "If Lady Muck was screaming, it was prob'ly because she discovered the olive wasn't to her taste."

Mrs. Pickleberry spat on the ground expressively, then with a swish of her rolling pin felled a marauder who'd made the mistake of charging at her while swinging a morning star around his head.

"I've never seen Viola so much as look at a cocktail in her entire life," protested Sylvester.

"Well, yes. I was exaggerating a bit. She went off near an hour ago to fetch herself some lunch – as if her mother's individually home-baked pies weren't good enough for her." Sylvester, who'd had one of Mrs. Pickleberry's pies and understood Viola's point entirely, did his best to look appalled at the girl's effrontery. "She hasn't come back yet," concluded Mrs. Pickleberry. "She's had her head turned, I'll warrant, by some smooth-talking—"

BANG!

For a moment, Sylvester and Mrs. Pickleberry just gaped at each other, ears ringing.

"What in the heck was that?" gasped Sylvester before he realized Mrs. Pickleberry couldn't hear him.

He could barely hear himself.

BANG!

He registered the second explosion only in a sort of muffled way, thanks to the residual effects of the first.

The marauders didn't seem concerned by the interruption or by the smell of rotting eggs hanging in the air, but carried on looting and vandalizing much as they had been.

Mutely, Sylvester pointed past Mrs. Pickleberry towards the door of the Snowbanks Inn.

Standing there, holding a strangely shaped metallic apparatus and blowing smoke from its tip, was Fourfeathers.

His other arm was around the neck of a struggling Viola. As Sylvester's hearing returned he could make out the noise of her grunting and gasping as she tried to prize the bigger animal's muscular arm off.

"Take your hands off me you . . . you stinking heap of manure."

Mrs. Pickleberry growled.

Sylvester reached out and put a restraining paw on her arm. "If you move against him now," he whispered, hoping against hope she could hear him through her rage, "you'll have every single one of his cutthroat crew descend on you. You'll just get yourself killed and you won't be any use to Viola if you're dead."

Mrs. Pickleberry nodded reluctantly, but Sylvester could feel her muscles tensing as she fought the urge to go to the aid of her daughter. The same struggle was going on inside himself.

Robin Fourfeathers, or whatever his name might be, slowly and deliberately gazed in Sylvester's direction. Gone were the ragged, road-dusted clothes he'd been wearing yesterday. Today he was dressed in a black leather vest, black leather trousers and black boots. His arms, hidden by his jacket yesterday but now revealed, were covered with old scars and tattoos; he had half a dozen earrings in each ear. Despite himself, Sylvester conceded that the fellow cut a dashing figure.

"Oh, there you are," called the big gray fox chattily, as if they might be two acquaintances who'd run into each other at some social gathering. "Young Sylvester, my good friend and drinking buddy. How's your head feeling?"

"At least it's still on my shoulders," said Sylvester as loudly as he could. "Which is more than yours is likely to remain for long."

A loud hissing noise filled the square as the cutthroats sucked in their breath.

"E's bein' disrespectful at Cap'n Rustbane," said a voice somewhere. "The Cap'n don't like being disrespectfulled at – not at all, 'e don't."

But Cap'n Rustbane (assuming the big gray fox who'd called himself Robin Fourfeathers was Cap'n Rustbane) didn't seem disconcerted at all.

"Pluckily spoken," said the fox, as if solemnly adjudicating a competition, "and especially so in the circumstances. Remind me not to hang you after you've given me the map."

"Map?"

"Yes, map. Approximately one-third of it anyway. Don't pretend you don't know what I'm talking about."

Sylvester's mind was racing. He knew what a map was, because Celadon had told him, but he'd never actually seen one. All those little shapes and squiggles at the bottom of the torn sheet must be places, or geographical features of some kind – towns, perhaps.

"What's a map?" he said, stalling for time. Beside him, Mrs. Pickleberry's knuckles cracked audibly as she tightened her grip on the rolling pin.

Rustbane let out an exasperated sigh. "Sylvester, you are, are you not, the proud possessor of the job description, Junior Archivist and Translator of Ancient Tongues, no?"

Sylvester mumbled an admission that, yes, this was indeed the case.

"In which case," Cap'n Rustbane carried on without apparently paying Sylvester's mumble any attention at all, "it is inconceivable that you don't know what a map is. Kindly do not waste my time, and the time of everyone else here, by pretending otherwise."

His vocabulary has changed, thought Sylvester. *His accent too. He put them on as disguises when he was acting the part of Robin Fourfeathers, minor ne'er-do-well and trickster. I wonder if this is what he really sounds like or if it's just another disguise.*

Before Sylvester could respond to Rustbane, another voice cut across the square.

"Stop bullying the boy, whoever you are, and let go of the girl at once."

Rustbane's eyebrows seemed to darken as he shot a hard stare toward the newcomer. "And you are?"

"Celadon, the Chief Archivist and Librarian of Foxglove, but that's unimportant. Who I am is someone who doesn't require the back-up of half a hundred armed ruffians in order to persecute young people who have no weapons and can't defend themselves."

Sylvester could see something he never expected to see on the gray fox's face: shame. It was there for only a moment, but it was there.

Slowly Celadon advanced across the square. Every eye followed his progress. Even Viola ceased her struggles.

"Let the girl go," the Archivist repeated, more quietly this time.

"Why should I?"

"Because decency dictates you should do so."

The fox let out a guffaw of laughter. "Decency, you say? I ain't got a shred of decency in me, and I'm proud of that! Don't you know you're speaking to a pirate, oldster?"

"I'd guessed as much," said Celadon mildly. "Now, if you'll take your hands off Miss Pickleberry . . ."

"A swap is all I ask," said Cap'n Rustbane, still more amused than infuriated by the elderly lemming's challenge. "This Miss Pickleberry's life, virtue at least partially intact, in exchange for the map the renegade Levantes stole out from under my nose and gave to this naive little pal of yours. That's known as trading, that is. A business proposition."

"Don't be so stupid," said Celadon as conversationally as if the two of them were discussing the weather. "That's extortion."

"Most business propositions are, if the truth be told."

Celadon smiled, acknowledging the point. By now he was standing directly in front of the pirate captain. "Let's not quibble about niceties of terminology," he said. "Just release her."

"You think so?" said Rustbane.

"Yes."

"Well, *I* have a nicety of terminology I'd like to share with you."

Still smiling, Celadon leaned his head forward to hear what the buccaneer had to say.

Still gripping Viola firmly around the neck with one arm, Cap'n Rustbane carefully put down the metal apparatus he'd been wielding. He stepped toward the stooped figure of the ancient Archivist, who was only half the fox's size.

"Here's a terminological nicety for you."

Rustbane's arm moved so swiftly that Sylvester couldn't see it, but he knew the bigger animal must have backhanded the elderly lemming across the face, because Celadon staggered backward a few paces before collapsing on a mound of spilled potatoes.

His grizzled form lay there terrifyingly motionless.

"That does it!" snarled Mrs. Pickleberry.

Sylvester was too horrified by what had happened to his mentor to have the presence of mind to stop her. She marched straight up to the front of the Snowbanks Inn. Rustbane, who'd been exchanging some jocular comment with a couple of his crew nearby, all of a sudden lost the grin from his face.

"That's my daughter."

"It is?"

"Yes, and I want her back right now, you murderous scum."

"Big words."

Cap'n Rustbane looked as if he might be tempted to deal with Mrs. Pickleberry the same way he'd dealt with Celadon, but a call from one of the rats stayed his impulse.

"Take care o' that one, Cap'n! She got the sting o' a hornets' nest, she has!"

Rustbane picked up the gadget he'd laid down a few moments earlier. Even though it wasn't smoking any longer, he blew on it anyway.

"I offer you the same deal I offered the old geezer here." He gestured toward the sprawled figure of Celadon. Mrs. Pickleberry's gaze did not waver in the slightest, still probing the fox's own like a surgeon's scalpel. "Your daughter," explained the fox, as if further explanation were necessary, "for the map her boyfriend has."

"She ain't got no boyfriend."

Rustbane arched his eyebrows in a parody of astonishment. "Are you so very sure of that, Mrs. Pickleberry? Is there perhaps something the charming Viola's been failing to tell her loving mother?"

"She's gonna marry the Mayor. Mayor Hairbell. That's all signed, sealed and delivered."

Sylvester felt as if he'd been kicked hard in the stomach, not once but several times. What was all this about? Viola had told him the other night about Mayor Hairbell directing unwanted attention in her direction and about how her father liked the notion. She hadn't seemed to take it very seriously and so neither had Sylvester. To witness the evident approval with which Mrs. Pickleberry announced the planned liaison, and the lack of dissent from the captive Viola made Sylvester wish that he *should've* taken it more seriously . . .

No wonder my name got on that list for the next Exodus. It isn't to do with Mom at all. Hairbell knew or guessed about Viola's feelings for me, and mine for her, and he wanted to get me out of the picture. Celadon was being one stage too clever when he thought it was because I was asking awkward questions. Anyway, I hadn't started asking them by then; I hadn't even started thinking them. No, it was just a simple matter of sending me to my death so the field'd be clear for Hairbell.

The scoundrel!

The murderous scoundrel!

The expression on Rustbane's face became one of genuine surprise. "Then it's the young swain himself that she's been keeping in the dark," said the pirate, glancing across toward where Sylvester stood. "My sympathies," he added more quietly. Something in his normally highly animated gaze made Sylvester believe that the gray fox, for once, meant what he said.

Rustbane turned back to the bristling Mrs. Pickleberry in front of him.

"Watch out for that rolling pin o' hers, Cap'n," bellowed one of the ruffians. "It's already done seen to Ragshoes Sam. 'E'll nivver go to the lavs again without taking some painkillers first, I'll warrant; and Mutt the Billybong's gonna be drinkin' 'is grog through a straw the rest o' 'is life."

"Thanks, Pigface," called the fox in reply. "Please, Mrs. Pickleberry, I wonder if we might both put down our weapons so we could converse in a more civilized fashion, no?"

She nodded reluctantly. Synchronizing their actions, the two put down their weapons. Well, at least Mrs. Pickleberry did, the fox just stuck the metallic bang maker into his belt.

"Gimme my daughter," said Viola's mother as soon as she was upright again.

"Perhaps this Mayor of yours could facilitate the transaction?" said Cap'n Rustbane brightly. "I'm surprised he's not here already to rescue the apple of his existence from the clutches of the vile, foreign rapscallion."

"You likes the sound of your own voice a lot, don't you?"

"How perspicacious of you, Mrs. Pickleberry. That aside, where is your Mayor?"

For the first time since Sylvester had arrived in the square, Mrs. Pickleberry displayed a sign of uncertainty. "I'm sure he'll be along by and by," she said. "He's probably just busy gathering together a party of strong and sturdy men to drive you and your scummy band out of Foxglove for good and all."

"Indeed?" said Cap'n Rustbane with the kind of courtesy that indicated he didn't believe a word of it.

Neither did Sylvester. He'd bet the last thought in the minds of Mayor Hairbell and his crony, High Priest Spurge, was the noble defense of the town. They were probably hiding in a basement, hoping no one would come looking for them.

Sylvester was wrong.

"We got 'im, Skipper!" came a cry from one of the little alleys that led off the square.

Rustbane watched with interest as a couple of his otter henchmen dragged the struggling Mayor Hairbell into view.

"Bring him closer," said the fox in a tone of gentle encouragement, as a doctor might to the parent of a nervous child. "Let me see his face."

In fact, Sylvester caught a glimpse of the Mayor's face before Rustbane had the opportunity. It was a mask of naked terror. Even so, Sylvester could see, beneath the rictus of fear, the signs that Hairbell was, as always, scheming. In this case probably scheming desperately in order to find some way of preserving his own hide – whatever the cost to the rest of Foxglove might be.

"So this is your true love?" said Rustbane to Viola, once Hairbell was in front of them.

Viola looked as if she wanted to throw up.

"See?" murmured Mrs. Pickleberry beside Sylvester. "Told you. She loves him."

"It doesn't look that way to me," replied Sylvester, his heart soaring. "Looks as if she loathes his guts."

"That's just girlish flightiness, is all."

"Hm."

Rustbane, ignorant of this byplay, was regarding Hairbell with interest.

"He seems a trifle old for you, m'dear," he remarked to Viola.

Viola redoubled her efforts to free herself from the fox's grip.

"And just a little . . . how can I put this tactfully? A little, well, fat."

"I'll have you know—"began the Mayor before his mouth was gagged by the hairy paw of one of the otters.

"And, um, quite a bit too greasy, if you ask me."

"Mmmfle mmmf mmmfle," protested Hairbell.

"Perhaps 'slimy' would be a better word than 'greasy.' I defer to your judgement, m'dear," said Rustbane to his captive.

"Slimy," said Viola, then clearly regretted the impulse.

"'Slimy' it is then. And do my nostrils detect a whiff of . . .? Yes, I think they do. He must be *very* frightened, this true love of yours. I cannot imagine why. All of us here, myself most especially, we're simply concerned for your welfare and happiness, you charming young damsel."

Viola bared her teeth in a snarl.

They were very sharp teeth.

They gave Sylvester an idea.

"Mmmfle mmmf mmmfle."

"Let him speak," said Rustbane to the otter thug who was gagging the Mayor. "Oh, do let him speak, the poor fellow."

Mayor Hairbell, as soon as his mouth was freed, took a great whooping gasp. Clearly the otter had been blocking not just his mouth but his nose.

Once he had his voice back, he said, "Welcome, your most honorable excellency, to our humble town of Foxglove."

Rustbane's bushy tail switched, but he said nothing.

"If anyone has been offering you less than the best available courtesy and hospitality, I'll—"

"Tell me something, Mayor," said Cap'n Rustbane, making a little gesture with his paw as if to beg forgiveness for the interruption. That the paw in question still held the metal device that produced such impressive bangs somewhat detracted from the effect, but still the meaning was clear.

"Yes, your magnificence?" said the Mayor.

"What do they use to make candles here in Foxglove?"

For a moment Hairbell was speechless. "Um . . . I . . . Well I . . . I suppose they . . ."

"Do your folk use tallow, like everywhere else, or do they simply harvest Hairbell oil?"

It took another moment for everybody to realize what the fox had just said, and then the square was filled with the sound of laughter – the raucous guffaws of the pirates but also the reluctant chuckles of the townsfolk. Even Mrs. Pickleberry grunted with mirth.

Sylvester, grinning despite himself, glanced in her direction. She was eyeing her rolling pin speculatively where it lay on the ground. He could sense she was bracing herself for some dramatic, but doomed, attack.

"Wait," he hissed.

Mrs. Pickleberry shot him a skeptical glare, but her muscles eased a little.

"Now, Viola, I have a bargain for you. Would you like me to tell my men to skewer this mayoral paramour of yours on their cutlasses?"

Viola's eyes were begging him, *Yes, please,* but out loud she said, "No, of course not."

"That was not spoken with much feeling, Viola."

"No! Let him go. Leave him alone."

But the voice was not Viola's.

Rustbane started in surprise as Sylvester began pushing his way across the square.

"I have your accursed map here," Sylvester cried, pulling the tattered piece of paper from his vest pocket and holding it high above his head. "You can have it if you let Viola go."

"A reasonable trade," said the fox. "But not quite reasonable enough, methinks." He mimed performing calculations on his paws. "Let's say instead that you give me the map and yourself in exchange for the fair object of your heart's desire."

Sylvester gulped. Loudly.

"What guarantee do I have that you won't just kill me, and her, once you've got what you want?"

The fox's jaw dropped in mock astonishment. "Do you doubt my word as a fox of honor?"

Sylvester didn't bother replying to that.

The fox nodded as if he'd received the obvious answer. "Such a cynical and distrusting world we live in." He sighed. "Well, the truth is, young Sylvester, you have no guarantee whatsoever. But, if you don't give me the map, my men and I shall most assuredly slay your girlfriend, and you, and everyone you know and love, and then we shall raze this little burb of yours to the ground, so that not one stone is left standing. And, just to be especially rotten about this, we'll spare the life of Mayor Hairbell. Is that understood?"

Sylvester nodded mutely. He was no more than a couple of paces from Rustbane and Viola now. Trying to be as subtle as he could, he caught Viola's eye and touched his paw to his teeth. Then he held his paw in front of him with three claws extended.

She got the message.

On the count of three.

"Then let me have the map, please."

Still without a word, Sylvester held the scrap of paper out. Rustbane looked around him, tucked the silvery metal bang maker into his belt, and grabbed eagerly for the map.

"Excellent."

Get him relaxed, Sylvester thought. *Distract him. This is going to be tricky, and there's hardly a chance in a hundred I can get the timing right, but . . .*

"What is that thing?" he asked, pointing.

Cap'n Rustbane looked down at the gadget he'd just put in his belt. "This?"

"Yes."

"It's a flintlock pistol, since you ask. One of the only pair that's known in all Sagaria. I'm lucky enough to own both of them. The other's in my boot."

"What's a flantick . . . one of those?" said Sylvester, pretending ignorance. He knew exactly what a flintlock pistol was. He'd read about them in the writings of the ancients, perhaps about this very pair. You packed one end of them with an explosive called gunpowder, and when you sparked the gunpowder it drove a metal ball at colossal speed along the barrel and out into the open air. If the metal ball hit someone, it could kill them or at least horribly wound them.

Just like Levantes, he thought, finally making the connection. *It must have been this swine who killed him with a ball from one of those damned pistols.*

His heart sank momentarily, then rose. Flintlock pistols fired only once before you had to refill them with gunpowder and another metal ball. Rustbane had fired twice to draw attention to his presence, and he'd been in Sylvester's open view ever since. He'd certainly not had the opportunity to reload the weapons. However fearsome a flintlock pistol might ordinarily be, just at the moment these two were completely useless to Rustbane.

"A flintlock pistol," said Rustbane, "is the most wonderful armament ever invented. I'd be surprised if anyone ever invents a weapon wonderfuller than these two." He smiled that disconcerting smile of his that showed a great many teeth. *Too many teeth,* Sylster reflected. "I imagine that it will be the last thing you ever see, young Sylvester, if you try to thwart me as I and my men make good our escape from here back to the welcoming home of the good ship *Shadeblaze.* You'll be looking into the pistol's muzzle, a hole that'll get bigger and bigger as you watch it, and then you'll see the dark shape of the ball, for just an instant, before—"

"You haven't let Viola go yet," observed Sylvester.

"Oh, haven't I? You're right about that, you clever little hamster. I seem to have changed my mind about doing so."

"Lemming."

"Oops, so sorry. Clever little lemming. It's mighty hard to tell the difference between hamsters and lemmings. They're both small, hairy, irritating and a bit smelly."

Sylvester stared at Rustbane, forcing himself to appear unresponsive to the insult.

The fox seemed to realize he'd lost this particular duel of wits, because his gaze dropped momentarily.

Not yet, thought Sylvester, hoping that Viola might pick up the message.

She seemed to, because she made no move. If the two of them struck prematurely, everything could be lost.

"Of course, you're assuming I will let her go," continued the fox. "As I told you before, there's no particular reason why I should. Now that you've given me what I want, I might as well let my men have a bit of fun. It's been positively ages since they've had the chance to do any looting and pillaging."

"You said you were a fox of honor."

"I'm also a pirate. A pirate of honor? No, it doesn't sound right. A contradiction in terms. Besides, if Captain Terrigan Rustbane started keeping his promises of mercy, he'd stop being the most feared and dreaded fellow Sagaria's ever known. People might begin daring to speak his name without bolting all the doors and windows first."

Sylvester winked at Viola. *Get ready.*

"You're a very extraordinary person," he said to Rustbane. *Keep this self-inflated fool talking about himself. It'll make what I'm going to try a bit easier. I hope.* "Truly extraordinary," he added, hoping he wasn't overbuttering the pudding of his flattery. So, the fox had never planned anything but to massacre the population of Foxglove, including Viola and, not to mention, Sylvester himself – although that seemed merely incidental at the moment. Sylvester sighed inwardly. He'd expected no better of the pirate, who was obviously a creature consumed entirely by treachery, and indeed he'd based his plan on exactly such a betrayal. Still, it was somehow disappointing to see his expectations confirmed.

"How right you are," the fox was saying. "Truly extraordinary. A fighter without equal and a genius in the bargain. I possess powerful alchemical knowledge as well, the kind of arcane secrets that make ordinary magicians tuck in their skirts and run for the hills."

"Is that so?" *Just a few moments longer.*

"It is indeed. Not for nothing do some people call me Deathflash. Or Doomslayer. Or Warhammer. Or . . . well, I can hardly remember all the different names people call me – not even the ones you can mention in polite company, which is by far the minority – but you can be sure most of them attest to the enormousness of my powers."

Slowly, deliberately, making sure that Viola was observing him, Sylvester retracted one of the three claws he'd extended.

She nodded almost imperceptibly.

Message received.

One.

"You'll be in all the history books," said Sylvester.

"Certainly, certainly. I'm the richest, greatest, most powerful and most feared pirate king Sagaria has ever known."

Sylvester pulled in another claw.

Two.

"And because you've been good enough to acknowledge the fact, Sylvester, I'm going to grant both you and your sweetheart a quick and relatively painless death. Regarding the rest of your lemming compatriots I can't be so sure, but you two will hardly know what hit you. Isn't that kind of me?"

"Definitely." Sylvester tried to keep the tremble out of his voice.

This is it.

He withdrew the last claw.

Three.

Now!

Obediently, Viola opened her mouth with its razor-sharp teeth and chomped down viciously on Cap'n Rustbane's hand.

There was the muffled sound of her teeth scraping on bone.

The pirate screamed – more from shock than from pain, even though the pain must have been extreme.

"You little—"

Rustbane instinctively tried to shake Viola loose.

Since this was exactly what she wanted to be, she released his paw and fled like the wind. For the moment the cutthroats were too stunned by the suddenness of what had happened to pursue her.

Just as Sylvester had hoped and prayed, the other part of his plan came right as well.

Rustbane dropped the map.

It fluttered awkwardly as it began to fall.

With a skill he hadn't known he possessed, Sylvester plucked it out of the air.

Then he, too, was fleeing, in the opposite direction from the one Viola had taken.

"Get after them!" shrieked Rustbane in fury.

His ruffians started to obey, but still their movements were sluggish. Sylvester had darted down an alley before the first of the pirates had begun to give chase.

Thoughts raced pell-mell through his mind, scampering faster even than his feet beneath him.

Okay, what next?

His forward planning had gotten him as far ahead as this moment, but no further. In truth, he never thought he'd get this far without being spitted on a pirate sword. It was a surprise to him he was still alive.

He needed to put the map somewhere where he, and only he, could retrieve it. He knew in a general sense where that somewhere was. Where his planning had faltered was in determining the particular location he should make for.

On a warm day like today, there weren't all that many possibilities to choose from in Foxglove.

If, in fact, there were any at all.

The sound of his running footsteps and frantic breathing, for a brief period, had seemed to fill the world but were now inaudible due to the racket made by his pursuers. He daren't slow down long enough to glance back over his shoulder, but it sounded as if there must be about a hundred of them, each swearing and shouting more than the next, each wearing hefty hobnailed boots that made the echoes ring.

Sylvester found that, without any decision on his part, his feet were taking him in the general direction of Doctor Nettletree's surgery.

He grinned grimly to himself.

Come to think of it, that's as likely a place as any to find what I need.

The question was, could he keep ahead of his pursuers for long enough? They seemed very close on his heels. On the other hand, he was young and relatively fit, and he didn't spend each and every day sozzling himself in grog.

And he wasn't wearing those heavy boots the pirates seemed to think were so fashionable.

He thanked Lhaeminguas, even though he no longer believed in the Great Spirit, that Rustbane still hadn't had time to reload either of his flintlocks. Cutlasses and cudgels could be outrun but not, Sylvester imagined, bullets.

Then he remembered that a couple of the vandals at work in the town square had been carrying crossbows.

He sobbed in despair and tried to force his feet to sprint even faster than they already were.

Yet no crossbow bolt came whizzing in his direction. Cap'n Rustbane's shout rose above the racket made by his fellow pursuers, which revealed why.

"Seize him!" yelled Cap'n Rustbane. "I want him alive, I tell you. I want to be the one to send the little maggot to perdition."

Exactly how Sylvester reached Doctor Nettletree's cottage he could never remember afterwards, but he managed it. The motley rabble in pursuit could not have been more than twenty yards behind him as he turned into the little path that led up to the door.

Usually Sylvester would have knocked. Today, he simply barged through the door, blasting it from its hinges.

As he staggered across the little reception area he had a dizzying glimpse of Nurse O'Reilly rising from her post with a look of thunder on her hatchet face.

Of Doctor Nettletree there was no sign.

Nurse O'Reilly might be exactly what's called for here today, Sylvester told himself, amazed he was still capable of coherent thought.

But Nurse O'Reilly chose not to focus her bullying fury where it might have been useful, which was on the pirates who were milling around the front garden. Instead, she turned wrathfully on Sylvester.

"You, young Lemmington hoodlum! I always *knew* you'd come to no good!"

"Which side are you on?" gasped Sylvester.

"What do you mean by that?"

"I'm trying to save Foxglove!"

She snorted. "A likely—"

Her voice was silenced forever by the pirate blade that stabbed into the base of her back and ripped ruthlessly upward to her neck.

Sylvester closed his eyes as Nurse O'Reilly's blood spurted.

For all the wrong reasons, she's managed to do just what I wanted her to do, give me an extra few seconds before those murderers reached me. She has not sacrificed her life in vain. In time to come, Foxglove may remember her as a hero, a martyr.

Even so, those few seconds might not be long enough.

At the back of the reception area there was a wall. At the center of the wall was a hearth where the doctor generally kept a fire going, except on the hottest of days. It served two purposes. Firstly, for his patients who arrived shivering with fever and, secondly, to provide an immediately available, if somewhat rudimentary, means of sterilizing his various needles and knives. The joke around town was that it was Nurse O'Reilly who kept the fire going because it reminded her of home.

Sylvester felt a catch in his throat. There'd be no more jokes about Nurse O'Reilly, not after today.

Mercifully, there were no patients waiting to see the doctor. That was one less factor for Sylvester to have to consider. The doctor must still be out making his daily rounds. Perhaps he'd been caught up in the melee surrounding the town square, although Sylvester hadn't noticed him there.

Getting here, Sylvester had had the advantage of knowing all the nooks and crannies of Foxglove fairly well, whereas the pirates were operating in a town that was unknown to them. So much had been a part of his hastily cobbled together plan. Now he was here in Doctor Nettletree's surgery he discovered another advantage he had, one that he hadn't foreseen.

The reception area, like the rest of the cottage, was built for creatures the size of lemmings.

Most of the pirates chasing Sylvester were much larger creatures.

Only a few could fit themselves into this room. Even fewer because of Nurse O'Reilly's sprawled, still-bleeding corpse.

One of those few was, of course, Cap'n Rustbane.

The gray fox had to round his shoulders and tuck his head in under the ceiling in order to be able to stand upright. His tricorn hat had been lost somewhere along the way. Or maybe, recognizing where Sylvester was leading them, the crafty pirate had flung it to one side.

Rustbane, despite the discomfort of his stance, was wearing that fang-packed leer of his. He was holding an evil-looking dark-bladed dagger in one forepaw, and an equally evil-looking bright-bladed rapier in the other.

"This is the end of the line for you, you scurvy lubber," he sneered. "Give me the map, and you've still got the chance of an easy death."

Sylvester gave what he hoped was a reckless laugh.

"Stare defeat in the throat, scoundrel!"

He reached out the paw that was holding the crumpled map and—

Thwokkk!

Sylvester hadn't seen Rustbane's arm move, yet the dagger that had been in the pirate's left paw was now embedded deep in the wood of the wall . . . neatly pinning the sleeve of Sylvester's jacket.

He couldn't move his arm, no matter how hard he tugged. The pirate had thrown his knife so that the sharp edge of the blade was downward, so that Sylvester couldn't even use the sharpness to cut himself free.

"Please accept my apologies, young fellow," said Cap'n Rustbane suavely. "I didn't mean to miss you."

One of the pirates jammed into the room behind him cackled.

Oh yes you did, thought Sylvester. *That dagger went exactly where you wanted it to go, to the nearest fraction of an inch. If you'd wanted me dead, I'd be standing here with that blade right through my windpipe or my heart. You want to take your time disposing of me, don't you? But first you want to make sure the map is safe.*

Summoning up a huge effort, Sylvester suddenly threw himself backwards along the wall, away from the dagger that pinned the cloth of his sleeve.

There was a tremendous *rrrrriiipppp* and the seam of his jacket's shoulder tore apart. Still clutching the map firmly in his paw, Sylvester hauled his arm out of the tube of cloth, ignoring the pain as he scraped his flesh across the sharp blade.

Rustbane's eyebrows rose. "I underestimated you."

"Again," said Sylvester, breathing hard. "It's a mistake you seem to keep on making, isn't it?"

Before the pirate had the chance to react to what he was doing, Sylvester took a single brisk step and cast the map into the merrily bobbing flames of Doctor Nettletree's fire.

The next thing he knew, he was being hammered against the wall with the tip of Rustbane's rapier at his throat.

"Fetch it!" the fox was snarling to the pirates behind him.

A foul-smelling water rat stooped and plunged his paw into the flames. There was the pungent stench of burning fur.

"If the map is lost, you will be begging me to kill you," hissed the fox in Sylvester's ear.

"The map *is* lost," said Sylvester with as much courage as he could summon. "The flames will have destroyed it by now."

Sure enough, the water rat had withdrawn his paw from the fire and on it there was only a thin wafer of black ash. When the rat moved his arm, the wafer disintegrated and big black flakes fell to the floor.

"You fool!" the fox snarled to Sylvester. "Before you die, you'll watch the death of your pretty little sweetheart. It won't be a pleasant sight, I can warrant you that. Nor a quiet one."

"Then you'll never see your chart again."

The fox's green eyes widened. "You mean that wasn't the map you just burned?"

Sylvester looked deep into Cap'n Rustbane's eyes and for the first time he gained a glimmer of understanding as to how the pirate could compel such a murderous and ragamuffin gang into obeying his orders. It wasn't just that he possessed great gifts of charm and persuasion, although assuredly he did. There was more. The greenish-yellow eyes seemed to spark with a flame of their own. The pupils were openings into endless black wells that sought to pull you down into bottomless depths of despair. There, vile ruthlessness mingled with cunning, and extraordinary bravery with sly intelligence. Cap'n Rustbane was one of those rare people who could slip a dagger into your belly and you'd believe it wasn't there if he told you so.

Cap'n Rustbane was a very dangerous individual indeed.

As if Sylvester hadn't already known that.

Feeling that his life was hanging by a whisker, Sylvester said, "That was the real map that went up in flames, yes."

"Well?"

"But I still have a copy of it."

"Where?"

"Let go of my arms and I'll show you."

Warily, Cap'n Rustbane took a step back, freeing Sylvester.

"Here," said Sylvester, tapping the side of his head.

"You've swallowed it?"

"No. I have the whole map, well, that piece of it anyway, safely locked up in my memory."

"You're driveling."

"It's true. I'm a trained archivist and librarian, remember. I'm used to taking in a tremendous amount of information at just a single glance. Last night I was studying that map for quite a while. Even though I didn't know what it was, all its details are lodged securely in my mind."

"You're joking. You're bluffing."

"I'm not."

"So if I gave you a parchment and a pen, you could draw the whole map again, perfect like, from memory?"

"More or less, yes."

"Just 'more or less'?"

Sylvester shrugged modestly. "I'm not very good at drawing. But if you have an artist who could help me, I'm sure that between us, we could reproduce that chart exactly."

"Then I'm going to fetch me an artist right away."

"And kill me as soon as it's done? Now you're the one who's joking. I said I could do this thing. I didn't say I would. I'll reproduce your map for you only if I choose to do so."

"And that means?" But the fox knew the answer, he didn't need Sylvester to spell it out for him. "I spare the town," said Cap'n Rustbane thoughtfully. "I spare your darling poppet, Viola. Me and my men clear out of here and leave Foxglove behind forever. That the sort of thing you had in mind?"

"It's almost as if you could read my thoughts."

"If I could read your thoughts, I'd have had that map out of you and you'd be burning to a crisp on a bonfire far bigger than the one that paper perished in."

The words were spoken bitterly, but Sylvester could tell the pirate had already resigned himself to the deal. Of course, as soon as he finally *did* produce the map . . . but that was something he could worry about when it happened. For the moment, Foxglove was safe and so was Viola.

"Every detail, you say?" said the fox, still looking thoughtful.

"Try me."

"All right. At the top of the map there's the last part of a name. The first part, which is the only part I've seen, is on the adjacent section of the map and I can tell you for free. It's 'Ma,' spelled m-a. What's the rest?"

Sylvester looked up at the ceiling as if he were concentrating hard. In fact, he knew the answer immediately. The name had been in big, bold letters. It was some of the small stuff down near the bottom of the sheet that might give him a problem.

"Mararobe," he said at last. "'Mararobe I,' according to the map. I suppose the 'I' must stand for 'Island,' though I didn't know that at the time."

The fox slapped his thigh. "Mararobe! Of course, I should have guessed."

"Underneath that," said Sylvester, deciding the moment was right to impress his captor, "it says, 'Coordinates: Lat 12 07 00 N, Long 61 40 03 W.'"

"By the great gullet of the three-breasted goddess who lives in the moon's rear end," said Rustbane in wonderment. "You really *can* remember this thing in every damned detail, can't you?"

"I told you, I'm a trained archivist."

"I've probably made the same claim about myself a few times," said Rustbane. "When you've told people as many lies about who you are as I have, you do tend to sort of lose count of the individual ones, if you know what I mean. How the blithering bacon," he continued, his voice becoming steadily more peevish, "was I supposed to know you were actually telling me the truth?"

"It's not *my* fault you thought I was a liar," declared Sylvester hotly. "You shouldn't judge everyone else by your own despicable standards."

"I could slit your gizzard for that," shouted the fox, his nose almost touching Sylvester's.

"Um, Skip," said a pirate from somewhere near the door, "in point of fact ye can't. Well, I means, ye *can*, being as yer Cap'n Terrigan Rustbane an' can do whatsoever ye pleases like, but if the 'amster's snuffed ye can't get the bleedin' map out o' him, yer'll pardon the strong language I'm sure."

"I . . . am . . . perfectly . . . well . . . aware . . . of . . . that," said Rustbane steadily, each word like a crossbow bolt aimed at one of Sylvester's vital organs. A *red hot* crossbow bolt.

Then the fox's whole body relaxed. He gave a chuckle and patted Sylvester on the shoulder.

"I like a victim with a bit of spunk."

Sylvester didn't deign to reply. Instead he turned to the pirate who'd spoken. "Lemming. Not hamster, lemming. Get it right, if you don't mind, or I shall refer to you as a duckling."

There was a gale of laughter, amid which the speaker despairingly protested, "Ducklings can be real mean an' nasty! Them's can! Them's can!"

"All right," said the Cap'n, evidently making up his mind.

He turned away from Sylvester, motioning to a couple of his cronies that they should grab the lemming and bring him along behind. Rustbane himself walked briskly to the door then hunching over, he went through it to where a band of fifty or a hundred of his crew were milling around, waiting without any clear idea of what exactly it was they were supposed to be waiting *for*.

"Here's what we're going to do," cried Rustbane, flinging one arm back and putting the fist of his other forepaw under his chin, in the manner of an orator who anticipates that the delivering of his forthcoming speech might well, in years to come, be depicted on collectible commemorative crockery. "Gather round here, my hearties, and meet your newest crewmate aboard that jewel of the eternal seas, the *Shadeblaze*, bless her and all who sail upon her. His name's, what did you say your name was? His name's Sylvester Lemmington, and be very particular as to how you address him, because he's a lemming, not a hamster. Call him a hamster and you might very well wake up the next morning to discover the worst has happened. He's gone and told your mom on you."

The assembled cutthroats let loose with roars of mockery and a few cheers. After a moment, standing there blinking against the bright sunlight, Sylvester realized to his surprise that there was no real derision or malice in the laughter. Clearly this form of ragging was just something that happened to everyone who was recruited (or abducted) to be part of Rustbane's crew.

Rustbane held up a paw to bring quiet to the crowd. "So don't mock him, my lubbers, even if you do see him filling his boots from time to time with stuff you have to hold your nose against, because the reality is that Sylvester here is fierce and tough and as courageous as an ox. It's just he don't often like to show off about it."

More of the strident mirth.

"And especially," added Rustbane, pointing a single claw skyward to emphasize his words, "do not accidentally hang him from the yard arm under the misconception that he's your freshly laundered underwear that needs to be put out to dry. You can easily tell the difference between young Sylvester and your filthy underwear if you just remember one important thing. Your underwear's the one that wriggles harder."

The clouds in the skies cringed at the uproar sparked by this last declaration of Rustbane's. Sylvester was at least three-quarters convinced his eardrums were going to burst under the strain.

At last, though, the noise died down.

"I think I did that rather well, don't you?" murmured Rustbane to Sylvester.

"Just about the only thing you didn't insult was the virtue of my mother," said Sylvester resentfully, his arms still pinioned by a pair of burly skunks.

"I'm saving that for later." The pirate leader looked at him breezily. "And now it's time to go. Lucky Foxglove, spared the sword and flames because of the craftiness of one of its more youthful inhabitants. And *not*, let it be said, because of the redoubtable courage of its Mayor – whose job it is to repel attackers and get immolated for his pains. In fact, so far as your Mayor's concerned, redoubtable courage seems to be a quality noticeable only for its shortness of supply. Are you sure you wouldn't like me to send a couple of my men back into town to treat his gizzard in a buccaneerly fashion?"

"No, of course not! Perish the thought." Later, Sylvester would be appalled at the fact he'd hesitated for a moment before replying.

Cap'n Rustbane gazed at him for a long moment with an eyebrow cynically arched, then turned on his heel and began leading his crew along the road from Doctor Nettletree's cottage toward the outskirts of town.

"Yer gonna be a good little captive, aren't ya?" said one of the skunks throatily in Sylvester's ear as they trudged along somewhere in the middle of the pack.

"What do you mean?"

"If we let go of yer arms, yer not gonna run away, anything stupid like that, are ya? I meanter say, yer one of *us* now, one o' the valiant crew o' the jolly ship, *Shadeblaze*. Wouldn't look good, yer started trying to make a break for it."

Sylvester gaped at the walls of sweaty bodies on all sides of him. It wasn't just that most of the creatures who made up Rustbane's crew were bigger than lemmings, it was that all of them were significantly more muscular than archivists.

"I think you'd be safe enough to release my arms."

"Good," said the other skunk. They unhanded him. "Try anything funny, though, and ya get to share a bunk for a month with Two-Tooth Percy."

This notion seemed to strike the skunks as extremely funny, because they laughed long and loud.

"What's so special about Two-Tooth Percy?" said Sylvester, trying not to sound as if the prospect of sharing a bunk with *anybody* didn't fill him with disgust. "Does he snore, or something?"

"Every pirate snores," said the skunk on his left, as if explaining the obvious. "It's part of the job description, like. Naw, Two-Tooth Percy's the bunkmate all o' us avoid like plague for quite a different reason."

Again the pair guffawed.

"And what's that?" said Sylvester. *On second thought, I'm not so sure I actually want to know*, he decided.

"Two-Tooth Percy . . ." began the skunk on his right before breathless mirth stopped him.

He tried again.

"Two-Tooth Percy, see, 'e's a porcupine!"

◈ ◈ ◈ ◈

This is the last time I'll ever see you, dear Foxglove, thought Sylvester for the hundredth time.

They were coming to the town gate; beyond it was open country and then the sea. Sylvester had lost all sense of how big the throng had become, what with cohorts of further pirates joining the stream from other parts of town,

He'd never known anything other than this town and its immediate environs. He'd always been aware, of course, that there was a wider world beyond it, but he had rarely allowed that fact to obtrude into his consciousness. It would never have occurred to him that he, Sylvester Lemmington, would one day venture out to see that wider world for himself. Now that it was actually happening he found that, although there was certainly some sadness in him that he was saying farewell to everything and everyone that ever had meaning for him, there was also a sort of bubbling exhilaration, and eagerness to throw himself into the arms of the unknown.

He might have begun to skip along between the two skunks were it not for one thing.

Amid all the rest that he was leaving behind, there was Viola.

Yes, it was painful that he would never see Mom again. Yes, the uncertainty of his dear mentor Celadon's fate (had the old fellow survived Cap'n Rustbane's brutal blow?) was an itch that Sylvester suspected would never go away.

But the loss of Viola . . .

Someone had made a vicious blade of shattered glass and thrust it into Sylvester's heart.

The only solace he could think of was that, after the slimeball's display in the town square, surely not even Mrs. Pickleberry would insist that Viola marry Mayor Hairbell. At least his true love had been spared that vile destiny.

And perhaps, on nights when the moon rose high in the mysterious sky and the heavens were filled with a richness of stars beyond all number, Viola would stare up at the universe's infinitude and feel herself wrapped in the eternal love of the one lemming whose heart for her had always been a pure and gleaming . . .

Sylvester shook his head angrily.

If his thoughts got any mushier he was likely to fall into them and drown.

He hoped Viola would be able to find someone else to fall in love with who would fall in love with her, and that she'd soon forget Sylvester. She'd be happier that way.

Hm. Still pretty high on the mushiness scale.

There was no sign of any guard as they passed through the town gate.

No wonder.

No one but a lunatic would put themselves in the path of a hundred or more bloodthirsty pirates.

Actually, I damn well don't hope Viola quickly finds some other lemming to love her. I hope she's miserable about losing me for a good long time and that, even if she eventually marries and has someone else's kids, it's always the name "Sylvester" that's on her lips as she drifts off to sleep. Because I'm not going to give up on her the moment she's out of sight. I'm going to be carrying a banner for her in my heart for the rest of my life. One day, however improbable it might seem now that I won't end my life at the bottom of the ocean, perhaps capricious fate will bring me back to Foxglove and I'll find her still waiting for me, those magical eyes of hers still filled with love for me . . .

He emerged from under the gate's shadow to discover that Rustbane had pushed back through the jostle of bodies to find him. The pirate had retrieved his tricorn hat.

"How're you bearing up, me hearty?" cried the fox. He attempted a piratical swagger but there really wasn't room for it in the mob.

"I'm, er, ready to look into the gaping jaws of Davy Jones himself and, um, laugh at fear," Sylvester essayed. That sounded like the sort of thing a derring-do buccaneer should say.

Maybe I should have added a cussword or two, he fretted.

"That's the spirit, me bucko!"

The comradely whack Rustbane delivered between Sylvester's shoulders was enough to send the lemming staggering.

"We've got a nice surprise for you." The fox winked. "Oh, you're going to be thanking Captain Terrigan Rustbane for this one, let me tell you."

That wink was a bit . . . well, vulgar, if truth be told. Lewd. What in the world can the fellow be talking about?

About fifty yards beyond the gate stood a little posse of pirates. One of them was sporting a rapidly blackening eye. Another was bleeding from the nose. A third, lying curled up hugging his hind legs in the middle of the road and covered in a sheen of cold, oily sweat, was moaning softly.

Sylvester's brow furrowed. Whatever could be going on?

Then the little knot of waiting pirates opened up and he could see, standing among them with her forepaws tied together, the person he'd just been thinking about.

"Viola!" he cried.

And one other.

"Mrs. Pickleberry," he cried as an afterthought, hoping his voice managed to convey the same degree of enthusiasm.

Rustbane seemed as surprised as he by the presence of Viola's mother. The fox did a double-take, then put his paws on his hips and began tapping his foot angrily. The pirates who'd been marching on all sides of him chose to discreetly melt away.

"What the devil did you bring the old trout for?"

"Lemming," corrected Sylvester automatically, before he could stop himself.

The Cap'n turned an irate glare in his direction.

"Er, not trout. She's a lemming," said Sylvester weakly, wondering if he were pulling himself out of the hole or digging it deeper. *At least so long as I'm still talking I know I'm still alive.* "Lemmings have four legs and hair, you see. And, ah, trout have . . . well, they—"

"For the triple-breasted goddess's sake, will you stop your gibbering?" Rustbane turned back to the battered little band who'd been awaiting them. "Couldn't you simply have got rid of the old bat?"

"Not bat," began Sylvester, then pretended he'd just been coughing.

"Well, we tried, Skipper," said a possum who looked as if he'd seen better days and was wishing he still could. "But, like, she 'ad her rolling pin with 'er."

Rustbane nodded, apparently accepting this as sufficient explanation. They'd all witnessed the lethalness of Mrs. Pickleberry's rolling pin.

"An' she'll make a fine pirate," added the possum hastily, pushing his luck.

"Hmmf," said Rustbane.

The possum rubbed his forepaws together in an ingratiating way. "Got to find her a good piratical nickname, mind. Summat fitting, like. Too bad 'Pigface' is already took, innit, cuz it'd suit her right down to the—aargh!"

"Definitely not 'Pigface,'" said a raccoon pirate quickly as the echoes of a very loud *thwokkk* slowly faded. He gazed sickly down at the writhing form in the dust and did his best to look as if he'd never seen the possum before in his life.

Rustbane made up his mind. Earrings jingling, he delivered to Mrs. Pickleberry the most elaborate bow Sylvester had ever seen.

"A thousand welcomes to the crew of the doughty vessel, *Shadeblaze*, sweet matron."

"Grmmple," said Mrs. Pickleberry, fixing him with a skeptical stare.

"Sylvester," called Viola softly, straining at her bonds.

Beside him, the two skunks tensed, ready to seize him again if it looked as if he might run towards her.

"Oh, let him go. Let the lovers unite," said Rustbane in a disgusted sort of a way as he straightened up from his bow. "I'd hoped this might strike terror into young Sylvester's heart, and instead what do I get? The kind of scenes that'd have put even my sentimental old granny, whoever she was, off her supper. Go on, Sylvester, go on. Get your slobberfest over with so the rest of us can start concentrating again on being the scourge of the Seven Seas. I thought the presence of the luscious Miss Pickleberry among our company might help hone your memory of the map's details during our voyage."

Sylvester ran to Viola and held her tightly to him.

"I'll find some way of setting you free," he whispered into her ear.

"Don't you dare!"

"What?"

"D'you think Mom would've allowed them to catch me if I hadn't insisted?"

"Huh?"

"It was touch and go, I can tell you. In the end she only agreed if she could come along too as chaperone."

"What's a chaperone?"

"I'm not sure. I think it's a type of pirate. Now, kiss me again, will you?"

It was difficult, under the searchlight of Mrs. Pickleberry's icy gaze, to kiss Viola with the full intensity the occasion demanded, but somehow Sylvester managed it.

"Why didn't you just run for the hills?" he said when finally, on the verge of asphyxiation, they pushed each other apart.

"And leave you unprotected at the tender mercy of a mob of murderous cutthroats?"

"I thought that was . . . I mean to say . . ."

She grabbed his ears and shook them affectionately. "You're going to need someone to look after you, Sylvester Lemmington. Otherwise you'll get yourself into all sorts of perilous scrapes. You're such a noodle, you know. No one's doubting your manly courage, of course," she patted him on the chest, "but you need someone alongside you to be the brains of the operation, don't you?"

"Oh."

"So—"

Sylvester kissed her yet again before he could say anything stupid.

"Daphne."

With difficulty, Sylvester pulled himself away from Viola.

"Sorry?"

"Daphne," repeated Mrs. Pickleberry.

Still Sylvester was baffled.

"My name," she explained gruffly.

"And . . .?"

"Since we're about to be shipmates, you'd better start calling me by it." She turned her gaze to Viola. "You too, you little flibbertigibbet."

Viola looked dismayed.

"Aw, Mom."

"Can't have your pretty boy here trying to stutter his way through 'Mrs. Pickleberry' if there's an emergency in the rigging and all our lives hang in the balance. He's likely to strangle himself with his own gizzard halfway through the third syllable. Calling me 'Mom' won't be no use either, since half these blaggards don't know who their real mom is and are likely to get confused. See?"

Sylvester felt his eyes slowly crossing as he tried to follow the logic of this.

Rustbane, who'd been eavesdropping, chipped in. "Daphne 'Three Pins' Pickleberry! A fine piratical name. I like it. I like it a lot. Now, you fine fellows and, er, fellowesses, shall we continue on our way to the *Shadeblaze*, just in case our friend Mayor Hairbell manages to round up a posse of sturdy folk to pursue us?"

"This is your last chance," Sylvester murmured to Viola. Mrs. Pickleberry – Daphne – could fend for herself. "If you're going to make a bolt for it, now's the moment."

"But why should I want to?"

"We're going on a long journey, and the chances are slim that we'll ever come home. Danger will lurk around every corner. It's not just foes we'll need to be wary of, but our so-called friends." He waved his arm to indicate the pirates surrounding them, who conveniently chose this moment to reinforce his point by looking as malignant and untrustworthy as possible. "We're going to see strange new places where every step we take could be our last. We're going to see horrors that'd turn the stomach of the toughest of lemmings. We're going to—"

"Oh, Sylvester," interrupted Viola. She clutched her forepaws together in front of her chest and gazed at him with rapturous eyes. "That all sounds just wonderful!"

Sylvester knew when he was beaten.

"To the *Shadeblaze* it is, then," he said resignedly to Rustbane.

"To the *Shadeblaze!*" cried the pirate king.

His men cheered, and began once more to stamp their heavy way along the road to the shore.

THE *SHADEBLAZE*

A couple of hundred yards out from the shore there floated a monstrous object unlike anything Sylvester had ever seen. It was made mostly of wood, or seemed to be, and there were windows in the side. It could have been a house bobbing upside-down in the water, except there were long, sharp bits sticking out both ends and three even longer poles sticking up from its top (or bottom) – if in fact it *was* an upside-down house, which Sylvester was pretty certain it wasn't. He was guessing this was what Levantes, and later Cap'n Rustbane, had called a ship – the *Shadeblaze*, no less.

From the upward-pointing poles there hung what appeared to be gray sheets.

It's obviously laundry day aboard the pirate vessel, thought Sylvester, smug in his growing knowledge of nautical matters. *What very big beds they must have.*

"The *Shadeblaze*," Cap'n Rustbane confirmed at his shoulder. "Doesn't she look magnificent?"

"Why, yes, she does," said Sylvester courteously, wondering why the black kitchen towel hung up to dry at the very top of the longest of the three poles had a skull and crossbones embroidered on it.

I hope Rustbane doesn't expect us to wash all the dishes, he thought.

Viola was regarding the ship with the same wide-eyed rapture she'd shown when he was telling her about the adventure awaiting them. Even Mrs. Pickleberry—*oops, I must learn to call her Daphne or, even better, Three Pins.* Even Daphne seemed impressed, although trying very hard not to be.

"It's a house on the water," breathed Viola adoringly.

"Aye," said Cap'n Rustbane. "That's exactly what it is, a house, a home. It's *my* home, you see, and you three are going to be my houseguests, in a way. Working houseguests, like. You three'll be working your furry little butts to the bone, I can warrant you that."

"You mean we'll be pirates," said Mrs. Pickleberry.

Rustbane gave her a big confirmatory grin. "Or corsairs, if you prefer. Sounds a lot better over afternoon tea if you say you're a corsair than you're a pirate."

Along the beach were drawn up a score or more of long, thin objects that Rustbane told them were longboats. They'd use the longboats to get out to the *Shadeblaze*, since the option otherwise was swimming.

"Pirates can't swim," he confided. "It's a law of nature."

Sylvester remembered how poor Levantes had been at swimming. At the time, Sylvester had thought it was just the ferret's injuries that had made him that way, but perhaps pirates weren't supposed to swim.

"If we discover a pirate can swim," continued the Cap'n, "we make him walk the plank. That gives him a chance to go swimming all right!"

Puzzled, Sylvester decided not to ask what walking on a plank had to do with swimming. He'd get to the bottom of the mystery soon enough.

He also decided not to tell Rustbane that he, Viola and Mrs. Pick—Daphne could, as lemmings, swim very proficiently. Their survival depended upon them playing the part of swashbuckling pirates, although what you actually did to swashbuckle was yet another thing Sylvester did not know.

This voyage is going to be extremely educational, if nothing else, he reflected.

Some of the pirates were beginning to leap into the longboats, and Cap'n Rustbane indicated to the three lemmings they should do likewise. The skunks who'd been escorting Sylvester jumped into the nearest boat and beckoned to him. As soon as the lemmings got close enough the skunks grabbed them and hauled them aboard, dumping them unceremoniously in the long pool of salty water in the bottom of the boat.

Rustbane decided to travel in this boat too. He waited until the vessel was packed with as many pirates as it could safely hold, then sprang aboard with a flourish, walking across the shoulders of his crew until he reached the bow.

"Cast off!" he cried.

Some of the pirates still left on the beach pushed the longboat out through the shallows until, heavily laden, it was afloat.

"Arm them oars," ordered Rustbane.

Obediently, pirates grabbed the ends of long poles Sylvester hadn't paid much attention to. He saw now, as the crewmen swung the poles around, that the other ends were flattened out. The poles – or oars, as Rustbane had called them – fitted into little cups fixed along the sides of the boat.

Sylvester suddenly realized how these things worked. If you put the flattened ends into the water and pushed on the other ends, the flat bits would act like paddles to propel you along.

Moments later, his guesswork was substantiated, although the pirates pulled rather than pushed on the oars.

By now, all three lemmings had found a place where they could peer over the side of the boat and watch what was going on.

"*Heeeeaaaaave!*" yelled Cap'n Rustbane every couple of seconds and "*Heeeeaaaaave!*" responded his rowers in unison as they hauled on the oars and the longboat sluiced through the water.

As the longboat pulled farther and farther from the shore, they saw a few ascending strands of chimney smoke, then the rooftops of Foxglove came into view. Sylvester could identify the temple and, lower and a little more distant, the Library where he'd worked for so many years – for the most part happily. He hoped Celadon had suffered nothing more than a sore head, something to give him a good excuse for grumbling until the bump went down, and perhaps even longer than that. Then all thoughts of Celadon and even his own mother vanished from Sylvester's mind as the longboat entered the pool of darkness beside the *Shadeblaze*.

Viola slipped her paw into his and squeezed tightly. Whether she was trying to reassure him or seek his reassurance Sylvester did not know.

🜚 🜚 🜚 🜚 🜚

The smacking of waves against the hull and the creaking of the masts woke Sylvester early the next morning.

For a few moments he lay on his hard bunk wondering where in the world he might be, then all the memories of yesterday came flooding back to him: the fighting in the town square, the murder of Nurse O'Reilly, the march to the shore, the trip in the longboat out to where the *Shadeblaze* lay at anchor.

Viola.

Mrs. Pick—Daphne. Three Pins.

Setting sail.

Foxglove sinking out of sight beneath the horizon.

The realization that it was not in fact laundry day aboard the *Shadeblaze*, that those weren't big bedsheets and that the topmost piece of flapping cloth most emphatically wasn't a whimsically embroidered tea towel, and the relief that he hadn't let slip any remarks that might have betrayed his ignorance.

Supper. The discovery of what the pirates called "hardtack," a supposed foodstuff that hovered uneasily on the borderline between edible and poisonous. The discovery of what the pirates called "grog," which after a while made hardtack not just edible, but actually quite palatable. Grog was rather like Foxglovian apple wine, although it had a kick that was at least three times as ferocious.

There had been other events last night, Sylvester knew, but they were all rather muddled. That lemming dancing on top of the compass table, surely that couldn't have been himself? His mind insisted on putting the face of Mrs. Pickleberry on the lemming dancer, which seemed even more impossible.

It was, however, a thought horrific enough to thrust Sylvester firmly out of any remains of sleep he might have been luxuriating in.

That was a pity because, now that he was fully awake, he made another discovery about life at sea.

Years ago, when he'd been small and while Dad was still alive, Mom had shooed the two of them out the door into the back garden one afternoon, telling them they should go and do some "father–son bonding," as she'd put it.

"That means we've got to play together, son," Jasper Lemmington had said glumly. He'd just been settling down with the newspaper when the instructions arrived.

"Bladabladabingbingaboo," his infant son had replied, that being his favorite word at the time (among the three he'd mastered).

Clenching his teeth yet more firmly on the stem of his pipe, Jasper Lemmington had dumped the eagerly squirming Sylvester on the seat of the little wooden swing in the garden. He made sure the boy was securely strapped in, and begun rhythmically pushing him.

It was at this moment that their neighbor, Mr. Frampington, emerged from the next-door house into his own garden.

"Fine day, Jasp," Mr. Frampington (whose fault Mr. Lemmington afterwards claimed it all was) said.

That was the start of it.

Of course, Sylvester was far too small to understand anything the two older lemmings talked about, but he did know their conversation lasted an interminably long time.

And all the while his father continued automatically to push, push, push on the swing, steadily, steadily, steadily . . .

After more than an hour, Mrs. Lemmington came out to see how father and son were getting along, and found her husband leaning with one arm on the fence, the other dutifully pushing the swing, while he and Mr. Frampington conversed absorbedly about issues of the day.

Meanwhile, grinning grimly because he knew he was supposed to be enjoying himself, the infant Sylvester was clutching one rope of the swing like a lifeline and displaying a face the color of lime juice.

Sylvester, even though he was too young to really know what was going on, would never forget the eruption that ensued when Mrs. Lemmington made this discovery. She had always been regarded as somewhat demure in her demeanor, but not today. In the distant temple, priests ceased their chanting to wonder what the sound might be. Jasper Lemmington limped for a week.

But there was another eruption even more indelibly imprinted on Sylvester's mind.

Released from the fastenings of the swing by his raging mother, he'd been put down on the grass while she belabored her husband.

Walking had been a relatively new skill for Sylvester at the time. It was something of a hit-or-miss affair. Even so, he'd been aware that it had never been quite like *this* before. The world seemed to pulse closer then farther from him in the same rhythm of the swing. He attempted to put one foot in front of the other in the approximate direction of the back door beyond which, he reasoned, lay security.

The net result, he was later told, was that he walked around in a perfect circle, once and almost twice, then fell flat on his face and, well, *that* had been lime-green, too.

Even after he'd been put to bed following an extremely necessary bath, the world had continued to fluctuate in the same stomach-wrenching fashion. There had been no question of his having supper, of course. His stomach felt like a raw wound.

Matters were not helped by the fact that Mrs. Lemmington was not entirely finished with her criminally negligent husband, not yet. The ringing walls of the Lemmington home made it hard for Sylvester to find the sleep that would release him from the agony of his insides.

It was the first time he'd ever prayed to Lhaeminguas, even though he couldn't pronounce the name.

Now, aboard the *Shadeblaze*, he was feeling similar in every respect to the way he had that long-ago night. He couldn't work out if the aftermath of the grog was making things better or worse. Better, perhaps, because it was insulating him from how he'd otherwise be. It was the bobbing of the ship to and fro on the water that did it, as had been explained to him last night, not long after the nausea had begun. Explained to him none too sympathetically by a bevy of drunken pirates as he'd hung his head over the taffrail. It was just the same as the to-ing and fro-ing of the garden swing, only worse, because there was no getting away from it.

Sylvester pushed himself up on his elbows and stared out moodily through the porthole just above his bunk.

He saw an eternity of sea, its gray surface moving up and down.

That was a bad idea.

Flat on his back on the bunk once more, he looked at the splintered ceiling. *Nice ceiling. Pretty ceiling. Friendly, stay-in-the-same-place ceiling.*

Outside, the boat hit a roller, a bigger wave than usual.

The whole vessel shuddered from the impact.

Not one part of the *Shadeblaze* shuddered more than Sylvester.

"Oh, this is misery – misery!" he cried.

There was a knock on the cabin door.

"I'm dead," he called weakly.

Dead or not, he managed to turn his head enough to see that the person opening the door was Viola. The sight was cheering enough to raise his state of health to mere terminal illness.

"Good morning," she said, bustling across the cabin to lean over his bunk and wrench the porthole noisily open. A strong smell of salt water and dead fish rushed into the room.

"Bleurgh," moaned Sylvester.

"That's better," said Viola. "A bit of fresh air'll see you right as rain in no time."

"Bleurgh," Sylvester agreed.

"I wonder what'll be for breakfast."

"*Bleurgh!*"

She sniffed the air. "No cooking smells yet. I hope it's going to be something nicer than that horrible hardtack they made us eat last night. Oh," she added, "what's the matter, dear Sylly?"

"Bleurgh."

"Oh, you old fusspot. You know I only call you 'Sylly' when I'm feeling especially fond of you."

Desperately racking his brains for something to say instead of "bleurgh," Sylvester tried to muster a few words.

"What's that you said?" asked Viola, leaning towards him.

"I said, 'That's kind of you, dear, but I really don't like the name.'"

"I can tell a night's sleep out on the ocean waves hasn't improved your temper any, you old crosspatch."

First a fusspot, now a crosspatch, and both of them *old*. Even through the miasma of his intestinal controversy, Sylvester saw he'd better do something to improve his "desirable boyfriend" image. He should be saying something both suave and incredibly witty, he knew, but in its current state, all his brain was capable of doing was wondering if he might be able to fit his head through that porthole . . .

He was rescued from his quandary by the cabin door being opened again.

The new arrival was an old sea rat with an eyepatch that had once been black but was now spotted with green mold, as if behind it one might find an exceptionally ripe cheese. The rest of his face was little better. All in all, disgusting as his eyepatch was, it was difficult to look at him and not wish it were bigger. He was, nonetheless, a friendly soul as Sylvester, Viola and Three Pins had discovered last night. He'd taken them under his wing, making sure they got some supper and weren't shoved to the back of the grog queue. This morning, Sylvester rather wished he had been kept at the back of the grog queue, but that was no reflection on the elderly rat's kindness.

"Hello, Cheesefang," said Viola brightly.

It seemed that Cheesefang, too, might have partaken too liberally of the grog, because his good humor of the night before had apparently evaporated. Rather than reply to Viola, he just scowled evilly at her.

"Cat got your tongue?" Viola gave the pirate one of her most charming smiles. Sylvester had never seen her this early in the morning before, and was dubious as to whether he ever wanted to again. There's something about early-morning irrepressibility that makes ordinary people want to hit things.

The rat's scowl deepened. "'M here on offisherl business."

"Official business? My, that sounds important, Cheesefang."

"Sharrap, wench!"

"Oo, you—"

"Sharrap, I said. 'M not here fer you."

"Then who *are* you here for?"

"Fer 'im." The rat pointed an ancient and pitted cutlass toward where Sylvester lay on his bunk.

"Me?"

"Yes, you. Gerrup. The Cap'n wants ter see yer, right 'way."

The news cleared Sylvester's head like nothing else might have done. That Cap'n Rustbane wanted to see him at this hour of the morning, and had sent such a no-nonsense emissary to fetch him, seemed to Sylvester to bode no good, no good at all.

"I'll be right with you," he said hurriedly, rolling himself from the bunk to the floor.

"Good," said Cheesefang curtly. He gave Viola a look of purest venom. "As for you, ye bilge ra—er, bilge lemming, ye c'n just stay 'ere and rot for all I cares."

The look she returned him made his own seem positively innocuous, and he cowered instinctively.

"Er, forget I said that, ma'am. It's just me piratical ways, see?"

"Hm."

"I'm ready," said Sylvester, patting himself down. "Shall we get moving?"

The rat looked delighted to be given a reason to escape Viola's steely gaze. "Yep. On the double. Can't keep the Cap'n waitin'. Mornin's ain't his best time, if ye sees what I means."

Then why the heck has Rustbane asked to see me now? thought Sylvester. *Why not leave it until the afternoon?*

This was seeming worse and worse. As he followed Cheesefang out of the cabin, Sylvester paused in the doorway and looked back at Viola. Now that he'd vacated the bunk, she was sitting on the edge of it, worrying her forepaws together. She looked up and saw Sylvester's eyes on her.

"It'll be all right," she mouthed. "I'm sure of it."

"Gerra move on!" yelled Cheesefang. "'Less you want me ter skewer ye where the sun don't shine."

THE CAP'N WOULD LIKE TO SEE YOU IN HIS CABIN

urching across the deck, the point of Cheesefang's cutlass at his back, Sylvester began to wake up properly. As the *Shadeblaze* plowed her way through the waves, periodic showers of icy cold spray hit Sylvester in the face, revitalizing him. All over the deck, pirates were busily working: coiling ropes, repairing rigging, gutting fish, doing any one of half a hundred other tasks that Sylvester couldn't even begin to identify. It was a far cry from the scene of festivity and merrymaking of the night before. When a blast of spray made him tilt his head back, Sylvester saw a bat far overhead, suspended from the crow's nest, spying this way and that with a long black telescope. Above the crow's nest fluttered the flag that last night Sylvester had learned was called the Jolly Roger.

He and Cheesefang were heading toward the bow of the vessel, where the Cap'n's cabin was housed.

There's something about all this feverish activity on deck that's not quite right. It's as if Cap'n Rustbane is keen that everyone is kept constantly busy, busy, busy. Even if there isn't in fact anything much that needs to be done. Most of it seems to be just make-work. Perhaps his idea is that the more people work, the less time they have for thinking – something he doesn't want them doing too much of. He's *the one to be doing the thinking, Cap'n Rustbane himself. I must remember, Cap'n Rustbane's the king on board this ship – in this world within a world. If I forget that, I'm likely to find my head separated from my shoulders, map or no map.*

"Down 'ere," said Cheesefang gruffly behind him.

They went down half a dozen wooden steps to face a stout oak door that hung slightly crookedly on its hinges. In the middle of the door was a copper plate, green with corrosion, in the shape of an anchor.

The rat shouldered Sylvester aside and knocked on the door.

"Enter," came Rustbane's voice from within.

"That means "Go in,'" said the rat to the hesitant Sylvester.

"I know that."

"Then do it."

He did. The rat waited until he was inside and then slammed the door shut behind him.

Sylvester found himself in a large and comfortably furnished cabin, all polished oak and shining brass and overstuffed black leather upholstery. Hung around the walls were a dozen or more gilt-framed portraits of what Sylvester guessed must be pirate captains of yore. There were otters, minks, rats and even a human, and none of them seemed to have a full complement of limbs or bodily organs. What they had in common, Sylvester thought as he gazed around at the gallery of nightmarish faces, was that they all seemed to be sneering at him.

Where the walls weren't adorned with pictures, there were bookshelves galore, all of them stuffed to bursting point with leather-bound books. Sylvester felt the Junior Archivist and Translator of Ancient Tongues within him begin to stir. This collection of books was far beyond anything the Library back in Foxglove could hope to offer. Even Celadon had only rarely seen a bound book; Sylvester knew them solely from Celadon's lovingly fastidious descriptions. Squinting, Sylvester could make out a few of the titles and his eyebrows rose. These weren't just tables of the tides or nautical manuals, although there were a few of those as well. Instead, Cap'n Rustbane's library was made up of poetry, novels, plays and treatises on the sciences: physics, mathematics, chemistry, astronomy . . .

Sylvester realized he was going to have to revise his opinions of the Cap'n. This wasn't the library of a scapegrace sea dog, but that of a scholar.

In the middle of the cabin was a great oak table covered with heaps of books and papers. Cap'n Rustbane stood at the table poring over something, his back to where Sylvester stood at the door. Hanging from the ceiling above the table, a brass lantern swung lazily from side to side with the motion of the ship. The cabin had no windows, and so the lantern was lit, even though it was broad daylight outside. The lantern light, as the ship rocked, created ever-changing patterns of shadow all over the floor and walls.

"D'you know how long I've been searching for this treasure, young Sylvester?" said the fox, not looking up from his task.

"No."

"Most of my life. All of my life, it sometimes seems."

Sylvester made a noncommittal sound.

"Yes," said Rustbane, "treasure. Glorious, wonderful, fabulous treasure. Treasure beyond all the riches a person could ever dream of. The kind of treasure that decides the fate of nations, of dynasties, of entire *worlds*. A treasure so splendiferous it could pave every street in all Sagaria with gold. A treasure for which whole armies have lost their lives and gladly so. A treasure that's fit to make the mountains hang their heads in shame as it o'ershadows them. A treasure that—"

If I sort of sidle over to the shelves as quietly as I can, thought Sylvester, *I should be able to get a better look at some of those jolly interesting looking books.*

"—in its radiant splendor makes the sun seem dim by contrast. Where are you going, young fellow?"

The lemming froze. Cap'n Rustbane still had his back to him and was earnestly scrutinizing some papers on the big oak table. Sylvester was certain the cautious movements of his feet had made not a single sound, yet somehow the pirate knew.

Sylvester had once had a schoolteacher like that. Bat Ears Thornapple. It was rumored that Bat Ears Thornapple had an additional pair of eyes in his hindquarters. He had also possessed a long wooden ferrule with which he'd delighted in rattling the paws of young lemmings he discovered moving or whispering behind him while he was writing on the chalkboard. Sylvester's knuckles still throbbed nostalgically any time he thought of Bat Ears Thornapple.

"Er, just moving one from one foot to the other. Pins and needles, you know."

Now Cap'n Rustbane did turn around to look at Sylvester. There was a crazy glint in the fox's eyes. Sylvester reminded himself that the pins and needles excuse had never worked with Bat Ears Thornapple, either.

"Terrible thing, pins and needles," said the pirate with sinister softness.

"Ye–yes. It is."

"The only known cure, I think," said Cap'n Rustbane, "is amputation of the affected extremities."

"That's odd," said Sylvester. "My case of pins and needles has cleared up. Just like that."

The pirate snorted. "And that, of course," he said, "is the *other* cure."

Sylvester inwardly cowered. This was exactly like Bat Ears Thornapple, only worse.

"Now, where was I?" the fox said.

"You were talking about the treasure."

"What an excellent thing to have been talking about. I must do it again sometime soon."

"Oh, yes, please," said Sylvester, his eagerness sincere. Anything to get the pirate off the subject of amputation. Sylvester, despite himself, began ranging over all the pieces of his body that could be amputated – that seemed almost designed for convenient amputation, in fact. Whoever had put his head on the end of a neck, for example, had clearly had easy severance in mind.

"Oh, all right then. You've persuaded me." The fox drew a deep breath. "I lost far too many years of my youth to ... to other things when I could have been hunting for this treasure, you see."

"You did?" said Sylvester, expecting to elicit a few seedy confessions.

"Yes. I was, I'm embarrassed to say, a rather amateurish sort of a pirate when I first began."

"You were?" Sylvester couldn't imagine Cap'n Rustbane being amateurish at anything, least of all piracy.

"Yes. Oh, I was pretty good at the actual buccaneering itself, you understand, and in fact I devised a couple of new techniques of pillaging that are still in use today, but I had the unfortunate habit of getting caught."

"But didn't they—"

Sylvester stopped himself short. *Under no circumstances remind this crazy fox of amputation,* he told himself sternly.

"No, they didn't. I played on their sympathies, of course. Told them I was a very young fox – which I was – and that I'd reluctantly been forced into a life of crime on the high seas by the need to look after my ancient invalid mother. I tell you, by the time Terrigan Rustbane had finished with a court of law, even the most notorious hanging judges were weeping on each other's shoulders." Cap'n Rustbane drew himself up to his full height, the fringes of his ears nearly touching the cabin's ceiling. "Many of them wanted to set me free, there and then, so I could run home and make an extra pot of chicken soup for my dear old mom, but The Law wouldn't let them." The pirate succeeded in pronouncing the capital letters of "The Law."

"But I thought—"

Cap'n Rustbane raised a paw. "You might have thought judges had the final word on what happens to the unfortunates brought before them, and for all I know this may be true in Foxglove. But in most of the rest of the world the judges are themselves under the direction of The Law. And The Law decrees that people found guilty of piracy on the high seas, no matter how well-intentioned, must be punished. So I spent more of my youthful years than I like to remember languishing in prison cells here, there and everywhere. I swear to you, Sylvester, I began to think the true color of the sky was blue with dark vertical lines.

"Still, my times of incarceration were not wasted. They taught me the error of my ways."

"But ..." began Sylvester, looked around him, mystified.

Cap'n Rustbane realized what his guest must be thinking. "Oh, no, I don't mean *that*. I don't mean they taught me to give up my life of crime. No, what they taught me was what an infernal nuisance it was getting caught. Sitting there behind bars for all that time, I recognized that the reason I kept getting caught was I kept leaving behind me people who'd seen me, and who could tell others what they'd seen. This was the single weakness in my *modus operandi*. The solution to my dilemma seemed such a simple one, once I'd discovered it."

Sylvester gulped.

"I see you're ahead of me," continued the fox with a smile that Sylvester wished he hadn't seen. "So, ever since then, I've made sure I don't leave behind me any surviving witnesses."

Sylvester gulped again, louder this time.

Cap'n Rustbane clapped his forepaws together. "And it works!" he cried gleefully. "As soon as I instituted my new practice, I stopped getting caught, and that meant I stopped having to spend long, boring periods in jail. From there it was but a single step – well, more accurately, a single swashbuckling bound – to becoming captain of my own ship, and I've never looked back."

"I, ah, can imagine," said Sylvester.

"I'll tell you about that swashbuckling bound another time," said Cap'n Rustbane in a softer voice, beckoning Sylvester to join him at the table. "Now, what you were really wanting to know about was the treasure, was it not?"

"Oh, yes," said Sylvester. "The treasure. Lots and lots of treasure, you were saying."

"I quite imagine I was. People who've heard about the magical chest of the Zindars – and exceedingly few people have, let me tell you – are apt to talk about treasure at length. Sometimes, dare I say it, to the point of tedium. But I shall be careful not to do that today, my little friend."

Cap'n Rustbane put his arm across Sylvester's shoulders as if the two of them were lifelong buddies. He lowered his voice yet again, looking around him furtively as if all the portraits on his cabin walls might be trying to eavesdrop.

"You see, my boy," he said at barely more than a whisper, "the magical chest of the Zindars is thousands of years old. It's been the ultimate prize for seafarers for as long as there has been avarice in people's hearts – which is, I should think, for about as long as people have had hearts to put avarice into."

"Who were the Zindars?"

The fox smiled. "I'll be laying a wager that's something you'd like to know. Maybe I'll tell you another time, once I've decided I can trust you. And maybe, contrariwise, I'll come to the decision that I can't trust you after all, and you'll be dancing on the end of a rope or swimming among the sharks at the bottom of the ocean. We'll just have to wait and see, shan't we?"

The conspiratorial smile he gave Sylvester seemed to reveal more teeth than ever before.

"What I can tell you is this," said the Cap'n, straightening up. He tapped the stack of papers in front of him with a very long and sharp-looking claw. "About fifty years ago, the greatest pirate to ever sail the seas of Sagaria – that is, until I came along, of course – the *second* greatest pirate who ever sailed the seas of Sagaria, one Cap'n Josiah 'Throatsplitter' Adamite, heard a rumor borne by the wind of where the Zindar chest might be found."

"It was just a rumor?" interrupted Sylvester. He was annoyed to find his own voice had instinctively dropped to a whisper to match Rustbane's.

The fox patted the side of his gray nose with the side of his paw.

"There's rumors and there's rumors, young Sylvester. This was one of *those* rumors."

"Ah," replied Sylvester wisely, as if he knew what Rustbane was talking about.

"By listening to the rumors, old Throatsplitter got himself as clear an idea as could be as to where the treasure of the Zindars was hidden, and he set down the results of his research in the form of a map."

"Ah," Sylvester repeated, shrugging guiltily. This time he did know what Rustbane was talking about. He wished he didn't.

"I see you know what map it is that's pertinent to this here discussion," said Rustbane, his yellow–green eyes looking sad.

Sylvester was keen to change the subject. "What happened to Cap'n Adamite? Didn't he ever get to look for his treasure?"

The fox sighed. "The ways of the ocean can be tragic ones, dear Sylvester, as you'll learn in the days and weeks to come. Old Throatsplitter, who was as kind and generous a man as ever disembowelled his granny, came to a sorrowful end. I was there to witness it myself, oh rue the day."

"Was he," Sylvester searched for something appropriately pitiful, "eaten by a shark? Or drowned trying to save a child's life?"

"Well, no," said Rustbane, looking annoyed at the interruption. "Not in veritable point of fact, no. I stuck my cutlass into his liver and twisted it about a bit, is what actually happened. And still he wouldn't tell me what he'd done with his map, see? He died with a horribly supercilious sneer on his face, as if he'd won out by dying. Which in a way," Rustbane hurried on, "he had. He'd gone to his watery grave. Well, it was watery by the time we'd given him the old heave-ho over the side of his ship, this very same *Shadeblaze* as has become your home. He'd gone to his grave knowing the secret of the treasure, and leaving me behind not knowing even what had happened to his sea chart showing the chest's location."

"That must have been very frustrating for you."

"Frustrating isn't the word. It was . . . It was . . ."

Cap'n Rustbane evidently found himself unable to speak.

"So, how did you find out what he'd done with the map?"

Rustbane's face cleared of its fury like sunshine bursting through an overcast sky.

"Ah, that, young fellow," he said, "involved some cunning. And, as many people will no doubt have told you, there ain't no one cunninger above or below the high seas, nor even on land, as your good friend, Cap'n Terrigan Rustbane."

The pirate let the final words hang in the air between them as if they explained everything.

Eventually, Sylvester broke the silence. "Yes, but—"

"Oh, I'm so terribly sorry. I'm quite forgetting my good manners. You can't have had breakfast yet. Let me summon the ship's cook to fetch you something appetizing from the galley. I haven't eaten anything myself this morning, so I'll join you in the repast. What's the saying? 'The condemned lemming ate a hearty breakfast'?"

Refusing to hear Sylvester's words of protest, Cap'n Rustbane picked up a little brass bell from the midst of a snowdrift of tidal charts on the table and rang it. Immediately, the door burst open and Cheesefang appeared, cutlass tremblingly at the ready.

"Yer wantin' me to rip out 'is innards, Skip?"

"Er, not quite yet, my good man. Later perhaps, if you're good. In the meantime, perhaps you'd be kind enough to ask Bladderbulge to bring up breakfast for two from the galley."

Looking disappointed, Cheesefang retreated. "Nothin' personal, mind. Just business," he muttered to Sylvester through the closing crack of the door.

"Bladderbulge?" said Sylvester, not immediately recognizing it as a name.

Cap'n Rustbane rolled his eyes expressively.

"Yes. It's so terribly unfortunate, especially for a cook. Heaven knows what was going through the mind of his mother when she named him. Not much, I'd expect. Whatever, he's the only sailor in the whole of the *Shadeblaze*'s crew who doesn't have a piratical moniker. Every time we try to invent one for him we, ah, fall short, as it were."

During the few minutes it took for Cheesefang to fetch the breakfast-bearing cook, Bladderbulge, Cap'n Rustbane resisted Sylvester's timid efforts to extract further information about Adamite's map, brusquely fobbing him off with remarks like "Can't talk sensibly on an empty stomach, m'boy" and "Sausages! Sausages! I do hope he'll bring sausages!"

On one of the latter occasions, Sylvester, in frustration, asked the Cap'n his views on sausages and was treated to a learned philosophical discourse on the relative virtues of sausages made with different piquancies of spice. Sylvester had never thought he'd be glad to see Cheesefang again, but it was a relief when the rat arrived with Bladderbulge, interrupting Cap'n Rustbane's sausageophiliac flow. Bladderbulge proved to be indeed bulging. He was a rotund badger with a wooden hind leg and he sported a stump where a tail should have been.

With an imperious swing of his arm, Rustbane swept the books and papers from one end of the table onto the floor and indicated to Bladderbulge that he should set down his tray of steaming food there. Sylvester was surprised to see that each of the several plates on the tray had a shiny metal covering on it.

Bladderbulge lifted these off one by one with the air of a conjurer revealing that his scantily clad assistant has not, after all, been sawn in half. The smell of hot, spiced meats filled the cabin.

There were plenty of sausages.

"Good," said Cap'n Rustbane firmly, seeing this. He pulled out a pair of low stools from under the table and sat himself down on one of them. Being so much smaller than the fox, Sylvester had difficulty clambering up on his, and even then the edge of the table was only at his chin level.

"You could try eating standing up," suggested Rustbane, who was already halfway through his second sausage and was eyeing the heap of sardines on Sylvester's plate in a speculative way.

So, Sylvester stood on the stool and ate like that. He hardly noticed the food he was consuming, so intent was he on finding out more about Adamite's map. The very fact that he was eating anything at all was a small miracle he realized afterward, bearing in mind how he'd been feeling when he'd reached the Cap'n's cabin. The greasy food settled his stomach, and for the first time this morning – in fact, since coming aboard the *Shadeblaze* – he began to feel like his normal self.

The food seemed to change Rustbane's mood too, but not for the better.

As soon as Bladderbulge had cleared the plates away, the fox began to pace from one end of the cabin to the other, occasionally paused to dart a furious glance at Sylvester, then resuming his restless striding.

When at last he spoke, it was in a voice filled with harsh bitterness.

"Yes, I remember it all too well, those long months spent locked up with hard rock beneath my feet rather than the comforting sway of Mother Ocean."

"It must have been miserable for you," said Sylvester.

Cap'n Rustbane didn't hear him.

"The cell I was in had one tiny window, high up in the wall. I could perhaps have jumped up and clung on to the bars somehow to look out at the world, but the bastards had shackled my feet to the floor with just enough chain for me to reach the privy in the corner, which stank. All I could do, day in day out, was gaze longingly up at that tiny rectangle of light, made even tinier by the height of the wall, and imagine what was happening underneath the pathetically small fraction of sky I could see. There was a dark cloud there ... Were people putting up their umbrellas and chasing each other laughingly through the rain or marching along, heads down with grim faces watching the water splash on the road in front of them? Ah, the scrap of sky is blue today ... Is everyone out playing ball on every available patch of green grass, or are they fanning themselves with their hands and wishing they didn't have to work on such a hot day as this? You see what I mean?"

The fox halted abruptly and turned blazing eyes on Sylvester, who cringed as if Death itself had snuck into the cabin.

"You see what I mean?" the fox thundered again. Clearly, he wanted no answer. "There was nothing a person could do, trapped in there, except think of how he was going to avenge himself once he'd finally been released from that hellhole. Oh, I tried all the usual means of escape and just about all of the unusual ones too. Didn't I tell you we foxes are cunninger than just about any other creature? But they were no use, as I'd known before I tried 'em. So, all I could do was wait and do my best to count the days, and think of what I was going to do when those days were ended. The higher and higher the number of days I counted, the nastier and nastier the things I plotted to do to more and more people. That's how prison affects a fellow, you see."

He paused again, swiping the side of his face lightly with his paw. "No, of course," he mumbled, "you probably don't see, being a lemming. Lemmings aren't naturally vicious creatures, like foxes."

Sylvester could have corrected him on this (it was obvious Cap'n Rustbane didn't know much about lemmings!) but decided it was safer to stay silent.

"The first time I was let out of prison, there were crewmates waiting to welcome me," the fox continued, pacing once more. "Risking their lives, they were, because if the peelers – that's the name for the coastal police, in case you didn't know – had known who they were they'd have found themselves dancing from a yard arm quick as blinking. But they came anyway and hauled me off to a tavern and filled me full of good grog to celebrate my freedom, and when I told them my plans for vengeance they shook me by the shoulders and told me not to be so damn stupid. The best thing I could do, soon as I'd thrown all that good grog up again and could walk on my own two hind legs (well, with my shipmates to support me, leastwise), the best thing I could do, they said, was put as much of the world between me and the prison – and the people who'd put me there – as I possibly could, and as quick as I could.

"So, I took their advice, and off we sailed on the big blue sea, and I tucked my memories of that foul hole away at the back of my mind and thought I'd never see them again.

"That was the ending of my first time in jail.

"But then, like a numbskull, I only went and got myself caught again, didn't I? Luckily, it was in a different country, with a different judge, or I'd've had my neck stretched for sure. Because you can blather your way out of just about anything in front of a judge the first time, but you try it again he's going to see right through your blandishments and be twice as hard on you as otherwise. Whatever, even though the crowd was baying for blood, the judge took pity on my youthful innocence and off I went to jail again. If they hadn't told me it was a different prison and a different cell, I'd never have known. Same tall walls, same tiny barred window, same jakes as stank to high heaven no matter if I used it or not.

"And I plotted and schemed, and my dreams were full of satisfying cruelty and gore . . .

"The day I was let free, though, there were my old muckers from the pirate ship, and off we went to the tavern, and I had a headache and an acid gut for a week but I never hurt anybody for having put me away.

"Same goes the third time I was incarcerated – which was what I had been the first two times, only I hadn't known the word. They was a lucky judge and jury, lucky peelers . . .

"Then there was the fourth time. Ah, me, yes, the fourth time."

The gray fox stopped at the side of the desk and leaned on his hands against it, looming over Sylvester like some enormous bird of prey. Looking into Rustbane's eyes, Sylvester could see deep pits of agony. Fury, yes – a crazy rage. Bitterness. A writhing serpent of vindictiveness. But, most of all, what Sylvester saw behind the screens of yellow–green was *pain*.

"The fourth time, it wasn't just me. The soldiers and peelers had caught near the entire crew of the *Mollie O'Grady*, which was the sweet vessel I sailed in under Cap'n Bosseye Skankangle, may his fine and twisted spirit be blessed in memory. There was sixty or more of us hauled into the assizes at Swivern. That's in Tarngonia, which is mongoose country, case you don't know. The judge was this little mongoose who was viciouser even than Bosseye, but all dressed up in long robes and finery so his viciousness looked civilized. The jury was worse – not that most of the judges I've come across pay much mind to what juries think. The chief of the coastal police stood up in front of everyone and told them there was no sense making much of a trial out of this, since we was all pirates and had been caught with our paws elbow-deep in booty and gore. Just string 'em all up, said this pillar of justice, 'less you want to boil a few alive for sport.

"The judge, peering over the top of the stupid little spectacles he affected, agreed with the police chief, and the jury and the audience obviously did too, because they were yelling and cheering and calling out for us to be torn limb from limb, not just hanged.

"Me, I squirmed my way to the front, and laid the most innocent gaze you ever did see upon the judge, who couldn't help but notice it. I swear to you, Sylvester, I made myself look so youthful and guilelessly misled that day it's a wonder no one offered to change my diapers. The judge hammered on his bench for quiet and sooner or later he got it. Of all the crew of the *Mollie O'Grady* I was the only one who got the opportunity to speak my piece in front of the court.

"And what I told them was all about my poor sick mother (I'd got *that* little speech down pat, all right!) and my half-dozen little brothers and sisters, some of 'em barely able to walk as yet, whose cute little furry tummies was empty and echoing. If I didn't want to just sit back and watch 'em all starve to death, the only thing I could do was to go to sea in search of wages so I could feed 'em. And how was I to know that the gentle sailors who offered me a job were really cutthroat pirates?

"I tell you, by the time I'd done there wasn't a dry eye anywhere to be found. Even some of my crewmates were bawling like babes on each other's shoulders. As for the judge, he'd had to take his little spectacles off a score of times to dry the insides so he could see.

"And the end result of it was that, while Bosseye and all the rest of the fine seafarers of the *Mollie O'Grady* were dragged off to the gibbet, I was thrown back into that same identical prison cell with the tall walls and the dinky little window and the lav in the corner that I swear they stunk up extra while I was sleeping at nights.

"That was the longest time I ever did spend in prison. And the last, by the belly of the triple-breasted goddess, the last!

"The day I was released, there was no one at the gate to meet me.

"They'd all swung, see? All my crewmates, all the people there were in the world that I could call 'friend.' Back on that dreadful day when I alone had been tossed behind bars, they'd met their makers at the end of a rope.

"I went on my own to a tavern and got drunk on grog, but my heart wasn't in it.

"All the time I was sitting there drinking, I was remembering the smug face of the chief of the coastal police, and the beady little hypocritical eyes of the judge who'd passed sentence on us, and the bloodthirsty looks on the jurors, and the braying of the townsfolk who wanted to see us all dangle. And most of anything, I remembered what my dreams and schemes had shown me doing to these scum.

"So I went into the hills and I found me a band of outlaws, and I beat them into taking me as their leader. I had to kill a few with my bare hands, but that was what was needed to get the rest to fall in line. I trained them how to use the swords and cudgels we got by murdering wayfarers on the lonely roads out there, and I bided my time until the wrath was banked back inside me, glowing white hot but fully under control.

"One night, when the moon was shy of the sky, me and my twenty cruelest cutthroats crept into the town where the courthouse was, and—"

Cap'n Rustbane stopped speaking abruptly, noticing Sylvester's presence for the first time in a very long while.

"You've put your paws over your ears," he said. "What in the world possessed you to do that, young Sylvester? We're just getting to the best bit."

"I don't want to hear what happens next." The words came squeezing out of Sylvester's mouth as if they'd rather have stayed inside him.

"What?"

"Blood and guts may be all right for you, but I'm a peaceable fellow and—"

"Are you too lily-stomached for tales of mayhem?"

"Yes! That's exactly it. Think what you like of me, but—"

"But it's the gore and grue and the shrieks of the women and the spurting of blood that thrills the soul of any buccaneering boyo!"

"Then I'm not a buccaneering boyo."

Cap'n Rustbane chuckled. It was a sound that could have made the flames of hell freeze in fear.

"But you're learning my ways." The fox's voice was so quiet that it could barely be heard over the creaking of the ship's timbers. "D'you think you're frightened at the moment, young Sylvester?"

"Ye–yes!"

"Then imagine how frightened you'd be if it weren't just at the thought of me *telling* you about hacking people to death – slllloooooowwwwly, so I could savor their pain – but because I was just about to do all of these things and many, many more . . . to *you*!"

The last word was delivered no more than a finger's width from Sylvester's nose.

He thought he was going to fall off the too-high stool.

He thought he was going to faint clear away.

Billows of blackness encroached from all sides of his vision, converging in towards the center and seemed destined to blot it out entirely, but somehow he clung on to consciousness.

He stared Cap'n Rustbane straight in the eye with what he hoped was a reasonable imitation of defiance.

"I'm a peaceable person, as I've said, and I've no stomach for bloodshed or cruelty, but that doesn't mean I'm a coward. I'd ask you, sir, to remember that."

For a moment, Sylvester knew, his life hung by a strand from a spider's web.

Then Cap'n Rustbane guffawed with laughter, slapping Sylvester on the back, which lifted him and sent him sliding across the table in a flurry of charts and pens.

"Only a hamster, and you've shown more courage to my face than any man-jack of my crew has done for a bucketful of years. I like you, young Sylvester. I knew from the first I was going to, and Cap'n Terrigan Rustbane is never, ever wrong about a thing like that."

"Lemming," said Sylvester.

"Whassat? Speak up!"

"*Lemming.*"

"Explain yourself." The pirate's grin seemed to span the cabin wall to wall.

"I'm not a hamster," said Sylvester with as much dignity as he could muster while lying flat on his stomach, his nose acting as an impromptu bookmark for what appeared, in the instant before impact, to be *A Voyage to the Atolls of the Great Western Ocean*, by Sir Perceval Montiffew. "I'm a lemming. I've told you before."

"You have indeed," cried Cap'n Rustbane, reaching out a paw to help him up. "And it's magnificently sorrowful I am to have made this same error yet again. Please accept my humblest apologies."

"Apology accepted," said Sylvester, hoping he didn't sound too prim. The fox was, after all, helping him to his feet and dusting him down.

"Good, good. Now, where was I?"

"Somewhere I'd rather you didn't go back," said Sylvester.

"Oh, yes. Me and my band of hoodlums were—but you wanted me to skip over the good part, didn't you?"

"Yes." Uneasily, Sylvester wondered if Viola would have given the fox the same answer.

Again, Cap'n Rustbane laughed. "You see, young Sylvester, the point of my telling you the story wasn't to impress you with the terrible things I've done during my time upon this mortal coil. That's a story too long to be told at a single sitting. What I'm trying to get through to you is the way a good pirate captain – and you don't find pirate captains any gooder than me, in a manner of speaking – makes sure of the unswerving loyalty and obedience of his crew, even their love. That'd be not too strong a word."

"You still haven't told me how you learned about Cap'n Adamite's map," Sylvester put in. He was sitting on the edge of the table now, his hind legs dangling beneath him.

"I haven't!" The Cap'n smote his brow histrionically. "And I was going to do that too, wasn't I? Whatever is happening to my brain? Sometimes I think I'd forget my head if it wasn't fixed on."

"Yes, you were. Going to tell me about the map, I mean."

"Telling you about the map's important, isn't it?" A sort of quiet reasonableness entered the fox's voice. Sylvester wasn't sure he liked the sound of it. "But then," Cap'n Rustbane went on, "the lesson I'm in the process of teaching you is important too. Yes. I think it's the more important of the two things. Remind me about the map later."

"Surely," said Sylvester as if that was what he'd intended all along.

"Good. Now, my fine young friend, I was talking about fear and I was getting to the stage of telling you about what fear can do to a person, even someone who, like your good self, is no coward. Fear, true fear, isn't listening to something appalling, and oohing and ahing about how ghastly it all is. Fear is when it's about to happen to *you*."

From nowhere a razor-sharp dagger had appeared in the fox's paw. Sylvester might have been better able to appreciate the legerdemain involved were it not for the fact that the paw in question was unnervingly close to his own throat.

"It's fear that enables me to rule the roost aboard the *Shadeblaze*," explained Cap'n Rustbane, turning the blade over and over so that in the light from the lantern above the metal seemed almost liquid. "Some of them scurvy creatures out there are bigger than me, and there's even a few of them that are tougher than me and better in a fight, but there ain't none of them *meaner* than me. Ain't none of them crueller than me, or readier to cut out a tongue or an eye or a heart if I don't like its owner."

Cap'n Rustbane let the implications of this sink in, then carried on.

"Aboard this ship, see, young lemming, I'm the judge and jury, and I've got a heart harder by far than that old mongoose back in Swivern. I know, because I saw *his* for myself as I held it in my paws and watched as it stopped beating. My word is law anywhere on the *Shadeblaze*, from the bottom of the keel to the topmost tip of the mainmast. It's law, as well, wherever my crew might chance to be on land or sea, even if they're not aboard the *Shadeblaze*. If anyone wants to go against my word, to break my law, why, he finds out the difficult way what it's like to raise the hackles of Cap'n Terrigan Rustbane."

With a dexterous flick of the gray fox's paw, the dagger vanished again.

Sylvester suddenly noticed he must have stopped breathing a while back without realizing it. He filled his lungs with a panicky gasp.

"Is that understood?"

"Cer–certainly," said Sylvester.

"The same goes for everyone. You included. That pert miss of yours too."

Sylvester could almost hear the gears turning over in Cap'n Rustbane's mind.

"And almost certainly for that mother of hers, Three Pins. I hope."

The dagger reappeared for a glittering split second. When it vanished again, Sylvester realized that a neat half-inch had been trimmed from his whiskers on both sides.

"Understood?" the fox repeated.

"Oh, absolutely."

"Obey my orders and you live. Disobey, and . . ."

Cap'n Rustbane drew his finger across his throat eloquently.

Sylvester tried to give a sophisticated laugh. It came out as if someone had strangled it.

Once more, the dagger was in Rustbane's paw. "Remember how I threw this, back in Foxglove, and missed you?"

"Yes."

"I don't often miss."

He flipped the dagger end over end, so that he was holding it by the blade rather than the hilt, then in the same movement gave it another flip.

Sylvester felt the wind as the weapon whistled past his cheek. A tiny coolness told him that he'd lost more whiskers. Behind him, there was a *thunkk* as the dagger lodged in the cabin wall.

"Your life's mine to do as I like with, you understand?"

"I do."

"Then remember it. *Fear me.* Your life depends upon it."

Yet again, the fox's mood visibly shifted, as if the shadow of a cloud were lifting off a grassy field.

"But you were asking me about the map, were you not?"

"Er, yes." Baffled by the fox's newly regained amiability, Sylvester suspected a trap somewhere. Cap'n Rustbane's constant shifts of humor made Sylvester feel as if he were walking on slippery ice. At any particular moment he was managing to keep himself upright, but always with the awareness that the very next moment might, without any advance warning, see him painfully dumped on his rear.

"Well," said Rustbane, uncannily perpetuating the theme of Sylvester's thought, "you're sitting on it."

The fox laughed uproariously as Sylvester, horrified, tried to look underneath himself without falling off the edge of the table.

"Not quite, dear Sylvester, not quite. But a little more to the side and you would be."

Sylvester's gaze turned towards where Cap'n Rustbane was tapping a long, sharp claw on what looked, at first glimpse, like some old paper someone had crumpled up to throw away, then relented and tried to flatten out again. Age had turned the paper that mellow brown Sylvester knew so well from his work at the Library in Foxglove. The irregularly shaped piece of map that he'd burned had been this same yellow.

"Take a look, dear boy."

Sylvester shuffled along so he could see the paper better. It was obvious at a glance, even though the job had been done with painstaking skill, that the sheet had been formed by gluing two roughly triangular sheets together along one edge. The result was a rectangle from which one large shape was missing. It didn't take a genius to work out what that piece of the jigsaw puzzle had been, especially since the remaining portions were covered in the same squiggles as the one Sylvester had destroyed.

On one of the pieces there were even more squiggles running diagonally across the top right-hand corner and then turning to follow, in an irregular fashion, the right-hand side of the paper for about three-quarters of the length of the sheet before disappearing off the edge. A sudden flash of insight told Sylvester this must be a section of coastline of a larger landmass.

One of the sheets of parchment was significantly filthier than the other, and than the sheet Sylvester had been given by Levantes. It looked as if someone might have been using it as a handkerchief – someone with a very bad cold. And that was the polite version of what seemed to have been done to it.

"The last time I was in jail," breathed Rustbane into Sylvester's ear, "back in Swivern that was, you'll remember. The last time I was rotting in a prison cell there was a poor wretch of a squirrel in the cell next to mine. It was strictly forbidden for the two of us to talk, on penalty of a flogging, so o' course we did. Not the way the guards thought we'd have to, mind, which was shouting out loud enough for the other one to hear us through the thick stone walls. No. Over the years, before we'd gotten there, there'd been other prisoners in these two cells and they'd dug into the mortar between the stones with their suppertime forks and spoons and whatever else came to hand, I have no doubt, even their fingernails. By the time I was thrust unceremoniously into that cesspit, there was a tiny hole all the way through the mortar into the next cell.

"The hole was just big enough to carry a whisper."

The gray fox stared off into the unknown distance, clearly reliving those times.

"Now," he said, "any two amateurish jailbirds'd have done their whispering at night, when even the tiniest whisper can be heard at the other end of even the tiniest hole. But me and Hamish – that was my prisonmate's name – we were wiser jailbirds than that. Think of it: at night, when it's really quiet and nothing's moving, a whisper's likely to be heard all over the prison, see, and most partic'larly by a guard just outside in the corridor. If such a whisper had been heard, it'd have been the flesh of me and Hamish that'd have paid the price, cut to tatters by prison whips. So, what we did was we whispered during daylight hours, when everything about the prison was hustle and bustle and the screaming of the luckless whose turn it was in the torture cells beneath was at its loudest.

"I didn't tell you there was a lot of torturing going on in that prison, did I? Some of the prisons I've been in have been all right in that respect but, remember, I was in mongoose country and mongooses can be cruel creatures. Luckily, my crime hadn't been deemed worthy of the time and labors of the torturers, but Hamish was less fortunate."

Cap'n Rustbane put his paw alongside his nose in the gesture Sylvester had come to recognize as indicating the pirate was preparing to impart some secret or item of received wisdom.

"The peelers in Swivern, you see, had got wind of the fact that Hamish knew something of great interest. He'd served for forty years as a midshipman under Cap'n Josiah Adamite, no less. Although the good Cap'n had placed a clamp of iron over the lips of his crew, fig'ratively speaking, somehow word had sneaked out that he'd discovered the location of the magical chest of the Zindars, and drawn himself a map of it. But more than that no one knew, 'cepting some of his crew, o' course. And here was poor Hamish, who'd been one of the fine seamen serving under Adamite, trapped in a Swivern jail and so under the mongoose thumb."

"I didn't know mongooses had thumbs," interposed Sylvester.

"Do you know how to do joined-up writing?"

"Well, er, yes, I do, as a matter of fact."

"Then you know enough to be able to recognize a figure of speech when you see one, right?"

"Um, yes, I, um—"

"It is not of relevance to this story whether mongooses do or do not have thumbs."

"That's true."

"The only possible pertinence might be if you were wanting to know the details of the tortures the mongooses perpetrated upon poor Hamish."

Sylvester scratched his head. "Would it?"

Cap'n Rustbane looked at him impatiently. "If mongooses don't have thumbs, it's hardly likely they'd have invented the thumbscrew, is it?"

"*Did* they invent the thumbscrew?"

"I don't know. Hamish never told me. It's likely he didn't know himself."

"But wouldn't they have—oh."

"That's right. Whatever the truth about mongooses, there's one fact I know for sure: *squirrels* don't have thumbs. Not much point waving a thumbscrew in a squirrel's face and telling him you're not afraid to use it."

Sylvester could imagine only too well the uses to which a thumbscrew might be put on even a thumbless victim by someone dedicated to the creation of pain (there were plenty of fingers and toes you could use instead) but he decided not to contradict the Cap'n. After all, as Rustbane had just been explaining in emphatic detail, Sylvester was completely at the pirate's mercy here aboard the *Shadeblaze*. And Sylvester was more than sure that the pirates had a lot worse than thumbscrews they could use on whomsoever their Cap'n told them they should.

Cap'n Rustbane waved a paw dismissively. "Forget about mongoose thumbs," he instructed.

"Right you are."

"Although," added the fox in a ruminative fashion, "there is one mystery about mongooses you might care to ponder in your leisure time, young Sylvester."

"What's that?"

"Why in the heck aren't they called mon*geese*?"

"Because they—"

Sylvester stopped short. It was one of those infuriatingly irritating questions that you wish you'd never heard asked. Indeed, why weren't they called mongeese?

He shook his head crossly. And Cap'n Rustbane had berated *him* for asking irrelevant questions that got in the way of the story!

"So what did the torturers manage to extract from poor Hamish?"

Cap'n Rustbane's eyes narrowed in amusement, then became serious again.

"Nothing," he said. "Nothing at all."

"Then why are you—"

"Which," the Cap'n's voice grew louder, overriding Sylvester's, "doesn't mean to say Hamish didn't tell *anyone* anything. He was loyal to Cap'n Adamite as only a true, black-hearted pirate can be to his skipper, so, the more they twisted the tongs or heated the daggers white-hot, the more firmly did Hamish fasten his lips. But then after each session of agony, once what was left of him had been tossed back into his cell like a sack of unwanted rubbish, he would whisper to me through the chink between our cells all that he hadn't told the torturers. And what I learned from him, in dribs and drabs over the weeks and months before poor Hamish died, was that Cap'n Adamite had decided, for the safekeeping of the treasure whose location he had deduced, to commit the map to memory, much like you've done more recently, young Sylvester. However, knowing that bad things might happen to him and not wishing the chest of the Zindars to be lost forever should his gizzard be slit, or some such, he decided that, rather than committing the map to the flames or casting it to Davy Jones's Locker, he divided it into three parts, which he consigned to three different areas of Sagaria."

Sylvester, engrossed, found his paw was straying to his mouth. Vexedly, he straightened his arm again and hoped Cap'n Rustbane hadn't noticed the telltale of the childish habit.

"Those three areas? Ah, yes," said Rustbane as if Sylvester had just asked him the question. "Hamish wasn't supposed to know but he did, and he told me. For many years it was a secret I carried close to my heart, telling no one, and it seems strange that today there's no reason to keep that secret any longer – least of all from you. Two parts are here on the table, and the third one would be if it weren't for your actions yesterday. Besides, the third one will soon be here, either supplied by you voluntarily or tortured out of you.

"What Hamish told me was that old Josiah had sent the first part of the map, this bit here" – Cap'n Rustbane jabbed a claw at the top-left section – "into the heart of worg country. There's no worg alive that has the brains to read his own name, let alone a sea chart, so Cap'n Adamite knew the meaning of the map was safe from discovery there. At the same time, there's no more possessive creature than a worg, they'd die rather than give up even the most worthless trinket that's caught their fancy. So Josiah knew too, that the map was as well hidden from more intelligent eyes as it could possibly be.

"Then there was the second bit," he said with another tap of the claw. "According to Hamish, there was something of a mystery about how it got there, but Cap'n Adamite knew it was on Booty Island. Knowledge of its exact ownership on that fair isle was not altogether possible. Of course, it being a pirate island, anyone known to be in possession of a treasure map would sure as fate be dead within the hour, if lucky enough to live that long. However, as Hamish said wisely, 'Anything worth killing for on Booty Island will sooner or later find its way to Darkwater, and anything worth killing for in Darkwater has a habit of making a beeline for a hellhole tavern called The Moldy Claw.'

"As for the third part of the map? Ah, there rested the ultimate enigma. Where could it have gone to? Even Hamish hadn't the first glimmer of a clue. It was a secret the old blackguard, Adamite, had kept clutched tightly to his chest. Aware perhaps that, despite threats as to what he should do if they told of his disposition of the first two pieces, one or two of his rapscallion crewmen were bound to find themselves loose-tongued at the wrong moment and cough up the information to willing ears. Well then, one can imagine the old curmudgeon reasoning that, in that case no one at all, not even his most trusted cronies, would know what he had done with the final segment.

"It was a secret that even my dear friend Hamish, who'd been like a brother to the Cap'n, died without learning."

"How did poor Hamish die?" asked Sylvester, becoming misty-eyed as he thought of the bravery of the imprisoned pirate, resisting his torturers to the last. "Did his tormentors finally put too great an imposition upon him?"

"Not precisely," said Cap'n Rustbane. "He was still alive when the day came that I was adjudged to have served my sentence."

"When you were released, you mean?"

"*Exactamente.* I was halfway to the jailhouse exit when I realized that, after my departure, there was nothing to stop my erstwhile pal, Hamish, from confiding through the chink in the wall to the next occupant of my late prison cell everything he'd been so intent on confiding to me."

An appalling conviction spread slowly through Sylvester. "You don't mean you—"

Cap'n Rustbane spread his paws, pleading for understanding. "Well, honestly, old fellow, what in the world *else* could I have done? Hamish had entrusted me with a large part of the secret of what Cap'n Adamite had done with his treasure map. Far more, I was willing to bet, than I could ever have hoped to extract from the grizzled old corsair myself. The thought was intolerable that he might convey the same information to anyone else, was it not? Then there'd be two of us after the map, which, as any mathematician would tell you, would be one too many."

"But there are two of us now who know about the map," said Sylvester and then wished he hadn't.

"Indeed," said Cap'n Rustbane very quietly. His voice in that moment reminded Sylvester of one of Doc Nettletree's finely honed scalpels. Sylvester wondered for an instant how Doctor Nettletree and the rest of the folk in Foxglove were getting along, then realized it was just a way of avoiding facing the reality of the peril he was in, and he switched his mind back firmly to the present.

Rustbane shrugged. "No sooner thought than done. I bribed the warder who'd been charged with releasing me and he allowed me into the cell of my dear, dear friend for just thirty seconds. Just thirty seconds? It was five times as long as I needed, though the only weapons I had with me were my bare paws and teeth. Look on it this way, I was putting him out of the reach of his daily tormentors. I was doing him a kindness really. Maybe for once Cap'n Terrigan Rustbane isn't such a blackhearted rogue as you think, eh, Sylvester?

"Anyway, within the minute I was on the street, with no one the wiser. Apart from, of course, the warder, except I'd not wasted my spare time in Hamish's cell, so the warder was strolling alongside Hamish in whatever afterlife they'd found together . . . Where was I again?"

"You were leaving prison," prompted Sylvester, feeling more than a little sick.

"Ah, yes. Footloose and fancy free." A lighthearted smile crossed the gray fox's lips, and he executed a few steps of some formal dance across the cabin's slightly unsteady floor to demonstrate how footloose he'd been.

"It didn't take long," he continued, returning to join Sylvester at the table, "to find myself a berth on Cap'n Adamite's trusty vessel, the *Shadeblaze*, as it was called then and is called now. There were, after all, a few vacancies for experienced seamen, seeing as how Hamish and those of his crewmates who'd been captured with him weren't going to be coming back. I served him well for a good long time, waiting for the moment to be ripe. Then I weaned the crew away from Cap'n Adamite, or at least enough of the crew to mount a successful mutiny. Those who objected, well, let's just say that the sharks off Pountlemont Island were burping happily for quite some time. To make myself the new skipper was a challenge of little difficulty for someone as skilled in the art of manipulation as your ol' pal, Cap'n Rustbane. And the rest you know. Or, if you don't, at least you'll have guessed, an intelligent young hamster like you."

"Lemming," corrected Sylvester, but his heart wasn't in it.

"But the truth of it is," said Cap'n Rustbane, his voice adopting a musing tone, "that no matter what I did to him – and I did a lot, as you can imagine – that old buzzard, Cap'n Adamite, wouldn't tell me one single teensiest hint of where he'd despatched the third section of his goddess-blasted treasure map. The third part. The *important* part. The bit with—"

"The bit with the big, bold 'X' marked on it," Sylvester completed for him.

The gray fox cocked his head to look down on Sylvester. For just a moment there was something oddly bird-like about those yellow–green eyes.

"So, you weren't kidding me, after all," said the fox.

"Of course I wasn—"

Sylvester's voice came to an abrupt halt. *Damn him!* he thought. *He's right about his skills of manipulation, or whatever it was he called them. He's just negotiated me, very neatly indeed, into confirming what he wanted to know.*

"Care to tell me anything else about your piece of old Adamite's map?" Rustbane was saying, inspecting the claws of one paw as if the matter of the map was no more than a casual concern.

"Not right now," responded Sylvester. "By the way, Cap'n Rustbane, just out of interest you understand, how was it your famed powers of manipulation didn't work on Cap'n Adamite?"

As Sylvester half-expected, the pirate ignored the question. "Come here and look at this, boy," he said.

Sylvester maneuvered himself clumsily across the table to look directly down at Adamite's chart.

"See, boy," said Rustbane, "we're *here*." He touched his paw to a place near the upper corner of the map, close to the irregular line that ran down the document's right-hand side. The line Sylvester had earlier deduced represented the coast of some larger landmass.

That's not just any old landmass, he thought now. *That's the landmass which happens to have Foxglove on it, Foxglove and the whole of the world I knew until yesterday. Yet Cap'n Adamite didn't even think it was worth marking Foxglove on the map.*

"Where we're going to," continued Rustbane, "is down *here*."

He traced his claw down the page, at the same time moving it progressively farther from the squiggly coastline. When the claw came to a group of four medium-sized shapes and several smaller ones, all roughly oval but with, again, irregular outlines, Cap'n Rustbane began to tap it.

"They're the Caraya Islands. Take us a couple of weeks to reach 'em, I reckon. They're hotter 'n the triple-breasted goddess's underwear, they are, lying across the tropics the way they do. There are the four big ones, as you can see. The rest aren't hardly worth thinking about. The old ocean lore has it there's a million of the Carayas, some of them no bigger than a sea lion's rump, but I don't hold with that. We'll put into Hangman's Haven on the biggest of the Carayas – Blighter Island, that is. We'll pick ourselves up some supplies and maybe let the crew blow off a bit of steam, if I'm feeling of a generous cast of mind. Then" – the claw began to move again – "we keep going southwest until" – the claw ran off the surface of crumpled parchment and onto the polished wood of the desk – "we find ourselves sailing through the uncharted waters of *your* map, Sylvester."

Sylvester squinted at the paper beneath his nose. That was right. The picture he could bring up from the back of his mind made a perfect fit with these other two pieces. He could see the *Shadeblaze*'s passage quite clearly. The ship was going to miss the "X" by a long way unless he told Cap'n Rustbane to alter course appropriately.

He began to say as much, then paused.

Was he yet again being manipulated by the pirate into telling him more than he wanted to?

Then Sylvester shook his head, impatient with himself. It was in his own interest – and Viola and Mrs. Pickleberry's – not to withhold too much from their captor. Unless Sylvester kept feeding Rustbane at least a few bits and pieces of genuine information from time to time, with some of those being substantive rather than incidental, the pirate's patience could at any moment snap. He'd probably have the self-control not to kill Sylvester, although he was perfectly capable of doing the most excruciating damage to Sylvester's body without actually killing him, but Viola and her mom's lives were by no means so guaranteed.

Give him a little now, Sylvester instructed himself. *Otherwise . . .*

"That's the wrong direction," he said aloud.

"Good fellow!" cried Cap'n Rustbane.

Timorously, Sylvester reached out and put his paw on the back of the gray fox's much larger one. He was startled by the softness of the fox's fur. He'd expected it to be stiff and prickly like a lemming's, only if anything more so. Instead it was almost downy.

"More *this* way," said Sylvester, pushing at Rustbane's paw.

"More like south-southwest than southwest itself, you mean?"

"If you say so," said Sylvester, not being sure of how the geographical directions translated themselves on to the map.

Rustbane was no fool. He immediately grasped Sylvester's difficulty.

The fox made two quick movements of his paw. "That way's south and that way's west. Southwest's halfway between 'em and—"

"South-southwest's closer to south than to west," said Sylvester eagerly. "Yes, I get it."

He did too. Up until this moment he'd been looking at the map as merely a type of document with which he was unfamiliar, a source of valuable information that was fascinating to him because it conveyed that information in a way quite unlike the way the words in the old scrolls did. But now, now it was a *map*, something very special and exciting. It was as if a map could take a whole region of the world, fold it up until it was tiny, then stow it away in a drawer where it would lie waiting, trembling with concentrated latent magic. Ready to be opened out again and become the full-size geographical area once more, complete with the winds and the scents and the splashings of cold ocean spray on your face.

There was beauty in this whole fresh *map* concept, but it wasn't the beauty that attracted Sylvester so much.

It was the magic that the map, that all maps, possessed.

The power.

"The place marked 'X' is more down here," he said, pointing, but he wasn't really listening to his own words.

Back at the Library in Foxglove, with kindly old Celadon breathing down his neck, Sylvester had read about books that had power – magical books that might or might not be grimoires. But he'd never dreamed that maps could contain that same pulsing quality. And it wasn't only special maps that had it, like only special books did, it was *all* maps. Anything capable of creasing up a part of the world until it was tiny enough to be put in a pocket was surely filled with magical power, was it not?

And there was one of them in front of him, made all the more powerful by the fact that a part of it didn't exist in this physical world.

He became aware that Cap'n Rustbane was watching him very quietly so as not to interrupt his chain of thought. When the pirate noticed Sylvester was returning from his reverie, he gave a little chuckle.

"You and me," said the fox, "we're going to be friends, my lad. Mark my words, but that's true."

Somehow, Sylvester doubted it, but while Cap'n Rustbane was speaking the words, they seemed plausible.

"Once we've found the treasure," Sylvester said, his voice sounding dismayingly thin, "we'll be—I mean, Viola and her mom and me, we'll be free to leave won't we?"

"As free as seagulls," replied the pirate grandly. "You have my word on it, as a fox of honor."

A fox of honor.

Sylvester remembered how much Rustbane's previous use of that oath had meant to the pirate.

Nothing.

Perhaps even less than nothing.

And he suspected the Cap'n regarded their lives in much the same way.

I have to be careful, thought Sylvester, *about everything, literally everything, I say or do from now on. However much Rustbane may make me believe from time to time he's good-hearted underneath it all, that he's a diamond in the rough, I have to remember he isn't that at all.*

He's a villain.

And we're at his mercy . . . the mercy he doesn't have!

THE ONLY LANGUAGE THEY UNDERSTAND

The rest of the day passed in fits and starts, time speeding up and slowing down in response to Sylvester's level of interest or boredom as Cap'n Rustbane showed him around the *Shadeblaze* and introduced him to the realities of seafaring life. Sylvester would never have believed there could be so much to learn, or that he'd take so many hours learning it. Every time he thought his head was on the verge of exploding because of the amount of new information that had been stuffed in there, Cap'n Rustbane (usually with the redoubtable Cheesefang in attendance as a combined bodyguard and straight man) would come up with something new to tell him. The science of navigation alone, Sylvester came to believe as he handled the ship's sextant or marveled at the hundreds of finely ruled gradations around the perimeter of the *Shadeblaze*'s compass, merited a lifetime of dedicated study. Rustbane managed to pack its rudiments into a couple of hours or less.

Navigation was possibly the most interesting of all the topics they covered that day. It was also the one where Sylvester's learning was most often disrupted by sudden bouts of daydreaming. Talking about navigation naturally led him often to start thinking about maps, and from there it was but a short step from going off into a reverie of wonder at the fact that one of these amazing, magical, powerful entities was contained right inside his very own head!

Every now and then he'd think about Viola and his mind would cloud with guilt that he wasn't thinking about her more often. She must be safe, he told himself. He wondered how she and Mrs. Pickleberry were occupying their time. Then Cap'n Rustbane would present him with some new marvel and they'd slide out of his thoughts again . . .

. . . until next time they appeared, when he'd feel guilty all over again.

There was one deeply disturbing incident during the day, followed by a series of events that would cloud Sylvester's happiness for a very long time to come.

It occurred not long after he and Rustbane had consumed their luncheon, back in the Cap'n's cabin for the meal.

There was a knock on the door.

"Enter if you really need to see me," cried Rustbane impatiently. "Otherwise you'd be better off just to creep back where you came from."

Under the circumstances, Sylvester thought, whoever was at the door would have to be a very brave person indeed if they entered the cabin.

So he was surprised when the door opened, and even more so when he recognized the opener.

"Sorry to disturb ye, Cap'n," said the mangy-looking ocelot whom Sylvester had last seen, back in Foxglove's town square, being thrown face first into a wall by an enraged Mrs. Pickleberry. Perhaps the ocelot had lost a few teeth during the encounter, perhaps not. It was hard to tell which of the gaps in the rotting array his mouth presented were new ones, and which had been there for a long time.

"Ah-hem?" said Rustbane. "Then why did you, Jeopord?"

"We seem to have a bit of trouble, Skipper."

"Spill it out, man!"

"It's Threefingers Bogsprinkler, sir."

What weird names some of these pirates do have, reflected Sylvester.

"What about him?" Cap'n Rustbane was saying.

"Well, sir, you know how I've been suspecting him of pilfering gold from the treasure room?"

"You may have told me, my Jack o' Cups. If so, I've forgotten about it."

You never forget anything, you rogue, thought Sylvester. *You've got a mind like a clamp.*

Jeopord made a little gesture with his hands as if to say he was thinking exactly the same thing but didn't dare speak it out loud.

"What about it?" prompted the Cap'n.

"Today, while he was on deck as one of the party deputed to do patches for the topsail, Skip, I searched his bunk and its environs."

"And?"

"And I found an oilskin packet wi' a dozen doubloons inside it hidden under his mattress, sir."

"You're sure someone else didn't plant it there?"

"Sure I'm sure." The ocelot gave a wide grin to show how sure he was. The room seemed to fill up with black and broken stumps. "But we're planning to find out the truth the traditional way, sir."

"Then you're right, I ought to be in attendance. We owe the fellow that, at least. Come along, Sylvester."

Back up on deck, the four of them – Cheesefang and Jeopord leading, Cap'n Rustbane and Sylvester in their wake – made toward the bow of the *Shadeblaze*. There, they found what seemed to be the entirety of the *Shadeblaze*'s complement gathered around two wolverines, who were holding between them one of the very few human beings belonging to Rustbane's crew.

The man looked terrified, his face as pale as one of the ship's sails. Every now and then he flinched with pain as a one-eyed beaver skipped behind the two wolverines and nipped the man in the leg.

The captive, Sylvester mused, must be the oddly named Threefingers Bogsprinkler. Sylvester tried to see if indeed the man had only three fingers, but the fellow's arms were being held behind his back.

Until yesterday, Sylvester thought, amazed at the rapidity with which he kept accommodating himself to the remarkable, *I'd never seen a human outside of an illustration in a book, and was only half-convinced they actually existed, that they weren't just mythical creatures like three-headed snakes with faces in their midriffs. Now I've become so blasé about humans that all that interests me is the number of fingers this one has.*

Cap'n Rustbane left Sylvester behind with Cheesefang while he and Jeopord pushed their way to the front of the crowd.

The Cap'n hopped up onto a barrel so that he came a bit closer to the same height as the frightened man. Aware that he was the focus of all eyes, but most especially Bogsprinkler's, the Cap'n very slowly pulled a pair of long black leather gloves out of the embroidered pocket of his jacket and pulled them on. Sylvester wasn't sure what the donning of the gloves implied, but it obviously meant something to Bogsprinkler, because the man shivered in stark dread.

"So," said the gray fox as if picking up in the middle of a continuing conversation, "you're not happy with the share I give you of the spoils we capture, eh?"

The words came bubbling out of the hitherto-silent man as if they'd been held inside him by a firmly jammed cork that someone had now pulled.

"'Tain't that! I was just, like, borrowing a little 'til nex' payday, Skip, honest I was."

"Avast!" said Cap'n Rustbane in a voice like ice. He held up one black-gloved paw. There was a terrible silence on the deck of the *Shadeblaze*, broken only by the creaking of timbers and the slapping of the sails. "Don't insult me with such tomfoolery! Save me your pathetic excuses, ye lice-infested scum!"

In a heartbeat his voice had gone from frigid to thunderous, his tone from calmly civilized to the coarse bellow of the dockside. It was the sudden alternation between these two facets of Cap'n Rustbane's character that would,

Sylvester thought, forever mystify him no matter how long he associated with the pirate captain.

Shivering in his ill-fitting boots, he hoped it wouldn't be long.

"Is there any reason I shouldn't have ye flayed alive?" snarled the gray fox. His claws, fully unsheathed, were scything rapidly through the air as if the flaying might be a task he'd undertake himself . . . with enjoyment.

"It-it-it wasn't my idea," stammered Bogsprinkler. His eyes, swiveling around desperately, fixed on the face of one of the spectators, seemingly at random. "It was him. Bluespot! It was Bluespot made me do it! It was his idea."

"Shaddap, Threefingers, ye accursed liar." The pirate called Bluespot was a big raccoon with a mightily scarred face. As other crew members shied away from him, clearing a space, he spat on the deck and pulled a dagger from the filthy red scarf he wore tied around his waist. "Lie about me, would ye? Blame me for yer own crimes to save yer lily-white skin, would ye? I'll gut ye like a fish!" He threw himself at the pinioned human.

"Seize him!" cried Cap'n Rustbane, staring at Bluespot with sneering disdain.

The leaping raccoon was plucked out of the air by several sturdy, heavily tattooed arms and thrown onto the splintery boards of the deck, where he struggled and gasped and cursed.

"Keep your tongue still," snapped Rustbane. "Or, swelp me, I'll make sure you don't have a tongue in your head to waggle any more."

Bluespot abruptly stilled.

"I'm weary of this spectacle," said the gray fox with a theatrical sigh. Once again, his voice had reverted to its habitual tone of mock sophistication. "Spare me any more of it, you two, will you?"

Impossibly, Bogsprinkler's face grew even paler.

Rustbane's voice dropped to a deadly hiss. "Threefingers, you know the penalty for stealing from the treasure room, don't you?"

"Ye-ye-yes, sir."

"Tell me what it is."

It appeared as if Bogsprinkler would more likely lose consciousness than be able to get the words out.

The gray fox's face adopted a look of deep sympathy. "I see your predicament. Then I'll say it for you. The prescribed penalty for stealing from the hoard is severe, and rightly so. For it's not just from *me* you're stealing, you despicable cur, but from all your hard-working crewmates."

There were shouts of agreement from the surrounding pirates.

"So, what we do, you see," continued Cap'n Rustbane, raising a paw to restore quiet, "is we boil treacherous thieves like you alive."

This time, Bogsprinkler did faint, collapsing between the two wolverines, without whose grip on his arms he'd have fallen full-length on the deck. They shook him roughly until he recovered his senses.

"But I'm a merciful man, or, rather, fox." Cap'n Rustbane turned to look around at his crew, a big, ferociously toothed grin on his face. "Ain't I just, me hearties?"

"YES!" they roared in return.

"So, I'm going to let you off the boiling, Threefingers," the fox resumed, "although, if you don't mind me saying so" – he made a show of sniffing the air – "a piping hot bath might do you a world of good. Instead, I'm going to have you keelhauled. There's a very good chance you'll survive it, although that pretty face of yours'll no longer be attracting the ladies, and any future Mrs. Bogsprinkler may find herself faced with an unwelcome surprise when the lights go down on your wedding night. But you'll bless my name every morning that you wake up still alive, Threefingers, I'll warrant you that. And you'll never steal again from the *Shadeblaze*'s treasure room, will you? I'll warrant you that too."

The fox drummed a hindpaw on the top of the empty barrel, to make an ominous booming noise.

He turned to Jeopord.

"Take him away and do it."

Sylvester wondered what keelhauling involved. It was obviously something pretty dreadful, to judge from what Cap'n Rustbane had said and how Bogsprinkler had reacted. He'd have to ask the Cap'n later.

"As for you," said Cap'n Rustbane, turning to the prostrate Bluespot.

"Have mercy upon my 'umble soul, Skip," moaned the raccoon, but without much noticeable hope.

"You jest, I trust," said the fox. "For you, there'll be thirty kisses from the gunner's daughter."

Sylvester looked around for a gunner. He couldn't see one, and certainly there was nobody on deck who could possibly qualify to be anyone's daughter. So far as Sylvester was aware, the only females on board the *Shadeblaze* were Viola and Mrs. Pickleberry (with the latter, in Sylvester's estimation, having only a sort of provisional female status).

"Thirty lashes?" shrieked the raccoon. "But I had nothing to do with—"

"Oh, all right, then," said the fox, seeming bored. "Make it forty."

"*Forty?* Bu–but—"

"You want me to round it up to an even fifty?"

"N–No!"

"Then thank your lucky stars your skipper's an amenable sort of cove." Cap'n Rustbane gestured to Jeopord. "See to it, First Mate."

The ocelot whom Rustbane had nicknamed Jack o' Cups sprang into action, issuing instructions to various ruthless-looking crewmen. Threefingers Bogsprinkler tried pleading with the wolverines for mercy, but the expression on their faces soon silenced him.

Cap'n Rustbane, who'd leaped down from the barrel as soon as he'd issued his sentences, took Sylvester's arm.

"I trust this will serve as a salutary lesson, young friend," he said as pirates bustled and jostled around them. "A salutary lesson in how to run a pirate vessel. These things have to be done, and they have to be done right."

And you think I'm going to believe that? thought Sylvester, looking into the fox's eyes. In them he saw not the regretful severity of a strict master, but a dancing cruelty. The fox enjoyed ordering the infliction of suffering.

The Cap'n must have read something of this in Sylvester's eyes, for he turned abruptly away.

"Cheesefang!"

"Yessir?"

"Show our young companion, Mr. Lemmington, to his cabin. I think he's had his fill of fresh sea air for the day."

"Yessir."

There was no trace left of the person who'd befriended them last night. Clearly there was the Cheesefang who displayed kindness to strangers and who emerged only when Cap'n Rustbane wasn't around, and another Cheesefang who did his skipper's bidding and was as pitiless a pirate as any. It was the second Cheesefang who grabbed Sylvester by the shoulders and turned him in the direction of his own cabin.

Sylvester obediently started walking in that direction.

Not obediently enough, it seemed. There was a sudden agonizing pain in his rear, and he realized as he clutched at himself that Cheesefang had jabbed him viciously with the point of his cutlass.

He turned toward the sea rat, enraged.

"Why, you—!"

"Cap'n's orders," responded Cheesefang smugly.

"He never ordered you to do that."

"He would've if he'd thoughta it."

Sylvester began to speak, then stopped. There was no arguing against that sort of logic.

Past Cheesefang he could see Cap'n Rustbane standing apart from the rest of his crew, who were moving about in organized chaos as they prepared to enact the punishments the Cap'n had specified. The fox looked vaguely lonely for a moment, but Sylvester knew any fleeting sympathy would have been misplaced. This was the way the gray fox preferred things to be. He was in his element. He had created his own world aboard the *Shadeblaze*, a world designed to be exactly how he wanted it.

"Bladderbulge!" the Cap'n was bellowing. "Where in the blazes is that blasted badger?"

"Right 'ere, sir."

"Ah, good. As soon as we've done with these two scoundrels, have my supper ready for me in my cabin, d'you hear?"

"Aye, aye, sir."

"And make sure it's nice and spicy."

"Aye, aye, sir."

"And piping hot, too. The muck you served me last night was hardly more than lukewarm."

"Aye, aye, sir."

"You get it right, Bladderbulge, or one of these days it's yourself you're going to be cooking for my breakfast, understand?"

"Aye, aye, sir."

"And no blasted broccoli, either."

"Aye, aye, sir."

"And stop saying 'aye, aye, sir' to me the whole blasted time."

"Aye, aye—aye'll remember that, sir."

"Good. Now get moving, you fat oaf."

"An' you git movin' too," growled Cheesefang in Sylvester's ear. "'Less'n you want another jab fro' Old Molly here."

Old Molly, Sylvester realized sickly, was the infernal sea rat's cutlass. No, Sylvester didn't want another jab from its rusty point.

He got moving.

⚓ ⚓ ⚓ ⚓

Both Viola and Mrs. Pickleberry were waiting for him in his cabin when he reached it, sitting side-by-side on his narrow bed and looking worried.

"Where in the world have you been?" cried Viola, leaping to her feet as the door opened.

Taking both her forepaws in his, Sylvester told Viola and her mother how he'd spent his day. It took him surprisingly little time. Surprisingly little because, as he realized almost at once, if he'd tried to give them even the most rudimentary explanation of the many things he'd done and gadgets to which he'd been introduced, it would have taken him hours.

"Then, just before he sent me down here," Sylvester concluded, "the Cap'n told one crewman he was going to be keelhauled, whatever that means, and another that he was," Sylvester felt a blush begin to spread across his face, "going to kiss one of the gunner's daughters a lot."

Mrs. Pickleberry, still sitting on the bunk, looked at him grimly.

"I know what keelhaulin's all about," she said. "Cheesefang told me about it. It ain't no summer stroll in the grasses, I can assure you, young Lemmington. No, that it ain't."

"Ain't—er, isn't it?"

"Nope."

"Then what exactly *does* it involve?"

As if in answer to his question, somewhere beyond the open porthole screaming started.

Very loud screaming.

"They've started," announced Mrs. Pickleberry. "Started keelhaulin' the poor beggar."

"Oh."

"He'll be lucky he has any skin left on him, when they're done."

Mrs. Pickleberry carried on to explain what happened during a keelhauling. By the time she'd finished, it was she who was standing and Viola and Sylvester who were sitting on the bunk, leaning against each other for comfort, holding each other's paws and significantly green in the face.

"As for kissin' the gunner's daughter," said Three Pins Pickleberry, "that means gettin' lashes from the cat-o'-nine-tails."

"There's a cat with nine tails?" said Sylvester dazedly. "I didn't see any cats out there at all."

"It's a type o' whip, see?" said Viola's mom with a certain amount of unconcealed relish. "It's got nine . . ."

That explanation didn't do much for Viola's or Sylvester's digestive comfort either.

"We've got to get off this accursed ship and far away from here," said Sylvester gloomily. "We've got to escape. Got to."

Viola sighed. She gestured toward the porthole, through which could be seen an endless expanse of choppy ocean.

"Yes, but how?"

A SOGGY DISCOVERY

en days passed.

The three lemmings had seen or heard nothing of Cap'n Rustbanc since the day the two pirates had been sentenced to keelhauling and a flogging respectively. For almost all of every day, the only contact the trio had with the outside world was an occasional visit from Cheesefang, who alternated unpredictably between kindly affability and foul-mouthed unfriendliness.

After a while, Sylvester noticed something peculiar. The grizzled old sea rat lost his acerbity and, especially, his atrociously bad language whenever Mrs. Pickleberry was around.

Briefly, Sylvester wondered if there might be some kind of unspoken romance in the air.

But no, that was impossible. Cheesefang was a sea rat, not a lemming. Viola's mom was a lemming, not a sea rat.

Then Sylvester made the obvious connection. Rustbane terrified Cheesefang, who accordingly, in the Cap'n's presence, behaved how he believed the Cap'n wanted him to behave. Mrs. Pickleberry terrified Cheesefang too. It was obvious, from the way she bristled and tutted every time the sea rat came out with yet another of his paint-blistering oaths, that she wanted him to behave just a trifle more like a gentleman ought toward a lady: with some respect and, unless Cheesefang wanted to find himself getting his mouth scrubbed out with soap and water, a certain temperance of language.

The sea rat was doing his best to comply with her wishes.

At the moment, he was attending to other duties around the ship. Mrs. Pickleberry was having "a little lie-down" in the cabin she shared with her daughter. She'd gotten into the habit of taking an afternoon nap and sometimes a morning one too, because there wasn't much else to do. Sylvester was taking advantage of Cheesefang's absence to score another line with his claw on the cabin wall, just above the lintel of the door.

"That makes ten," he said, standing back when the brief task was done. "Ten days at sea. We're becoming real seafarers now, aren't we, sweetheart?" he added, trying to cheer himself up as much as Viola.

"I suppose so," she replied dolefully.

"Look on the bright side."

"I have. It's just as boring as the dim side. Boringer, actually. At least the dim side's broken up a bit by having to be sea sick every now and then."

"We'll soon be there."

"Where?"

"The Caraya Islands."

Sylvester tried to keep the exasperation out of his voice. He must have told Viola this a dozen times or more during the past two or three days. Hadn't she been paying attention? Then he realized she was asking him the question just to have something to say. Speaking was her way of keeping her morale up, or at least of stopping it from plummeting, even if what was being said was the same thing over and over again.

"The Caraya Islands," he repeated, his tone softening. "You remember. I told you about them. The Carayas are that group of islands – an archipelago, to use the proper term – that runs like a chain parallel to the equator. I saw them on that piece of the map I had before I burned it."

For once, Viola said nothing, just looked at him sourly and crossed her arms ever more tightly across her chest. Her meaning couldn't have been clearer. *If you hadn't burned that map, we would all be back in Foxglove, not incarcerated on board a vile old pirate ship where the boards seem to leak mold and you keep expecting something with a lot of teeth to leap up from under you when you're using the lav.*

Sylvester stared back at her. *The truth is, and you know it, that if I hadn't destroyed the map there'd be nothing left of Foxglove now but a few bits of blackened timber, nothing left of us but the faint smell of roasted lemming still lingering in the air.*

Finally, Viola's gaze dropped. She knew he was right. She just didn't have to like it, that was all.

"Once we get to the Carayas, Cap'n Rustblaze plans to put into harbor for a while," said Sylvester. "Maybe we'll have the chance to escape then."

Not, he added silently, *that the idea of escaping into a port called Hangman's Haven seems exactly enticing. Cutthroats on every corner, I should imagine. An awful, lawless place, but it's the same here on the Shadeblaze. At least when we're off the ship there'll be the chance of running away from people who want to slit our gizzards without running smack into a bulkhead before we've properly got our speed up.*

Viola looked up at him again. He could tell she was thinking exactly the same thing. He suddenly wished Mrs. Pickleberry were here. Viola's mom would probably relish the prospect of Hangman's Haven, so long as she had her rolling pin with her.

"Dry land seems a long way away," said Viola quietly, "however you look at it. And every hour on board this stinky ship seems to last a year or two at least. Oh, if only there was something we could do *now*. We could untie one of the longboats from the poop deck and—"

"We'd never get away with it. Who would lower the longboat into the water?"

"Mom."

"Then she'd be stuck aboard the *Shadeblaze*."

"She could jump in after us."

"The crew'd hear the sound of the winches. Remember how the gears squeaked and squealed when the longboats were being hauled aboard? We'd have half a dozen pirates on us before the boat was halfway to the water. Even if we could escape, your mom would be cut to ribbons."

Viola sniffed as if she wasn't sure how important that was.

"Then the pirates would come after us," Sylvester continued, "and catch us, and cut *us* to ribbons."

"We could go at nighttime."

"What difference would that make?"

"In the dark they'd not know where to look for us."

"These are mariners, Viola! They've been learning the mysteries of the sea longer than either you or I have been alive." *Possibly, looking at some of them, longer than even Mrs. Pickleberry's been alive.* "They know how to get around little problems like that. They have mirrored lanterns that can send a beam of light a hundred yards or more. They'd catch us in no time, don't you doubt that at all."

"I'd rather be dead than stuck on this rotten heap a day longer."

"It only seems that way. You don't really think that."

Silence loomed between them.

"Do you?" added Sylvester in a small voice.

"What do you think?"

His mind groped for an answer.

After what seemed like too long, Viola spoke again.

"I'd give anything for a bath," she said wistfully.

"Wouldn't we all?"

"A long, long bath."

"Hot too."

She nodded. "Hot. With lots of that bubbly stuff that smells like a house of ill repute."

"What's a house of ill repute?"

"*You* know. A house where females who smell like that bubbly bath stuff live. Loose females."

"Um, Viola, if you had a bath in that goo, would you have to live in house of ill repute?"

"It's just a figure of speech, Sylvester! Don't be so literal about everything."

Not long ago I knew what this conversation was about, Sylvester thought. *Now I'm floundering.*

"Are there any houses of ill repute in Foxglove?" he said.

"Possibly," Viola murmured darkly. "Have you ever been, you know, just walking along and suddenly the scent of bubble-bath goo has come wafting out of nowhere and . . . and assailed your nostrils?"

Sylvester thought back. "I can't rightly say that I have."

"What a very sweet and innocent person you are, Sylvester."

"I am?"

She giggled.

Sylvester was pretty certain the giggling was about him, but he didn't mind. Anything, anything at all so long as the gloom lifted from Viola's mood.

"Besides," said Sylvester, "even if we did manage to escape in the longboat, and even if we did manage to lose the pirates' search party somehow, how'd we be able to get all the way to dry land?"

"You'd navigate, of course. Weren't you paying attention when Cap'n 'I'm So High And Mighty' Rustbane was telling you about navigation?"

"Yes, but I don't have a sextant."

The faintest glimmer of a grin was beginning to twitch the corners of her mouth. "That's your problem."

"Or an astrolabe."

"Pity Doc Nettletree's not here. Sounds like you need some urgent attention."

"Even if I could navigate us to dry land, how's the boat going to cross hundreds and thousands of leagues to get there?"

Viola snorted. "It's not that far."

"However far it is, the boat's not just going to go there on its own, is it? And those longboats don't have sails, not so's I've noticed anyway."

"Easy, you'd row us."

"I'd row us? But I'd be too busy navigating to pick up an oar." Sylvester shook his head sorrowfully. "No, no, no, Viola. The person who'd have to do the rowing would be—"

The pillow she threw hit him full in the face.

At first, Sylvester thought she must have thrown it with phenomenal force, because he staggered uncontrollably backward and crashed against the far wall of the cabin. The rear of his head struck the wooden wall hard and he slid to the floor, lights flashing on and off in front of him.

For a moment, he couldn't speak and was barely aware of anything going on around him except for a high, thin wail that he eventually identified as Viola screaming.

There was a puff of brightness, a whiff of scorching.

"*Fire!*" bawled Viola.

The single word was enough to make Sylvester recover consciousness fast. "Where?" he said groggily, pushing himself up onto jelly-like legs.

"Right in front of you, you idiot," she snapped.

A glance was enough to tell him what had happened. Whatever had jolted the ship and thrown him across the room had also dislodged the lamp that had been hanging from the ceiling. The lamp had fallen and smashed. Its oil had sprayed across the floor and caught fire, also setting alight the underside of a wooden chair in the corner that no one ever used because it creaked and groaned as if it were going to collapse at any second.

"Water!" yelled Sylvester, taking control of the situation.

"We don't have any."

"But of course we must have, we're in the middle of the—*oh, heck!*"

The door was flung open.

"Cheesefang!"

Sylvester wished momentarily that Viola's cry hadn't sounded quite so welcoming, then forgot about it as a tongue of flame seemed to show an interest in his foot.

The rat dumped a brimming bucket just inside the cabin.

"More buckets at t'end of the companionway," he grunted then turned to go.

"Wait!" yelled Viola.

The sea rat paused, looking back over his shoulder. "Yeah?"

"What about my mom? Er, Three Pins, I mean."

"Three Pins is okay. I got my eye on her."

The rat vanished along the corridor.

It didn't take long for Sylvester to put the fire out. Some spare clothes Cheesefang had given him not long after they'd come aboard were singed beyond rescue, and Viola got rid of them by thrusting them out the porthole. Soon, there was no trace of the fire except a grayness in the air and a poignant stench that reminded Sylvester of his mother's traditional home cooking.

How, he wondered miserably as he put the nearly empty bucket back out into the corridor, trying not to slosh its remaining contents onto his feet, *are you getting along without me, Mom?*

All the while, the ship was bucking and heaving underfoot as if some giant had picked it up and was shaking it to see if the contents rattled.

"What's going on?" said Viola. She'd been a model of competence from the moment Cheesefang had delivered the water to them, but now she was beginning to give in to fear again.

"A storm. That's all it is. A storm at sea." Sylvester hoped he sounded calmer than he felt. "They have 'em all the time in this part of the world. It's the tropics, you see. It's a sailor's way of knowing when you're getting into them, a storm is. Nothing to worry about."

"We're doomed, doomed, *doomed!*" came Cheesefang's voice from the companionway outside.

The sea rat stuck his head round the door.

"Jus' kiddin', like."

Viola said something unladylike.

"My!" said Cheesefang and vanished, shutting the door behind him.

Through the crashing of the waves and the sudden howling of the wind they could hear voices from above.

"Stem the tide and make the course good." That was Cap'n Rustbane.

"Rat overboard." Jeopord talking, at a guess.

"Good." Rustbane again. "He was three sheets to the wind."

I wonder if I'll ever get the hang of these nautical terms, thought Sylvester.

"But Cap'n," said a different voice, "I dinnae ken if—"

"She can and she will." There was a cold core of determination in Rustbane's declaration. "No turning back. We're going through it."

"Aye, aye, Skip."

There was a pause. Viola and Sylvester could hear, directly above their heads, the sound of countless feet scuttling this way and that as the pirate crew took measures to protect the *Shadeblaze* from the worst effects of the storm.

A sudden crash made the two lemmings start.

"I think that was a hatch being battened down," said Sylvester.

"Rat back on board," came a call from above.

"Jus' a lucky wave," said a smug voice they'd not heard before.

"So Davy Jones 'as spared yer. Now grab this spar, yer lubber!"

The caterwauling of the wind rose to a crescendo. The nameless giant seemed to be shaking the *Shadeblaze* harder than ever. The voices were lost to the cacophony of the elements.

Sylvester gave Viola a significant look and she returned it. They could swim, all lemmings could, but could they keep themselves afloat for long enough to have a chance of rescue?

His gaze strayed from her, creeping up the hull to the porthole. The black waves out there seemed as tall as the tallest pines and as broad as eternity.

It struck him, for all he'd said to reassure Viola, that the ship might founder and they might die in this storm.

The giant suddenly punched the underside of the vessel.

There was a crack like that of the cat-o'-nine-tails.

Sylvester, thrown upwards, hit his head on the ceiling.

Darkness descended.

Loudly.

⚓ ⚓ ⚓ ⚓ ⚓

What woke him were Mrs. Pickleberry's boots.

Viola's mom had never been the lightest-footed of lemmings but, ever since she'd donned the heavy mariners' boots Cheesefang had given her when she came aboard the *Shadeblaze*, her progress around the ship had been marked by what sounded like an orchestra of drunks falling downstairs, complete with their musical instruments.

It wasn't just that her boots were individually noisy. It was that there were four of them.

Viola was hanging on to her mother's shoulder as Sylvester's gaze came grayly into focus.

"Do you think he's dead, Mom?"

"No such luck."

"Just because you've never liked—"

"His eyes are opening."

"Oh, so they are! He's going to be all—"

"Little piggy eyes, they are. Like pigs have, only littler."

"Well, of course pigs have piggy eyes, Mom! That's what pigs are for. Oh, I was so frightened."

This last was to Sylvester, beside whom Viola was now kneeling.

"You were frightened? I thought I was—"

"There, there, sweetheart." Viola's voice adopted a new, soothing tone, which, after a moment Sylvester recognized. He'd heard Doctor Nettletree use something very like it when dealing with people who'd been out in the sun too long.

"I'm going to be fine, I tell you," he said irritatedly, trying to struggle to his feet.

"Are you sure?"

"Of course, I'm sure," he snapped. "Mind you," he added more quietly, rubbing his head, "I've got the most enormous bump back here. What happened?"

"Damn stupid ship hit a damn stupid monster wave," said Mrs. Pickleberry as if that explained everything.

"Do you remember the storm?" said Viola, looking anxiously into his eyes.

"A bit of it," Sylvester said. "We were talking about . . ." He glanced nervously around in case any of the crew might be nearby. "We were talking about how we might escape," he whispered.

"Then, like Mom says, the *Shadeblaze* went nose-first into what must have been the biggest wave the sea has ever known, and . . ."

How does she know how big the wave was? thought Sylvester, still woozy. *And how does she think she knows how big a big wave is? Not long ago, the closest she'd been to the sea was watching it from the top of the cliff. Now she thinks she's some kind of master mariner?*

He shook himself. Where were waspish thoughts like that coming from? His head ached, not just the bump on the outside of it but the inside of it too, as if someone had challenged his brain to a boxing match and won.

"Thought the whole ship was goin' ta come apart at the seams," confirmed Mrs. Pickleberry.

She's starting to talk like a pirate, Sylvester thought. *When she's been talking with the crew, it must have rubbed off on her somehow. On the other hand, Mrs. Pickleberry's way of talking in general was not all that different, come to think of it. Her temper didn't differ much from a pirate's either*, he concluded. *She would be a perfect pirate.*

"Nails poppin' out everywhere," she continued. "Half the scum who keep this scurvy tub afloat were on their knees on the deck prayin'. And not," she noted darkly, "to the Great Spirit Lhaeminguas, I'll be bound."

Now that Mrs. Pickleberry had made him aware of it, Sylvester could hear a great clattering of footsteps overhead and much shouting of orders and curses like, "Avast behind!" "Man the bilges!" and "Bottle the spinnaker!" Clearly, now that the *Shadeblaze* was through the worst of the storm, the crew had a major job of clearing up and repairing to do.

"They'll not be disturbin' us a while," Mrs. Pickleberry continued.

"Is that good news?" said Sylvester. Perhaps he needed some medical attention. A bang on the head could be a dangerous thing, he knew. He'd be a bit nervous about putting his well-being in the paws of any sawbones who might be part of the complement of a pirate ship, of course (they would be better at hacking off injured limbs than at treating cases of the vapors, no doubt) but this once he'd be prepared to chance it.

Perhaps a nice restorative tisane would set him right.

Mrs. Pickleberry gave a derisive snort, as if she could read his mind and didn't much like the headlines.

"Somethin' happened when that wave hit," she said. "Somethin' the scumrats don' know 'bout yet."

Sylvester and Viola looked at her blankly and she responded with a self-satisfied smile.

"But they'll find out soon as one o' them thinks ter come down here an' check up on us. That'd be that oaf Cheesefang, 's my guess. So we'd best get movin' if we wants ter investigate."

"Investigate what?" cried Sylvester and Viola in exasperation.

"The secret passage, o' course."

"What secret passage?" said Viola. She looked as if she were accustomed to dealing with her mother's obtuseness. Sylvester hoped he'd never need to become likewise.

"Come see," said the older lemming enigmatically, going to the door and cracking it open a pawsbreadth so she could check the corridor outside. Satisfied, she beckoned them to follow her.

"I didn't know ships had secret passages," murmured Sylvester to Viola as they left his cabin. "I thought it was just old haunted houses and that sort of thing that had secr—"

"Hush yer trap, will ya?" hissed Mrs. Pickleberry back over her plump shoulder.

The storm might be past, but the *Shadeblaze* was still shuddering and swaying underfoot. As they made their way along the passage, the three lemmings lost count of the number of times they bumped into the walls. There was a new smell too, in addition to the lingering odor of unwashed undergarments that tended to hang around the ship's living quarters. A post-storm smell, Sylvester concluded, a mixture of fresh brine and rotting organic material. He couldn't decided whether he liked it or not.

He hadn't before been into the cabin the two Pickleberries shared, and he was somewhat hesitant about following Viola in there now. He tried to keep his gaze fixed firmly on the back of Mrs. Pickleberry's head in case he might, out of the corner of his eye, spot some item of intimate feminine attire left inadvertently lying around. Of course, this made it very difficult *not* to be alert to the sight of anything wispy.

What he did notice out of the corner of his eye was that Viola was grinning at him.

He wondered if he'd started blushing.

Viola was depressingly good at making him blush.

"See?" said Mrs. Pickleberry.

"See what?" said her daughter.

"What I'm pointin' at, yer lummox."

Between two of the vertical planks that made up the cabin's rough walls there was a long, black triangular gap. The boards must have heaved slightly apart when the ship was being tossed around by the heavy seas.

"It's lucky that wasn't an outside wall," said Sylvester, wondering if he had the terminology right.

Mrs. Pickleberry looked at him in exasperation. "Then there wouldn't be a secret passage on the other side o' it, would there? There'd just be a lot o' cold salty water, an' you'd be drowning in it. Which," she added *sotto voce*, "might not be a—"

"Mo–*om!*" said Viola.

Sylvester wasn't paying any attention. He'd inched forward, past Mrs. Pickleberry and had glued an eye to the gap between the boards.

Viola's mom was right. There *was* a bigger space behind here than there ought to be. He couldn't see enough of it to tell whether it was a secret passage precisely. He tried to visualize the corridor they'd come along to reach the females' room, to work out if there'd perhaps been a door or two fewer than there should have been, then twitched his head crossly. It was a hopeless exercise. He hadn't been paying attention.

Behind him, the two Pickleberries were still exchanging recriminations and gasps of outrage.

"Come have a look," said Sylvester.

At first, neither of them heard him. Then Viola saw his beckoning paw.

"What?"

It wasn't said in the friendliest of fashions, but Sylvester decided not to let his inner bristling show.

"Your mom was right."

"She was?"

"There's what looks to be a room behind here."

"Yes?"

"'Course, it could just be a broom cupboard."

"Doubt it," said Mrs. Pickleberry tersely, joining the conversation. "Pirates don't use brooms. Filthy bunch of bilge rats, if you ask me."

Sylvester tried to be conciliatory. "Or a lavoratory facility."

"Doubt that too. Pirates don't use a privy."

"They *do*," Viola chipped in.

"Only when they *has* to," responded Mrs. Pickleberry with the air of One Who Knows.

It was clear Viola and Mrs. Pickleberry were brewing up for a resumption of their spat. Sylvester didn't know what exactly had gotten into them but he wished it'd get back out again.

"Do you two not want to discover what's behind the panels?" he said, clapping his forepaws together.

Two uncannily similar pairs of eyes turned in his direction.

"S'pose we do," Mrs. Pickleberry said grudgingly, for both of them.

"Then watch," said Sylvester, not at all sure he was going to be able to do what he was about to try to do.

He reached a paw up to the top of the left plank of the two that had been jerked apart and dug in his claws. The end of the plank was just wide enough for him to get a good grip. He yanked on the end of the board as hard as he could.

There was a noise like someone ripping canvas apart.

The plank Sylvester had pulled came away from the wall in a shower of, firstly, dust then secondly, the husks of dead insects and thirdly, rusty old nails.

Behind it was a pool of blackness that yielded only reluctantly to the incursion of the cabin's lantern light. Motes swam amid air that seemed to have been lifeless for a very long time. There was a strong smell of damp mold.

"Wow," said Viola at Sylvester's shoulder. All trace of the animosity between her and her mother had evaporated.

"Wow, indeed." He smiled at her and looked back into the cabin. "Let me see if I can unhook that lantern from the ceiling."

"Already done." Mrs. Pickleberry handed it past Viola to him. "Mind yourself on the lamp, it's hot."

It was too. Sylvester could feel the tips of the hairs on the back of his paw singeing as he held the lantern in the gloom.

Viola's breathing loud in his ear, he gazed at what the glow of the oil lamp revealed.

"It's another cabin," she whispered. "A cabin that people must have sealed off years ago, *decades* ago. I wonder why in the world they'd have wanted to do that?"

"Plague," said Mrs. Pickleberry matter-of-factly.

"Ugh, Mom."

"S true. That's why people generally seal off places. Because there's a deadly disease in there that'd spread like wildfire through the very air itself, cutting adults and children down alike with its toxic scythe, sparking painful, suppurating buboes all over their tormented flesh Shriveling up their secret organs until—"

"Shut up, Mom!"

"Only sayin'."

"Well, stop."

Paying little or no attention to their bickering, Sylvester had squeezed in through the splintered opening he and the storm had created, and was now standing in the center of what must once have been quite a splendid cabin. Along one wall, a row of portholes had been overgrown entirely by sea mosses and barnacles, so that only a sinister dark green light shone in from the outside world to supplement the radiance his lantern cast. The smell of mold and mildew was far stronger than it had been in the females' cabin; it was almost overpowering.

Sylvester took an extra step or two into the fuzzy green dimness. His feet sloshed through cold, shallow puddles that swayed from side to side with the rocking of the ship. He had to move carefully for fear of slipping. Looking down, he saw slick black water where a few unhealthy looking shellfish seemed to be trying to eke out an existence among swashes of what, at first he thought must be long hanks of hair shed by the head of some monstrous creature but which he soon realized, was seaweed. Somewhere near this part of its superstructure, the *Shadeblaze* must have sprung a leak many years ago. A leak not large enough ever to cause a threat to the vessel's seaworthiness, but enough to allow a slow, progressive invasion of small creatures and, of course, water. These had shared the interior of the cabin with what was already there, rather than replacing it entirely, so that it wasn't too hard for him to discern what the room must have been like at one time.

"It was a captain's cabin," he breathed. "That's what it was. A captain's private cabin. I'm sure of it. This was the place where the captain who was master of the *Shadeblaze* before Rustbane used to come to relax or study."

"But how could it be a—" Viola began, then stopped as her own eyes took in the scene.

In one corner stood a writing desk that must have been, in its day, a magnificent piece of furniture and still, even through its lumpy veneer of shellfish and rot, spoke of expense. Just as in Rustbane's larger and more public cabin up on the main deck, there were pictures along the walls, neatly spaced between the portholes on the hull-side wall and in almost a solid line on the other three. Time and the elements had taken their toll on the pictures themselves, but Sylvester thought he could make out traces of coastal landscapes where great sailing ships stood just offshore. The fitful light of the lantern made the flags and sails of the ships flutter, and the trees of the shoreline wave in the salty breeze.

Opposite the writing desk was a chest of drawers, and on the floor in front of the chest of drawers was a sodden mass Sylvester recognized with some difficulty as a pile of discarded clothing. It was as if the long-ago captainly occupant of the place had been picking through his most splendid garments, trying on one and then another, but was never being quite satisfied with any of them. Then, some alarum had caused him to sprint from the cabin wearing whatever he'd had on at the time. Sylvester had seen the look before, in his mother's bedroom when she'd been preparing herself for some social function or other where she'd thought it important she look her best.

Holding the hot lantern carefully away from himself, Sylvester bent down and picked up a splintered spar of rotting wood from the cabin floor.

"What're you doing?" hissed Viola.

"He's going through them old raiments is what he's doing," answered Mrs. Pickleberry, who'd by now joined them and was looking around her, hands on her waist, as if she longed for nothing more than to give this place the kind of cleaning and tidying it'd not forget in a hurry. "Maybe he thinks he can salvage a nice pair of underpants."

"Oh for—"

Sylvester was stopped from saying whatever he'd been about to say by Viola's paw on his forearm.

"It's just her way. You mustn't mind her."

The spar broke in Sylvester's paw as he tried to use it to lift the topmost layer of saturated cloth.

"You could make yourself useful," he said to Mrs. Pickleberry, marveling even as he did so at his own courage.

"Yeah?" Heavy on the sarcasm, light on the promise of cooperation.

"Yes. You could go and fetch that rolling pin of yours."

"Elvira, you mean?"

"*Elvira?*"

"Yep."

"You mean your rolling pin has a name?"

"Don't everybody's?"

Sylvester couldn't think of a reply.

"Er, could you bring Elvira then, please?" he mumbled lamely.

"I'll ask her," amended Mrs. Pickleberry, retreating into the main cabin.

"Your mother ever found a need to have long conversations with Doctor Nettletree?" asked Sylvester once she'd gone.

"No," said Viola, looking mystified. "Why should she?"

"Oh, nothing. Just wondering."

Mrs. Pickleberry splashed back into view, clutching Elvira.

"Whass so int'resting 'bout a bunch o' moldy ol' clothes anyway?" said Mrs.

Pickleberry as she handed the rolling pin over.

"Camouflage," Sylvester replied.

"Eh?"

"In your bedroom, where do you put things you don't want anyone to find? To keep them safe from burglars, perhaps." As soon as he'd spoken he wished he hadn't asked. Aside from anything else, it was many years since last there'd been a case of burglary in Foxglove, and the culprit in that instance had proved to be not a genuine criminal, but an unruly young jackdaw.

"In the chamberpot," Mrs. Pickleberry said promptly. "No one'd ever t'ink of lookin' in there."

No one would ever want *to*, thought Sylvester.

"Or?" he prompted.

"Or, if they *did* look in there, me an' Elvira'd clobber 'em."

Sylvester moaned inwardly. This wasn't quite what he'd meant.

"What I'm saying is," he tried again, "if there isn't a chamberpot to, er, to *hand*, as it were, where's the next best place in a bedroom to hide things?"

"Under yer kegs," said Mrs. Pickleberry. "Like Viola does."

"Kegs?"

"Yer smalls."

Ah. Sylvester grinned happily. That was more like the answer he'd been searching for.

Viola looked fretful. She glanced at her mother. "I didn't know you'd worked out that—" she began.

"Precisely," Sylvester said, cutting her off. "Underneath some dirty underwear. If whoever was the inhabitant of this cabin – and I'm pretty sure I know who it was, from what Rustbane was telling me the other day – if whoever he was wanted to hide something in a hurry before rushing up on deck because of an emergency, where better than under a heap of dirty clothes?"

"Blimey," said Mrs. Pickleberry. After a long moment's cogitation she added, "Yeah, but, even if folk afterwards had a nat'ral whatjacallit, a nat'ral reticence about pokin' around in his smelly undies, don't yer think that eventually someone'd have done it anyway?"

Sylvester rocked on his heels. *Damn, I hadn't thought of that. These are cutthroat pirates we're talking about, not milksops. They'd not be deterred for long, no matter how filthy the—*

"I don't know," he said, shrugging. He glanced at the rolling pin in his paw, then at the fungus-girt mass of clothing by the chest of drawers.

"They could have been a whole lot worse many years ago," said Viola dubiously.

"That must be it. Over time their initial, ah, virulence must have abated somewhat, so that—"

"Oh, gimme 'ere, yer great buttockbrain!" said Mrs. Pickleberry, grabbing back Elvira. "I brought up children o' me own, ya know. I seed a lot worse'n this in their bedrooms."

Soon there were items of clothing, and bits of items of clothing, all over the cabin floor. Some were indeed not so savory as one might have preferred.

"Nope," said Mrs. Pickleberry with finality after a while. "There ain't not nuffink of value 'ere."

Sylvester, having been a little hopeful despite the unlikelihood of actually finding anything having fought his way through the thicket of negatives, gave a little sigh of disappointment. Then something caught his eye.

"Wait a moment."

"Wot?"

He went down on his knees, ignoring the cold slimy water that splashed on to him.

"Look!"

"What is it?" said Viola.

"It's a chest."

"A chest? A *treasure* chest?"

"Who knows? Who can tell until I get it open," cried Sylvester, his excitement rising. Forgetting about what he was putting his paws into, he scrabbled away at the last of the clothing.

"'S a very small chest," said Mrs. Pickleberry staring at it critically, her head cocked to one side.

"Sometimes it's the smallest things that're the most valuable," observed Viola, looking eagerly at the little chest.

"Thass what yer father keeps sayin'," muttered Mrs. Pickleberry.

Their discovery was made of wood, with iron bands hooping around it in both directions. The bands had severely rusted, as had the lock that held the lid down. Even if the discoverers had possessed a key, it was clear the only way they were going to get inside the box was by brute force.

"Lemme at it," said Mrs. Pickleberry, as if on cue.

Elvira rose and fell with brutal effectiveness, then rose and fell again even more devastatingly. Sylvester found himself shuddering in sympathy with the wooden chest or, at least, what was left of it.

"Yow! I've got a splinter in my leg," wailed Viola, putting a forepaw on Sylvester's shoulder to balance herself while she reached for the offending area.

"I'm just surprised we don't all look like porcupines after that little display," said Sylvester too softly for Mrs. Pickleberry to possibly hear the remark.

She heard it anyway.

"You got any complaints, punk?"

"Not quite."

"Then keep 'em to yerself, unless you wanna end up lookin' like that box o' yours."

"Certainly."

By this time, even had Sylvester been remotely in the mood for an argument, his attention would have wandered. Lying in the blistered wreckage of the wooden chest was a shape Sylvester recognized only too well from his time in Cap'n Rustbane's cabin.

A book!

Not a scroll, like those in the Foxglove Library, but a book with binding and pages you could turn and a spine with lettering on it.

Well, not much by way of lettering. Age and disrepair had more or less eradicated the gilt altogether. Still, who cared about minor details like that when one had a book that looked like it hadn't been read for decades!

"Let's get this back to my cabin," he said with sudden decision. "Clearing up the deck in the storm's wake isn't going to take the crew forever, is it? The sooner we're out of here and have hidden any trace of this secret room the better. Agreed?"

The other two saw his point.

Within ten or fifteen minutes the three lemmings had managed to conceal the hole in the cabin wall sufficiently to pass a casual inspection, and who was likely to give the cabin anything more than this? Not Cheesefang, that was for sure. The temperamental old rat was clearly intent on doing only as much as he had to in order to pass muster in the Cap'n's eyes, and not one iota more. Sylvester pushed the boards together – their dampness made them stick to each other as if coated in a weak glue – then the two females pushed the clothes cupboard that had been near the porthole over to cover any trace there might be of Sylvester's repair job.

"I think that'll do," said Sylvester, puffing, at last. "What in the world have you two *put* in that wardrobe?"

"None o' yer business, whippersnapper."

His mind filling with images of extremely heavy metal strengthenings for various inscrutable items of female lemming underwear, Sylvester led the way back along the passage to his own cabin.

Once the three were settled there, Viola and himself sitting on the bunk while Mrs. Pickleberry appropriated an old sea chest on which to deposit her ample rear, Sylvester opened the book.

It was, as he'd suspected, a journal or log. What made him whistle, however, was the inscription on the flyleaf:

Logbook of
CAPTAIN JOSIAH ADAMITE
Skipper of the Good Ship *Shadeblaze*

Beneath this there was an inscription that Sylvester couldn't read. The long confinement in the damp of the secret compartment had made the old sea dog's ink run. Sylvester hoped this wasn't going to affect any pages but the outer ones. After being granted such an incredible stroke of luck as to discover the logbook in the first place, it would be too cruel a stroke of fate if much of it was illegible.

Cautiously, he riffled through the next few pages. Phew. It looked as if the writing on them was perfectly readable, or as readable as Adamite's crabbed hand had ever been.

"What does it say?" urged Viola, nudging him in the ribs.

"Patience, patience. I'm just getting to that."

"I got a passin' interest in the subject meself, laddie," said Mrs. Pickleberry from the corner.

"I know, but this book is very old and it's been kept in lousy conditions. I don't want it to fall apart in my paws. We've got to be careful with it. There could be invaluable information in here, information even Cap'n Rustbane doesn't know!"

"You goin' to tell it to him?" said Mrs. Pickleberry fixing him with a gimlet gaze. "You bein' so matey with the verminous skunk an' all?"

"Fox," said Sylvester tiredly.

"Eh?" said Mrs. Pickleberry and Viola.

"He's not a skunk," Sylvester explained. "He's a fox."

"Like we're not hamsters?" said Mrs. Pickleberry.

"Same principle."

"Oh, shaddap, yer dingbat."

"Lemming," said Sylvester. "Not a—oh, look," he added hastily, "here's the first page Cap'n Adamite wrote in this volume of his diary."

It was a pity, Sylvester ruminated as he pored over the small, angular handwriting, that he'd been unable to make out the date on the flyleaf. They had no way of telling how old this diary was. Presumably, it was the last set of records the old buccaneer had committed to paper before his untimely demise at the end of Rustbane's cutlass. For a moment, Sylvester wondered if trunkloads of earlier volumes of Cap'n Adamite's writings might exist elsewhere aboard the *Shadeblaze*. Then he realized the inevitable truth: all Adamite's earlier diaries must have been discovered after Rustbane's mutiny and cast overboard like their author. No, thrown to the flames, more likely, lest any of them should somehow survive the ravages of the ocean and come to the attention of other eyes.

However minuscule that possibility might be, Sylvester thought, *Cap'n Rustbane is not a person ever to take even the slightest chance unless he has to.*

Even so, Rustbane *had* taken a chance, without knowing it.

He and his crew hadn't searched the vessel that they'd stolen from its master carefully enough. Cap'n Adamite had outwitted the gray fox, something few could ever boast. This final volume had survived.

"Gerra move on, dammit," growled Mrs. Pickleberry.

"I'm just adapting my eyesight to the handwriting," pleaded Sylvester. "It's very small and blurry and the ink's faded. And the spelling's *awful*, it's hard to make out what Cap'n Adamite meant some of the words to be, his spelling of them's so weird."[1]

"Yeah, right. Excuses!"

"Oh, *Mom*."

"Hmmf. Infatuated, that's what you are. And why?"

The bickering between the two Pickleberries, which had diminished to a minor trickle for fully ten minutes or so, now threatened to become a mighty torrent once more.

There was one possible way of stopping it, Sylvester decided.

Holding the open book up toward the lantern, he began to read aloud words that had been written decades ago by a buccaneer who'd willingly shed the blood of the innocent all over the seas of Sagaria, whose flinty heart had been a stranger to mercy, and yet for whom Sylvester now experienced a strange stirring of fellowship, in that they shared a single adversary, an adversary called Captain Terrigan Rustbane . . .

---

1 Thanks to a kindly editor Cap'n Adamite's spelling, which was indeed bizarre, has for the sake of preserving the reader's sanity, been corrected in the extracts that appear over the next few pages of this narrative. All of us should be so lucky.

DEAD MAN'S TALE

hat better time to start a new volume of my logbook than now, when I have reached a turning point in my piratical life?

From the very first moment I heard those wonderful, dream-inspiring words "the magical chest of the Zindars," I have known that somehow my fate and that of the chest were to be intertwined and, sure enough, that is what has come about. It was by something of a miraculous happenstance that I heard about the chest at all, for few have done so and fewer still have lived to tell the tale. I am in the process, wherever I can, of rendering that number even smaller.

I can still remember that night at The Moldy Claw in Darkwater, many years ago, as if it were only yesterday. Such are the illusions that the mind plays to trick a man, even as scurvy a knave as this old dog of the open sea! I was in the tavern for the simple purpose of wetting my whistle, with a few of my men alongside me for—

"He was a dog then?" said Viola.

Sylvester stopped reading and looked at her in bafflement.

"Who?"

"This Cap'n Adamite of yours."

"I, ah" – he looked down at the logbook, where his claw was marking a place that was still far too close to the beginning – "I don't know what particular type of animal old Adamite was. Now I come to think of it, it was something Rustbane didn't tell me that day in his cabin."

"But Adamite himself just said it."

"Hm?"

"He called himself an old dog. I remember." Viola jostled Sylvester as she peered over his shoulder at the journal. "See? There it is, an 'old dog of the open sea'!"

"I heard it too," said Mrs. Pickleberry. "Ain't no gettin' out of it, young Lemmington."

"I think—" Sylvester began wearily.

"Don't matter what *you* think," said Mrs. Pickleberry, pulling a pipe from her pocket and looking around for some means of lighting it. "If there was one person best placed for knowin' what sort o' a creature Cap'n Adamite was, it'd bin Cap'n Adamite hisself, the ol' bastard, and he said he was a—"

Sylvester put up a paw to stop this madness. "He just said he was an old sea dog."

"'Xactly."

"It's an *expression*."

"So you says."

"He was just saying he'd been at sea most of his life, that's all. That's what's meant by 'sea dog,' just 'sailor,' really. I mean, if I'd spent years at sea I could call myself a sea dog, even though I'm not a dog at all, I'm a—"

"Lemming," said Mrs. Pickleberry for him. "Not an 'amster. We knows. You keep tellin' us."

Sylvester drew a very long, very noisy, very deep and, in the end, wholly unsatisfactory breath. It did, however, serve its purpose which was to stop him from beating Mrs. Pickleberry to a bloody pulp and possibly, however much he might love Viola, doing the same to the younger lemming.

"Look," he said when he thought he'd probably be able to keep his voice under control, "if I keep being interrupted every few lines, we're never going to get the journal finished, are we?"

"Who's doin' any interruptin'?" said Mrs. Pickleberry, glaring around the cabin as if there might be culprits hiding under the furniture. She'd managed to get her pipe lit, which somehow made her bulging-eyed glare even more intense. It was also turning the air in the cabin a virulent-looking yellow-gray. The lantern chose that moment to flicker. Sylvester wondered if the flame was about to expire through lack of oxygen. "I can't see no one," she said.

He sighed again. "Let's just try to get through the rest of the logbook in one go, shall we?"

"Why not cut ahead to the interesting bits?" said Viola, clearly thinking she was being helpful.

"That was one of the—"

Realizing the trap he'd been just about to walk into, Sylvester tried the conciliatory approach.

"Perhaps we can learn something from Cap'n Adamite's account of how he first learned of the magical treasure chest of the Zindars?"

"Hmmf," was Mrs. Pickleberry's acerbic response, but she seemed ready to let him carry on. With any luck, she'd fall asleep soon. Surely it must be about time for her afternoon nap by now?

"Where was I?" Sylvester muttered. He must have moved his paw during the disputation, but soon he found his place again.

> *. . . with a few of my men alongside me as a safeguard and for company, couthless though it might be. The atmosphere in the tavern was if anything more pungent than ever, which, I might tell you, took some determined pungenting. My trusty midshipman, Hamish, was with me, as he always was when there was ale to be had and the prospect of a wench between the sheets, as was my first mate Jeopord . . .*

This time it was Sylvester who wanted to pause, although he knew any hesitation on his part would be pounced upon gleefully by Viola and Mrs. Pickleberry as setting a precedent for the future. He pretended there was an extra bad smudge of the ink, holding the page closer and screwing his eyes up as if struggling to decipher the words.

> *Jeopord . . . I know that name! He's that ocelot who carries out Rustbane's orders with such gratuitous willingness. So, he was old Adamite's first mate as well, was he? That means that at some stage Rustbane must have leapfrogged him in the* Shadeblaze's *pecking order, doesn't it? It's a wonder Jeopord is happy with that situation – getting rid of the old master simply to find himself serving a new one. Perhaps there's resentment still there. I must bear it in mind in case it's something I can explore to our advantage later.*

"D'yer want me to do the readin' fer yer?"

"No, no, no, Mrs. Pickleberry. I'll be fine. Just a, heh heh, tricky bit, that's all."

> *. . . as was my first mate Jeopord, with whom at the time I'd have entrusted my soul, so confident was I of the fellow's loyalty. But, as the old saying goes, the only ocelot you can ever trust is the one whose pelt you're wearing, and that certainly has proved to be the case with Jeopord, damn his guts. I can still use him for a while yet, so long as I keep a vigilant eye turned on him, but the time must surely come when either he or I must walk the plank. 'Tis a pity I ever took that mangy fox, Rustbane, aboard, for it's him I blame for the turning of Jeopord's allegiance from me!*
> *But enough of this. I lose track of my own musings . . .*
> *We were in the Moldy Claw, all those years ago, the three of us and a few*

others from the Shadeblaze besides, and I make no apologies for the fact that the drinks were chasing each other briskly enough down my throat. I've always had a hard head for drink, but this night . . . well, let's just say I was glad enow that we'd brought a youthful second mate with us to act as our Designated Stander and make sure those of us who wanted to got home.

When the ales had caused their usual consequence, I decided to brave the rigors of the shack that's out the tavern's rear. Something I'd never have done had it not been for those same ales, mark my words! I wobbled past rogues from every corner of Sagaria as I made my way to the door of that crowded room, and was dampened by so many spilled drinks of so many kinds, that e'en at the best of times I'd have not been able to put a name to all of them.

On coming out into the colder air of the night, I stood there motionless awhile, hoping the chill might reduce the befuddlement of my brain.

After I know not how much time, although I'm sure it cannot have been long, I found myself with my arms wrapped around a lantern post, grinning inanely at the full moon above.

It was then, in that dingy, misbegotten light, that I heard the voices.

No, dear reader (should this private journal ever have a reader other than myself), I do not mean I heard those voices that sometimes speak to a body when he's been oversupping ale! These were genuine voices, not fancies. They came from the opposite corner of the courtyard in which I stood. Either, the speakers had not noticed my emergence from the inn or they'd assumed I was just a harmless drunk in front of whom they could speak as freely and with as little concern for privacy as they might in front of a trunk of wood or a block of stone.

Of course, me being Cap'n Josiah Adamite, the blackest heart of any blackheart that ever sailed the ocean, while drunk I might be – and that I willingly confess – harmless I most certainly was not, nor ever shall be.

"'Tis the greatest treasure that's ever been known," said the first of the voices. My mind honed itself to razor-sharpness the instant I heard that word "treasure," I can tell you.

"Hist!" said the other voice.

Both of the speakers, whom I could identify only as grayer shapes in the smoggy, cloying, darkness of the Moldy Claw's back courtyard, froze.

As for me, I did the opposite of freeze. I was just a mud-brained drunk, wasn't I? What mud-brained drunks generally do is make quite a lot of noise. Besides, I'd come out of the boisterous warmth of the tavern's interior for a purpose, and it might well behoove me to fulfill that purpose even as I spied upon the locutors.

"He doesn't half rattle on with this ever-so-posh hoity-toity lingo of his, doesn't he?" Viola complained.

"Shut yer trap," said her mother crossly. "This is beginnin' ter get good."

Even so, Sylvester decided, in order to spare his companions' delicate female sensibilities, to skip the short paragraph in which Cap'n Adamite described, in some detail, the satisfaction he gained from "fulfilling his purpose."

I think it was the fact that I'd drenched my right foot (not, in fact, a deliberate camouflaging effect on my part, but a happy accident of which I took full advantage) that convinced the pair I was no more sinister than I seemed. Just in order to cement this notion in their minds, I gave a hefty moan and leaned against the nearest wall as if my innards were in rebellion. The two strangers hastily retreated a couple of precautionary steps, but then seemed content to leave me to my own devices.

"The greatest treasure of all time," said the second stranger. "'Tis a marvel such a thing should exist."

"Beyond gold," said the first. "Beyond jewels. Beyond the powers of coinage to equal. Beyond life itself."

"What can this marvel be?" wondered his fellow.

"'Tis just this . . ."

"Yes?"

"'Tis the magical chest of the Zindars!"

"The magical chest of the . . . Who was that again?"

"The Zindars."

"And they were?"

"You know."

"Um, no."

"They were the—wait a moment, what was that?"

"What was what?"

"That sound."

"It was just the old drunk over there by the door."

Of course, the "old drunk over there by the door" was none other than Captain Josiah Adamite – me, at your service, old Throatsplitter himself – and I was getting rapidly less drunk with every passing moment. I too had heard the sound. It had come from somewhere beyond the courtyard's wall, somewhere beyond the miasmic shed where drunks more courageous than I might risk relieving their ale-wrought pressures.

"A cat," said one of the speakers at last, the one who had been about to explain the provenance of the Zindars.

"If you say so," said the other, sounding not entirely convinced. "Now, about these Zindars of yours . . ."

The first speaker's voice dropped even lower than before, so that it became even more difficult for me, trapped by my subterfuge on the far side of the courtyard from where the two strangers conversed, to hear what he was saying. Yet never let it be said that Captain Josiah Adamite is without guile and resource! I gave a louder groan than before, then staggered to where someone had left an empty beer barrel in the midst of the area, presumably in a doomed attempt at capturing "ambience." I sat myself down on this object and let out a piteous bellow.

It was enough to convince the speakers they had nothing to fear from me.

"No one knows for sure," said the individual who had initiated this discourse, "precisely who the Zindars were, nor when they walked the world. What is known, however, is that they built a civilization far beyond anything Sagaria has seen. In the arts, the Zindars were paragons. They made music that could conjure the souls of singing birds from the air and weave them into tapestries of harmony which so delighted the ear that even the sound of a lover's words became drab. Their poetry was so emotive that its words smoldered upon any page which attempted to contain it, while the triple-breasted goddess herself became jealous of their paintings and sculpture, which she rightly saw cast even her own legendary beauty in a shadow of ordinariness. But, if they were prodigies of the arts, the Zindars were yet more than that in their scientific endeavors. They had vessels that could cruise not the seas but the skies and, 'tis said, might go yet farther than this, to sojourn among the stars! They built devices such that a Zindar could talk in one continent and be heard by his fellows in another, and not just heard, but seen as he was speaking. They had wheeled machines that could—"

"What's a continent?" said Viola, who'd obviously been finding the mental strain of not interrupting difficult to tolerate.

"I think it's an exceptionally big piece of land," said Sylvester.

"Sort of like Mugwort Forest, you mean?" she said, referring to the dark, forbidding woodland onto which Foxglove rather tremulously backed.

"A lot bigger than that," replied Sylvester. "A very, *very* lot bigger than that." Viola's eyebrows rose. "Oh, my."

"Where was I now?" said Sylvester, hoping his change of subject was adroit enough. "Ah, yes, here we are . . ."

". . . They had wheeled machines that could travel faster than the fastest horse, bearing not just a single rider but as many as dozens, hundreds even, or so the

story goes. They could—"

"Yes, yes," said his comrade. "This all sounds very wonderful and all, but what about the treasure?"

"I'm a-getting to that," said the other haughtily. "All in good time, my friend." He sounded to me as if he didn't know whether to throw a tantrum or burst into tears.

To be honest, his fellow wasn't the only one who was tiring of accounts of proverbial wonders. Ancient flying machines and their like are all very well, but they aren't exactly the sort o' things you can go out and spend, are they?

"Beyond all of these marvels what I have recounted to your ungrateful ears," the chap restarted, "there was one more marvelouser than any other feat the Zindars had accomplished. It was splendider than e'en the Mountains of Molgarvid or the Waterfalls of Helgioratha. It was tremendouser than the crystals of purest diamond that make up the coronet worn by—"

"Oh, by the unseen fourth breast of the goddess," muttered his listener in disgust. "Can't we just take it for granted that the Zindars were pretty damned fine in all directions? What was it that they put in their chest?"

"Ah, if only the answer were that simple, my callow buddy. If only I could—ow!"

"You see this dagger?"

"Er, yes."

"You see the tip of it?"

"Er, no."

"That's because it's under your chin. Could you possibly get to the point?"

"Er, I'll try."

You'll understand that by this time I was, as it were, silently cheering on the beezer with the dagger.

"What was it that the Zindars put in their magical chest?"

"Well, that's the trouble, you see."

"Eh?"

"Nobody actually knows for certain."

"They don't? Then why in the name of the triple-breasted goddess's gauzy lingerie are you wasting my time with—"

"But what we do know," began the other in the tone of voice of someone who's staring Death in the eyes and not much liking what he sees, "what we do know is that . . ."

"Yes?"

"Is that the Zindars themselves thought it was the most precious thing their civilization had ever produced or ever would produce, for that matter."

"Oh, blasted heck![2] For all we know it could be some blasted[3] sonnet! 'Hello sweet flutt'ry bluebirds that do flit among the glades' sort of thing."

"I think that's most improbable."

"You do? What makes you say that?"

"Because later historians, while being coy about the precise nature of the treasure itself, did specify that the Zindars had wrapped it up, before hiding it in the chest, in layers of gold, rubies and diamonds."

"Ahhhhh, now yer talkin', me bucko."

"I cannot imagine anyone doing that for a sonnet," said the other, his voice beginning to fill with relief. Clearly his confederate had lowered the dagger a few inches.

"Who cares if the Zindar treasure is a sonnet? Ol' Chainfist Garth here'll be contented with the wrappings, that he will."

So, at last I had a name for one of them: Chainfist Garth.

"My thoughts exactly," the other agreed, reluctantly, it seemed to me. "While, without a doubt the cultural treasures of the Zindars must be of immeasurable value, it is true there is something to be said for artifacts of a rather more worldly value, if you know what I mean."

"Jools," assented Chainfist Garth with a cackle.

"Assuming their settings have been crafted with a certain modicum of artistry, yes."

"An' gold! I can feel the gold running through me fingers already. Can't you?"

"Not really, old boy. You see, there's one difficulty about witnessing the glories of the magical chest of the Zindars."

"And that is?" said Chainfist Garth, suddenly reverting once again to a threateningly aggressive tone.

"Finding it."

"Why, I'll—"

There was that distinctive swishing noise a dagger makes when it's being brought speeding through the air to within less than a hairsbreadth of someone's gizzard. Rather like a cobra striking, only infinitely more menacing.

---

2 Here Sylvester really did find Cap'n Adamite's spelling incomprehensible. Perhaps fortunately.
3 Here too.

The individual whose gizzard was the focus of the said dagger's attention, so to speak, gulped audibly.

A hazardous thing to do, under the circumstances, but it was, after all, his gizzard to hazard.

Then he spoke, which must have taken a steely courage as well.

"But there is a map."

"A what?"

"A chart. A map of how to find where the magical chest of the Zindars was buried out of the world's sight."

"A treasure map, you mean?"

"Nothing other."

"And I suppose the location of this treasure map is as enigwhatsit as the location of the treasure itself, is it?"

"Not at all, Chainfist."

There was a long pause, during which you could just hear the far quieter sound of a dagger being slightly retracted from a gizzard.

"Then where the flipping Matilda is this map?"

"You have it."

"I have it?"

Chainfist Garth started to laugh, always a foolish thing to do when you're holding a dagger close to the throat of someone who possesses knowledge you rather wish you possessed yourself. Either their gizzard's a goner, in which case you feel mighty stupid, or—

"What's this?" said Chainfist Garth, his voice becoming suddenly a deal more solemn.

"It's your dagger," said the other.

"And it's pointing at my—"

"Your gizzard, yes."

"And from very close up, I'll be certain."

"Wisely so."

"Ah."

There was another of those long silences. Quite clearly both of them had forgotten the drunk who'd come stumbling out into the courtyard and then made such a malodorous exhibition of himself. This was a good piece of amnesia, so far as I was concerned. What did worry me was that some other drunk might come charging out here on a similar mission. I had reasons of my own for wishing that Chainfist Garth's nameless informant would speed things along a trifle.

"So, ah, so where is this map of theirs?" said the supposedly chainfisted one with a nervous would-be laugh.

"Earlier today, you bought yourself a new coat from a beggar down by the docks, did you not?"

"Well, er, 'bought' is perhaps not the best word."

"I euphemized. You obtained it, shall we say?"

"Yes, 'obtained' is a good word," Chainfist Garth hurriedly agreed. "In context."

"You obtained this beggar's coat, and no wonder. Your old one was, well, how to put this tactfully?"

Chainfist Garth mumbled something.

"I'm sorry," his companion said. "You're going to have to speak louder than that. I couldn't hear you."

"I got a job in a fish-gutting factory and was wearing me work clothes. No shame in that, I say!"

"No shame in that at all, if it were true. I find it hard to credit that you've ever had an honest job in your life, Chainfist."

"Wot's so special about this beggar's coat anyway?"

In the gloom I could make out the shape I'd identified as Chainfist Garth spreading its arms and looking down on itself as if the map might be printed on its front.

"Something the beggar himself didn't know."

"Poor ignorant beggar."

"That coat had previously belonged to a buccaneer groundhog named Barterley Smitt. Barterley Smitt was the first person in the modern era to discover the location of the magical chest of the Zindars. He did this after he'd been marooned on a desert island for showing an undue interest in the daughter of the captain of the vessel aboard which he was second mate. Are you following this?"

"In bits."

"Good. On this nameless island in the Sea of Misery, Barterley Smitt, who was reduced to digging up worms and eating them in order to keep his body and soul together, was one day having to dig deeper than usual for his supper (the worms were getting wise to his game), oh yes – when he came across a piece of shale upon whose flaky surface someone had long ago scratched a map. On this map were five islands shown, and one of these was marked with a big arrowhead."

"Arrowhead Island."

"Eh?"

"Arrowhead Island. I know it well. Just off the coast of Dumbalaia."

"No, fool! It was marked with a big arrowhead to show it was the important one on the map."

"So? Doesn't mean it couldn't also have been Arrowhead Island. It stands to reason."

"Chainfist, my mindrottingly literalist friend, let me ask you one question."

"Ask away."

"Why is Arrowhead Island called Arrowhead Island?"

"I have not the first idea. Why is Arrowhead Island called Arrowhead Island?"

"Because it's shaped like an arrowhead."

"I knew that."

"And this particular island, the one marked with an arrowhead on the map on the piece of shale what Barterley Smitt dug up, wasn't shaped like an arrowhead at all. It was shaped like a ripe cheese with a wedge cut out of it, as a matter of fact. It certainly wasn't Arrowhead Island."

"The tide could have been in?"

It was apparent to me, even at my distance from the pair, that Chainfist Garth was becoming forgetful of the proximity of his companion's daggerpoint to his gizzard. This must have occurred to his companion too, because his arm gave a small twitch and there was a cry of pain from Chainfist Garth.

"Okay, okay, have it your way. It wasn't Arrowhead Island!"

"Good."

"So, when this Barterley Smitt got off the island where he'd been marooned, he knew where the magical treasure chest of the Zindars was, did he? How did he know the arrowhead referred to the chest of the Zindars?"

"Because whoever had scratched the map had also scratched the words 'Chest of the Zindars Lieth Here' alongside the arrowhead."

"Barterley Smitt could read?"

"Many people can."

"Blimey."

"Yes."

"So," said Chainfist Garth eventually, "why didn't Barterley Smitt go and dig up the treasure and live happily ever after then?"

"Because there were only five islands shown on the map."

I could have sworn I heard the sound of brows furrowing in puzzlement. "That was four more islands than he needed to know about, wasn't it?"

There was a long sigh from the taller shadow. "His problem was, dear Chainfist, that he didn't know where the five islands were. They could have been anywhere in all the broad seas of Sagaria."

The sound of furrowing brows was replaced by that of fog clearing.

"Ah, I see. He had to sort of narrow it down, like."

"Quite so. After eighteen years he was rescued from the island by a passing merchant ship, whose entire complement he ate simply because they weren't worms. It's surprising the extremes to which eighteen years of a monotonous diet can push a man. He then sailed the ship to the first port he could find, which happened, luckily for him, to be Malmesduke, seat of one of the foremost universities in the world. In the library there, he laboriously compared the five islands of the shale map with every sea chart he could lay hands on, until—"

"Until he found the ones he wanted!"

"Yes. Making sure that no one was watching him, he folded up the relevant sea chart and smuggled it from the library. Once home – if a hotly fought-for portion of a ditch on the outskirts of Malmesduke can be called home – he was able to indicate the relevant island with a big, bold 'X.'"

"Not an arrowhead?"

"He might have done that, but he didn't."

"Why not? Ouch!"

"He'd hardly finished drawing the 'X' when he realized the map was a potentially explosive piece of property, and that anyone known to possess it might consider himself a marked man. Up and down the corridors of history, people had talked in hushed voices of the magical chest of the Zindars. If it were rumored that Barterley Smitt owned a chart that might lead its bearer to . . . well, need I go on?"

"He'd have found a bayonet up to the hilt in his guts before he could say lickety-split."

"Just one bayonet? Ha! Within seconds of the news getting out, Barterley Smitt would have resembled a porcupine. So, with some difficulty – needles and thread being in somewhat short supply in ditches, even the upper-crust ditches of Malmesduke – our good fellow, Barterley, sewed the map into the lining of his coat."

"And to think I thought he was just a beggar," said Chainfist Garth.

His companion laughed. "Oh, no, dear Chainfist. That wasn't Barterley Smitt. The beggar whose overcoat you requisitioned this morning was just an ordinary beggar. Well, not quite ordinary. A rather murderous beggar, if truth be told. It never crossed the mind of Barterley Smitt, who had a somewhat sheltered childhood for one who would turn out to be a pirate, that he might very well be murdered for the sake of not the map but the coat. Yet, that was precisely what your beggar did a few years ago, and then today, of course, history repeated itself when you killed the beggar so you might replace the disgustingly fishgut-smeared monstrosity you'd been wearing."

"It's called 'recycling,'" said Chainfist Garth defensively. "A very responsible thing to be doing, so the nobs keeps telling me."

"How virtuous of you." His associate's voice was dryer than talcum powder. "And now, I must display comparable virtue."

For a long moment Chainfist Garth, not the quickest-witted of fellows, even for habitues of The Moldy Claw, didn't cotton on to the implications of this final cold statement, and by the time he did do, it was too late for him.

The Moldy Claw's courtyard had witnessed a succession of distinctive noises within the past few minutes: a brow furrowing, a fog clearing, but now there was a sound clearly recognizable to any pirate from one end of the ocean to the other.

I refer, of course, to the gurgling rustle of a gizzard being slit.

Two gizzards, in point of fact, because I had not been idle all this while. As soon as Chainfist Garth was sent off to meet his Maker, who must have been hoping the encounter could be put off indefinitely, he was followed, courtesy of my good self, by the very individual who'd despatched him along that road. An individual whose name I never did learn, even though, as I returned into the roistering coziness of The Moldy Claw's taproom, I thanked him silently for all the information with which he'd supplied me.

I was greeted by Jeopord.

"A new coat ye've got yerself, Skipper?" he said.

I touched the side of my nose in that universal gesture to indicate things better left unsaid. "I found myself getting a touch cold out there. Now, be there any o' that fine mulled ale I might sup to warm my soul a fraction?"

The ocelot laughed and asked me no further. Yet, often since that night I've asked myself if his suspicions were more roused than was at the time apparent. I have never been by nature much fussed about the prescriptions of fashion, nor about the stylishness of my own apparel. Leave such considerations to eyebrow-plucking fops like Rustbane, I say, while the rest of us boyo buccaneers get on with the serious business of pirating. But it must have seemed odd to more than merely Jeopord that I should depart the taproom with moderately respectable attire and return clad in a coat which had clearly been disreputable for many a long year and was now further disreputablized by the recent addition of a few knife holes and an effusive outburst of fresh bloodstains.

That I should have taken so long acquiring this novel garment must also have been fit matter for curiosity among my fellows, I think.

Still, none of them questioned me further at the time, and I assumed the matter must have been soon forgotten.

"He assumed wrong, the dunderwit," said Mrs. Pickleberry tersely.

Sylvester had become so lost in the narrative by the old buccaneer, so completely transported into that long-ago courtyard where blood flowed as miscreants died, that the sudden, grating intrusion of Mrs. Pickleberry's voice made him start and almost drop the logbook.

"What do you mean?" he said once he'd got his breath back.

"Ain't it obvious? Jeopord remembered that night all too well, and, if he didn't, his crewmate, Hamish, did. Perhaps lots o' other crewmates too. They musta been talkin' all over this sorry barque about the night their Cap'n got his" – she waggled her fingers at her throat to indicate heavy sarcasm – "new coat. New coat my—"

"Mo–*om!*" said Viola.

"So that by the time Rustbane got to the *Shadeblaze*, whenever that was," said Sylvester excitedly, "people like Jeopord were all ripe for his talk of mutiny."

"That's the way I'm reck'nin' it," asserted Mrs. Pickleberry her pipe clamped more firmly than ever between her jaws. Fortunately for Viola and Sylvester, it had gone out some while earlier, and she'd been too engrossed in Adamite's narrative to remember to light it.

It was vital, Sylvester suddenly realized, that she be *kept* engrossed. Accordingly he seized up Adamite's journal and started to read once more . . .

I had thought that, with the map in my possession, it would be a matter of mere moments before I was able to plot a course for the last hiding place of the magical chest of the Zindars, but few things ever go as smoothly as we anticipate them going. When we finally got back aboard the Shadeblaze after our carousing at The Moldy Claw, dawn was already fumbling its way over the horizon. Besides, I was too confused of wit by the strong ale I had been consuming to do anything more than fall into my berth and hope as I fell that no one had moved it in my absence. It occurred to me as I slumped off into sleep that my life might depend on my keeping it a secret from my men that I had come into the possession of a treasure map, at least for a while. I knew I had their steadfast loyalty, because any who'd exposed himself as insufficiently loyal had long ago departed for Davy Jones's Locker, but at the same time I was as aware as any that the loyalty of a pirate becomes a malleable entity when the prospect of undiscovered treasure is in the air.

Was there any among them I trusted enough to guard my back?

This was the question that plagued me the following morning, and what plagued me even plaguier was the answer, which was a resounding, "no." Not even Jeopord, to whom I had given everything that he regarded as precious in life, not even him (and I was right in this, was I not?).

My analysis of Barterley Smitt's map was something that must be done under conditions of strictest privacy. Although all of the crew were under instructions never to enter their Cap'n's cabin without first knocking and seeking permission, I knew of old that secrets stored there did not remain secrets for long. There were too many comings and goings, especially in the times when I was elsewhere and going about my duties, for the place to be secure. If I started putting it under padlock and chain, the gossip would soon be racing like wildfire as to why I had taken this precaution, and again any hopes of secrecy would rapidly be forfeit.

There was only one option open to me.

I called to me the ship's carpenter, a scurvy ferret by the name of Levantes, and impressed upon him, under threat of a horrifically prolonged and extraordinarily gruesome death, that everything transacted between himself and myself should go with the pair of us to our salty graves. He knew my threat was not an idle one. Like any of the buccaneers of the good ship Shadeblaze, he'd seen the inventiveness of the punishments I meted out when my wrath was sufficiently roused, and he'd no wish that the same sort of fate should become his own. O' course, I had no intention whatsoever of keeping Levantes along for one moment longer than it took him to complete the task I had in mind, but I did not explain that to him. Besides, at least this way his death would be quick, quiet and relatively painless as opposed to slow, screaming and filled with unbearable agony.

What I wanted Levantes to do was this: If my own cabin could never be made a secure enough place for me to enact my studies of Barterley Smitt's sea chart, then I must have me another cabin made, a cabin that was itself secret. There were various places I knew about within the structure of the Shadeblaze that had been built by the shipwright as hideouts for the captain and his officers should the ship be boarded by foe. I was certain none other than myself knew of these – none other than myself and, now, Levantes. To him I revealed the location of one of these hideouts and gave my instructions as to how I desired it to be converted into a pleasant, but covert, study for my own personal use. This meant that not only must its existence be cloaked, but my access to it and exits from it be capable of complete concealment.

He was a fine carpenter, that ferret!

I sent all of the crew ashore for a long weekend in the fleshpots of Darkwater. All of the crew except a skeleton complement of perhaps half a dozen, the minimum necessary to keep the Shadeblaze afloat. Then I set Levantes to work constructing the new chamber. Since I might be spending long hours therein, I was determined that it be not overly spartan; his first

instruction concerned an en suite jakes. That completed, I gave him a list of
furnishings and accoutrments that included . . .

"He does rather go on for a bit here, the old rogue," said Sylvester, breaking off from his reading to paw his way through the next few pages of the Cap'n's spidery, blotted handwriting. "There's a long list of everything he insisted should be incorporated into his new . . . his new *den*, really, because it's obvious he'd begun thinking of it as a secret personal luxury far beyond any strict utility it might have in connection with his research into the . . ."

He looked up and saw that Viola and her mother were staring at him, jaws slack.

"Oh, I'm sorry. I'm beginning to talk like old Josiah wrote, amn't I?"

"Uh-huh," Viola concurred.

"It's a bad habit of mine."

"Uh-huh," said Viola again.

"Celadon's commented on it more than once."

"Uh-huh."

"I get the same way when I've been perusing musty old annals for too long, you see, and—"

"Sylvester."

"Yes?"

"Just skip the old buzzard's list of household knick-knacks and get back to the story. I'm bursting to find out what happens next!"

"I'm just bursting," interposed Mrs. Pickleberry sourly. "'Ow many more pages o' that thing yer got still to go?"

"Um, quite a lot."

"Well, just wait yerselves up for me while I go and get my nose powdered."

With rather more bustle than was strictly necessary, Mrs. Pickleberry left the room.

It wasn't long before she was back. If she noticed the blush that had invaded her daughter's cheeks she made no comment upon it.

"Get a move on then, laddie."

Mrs. Pickleberry settled herself back onto the cabin trunk she'd been using as a seat, fastened her lips aggressively around the stem of her pipe, and focused upon Sylvester the incandescent stare of an audience that's been forced to wait too long for the star attraction to come onstage.

"Ah, right," said Sylvester. He leafed through a few pages until he found where Captain Adamite's list ended, cleared his throat, and resumed reading . . .

The last item that Levantes installed in my new cabin was the great lantern.

Without it, study of Barterley Smitt's map would have been impossible, yet I had sentimental reasons for not commencing that study until my cabin was fully rendered. Not to mention the very pragmatic one that, before I risked removing the map from the lining of the old and bloodstained coat, it would be wisest if my little friend, Levantes, were feeding the fishes. That way he couldn't inadvertently, in his cups or out of them, betray the existence of my secret chamber.

The lantern itself was a masterpiece, a rare antique that I had picked up many years ago during my voyage to the Great Misunderstood Continent. It took the form of a . . .

"More boring stuff here about the Cap'n's sense of interior decor, yah-de-yah-de-yah-de," lied Sylvester, hoping it wasn't obvious to the two females that he'd begun to sweat profusely. If the continent's artisans designed all their furnishings like *that* it was no wonder the place was misunderstood.

"I'll just skip past this bit," he said, "and . . ."

"But I've always been interested in design," said Viola, eyes aglow.

"Not *this* design, I can assure you," Sylvester muttered hastily, turning a page or two.

"Later?"

"Later, perhaps. For now . . ."

I had underestimated the ferret. Not just in the sense that his craftsmanship in the construction of the secret cabin surpassed anything I would have deemed him capable of, but also that he successfully pre-empted my disposal of his poxy carcass. Less than an hour after he'd accomplished his task, I crept to his bunk with my trustiest garrotte in hand, only to find he'd skipped his passage. Jeopord had returned from Darkwater prematurely, and so the ocelot and I combed the Shadeblaze from stem to stern in search of the little rodent, but we found neither hide nor hair.

"Where in blue blazes could he have gone?" wailed Jeopord petulantly at last. "And why?"

I had, of course, declined to take him into my confidence about the new cabin.

At last, I had to concede defeat. Wherever Levantes had taken himself, it was someplace we weren't going to find him, not if we searched for half a year. Darkwater had swallowed him up, the way that foul port had swallowed up so many.

"Never mind," I said to Jeopord. "Carpenters aren't hard to come by. It's

just that Levantes was especially skilled at his task."

Jeopord gave me what was, with hindsight, a look of askance, but he said nothing.

Two days later, we set sail from Darkwater, heading due south toward the equator.

It was as good a direction as any.

Still I had not had the opportunity to look at Barterley Smitt's map. The coat lay over the back of the leather armchair that stood in front of my secret writing desk in my secret study, but I dared not start unpicking the seams while we were still within sight of port lest someone spy me in the act, seize the chart and vanish as Levantes had vanished.

That night, as the last images of Darkwater sank below the horizon behind us, I waited until all the crew bar the nightwatchmen were asleep, then, a guttering candle held high above my head, I furtively crept down the companionway from the main deck to my secret chamber. There was something in me of shame, I confess, that the all-powerful captain of a corsair vessel should be slithering thus in subterfuge aboard his own craft. Yet, there was also tumultuous exultation bursting in me like mighty ocean breakers come halfway around the world to crash upon the sand, for was it not this very night that I would—

"Aw, come off of it, Josiah!" cried Mrs Pickleberry, sitting bolt upright on her sea chest as if emerging from a trance, her pipe held in front of her like an offensive weapon (which was, Sylvester saw in a moment of insight, in a sense what it was). "We don't need to know about yer innermost motivations and junk like that," Viola's mother continued. "Enough already!"

"I think he's just about to get back into the thick of things," Sylvester nervously assured her. "He seems just, er, to have got a bit carried away there."

Mrs. Pickleberry wrinkled her nose. "Well, get along with it then, you great lummox."

The stitched seams of that antique coat did not long resist my ruthless dagger tip, and it must have been less than a minute before I had the garment reduced to its component pieces in front of me. And there, just as Chainfist's assassin had promised back in the courtyard of The Moldy Claw, was the map Barterley Smitt had secreted within. But what that worthy had not elaborated, for indeed he could not have known, was that someone's blade (perhaps that of the beggar who had slain Smitt, perhaps that of Chainfist when in turn ridding the beggar of the garment, perhaps both) had sundered the map twice, slicing it into three neatly separated portions. Those same lunges had covered the yellowing parchment with copious flows of blood, which it was going to be my task to leach out of the fabric so the lines and inscriptions would be legible once more. I knew this could be effected; I also knew it would take me many long hours and my full reserves of fastidious patience before the chore was done, but seeing the map in three gave me a notion.

When the three parts were together, it was only then that they posed a danger to the one who possessed them, for anyone who bore the map entire had the complete route to where the chest resided, but if the three parts were kept widely separated . . .

Firstly, I had to rid the parchment of those gruesome stains of blood . . .

"There's a long technical explanation here," said Sylvester, leafing through quite a few more pages of the journal. "Interesting if ever you want to get blood out of parchment, which would be quite a useful thing to know when I get back to Foxglove and the Library, but—"

"A moist compress of Spongewort and Drunkard's Breath," said Mrs. Pickleberry, addressing the empty air in front of her as if it were some kind of simpleton. "Gently press it on the affected article, avoiding any possible running of the colors in the article by use of a paste of Lime Ankleberry and Mutton Aloe. Then—"

"How did you know all that?" cried Sylvester.

"Everyone who has had to do the laundry for a family knows it," said Mrs. Pickleberry with a sniff. "Obviously that's a chore you've always just lef' for yer poor mother to do, Sylvester, Lhaeminguas bless her bones. And as for little Miss High 'n' Mighty here, o' course—"

"Mo-*om!*"

"So we can assume he got the map clean all right." Sylvester continued to turn pages. "Ah, yes, here we are. He finally has it in a condition where he can read it clearly enough, even though it seems Barterley Smitt's handwriting wasn't much better than the Cap'n's own. He talks about sitting at his writing desk with the map in front of him, memorizing every 'nook and cranny,' as he describes it, but most particularly the lower section of the sheet, the one that has the island marked 'X' on it. There's a lot for him to memorize. Some of the waters through which any vessel must pass on its way to the island are mighty treacherous. But he knows this task must be completed before he so much as hints to his crew that they'll be going off on a treasure hunt, so he applies himself to it every opportunity he has. Once he's gotten himself to the stage where he can . . ."

The day dawned bright and early. The previous night I tested myself to make sure the image of Barterley Smitt's chart was firmly engraved on my mind, and I think the process engraved it even more deeply. I put the map away in a drawer, took a fresh sheet of parchment, and on this prepared the best representation I could of my mental etching. When I was satisfied, I compared the two versions of the map side-by-side to assure myself they were as near identical as made no matter.

This accomplished, I reduced my newly drawn map to finely powdered ashes in the lantern flame, then repeated the whole process, again creating a rendition of Barterley Smitt's penmanship on a virgin parchment. In all I did this three times before I was done.

Assuring myself thus that the map was in its entirety reserved within my memory, I determined to scatter the three portions to widely separated areas of Sagaria. The first of these, and perhaps the cunningestly chosen, was back where I had first clapped eyes upon the map and its previous owner: the tavern called The Moldy Claw in the port of Darkwater. I sent my trusty crewman, Hamish, there with it, little knowing that, alas, I would never see him again. For a while I thought dark thoughts about him, but much later I learned he had fulfilled his task right readily and then, the duty accomplished, had suffered the ill fortune to be shanghaied aboard a mongoose vessel out of Tarngonia. Not long after, he was captured by Tarngonian peelers and jailed for his pains . . .

"Then," said Sylvester, skipping ahead nervously once again – it was clear from the expressions on the faces of his two companions that if he wasn't careful there might be a mutiny in this very cabin – "old Cap'n Adamite details how he disposed of the three parts."

Sylvester paused hither and thither, digging his nose into the journal, oblivious to its old seaweed stench as he devoured nugget after nugget of information. So, Cap'n Rustbane had been wrong when he'd thought the relevant section of the map had just "somehow" made its way to The Moldy Claw. Adamite had taken it there deliberately, believing that'd be a safe hiding place. Sylvester thought he understood the logic. If everybody's squabbling over something, fighting and killing each other for possession of it, then effectively it never belongs to anyone. But somehow, Levantes had gotten hold of it anyhow. Perhaps Levantes had known a lot more about what was going on aboard the *Shadeblaze* than Cap'n Adamite had realized, giving the ferret a big advantage when it came to the murderous tussle for the map's ownership.

Then Sylvester cursed his own stupidity.

No, that couldn't be it. The fragment of Barterley Smitt's map that had come into Levantes' possession was the biggest and most important – the one with the island marked "X."

Cap'n Adamite would never have dared let that fragment loose in Darkwater, where too many expert mariner eyes might come across it and recognize the pattern of islands depicted there.

"Is that it then?" said Mrs. Pickleberry. "All done?"

Sylvester became aware that he'd left the two females in silence for rather too long a time.

"Er, no," he said. "There's more."

"Then get a move on, will you?"

"Yes, Sylvester." Viola confirmed her mother's instruction. "We haven't got all day."

They probably had, but Sylvester chose not to contradict her.

As for the second portion, I sent one of my crew, a gray squirrel whom I trusted not at all, with it into the heart of worg country, telling him that under no account must he be tempted to sell it to the highest bidder. For is it not a well-known fact that worgs will purchase even the most useless of objects and treasure them forever more if only they can first be persuaded the items in question are desired by others? Of course, no sooner had my rapscallion squirrel gotten to the land of the worgs than he started himself up an auction for this tatter of paper. Within minutes he'd started a battle amongst various worglords who each coveted the piece merely because the others did. After immense bloodshed, the piece of the map ended up in the possession of a certain Growgarth, one of the most powerful of all his kind and reputed to be indubitably the wartiest.

And what of my treacherous squirrel? Ah, just as I'd planned, he was roasting on somebody's spit even before the battle had properly started, and so died the only person in the land of the worgs who had the first idea of what that scrap of parchment actually was.

The third and most significant portion of the map?

Ah, that piece I'll keep . . . for now. Despite the tests I have carried out on my own memory, I must not be satisfied until I have performed the memorizing exercise a hundred times more! Remembering the general location of the islands where the treasure is hidden is easy enough. Far more arduous is memorizing all the currents and shallows that protect the resting place of the magical chest of the Zindars from accidental discovery.

Content that two of the thirds were beyond the powers of any to discover, I summoned a meeting of the crew on the main deck. Many of them had become aware that their old cap'n was hatching some new scheme and were eager to hear it explained for them. I kept them in suspense a mite longer while I issued instructions to the helmsman to set a new course.

Then I gave to my hearties some news that at first they had little wish to hear.

There have been those who, over the years, have accused that brothy buccaneer, Cap'n Josiah Adamite, of lacking a sense of humor. Most of 'em, if they've been near enough when they've committed this libel, have found themselves pondering the hilarity of lacking their ears and fingers.

When old Throatsplitter jokes, he jokes for keeps, you see.

So I stood up there on the deck and I looked at all their expectant faces and I announced I was giving up the piracy business.

This caused such consternation that I thought I might have a mutiny on my hands right there and then.

More than this, I said, I was going into a new business. I'd determined to become an entrepreneur trading in rare and valuable items that were currently, ahem, buried for safekeeping.

One or two of the sharper-witted amongst them (and there were only one or two, because I don't recruit my crew members based on their sharpness of wit!) cottoned on to the implications of what I was saying and began to grin. The rest looked just as mystified as ever they'd been.

Until I explained it to 'em.

Well, that, of course, changed everything.

Treasure hunting is something every red-blooded pirate in the world can heartily approve of!

Those fine boyos of mine cheered me to the rafters – or to where the rafters would have been had there been any above the open deck o' a pirate ship at sea! Then, when they'd done cheering me, they started cheering me all over again. The more I told them about the treasure, the more they cheered. Jeopord, at my instruction, broke out the grog and afore long there were pirates a-dancing and a-singing and a-puking all over the Shadeblaze.

One or two of the crew expressed their doubts, sayin' that mayhap we should stick to pirating rather than searching for hidden contraband, so even the sharks were happy.

I have to confess I swilled back plenty of the ship's supplies of good strong grog myself that day, and on the morrow I was to curse my weak-willedness in doing so, but at the time it seemed fitting. This was a moment for a captain and his crew to share.

Even despite the blurring of my wits by the booze, though, there was something that disturbed me, some element of the celebrations and festivities that didn't ring one hundred per cent true. For a long time I couldn't think exactly what this might be. I mentioned my unease to Jeopord, but he was in an even sorrier state from the grog than I was, and I think had fallen asleep by the time I'd properly finished my explanation.

Looking back now on that day, and with the benefit of more recent events, I know what it was that perturbed me.

There was a crewman who had but recently joined us, a fox who'd emerged from the scummy underworld of Darkwater – or so he claimed. He had proven himself to be such an excellent and knowledgeable seafarer, not to mention an excellent and knowledgeable cutthroat, that I had not a moment's pause in hiring him to be part of the complement of the Shadeblaze. Although he was as demonstrative as any in his rejoicing on the day I announced the start of our quest for buried booty, there was something just a trifle off-key in the tone of his celebrations.

This I would not have noticed in the ordinary way. The fox, whose name was Rustbane, was after all just another crewman and I had those in plenty. There was nothing in particular to distinguish him (or so I thought), nothing to make me notice one way or the other how he was reacting to my happy news.

It was just the briefest of glimpses of something that drew him to my attention. I was well and truly soused in grog when I noticed him vanish behind the poop area. Gone to answer the call of nature, I thought and, since nature had been calling me too rather insistently for some while by now, I followed in his footsteps. As I rounded one of the main guns I saw that he was not contributing to the ocean's swells. Indeed, he was not by the rail at all. Instead, he was standing next to where one of the longboats hung tarpaulined.

And he seemed to be speaking to it!

Fascinated by the notion of a talking longboat (I may have mentioned that I'd imbibed more than my share of grog by this time), I made to approach him.

He looked up and saw me.

"Ahoy there, Cap'n," he said in a cheerfully loud voice.

Not just cheerfully loud, I later thought, but suspiciously sober.

"Ahoy there," he said again, even more loudly, as if I might not have heard him the first time.

He advanced upon me with his arm out in a companionable fashion, as if concerned I might tumble over the side. As this was not an entirely impossible event, I was grateful enough to accept his support.

"Speaking to longboats, eh?" I said.

He grinned broadly.

"Fine grog you serve aboard the Shadeblaze, Skipper" he said. By contrast with a moment earlier, his voice now sounded considerably lubricated.

Arms around each other's shoulders, we sang a song badly together as we made our way back to join the rest of the crew.

Again, it was only in later recollection that I perceived what had been truly odd about the entire little incident.

For a fox to speak to a longboat is unusual, but by no means extraordinary, especially considering the likely inebriation of the fox.

No, what was truly bizarre was that I'd heard the longboat answer him back!

Just a word or two, mind. And, although I'd heard those words, I had not heard them clearly enough to understand what they were.

But I had been able to discern something about them.

They'd been spoken in the unmistakable tones of a ferret!

"Levantes!" said Viola, startling Sylvester, not just with the sudden interruption but by the fact she'd been paying attention. "It has to be."

"I rather think you're right," he replied, stroking his chin with his paw. "Just like Adamite realized the best place to hide a piece of the map was somewhere so obvious no one would ever think to look for it there – The Moldy Claw, in other words. So Levantes must have decided the safest hiding place for himself was aboard the *Shadeblaze*. Adamite thought the ferret had put as much distance between himself and his old captain as possible but, in reality, Levantes was hidden right under his nose. He must have been a stowaway for *months*. He knew there was treasure at the end of the trail, so it was worth his while to stick as close to Adamite as he could."

Viola's eyes were glowing with the thrill of the chase. "And Rustbane must have found him and made him his accomplice."

"I think we can be sure of that," said Sylvester. "Later on, something drove them apart."

"Rustbane's habit of never leaving any witnesses alive," suggested Viola.

"Most probably so. Whatever, at the time of which Cap'n Adamite was writing they seem certainly to have been the closest of allies."

"Figgers," said Mrs. Pickleberry enigmatically. "Keep readin', youngster."

Sylvester turned the page. "There's not much more to read," he said, holding up the book so the other two could see where Cap'n Josiah Adamite's tiny, spiky handwriting came to an abrupt halt halfway down the right side.

"All the more reason to read what's there."

Sylvester peered at Mrs. Pickleberry. What she'd just said didn't seem to make any sense. Still, he wasn't going to argue about it now. Instead, he turned his attention to the last two pages of Cap'n Adamite's journal, perhaps the last two pages the old buccaneer had ever written.

Weeks have passed since then, and it sometimes seems hard to remember the merriment with which we set out on this voyage. Two days ago we watched Cape Waste sink below the horizon behind our stern. Ahead of us is a voyage at whose end might lie, perhaps, riches beyond the dreams of any mortal alive in Sagaria.

Yet it is a voyage that I fear I shall never see.

For weeks now I have been ailing. At first I thought it must simply be one of the illnesses that can strike down seafarers unpredictably, powder monkey and cap'n alike. Yet, slowly my suspicions grew that my malaise had another cause and now I am convinced of it.

I am being steadily and systematically poisoned.

And the person doing the poisoning is that accursed fox Rustbane.

Woe the day I ever clapped eyes upon him!

Tonight I shall slip away from the Shadeblaze. I shall steal a longboat and row it into the concealing darkness of the night. I suspect this is how the dastardly creature Levantes finally escaped the Shadeblaze, however long ago that was.

Let Rustbane and those scum of the seas I once thought were loyal to me sail on, searching for the magical chest of the Zindars. Even if they find it, I doubt they will be satisfied in the discovery, for just within the past few days I have encountered in my research an account that says the Zindars' treasure is nothing that we would recognize as riches at all. That the tales of it being wrapped in precious jewels are simply myths.

Needless to say, I have not conveyed this information to Rustbane.

And there is more.

Barterley Smitt marked the island where the chest is buried with an arrowhead.

When I came into possession of the map, I carefully erased the arrowhead and replaced it with an "X."

A trifling alteration, you might think. A mere cosmetic change.

Except for the fact that I put my "X" alongside the wrong island.

The true location of the treasure?

Let me commit to writing no more than that it can be seen only through the fall of the Ninth Wave.

Rustbane's a cunning one. His cunning may one day lead him to the magical chest of the Zindars, I'd not be surprised at all if this were so.

But, if he achieves this feat, it shall not be for any help of mine.

And, when he makes his great discovery, I will be waiting there for him.

Now it is dark. Even though the cramps created by Rustbane's poison make it seem as if my guts are being slowly ripped apart, I must tiptoe from this place, sealing the entrance so none can tell it even exists and make my way up to the longboats.

I wish I could take you with me, dear journal. You, who have been my solitary friend for longer than I can now reckon, but I must leave you here. There is a good chance I will be caught before I can effect my escape, and in such an event it would be fatal if you were discovered about my person. For then all of my inmost secrets would become known to the vile fox. Better that you remain here, hidden away from mortal sight.

Enough!

I must be on my way!

Wish me good fortune, dear journal . . .

ESCAPE!

"**D**id he escape?" asked Viola urgently, leaning forward eagerly on the bunk bed. Again her eyes were aglow.

"I don't know," Sylvester replied, once more tipping the open book in her direction so she could see where the writing stopped. "That's the end of the old sea dog's reminiscences. Cap'n Rustbane told me he'd killed Adamite himself, stuck him through the liver with his sword" – Sylvester shuddered graphically – "but I'm becoming less and less certain whether I should believe a single word Rustbane tells me."

"Still, it's the most likely thing, isn't it?" murmured Viola. She gazed wistfully at the mildewed journal. "He won't have been able to move very quickly, not if the poison was paining him as much as he says. He can't have had much of a chance of making it to the longboats undetected. Poor old soul."

Sylvester stared at her disbelievingly.

"Poor old soul?"

"Why, yes. I mean . . ."

"Poor old soul! One of the cruelest hearts the seas of Sagaria have ever seen? A mass murderer? A sadist who took the greatest delight in subjecting his enemies, or anyone who offended him, to the most excruciating agonies as he watched them die? And you call him a poor old soul?"

Viola shifted uneasily. "Well, yes. I mean, hearing his account of himself, didn't you rather get to like him? Especially by comparison with that horrid Rustbane?"

Despite himself, Sylvester was forced to admit she had a point. It was hard to think of any redeeming characteristics old Josiah Adamite might have had, but alongside Cap'n Rustbane he had a certain brutal straightforwardness that one could perhaps learn to appreciate.

"That was one vital thing the old buzzard be lettin' slip," observed Mrs. Pickleberry.

"It was?" said Sylvester, pleased to change the subject.

"'Bout him having put his "X" alongside of the wrong island, I mean," Mrs. Pickleberry explained. "Ten to one that Cap'n Rustbane friend of yours don't know about it, even after all these years. So we know somethin' the gray fox don't know, and that gives us one mighty great wallopin' advantage, it does."

"You're right," agreed Sylvester slowly. They could do with any advantage they could get, if they weren't going to end their days being chewed by the fishes at the bottom of the ocean. Even so, he couldn't imagine what help it was going to be, aside from a sort of gleeful, vindictive *schadenfreude* to know that, even if Rustbane *did* lay his rotten little paws on the third portion of the map, he was going to waste weeks and months and possibly forever digging up the wrong island.

"So it's important," continued Mrs. Pickleberry, "that we keep it a secret from the fox until we escape."

Sylvester nodded seriously. "Quite so."

How many days now until we reach Hangman's Haven? he thought. *And, once we get there, do we realistically have more than the slightest chance of escaping?*

Very deliberately, he closed Cap'n Josiah Adamite's book and stuffed it under the mattress of his bunk.

Whatever you do, Sylvester old fellow, it's important you put on a brave face when you face the world. If ever Viola and Mrs. Pickleberry realize how utterly terrified you are, they might crack up completely.

Viola, watching him, could deduce most of his thoughts.

She glanced across at her mother.

The two Pickleberries rolled their eyes at each other.

A few hours later, the storm had died away and the crew of the *Shadeblaze* had finished making the myriad minor repairs and adjustments necessary in the wake of the elements' wrath. There was now a grog-swigging party in full flow on the main deck. The three captives had been invited to join in and Mrs. Pickleberry, in her persona as Three Pins, Scourge of the Sagarian Seas, had accepted the invitation with gusto. Sylvester and Viola had been a little more fastidious ("prissy!" according to Mrs. Pickleberry) and were now standing on the sterncastle, looking out at a moonless night studded with more stars than could ever be counted.

Every now and then, the rasping sound of Mrs. Pickleberry's voice, raised in song, floated up to them and Viola shuddered in embarrassment.

"She gets like this sometimes," murmured Viola.

"Don't they all?" responded Sylvester in an attempt to reassure her, although ,in fact, he couldn't imagine his own mother ever behaving this way. Hortensia Lemmington had always, he was sure, been demure and ladylike.

He leaned forward on the rail, acutely conscious that his elbow was barely more than a hairsbreadth away from hers – a very thick hair, to be honest, but it was the principle that counted. An amiable silence descended between them into which even the boisterous carousing of the pirates could penetrate only in a sort of muffled way, as if heard through a couple of layers of cotton wool.

"Do you really think we'll be able to manage it?" said Viola softly after a while.

"Eh? Manage what?"

"Escaping from these frightful people, I mean."

"Of course I do." He paused to admire the confidence in his voice. "We're lemmings of Foxglove, after all. There's nothing we can't do once we've set our hearts on it."

"That's what worries me," continued Viola, putting a paw on his arm. "We're lemmings. We're not foxes or weasels or ferrets. We don't have the inbuilt viciousness some of the pirates have."

Sylvester turned to look her in the eyes. He wished there were some moonlight. As it was, he could barely distinguish her face, let alone the eyes within it. He felt certain the darkness was ruining his intended effect.

"Trust me."

"I do, Sylvester, implicitly. Of course I do, but . . ."

He wished she hadn't added that querulous "but . . ."

"Please."

"Oh, Sylvester, if ever there was a lemming who could become a hero it would be you."

"That wasn't what I meant."

"Oh?"

"You were comparing lemmings to other creatures and implying we can't be as vicious as them."

He heard rather than saw her shift from foot to foot.

"Well, yes."

"Think of Mayor Hairbell."

"Must I?"

Sylvester gave a snort of laughter.

Viola joined in. "If I had to choose between Mayor Hairbell and Cap'n Terrigan Rustbane . . ."

"You'd choose neither."

She hooted. In the darkness, Sylvester grinned. It was good to hear her laugh so freely, as if, for a moment, she'd forgotten the terrible dangers around them, the perilous future that awaited them.

"But you saw it yourself," Viola said, sobering. "Back in Foxglove. If there were a fight between Rustbane and Hairbell, there's no question who'd win. It'd be over in seconds and then Rustbane'd be kicking Hairbell's head around as a football."

"That's only because Rustbane is bigger and stronger and has sharper teeth and claws. Hairbell is the meaner and viciouser. Well, he's *as* mean and *as* vicious anyway. We lemmings, Viola, we're not the cuddly creatures people tend to think we are. That's a big advantage we have. Folk tend to look at us and assume we're not going to create any trouble, and the next thing they know they're lying in the gutter counting their broken bones."

"Do we have to talk about this?"

"Yes, Viola, we do have to talk about these things. Our lives might depend upon it, in the days to come. Any one of us might have to hurt someone. We might even have to kill someone."

He'd expected her to gasp with revulsion at the possibility. She didn't.

"Besides," he added, "if you're not overly impressed by the idea of a duel to the death between Cap'n Rustbane and Mayor Hairbell, trying imagining a fight between Rustbane and your mom."

"That," said Viola, "is another matter entirely."

Sometime later, she kissed him.

Suddenly there was a moon in the night sky, after all.

✥ ✥ ✥ ✥ ✥

Two more days went by.

Very slowly.

Almost reluctantly.

Days are like adolescents.

It's not so much what they say as the *way* they don't say what they *would* say if they *did* say anything.

These two days didn't approve of the delay.

Neither did Viola's mom.

Strong stuff, that pirate grog. Got a kick like a mule.

Worst of all, with every hour the *Shadeblaze* traveled southward the air got hotter.

Viola was sharing a cabin with her mom.

Poor Viola.

"Land ho!"

"Huh?" said Sylvester.

He breathed in, then recognized the stuff that was filling his mouth wasn't air but the corner of his pillow.

He spat it out and pushed himself up on his elbows.

"Land ho!" repeated the invisible pirate obligingly, somewhere beyond the porthole. Sylvester had opened it last night in the wan hope some cooler air might drift into his cabin. Despite his efforts, the atmosphere in here was so hot it felt like boxing gloves battering against the sides of his head.

There was a knock at the door.

"Whazza—" he said.

"Sylvester?"

Viola's voice. She sounded dreadfully cheerful. Her mother must have dropped off to sleep.

"Yeeurgh," he said.

"Did you hear that?"

"Hear what?"

"Land! We're just about there. The Caraya Islands."

"You sure?"

He wallowed in his bunk. Knowing Viola, she'd probably brushed her teeth on the way to his cabin. His own breath, he felt certain, must smell like a compost heap. That was what hot weather did to you.

Well, did to you if you weren't Viola, that was.

He groaned.

"Can I come in?" she hissed through the wooden door. "I mean, are you decent?"

He could have done without the coy, girlish giggle that followed the question.

"I'm . . . ah . . ." he replied.

She dropped her voice to a penetrative hiss.

"The *Caraya Islands*, Sylvester. Don't you remember? Hangman's Haven? Our big chance of escaping?"

"Ah, yeah."

He knew he was being stupid and hated himself for what he must be making her think about him. It was this accursed heat. It seemed to rot away his brains until there was nothing left to think with.

Pull yourself together, Sylvester! Your life may depend upon it.

With a conscious effort, he was able to focus his gaze upon the wall on the other side of the cabin. There was a knothole there the shape of a rat's head.

"I'm coming," he said, rolling out of bed. He opened the door to find Viola looking, to his horror, even fresher and more adorable than when he'd last seen her.

"What's that word my mother uses? Lummox?"

"That's it."

"Well, you're one of those, Sylvester Lemmington."

"Thanks."

Despite the awful taste in his mouth, the sight of her was making him feel better by the moment.

"Have you been up on deck yet?" he said.

"Since they started shouting about land ho, you mean?"

"Yes."

"No. I was waiting for you."

"How's Daphne? Three Pins, I mean."

"Dead to the world. I was going to wake her, but then . . ."

"You didn't." Who could blame her? Her mother had been like a thwarted hornet these past two days.

"I didn't," agreed Viola. "You ready?"

"I suppose so."

She grabbed him by the paw and tugged him toward the nearest companionway. A moment or two later, Sylvester still blinking as if daylight was an entirely novel concept to him. They were standing on deck looking out across a stretch of impossibly blue water to a distant gray smudge.

"That's land?"

"Oh, stop being so grumpy, Sylvester."

He screwed up his eyes, hoping that somehow the smudge might get bigger and clearer.

It didn't.

"Here," she said.

"What?"

He looked down. She was holding a leather flask in front of his whiskers.

"Water," she said.

He grabbed the flask and took a long pull. The contents were warm and brackish, like all the water seemed to have become aboard the *Shadeblaze* the farther they got from land. Even so, the liquid refreshed him, made the morning seem somehow more approachable.

"Thanks."

As they watched, the bow of the *Shadeblaze* slowly turned until it was pointing in the general direction of that distant gray mass. There could be no doubt as to the ship's intended destination.

"That must be Blighter Island," said Sylvester.

"None other," Viola replied.

"Hope it's better than its name."

"Me too." She took his paw in the pair of hers.

For the next couple of hours they watched as the island came slowly closer. For some reason none of the pirates thought to disturb them. Sylvester guessed the crew had other things to do in preparation for landfall.

As the details became more visible, so did the sounds. The first ones Sylvester was able to identify were bird calls, but these were birds and calls the like of which he'd never seen or heard before. There were other shrieks and cries, too. Noises he didn't believe could be produced by a bird's throat. Despite the baking heat of the day, those cries made cold flutters of fear run up and down his spine.

Viola must have been feeling the same, because she shivered and pulled herself closer to him.

Over the next few hours the *Shadeblaze* swung slowly around the island until a town came into view, with scores of little houses clustered on the hillsides surrounding a big, semicircular bay. The trees and plants that grew around the houses, pressing up close against them as if attempting a passionate embrace, weren't at all like those of Foxglove. Their forms were somehow squatter and fleshier, and they were a paler and brighter green than Sylvester had ever seen plants before, as if they weren't real plants but ones in a picture painted by a very young lemming.

In the bay were moored a dozen or more sailing ships though none of them, Sylvester was illogically proud to observe, as large or as splendid as the *Shadeblaze*.

He wasn't the only one to notice this. Here and there along the dockside people were pausing in their activities to stare at the new arrival. There were stoats, foxes, weasels and bobcats there, Sylvester saw, as well as a couple of animals he didn't recognize at all that must be native to these far southerly climes.

No lemmings, though.

The fact that there weren't any other lemmings in sight was an unwelcome reminder of how truly far from home he and the Pickleberries were.

A large paw fell on his shoulder.

Cap'n Rustbane.

Sylvester almost jumped out of his fur.

How had the gray fox managed to creep up behind him and Viola without either of them having the slightest suspicion of his approach?

Rustbane chuckled, reading Sylvester's mind.

"How are you, me hearties?"

"Ve-very well, thank you. We were just w-watching—"

"Blighter Island," the pirate captain completed for him. "None other, and that's the pretty little burg of Hangman's Haven you can see in front of ye."

He settled his elbows on the rail alongside Sylvester's, ignoring Viola's hostile glare.

"The place got its name because it was once said that, if ever a hangman could survive in it more than five minutes without finding a dagger in his back, there wouldn't be a single person there – male, female, grown-up or whelp – who'd not qualify for his noose. There are no laws down in these parts, see. Leastwise, no laws that anyone can remember to obey. Perhaps it's because the Caraya Islands are so close to the equator and the heat stifles the growth of laws. I don't know, I'm just a humble pirate."

He chuckled again. The meaning of his chuckle was clear. If there was ever a pirate who was humble, it wasn't Rustbane.

The gray fox was dressed in his full piratical finery today, from his black cocked hat to the toes of his highly polished black leather shoes, their brass buckles gleaming in the sunlight. He'd chosen a fiery red tunic and jacket, the seams embroidered in gold thread. A few brightly ribboned medals sparkled on his chest. Medals, thought Sylvester sourly, that the pirate must have stolen from victims of his treachery.

Topping off the whole dazzling assemblage was Rustbane's broad grin. There seemed to be even more teeth in his mouth than ever before.

"Looks pretty enough from here, Blighter Island does, don't it?" he remarked. "You can't tell at this distance that yer throat wouldn't be safe one instant in those cute little streets. Not if anyone thought you might have a wallet to steal or a gold tooth they could prize from its socket and sell for a farthing. Why, you're safer aboard a pirate ship than you'd be in Hangman's Haven."

The hint was thunderingly obvious. Sylvester pretended to take it at face value.

"Lucky we won't have to go ashore then, isn't it?"

"I wouldn't even think about it, if I was you."

"How long are we going to be here, with that" – Sylvester offered a histrionic shudder – "hellhole just the thickness of the hull away from us?"

"Three days."

"That long?"

"We got to pick us up supplies for at least three months, I reckons."

"Three *months*? How far do you think we're going to be at sea?"

"It's not how long it'll take us to reach the island where the treasure's buried that counts, young Master Lemmington, it's how long it'll take us to find the treasure once we get there. It also matters what the island's got to offer. If we're lucky, the trees'll be bowed down by the weight of bananas and coconuts, not to mention all the fat pigeons nesting there. But if we're unlucky it'll be some stony, barren shore with nothing but crabs to catch and seaweed to dress 'em with. So I'm laying in plenty o' salt pork and oranges and barrels o' water. And grog, o' course. A pirate cap'n must always make sure he has rivers o' grog to feed his crew or the next thing he's likely to find is himself wishing he'd made sure the barnacles were cleaned off his keel. You savvy?"

"We savvy," said Viola.

Rustbane shot her a glance, clearly not liking the cold detestation dripping from her voice.

"O' course," he said quietly, "there's another animal a pirate crew's more'n happy to eat if provisions run short and that's a lemming."

"You so sure about that?"

Rustbane just grinned in reply.

"How many of your men would be wanting to eat their good buddy Three Pins then?"

The pirate's grin faltered. "There are lemmings and lemmings."

"Or Three Pins' daughter?"

It was fun, Sylvester decided, watching Cap'n Rustbane realizing he'd been outflanked. The pirate looked this way and that, as if someone might come to rescue him, but there was no one to come and it was clear he was at a complete loss for words.

Rustbane made up his mind to abandon this topic of conversation. He directed his gaze toward Sylvester.

"Three days before we set sail. Not a lot of time, young Lemmington. Not a lot of time for you to make sure you have every last piggly detail of that map engraved on your mind. Even Three Pins's best friend among the crew'd not be in any mood to show mercy to her if the *Shadeblaze* sailed and sailed until it was obvious we was on the wrong course. And if my brave boyos would be cruel to Three Pins, it don't bear imagining what they'd do to Three Pins's daughter and, worst of all, to Three Pins's daughter's paramour, him that'd got everyone into this mess in the first place."

The pirate stared out into the limitless sky beyond Blighter Island and spoke quietly, as if to himself.

"There ain't nothing more pitiful than watching a brave fellow, or lemming as it might be, trying to stop hisself screaming long enough to beg to be fed to the fishes."

"You're good at threatening people weaker than yourself, aren't you?" said Viola, her voice, if anything, even icier than before.

Rustbane laughed. "That's what life is all about. The strong win out, and the weak lose everything. The wages o' kindness is misery, the wages o' cruelty is wealth and happiness. You don't need to be one o' they famous philosophers to work that out."

"You poor sap," commented Viola, dropping her words like icicles into the frigid pond of the silence that had followed Rustbane's remark.

He snorted. "Me? Poor? Sap?"

"Yes, you. What have you gained from your life of cruelty and murder and theft?"

Rustbane's gesture embraced the proud ship on whose deck they stood and his own magnificent attire. The pearl handles of his flintlock pistols shone, but even they seemed almost tawdry alongside the splendor of the jewels encrusting the pommel of his evilly curved cutlass.

"Quite a lot, I'd say."

"You would?" said Viola, feigning incredulity. "There's more comfort in the poorest Foxglove cottage than there's to be found on board this cesspit of a ship. Oh, sure, it looks fine and dandy when you see it from afar, with its flags fluttering and its sails full, but as soon's you come close you start smelling the stench of its bilges. And there's better food on the table of that Foxglove hovel than ever you'll eat on the *Shadeblaze*. Fresh nuts and vegetables, not cabbages that've been rotting a month and more."

Rustbane looked nettled.

The cabbages were a sore point, and by tacit agreement everyone aboard the *Shadeblaze* resisted the temptation to talk about them. Long before the ship had come to Foxglove, its captain had struck what he'd thought was a fine bargain with a trader out of Winter Isle for a large consignment of cabbages. Food enough to keep the cold out for the next three voyages, the trader had claimed before making himself scarce with the gold Rustbane had given him. For the next week, the crew of the ship had eaten cabbage with every meal. By the end of that week, even the pirates who'd started out being rather partial to a spot o' cabbage, doncha know, were in a mood fit to kill anyone who even suggested the possibility of ever eating the vegetable again.

So the huge consignment, barely marked by the incursions made upon it by a full week's worth of eating by the *Shadeblaze*'s complement, sat in the ship's hold.

Moldering.

Six days ago, Cap'n Rustbane, in one of his rare misjudgments of the mood of his men, had insisted that, waste not, want not, it was time once more to have a meal of cabbage.

He had been deaf to the protests of the ship's cook, Bladderbulge, that the heap of vegetables had by now become more liquid than anything else. Rustbane had paid for this fodder, hadn't he? Who was Bladderbulge to be suggesting the captain's investment should be pitched over the side?

Sylvester remembered that meal, remembered it only too clearly no matter how hard he tried to forget it.

So did everyone else on the *Shadeblaze*.

And no wonder.

They'd all seen it twice. Once on the slow, reluctant way in and a second time, not long thereafter, as they clung to the ship's side wishing sweet death would come down from the skies to claim them as it forcefully propelled itself from parts of their digestive system they'd never known they had.

As soon as enough of the pirates had regained their strength, the remainder of the squelching heap of cabbages in the hold had gone the same way as the stuff Bladderbulge had cooked up, being abandoned as a green, poisonous scum spreading across the ocean surface behind the *Shadeblaze*'s rapidly receding stern.

Surprisingly, Bladderbulge hadn't gone into the sea alongside it.

To give Rustbane credit, thought Sylvester, the gray fox had headed off the vengeful mob of pirates that was in search of the cook's hiding place and persuaded them Bladderbulge was not to blame but, instead, he himself was.

Somehow mutiny had been averted.

No one mentioned the word "cabbages" again. Not outside their own nightmares, anyway.

Now Viola had.

No wonder Rustbane's eyes flashed venom.

"You've got some serious thinking to do, Sylvester," he said tightly. "Three days to remember every last detail. And if I'm not satisfied that you've done exactly that, then you're going to find yourself swinging from my high yardarm with," he gave a bitter mock-courteous nod towards Viola, "your lady friend dancing alongside you. Understood?"

"Understood," said Sylvester, trying but failing to match the pirate's stare.

"Good," snarled the gray fox.

He turned and stomped off down the deck away from them.

A squawking gull flew down towards him, perhaps hoping the pirate might feed it some tidbit.

The bright steel blade of Rustbane's cutlass flashed.

The two halves of the bird fell like stones into the churning dark water below.

$\phi \ \phi \ \phi \ \phi \ \phi$

"Darkness at last," said Viola.

More hours had passed. The three lemmings sat in the cabin Viola shared with her mother. Luckily Mrs. Pickleberry agreed with the two younger lemmings that flight from the ship was their best option. Sylvester had been worried she might have grown to enjoy the pirate life and would prefer to throw in her lot with Rustbane and his nefarious crew.

But Mrs. Pickleberry had no better plan for escape than Sylvester had managed to conjure up himself, which was no plan at all.

They'd all agreed any attempt to escape should wait until nightfall.

And now Viola was pointing out that, indeed, night had well and truly fallen.

"Any suggestions as to how we're going to set about this?" Sylvester said desperately, not looking at either of his two companions but instead at the paneled wall on the far side of the cabin.

"Not nuttin'," said Mrs. Pickleberry glumly.

"It's not as if we could just walk out the door," said Sylvester.

"Or even the window," added Viola, significantly not looking in the direction of the open porthole. She and Sylvester would have been able to squeeze through that aperture, but her mother was a middle-aged lemming with a middle-aged lemming's amply spreading girth, and . . . Best not even to think about it in case Mrs. Pickleberry heard your thoughts.

"On the other paw . . ." Viola continued, her voice growing more thoughtful, even dreamy. "Yes, the window's the answer, isn't it?"

Sylvester darted an incredulous look in her direction.

Viola intercepted it and smiled merrily.

"Listen," she said, beckoning the other two to bring their heads close to hers. "Listen, here's what we'll do . . ."

$\phi \ \phi \ \phi \ \phi \ \phi$

Cheesefang tended not to bother knocking on doors, especially doors behind which were confined females who might or might not be changing their attire. Instead, he either kicked doors open or, if he was carrying a heavy tray laden with steaming plates of tucker, as he happened to be doing right now, he turned and burst doors open with a mighty clout from his threadbare rear end.

The door satisfyingly crashed against the cabin wall.

"Here ye are, ye stinking landlubbers. Here's a supper ye don't deserve, scumbags. Ye c'n spend the whole time yer eating wondering which is the plate inter which I've gobbed, heh heh. Ye c'n—oh, by the lips of the triple-breasted goddess, I'll be dancing to the tune of the hempen jig for this!"

The cabin was empty.

The porthole gaped wide open.

The tray clattered to the floor.

"Emergency!" yelled Cheesefang, his claws rattling on the steps of the companionway as he sprinted up to the main deck. "Alarm! Tarnation! The prisoners is escaped!"

Below, barely daring to breathe, the three lemmings huddled inside the secret study that Cap'n Josiah Adamite had built for himself.

The sound overhead of Cheesefang's claws scuttling this way and that was joined by other noises of panic.

Half the pirates were drunk already on their nightly ration of grog, which did nothing to increase the coordination of the response to Cheesefang's discovery.

Sylvester permitted himself a tense little giggle. There was a long way to go before the lemmings would be out of the wood or, more accurately, free of the *Shadeblaze* but this was an excellent start.

He nudged Viola. "Did I ever tell you you're brilliant?"

"Can't remember."

"Well, I'm telling you now."

"Gosh. Thanks."

"Don't mention it."

"Shaddup, you two spoonin' lovebirds, afore I chucks me load."

Sylvester shrugged in the darkness. Maybe it'd have been better, after all, if Mrs. Pickleberry had decided to stay with the crew.

Too late for that wish now, though.

"Time we were making tracks," he whispered to Viola.

Together they threw their shoulders against the planks that had been concealing their hiding place from view.

The three lemmings tumbled into the cabin. The door was still swinging open, as Cheesefang had left it.

"Help me," grunted Sylvester, picking up one of the planks from the floor.

Viola gaped at him. "What're you doing?"

"Boarding up the den again. We" – how could he explain this? – "We owe it to old Josiah. Something like that. We can't let Rustbane and his thugs go pawing their way through the old rogue's secrets, can we?"

"There's not any time for sentiment, you idiot!"

Mrs. Pickleberry was already vanishing out through the cabin door.

Sylvester didn't bother answering Viola's angry hiss, just maneuvered the first of the boards back into its place in the wall.

"Oh, all right," she said. "You're an idiot, but you may have a point."

She passed him the second plank and he struggled to fit it into its slot.

"Done," he said at last, when he was sure Cap'n Adamite's study was as safe from rediscovery as it was ever going to be. "Now, let's *fly!*"

He grabbed Viola's paw and darted out of the cabin.

They peered up the darkened companionway. They could just see Viola's mother at the top, peering back down at them.

"The coast's clear," said Mrs. Pickleberry, "but who knows how long it's gonna stay that way? Get a move on, yer two great lardlumps."

They hardly needed any urging. Quicker than thought, they were by Mrs. Pickleberry's side.

Sylvester was glad to notice she'd remembered to bring Elvira, her rolling pin, with her. Depending on how things worked out, the weapon might prove to be the difference between success and failure, between escape from the clutches of the pirates and . . .

. . . and death.

Better to get it right out into the forefront of his mind, Sylvester thought. This wasn't just a game. The penalty the three of them would almost certainly pay if Rustbane or any of his crew clapped eyes on them as they fled was death.

And a lingering, tormented death at that.

He gulped.

If it came to it, he must be prepared to face such an agonizing fate if it meant that Viola could go free.

Viola and her mother, he told himself less confidently.

He suspected Mrs. Pickleberry was far better than he'd ever be at looking after herself.

"Anyone around?" he asked her now in an urgent whisper.

"Told you, the coast's clear. Ain't no one anywhere near."

"So where are they all?"

"They's combin' the dock from one end to the other. Reck'n Cheesefang must of swallowed hook, line an' sinker the illusion we'd gone out the porthole, and convinced the rest o' those scurvy cutthroats we was long gone from the ship."

Now that Mrs. Pickleberry had mentioned it, Sylvester could hear the hue and cry as the *Shadeblaze*'s crew carried out their search of the harbor surrounds. Not all of the locals were happy about what the strangers were doing. There were shouts, curses, occasional clashes of steel and, a couple of times, the abrupt cutting short of a strangulated scream.

This was both good news and bad news.

The pirates' activities offered the fugitive lemmings perfect cover. No one in Hangman's Haven would think twice about an extra stranger or three.

The only trouble was, of course, that the pirates might actually be doing a proper job of the hunt, and succeed in catching the lemmings in the net they were casting.

Or a Blighter Islander might have become sufficiently enraged by the pirates as to slaughter the lemmings on sight as just another three of those boorish, violent, inconsiderate foreigners.

Sylvester squared his shoulders.

Always look on the bright side, as his mother used to tell him.

He was pretty sure she had, anyway, even though he couldn't remember her doing so.

"Let's get going," he said.

"That's what I bin tryin' to tell you," insisted Mrs. Pickleberry, "but instead you just bin standin' here with yer mouth openin' and shuttin' like you was a fish in a bowl."

"Okay, okay," said Sylvester.

"You great—"

"Mo–om!"

"And as for *you*, you—"

"Mom!"

"Yeah?"

"Just stow it, will you?"

"Why, you young—"

"Put a sock in it."

"You—"

"Stuff your head up your—"

"Could you two save the invective for later?" intervened Sylvester nervously. "Like, you know, after we've gotten ourselves to somewhere we don't have a hundred buccaneers wanting to cut us to pieces?"

"Right," said Viola sullenly. Her mother didn't deign to say anything at all, but Sylvester could see the older lemming's lips moving.

"On the count of three," Sylvester said, taking Viola by the arm.

"How original of you."

"One."

"You're always so macho when you're counting."

"Two."

"That's higher than you've ever managed before."

"Thr—look, dammit, Viola, just whose side are you on?"

"Go!" said Mrs. Pickleberry.

She went, went so fast that all Sylvester could detect of her was the blurred impression of a rolling pin wielded on high as she darted down the gangplank to lose herself in the shadows alongside one of the harbor's decrepit warehouses.

"Wow," said Sylvester, unable to stop himself.

"C'mon," snapped Viola.

He could almost hear the air whistle as she vanished in the direction her mother had taken.

She's never run as fast as that when we've been racing each other on the hill, he mused, then became immediately angry with himself for having been so stupid as to waste time on the thought.

He ran as fast as his feet would carry him. Then, down the gangplank, across the dirty cement of the dock, and into the shadows.

There.

Done that.

The only trouble was that none of them had noticed the pirate who'd been stationed at the foot of the gangplank just in case the escapees, whom Rustbane assumed to have already made it ashore, tried cunningly to smuggle themselves back aboard the *Shadeblaze*.

The pirate, for his part, hadn't noticed either of the Pickleberries scuttling past him, so swiftly and light-footedly had they been moving. He was a big, fat groundhog whom Sylvester had seen around on the *Shadeblaze*. It wasn't any wonder the two female lemmings' rapid progress had eluded the slow-witted animal's attention, especially since he'd been taking the opportunity of being left on his own to help himself to a bolstering swallow or two from the flask in his pocket. But Sylvester's heavier lumber was another matter altogether.

"Oi!"

"Well, darn it," said Viola's mom. "You great clumsy oaf, Sylv—"

"Oh, stow it 'til later, you old bag," Sylvester hissed back at her.

For the first time in a very long time, Mrs. Pickleberry was stunned into silence.

"Oi!" the pirate cried again, far more clearly than before, when his shout had been partly smothered by the glug of grog he'd been clandestinely trying to swallow at the same time. "Fugitives sighted! This way! This way!"

There must still have been a few pirates left aboard the ship, too, because suddenly the *Shadeblaze*'s bell started clanging.

Blang! Blang! Berrrr-laaaang!

The groundhog began lurching across the dock toward them, drawing his sword laboriously from his belt. "I got the scum in me sights, Cap'n!" he bellowed. "This way! This way!"

Sylvester darted his eyes this way and that.

The dock was almost entirely in darkness except for the lights shining onto it from the ships moored there. Farther along, though, perhaps a couple of hundred yards from where the three lemmings cowered in the inky shadows, there was an outburst of light and sound.

A tavern!

A dockside tavern!

If only Sylvester and the other two could reach it, maybe they could lose themselves among the carousing throngs?

Some fat chance.

But, right now, it looked to be the only chance they had.

Beggars can't be choosers.

"Follow me," he hissed at Viola.

"But—"

"No arguments. Just follow!"

"This way! This way!" bawled the oafish groundhog again. He had a patch over one eye. The other looked rheumy from an excess of grog. The fact that Sylvester could tell this meant the pirate had gotten far too close to them.

"Now!" Sylvester yelled.

He ran like the wind in the direction of the brightly lit tavern.

Behind him he could hear the rattle of claws on stone as Viola sprinted in his wake. He hoped her mother was doing the same and hadn't stupidly stayed behind in the hopes she could win a fight with a groundhog. The pirate was stupid and half drunk and addle-brained, but he was twice the size of Mrs. Pickleberry. When it came to a brawl between a lemming and a groundhog, there could only be one winner, and it wasn't the lemming.

Rolling pin or not.

The two hundred yards seemed to get longer and longer the farther Sylvester ran. His breathing was like a thunderstorm in his ears. Ahead of him he could see the front of the gaudily illuminated pub as if through the wrong end of a telescope, like a tiny but preternaturally bright image at the far end of an extremely long tunnel whose dark walls were pressing in on Sylvester's eyes.

Out of his peripheral vision he became aware that Viola was pulling up alongside him.

"Soon be there," he gasped, not sure if he believed his own words.

"Keep running!"

It was almost a satisfaction that she seemed as puffed as he was.

"Daphne?" he forced himself to ask.

"Behind us."

"Okay."

"Run!"

He was already running, he thought resentfully, as fast as he was able.

Which was faster than the drunken groundhog. Sylvester could hear the pirate calling, "This way! This way!" still, but from a distance that grew increasingly larger each minute. For sure, the other pirates must be scuttling to try to intercept them, but so far there was no sign of them. Maybe the lemmings had been lucky and all of Rustbane's verminous crew had happened to be on the far side of the harbor when the lemmings had chosen to make their dash for freedom.

Maybe.

Unlikely, but anything's possible, isn't it?

Sylvester could now make out the name written on the sign that hung out in front of the tavern.

The Monkey's Curse

I didn't need to know that, he thought wildly. *I could have put all the effort of reading those words into trying to run a bit faster. I could have . . .*

He realized he was thinking nonsense and just concentrated on trying to get to The Monkey's Curse as quickly as he possibly could.

Now there were indications of the other pirates in hot pursuit. Shouts. Cries. Heavy footfalls.

"There they go! Catch 'em!"

Rustbane's voice commanding his men, but from a good distance away. There were other pirates far closer, though. It was going to be touch and go who made it to The Monkey's Curse first.

Just to this side of the tavern was a vertical slit of darkness.

An alley.

You couldn't even see it was there until you were almost on top of it.

Sylvester let out an unintelligible grunt and jerked his head towards the black streak.

Viola drew up beside him, her eyes flaring. She'd seen the alley too. They were just going to have to trust luck and the Great Spirit Lhaeminguas (or perhaps even the triple-breasted goddess?) that Mrs. Pickleberry, trundling along in the wake of the two younger lemmings, had spotted the dark haven likewise. And that none of the pirates had. That was a lot of luck to be calling on. Especially when your heart was about to burst through your ribs.

Then Sylvester and Viola reached the alley. They ran at full speed straight into pitch blackness, and tripped over a heap of debris and garbage cans, which sounded like a bomb going off in the middle of a hardware store.

"*Yaaaaaarrrrrgggggghhhhh!*" screamed Viola as her mother landed at full tilt on top of her, rolling-pin end first.

Sylvester could hardly hear them. His ear was jammed hard up against a half-cooked pumpkin someone had wisely thrown out when it got too old. He had the suspicion that a single feather's worth of extra force and his head wouldn't be on the outside of the pumpkin any longer.

A horrible *faux* quiet descended on the interior of the alley. A *faux* quiet broken only by the painful gasping of the three lemmings and the *pocka pocka pocka* as one last can lid settled itself down flat on the ground.

It wasn't a real quiet, but when the lid stopped moving it seemed like it was real.

It was *faux* because nowhere this close to a pub like The Monkey's Curse could ever be truly quiet, even when the pub was empty.

Despite the cacophony of the lemmings' arrival, it was obvious no one inside the tavern had noticed a thing.

But the pursuing pirates had, though.

"See that?" said a voice from the end of the alley.

It wasn't the voice of the groundhog, alas. This was someone who sounded much brighter. And soberer.

"It's where they put the trash out from the pub," said a companion of the first speaker.

"And those horrid little hamsters just went full pelt, hell-for-leather into it, din't they?" said the first.

"That's my guess too. You got a lantern?"

"Naw. Here's Toadsbreath with one, though. Hiya, Toadsbreath."

A glimmer of light crept into the end of the alley. Sylvester could just make out a tangle of furry limbs that he assumed must be Viola, Mrs. Pickleberry and himself.

And what looked like a ten-year accumulation of rotting food and empty bottles and cans.

"We're not hamsters," he muttered angrily under his breath. "I keep telling you, we're lem—"

"Shut up, you halfwit," said Viola hotly in his ear.

The three of them stayed very, very still.

Disconcertingly, the garbage stayed rather less so.

Maggots.

Sylvester prayed Viola wouldn't realize that's what those clammy little movements were.

"You going in after them, Toadsbreath?"

"How stupid d'you think I am?"

"You want the long answer or the short one? *Oof!*"

For a moment the lantern's beam darted here and there all over the alley walls, and then it steadied again.

"Now listen, Viola," said Sylvester as quietly as he possibly could and still let it be possible for her to hear him.

"What?" she answered in the same, almost silent tone.

"I'm going to create a diversion."

"You're *what?*"

"Create a diversion, so the pirates all start chasing me. In the confusion, you and your mom'll have a chance of making good your escape. Okay? On the count of—"

"Don't be such a complete gormless lamebrain, Sylvester Lemmington, you hear me?"

This wasn't quite the reaction he'd been anticipating. "My hero, my hero, my hero, pardon me while I swoon," had been more the sort of thing he'd had in mind.

"Now *you* listen to *me*, Sylvester Numbnuts," Viola was saying. "We're all three of us in this together. There's going to be no heroic sacrifices. Got that?"

"But—"

"No buts."

"Ess zere somepatin ze matteur?" said a squeaky voice that was totally unknown to any of them.

Sylvester was the first to recover his wits.

"Huh?" he said.

Well, some wits, anyway.

"You een need of a little sanctuary from ze big bahd piratical goons, yes?"

"You could say that."

"I jus' did, *mon ami.*"

"No, what I meant was—"

"Stop messing around, Sylvester," said Viola. "If this person can help us lose Rustbane and his louts we should listen to him. He probably knows this island and we don't."

"Yes. We'd be glad of your help," said Sylvester.

"Zen follows me."

"How can I do that?"

"Well, all you needs to do, *mon ami*, is put ze one leg in fronts of ze other one and—"

"No," Sylvester whispered urgently. "What I mean is I can't see you. If I don't know where you are, I don't have much of a chance of following you, do I?"

"Ah, yes. How silly of *moi*. 'Ere, Mr. Lemming. You take my paw and I will guide you."

The paw that slipped into Sylvester's was small, hardly larger than that of a newborn lemming. Sylvester wondered if it could possibly be a child who was trying to save them. But no, that didn't make sense.

For his own part, he took Viola's paw. He could feel her adjusting herself so she could grab Mrs. Pickleberry's.

"Iss we all set now?" said the perplexing, heavily accented little voice out of the blackness.

"As ready as we'll ever be," replied Sylvester.

"Good, *mon ami*. Then 'ere we go."

⚓ ⚓ ⚓ ⚓

Later, Sylvester did his very best to forget the nightmarish journey they took from the darkened alley to something approximating safety.

The journey didn't last long and it didn't take them very far, not in terms of sheer physical distance, anyway, but it left deep scars upon his soul.

He'd expected their invisible savior to lead them farther back into the alley, or perhaps to one side of it or the other. Sylvester wouldn't even have been too surprised if their route took them upwards, perhaps to a high window concealed from the ground by the angle of the wall.

Instead, though, the route led down.

Down through layers of wriggling maggots, putrescent meat, vegetables liquified by rot, more maggots . . .

And those were only the identifiable bits.

The *un*identifiable bits were worse.

They smelled a lot worse, anyway.

"Where are you taking us?" Sylvester began to say to the insistently pulling guide beneath him, but he got only as far as "Where are you gwish schwabble bleeuch" before his mouth filled up with some lukewarm, jelly-like substance he resolved to take particular care never to taste again.

A few moments later he could hear Mrs. Pickleberry, who'd been muttering away in a semi-audible stream of complaints and curses, getting a mouthful of the stuff as well, which silenced her, so the news on the jelly-like goo front wasn't altogether bad.

By now, the four creatures had shifted themselves so that each, with the exception of the stranger with the bizarre accent, was reaching out with one paw to grab an ankle of the person in front. With their free leg and free arm they sort of half-hauled themselves, half-swam down into the squishily resistant filth.

After a minute or two, Sylvester discovered to his surprise he no longer especially noticed the stench of the garbage. He'd never have believed he could become acclimatized to it. Then abruptly they were falling out of the greasy embrace of the slick refuse and into open air.

Luckily, the drop wasn't a long one.

Sylvester lay on his tummy on an earthen floor, heaving a long sigh of relief that against all the odds he was still alive, when a sudden enormous impact in the middle of his back told him he should have had the presence of mind to roll over out of the way of Viola.

"You darling," she said quietly, sounding a little winded. "You lay here to break my fall."

That was when Mrs. Pickleberry landed on top of her.

"We iss all apresenta and correcta, yes?" said the small voice.

"I think so," said Sylvester, extricating himself from under the two Pickleberries. He reached gingerly upwards and discovered that the ceiling of wherever they were was quite low. Standing would be out of the question, and it would be wise to be cautious about sitting up too impetuously.

From above, he could hear the muffled noises of some very heavy somebodies rootling around clumsily in the spilled garbage. Also from above, but off at an angle, there were the sounds of drunken revelry: out-of-tune singing, shrieking, perhaps a fight. The Monkey's Curse was obviously doing a whale of a business this evening. Sylvester hoped it'd carry on doing so once Rustbane's mob of ruffians invaded the premises in search of three fugitive lemmings. The *Shadeblaze*'s crew would be certain the runaways must be hiding somewhere among the motley crowd of drunks and could waste hours before becoming convinced otherwise.

Misdirection, thought Sylvester, listening as his breath grew easier and more regular. *It'll be the second time tonight we'll have used it to our advantage.*

Unless, of course, we're nuts to be doing that.

We don't know who it is who's brought us here.

Frying pans.

Fires.

Out of one and into another.

Hope not.

Just then there was a faint gleam of light, and for the first time Sylvester was able to clap eyes on the person who'd led them out from under the very noses of the pirates.

A mouse.

He stifled a laugh.

Among lemmings, mice were generally considered the lowest of the low. Put it this way, for a lemming there isn't generally a way to look at the rest of the rodent brotherhood that isn't up. Rabbits and groundhogs and beavers are bigger, *way* bigger, and in the archives at the Library in Foxglove Sylvester had read of rodents called coypus that made even rabbits, groundhogs and beavers look pretty paltry. Rats and squirrels are quite a lot smaller than lemmings, but they're also generally regarded as quite a lot cleverer and more resourceful. Rats in particular have a streak of cunning ruthlessness that makes lemmings seem positively benign. So, if a lemming wants to look down the not terribly impressive length of its coarsely haired nose at anyone, who of the rodent persuasion does it have left?

Mice.

That's about it.

And chipmunks, of course.

Except chipmunks, damn them, are so damned *cute*.

And they're bright too, the little stinkers. Bright enough to run rings round the average lemming.

So that just leaves mice.

For a lemming brought up in a conventional household, as Sylvester and Viola and Daphne and, in fact, every other lemming he'd ever known had been, the prospect of being rescued from seemingly inevitable death by a *mouse* ranked about as low on the scale of ignominious circumstances as you could ever dread reaching.

Yet that was exactly what had just happened to Sylvester and the Pickleberries.

They were going to have to learn a different way of judging those around them, that was all.

Sylvester didn't mind the prospect of philosophical readjustment. He'd read enough in the Library to know that whoever judges others by outward appearance is doomed to a sticky and well-deserved end.

He wondered how Mrs. Pickleberry was going to react to the notion.

Mrs. Pickleberry reacted to the notion by waddling straight up to the small black mouse who'd saved them, picking him up and planting a great big slobbery kiss on the little creature's cheek.

"Thank you, thank you, thank you," she breathed. "If ever I needed a hero, that was the moment, and you came along just in the nick of time."

So much for preconceptions, thought Sylvester wryly.

"What's your name, you sweetheart?" Mrs Pickleberry was asking the mouse.

"Zey calls *moi* Rasco," said the little black mouse, cleaning his whiskers with an industrious paw. "Zat is because it is my, 'ow you say, *nom?*"

"Love that accent," said Mrs. Pickleberry.

"Mo–*om,*" said Viola.

"You're called Rosco?" said Mrs. Pickleberry, ignoring her daughter.

"Rasco. An easy enough mistake to make. *Mon Papa* 'e was so delighted when myself and my seventeen siblings were born, 'e went out and drank 'imself a 'ole glass of cognac before going down to ze offices to register us. 'E was *trying* to call me Rosco but it came out as Rasco, so Rasco is ze name I 'ave to zis day, no? 'Ave pity on my little bruzzer, 'oo was supposed to be called Farthing."

Sylvester decided it was about time he made a contribution to the conversation.

"I think all three of us would like to thank you from the bottom of our hearts."

The mouse bobbed his nose in friendly fashion, giving Sylvester a narrow-mouthed grin. He was wearing a shirt and shorts dyed in such garish, clashing colors that, even in this dim light, it made Sylvester's head hurt to look at them. On his rear feet were sandals that seemed designed to show off his claws to best advantage. The fur on his pate had been elaborately coiffed into a ball so big it looked almost like an ancillary head.

"You could not have found better zan to find yourself in the embrace of ze *famille des* Roquettes," he said.

"We couldn't?"

"Would you like a little more light?"

The three lemmings nodded. Lemmings have rather poor vision at the best of times. The weak glow down here in what Sylvester was becoming increasingly convinced was an earth cellar was making their heads hurt.

"It iss, 'ow you say, easy enough to do."

Rasco stepped over to the wall and drew a little farther open what Sylvester realized was some kind of a curtain. There was a crack there, a crack that ran along the bottom corner of a wall in one of The Monkey's Curse's bars and, correspondingly, along the ceiling of the earth cellar. Someone, one of Rasco's ancestors if not Rasco himself, had rigged up a curtain on a high rail so that the crack could be used as an adjustable source of illumination.

And as a way of spying on whatever was going on in the bar of The Monkey's Curse.

You couldn't see much through the crack, of course, except people's feet and the occasional spittoon that might float within eyeshot.

But you could hear plenty.

What the three lemmings and the little black mouse could now hear was the incursion of a half-dozen or more of Cap'n Rustbane's cutthroats into the midst of the convivial crowd of The Monkey's Curse.

"You scurvy knaves seen anythin' o' a bunch o' lemmings?"

There was the sound of breaking glass, followed almost immediately by the sound of someone landing very heavily in the street.

"You, ahem, fine gentleman noticed anyone entering within the past few minutes?"

A sophisticated ear could have told that the glass broke less violently, but the impact of a body on the street was, at best, undetectably lighter.

"Free drinks, anyone?"

The last was Rustbane's voice, and it drew instant cries of approval.

Rasco looked worried.

"Zey are my friends, up zere," he said. "But zey are like anyone else in 'Angman's 'Aven outside ze Roquettes and zeir closest relations."

"You mean—" said Sylvester.

"Zat's right. Any one of zem could betray our presence 'ere at any, how you say, moment. It is best we move ourselves away from here as *vitement*, I mean fast as possible."

Overhead, Rustbane had clearly cornered one of the regulars at The Monkey's Curse. From here, the voices sounded crystal clear.

"Far as I can see, old chap," said Rustbane, belching discreetly, "those infernal lemmings vanished as if by magic from the middle of a heap of" – a sudden drunken shout drowned out his next word – "in that alley that runs up the side of the tavern."

"An' what these lemmings ever been a-doing to you?" said the other, clearly trying to show he wasn't such a pushover as everyone thought. "Another pint o' mead, I'll trouble you for," he added in a lower voice, indicating that in fact he was.

If the entrance from the alley into the earth cellar was widely known among the tavern's habitués, Sylvester and the Pickleberries were as good as dead. Rustbane's persuasive charm would have the secret out of someone, probably this old sousehead, within the next few minutes at most.

"We 'ave to be moving," said Rasco.

"You said it," confirmed Sylvester.

"What's your accent?" said Mrs. Pickleberry with the air of someone who's been locked out of a conversation quite unreasonably and for far too long.

"It ees irresistibly *exotique*, zou are zinking, *non, ma charmante*?"

"No," said Mrs. Pickleberry, looking wistfully at the rolling pin she'd managed to keep firmly clutched in her fist all the way through the rigors of their escape from the alley. "I was thinkin' more along the lines of how it was infuriatingly difficult to understand."

"But, *ma belle*, 'ow could you zay such a thing?"

"Easier than you might imagine," replied Mrs. Pickleberry ominously.

"Um," said Rasco.

All four waited for someone to make the first move.

No one did.

"Truth is," admitted Rasco after a pause, "the exotic accent is expected of us folks who live out here on the islands."

"It is?" said Sylvester, intrigued. He'd never heard of anything like this before.

"Yeah," said Rasco. "See, the job most of us mice have is to make the females who come here on the tourist ships feel at home. *Right* at home, if you know what I mean?"

"Your job's to be a holiday fling?" said Mrs. Pickleberry, looking at the little black mouse suspiciously.

"You have hit the nail right on the thumb," said Rasco, nodding vigorously. "I'm the cutie-pops every gal dreams of spending a week with, then never having to see again no matter how long she lives. You'd be surprised how many gals are prepared to pay just for the privilege o' swanking me around in front of the other gals, y'know, the gals that are supposed to be their friends."

Mrs. Pickleberry started to giggle.

"Bit of a dreamboat, aincher?"

"That's the general idea, Mrs. P."

She cackled again.

"Now," said Rasco, "I really do think we ought to be getting out of here. Right now. Not a moment more's delay."

"He's right," Sylvester said to Viola and Mrs. Pickleberry.

"Good. We's all agreed then," said Rasco, clapping his paws together.

"Only," he added, "where do you guys think it might be a good idea to escape to?"

🐾 🐾 🐾 🐾 🐾

It took a long time for Viola and Sylvester, between them, to tell Rasco the story of how they had been bamboozled then seized by the dastardly Cap'n Terrigan Rustbane and his equally vile crew. In a way, the pair of them realized as they were telling it, it was a story with everything: violence, pathos, remorse, romance, comedy, tragedy . . .

"Blimey, mon," said Rasco when at last their narrative petered out, "that ain't half an epic, ain't it?"

"Well, I, ah . . ." said Sylvester, aware he was sounding even more of a pompous ass with each extra syllable.

"This Rustbane o' yours," Rasco cut in, covering up Sylvester's confusion gracefully, "he sounds more than a smidgen like someone who's made himself a bit of a legend around here. But the one I'm thinking of isn't called Rustbane." He tapped his chin with little sharp claws. "His name is, ah, that's it, his name's Deathflash."

By now they were some considerable distance from the wine cellar of The Monkey's Curse. At least, Sylvester hoped they were. Rasco had shown them a tiny opening at the join between wall and floor, concealed behind a large tun of malmsey.

"Malmsey?" said Mrs. Pickleberry with a grin, pausing to sniff appreciatively at a puddle of the stuff that had leaked out onto the floor.

"Away with you, Mrs. P.!" cried Rasco, laughing, pulling her away from the heady liquid.

The crack in the clay seemed barely large enough for a mouse to get into, let alone a full-grown lemming (not to mention a full-grown, rather plump lemming like Mrs. Pickleberry) but Rasco vanished into it with an adroit wriggle and clearly expected the others to have no difficulty following him. Sylvester looked at Viola, who shrugged, so he shrugged too and they both looked at Mrs. Pickleberry.

"Hold Elvira, there's a dearie."

Viola took the rolling pin and the two younger lemmings watched in amazement as Mrs. Pickleberry disappeared into the gap with the same ease Rasco had displayed.

They had more difficulty getting the rolling pin through the crack than its owner seemed to have had.

Viola went next.

"It's not as difficult as it looks, Sylvester," she called back to him.

Skeptically, he put his forepaws on the two edges of the crevice, then pushed his nose into it, then gave a little thrust with his back legs just *so* and . . . got firmly stuck. It felt as if some monster had snatched him up in its mouth and was slowly tightening its teeth around his midriff.

The worst of all was that he could see his three companions watching him with perfect calm. Rasco had produced a lighted candle from somewhere and was holding it high above his head. The two lemmings and the little black mouse were standing in a cavern that, though not as big as the wine cellar, was plenty spacious enough for them. The floor was comprised of old crumbly brick. It was harder to see the walls in the flickering shadows created by the candle, but Sylvester could discern just enough of them to know he didn't want to see them any more clearly. There was a definite sense of evilly fluorescing fungal ooze and clammily lurking spiderwebs.

Not that he had much brainpower left over right now to spare for thoughts about carnivorous fungi. Right now, he was firmly stuck in a sharp-edged hole and it seemed as if the only way he'd ever get through it was to leave his rear half behind him for the pirates to find.

"Just give one great big heave," said Rasco helpfully.

"I've already tried that," gasped Sylvester. "Several times," he added.

"Pizza," said Viola.

"Eh?" said everyone.

"Pizza," she explained. "Sylvester tends to eat too much of it. I've told him and told him. Mom, why're you looking at me like that?"

The final question seemed to be addressed not so much to Mrs. Pickleberry as to Mrs. Pickleberry's rolling pin.

Through the red haze of his own panic, Sylvester saw Viola's mother come to some sort of decision.

"Sylvester," said Mrs. Pickleberry.

"Yes?"

"You ever been bit by a rattlesnake?"

"Er, no." *What in the world,* thought Sylvester in a rare moment of clarity, *is the daft old bat talking about?*

Like all lemmings, he had a distinct aversion to snakes of any sort. Rattlers weren't the worst, that'd likely be cobras, but at the same time they weren't far from it.

"A *rabid* rattlesnake?" probed Mrs. Pickleberry.

"Most certainly not!"

"Cos I think there's one o' them rabid ones back in that wine cellar wot we just left, and he's got his fangs all shiny and eager and his greedy little eyes on yer bum. In fact, I think if yer lissens real careful yer can just hear his dinky little rattle-rattle-*rattle* . . ."

"Oh, hello, Sylvester," said Viola, surprised to find him standing beside her, puffing and panting a lot. "How did you get yourself out of that hole in the wall?"

"I haven't the faintest idea," answered Sylvester, honestly.

Mrs. Pickleberry cackled irritatingly.

"Are we ready to get a move on now the pantomime's over?" said Rasco in a bored voice.

"Just let me catch my breath," Sylvester replied.

"Or the pirates catch you," said Rasco pointedly. Without waiting for any further response he turned and, holding the candle aloft in front of him, scuttled toward the darkness at the rear of the cavern.

After a moment's pause, Mrs. Pickleberry chased after him, with Viola and Sylvester, arm in arm, coming along behind her.

The next hour or so was a bit of a blur in Sylvester's memory, but at last they found themselves in the sanctuary of a small cavern that smelled of lots of warm mammalian bodies snuggled closely together. Of that and, just faintly, of mature cheddar cheese. Miraculously, Rasco's candle was still flickering happily. He'd used the candle's own hot wax to stick it firmly upright in the middle of the cavern floor, and the little gang had sprawled around it like explorers might sprawl around their nighttime campfire.

"Deathflash," Rasco repeated, staring at the small flame.

Sylvester was sure he'd heard the name before but he couldn't remember quite where or when. Then he remembered! Back in Foxglove, what seemed like a million years ago, when he and Viola had been pretending to listen worshipfully while letting Rustbane brag away about his own magnificence. What was it the gray fox had said? "Not for nothing do some people call me Deathflash. Or Doomslayer. Or Warhammer. Or . . . well, I can't hardly remember all the different names people call me, not even the ones you can mention in polite company, which are by far the minority, but you can be sure most of them attest to the enormousness of my powers."

"That's him!" Sylvester exclaimed, leaning forward enthusiastically. "That's Rustbane, sure enough. It's one of the names people have given him or he's given himself, more like. Such a boastly fellow, he is."

"If it's Deathflash we're up against," said Rasco slowly, looking off into the moving shadows in a corner of the room, "then we sure got ourselves a problem." He shuddered theatrically. "They say even the monsters of the ocean depths are terrified of the gray fox, despite the fact he feeds 'em so well with all the corpses he casts their way."

"Thanks," said Viola, pressing herself close up to Sylvester's side. "That's cheering." But, glancing sideways, Sylvester could see her eyes were gleaming.

"I thinks," continued Rasco, paying them no attention, "we ought to go consult my grandma."

"Your grandma?" said Viola's mom.

"None other, Mrs. P."

"And who is this grandmother of yours, dearie?"

"My grandma, Mrs. P, is Madame Zahnia."

The mouse paused for effect – an effect that did not come. The three lemmings just stared at him expectantly.

"You haven't heard of Madame Zahnia?" said Rasco.

"Not entirely," Sylvester said after a brief, embarrassed pause.

"The greatest voodoo priestess this side of the yawning chasm between the living and the dead?"

"The name rings a bell, I'm sure it does," lied Sylvester.

"Does she write a newspaper column?" asked Mrs. Pickleberry, brows wrinkling.

"She could," Rasco assured her, "but in point of fact she, ah, doesn't. Instead, she is content to accept the reverence of every god-fearing mouse in the Caraya Islands – and many a rat and porcupine too. She is a woman of" – he sucked in his breath and looked at each of their faces in turn – "of *power*."

"Oh," said Sylvester.

"My sisters are likewise all trained in the finer and subtler arts of voodoo," Rasco carried on after a dramatic pause, "but not one of 'em is a patch on me old gran. She is mighty wise, is Madame Zahnia, and there ain't a voodoo-practicing mouse under Sagaria's blue skies that don't respect her. I'm sure that, if anyone can, my gran can help you."

The three lemmings glanced at each other. When Viola spoke she knew she was speaking for all of them.

"Thank you, Rasco. We'd really like to meet your grandmother, as you suggest. Where does she live?"

"Quite a distance from here, in the middle of the jungle."

"How are we supposed to get there?"

Rasco looked down the length of his hindlegs to the feet at their ends and curled the claws there.

"On foot?" said Mrs. Pickleberry.

"You got it in one, Mrs. P."

JUNGLE BUNGLES

ow much longer?" gasped Sylvester. Fortunately, there was no one to embarrass him by being within earshot. Even more fortunately, one of the people who wasn't there was Viola.

Somewhere far above, amid the canopy of foliage that hid the sky from view, a leaf tilted to send a drop of sap plummeting toward the thick, moldering sludge of the jungle floor. The droplet hit the back of Sylvester's neck just before reaching its intended destination. By that time, it had cooled down to a temperature not significantly above boiling point.

"Owwwwww!" Sylvester wailed in misery.

He was glad Viola wasn't near enough to hear him say that, either.

"Jungle life isn't all it's cracked up to be," he muttered crossly to himself, as the sap peeled painfully from his hairy neck and he began pressing his way forward through the vegetation once more. "I wonder if that's just a big root or if it's a huge snake planning to squeeze me to death and then swallow me whole?"

The question seemed, in his current state of abject exhaustion, to be more of academic interest than anything else.

He felt like it had been forever since Rasco had led them to the place where they could escape from the block of buildings of which The Monkey's Curse was a part. By then the whole night had gone by and the sun was already drifting clear of the horizon.

The little mouse had gestured them to stay back. "We wait until nightfall," he said firmly.

"But that's *hours* away!" cried Viola. "We can't wait that long."

"Better to wait a while than to find ourselves fried by the noonday sun," Rasco told her, lowering his voice ominously. "If we even live that long."

All he got from Viola by way of reply was a gasp.

"Predators?" said Sylvester, trying to maintain his cool.

Rasco nodded. "Back where you folks come from, perhaps they don't have boa constrictors, rabid crocodiles, venomous spiders the size of hunting dogs . . ."

Sylvester had the obscure feeling he ought to stick up for the dangers of living in Foxglove.

"We do have some very fierce sheep," he said.

Rasco looked at him from under deeply drooping eyelids. "And soldier ants that can strip a lemming down to the bone in less time than it takes to hiccup," he added.

"How hot does it get out there?" asked Mrs. Pickleberry, clearly bored by this display of bravado by the two males.

"As hot as a furnace," said Rasco. "Hotter. The sun's rays can have the blood boiling out of your veins in fountains soon as look at you. That's why we should stay here until darkness and get some sleep, rather than take the risk of being caught out in the open at midday."

Sylvester recognized there was no point in arguing. If Rasco didn't want to go any farther until evening fell, then no one was going anywhere. The lemmings wouldn't last ten minutes in the open in this strange and vicious town. Anyway, they'd never be able to find Madame Zahnia on their own. So, the four of them made themselves as comfortable as they could, sneezing in the dust of a dark cavity, and soon dropped off to sleep.

To Sylvester's surprise, none of them woke until the outside world was growing dark once more. The mouse and the three lemmings, noses in a neat row, peered beneath a ledge of brickwork that hid them from the sight of anyone who might pass on the sidewalk.

"Do you," whispered Viola, "think Cap'n Rustbane will have abandoned the search for us?"

Sylvester fought the impulse to snort derisively. "Some chance," he said. "Not if I know Rustbane. He'll still be hunting us, up one street and down the next, and he'll not give up unless there's something that forces him to."

"Oh," she said in a very small voice. "That's not terribly good news, is it?"

"Not really," cut in Rasco with an attempt at joviality, "but it could be worse, couldn't it?"

"How?" said Mrs. Pickleberry.

"Oh, look," said Rasco. "See that pretty moth over there?"

"Well, let's get ourselves out of Hangman's Haven, anyway," said Sylvester. "Once we're in the jungle, surely he'll never be able to find us. Not once we're under the protection of your famous voodoo grandmother, at least," he added as a courtesy to their guide.

"I'd almost hope Deathflash *did* track us down to grandma's place, mon," said Rasco darkly. "She'd put paid to him and his murderous scheming, she would. A strong dose of voodoo would do for him, you can be sure, and if it didn't she could get some of her zombies to eat his brains."

There was a horrible stillness of soul among the lemmings.

"Your people do much of, ah, that?" said Sylvester at last, wondering if that really was his own voice that had said the words.

"Much of what?"

"Eating, ahem, people's brains."

"Not as a matter of course, no. It's just, like, when a zombie gets hungry, you don't want to be standing between it and the nearest head, is all."

"Ah."

"And you most *particularly* don't want to be the owner of that nearest head, see? The zombies ain't too fussy about making sure you're dead before they start crackin' your skull open."

"I think I'm going to—" began Viola.

"Me too," said Sylvester.

There was a sort of faint gulping noise from Mrs. Pickleberry before she added, "I already have."

"Then that's a second reason we want to get out of here as quick as we can, ain't it?" said Rasco in a reasonable tone of voice. "Come on, let's go."

He shot out of the narrow gap like a bullet from a gun, and the next time Sylvester saw the little mouse as anything other than a disconcerting blur, Rasco was standing on the far side of the street, waving at them urgently to join him.

"You next," said Sylvester to Daphne.

"I can't run that fast."

"Me neither."

"'Specially with me rolling pin to weigh me down."

"I'll carry it."

"You better not lose it."

"I won't."

"Okay. Here goes."

If Mrs. Pickleberry made it to the other side of the street any more slowly than Rasco had, Sylvester's eyesight was too insensitive to detect the difference. He looked at the rolling pin in his paws and wondered how in the heck he'd been so stupid as to allow himself to be lumbered with it.

"Now you," he said to Viola, hoping she'd assume the tremble in his voice was brought on by adoration.

"You scared?"

"Scared? Me? Nah."

"Okay, you go first."

"Ahem. I think it's the role of the male to hold himself in readiness to come to the rescue of the lovely ladies in distress."

"You *are* scared."

"I am?"

"Never mind, though. So am I."

And with that she was gone from his side. The next he saw her, she was standing between Rasco and her mother and, like them, beckoning to him. Even more startlingly, she was holding her mother's rolling pin in her non-waving hand. Sylvester looked down at his paws. He'd never even noticed her taking it.

Oh, well, Sylvester Lemmington, he thought feverishly. *This is the moment. This is where the adults get sorted from the children. When the tough get going the going gets tough. Now ain't that true and reassuring? Wait a moment, I think I got that the wr—*

Without his brain having given them any command to do so, his plump little legs were running out of the shadows of the overhanging wall and into the full brightness of a pair of streetlamps, and a full moon that chose precisely that moment to emerge from behind a cloud.

Sylvester was certain he must be making a riveting sight for the entire population of Hangman's Haven. Who could fail to notice the spectacle of a not so slender lemming, already beginning to gasp for breath, as he stumbled and skittered on the first part of a journey that had unanticipatedly multiplied many times over in length?

As if in answer to his question, something was going awry with his legs. Well, it wasn't really his legs' fault, so far as he could ascertain. Ascertain without looking down, that is, because he knew that if he looked down he'd certainly trip and fall flat on his face. It felt as if, in place of ordinary air, the ground had become covered in honey or molasses. His feet were definitely sticking to the sidewalk every time he tried to lift them up, and his lower legs were struggling to make progress through a liquid so viscous it was the very next thing to solid.

He wasn't running. He wasn't even walking. He was swimming – and not so much faster than a fly stuck in wet concrete. Surely everybody must be watching him, their hands on their hips as they guffawed with laughter at his predicament. He was the object of derision for every cutthroat and miscreant in Hangman's Haven on the whole of Blighter Island. They'd be talking in the taverns for years about the plight of the fat little lemming that got himself stuck in an ocean of syrup and kept flailing away until he hadn't any strength left to flail with and how, at that point, Cap'n Terrigan Rustbane had stepped in and announced the most sadistic and revolting method of execution he'd ever devised—

Cap'n Terrigan Rustbane!

The three words went through Sylvester's consciousness like a red-hot wire through butter.

Legs that, until an instant before had been made of solid lead, were now suddenly light as a feather.

I could run along the surface of this molasses lake!

No sooner said than done.

"I think you got across here quicker than any of us, darling," said Viola. "That's twice you've done that. Moved faster than the eye can see. You must tell me how you do it. But," she added as Sylvester puffed out his chest and began to preen himself in preparation for a long, not entirely self-effacing explanation, "not now. At the moment, dearest, we have to make tracks for the jungle."

For the jungle! While the three words "Cap'n Terrigan Rustbane" had struck the most fiendish form of terror into Sylvester's heart, the three words "for the jungle" filled him with exhilaration. There was a strange whiff in his nostrils, an odor he'd smelled somewhere before, and it took him a moment to recognize it for what it was: the salty tang of brine as the sun begins to rise over the horizon of a brand new day at sea.

For a moment, he thought one of the pirates must have crept up on them, but then he realized what he was smelling was his own excitement.

"For the jungle," he echoed, then began to wonder what being in a jungle could possibly be like.

He was to learn soon enough. It was a place where molten balls of sap fell from the skies onto the necks of perfectly innocent, unsuspecting lemmings, and where tree roots looked like giant boa constrictors.

But first they had to get out of Hangman's Haven.

Rasco was a sure guide, but he was small and swift-moving and very much the same color as the shadows – of which there were more of than there were sunlit patches. He had a habit of getting a long way ahead and then wondering why they hadn't caught up yet. After a while, the little mouse started becoming less prone to committing this error. Well, after the couple of times when Mrs. Pickleberry had been the first of the lemmings to reach him, in any case. Even so, he was still infuriatingly easy to lose, especially after they'd left the center of Hangman's Haven behind and were making their way through the more sparsely housed outskirts. There, the lights came only from windows and the homes were few and far between that hadn't boarded up their windows in self-defense.

Come what may, though, the three lemmings couldn't afford to lose him. As complete strangers in this town where lives were worth less than spit in the wind, they were more vulnerable than they'd ever been before – even when Cap'n

Rustbane had them in his merciless grasp. Without the mouse, it would be only a matter of time before their corpses joined the long, somber line of those floating down the dark gutter that leads to oblivion.

Sylvester tried to say something of this to Viola at one stage when Rasco had allowed them to pause to regain their breath.

"You mean we're dead as doornails unless we stick close to the little—"

Sylvester clamped his paw over her mouth, hoping she'd not bite. "Sssh."

"She's right," said Rasco brightly. "I *am* little. I know it. There's no need to be so sensitive 'bout me feelings."

Sylvester gave him a watery grin.

Then they were off again.

What was worrying Sylvester all this while was that there were no signs of pursuit by Cap'n Rustbane and his bloodthirsty cronies from the *Shadeblaze*. Surely the pirates wouldn't have given up this easily? Surely they would be combing the town for the fugitives, especially since those fugitives had already made them look foolish. Sylvester's estimation of the pirates wasn't all that high, and he knew for certain many of them would have been happy enough to call it a day early on and head back to the *Shadeblaze* to spend a few hours in the muzzy grip of a quadrupled grog ration. But Cap'n Rustbane himself – and Jeopord, plus a few others – were made of totally different stuff, and they'd not rest until they'd tracked down the lemmings and extracted horrific revenge for crimes real and imagined.

So, where were they, the pursuers?

He tried to ask this question of Rasco at another moment when the mouse stayed still long enough for speech to be possible.

The little fellow shrugged. "I just live here."

"Yes, but—"

The worst moment of the whole night, Sylvester later decided (at about the same time as he was deciding that nothing which had happened to them during the escape from Hangman's Haven was even on the same page as the horrors they discovered in the jungle's lush, overpoweringly fecund embrace), was near the end of it. The air was full of bizarre cries and unearthly screams, all coming from the miasma of blackness that lay between the runaways and the first paling of the eastern skies. Rasco had left the lemmings on their own for a few minutes, sheltering in the lee of someone's gateway, while he scouted on ahead. He was sure, he told them, that he knew some people hereabouts who'd give them a safe haven and some food while they recuperated from their hours of flight.

"We'll soon be there," said Sylvester, trying to sound comforting, hoping neither of the Pickleberries would think to ask him where "there" was.

"Soon be where?" said Mrs. Pickleberry, on cue.

"Soon be with young Rasco's grandma," said Sylvester.

"Hm."

Just then the faint light in the sky seemed to get hugely brighter.

"What was that?"

"Ssh," said Viola forcefully.

There was a long, low, ominous creaking noise that seemed for a moment to be coming directly from the ground beneath their feet. In blind panic, Sylvester clutched Viola to him, then discovered it was Mrs. Pickleberry he'd grabbed by mistake.

The rasping sound wasn't coming from the ground, he realized. It was coming from directly behind where they were standing, in the lee of the ponderous, peeling-painted wooden gate.

"Someone's coming out of the house," hissed Viola.

Sylvester didn't even bother thinking before he spoke. "Run!"

He and Viola fled across the open but fortunately deserted roadway. There was no one around at this early hour of the morning except whoever was opening the gate they'd been lurking behind but, even so, Sylvester felt once again as if the moon's silvery rays must be picking him out as if he were a dancer hogging the spotlight. With every pace he took, he expected to hear a shout of fury as the alarm was sounded.

But no bellow split the night air.

The only sound was heavy, labored, wheezy breathing and the long *crrreeeaaaakkkkk* of the gate being opened.

Sylvester and Viola cowered together, trying to make themselves invisibly small. The moon was enthusiastically washing light over the whole area where they stood. Where were clouds when you needed them?

And, now that Sylvester thought about it . . .

"Where's your mom?" he whispered.

He felt Viola's shoulders shrug beneath his embracing arm.

"Dunno. I thought you had her."

The figure emerging from the gate was still hidden by shadow. There was plenty of shadow, Sylvester noted sourly, on *that* side of the street. Here, by contrast, where he and Viola could have done with as much as possible, there was nothing.

Worse than that, there was dew on the ground. The moonlight was making it look like a trillion tiny diamonds, each one of them intent on making the presence of the two lemmings even more obvious than it must already be.

"She'll be all right," said Viola into Sylvester's arm. "She always is."

He wished Viola's voice sounded a little more confident.

Then he spotted Mrs. Pickleberry.

The older lemming was about as far from all right as it was possible to be. She must have tripped almost immediately once the three of them started running – caught a claw in a crack, perhaps, or got her rolling pin snarled up between her hindlegs. She was lying in a heap on the sidewalk not half a yard from where the unknown stranger was now turning to close the gate behind him.

The unknown and exceptionally *bulky* stranger. In the darkness, all Sylvester could make out was what seemed to be a vast, bizarrely shaped mountain of musclebound sinew, with haphazardly placed bulges which he assumed were extra-large muscles. One of those bulges, to judge by its position, was the stranger's head. It seemed as muscular and sinewy as the rest.

At least Mrs. Pickleberry wasn't out in the open moonlight. Sylvester started thanking the shadow whose fickleness he'd a moment ago been cursing.

Far overhead, the cloud shifted a little.

For the first time, Sylvester and Viola could see the person who'd opened the gate.

"Oh no," breathed Viola.

At first glance, Sylvester thought the individual must be a human being, like Threefingers Bogsprinkler and one or two others of Rustbane's piratical crew, but there was something wrong with the shape of the body. The arms were longer, the neck shorter, the shoulders more slumped, the legs stockier and more bowed. Sylvester dredged through his memory, trying to recall where he'd seen pictures of creatures like this.

Then he had it.

"A chimpanzee," he murmured in Viola's ear.

The name meant nothing to her, he could tell.

"Smaller than one of the human creatures but far, far stronger," he explained. In fact, either this particular chimp was still not fully grown or it was a member of one of the smaller chimp species – Sylvester had no way of telling. The primate was wearing work clothes, an overall made out of some rugged canvas-type cloth, and had a sleepy expression on his face. He paused outside his gateway to focus on lighting a stubby little pipe with a match struck on the seat of his pants. The flare of the kindling tobacco lit up his face.

He looks friendly enough, thought Sylvester, relaxing a little.

Viola must have understood the relaxation of his body, because she trod firmly on his foot to stifle any impulse he might have had to start staggering across the road, paw held out in greeting, saying to the chimp, "Hello there, my friend.

We're strangers in these parts and . . ."

Satisfied his pipe was properly lit, the chimp tucked away his matches in one of the pockets of his overalls and, from another, pulled a long, curved object that Sylvester recognized.

"That's a banana," he told Viola.

"Makes two of you," she muttered, her eyes on Mrs. Pickleberry, who seemed to be holding herself very, very still.

There was the tiniest of squeaks from just behind Viola.

"Is that—" Sylvester began.

"It's me," said Rasco in a low voice. "What kind of mess have you folks got yourself into this time? Really! Can't turn my back on you for one moment without—"

"Oh, shut up!"

Sylvester's eyebrows rose. Viola's angry exclamation had been all the more threatening for being spoken so quietly. It had clearly scared Rasco into silence.

The chimp finished peeling the banana and, still puffing contentedly on his pipe, stared toward the center of town while scratching his rear end noisily. Mrs. Pickleberry was no more than a few inches from the chimp's right foot.

Viola's mom shifted her position ever so slightly and the end of her wooden rolling pin tapped the surface of the road. By a quirk of fate, it did so just at the moment that the chimp stopped his noisy scratching. The faint *click* of wood meeting road sounded clearly through the cold dawn air.

"Uh-oh," whispered Viola.

Sylvester was transfixed by the horror of the sight, and could only watch as the chimp looked down and saw, not far from its toes, the huddled dark shape that was Mrs. Pickleberry.

What the chimp thought he was seeing was anyone's guess. It was surely too dark for him to be able to tell there was a terrified lemming looking straight back up at him.

He might have shrugged and ignored the blob on the roadway had Mrs. Pickleberry not decided to make a run for it.

She stood up, gathered her skirts around her and started to scuttle toward where Sylvester and Viola lurked on the far side of the road.

The chimp grunted in surprise.

His long, powerful foot rose, preparing to stamp down viciously on the fleeing creature.

The foot began its rapid descent and—

"Oi!" bellowed Sylvester, shoving Viola violently away from him, so that she was lost in a clump of weed that grew out of the bottom of a neighbor's fence.

The chimp paused with his foot in midair, staring across to where the shout had come from.

Claws scraping on the hard road surface, Mrs. Pickleberry scrabbled to get away from him. In her terror, she wasn't making much progress.

It was the first time Sylvester had seen her truly frightened, but he was in too much of a funk to relish the experience. What in the world had possessed him to draw the chimp's attention like this? It was suicide, plain suicide. What would his mentor, Celadon, be thinking if he could see Sylvester now?

"Good move," said Rasco from somewhere near Sylvester's elbow. "I'll go and help the ol' girl."

From the corner of his eye, Sylvester saw a small black streak propel itself across the road toward the struggling older lemming.

"Come and get me, fatface," he heard himself taunt the chimp.

"Why, you—!"

The chimp threw its pipe aside.

"Mneh-mneh-me-mneh-mneh!"

Ahead of Sylvester was the wrathful primate, now beginning to move in his direction, mouth drawn open in fury to reveal irregular but powerful-looking teeth. Behind Sylvester was the solid wooden fence belonging to the house opposite the chimp's, with Viola flailing somewhere in a knot of weed. There were only two ways Sylvester could think of running from the vengeful primate. Down the street back toward the center of town, where Cap'n Rustbane and his band of pirates would surely still be combing the streets in search of the fugitives, or the other way along the street, heading for the unknown jungle and all the horrors it might contain.

Sylvester knew very little about those horrors . . . as yet.

Toward the jungle it was, then.

Twice before, during this flight from the pirates, he'd managed to gear himself into a special frame of mind that had allowed him to cover distance faster than any mortal lemming could run, in particular, faster than a somewhat portly assistant librarian lemming could run. It was a knack he could do with being able to reproduce now. The other two times he'd been terrified, yes, but there had been something more than that, something beyond the ordinary limits of terror, something that—

The chimp roared.

That helped. Sylvester felt his legs gathering strength underneath him.

But if he fled, what about Viola? She'd be left here on her own . . .

He dithered.

The chimp's banana, furiously hurled, whistled past Sylvester's head, missing by a quarter of a millimeter at most, and splattered to annihilation against the painted wooden fence behind him. He felt liquified banana cover his back in a thin, uniform layer and staggered forward from the impact into air yellowed by other rebounded banana droplets.

Fear made him do it. He roared right back at the chimp.

Lemmings don't have the lungs to produce a very impressive roar. What came out of Sylvester's mouth was more of a snarl than anything else, but it nonetheless conveyed a level of savagery that startled even Sylvester himself.

"Huh?" said the chimp, again balancing on one foot, the other poised halfway through the creature's first step towards Sylvester.

There was a commotion beneath the larger animal. Sylvester was barely aware of it, unable to unlock his own gaze from the chimpanzee's.

He roared again. He made as if to pound his chest but then realized this wouldn't look too impressive, so instead he just jutted out his jaw.

"Come and get me, dumbbutt."

"I'll—"

Crrrrrack!

"Aaaaargh!" shrieked the chimp, the expression on his face changing instantly from aggression to agony. Still staring at Sylvester, but now as if imploring him for mercy, the big creature began slowly to topple over sideways, reaching one hand toward his ankle.

"Gotcha!" squeaked Rasco in triumph. He was holding Mrs. Pickleberry's rolling pin in his arms, staggering under its weight.

Then he looked upward and realized where the falling chimp was going to land.

"Run! *Run!*"

Sylvester turned to the thick weeds. Viola was just beginning to right herself. He grabbed one of her hands and pulled hard. She shot upright and cannoned into him, almost knocking him off balance.

"What—?" she began. One glance past him at the stricken chimpanzee was enough to answer all her questions and she shut her mouth firmly.

"Come on," he cried.

"Mom!"

"Rasco's helping her."

Even as he spoke the words, Sylvester recognized their falsehood. Rasco was tough but he was far too small to be of much use helping Mrs. Pickleberry to her feet, let alone dragging her out of danger if that proved necessary.

Sylvester darted straight toward the chimp, who was now flailing his arms in the air in a doomed attempt to stop himself from crashing to the ground.

Rasco had dropped the rolling pin and was throwing his full weight against Mrs. Pickleberry, trying to get her to move out of danger. Without success.

The whatever-it-was that had helped Sylvester move at unnatural speed earlier now suddenly decided to make its presence felt. Not caring about the antics of the chimp overhead, he darted straight toward the prone lemming.

"Run for your life," he commanded Rasco.

The mouse looked at Sylvester's face and vanished in a flurry of black fur.

Sylvester barely paused as he scooped up Mrs. Pickleberry from the ground. The darker moonshadow of the falling chimp was getting larger and larger on the roadway all around them. Mrs. Pickleberry seemed barely conscious, which was a blessing. She was in no condition to struggle or protest as Sylvester threw her over his shoulder like a sack of seeds.

On the other side of the road, where Sylvester had been just a split second before, Viola was making good her own escape. He could see, in the moonlight, the glitter of her wide eyes as she scampered away parallel with the fence. Luckily, she was going in the same direction Rasco had taken – away from town, toward the jungle.

The jungle was just beginning to come awake with the dawn. The air was full of screams and shrieks and caterwauls. Most of them sounded hungry.

Don't think about it, Sylvester told himself. *Solve one problem before you start worrying about the next.*

Limp and uncooperating, Mrs. Pickleberry was a lot heavier than he'd expected. He guessed she was a lot heavier than she'd ever have admitted in mixed company. Would Viola become like this when she was a bit older? It was an unnerving thought.

So stop thinking it!

I should be running!

Running like the wind!

Running so fast that . . .

Confused, he looked around him. The *kerthump* of the chimpanzee hitting the road, and the ensuing torrent of curses, seemed strangely distant.

That was because they *were* strangely distant, a full fifty yards away.

Sylvester had no recollection of covering the intervening distance. He had no conception of how he'd been able to do so, burdened as he was by about a ton and a half of lifeless Mrs. Pickleberry.

Viola came puffing up to him. He must have overtaken her on the way. All around, lights were coming on in the houses as the chimp's screams of anger woke the neighbors. In a few moments there was going to be a mob out here, a mob that'd think nothing of ripping a few foreign lemmings limb from limb.

"My hero," gasped Viola, looking as if she were about to fall into Sylvester's arms, even though they were already full.

"Keep running," he cried. "Keep running for your life. We're not out of the woods yet."

"You mean we're not *into* the—oh, never mind."

They ran.

⧫ ⧫ ⧫ ⧫

They stopped running when Sylvester tripped over a root and went flying, Mrs. Pickleberry shooting out of his arms to fly even farther. Fortunately, they both landed sprawling on soft, mushy ground.

"You all right, boss?" said Rasco hoarsely in Sylvester's ear.

Sylvester swallowed a mouthful of mud and jungle-floor compost. The fall hadn't hurt. Having just run flat-out carrying the heavy Mrs. Pickleberry for at least five hundred miles was what was hurting him. Well, maybe it hadn't been *quite* five hundred miles. But a pretty hefty distance, anyway.

"I'll be all right," he managed to say. "I hope. See how Daphne is."

"I'm all right," said Mrs. Pickleberry from a few yards away. Sylvester was dimly aware of her sitting up in the moonlight. She cackled. "Wha'ever made you think I wun't?"

"You were uncon—oh, never mind."

"Me? Unconscious? Not me, I wasn't, but why should I tire out me old legs when there was a young gemmun prepared to tire out *his* legs fer me?"

She's lying, thought Sylvester dully, nestling his head on a lump of something squishy. *She was out cold. The fall must have jolted her awake again. Why's she lying about it? What's she trying to hide?*

"Mom?" said Viola in a worried tone of voice. Sylvester couldn't immediately tell where she was, then heard her sit down heavily beside her mother. "Are you all right?"

"'Course I'm all right, you young nincompoop."

"Mo–om."

"No need to be bothering your head about an old baggins like me."

She must be all right, thought Sylvester, shutting his eyes firmly. *They're bickering again.*

"Don't go to sleep on me," said Rasco urgently. The mouse tugged at Sylvester's ear – hard. "We're not safe yet."

"Um-hm."

"Wake up!"

Sleep seemed an excellent idea to Sylvester. Sleep was an enormous puffy mattress, half the size of the world, and it smelled something like fresh straw, something like warm puppies. He'd just climbed aboard the edge of the mattress, and was now walking in long, bouncy, restful strides towards the center of it. With each new stride he took, his legs bent just a little more than they had the last time, and moved a little more slowly, so that very soon he was going to be crawling along on his tummy and then, perhaps, at last he'd be allowed to . . .

"Wake up!" Rasco repeated, much louder than the last time. "We can't stop here. We got to get ourselves farther into the jungle than this."

"Wazzat?"

The mouse called over to the other two. "Hey, you!"

Viola and Mrs. Pickleberry barely paused in their squabbling.

Rasco made a curious noise in his throat. After a moment, Sylvester realized the mouse was growling. The effect of the growl was to make the mattress Sylvester was bouncing along just a little firmer. When Rasco growled a second time the mattress became positively lumpy.

Sylvester shook his head. The mouse was right. However tempting it might be to rest, they were still in danger. If the chimpanzee and his neighbors were still searching for the intruders, they couldn't be far away. Even if they weren't – and through the thunder of blood in his ears Sylvester could hear no sounds of pursuit – by the time the sun was fully up anyone would be able to look in here from the road and see the little party.

It seemed like the biggest effort he'd ever made, even bigger than carrying Mrs. Pickleberry, but he forced himself up from the ground and stood unsteadily on legs that seemed to be made out of custard.

"You two," he said harshly in the general direction of the Pickleberries.

To his astonishment, they quit their wrangling immediately and stared at him, eyes wide, mouths open mid-insult. It would have been better, he thought, if he could have seen a little respect for his leadership in their eyes, or at the very least a preparedness to listen to what he was about to say. Instead, all he saw there was irritation, as if Viola and Mrs. Pickleberry were impatient for him to get the words out so they could keep going from where they'd left off. But at least they'd shut up.

"We've got to keep moving."

"We have?" Viola's voice was very flat.

"We have."

"The boss is right," chipped in Rasco.

"So we're taking orders from a mouse now, are we?" said Viola.

"This mouse has survived in these parts for the whole of his life," Rasco pointed out, his forepaws on his hips. "If it hadn't been for him, you lot'd be dead by now. You don't know diddly-squat about a *thing* here on Blighter Island. I don't know why I didn't just let you all be killed by the pirates, I don't. It'd have been a lot less trouble for me if I had. I could be curled up all safe in my nice warm wine cellar right now, but no, I'm stuck in the jungle with a mob of angry primates after me blood and a pair of spoiled brats arguing with each other like chipmunks, and what thanks do I get? I ask you, what thanks? I don't know why me and Sylvester here don't just leave you two where you are and go off and find me gran and put a few drinks inside us and—"

"Oh," said Viola.

"Yeah, right," said Rasco, looking as if he might, should she utter so much as a single further syllable, leap straight down her throat and tie her vocal cords in a knot.

She shut her mouth.

"Now," said Rasco less pugnaciously, "we gotta do what the big guy says. We gotta get well away from the edge of the jungle. There are trails in here that only the natives know, that only the natives, like me, can even see. I can guide you to my grandma's place, and I can keep you out of the clutches of them brigands want to fry you alive, but only if I get a bit of cooperation. Right? Is that understood?"

Viola looked at Rasco as if she was about to burst into tears. Mrs. Pickleberry stared at him as if she wanted to rolling-pin him until he was just a furry puddle. But neither of the two lemmings said a word. He'd won the argument.

Rasco grinned up at Sylvester.

"Ready to get going, mon?"

"Mon?" said Sylvester.

"Yes, well, ahem, I sort of picked it up on Bojingle Island. I heard that there was a lot of beautiful *mademoiselles* there."

"*Mademoiselles?*"

"It means young ladies," explained Rasco. "It's a word I picked up in another place. Anyway, I was a stowaway on a ship heading to Bojingle and, wow, were those young ladies a sight! I stayed there for quite a while so I picked up the accent somehow. There you have it . . . mon."

❖ ❖ ❖ ❖

For some hours, Sylvester felt as if he was indeed the leader of the quartet, that Rasco was merely his lieutenant and, well, enforcer. The little mouse was able to detect jungle trails where anyone else, glancing inexpertly, would have seen merely a thick tangle of vegetation. The only trouble was that very often obstacles of one kind or another had fallen across their path. Luckily Sylvester, being bigger, was able to shove most of these out of the way or at least help the others climb over them.

"Gee, thanks," said Rasco about the tenth time this happened. He and Sylvester stood together waiting for the Pickleberries to catch up. Viola and her mom could probably clamber over this fallen branch without Sylvester's assistance, but he wanted to be there just in case Viola should chance to get into any difficulties.

"You're besotted with that so-called babe, ain't you?"

Rasco's question interrupted Sylvester's dreamy thoughts.

"Ah, and, er, which particular babe might it be you had in mind?"

"The one you go all googoo-eyed over. Miss Prancy-Dancy. Viola."

"Oh, *her*, you mean?"

"None other."

"Well, she is, in a manner of speaking, quite lovely, you know."

"Not to me, she ain't."

Sylvester beamed down at his smaller companion in a patronizing fashion.

"I don't expect she would be. A bit much for a little fellow like you to handle, I'd say."

Rasco glowered. "Not just that, puddinghead. There's also the fact that I'm a mouse and she's a—say, what kind of creatures are you folks, anyhow? I never thought to ask."

"We're lemmings," said Sylvester, hoping he didn't sound too pompous.

Rasco snickered.

Sylvester's gaze narrowed. He didn't like the sound of that snicker. It hadn't seemed sufficiently . . . respectful. It had been more like, well, downright derisive. "What's so funny?"

The mouse rolled his little black eyes. "*You* know. I asked you a question and the answer is a lemming."

"I don't get it."

Rasco shrugged. "Never mind. Ask someone to explain it to you sometime."

Sylvester twisted his lips. The mouse's response didn't seem very satisfactory, but he suspected it was the best he was going to get.

Ignorant of Sylvester's thoughts, Rasco continued, "I've heard about you lemmings. Never seen one, o' course, until you lot came stumbling along."

A warm glow filled Sylvester's chest. "So the renown of we lemmings has spread as far afield as Blighter Island, has it?"

Rasco nodded, staring back along the path. It was beginning to be worrisome that the two Pickleberries hadn't yet appeared.

"'At's right. Me grandma was talking about your folk a while back. Let me try to remember what it was she said." He scratched the back of his small head. "Oh, yes, something about the whole caboodle of you being obsessed with suicide."

Sylvester chuckled. "I'm afraid your grandmother's got hold of the wrong end of that rumor. That's not the way we are at all."

"You're not? Not constantly looking for cliffs to jump off?"

Sylvester's chuckle broke into a full laugh. "Naturally not! We just—"

His words came to an abrupt halt. If you looked at it from the right angle, which was the *wrong* angle really, then it was true to say that the inhabitants of Foxglove did spend quite a lot of their time obsessing about jumping off a cliff. It wasn't that they were suicidal, of course. They were as fond of life as the next creature. It was just that . . .

He winced.

"Look, it's all a matter of context," he said.

"It is?" responded Rasco absently. "Them gals of yours is taking their time, ain't they?"

"I wouldn't think there's anything to be alarmed about," Sylvester reassured him. "It's probably just that one or other of them has had to stop for a few moments to . . . powder her nose."

"In the jungle?" said Rasco, wrinkling his brow as one might on discovering one's sardine was rather more elderly than anticipated.

"I didn't actually mean they were powdering their noses. I meant that—"

"What you said was—"

The mouse broke off suddenly, holding up an open paw to tell Sylvester to hush as well.

"Can you hear?" whispered Rasco after a few seconds.

"Hear what?"

"Voices. Listen."

"It's just Viola and her mom."

"Ssh! It's not them."

Sure enough, Sylvester was beginning to be able to make out a faint sound himself. Those weren't the voices of female lemmings. They were the voices of . . .

"I know who that is," he said to Rasco, fear making him speak so quietly that for a moment he thought he might not have spoken at all.

But Rasco heard. "Who? Not Deathflash, is it? The ruffian you call Rustbane?"

"No, not him. One of his men. That's why the others haven't got here yet. They must have recognized his voice and taken cover. A wise move. We should do the same."

"Okay. Over there."

Moving as quickly but quietly as they could, the mouse and lemming secreted themselves behind a strange plant that looked more like something out of a nightmare than anything that could actually grow.

"Don't touch them spines," instructed Rasco just as Sylvester was about to prod one inquisitively. "Them's poisonous."

"They are?" said Sylvester, recoiling.

"Too right, boss. Stick yourself on one o' them and . . . best I not tell you what'd happen, but you'd not be having any little Sylvesters in a hurry. Now *hush*."

The voices had been getting closer all this while and now, their owners came into view. Although Sylvester already knew who one of them was, he still sucked in his breath in a little hiss of dismay when he recognized the big figure of Jeopord, Cap'n Rustbane's first mate aboard the *Shadeblaze,* the ocelot whom the captain affectionately referred to as his Jack o' Cups. And now Sylvester recognized the other pirate too, a raccoon with an ear missing and a permanent snarl on his face, although he'd never learned the fellow's name. He didn't have long to wait to discover it.

"That should be far enough," said the raccoon, looking back the way they'd come. "The rest of 'em are searching 'way to the south o' here for those infernal lemmings, God rot 'em."

Jeopord shook a paw as if shaking a fly off it. "The lemmings aren't of any consequence, Bellowguts," he said. "You ask me, they're just another of the old buzzard's distractions. Summat to keep the hearties busy so they'll forget there's still no more of a sign of Adamite's treasure than ever there was."

Bellowguts sniggered, wiping his nose on the back of his paw. "Still an' all, Rustbane'll not let them escape. He don't not never let no one escape, he don't."

Jeopord guffawed. "Sure as rain is rain, you've got that right, me old faceache!"

The two pirates laughed long and loud together, though for the life of him Sylvester couldn't see what was so all-fired funny.

"But, truly," said Jeopord at last, drying his eyes much as Bellowguts had wiped his nose, "the lemmings needn't concern us. And, by the time we're done with him, Rustbane won't be bothering them either."

Again the two cutthroats gave themselves up to laughter.

"Seriously, though," said Bellowguts eventually, "what if something should go wrong? There's been times a-plenty folk 'ave tried to put an end to Rustbane's charmed existence, and all of 'em have found theyselves swingin' from the yardarm while diverse bits of they's anatomy is already feedin' the fishes."

"Not this time, me old blaggard, not this time," replied Jeopord, rubbing the side of his nose with an evilly long claw. "You mark my words on that."

"Ye so sure?"

"Aye, I'm sure. There be fifty of us, maybe twice that, and Rustbane, damn his eyes, is growing old. He ain't half the fox he used to be, and that was even afore his vision went all cloudy over this tomfoolery about the magical chest of the Zindars."

"Ye don't think there's any such thing, do ye, eh, Jeopord?"

There was something in Bellowguts's eyes that told Sylvester the raccoon knew a bit more about the treasure than Jeopord thought he did. If the ocelot saw that cunning little light, he paid it no attention.

"A bit o' mythology, mate," said Jeopord. "That's all it is, a bit o' mythology."

Sylvester, still watching Bellowguts's eyes, saw something change as decisively as if a switch had been turned from on to off, and wondered if he'd just observed Jeopord's death sentence being signed. The ocelot was not nearly so clever as he thought he was, and the raccoon far cleverer.

Aside from that little flicker in the eyes, Bellowguts gave no sign he was anything but Jeopord's gullible acolyte.

"When are ye going ter brief the crew, Jeopord?"

"When I'm good and ready, is when." The ocelot put the heel of his paw on his cutlass's pommel and strutted up and down the little clearing where the two had paused. "This ain't going to be a plan that gangs agley because too many people know about it ahead o' time, oh no it ain't, not with good old Jeopord in charge o' things, it ain't."

Before he could stop himself, Sylvester let out a tiny hiss of disbelief at the pirate's vanity.

"What was that noise?" said Jeopord, stopping suddenly mid-strut.

"I 'eard nothin'." Bellowguts's reply was very quiet, dangerously so. Already his own sword was in his hand, its tip dancing a menacingly casual dance in the air in front of him.

"A hissing noise," said Jeopord. His sword was circling in the air too, as his gaze searched the foliage around him.

Rasco and Sylvester stayed as still as stone, not daring even to breathe.

"It came from . . . from over 'ere, I think." The ocelot's eyes seemed to focus on the chubby leaf directly in front of Sylvester's nose.

Cutlass raised on high, Jeopord pounced forward.

Sylvester shut his eyes tight, expecting this moment to be his last.

He waited for the blow to fall.

It never did.

At least, not on him.

There was a *swwwiiiissssh* as something whistled through the air next to his face, almost close enough to take off a few whiskers, and then there was a commotion just a few inches from where his toes lay quivering in the jungle mulch.

"Got it!" crowed Jeopord loudly, the shout sending brightly colored birds high above into a new cacophony of chattering and squawking.

With a courage he'd never known he possessed, Sylvester managed to prize one eye open.

Back in the center of the clearing, Jeopord, cutlass back in its scabbard, was proudly holding aloft the two dripping halves of a serpent that was as thick as one of his own arms and twice as long as one of his legs.

"Told you I'd heard something," the first mate informed Bellowguts triumphantly.

"A snake," said the raccoon.

"And not just any old snake." The ocelot laughed. "Don't you recognize the markings?"

From where Sylvester crouched trembling, the markings of the dead creature seemed as gaudy as the plumage of the jungle birds.

The raccoon peered. "Nope."

"That's a yellow-headed colonswallower, that is."

"It is?"

"Nastiest reptile in the whole jungle."

The raccoon looked suitably impressed.

"Yes," said Jeopord with affected casualness, casting the two halves of the snake away from him in opposite directions. Where they landed in the greenery there was a sudden commotion as jungle creatures moved in swiftly to fight over the fresh carrion. "It tends to lurk in latrines, that's the place it likes to haunt the most, and when it sees its opportunity it moves like a streaking arrow and buries itself, all unnoticed, right inside a fellow."

Bellowguts gulped. "Ye mean it . . .?"

Jeopord gave him a long, significant look. "Like a terrier down a rabbit's burrow."

Bellowguts gulped again, this time violently enough that Sylvester heard it distinctly. "An' then?"

"Slowly, over weeks, or maybe even months, it *gobbles him up from the inside out!*"

Sylvester had never seen a green-faced raccoon before. He did now.

"I'm gonna wear two pairs of trousers in future," muttered Bellowguts, looking around him suspiciously.

"Good idea."

"Three."

"Even better."

"Ah, Jeopord?"

"Yes?"

"Why did ye want to . . . call this meeting?"

"Because you are my best and most trusted fellow conspirator, o' course, Bellowguts."

"Ye said ye had something ye wanted to talk about."

"I did. I do."

"Well, we ain't talked about it yet."

"We haven't? Why, yes, Bellowguts, you're perfectly correct. What I wanted to talk about with you was . . . *this.*"

Faster than the eye could see, Jeopord's cutlass was back out of its scabbard and moving in a screeching arc toward the raccoon's exposed throat. Bellowguts reached for his own weapon but, too late, too late! The tip of Jeopord's blade seemed merely to nick the flesh of his crewmate's furry neck, but there was a sudden fountain of blood.

The ocelot stepped back sharply as, making a hideous bubbling noise through his torn throat, the raccoon slowly collapsed forward.

In an instant it was all over, and Bellowguts's body was still. The stillness of death. All that moved was the pool of blood in which the dead raccoon lay, its surface rippling in a small breeze that shifted sluggishly among the densely packed trees. The scent of blood's sticky saltiness was strong in the air.

"Thought you'd sell me out to the skipper, did you?" said Jeopord to the corpse at his feet. "Thought you could be his spy among us, then betray us at the last possible moment after we'd cast our die? Well, this is what happens to traitors. Just be thankful, wherever you are, I didn't have the opportunity to take me time over it and give yers a proper send-off from this scurvy life."

He drew back his foot to kick the dead raccoon, then obviously thought better of it. Instead, he wiped off his blade on some grass until it was shiny again, and put the weapon back in his belt. He gave off the air of one satisfied by a job well done.

But not completely done, not quite yet.

"I hear you!" cried Jeopord, turning slowly in a circle, addressing his words to the riot of vegetation on all sides. "I hear you!"

For a moment, Sylvester thought the pirate must be speaking to Rasco and himself, must have known all along that the quivering smaller creatures were spying on everything that had been happening, but no.

"You out there," the ocelot called. "You carrion-eaters. I know yer watching. Come here and have yer fill. Come and get rid of me evidence for me."

There was a rustling in the bushes, lots of rustlings in lots of bushes. The wild creatures of the jungles were waiting only for Jeopord to leave them alone with their meal.

And, if the dead raccoon didn't provide enough to sate their appetites, to what else might they look as provender?

"We best get out of here," whispered Rasco.

"I was thinking the same thing."

They both eyed the ocelot's back, *willing* him to leave quicker. He was clearly unaware of their mental urgings, because he sauntered slowly from the clearing, his forepaws hooked into his belt, whistling softly to himself as if he hadn't a care in the world.

"Get a move on," said Sylvester under his breath.

At last, Jeopord was out of sight. The rustling around them grew louder.

"You know where the gals are, mon?" said Rasco.

"You know I don't."

"We best find 'em."

"We had."

In the end they didn't have to find Viola and Mrs. Pickleberry – the two female lemmings found them.

"Did you see that?" said Viola, her eyes saucer-wide, as she ran into Sylvester's arms. "That . . . that brute just murdered the poor raccoon."

"I'm not certain the 'poor raccoon' was exactly a little innocent," murmured Sylvester, but not very loudly, not loudly enough for Viola to hear, in fact. It felt good having her in his arms and her head on his shoulder, and there was nothing he was going to do to end that situation sooner than he had to.

Then his eye fell on the corpse of Bellowguts. Already the sight of it was largely obscured by the clouds of fat, shiny black flies that had descended upon it. A couple of small creatures had dared to slither out of the undergrowth, their beady eyes intent on the raccoon's flesh. They seemed to have teeth larger than the rest of their bodies. Holding Viola tight was a luxury he'd have to save for later.

"Let's go!" he cried.

Mrs. Pickleberry was staring at him askance. "And none too soon, if you ask me."

"Um, yes," said Sylvester self-consciously, gently pushing Viola away.

"Sheesk!" said Rasco.

The single syllable summarized it all.

With the black mouse in the lead once more, the little party resumed their trek through the dense jungle growth. Viola was directly behind Rasco, then Mrs. Pickleberry with Sylvester taking up the rear.

I suppose I should be glad Rustbane's facing a mutiny, Sylvester told himself, holding up a paw to deflect a whippy branch that seemed determined to crack him across the face. *I suppose I should be glad that soon the murderous scoundrel will be walking the plank. Yet . . . somehow I can't make myself feel good about it. Yes, Rustbane's cruel and despicable and he's got more blood on his paws than a thousand tyrants, but he's also something more than that.*

Sylvester's thoughts ran back to the time he'd spent with the gray fox in the cabin aboard the *Shadeblaze*. Somehow, Rustbane had seemed as much at home in that book-lined place as he did when he was swaggering across the deck of a pirate ship, condemning some poor mortal to an excruciating death. *It's as if there are two people inside him, but one of them's hardly ever allowed to show his face.*

Phew, but it was hot here in the jungle. Even though it was still early in the day, the air was like that in front of a just-opened oven door. Sylvester felt as if he were in danger of being cooked alive. It was difficult to walk and think at the same time in this baking heat, especially when the ground underfoot was a treacherous maze of snaking roots and grasping grasses, all of them eager to trip up an unwary lemming and send him sprawling.

Perhaps I should try to work out some way of warning Cap'n Rustbane of what's going to happen?

Without having made any conscious decision to do so, Sylvester found he'd paused on the track and was leaning against a conveniently situated tree trunk.

Idly, he wondered how long he'd been here.

And where the others might have gotten to.

He was on his own.

Snakes.

Lizards.

Poisonous insects.

Wild carnivores.

"How much longer?" he wailed.

VEGGIE MUSIC

"Quite a lot longer, mon, if you're proposing to just lean against a dead tree until a boa constrictor comes along to ingestify you."

Rasco's voice, coming from thick undergrowth almost next to Sylvester's ear, startled the lemming. He kept his balance with difficulty as he pushed himself away from the tree.

"Don't creep up on me like that," he hissed.

Rasco made the sound of a shrug. "There was no creeping up involved, mon. You were looking to me like someone who done fallen asleep with his eyes wide open."

"I was?"

Now Rasco stepped daintily out of the vegetation, dropping from a gnarled but hideously fecund-looking root onto the mushy forest floor. "You were."

"Where are the others?"

"Waiting for us." Rasco indicated, with a twitch of his nose, the jungle behind him. "Waiting in a small clearing where the insects buzz as they decide which bit of you to bite next, and where that log in the swamp could as easily be an alligator as a log, only you'll never find out until you trustingly put your foot on it. That kind of waiting."

"We'd better join them at once, hadn't we?" said Sylvester, looking anxiously from one side to the other, as if an enemy could spring out at them any moment.

Rasco sighed. "I was hoping you'd say that. Come on now."

Heart pounding, Sylvester followed the mouse through a maze of snaking greenery until finally, just as Rasco had described it, they came into a clearing where Viola and Mrs. Pickleberry stood. Neither of the females was displaying much by way of patience.

Mrs. Pickleberry was the first to notice their arrival. "You've found the stupid dope, have you?" she rasped.

"He had discovered something of interest," Rasco lied smoothly. He clearly subscribed to the notion that males should stick together in self-defense against the onslaughts of the supposedly weaker sex.

Viola gazed at Sylvester. "He'd discovered the sheen on a leaf or the sparkle on a butterfly's wing, you mean." The expression on her face finally opted for affection rather than exasperation. "Just my luck to fall for one of life's natural-born dreamers."

"I'll have you know—" Sylvester began.

"Leave it," whispered Rasco behind him. "You're ahead at the moment. Anything else you say's only going to dig you deeper into trouble, mon. Call her your darling honeybunch and be quick about it."

Sylvester wondered how old Rasco was. It was always difficult to tell with mice. He seemed to know much more about the ways of the world than Sylvester did himself, and to be so much wiser in them.

"Now that we have all had a rest," said Rasco, blithely ignoring the fact that he himself had not, "I suggest we push on as fast as we can. There is much of the day still to pass, yet we are a mighty long way from the home of Madame Zahnia, and I would not wish to be still out in the jungle wilds after darkness has fallen and the nighttime creatures have become ... ravenous. Do the rest of you have opinions on this matter?"

The lemmings let their feet do the talking. They scrambled to make as much haste as possible.

After an hour or so had passed, Sylvester began to notice a strange sound. Well, all the sounds in the jungle seemed pretty strange to him, and there were a heck of a lot of them to be shocked and bamboozled by: the screeches of birds that were rarely seen as anything more than a brightly colored blur out of the corner of his eye, the ghastly screams of small animals as they fell prey to larger ones, the lugubrious *plop plop plop* of unseen nectar dropping from high leaves onto lower ones, and so on. But this new sound, which seemed to be coming from somewhere ahead of them and yet at the same time to fill the jungle in all directions was, well, different.

He and Rasco were sitting on a branch waiting for the two Pickleberries to reappear from yet another foray into the darker depths for purposes unstated yet perfectly obvious.

"What is that noise?" said Sylvester.

"That is veggie music, *mon ami*."

"'Veggie music'?"

"Veggie music."

Sylvester nodded and for a few moments said nothing more. Then he realized the mouse's answer had explained exactly nothing to him.

"What in the world is veggie music, Rasco?"

"Music made with vegetables, o' course."

A few more moments passed. Then Sylvester realized, once more, that he was no wiser than he'd been earlier.

"Could you perhaps explain that a bit more fully, my friend?" he said.

Rasco started, as if his thoughts had been far away. "Oh, OK. See, Sylvester, the instruments are all made from dried vegetables, gourds and things. Our people hollow them out, then dry them until they're hard as wood, or maybe they do the drying first and the hollowing after, I'm not sure. I'm not so much of a musician myself. Whatever, once you got these hard, hollowed, dried-out fruits and veggies, you can make drums out of them, or put strings on them, or you can . . ."

Sylvester wasn't really interested in the details. What was important was that the source of the rhythmic, pounding music seemed to be not too far away from them.

"Does this mean we're close to where your Grandma Zahnia lives?" he demanded.

"Sure does," said Rasco, shifting on the branch. "In fact, I'm wondering where those womenfolk of yours might've gotten themselves to. Could be they've run into some of my kin. Be a bit embarrassing for them, I guess, if they've got their knick—"

"Sorry to have been so long," said Mrs. Pickleberry, appearing suddenly beside him. "Viola found a toad."

Sylvester was as underinformed by this as he had been by Rasco's explanations earlier. He thought about it briefly, but decided not to inquire any further. Whatever it was that had gone on between Viola and the toad didn't seem to have done her any harm. She put her arm through his and smiled brightly.

"How far do you think we have left to go?" said Sylvester, directing the question toward the mouse.

"You can see the village from here," replied Rasco, grinning.

The three lemmings looked ahead but could see nothing.

"Where are all the houses?" said Sylvester.

Rasco's grin broadened even further, if such a thing were possible. "I can see them. You should be able to as well."

Then Sylvester did see the houses. His jaw dropped open.

"Look," he said softly, nudging Viola and pointing.

She obeyed. "Wow," she breathed.

Their mistake had been to look for the village on the ground.

At first, Sylvester had thought the trees around here must be infested by unusually large spiders which had slung their webs from one branch to another and from one tree to another, and built big nests here and there in the crooks between branches. But, as he squinted against the bright flares of sunlight that stabbed through the jungle foliage above, he realized this first impression had been wrong. Those weren't nests, they were well-constructed wooden houses, perched precariously among the high canopy. And those thin strands weren't as thin as he'd thought – they were vines, placed as bridges to link the various parts of what was quite an extensive habitation. Along the vine bridges scuttled small dark shapes that he could barely distinguish from here.

Sylvester glanced sidelong at Rasco. Mice. That was what those quickly moving shapes must be. Lots of mice, just like their guide. They must have found Rasco's people at last.

One of the houses was larger than the others and sat a little apart from the others. As Sylvester stared at it, Rasco saw the direction of his gaze and said with a chuckle, "That's my grandma's house. Madame Zahnia's house. Welcome to Ouwinju. She'll be looking forward to seeing you."

Sylvester looked skeptically upward. It seemed a very long way indeed from where he stood to that wooden house in the sky. "But . . . but how are we going to get up there?" he asked.

Rasco winked at him. "Easy. We're going to climb."

"Climb?"

"That's what I just said, my friend."

Before Sylvester could ask him for any more details, Rasco put two claws to his mouth and let out a piercing whistle.

Above, all the moving shapes abruptly froze and Sylvester could sense that he and his friends were now subject to the scrutiny of hundreds of small, beady eyes.

Then the mice slowly resumed their business.

Not all of them, though.

"'Zat you, Rasco, y'old stinkyguts?"

"Sure is, Gasbag. You gonna let me come up an' see my grandma?"

"She got better things ta do 'an see a bumhead like you, no?"

"You want your features readjusted?"

There was a fusillade of crazed laughter from the mouse hanging upside-down under a liana a dizzying distance overhead. "You been takin' bodybuildin' classes?"

"Don't need to, a little runt like you."

"Yah-ha!"

"How long is this going to go on?" said Viola in a world-weary voice. "We could always turn around and throw ourselves on the mercy of the good folk of Hangman's Haven."

"Who're yer friends?" Gasbag called down.

"Three lemmings, need to see Zahnia."

"Lemmings?"

"That's what I just said. Lemmings."

"They too big for up here, man."

Sylvester privately agreed with Gasbag's assessment. The vine bridges and little wooden houses were all designed for mice, not for much larger and heavier creatures like lemmings. That was an important part of the village's defenses against invaders, he reasoned. Larger animals trying to make an attack would soon find themselves plummeting toward the ground in the midst of a cloud of splintery debris.

Gasbag cackled again, even longer and louder than before, and it was clear he'd just been making a joke. A moment later, he hurled something down toward the group on the ground. Sylvester flinched as the dark object unpeeled itself through the air until one end slapped into the sludge just a couple of paces away from where he and his friends stood.

A rope ladder.

A rope ladder designed for mice.

As Sylvester looked at the too-narrow, too-closely spaced rungs, he felt his stomach beginning to mount what promised to be a full-scale war of resistance.

"I ... am ... not ... climbing ... that," said Mrs. Pickleberry, speaking Sylvester's own thoughts aloud.

Bless you, Daphne!

"Oh, I don't know," Viola chirped. "It could be rather fun."

"Nope. No way. No how. Not a thing a lady should be doin'."

"But, Mo-om—"

"Little flibbertigibbet."

"Mom!"

"No better than you hadn't oughter be!"

Viola snorted and reached for the ladder. Within moments, she was hauling herself up it, an expression of grim determination on her face as she spun and swung crazily. From far above there was the sound of a branch creaking in protest.

"Hey, mon!" wailed Gasbag. "You done sent the fat one first!"

Viola climbed with even greater resolution. Sylvester would not like to be in Gasbag's shoes when she reached the top.

He was startled out of his aghast reverie by a chuckle.

Mrs. Pickleberry was giggling.

"How on earth did she get that fast?"

"Young fellow," she said, face covered in smiles, "you got a lot to learn about the best ways of handling that daughter o' mine. You ask her all sweet and kind to do something, you can be asking away until the sun's gone to bed and the moon's high in the sky and still Viola won't have moved so much as a hair. But you tell her she's on no account to do something, and it's done afore ye've had time to turn around. We'd never have *persuaded* her to climb up to this Zahnia person's lodgin's, but she gets strict orders from her crusty old ma to keep her feet firmly on the ground an' she's off up that ladder like a rat up a drainpipe, she is. See?"

Mrs. Pickleberry jerked a thumb skyward. Viola had already reached the branch where Gasbag awaited and was now looking, so far as Sylvester could discern from the ground, somewhat seasick. Perhaps the mouse would live to see another day after all.

There was only one problem, so far as Sylvester was concerned, with the stratagem Mrs. Pickleberry had deployed.

It meant that *he* was going to have to climb that rope ladder as well.

"Er, after you," he said to Mrs. Pickleberry, bowing slightly and gesturing with a paw toward where the lower end of the ladder jigged and hopped.

"You gotta be kidding."

"But—"

"And have the likes of you lookin' up me skirts? Dream on, buster."

"But—"

"Better just go, mon." They'd both forgotten briefly about Rasco. "If I had known what pains in the neck lemmings could be, I would have left you all to your fate in the basement of The Monkey's Curse."

"It's not that we mean—" Sylvester began.

Rasco gestured at him impatiently. "Go, dimwit."

Climbing a rope ladder isn't as bad as I'd expected it would be, Sylvester told himself a little while later. He kept his gaze focused on the rung directly in front of his nose and remembered the immortal dictum: whatever you do, just don't look down. *This is all going rather well. So far.*

"You're supposed to take your feet off the ground, you daft lummock," said Mrs. Pickleberry savagely, "not just stand there holding the ladder to stop yourself fallin' over."

"Ah, yes," replied Sylvester. "Just, ah, testing it, see?"

He tugged the side of the ladder as if to reassure himself it would take his weight.

Behind him, Mrs. Pickleberry gave a girlish shriek. "Oh, no! It's that poisonous snake from the pub basement!"

"Hello," said Gasbag, helping Sylvester pull himself up the last little way onto the branch beside Viola. "You got here quick."

"Ahem, yes," said Sylvester, attaining his balance and patting his chest clear of imaginary dust. "Climbing. Yes. Nothing like it, is there? Excellent sport. Something of a specialty among we Lemmingtons. I remember there was an uncle of mine, or was it a great-uncle? I always get conf—"

"Sylvester?"

"Yes, Viola?"

"Shut up."

Within a few minutes they'd been joined by Mrs. Pickleberry, huffing and puffing and swearing with sufficient skill that, Sylvester thought, even Cap'n Rustbane might have murmured a few words of congratulation. Apparently it was not at all easy climbing a rope ladder when you were encumbered by a rolling pin. She was followed almost immediately by Rasco, to whom the climb was clearly a matter of no consequence. He and Gasbag threw themselves into each other's arms.

Sylvester scratched his head. Not long ago the two mice had been trading dire insults and now they were the best of friends.

"Is Grandma Zahnia in?" said Rasco after the mutual welcomes were largely over.

"Sure is."

"Then lead the way, little brother of mine."

Walking along the branches and, from time to time, along the vine bridges between them was, Sylvester discovered, rather like trying to retain dignity while trampolining. Thank goodness Viola and Mrs. Pickleberry were quite clearly in the same quandary.

While the two mice cavorted around them emitting squeaks and whoops of encouragement, the lemmings made an unsteady and distinctly unstately procession towards the big house belonging to Madame Zahnia.

When they reached it, Rasco reached out a small fist and rapped on the gnarled wooden door. As the little group waited, Sylvester noticed uneasily that there was the skull of a shrew nailed to the lintel.

"Come in, Rasco," said a voice that seemed to be centuries old – murky centuries that had seen more than their fair share of evil-doings and treachery. "And you too, Gasbag, and bring your lemming friends with you."

"How did she—?" began Viola, still somewhat out of breath from their scramble across the branches.

"My grandma always *knows*," said Rasco. He tapped the side of his nose and looked mysterious as he pushed the creaking door open.

"Don't you pay him no mind," whispered Gasbag. "As soon as I saw you lot in the distance I ran an' told Madame Zahnia. That Rasco, he's all full o' bullshine."

The inside of the room was so gloomy that for a moment Sylvester could see nothing of it at all. As his eyes slowly accustomed themselves to the dimness, he was able to make out that the place was jam-packed with stuff, just like the inside of "Mother Brisket's Antiques & Curios from Around the World" back in Foxglove. An emporium that, despite the grandiosity of its name and the splendor with which the proprietress always presented herself, was actually a junk shop. Lanterns made from dried-out blowfishes with candles stuck in them hung from the ceiling. Wherever the walls weren't lined with shelves they were covered in decorations of all sorts, all crammed together as close as they would go with no apparent concern for artistry: seastars, glass balls, knotted driftwood, shells . . . The shelves themselves were at higgledy-piggledy angles, as if the carpenter who'd built them had been doing so in high seas and in a terrific hurry. The gadgets and trinkets littering the shelves seemed to be clinging to them rather than just sitting there.

Sylvester was reminded yet again of Cap'n Rustbane's cabin, back on the *Shadeblaze*. Although the two rooms had very different contents and, he realized, wrinkling his nose, very different smells, they nevertheless had a lot in common.

At the far end of the room was a wildly overstuffed plush armchair and sitting on it, with a plump red cushion at her side, was a large brown mouse. *Also wildly overstuffed*, Sylvester couldn't stop himself from thinking. Even in the half-dark, the dress Madame Zahnia wore was almost dazzling in the swirl and clash of its colors, and the cloth wrapped around her head was as anarchic. She had massive brass earrings and, on her arms, bore bracelets and bangles galore. As she raised her arm in greeting to Rasco, the bracelets jangled together to make a noise like an orchestra tuning up.

A very bad orchestra.

Just behind her head, its feet screwed to the back of the armchair, was a stuffed mantis which had once upon a time been green but was now primarily dust-colored. Sylvester wasn't certain, but it seemed to him as if the mantis moved its head in time to Madame Zahnia's, regarding the visitors through eyes the color of spiderwebs.

Rasco bowed deeply in front of her. She might be his grandma, but obviously the little mouse held her in awe. "At your service, Madame Zahnia."

She held up her arm again and once more there was that tuneless clangor. "Welcome home, Rasco," Madame Zhania said, "and welcome to you too, dear lemmings."

"Er, thank you, Madame Zhania," said Sylvester, still mystified how the round mouse could know they were coming. He decided not to ask.

"Is there something I can be of assistance with?" Madame Zhania said.

"Yes, Madame Zhania," Rasco said. "We—I mean them are in quite a fix."

Madame Zhania darted him a glare. "Please mind your tongue, young Rasco."

Rasco shot a glance back over his shoulder at the three lemmings, crammed into a room that had been designed for mice. "Forgive me, Madame Zahnia."

The old mouse's brightly painted lips twitched slightly in a polite imitation of a smile. "It's of no matter. Tell me why you are here."

So, with some help from Sylvester and Viola, Rasco told her.

✦ ✦ ✦ ✦

"The short and the long of it, *grandmère*," he said at the conclusion of his story, "is that they need to get off the island and far away before they're captured by Deathflash and his crew and put to the most hideous of deaths."

"I can see that," Madame Zahnia murmured. For a long moment she sat in complete silence, her face creased in thought.

When at last she spoke, it was directly to the lemmings.

"I have heard that Deathflash, or Rustbane or whatever it is you wish to call him, has returned to these unfortunate shores. The monkeys told me about it. Wherever Deathflash goes, evil deeds and dire happenings must surely follow. He is one of the accursed and his presence is like an onslaught of the plague."

Sylvester shrugged mentally. They knew that. If this was all Madame Zahnia was going to tell them . . .

"Don't be so impatient," the old mouse told him. "All will be revealed in good time."

He gulped.

"What should we do, Madame Zahnia?" Viola's voice was filled with courtesy.

"I think the time has come for me to consult my Revealer."

"Your Revealer?"

"Yes," said Rasco. "That's the best of ideas, *grandmère*."

What Madame Zahnia did next would feature occasionally in Sylvester's nightmares for the rest of his life.

Turning swiftly around in her seat, she grabbed the head of the mantis with a firm paw and twisted it right round backwards.

There was a loud squeak, as if of agony.

Sylvester squinted at the mantis. *It can only have been an illusion that it was alive,* he told himself but he felt his heart thumping heavily at the back of his throat. *It was stuffed, after all. Oh, please let that insect have been already dead.*

"Thank you, Nero," said Madame Zahnia.

In the gloomy depths of the room behind her there was another noise, a slow creaking, like that of a door being opened that had been kept firmly shut for a thousand years. Sylvester gripped Viola's hand tightly.

"Come with me," said Madame Zahnia, pulling herself ponderously to her feet. "Rasco, give me your arm, will you? You're a strong young fellow and your grandmother is old and frail."

She reached out her hand and leaned against Rasco, who staggered but nobly tried to conceal it.

Slowly, the two mice shuffled toward the rear of the room, the lemmings behind them. Gasbag, who'd said not a word since they'd arrived at Madame Zahnia's house, was at Mrs. Pickleberry's side. He seemed to have taken an unaccountable liking to her.

On the far side of the hidden doorway they found themselves in another room, almost as big as the first, but this time circular and significantly less cluttered. In the center of the floor was a large round table, with chairs tucked under it. What caught the eye immediately, however, was the object in the middle of the table, a crystal ball about the size of Madame Zahnia's head. Unlike virtually everything else in this house, the ball was free from a surface layer of scummy dust. There was an opening in the roof directly above the table, allowing a column of sunlight to descend straight down onto the crystal ball which, in response, seemed to glow with all the colors of time.

Madam Zahnia went straight to the nearest chair and, releasing poor Rasco at last, plopped her ample rear end down onto it. Rasco took the chair next to her on the left and, slipping past the lemmings, Gasbag sat down to her right. Sylvester eyed the chairs, but there was no way they were big enough for the likes of a lemming. He and Viola settled down on the floor to the right of Gasbag, which meant they could still see comfortably all that took place on the table. Mrs. Pickleberry moved to Rasco's left-hand side but chose to remain standing, her shoulders humped over under the low ceiling.

"Don't be afraid," said Madame Zahnia. "Me and my Revealer won't hurt you."

Once everyone had assured her they weren't frightened, really they weren't, she continued, "Now, I want each of you to hold the hands of the person to either side of you."

With a certain amount of difficulty, people rearranged themselves to obey, with Rasco and Gasbag straining to reach each other's outstretched paws behind Madame Zahnia's broad back.

"Now," Madame Zahnia muttered, "jus' let me concentrate."

She began humming in a thin whine that Sylvester found almost intolerably spooky. Risking a nervous glance at her face, he saw that her eyes had taken on an uncanny luster, as if there was an extra layer of something masking them from the outside world.

He shuddered.

Madame Zahnia reached out both her paws to start stroking the big crystal ball in front of her, caressing it as if it were a pet or a beloved small child.

"There now, my little one. Your grandma is here beside you. You're in friendly company, Now, tell me what you see."

For what seemed like a long time there was no sound except her resumed high humming and the faint scrape of her rough paws on the smooth crystal surface.

"Oh, I see," she murmured at last.

"See what?" Sylvester whispered, leaning across to try to get a better look at the ball.

"Sh!" hissed Rasco.

"That's why Deathflash is here," said Madame Zahnia contemplatively. "Oh, the poor sorry fool that he is. He's always been prey to his greed, but now he's letting it devour him entirely."

"What's he doing?" said Rasco. The prohibition against interrupting the flow of Madame Zahnia's thoughts apparently didn't apply to him.

She didn't seem to mind.

"He's going after *it*."

"It?"

"The magical chest of the Zindars."

"I knew that," said Sylvester. Once again, Rasco silenced him.

"The magical chest of the Zindars," Madame Zahnia repeated. "Discovery of the chest could bring the greatest boon Sagaria has known for many a long millennium, or it could bring the final doom of the world. Who's to tell what the outcome could be? Best to leave the chest, and its contents, well alone forever."

Sylvester felt something stirring inside him. That was the attitude of far too many of the lemmings back in Foxglove. Indeed, it had been his own attitude until impetuosity had led him into the series of adventures that might all too easily kill him. Leave well alone. Things are all right just as they are, so don't rock the boat. What you don't take a risk on can't hurt you. The ways of our fathers are good enough for us. Who cares what lies around the next bend in the road?

He was in a bizarre and unusually terrifying jungle tree hut halfway around the world, and a pack of bloodthirsty pirates wanted to put him to the slowest and most agonizing death. Every now and then when he was having difficulty getting to sleep, he did – yes, he admitted, he *did* – think that possibly, just possibly, all this while he could have been safely tucked up in his own bed back home with his mother snoring gently in the room next to his. All of that was true. But, even if Rustbane never had showed up, think of all the excitement and joy he'd have missed out on.

Being seasick, just for starters.

Okay, maybe not that.

Seeing Viola's eyes sparkle when he told her something that made her laugh, or performed some feat of derring-do of which neither would ever have thought him capable.

Yes, that was something worth taking all the risks in the world for.

Madame Zahnia thought the magical chest of the Zindars should be left alone because its discovery might bring great risk with it, even though that self-same discovery might be the very best thing that had ever happened to Sagaria and all who lived there.

A little knot inside Sylvester rebelled against the old mouse's caution. If the magical chest of the Zindars was out there to be discovered, and if finding it could make the world a better place then he, Sylvester, was going to make every effort to find it before a murderous villain like Cap'n Rustbane did, even if he died trying.

He realized he was squeezing the paws of Viola and Gasbag far tighter than he should be, and grunted apologies to each of his two neighbors at the table.

"What are you trying to tell me?" Madame Zahnia was asking the crystal ball, her Revealer, still running her paws over its surface. "Speak to me, my old friend."

Suddenly, her arms stiffened.

"What? *What?*"

"What is it, Grandma?" Once again, it was Rasco who dared to speak.

"A voice, child. I hear a voice."

Gasbag rolled his eyes at Sylvester. It was clear Gasbag wasn't as completely convinced of Madame Zahnia's occult powers as his brother.

"I hear a voice," the old mouse repeated. "Speak louder to me," she commanded the air directly in front of her.

Sylvester strained his ears but could hear nothing. Madame Zahnia evidently did, though, because she nodded her head and then looked appalled, much of the color draining from her flabby face.

"*A curse,*" she breathed. "There is a terrible curse upon all of this, unless . . ."

Once more there was a short silence. The air itself seemed to grow heavy with dread.

"Ancient forces that should have been left alone are starting to move once more," said Madame Zahnia, her voice trailing off into the dusty air. "Ancient forces . . ."

"Yes? Yes?" said Sylvester.

She looked at him with eyes that seemed sightless. When next she spoke he had the impression she was talking to someone a long way behind him and in a different world that only she could detect.

"The course of events has already been set," she whispered. "It must be followed or catastrophe will be the inevitable consequence. The island that sleeps among the mists of misplaced time must be awoken, whether mortal beings think this is right or wrong. It is too late for the future to be changed. Too late! Aaaaaahhhhhh . . ."

With a final long sigh she subsided into her chair, her hands slipping off the surface of the Revealer. The crystal ball's glow faded.

For several long moments there was no sound except the breathing of those in the room and a flurry of squeaks from outside as two mice children argued about something.

"What did you see?" said Sylvester at last.

Madame Zahnia shook her head as if emerging from a confusing dream.

"I can't tell you too many things," she said softly. "Just enough, perhaps. If I told you too much, that would alter your actions and, in turn, that would affect the route of the future. What's going to happen must happen, I tell you!"

"Yes, but what *is* going to happen?" said Viola pointedly.

"And who were these blasted Zindars?" growled Mrs. Pickleberry.

Madame Zahnia chose to answer the latter question. She signaled to her guests that they could release each other's paws, and everyone made themselves comfortable as she settled into her tale.

"The Zindars, or the People of the Stars as many of the older people used to call them, were an ancient race who inhabited these islands thousands of years ago. They had knowledge that far surpassed anything we know today. Because they knew so much, they called the most arcane and powerful of all their secret magics, tech-*know*-logy. Nobody now remembers anything of this techknowlogy or what it could do, but folk say that, if only that secret magic could be rediscovered, the world could be a far, far better place . . . or could meet its fiery doom.

"Yet, few remember the Zindars now. Untold centuries ago they suddenly left Sagaria under circumstances shrouded in mystery, and they have never been seen again. Even the legend of the magical chest of the Zindars is known to a bare few, of whom your friend Deathflash – Rustbane – is unfortunately one and Cap'n Adamite, as bad a rogue as Deathflash if such a thing were possible, was another. It is a tragedy that two villainous pirates could have learned of this lore.

"The Zindars were respected as great teachers, and they were much loved by the peoples of Sagaria. However, what no one knew at the time, except the Zindars themselves, was that they had come to this world in flight from powerful malignant forces which had hunted them through many worlds far beyond this one."

Sylvester's jaw dropped. Not long ago his world had extended little farther than the environs of Foxglove. Then it had dramatically grown to include the whole of the realm of Sagaria. Now, here was Madame Zahnia talking of other worlds beyond Sagaria! He wasn't certain there was room enough in his brain for all these sudden leaps in the scale of the universe.

Madame Zahnia, oblivious to his racing thoughts, carried on speaking in that same slow, sepulchral voice. "The secret of their hiding place could not last forever, of course. At last, the enemies of the Zindars discovered their whereabouts, and they arrived in the skies of our world in a thousand great flying ships. They too had infinite reserves of techknowlogy, but it was *evil* techknowlogy. For long years, the evil techknowlogy of the invaders did battle with the benevolent techknowlogy of the Zindars, so that the surface of this world was rent and torn. Mountains were leveled to become desert plains, and seas boiled to float above the clouds. Somehow, the Zindars managed to spare the native Sagarians the worst effects of this great war, but even so, the death tolls were appalling.

"Then, at last, it just suddenly stopped. No one knows why. No one knows how. All we can guess is that the Zindars played one final techknowlogical trick that whisked them out of Sagaria and off somewhere else, far away beyond the curtain of the stars in the wink of an eye, and that they took the evil invaders with them.

"But, just before the warring races disappeared, something happened that will, the Revealer tells me, change the course of our world's future entirely ... *if* everything happens over the next few days and weeks in the way it has been preordained."

She paused again, as if trying to catch her breath. Sylvester, giving her a sidelong look, realized the old mouse was simply playing upon the dramatic expectations of her audience.

He cleared his throat.

Madame Zahnia took the hint.

"What happened," she continued, "was that a squadron of the evil invaders managed to trap the King of the Zindars and his closest guard of honor in a remote craggy valley high in the icy mountains of Carvenia. One by one the members of the guard of honor were cut down by lethal enemy fire, until none were left, save the king himself. He was putting up a brave battle against his attackers, but all knew it could be only a matter of time before he went to his final resting place, to where his guard of honor had loyally preceded him.

"It was then that a lowly human intervened to alter the course of Zindar history. There are more humans in Carvenia than you commonly find elsewhere in Sagaria. They're surprisingly good at eking out an existence among the hostile, infertile terrain of that forsaken part of the world. This man, barely more than a boy, really, a shepherd in search of a lost sheep, was drawn by the hissing sound of the techknowlogical weaponry being fired. He strayed into the valley where the combat was continuing. It didn't take him more than a moment to see how the wind was blowing, and it didn't take him more than *another* moment to snatch up a weapon that one of the dead honor guard had dropped and to run to the side of the King of the Zindars. Side by side and back to back these two fought off the attackers the rest of the day, and by the time the last rays of the sun were extinguished on the horizon they were the only two left standing.

"But the human lad was mortally wounded. He knew this, and the King of the Zindars could tell just by looking at him. The very last of their foes, with its very last gasp of this life, had let fire one final bolt of that blue-green techknowlogical fire they had which could cut through the thickest armor and even great city walls. The fire had burned away the shepherd boy's arm, leaving just a stump from which the blood showered like rain.

"The King of the Zindars cradled his savior's head on his lap and watched the last of the life light ebb from the lad's eyes. Then, as the boy went to that place from which there is no return, the King of the Zindars resolved that, even as his people fled back among the stars, they would leave behind them a gift for this world of Sagaria that had for so long treated them so generously.

"The gift the king decided they would leave was that, sometime in Sagaria's future, there would be the granting to a single mortal of a single wish."

Madame Zahnia raised a paw as if to fend off an interruption from her listeners. In truth, they were all too enthralled by her tale to be capable of breathing a word. All except Gasbag, who was snoring gently, his head face down on the table in front of him.

As Madame Zahnia lowered her arm she absently clipped Gasbag around the ear and the little zany mouse woke with a jolt and a snuffle.

"Wha—wha—?"

"Pay attention when yer ol' grandma's speaking to ye, you pesky little scapegrace."

"I *was* listening. Just *in my own way!*"

"Gnah!"

Smack!

"That doesn't sound like, well, very much," said Sylvester nervously, referring to the Zindars' gift.

"Oh, but it is," responded Madame Zahnia, her attention shifting to Sylvester and away from a grateful looking Gasbag. "It is. Whatever the wish, no matter how great it is, no matter how impossible it might seem, it'll be granted. That's the deal. You can wish for riches far beyond the wildest dreams of avarice, and they'll be yours. Or you can wish for your dreams to come true, for your grandest fantasies to be realized right here in the real world, in flesh and blood and stone, and that'll happen too. You could even wish for the stars to start going out, one by one, until the sky is dark and the world is cold and dead, and that'd come about just like you wished it. The only provision the King of the Zindars put in place is that, whatever it is you wish for, it's got to be of your own free will that you're doing it. If someone else tries to force the person who's been selected as the lucky wisher to wish for something else, then that's a wish that won't come true, and the treasure of the Zindars will just lie there like an inert lump, dead to us forever."

She sighed, then resumed her tale.

"The King of the Zindars took this gift and sealed it in a magical casket, and his followers buried the casket in a place where no one left behind on Sagaria knew where it was. When the time is right, so the Zindars said to the Sagarians, there'll be a person who's as right as the time, and that person will find his footsteps – or *her* footsteps, true, dearie," Madame Zahnia added hurriedly to Viola, "that person will find his or her footsteps guided infallibly to where the magical chest of the Zindars lies in its Hiding Place of the Ages" – *you can hear those capital letters,* mused Sylvester – "and will know how to act wisely with the gift that is found there."

Madame Zahnia placed both of her front paws flat on the table and looked at each of her visitors' faces in turn.

"You can imagine how much those who are of base heart would give to get their hands on a power like that," she said portentously, "on the ultimate prize. It is lucky that so few believe the legend. It is *unlucky*, as I said, that one of those few is that villain, Cap'n Rustbane."

She paused once more to let the full import of her words sink in.

Sylvester replayed those last few words in his mind. "Those who *believe* in it, you said," he observed slowly. "Does that mean you yourself don't? Believe in it, I mean?"

Madame Zahnia cocked her head and looked at him out of one glinty eye, like a bird. "My, you're the sharp-eared young feller, aren't you just?"

Sylvester felt himself blushing. "Well, it's just that you . . . that you . . . well . . ." he found himself stammering.

"It's hocus pocus, isn't it?"

"It surely does sound like hocus pocus," he agreed. "A lost race from somewhere beyond the stars. A war that tore up the face of the world and stitched it back together again. A magical power that has to be sealed in a treasure chest. The power to make all your wishes come true. It sounds like the sort of thing our mothers tell us to make our eyes grow wide when we're too small to know any better. And yet . . ."

"And yet you're all prepared to believe it, aren't you?" said Madame Zahnia, her voice sounding kinder that it had at any time since they'd been brought to her.

Sylvester spread his paws. "I . . . I do."

She reached forward and patted the back of his forearm. "Good for you, young . . . *Sylvester*, wasn't it you said your name was?"

"Sylvester," he confirmed.

"The legend of the treasure chest of the Zindars," she said, her voice low as if she were confiding in him, "is one of those legends that's true only so long as you believe in it. For all those people who dismiss it as nothing more than a load of old baloney, something only the credulous would fall for, then sure enough there's nothing in it. It's just a fairy tale. They could be given a map that led them to the exact site where the casket is buried, and they could dig there for a thousand years and still not find anything – not unless they believed in the truth of the tale with all their heart. They'd be trying to get their hands on the gold at the end of the rainbow, because they don't truly believe in that either. But for someone who does believe in the Zindar gift, someone who has a kind of conviction they can't explain that the magical chest of the Zindars is out there somewhere just waiting to be discovered. For them it's a different story, a different story altogether. If they search for it they may find it. And if they find it, then the chances are they're the right person to have done so, just like the old king foretold. And in that case they're the one who can make the greatest wish there's ever been and see it come true.

"Which is why Deathflash – Rustbane – can't be the one to find it. There's no one who believes in the legend more than he does, so he fits the bill that way, all right. But the kind of thing he would wish for, the kind of fate he'd desire to see falling upon this world and all who dwell in it, why it doesn't bear thinking about. It'd be worse than your worst nightmares, wouldn't it, young feller?"

Again she patted the back of Sylvester's forearm in that maternal way.

He gulped. "Yes."

Madame Zahnia held his gaze a few heartbeats longer, and then fell back into her chair, chortling and chuckling so the ripples of fat in her face ebbed and flowed like ocean waves.

"And here you are believing me," she said, wiping a little white dot of spittle away from the corner of her mouth, "a well-educated librarian and assistant archivist who should know a whole lot better than to be listening to the maunderings of a daft old jungle charlatan. And I *am* a charlatan, Sylvester, let no one deceive you otherwise. The advice I give the people who come to me is usually based on things I see or I feel, or that I've learned over many, many years in this world. I spice up common sense, traditional medicine and a passel of good education that no one around here knows I have with a few words of voodoo mumbo jumbo here and there, and everyone thinks I'm the great Voodoo Priestess. Even young Rasco and Gasbag think that."

She thwacked Gasbag upside the head again, not because he'd done anything new to deserve it, but presumably as a matter of principle.

"At least, they *think* they think it. Deep down, what they know is that it's all hocus pocus. But it's hocus pocus that makes them happy and that's what they pay me for – pay me willingly, and shower honors and gifts upon me even when I don't want them. O' course, my advice would be every bit as good without the voodoo hocus pocus, but it wouldn't be so enjoyable for them to swallow, like a pill someone'd forgot to put the sugar coating on. I can see, young Sylvester, that you're one of the few that can do without the sugar coating. What you don't know, my lad, is how much o' what I just been telling you is true and how much is," she gestured expressively, "hocus pocus."

"Then all this," said Sylvester, nodding toward the impressive crystal ball in the middle of the table. "All this is just a ruse?"

Madame Zahnia shook her head firmly. "Oh, no. I didn't say that everything I do is a fraud. I do have a gift. The gift I have is being able to see the future. I can't always see it very well, and I can't always see it very far and without the help of my Revealer," she patted it affectionately. "There's times I can't see into the future at all, but the gift's there, all right, and it's as real as you and me."

Sylvester, who occasionally wondered idly if he did exist or whether life was actually an illusion, took her words at face value.

"And the future you've seen for us all is what?"

"That I can't tell you," the old mouse replied. "The only way you can find out what the future's going to hold for you is to live through it yourself."

"Well, that's not much use," exclaimed Viola. Clearly, she'd been keeping a lot of emotion pent up for far longer than she'd have liked, because her voice was uncomfortably loud in the confined space. "What's the use of being able to predict what's ahead if you can't tell anyone about it?"

Madame Zahnia grinned inscrutably. "It's better than nothing, ain't it?"

Sylvester knew that wasn't the real reply, but it was all Viola was going to get. While Madame Zahnia and Viola shared one of those conversations that goes round and round in circles without anyone expecting it to ever actually get anywhere, Sylvester tried to recall something he'd read in Cap'n Adamite's journal was nagging away at the back of his mind and for a few minutes he couldn't for the life of him put a finger on what it was. Then, with a little gasp of relief, he remembered. He could see the dead buccaneer's scrawl as clearly as if it had been there in front of him (rather clearer, in fact, because his imagination cleaned off a few of the ink smudges created by the dampness of the journal's hiding place). What Sylvester read was this:

The true location of the treasure?

Let me commit to writing no more than that it can be seen only through the fall of the Ninth Wave.

He waited for the next gap in the increasingly waspish exchanges between Viola and the old voodoo priestess, then said shyly, "Tell me, Madame Zahnia, if you'd be so kind, what's the Ninth Wave?"

Madame Zahnia seemed to freeze mid-breath. Viola could tell she'd been dismissed instantly from the old mouse's attention and pursed her lips angrily.

"The Ninth Wave?" said Madame Zahnia quietly. "And where would a young feller like yourself have been hearing about that, eh?"

Sylvester looked evasively from side to side. Somehow he didn't think it'd be right to tell a near stranger about Cap'n Adamite's secret journal. "It was just in, er, idle chitchat, you know. Something I overheard in a bar one day. Can't think why it popped into my head just now."

It must be excruciatingly obvious that I'm lying, he thought. He dared a glance at Madame Zahnia and could see by the smile touching the corners of her mouth that she was seeing right through his clumsy subterfuge.

She chose, however, not to call him on the lie.

"The Ninth Wave," she said. "Ah, yes. It's a tale out of mythology, you know."

Now Madame Zahnia's the one who's lying, thought Sylvester, *and I'm the one seeing through her. She doesn't believe this is just a piece of mythology at all. She believes in it as much as she believes in the treasure of the Zindars, which is with everything she's got.*

The old seer was still talking.

"In everyday terms, there's the sailor's superstition that every ninth wave is bigger than the other eight, but I don't think that's what you mean. What the old myths say is that the boundaries of the mortal world are marked by a wall of . . . a wall of *something* that's called the Ninth Wave. On this side of the Ninth Wave, there's the world we know, and not just this world, but all the stars of the firmament too. On the far side of the Ninth Wave, though, ah, things are different there. That's the Otherworld, that is, on the far side of the Ninth Wave. It's where magic happens, and it's where the soul journeys in dreams, or after it's left behind this mortal realm."

And Cap'n Adamite believed the chest of the Zindars can be found only "through the fall of the Ninth Wave, thought Sylvester. *What in the name of goodness can he have meant by that? Did he mean the only way anyone can find the treasure is by dying first? But that wouldn't be much use, would it? Not a lot of fun having your wishes granted if you happen to be dead at the time.*

His confusion must have been written all over his face, because Madame Zahnia smiled at him sympathetically. "My answer hasn't been as helpful to you as you'd hoped, has it?"

"No."

"Answers have a habit of doing that," she said. "Especially the answers to the most important questions of all. And especially when those answers come from the lips of an old charlatan voodoo woman you ought to have better sense than to ask questions of in the first place. No?"

There wasn't any malice in her teasing, and Sylvester grinned back at her. "I expect you could tell us more if you really wanted to."

Her face grew serious. "No, I couldn't. It's like my telling you about what your future holds. I can tell you only so much. After that, it's something you have to find out for yourselves. I'm sorry, but that's the way it is."

Madame Zahnia suddenly clapped her forepaws together. "Now, it's getting late and you've a long journey behind you. You people must be tired and, if you're not, this old voodoo woman most certainly is. These pesky scamps of grandchildren it's been my evil luck to inherit will sort you out somewhere to sleep, and some good food to put in your bellies before that."

She turned a stern eye on Rasco.

"Hop to it, brat."

"Okey-dokey, surely I will, Madame Zahnia, oh mighty one, mistress of all the known universe. You can rely on your Rasco to—"

She aimed a half-hearted blow at his head. "Less of your impertinence, rascal."

Sylvester wasn't really listening to her. "Sometimes I wish," he began, speaking really to himself, "sometimes I wish it wasn't me all this was happening to but someone else. It'd have been easier if I'd never set eyes on that map."

Old she might be, but there was nothing wrong with Madame Zahnia's hearing.

"Don't talk tripe, Sylvester."

"What?"

"Tripe. Don't talk it. You're not a fool, so don't make yourself out to be one."

"Eh?"

"Throw a stone into the pond."

Sylvester looked around him. "There isn't a pond."

The fat old mouse rolled her eyes expressively. "Pretend there's a pond, dimwit. Do I have to explain everything to you?" She saw Sylvester looking down at his paw and added, "And pretend there's a stone as well."

"You want me to throw a stone that isn't here into a pond that isn't here?"

"You're a bit slow to catch on, young feller, but you get there in the end. Yes, that's exactly what I mean. Now, go ahead and toss your stone."

A little self-consciously, Sylvester mimed lobbing a pebble. "Splash," he said.

"Well, at least you didn't miss the pond altogether," said Madame Zahnia with a mock sourness. "Now, look at the ripples."

"I'm looking at the ripples."

"See them?"

"As clearly as I see you."

"All right, Sylvester, what I want you to do now is stop those ripples."

He took a half-pace forward, as if to the edge of the imaginary pond, then looked at her in bafflement. "What do you mean?"

"The surface of the pond is all covered in ripples because of the stone you threw in. I'm just asking you to make that surface smooth again."

"But I can't do that," he cried, his brow furrowing in mystification. What was the voodoo lady trying to tell him? "If I tried to get rid of the ripples, all I'd do was make more ripples, and more ripples on top of that. Every attempt of mine would just make the surface . . . ripplier."

"Exactly," said Madame Zahnia. "And that's how it is with life, too. The only way you can stop the ripples is not to throw the stone in the first place. But you've already thrown the stone – or discovered the map, it's the same thing really. You can't go back and change that. So, you're just going to have to live with the ripples until time makes the surface smooth."

"I've got to live with the consequences of my own past, you mean?" said Sylvester.

"Exactly. Like it or lump it, you've started along a road you're going to have to stay on until you reach its end. These good companions of yours" – Madame Zahnia indicated Viola and Mrs. Pickleberry, who were watching all that was going on as if it were a theatrical play – "they could abandon the route if they wanted to. But—"

Viola grabbed Sylvester's arm. "Who said anything about abandoning? We're all in this together."

Madame Zahnia stared at her. "You're certain of that?"

"Yes."

"Me too," chipped in Mrs. Pickleberry. "If I don't keep me peepers on those two there's no telling what they might get up to they shouldn't oughter."

"You're a mother after my own heart, Daphne," said Madame Zahnia warmly. "Now, as I said, I'm tired even if you three aren't. Let Rasco and Gasbag look after you, and don't eat the mango they offer you for your supper, even though Gasbag'll tell you it's perfectly fresh. He's been trying to get rid of it for a month now." Madame Zahnia waved them away carelessly. "Now, be gone with you."

BETRAYAL, DOUBLECROSS . . . AND WORSE

here was a monkey chattering directly outside his window. Sylvester propped himself up on one elbow and looked around him through blurry eyes. Last night, he'd slept better than he could remember doing in years, and certainly since leaving Foxglove. There'd been something about the combination of the heavy and surprisingly good meal their hosts had served up, then a bed made of a heap of mats and cushions, then the gentle rocking of his little hut all night long as the wind made the branches sway.

The only trouble was that he'd spent much of the night dreaming about Cap'n Rustbane, or at least of being back on board the *Shadeblaze* with Viola and Mrs. Pickleberry.

It must have been the motion of the branches making me think I was at sea, thought Sylvester crossly to himself, shaking his head to try to banish his dreams from his mind. He pushed the covers back and stretched his legs.

Someone threw something at the monkey, but it carried on chattering regardless. No wonder. Had it taken it into its mind to do so, the monkey could have easily killed a few of the mice, which were far smaller.

The mindless cacophony reminded Sylvester of something he'd heard last night as he was drifting off to sleep – or had it been another of his dreams? He'd heard – or imagined he'd heard – Madame Zahnia talking in quiet tones. He hadn't been able to estimate how far away she was – right outside his bedroom window or on a different branch altogether. In the stillness of the night, once all the mice and their guests were safely tucked up in bed, sounds were deceptive. Nor had he been able to make out any of the words Madame Zahnia had been speaking.

After a short while, the flow of words stopped altogether. There was the sound of wings fanning the night air, then silence.

He shook his head again and smiled ruefully to himself.

There was a scrabbling noise as the monkey suddenly shut up and scampered away through the foliage, attracted by the prospect of food, perhaps, or by another of its kind.

Sylvester breathed easier. The mice had told him not to worry about the monkeys, that the monkeys were trained not to harm anyone in the settlement, but even so Sylvester couldn't make himself trust long-legged, long-tailed creatures. They were *big* monsters, and their teeth were sharp.

Thinking about sharp white teeth made him think again of Cap'n Terrigan Rustbane.

He shuddered.

I wish I hadn't done that.

There was no sign of Viola or Mrs. Pickleberry, but someone had left a dish on the floor for him with a couple of bright red berry-like fruit on it. They tasted like sugar dusted with cinnamon, he discovered rapidly, and he wished his unknown benefactor had left him more.

A few minutes later he was standing at the bottom of the rope ladder, his hand in Viola's. She and her mother had been waiting down there with Madame Zahnia, Rasco and Gasbag. The plan, they explained to Sylvester when he'd appeared, was for Rasco and Gasbag to guide them to a port on the far side of the island, Skull Cove. Once there, with luck, they could stowaway on one of the merchant ships that, despite the constant threat of piracy, plied their trade in these waters.

"Now, my friends," said Madame Zahnia, all the bangles and gewgaws on her arms jangling discordantly as she adjusted her headdress, "it is time for us to be saying our goodbyes to each other."

Each of the lemmings leaned down so Madame Zahnia could embrace them around the neck. Her perfume seemed even heavier than it had last night, when it had been almost suffocating in the confines of her house.

Sylvester was the last of the lemmings she hugged and, once she'd done so, she looked at him earnestly.

"I wish," she told him, "there was something more I could give you as you leave Ouwinju than just the advice my Revealer relayed to you yesterday." She shrugged. "But that's the way my gifts work."

Her voice became so bleak and sympathetic that Sylvester stared at her, trying to read the meaning behind the words.

"Always remember," she was saying, "that the true path is seldom the one you'd like it to be, even though it's the one that leads you home quickest and safest. You still have much to do, Sylvester Lemmington, and many lives depend on you completing those important tasks correctly. Believe me when I tell you I'm acting in your best interests."

Sylvester wrinkled his forehead. *What in heck is she trying to tell us?*

"Uh, thanks, I guess," he said.

"You would do well to remember my words, all three of you, even though it may be hard to believe them in the days to come."

Sylvester felt his hackles rising. There was something very . . . amiss going on here.

"Thank you, Madame Zahnia," Viola said, her suspicions evidently unaroused. "Thank you for everything."

"You're welcome," said Madame Zahnia, pleasantly enough. "There's something else you should know. There may come a time when one of you has to make the greatest sacrifice of all, when one of you has to close the circle."

Everybody looked at the old seeress, expecting her to explain herself, but her lips remained closed.

"What do you mean?" said Sylvester at last.

"You'll find out soon enough," was all the answer Madame Zahnia gave him.

Rasco and Gasbag were looking at her in just as much confusion as the lemmings.

"What's you talking about, *grandmère?*" Rasco began. "It seems to me you—"

There was a sudden turmoil in the undergrowth.

"Ah, there you are!" said a dreadedly familiar voice. "Good to meet you again, Lemmington. So tiresome of fate to have pulled us apart the way it did, what?"

Sylvester looked up. Standing over him, a big grin on his face, was the one person he'd hoped never again to meet in his life.

"Rustbane!" he gasped.

"That'll be *Cap'n* Rustbane to you, my lad. Cap'n *Terrigan* Rustbane. You could add a few respectful words about me being the Scourge of the Seven Seas and the like, if you felt like being a little bit extra-courteous. No? I can see that my appeals for gentlemanly etiquette are lost on you. So sad. Maybe a few dozen lashes with the cat-o'-nine-tails will persuade you to pay a little more attention to social decorum. *Seize her, boyos!"*

The last cry was directed toward a bevy of his thugs, who'd come crashing out of the bushes behind him. Obediently, they leaped as one upon Mrs. Pickleberry,, who'd been threatening to do serious damage to their skipper with Elvira.

"Now, where was I?" said Rustbane a few moments later, when the din of the scrum on top of Mrs. Pickleberry had died down a little. "Ah, yes, I was dwelling upon the delightful prospect of watching Sylvester's miserable little furry hide being sliced to shreds by the cruel claws o' the nine-tailed cat."

Sylvester tuned the pirate's gloating out.

He looked at Madame Zahnia. The old, gaudily dressed mouse was standing there, her hands knitted in front of her copious breast, the rolls of fat on her throat overflowing the neck of her bright pink dress, her eyes closed as if the last thing in the world she wanted to see was Sylvester's accusatory glare.

When finally she spoke, it was in a voice entirely unlike any they'd heard from her before.

"Here's yer prey, Deathflash. I'd a trussed 'em up all neat and tidy fer ya, but there din't seem no need, wus there? Leastwise, that's what this old jungle priestess thought."

Madame Zahnia cackled like a she-devil and danced a little caper where she stood.

"If a fish coulda keep him mout' shut, it would neva get itself caught," she said with a further burst of shrill hilarity.

Cap'n Rustbane joined her laughter.

And now Madame Zahnia *did* open her eyes.

She stared straight at Sylvester, who stared straight back into the depths of her gaze.

What he saw there was an emotion entirely different from that in her voice or her words, or on her face. He saw what he could describe only as a frozen ocean, infinitely deep, eternally chill. There was sadness there, and pleading and a wisdom that seemed to belong not to any living creature but to come from somewhere far beyond all mortal understanding. It was, he realized, making a sudden intuitive leap, the wisdom of the Zindars, which had not disappeared from Sagaria when that ancient race had left but passed down from one Sagarian to another, preserved in such unlikely frames as that of a fat old mouse with atrocious taste in dress isolated in the middle of nowhere on a pirate-infested island. The Zindars had left behind two treasures, not just one. And who was to say which was more valuable?

Sylvester heard once more those enigmatic words of Madame Zahnia, spoken just a few moments ago, "Believe me when I tell you I'm acting in your best interests. You would do well to remember my words, all three of you, even though it may be hard for you to believe them in the days to come."

He nodded almost imperceptibly to the voodoo mouse and she nodded back. He thought he could detect, just for an instant, the hint of a smile in her gaze.

Then it was gone. She was the cruel mistress once more, the turncoat who'd sold them out to their pursuers.

"But here's a fish can't keep his mouth shut," said Cap'n Rustbane, beaming. He gestured, and two of his crewmen stepped behind Sylvester and started hobbling his legs. Out of the corner of his eye, Sylvester saw that Viola was being similarly tied. Nearby, Rasco and Gasbag were staring at their grandmother in complete shock. It was obvious this betrayal, if betrayal it truly was, was as much of a surprise to them as to the lemmings.

"How could you do this, Grandma?" said Gasbag, looking as if he was about to burst into tears. "How could you do this to our friends?"

"Never trust an old voodoo witch further than you can throw her," Cap'n Rustbane explained. "It's a maxim that'll guide you well in the future. Now get lost, small fry, unless you want to join your friends aboard my merry pirate vessel?"

The two younger mice melted into the undergrowth, so that within a moment it was as if they'd never been there.

"I thought so," said Cap'n Rustbane, picking at his teeth with a long curved thorn.

He took off his feathered hat and bowed deeply to Madame Zahnia. "I have you to thank for the successful conclusion of this search, my lady," he said. "Believe me, it is not something I shall forget early. Cap'n Terrigan Rustbane is well aware of how deeply he is in your debt, and be assured he will return the favor at some not-too-distant time."

Madame Zahnia gave an awful leer that was at least ninety-five percent scarlet lipstick. Sylvester, by now so well-bound he could hardly breathe, thought she was blushing. "Oh, go on with you, you old rogue," she said.

Cap'n Rustbane became businesslike, moving briskly around the clearing at the base of the rope ladder and issuing crisp orders to his henchmen. Mrs. Pickleberry had incapacitated five of them before being eventually overpowered, so arrangements had to be made to carry injured personnel as well as herself – the only way the pirates had been able to subdue her had been by beating her unconscious. One of them, Jeopord, was wearing her rolling pin in his belt as if it were an extra sword. Sylvester could detect no trace in the gap-toothed ocelot's demeanor of the treachery he was planning against his skipper.

At last, they were ready to depart for the long march back to Hangman's Haven.

"See ya soon, big boy," was the last they heard of Madame Zahnia.

Sylvester glanced back down the path along which he was being poked and prodded by his captors. The old fat mouse was standing beneath the treetop settlement of Ouwinju, which had become unnaturally still, as if the mice who dwelled there were horrified by their elder's perfidy. She was waving a large red and white-spotted handkerchief after them.

❖ ❖ ❖ ❖

Sylvester had no idea how much time had passed when the lemmings became aware from the rocking of the floor beneath them that the *Shadeblaze* was making its way out of Hangman's Haven.

The trek back from Ouwinju had been a nightmare of savage heat, exhausted muscles, and merciless lashing by the low branches and twigs that seemed to search out the captives as they stumbled along in the midst of the scoffing pirates. Once they'd reached the harbor, they'd been led immediately down into the deepest bowels of the corsair vessel. Deeper, deeper and yet deeper, until it seemed for sure they must burst through the planking of the *Shadeblaze*'s hull and emerge in the cold, murky water beneath. Instead, they'd been hurled into a cabin barely large enough for the three of them that smelled of stagnant water, mildewed timber, and rancid, well, best not to think of what it was that had gone rancid.

Mrs. Pickleberry had been unconscious but, after they'd been sitting there in the pitch darkness for an indefinite period, Sylvester and Viola heard her pull herself up off the soggy floor.

"Are you all right, Mom?"

Mrs. Pickleberry hawked and spat a few times before replying. When she did speak it was in a voice almost unrecognizable. "I'll be even better when I've nailed that blasted mouse's hide to the wall. With the blasted mouse still in it."

"Er, Madame Zahnia, you mean?" said Sylvester. He could hear Viola shuffling on her rear across the cabin floor to put her arm around her mother's shoulders.

"Who else? Viola, get your nose out of my ear, drat you, you clumsy chit."

"Mo–*om*." Threateningly.

"O' course I mean that fatty Madame Zahnia," continued Mrs. Pickleberry, clearly addressing Sylvester now. "Who else d'you think I mean? Though I reckon her hideous little grandsons are as bad as she is any day, if you give 'em the chance."

Tripping over his words, Sylvester tried to explain to her what he'd seen after Mrs. Pickleberry had vanished beneath a punching and grunting pile of pirates. "The two young mice were as dismayed by what she'd done as any of us. Besides . . ." He paused. How to explain in the darkness to a doubtless skeptical Daphne Pickleberry the expression he'd observed in the old voodoo priestess's eyes?

The odd thing was that, knowing all this, there was a part of him that still agreed with Mrs. Pickleberry. The knife of betrayal was still turning its blade remorselessly in his gut. He wanted to punch someone, and the only suitable candidates seemed to be the three mice.

Except, of course, they were countless miles away in the middle of the jungle, doubtless swinging happily along their rope bridges and sparing not a moment's thought for the three hapless lemmings who'd been delivered into the ruthless paws of the pirate.

"It could be worse," Viola was saying to her mother. "We're all still in one piece, aren't we?"

But for how long? thought Sylvester despairingly. He remembered all too clearly the promises Cap'n Rustbane had made to put a painful end to his life, and it was unlikely that Cap'n Rustbane's memory on the matter was any worse than Sylvester's own. And Cap'n Rustbane had never struck Sylvester as the kind of individual who failed to follow through on his promises.

"What was that you said?" Viola asked him sharply.

"Nothing, I just gulped."

"But you gulped very expressively."

"I did?"

"Is there something you're trying to tell us?"

Yes, there was, but at the same time he couldn't tell them. He couldn't tell them it had been criminal of him to allow them to accompany him on this madcap escapade. Most particularly, he'd been a fat-headed imbecile to let them, when they'd finally escaped from Rustbane's clutches, be captured once again. He tried to draw some reassurance from what Madame Zahnia had told them yesterday when she'd been reading the messages her Revealer showed her: that a successful result depended on all of them following the course of action that had already, somewhere, somehow, sometime, been predetermined and that this course of action might often seem to them to be doomed. If there was ever a situation that seemed doomed, Sylvester reflected sadly, now was it. But this might have been exactly what Madame Zahnia's Revealer was referring to.

Or she might be just a mad old mouse who'd sell her soul to the highest bidder, in which case . . .

Sylvester gulped again and hoped it wasn't as loud as the last time.

He didn't like to think about that "in which case."

"She could have poisoned us, you know," said Viola, sounding as if she were trying to sound cheerful.

"True," said Sylvester.

"Just about did, that supper they fed us," mumbled Mrs. Pickleberry. There was still something odd about the way she was speaking.

"Or," said Viola, "turned us into something. You know, something voodooish."

"She could," said Sylvester. "Except it was all mumbo jumbo. She told us so herself."

"You think it really was?"

"Of course." Sylvester wasn't at all sure it had been nonsense, but he decided the best way to reassure Viola and Mrs. Pickleberry was to pretend he was. "Always remember that the true path," he said, his voice warbling in a passable imitation of Madame Zahnia's, "is seldom the most likeable but it most often leads you home."

"You're bad," said Viola, beginning to giggle.

"Bloody awful, you ask me," said Mrs. Pickleberry.

They didn't.

Viola's giggling was infectious and soon, Sylvester found himself rolling around in the fetid bilgewater that covered the floor of this dungeon. With each new whoop of laughter that came out of him, Viola's laughter too became more uncontrollable. He knew there was more than a touch of hysteria in the way they were behaving, but he didn't care. It had been far too long since either of them had just let themselves go like this.

Mrs. Pickleberry was unamused. "Kids!"

When they finally calmed, Viola and Sylvester were leaning against each other, shoulder to shoulder. Neither knew how they'd managed to find each other in the dark, but they had. Sylvester thought it must be an omen or something – a sign they were meant to be together, whatever adversities life threw in their path.

"Are you thinking what I'm thinking?" he said to Viola.

"Quite probably," she said. "But unfortunately, my mother's here."

"I'm not deaf, you two!" roared Mrs. Pickleberry.

That set the pair of them off laughing again.

"You know what?" said Viola.

"What?"

"We make a pretty good team, you and me."

"We do?" said Sylvester, as if this were the most astonishing news in the world.

Mrs. Pickleberry coughed.

"And you too, Mom," said Viola quickly.

"Right."

"We're the most fearsome lemmings on all the Seven Seas," Viola continued.

"I don't think that's a particularly difficult status to achieve," said Sylvester. "For all we know, we're the only lemmings on the Seven Seas. The rest of our kind are probably still back at home in Foxglove."

"What about everybody who's thrown themselves over the Mighty Enormous Cliff?" interposed Mrs. Pickleberry. "What about them, eh?"

"True, true," said Sylvester evasively. Now was not the time to explore his theory that all of those brave lemmings had dived not to glory, but to their deaths.

"Even if they are sailing the Seven Seas somewhere," said Viola, "we're still the most fearsome, aren't we?"

Sylvester, his arm around her shoulders as she nestled against him, pulled her to him even more tightly.

"It's just that . . ." he began, then let the words trail away.

"Just that what?"

"Um."

"What is it with men and words? Spit it out, you idiot."

"Well, ah . . ."

"C'mon."

Sylvester thanked his lucky stars their prison was completely lightless so Viola couldn't see his face. He knew for a fact he was blushing. Blushing badly. Blushing redly. Blushing every which way a fellow could possibly blush.

Oh, *there* was a dreadful thought.

Was he blushing so luridly she could *see him in the dark*?

He couldn't hide his face in his paws, not under the circumstances. He'd feel such a fool if she found out what he was doing. Besides, one of his paws was otherwise occupied, being at the far end of the arm he'd placed around Viola's shoulders.

"You see—"

"See what?"

"Let me *finish*, will you? You're not helping."

"Oops. Sorry."

Was she laughing at him?

He took the plunge. "Look, Viola, it's nice of you to have faith in me as one of your 'most fearsome lemmings,' but I think you may have the wrong lemming. I mean, I may not be who you think I am."

"I hope you are."

"You do?"

"If you're not Sylvester Lemmington, then who's been cuddling me in the dark?"

"You're not taking this seriously."

"No, I'm not. You're starting to sound like a pompous oaf."

"I am?"

"You are," rasped Mrs. Pickleberry. "Worse than her father ever was, when he was your age, and believe me—"

"Mo–*om*!"

Mrs. Pickleberry's voice subsided into a froth of incomprehensible monosyllables.

His first attempt at taking the plunge having been thwarted, Sylvester decided to try again. "It's very *kind* of you to place such faith in me," he said solemnly, "but I really don't think I deserve it. I'm not a hero, you see, not anything like a hero at all. I'm just a humble little lemming assistant archivist who's scared stiff because he's strayed so far from home and . . ."

His voice petered out. The two Pickleberries had started speaking among themselves.

"Lor' love a duck."

"Where'd yer learn that sort of language, you saucy chit?"

"From you, Mom."

"Oh, right. Well, that's different."

"He's a dear but, if ever there's a cliché going by, trust Sylvester to throw a saddle over its back and ride it to extinction."

"He's still young. Maybe he'll improve. Could hardly get any worse, could he?"

"Mo–*om*, that's not fair and you know it!"

"Hmmf."

"Excuse me."

"Yes, Sylvester?"

"What do you mean about, about me and the clichés?"

"It's the oldest line in the book."

"What is?"

"The line about not feeling like a hero at all, being just an ordinary, fallible, weak, frightened milksop."

"That's me."

"It's what all the heroes say."

"They do?"

"Yes. They say, 'Oh, ai am such a pathetic lump of lard, not worth a monkey's cuss,' then they go out and slay a dragon or save the fair maiden, that sort of thing."

"Oh."

"Don't 'oh' me, Sylvester Lemmington. If any more proof was needed that you're a hero, you've just provided it."

"Out of the mouths of babes and numbnuts," confirmed Mrs. Pickleberry.

Sylvester wished she hadn't chosen this moment to agree with her daughter.

"So you think I should—" he said.

"Find a dragon? Yes."

"But it's pitch dark in here!" he said and chuckled.

"If there's a fire-breathing dragon somewhere around, it can't hold its breath indefinitely."

"What's that got to do with—oh, I see what you mean."

"Duh."

"But then we'd be toast."

"Shaddap!"

The forcefulness of Mrs. Pickleberry's sudden interruption startled both the others into silence.

Then they heard what she'd heard.

Footsteps.

Slow, heavy, dragging footsteps.

There was never good news to be had on the arrival of someone whose approaching footsteps sounded like this.

And approaching they most definitely were. Sylvester didn't notice when the pirates had brought them down here, but he was pretty certain this maritime dungeon they were in was the only possible destination in this particular bowel of the ship.

As if in answer to his thoughts, the footsteps came to a halt just a few feet from him, and there was the sound of someone fighting with a key that didn't want to turn in a rusty lock.

Finally, the newcomer, with a climactic volley of curses, succeeded in getting the lock's tumblers to cooperate.

There was a lot of heavy breathing and a little more swearing, then a dazzling vertical spear of yellow light as the cell's door creaked ajar by a claw's width.

"Cheesefang!" cried Viola.

The door opened fully.

It took longer for Sylvester's eyes to adapt than it had taken Viola's, but soon enough, he recognized the pot-bellied figure of the old sea rat. Cheesefang was fending off Viola, who apparently wanted to give him a big kiss of welcome.

"The Cap'n wants you lot. Up on the deck. Now."

Sylvester was obediently pulling himself to his feet when he glanced across at Mrs. Pickleberry. What he saw made him suck in his breath.

The damage she'd suffered in the skirmish with the pirates was far beyond anything he'd ever dreamed. No wonder her voice sounded peculiar. Her lips and chin were dark with dried blood and clotted fur. When she grimaced in a moment of silent pain, Sylvester could see gaps between her teeth – far too many gaps, and some of them still seemed to be bleeding.

"I'm sorry," he said to her quietly. "I hadn't realized."

She gave him a grin of such ghastliness he knew he'd see it in his dreams for years to come.

"Don't fret yerself, young Sylvester Lemmington, although I think the better of you for havin' thought to say it."

"Let me help you to your feet."

"No need. I'm on 'em already. But you could take the arm of an ol' biddy, if you'd like, just to save her from slippin' an' fallin'."

She stepped carefully across the wet floor to wrap her arm in his.

Viola had given up her attempts to welcome Cheesefang. Turning, she saw for the first time what had happened to her mother's face.

"*Mom!*"

"It's nothin', I tell you. There's not much you could do to this ol' mug of mine that wouldn't be an improvement, is there? You just ask your father."

Even Cheesefang seemed horrified. "I'm sure they didn't mean any harm, like," he muttered.

"Just take us to that pathetic scapegrace you're unlucky enough to have as your skipper," said Mrs. Pickleberry haughtily. Sylvester could feel the effort it cost her to draw herself up to her full height. "And look snappy about it, hear?"

⚓ ⚓ ⚓ ⚓

They found Cap'n Rustbane on the poop deck, standing with one foot on the boards and another on a small barrel, as if posing for a portrait. When he saw them approaching, he took off his hat and prepared to bow to Mrs. Pickleberry.

"Aw, stow it, buster," she told him.

The fox looked rather taken aback by the pre-emptive rebuff and said nothing for several seconds, instead staring out at a sea and sky so gray it was impossible to tell where one met the other.

"Your reaction, Three Pins, has made it easier for me to say to you three what I have to say," he said, turning back toward them at last.

"And that is?" Mrs. Pickleberry retorted.

"You'll have noticed none of you have yet been flayed alive."

"True."

"Hung from the highest yardarm."

"True again."

"Boiled in oil."

"Three out of three ain't bad."

"Keelhauled. Gutted."

"Still scorin' one hunnerd per cent."

"Far from slit, your gizzards are perfectly intact."

Sylvester felt it was time to contribute to the conversation. "Get on with it, Rustbane."

"That's *Cap'n* Rustbane to you, Lemmington." The pirate blew on the tip of his claws as if they'd suddenly heated up when he'd not been looking. "I'm so very, very disappointed in you."

"Good."

The gray fox arched his eyebrows as he shot a bolt of jade fury from those disturbing eyes of his. "Defiant to the last, eh?"

It was only then that Sylvester noticed the ship's carpenters had made an addition to the *Shadeblaze* while the lemmings had been incarcerated in the hull.

Jutting out over the water from the edge of the deck was a long, terrifyingly narrow piece of wood.

A plank.

Sylvester couldn't see the sea from where he and the others stood under the watchful eye of Cheesefang's rusty cutlass, but lemming instinct told him it was crowded with prowling sharks.

And he, Sylvester Lemmington from Foxglove, was going to be forced to walk along that plank and off the end, so that he plummeted into the mercilessly cold waters where, soon as anything, he'd be torn limb from limb by the mighty jaws of . . .

He shuddered.

Cap'n Rustbane chuckled. "I know what you're thinking, Sylvester Lemmington, and you got it all wrong. I ain't going to make you walk that plank, no sirree."

You're not? Oh, joy, joy, boundless joy!

"It's young Viola Pickleberry here I'm going to send along it," Cap'n Rustbane added.

WHAT?

"That is, unless you give me the coordinates I'm looking for," the pirate finished.

"You brute!" shrieked Viola.

Two of the crew, at a signal from their skipper, grabbed her.

Mrs. Pickleberry looked around her for some weapon she could use. There was none to be seen. The pirates had finally had the sense to confiscate her rolling pin and lock it inside Rustbane's cabin. Without it, she was nothing.

"You'll not get away with this, you f-fiend!" snarled Sylvester.

"Oh, yeah? And who's going to stop me. You, muscleboy? I think not."

"I'll . . . I'll—"

"Do what? Hold your breath and scream?"

"Don't fall into his trap!" Viola yelled, her voice half-muffled. She'd bitten deeply into the wrist of one of the pirates who'd been attempting to tie her up. It wasn't going to do her any good, but it was satisfying to hear the big stupid raccoon howling in agony. "It's a trap, Sylvester, I tell you, a trap!"

"I'm perfectly aware of that," said Sylvester, trying to sound calm. *A trap? Is it?*

"The moment he gets those coordinates out of you, he'll kill us all," Viola cried. Two of the pirates were arguing as to who should risk gagging her. Those little lemming teeth of hers had proven unexpectedly sharp. Meanwhile, the injured raccoon was leaning with his back against a lifeboat and trying to bandage his arm.

I suppose Rustbane could do that, thought Sylvester.

"But I won't let him," he said aloud.

"And what do you plan to do?" said Cap'n Rustbane. He'd produced a toothpick from one of his numberless waistcoat pockets and was casually putting it to use. He seemed amused rather than anything else.

Sylvester glared at him. "I'm not so stupid as to tell you in advance."

"Well, I'll tell you what you *could* do."

"What?" Any straw to grasp at.

"You could give me those coordinates and then we'd just forget the whole argument. How about that? It seems the easiest course to me."

"Don't let him trick you," shouted Viola. The two pirates had decided not to gag her after all.

"Don't worry." Sylvester gave what he hoped was a supercilious sneer. "I'm on top of this one."

Cap'n Rustbane smiled. "So you're going to give me those coordinates?"

Sylvester made a decision. He set his jaw. "Yes."

"You are?"

"I am. And after I've done that, you're going to set Viola and her mother here free. I want your word on that, your word as an old sea dog."

"Sea fox, to be precise. But, yes, I'll give you my word on that."

"Don't believe him, you nincompoop!" bellowed Viola. She was being forced out on to the plank by the two pirates, both of whom had drawn their cutlasses. The blades and points of the weapons looked horrifically sharp and horrifically close to Viola's exposed skin. Not that there was very much of it exposed. In their nervousness, the pirates had used about five times as much rope to bind her as was strictly necessary. She resembled nothing more than a windlass with a pair of feet sticking out the bottom and a head sticking out the top.

The ship rocked in the ocean swell and she teetered precariously on the plank.

"Don't believe him," she repeated, panic beginning to infect her voice. She glanced down at the waters beneath. Oddly enough, the sight seemed to calm her. "You can't trust the word of that monster. He'd sell his grandmother's soul for a pint of ale."

"A whole pint?" mused Cap'n Rustbane aloud. "You overestimate my love for dear old Grandma."

Viola staggered again.

A fresh crop of sweat broke out on Sylvester's brow.

"I'll tell you the coordinates," he said again.

"You will?" said Cap'n Rustbane, looking at him quizzically. "Even though you know you can't trust my promise further than you could throw it?"

"Even though I know I can't trust your promise further than ..." Sylvester ground to a halt. "Even though you're a lying sack of ... of ..." he amended.

"I'm so glad to hear it," said Cap'n Rustbane. He flipped the toothpick over his shoulder, and Sylvester lost sight of it as it went spiraling away over the deck rail into the ocean. In the same movement, it seemed, Rustbane produced from yet another waistcoat pocket a grubby piece of parchment and a pencil. He eyed the tip of the pencil critically, his eyes crossing as he held it up just in front of his nose.

"A bit blunt, if you ask me, but it should still be of service."

He scribbled for a moment on the parchment, then passed both it and the pencil to Sylvester.

"There, Lemmington. There you have the coordinates for where we are now, which, according to my calculations is exactly twenty knots due west of Cape Waste. I need to plot a course from here to the island where dear old Cap'n Adamite buried his treasure. You just write the coordinates of that island, as you remember them from the map, and we'll all be happy little sandpipers, won't we? Any attempts at delay or trickery, and your pudgy little sweetheart goes straight to the fishes, of course. And if you give me the wrong coordinates, thinking you should be able to find another chance of escape before I discover the deception, think again. You three furballs are going to be with me here on the *Shadeblaze* until the moment my spade, digging down into the sand, goes *thunk* on the top of Cap'n Adamite's chest. Are we understood on that?"

"We're understood on that," said Sylvester in a low voice.

"Then write down them coordinates!"

"Don't listen to him, Sylvester!"

Mrs. Pickleberry, who'd been uncharacteristically silent, pinned Cap'n Rustbane with a piercing stare. "If so much as a hair o' my daughter's hide gets harmed—"

"I assure you, Madame Three Pins, that not one of her hairs shall be harmed if only her tubby little paramour could get a move on and write down a simple string of numbers and letters for me." The gray fox spread his paws as if he were an actor appealing to some unseen gallery. "I ask you, what could be more innocuous than a few numbers and letters? They don't even join up together to make somebody's name."

"Be quiet," Sylvester snapped. "You're making it hard for me to concentrate."

The pirate made a big display of slapping his forehead and casting his gaze heavenward in shame for his own stupidity. "Oh, how enormously inconsiderate of me. What a knucklebrain I am. Of course you can't get the numbers and letters straight in your brain. You *do* have a brain, don't you? Just checking. Don't mind me. Where was I? Oh, yes, of course you can't get the numbers and letters straight in your mind if there's an empty-headed fox prattling on about inconsequentialities not half a yard from your earhole. How could you be expected to? It's a plain matter of common sen—"

"Shut up."

Shocked by the sudden authority in Sylvester's voice, Rustbane stopped talking.

"If you want your coordinates, keep your trap shut." Sylvester tried to focus his eyes on the sheet of parchment in front of him, but the numbers Rustbane had written seemed to be performing some madcap dance. The trouble was there'd been so much *more* on the original map than just the coordinates. In fact, it'd have been easier if Rustbane had asked him simply to draw the map.

"And get Viola off that plank right *now*."

Rustbane gestured to one of his crew, who lowered his cutlass and prepared to step on to the plank behind Viola.

"No," she said. Her voice was quiet but firm.

"Whaddya mean, no?" said the beaver who'd been sent to retrieve her.

"Don't come any farther."

"But the Skipper tol' me to."

"I don't care what your disgusting boss told you. Stay back."

The beaver looked over his shoulder to Rustbane for guidance. Before the gray fox could say anything, Viola spoke again.

"I've decided it's better for all concerned if I," she swallowed, "if I just . . . give myself to the waves."

These last words acted on Sylvester like a bucket of ice water thrown over him.

"Wh–what?" He gaped at her.

"If I'm gone," she said in Rustbane's direction, "there'll be no reason for Sylvester to give up the location of the treasure of the Zindars."

"Ahem," said Mrs. Pickleberry. No one paid her any attention.

"He can die in agony knowing it's for a good cause," Viola continued.

I can? thought Sylvester.

"Ahem," repeated Mrs. Pickleberry.

"You have something to contribute, Three Pins?" said Cap'n Rustbane, sticking his jaw out, a vicious glint coming into his green eyes.

"All this palaver ain't gettin' yer them map coordinates any faster, is it?"

"That's hardly my fault."

"Damn well is."

"Hmmf!"

"Get my daughter back off that plank, sit all three of us down somewhere comfy and give us a drink or three to relax us, then maybe young Sylvester'd be able to get his sorry apology for a brain in gear and give yer that info ye wants. Savvy?"

Cap'n Rustbane stroked his chin. "You may have a point. But the young, er, female seems not to want to be rescued from her watery fate. Does rather throw a spanner in your works, don't you think?"

"Then I'm goin' with her."

"Me too," said Sylvester.

The fox raised a paw. "Not you, Lemmington. By the nose of the triple-breasted goddess, any dying you're going to do is going to be considerably nastier than getting eaten alive by sharks. But I'm tempted to let Three Pins here have her chance as a shark snack."

Mrs. Pickleberry pre-empted him by pushing her way past the crewmen who'd been set to guard her and joining her daughter on the plank. Like Viola, she looked surprisingly cheerful in the face of imminent death.

"Look, you two, you don't have to do this," Sylvester yelled. "I'll give him the coordinates!"

"It's no use," Viola said. "We escaped once, and Rasco came to our aid. But lightning doesn't strike twice. To escape a second time from the cunning Cap'n Terrigan Rustbane? The very idea's preposterous."

"Farewell, cruel world," said Viola, rolling her eyes toward the sky. Quite deliberately, she stepped off the plank and vanished.

Cap'n Rustbane took off his hat and pressed it to his breast as he regarded the empty space where Viola had just been. He sighed. "So young to die. But at least she was able to call her mother. Someone tell Bladderbulge that from now on Viola's breakfast rations should be added to my plate."

"You monster!" said Sylvester.

"Perhaps," said Mrs. Pickleberry with a leer, "one o' these days you sewer rats will come to understand me."

With a bob of her head and a shake of an imaginary rolling pin at them, she too stepped off the plank.

Sylvester dropped the sheet of parchment. The ship around him and the surly, threatening pirates disappeared as his eyes filled with tears. Even though, a moment before, he'd been convinced Viola knew what she was doing, that she'd become aware of some way out of the impasse – other than going to a watery grave, it didn't reduce the tide of grief that hit him. So far as he could tell, she was gone. She could be dead or even worse, at this very moment suffering a hideous death as savage sharks fought over her limbs.

He threw himself down on the deck and let out a high, keening wail.

"By the beard of the triple-breasted goddess," swore Cap'n Rustbane. "I do so *hate* it when they blub."

"Aye, aye, Skipper," said Jeopord, looking down at Sylvester as if he'd discovered something on the underside of his shoe.

"And I hate it also," added Cap'n Rustbane, his voice rising, "when my captives despatch themselves. Where's the fun in that, I ask you?"

Sylvester started sobbing even harder, even though he was thinking fast. From the way Viola and Mrs. Pickleberry had behaved while casting themselves off the plank—

But any further thoughts he might have had along those lines were interrupted by a cry from far above, a cry from the bat who dangled from the crow's nest and scanned the horizon with a dilapidated telescope.

"Ship ahoy!" yelled the bat, pointing a wing. "Ship ahoy!"

A Ship of Her Majesty's Fleet

veryone looked upward to where the bat hung, even Sylvester. The shriek of the bat froze the tears in his eyes.

"Ship ahoy!" the lookout cried a third time.

"What the dev—" Cap'n Rustbane began, then interrupted himself. "Give me an eyeglass, damn you, Jeopord."

Obediently, the Mate passed over a copiously scratched brass telescope. Rustbane grabbed it and leaped round the forecastle to the far side of the *Shadeblaze*, the direction the bat's wing indicated. The other crewmen who'd been attending their skipper at the plank followed him.

Left alone for the moment, Sylvester got to his feet, dusted himself off and went to peer over the side of the vessel at the gray waters beneath. All he could see were the eddies of the *Shadeblaze*'s own motion. But something told him that Viola and Mrs. Pickleberry were somehow all right. He didn't know why he should be so certain of this, he just was.

He rubbed his forepaws together, then scuttled after Cap'n Rustbane and the rest.

"Well, smack me in the gob for sixpence," the cap'n was saying when Sylvester reached the group on the far side of the ship. The gray fox was holding Jeopord's telescope to his eye and, to judge by the expression on his face, positively glaring through it.

It wasn't hard to work out why the pirate was so incensed. Less than a mile away there was another ship, larger and in better shape than the *Shadeblaze*. Even from here, without the aid of the telescope, Sylvester could make out the banner flying proudly from the top of the new ship's mainmast. The design on the banner was of two lions rearing up on either side of a shield. Below the shield was a scroll with writing on it that Sylvester couldn't make out; above the shield were two crossed swords.

"Damn," muttered Cap'n Rustbane. "Damn, damn and double-damn twice over."

"We'll sink her, take whatever booty she carries and be on our way," said Jeopord casually. "What's so difficult about that?"

"What's difficult—" Rustbane began, then took a very, very deep breath before starting again. "What's *difficult*, as'd be obvious to anyone who didn't have guano for brains, is that ship, that *other* ship," he pointed dramatically, "is only the blasted *Queen of Spectram*'s ship, isn't it?"

"Ah," said Jeopord.

Sylvester nodded, as if to himself. He'd read much about the Queen of Spectram in the archives back in Foxglove. There were even whole books dedicated to her kingdom, and her predecessors on the throne there. Spectram was probably the most powerful and important kingdom in the whole of Sagaria. No other nation would be willing to stand against the Spectram army. In addition, the kingdom also had a navy, whose main task was to police the seaways, and it must be one of the ships of that navy which had gotten onto the trail of the *Shadeblaze*.

The lemming grinned inwardly. This could be the end of his captivity, his and the Pickleberries'. The Spectram crew would doubtless be only too willing to return the hostages to their home.

If, he thought, sobering, *Viola and Mrs. Pickleberry are still alive.*

Turning and lowering the eyeglass, Cap'n Rustbane saw Sylvester standing there. "Well, what in tarnation are you doing here?"

Sylvester couldn't think how to answer.

Luckily, he didn't have to, because Cap'n Rustbane spun impatiently on his heel and began striding away down the deck, the little band of sailors fluttering along behind him like the train of a bridal dress. Shrugging, Sylvester followed too.

"Is they after us, Skipper?" puffed Cheesefang, struggling to keep up.

"Whatever gave you *that* idea?" responded Rustbane sarcastically over his shoulder. "No, of course they're not! They were just sailing along on a honeymoon cruise in the middle of waters where there are more pirates than sharks, and they thought it might be friendly to invite us over for afternoon tea. Why the devil do you *think* they're here, you nincompoop?"

"Because . . . ah, seein' as you phrase it like that . . ."

Jeopord sneered at the rat, then addressed himself to the Cap'n. "They looked well armed," he observed.

"More than well armed," agreed Rustbane tersely, coming to an abrupt halt. It was only by dint of some energetic gymnastics that the others didn't go caroming off the back of him as he leaned once more against the rail and raised the telescope to his eye. "She has cannon up and down both sides of her, three levels of 'em, and all manned by plenty of Her Majesty's loyal subjects, I'll have no doubt. Hooks and grapples a-plenty too. I can see it all from here. We've a pretty fight ahead of us, mateys, I can tell you that. If we weren't the most courageous, blackheartedest pirate crew that ever sailed the seas, I'd be betting we'd be at the bottom of the ocean by nightfall. As it is, my hearties, it'll be the queen's men who're breathing with the fishes tonight."

His heavy laugh sounded a bit forced to Sylvester.

"We're all awaiting your commands, Cap'n," said Jeopord smoothly. There was something in the ocelot's voice that made Sylvester pay special attention to him. Surely it couldn't be possible that the treacherous First Mate had drawn the Spectrum vessel down upon them?

Cap'n Rustbane cackled again. "My dear friend and loyal shipmate, Jeopord," he said, "I've got a little something special for these lubbers this time, a little surprise that'll have them ruing their decision to put on clean underwear this morning."

Jeopord grinned back at him. "And this would be?"

"Just keep our course the way it is and let them catch up – but slowly, *slow-ell-ee*, mind, so it don't look to them as if we're doin' it deliberate, like. We want 'em to think that they're catching us because of their own skill in pursuit. We're setting a trap for them, you see, with ourselves as the bait."

The ocelot's eyes gleamed. "Understood, Skip."

"And while you're doing that, dear Jeopord, I'll be preparing my little surprise."

"Aye, aye, Cap'n."

"You two," said Cap'n Rustbane to a pair of rats, "Thickskull and Sneezeball, come with me and help me get things ready to teach those navy troopers a lesson."

He swirled his cloak about him and was just about to make an exit when his eye fell once more on Sylvester.

"As for you, Lemmington, you and I will resume where we left off, once I've sent all these soldier-boyos to the tender mercies of the waves. If you show yourself willing to fight bravely alongside my crew, perhaps I'll take pity on you and spare you a lingering death."

With that, he was gone.

✦ ✦ ✦ ✦ ✦

Slowly, the *Specter of Justice*, the great three-masted ship of the Queen of Spectrum, drew closer to the pirate vessel and then abreast of it. The distance between the ships as they sailed alongside each other was short enough that

Sylvester felt he could have hurled a stone across to the Spectram crew, whom he could see manning their various stations about the deck.

Two ships more different in appearance it would have been hard to find. The *Shadeblaze* was a scruffy denizen of the sea. Every part of her looked as if it had been patched and repatched a dozen times or more, and even then was kept from falling apart more by faith than by reason. Even so, she gave the impression of being a tough tyke of a vessel, one you wouldn't choose to pick a fight with. The *Specter of Justice*, by contrast, was immaculately tidy. Gazing at her, it was hard not to be reminded of the auditorium of some splendid theater, with galleries rising above galleries, all gilt paint and polished brass. This impression was enhanced by her officers, who were resplendent in their own right. Their uniforms were a dark salmon pink in color, trimmed wherever there was an edge to trim with impeccable gold braid. Brightly hued cockades ascended above their hats and swayed in the sea breeze. The hats themselves were shaped like upended soup tureens and seemed to be made of black velvet. Even the crew, scurrying hither and thither, were smartly attired – unlike their counterparts aboard the *Shadeblaze*, who couldn't have cared less about their appearances and often had to be reminded to dress themselves at all.

The Junior Archivist and Translator of Ancient Tongues within Sylvester yearned to be a part of the complement of the *Specter of Justice*, where everything and everybody seemed to know its correct place, rather than here aboard the *Shadeblaze* with its captain and crew of villains and cutthroats and its air of dilapidation and decay.

He sighed. Maybe after this battle was over . . .

Of course, the fact that the personnel aboard the *Specter of Justice* appeared to be human made it less than likely a lemming would be welcome.

The Spectram vessel was certainly the bigger of the two, and it looked to be the better equipped and armed, so there was every reason to think it would triumph in any encounter.

For the first time, it crossed Sylvester's mind that he might not survive the imminent battle. That, though innocent, he could all too easily be caught in the crossfire between the two hostile forces.

And how do I feel about that happening? he thought, leaning against the deck rail and gazing at his opposite numbers on the *Specter of Justice* with what he hoped they'd interpret as a friendly expression. *If it's the truth that Viola is dead, then how much does it matter to me that I might die too? The old superstitions say we live on after death in a better and happier place. If that's the case, then dying may be the only way for me to be reunited with her, and dying here would be the quickest and easiest way to bring that about. But no one with a lick of sense believes that sort of codswallop. When I go I'll . . . go. All I've got to look forward to is an eternity of nothingness.*

He brought himself up short, then resumed his musings. *Besides, I'm convinced Viola's still alive. As she dropped off the side of the ship she looked like she was starting out on some amazing prank, not as if she were going to her doom. And the same with her mother, although it's harder to tell with Mrs. Pickleberry – what with her face looking the way it does, beaten up by those bastards back at Ouwinju. It's enough to turn milk to cheese even at the best of times.*

He found that, despite the awfulness of the situation, he was smiling. If Mrs. Pickleberry could get even a hint of what he was thinking, he'd be picking rolling-pin splinters out of his skull for months.

Cap'n Rustbane had reappeared on deck while Sylvester had been lost in his thoughts.

The gray fox's timing could not have been better.

"Ahoy there, *Shadeblaze!*" came a voice across the water.

The voice sounded oddly thin as it competed with the brisk sea wind. Sylvester glanced over at the other vessel and saw that one of the Spectram officers had raised a big silver megaphone to his lips.

"Ahoy there in the name of the Queen of Spectram!"

The gray fox cupped his hands in front of his mouth. "You want me to tell you where you can put your ahoy?"

The officer lowered his megaphone and spoke briefly and inaudibly to the people around him. Whatever they decided it was impossible to tell, because when he hailed the *Shadeblaze* again it was simply to call "ahoy!" once more.

"Darned idiots!" snarled Cap'n Rustbane to Jeopord, beside him. "Whimpering little lapdogs. All of them doing what their mommy tells them. Impale me on my own mizzen if I ever *look* like doing the bidding of a woman."

Sylvester reflected that he wasn't the only one lucky to be out of Mrs. Pickleberry's earshot.

"We have a warrant for your arrest, Terrigan Rustbane," came the officer's voice again.

"You hear that noise like crossbones rattling?" called Cap'n Rustbane. "That's me knees, shaking in terror!"

"Prepare yourselves for boarders, *Shadeblaze!*"

Cap'n Rustbane put his paw to his mouth and made a great show of gnawing his claws in fear. "An' how're you planning to do the boarding, eh, my hearties? Swing across here like a bunch of monkeys? Grappling hooks and ropes? You'll all find yourselves swimming if you try that!"

"Cease your parlay, *Shadeblaze*. I repeat, prepare for boarders!"

Sylvester began wondering if he ought to display the better part of valor and find somewhere good and secure to hide. There was no point in being rescued by the Queen of Spectram's navy if he was dead already from the fighting. Cap'n Adamite's secret writing chamber seemed to offer as good an option as any, if only he could reach it without being spotted.

He was just about to tiptoe away when he was unlucky enough to catch Cap'n Rustbane's eye.

"And where are you off to, you piggy little furball?"

"The bathroom."

"The what?"

"The bathroom. Er, the head. The jakes. It's all the excitement, you know."

"A pirate never goes to the lav before a battle, does he, my lads?" cried Cap'n Rustbane.

"*No!*" yelled the crew around him loyally.

"He saves it for when it's really needed, don't he?"

"*Yes!*"

Sylvester's mind boggled. What in the world could Cap'n Rustbane mean?

"So, you just stay here beside me, young Sylvester Lemmington," said Rustbane, reverting to his normal voice. "You'll learn a lesson as good as any lesson learnt at sea could possibly be, a lesson in the way we scurvy knaves treat those pompous lords who would try to haul us home to face Jack Ketch."

He put his arm round Sylvester's shoulders as if to reassure him. Sylvester thought there could be no other gesture so threatening. Jeopord looked on with a sardonic smile twisting his lips.

"Just come a little closer, my beauty," breathed Cap'n Rustbane, addressing the Spectram vessel. The churning of the waters was becoming almost deafening as the *Specter of Justice*, charging through the waves roughly parallel to the *Shadeblaze*, drifted nearer and nearer to Rustbane's ship. "Come a little closer to your Uncle Terrigan. He's got a little gift for you."

"Keep your vessel on its course, Rustbane," hailed the Spectram officer unnecessarily.

"Is that so?" Rustbane called back. "I regret to say, Captain, that we have to leave you now."

"Don't make it even harder for yourself, Rustbane! You'll swing anyway, and your men alongside you, but there are worse things that could happen to you."

"And there are worse things that could happen to you too, my fine one!" bellowed Rustbane. "*Let 'er rip, lads!*"

For a moment, Sylvester thought the largest thunderstorm in the history of Sagaria must have crept up behind them unnoticed and suddenly let loose. The explosion was so loud his eyes watered from the pain of it. Surely no thunderstorm could be as noisy as this? Then it must be that Sagaria herself was splitting into a thousand pieces, erupting into a cold and merciless space. He staggered, clutching ears he was certain must have been torn apart from the explosion.

"What in the blazes was that?" he asked as the echoes reluctantly subsided, astonished he could hear his own words.

"Chain shot," said Cap'n Rustbane from somewhere close by in the gray, pulsating smoke. "Marvelous stuff is chain shot, if you use it at just the right time. And was there ever a righter time than the one we just used it at?"

Sylvester started coughing. The smoke around him was already clearing, but it still bit his throat like the fieriest spice. Through the haze he could see, in the direction of the Spectram ship, angry red glows where fires had started. There were smaller dark shapes he identified as Spectram sailors jumping overboard in the hope the water would be safer than the decks of their vessel. One larger dark shape, lurching fitfully sideways, he realized, was the *Specter of Justice's* mainmast toppling.

Beside him, Cap'n Rustbane chortled gleefully. "That'll teach the bluenoses to come searching for a fight with the triple-breasted goddess's own true free men."

The smoke was clearing rapidly now, as the two ships left most of it behind them. Quite how the *Specter of Justice* was still propelling itself through the water was a mystery to Sylvester, but Rustbane seemed to regard it as perfectly natural that it should do so.

"*Fire again!*" barked the gray fox, and there was another explosion from beneath where they stood, this eruption barely less loud than its predecessor. The chain shot had done awful damage to the Spectram ship, the chains scything down almost anything that stood in their way, including the ship's crew. Now the *Shadeblaze's* cannon were firing a more conventional load, the balls ripping huge holes in the side of the other vessel.

One of the largest holes was only half above the waterline. Sylvester watched sickly as water rushed into the great splintered wound, like an army descending on a city whose last defenses have just fallen.

"Surely, that's enough," he murmured to himself.

He must have spoken louder than he thought, because Cap'n Rustbane turned to look down at him, a deceptively friendly grin on the gray fox's face.

"But I've hardly even got started."

Sylvester stared into the fox's eyes, those oddly baffling greenish eyes that were prepared to reveal so little. "Why can't you just leave them alone now? They'll be lucky if any of them survive at all."

The green eyes narrowed. "Oh, they'd survive all right. There's no one better at saving his own skin than a Spectram officer, I can tell you. It's their naval training. They'll have the lifeboats broken out already, somewhere we can't as yet clap eyes on 'em, and we're not so far from port that the bluenoses won't be able to reach there. It's like we're dealing with a nest of ants, you see, Sylvester. The only safe thing to do is stamp the life out of the very last one of 'em. Otherwise, before you have time to turn around twice, there's ants all over the place again. You see what I'm driving at, don't you, boyo?"

"N–Not really," said Sylvester.

"Well," confided the gray fox, "to tell you the truth, it doesn't really matter whether or not you do, because after all this is over you're going to tell me what I need to know and then be feeding the fishes yourself."

He winked. Sylvester had never thought a wink could chill a person to the bone, but this one did.

Cap'n Rustbane let go of Sylvester's shoulders and turned to walk away along the deck, though the billowing smoke. His black leather coat whipped and flapped in the ocean wind, creating for a moment the illusion that he was a winged angel of death descended upon the world to suck the souls of the dead off to some place of eternal weeping. As Sylvester watched, Cap'n Rustbane reached to his belt and drew his two flintlock pistols.

Everyone's attention was suddenly distracted by a commotion as two smoking figures emerged from a hatch onto the deck. It took a breath or two before Sylvester could recognize them as the two rats, Thickskull and Sneezeball, whom Cap'n Rustbane had detailed to carry out his deadly orders. They must have been right next to the cannon when the chain shot was fired. Blood was pouring from their ears. They staggered a few steps across the open boards, then bumped into each other and fell.

"Fine work, my powder monkeys," said Rustbane, turning back in Sylvester's direction, the two flintlock pistols crossed beneath his chin like the bones crossed beneath the skull on the *Shadeblaze*'s flag. He appeared oblivious to the fact that the rats could hear not a word he said, that they probably would never hear anything ever again. "Well done! You've won the battle for us. Now it's up to your skipper to clear away the remnants so that we don't leave a mess on the sea behind us. Oh, and to have himself a little fun at the same time, o' course."

The air directly above the water had now largely cleared of smoke. Looking over the side of the *Shadeblaze* was like looking under a pillow. In the water there was a mass of floating wood, many of the pieces splintered and blackened. There were also more broken bodies than Sylvester wanted to think about, as well as a few sailors who, though hideously injured, were putting up a brave fight to stay afloat. And, miraculously, there were three or four people who seemed to have survived the onslaught of the *Shadeblaze's* cannon virtually unscathed.

One of these was the officer who had been hailing Cap'n Rustbane through a megaphone. Rustbane had addressed him as the *Specter of Justice's* skipper, and Sylvester knew of no reason to think otherwise.

As Sylvester watched, one of the *Specter of Justice's* lifeboats peeped into view beyond the bow of the doomed vessel. It was overladen already with rescued crew, but the Spectram captain, seeing it, began to swim determinedly towards it.

"Ah," said Cap'n Rustbane, beaming. "Target practice! This is going to be like shooting fish in a barrel."

He stretched out his arms in front of him and screwed up his face as he tried to squint along both barrels at once.

"You can't do that!" shouted Sylvester.

"Like hell I can't." The gray fox decided to concentrate on the pistol in his right paw. His arm steadied.

"He's defenseless!"

"More fool him."

"He's fighting for his life already. How can you be so cruel?"

"Quite easily. Just you watch."

"In the name of your . . . your . . . ah, yes, your triple-breasted goddess, show the poor fellow some mercy, can't you?"

"Shut your piehole and press the lid down firmly, why don't you?"

"But—"

"Mercy's for wimps. Mercy gets you killed. And mercy's no fun. Just wait 'til you see the fountain of blood when my bullets split his skull wide open."

Cap'n Rustbane claw tightened on the trigger.

Sylvester could stand it no longer.

There was a barrel of rum just behind the pirate. None of the crew was paying any attention to their sole remaining captive, not when there was the prospect of watching a few good killings.

Scuttling forward as fast as his legs would carry him, Sylvester launched himself, in what he was sure was a suicidal leap, to land on top of the rum barrel.

He landed there with a scrabbling of claws. More by luck than good judgement he managed to stop himself from sliding straight across the top of the barrel and falling off the other side.

From here he was same height as the gray fox.

"Watch out behind you, Cap'n!" he squealed.

Rustbane lowered the pistol he'd been about to fire and turned, an expression of bewilderment on his face.

"What's going on?"

"Take *this*, you murderer!"

Again, Sylvester launched himself crazily into the air, this time leaping toward a much smaller target than the barrel top – at the pistol still held in Cap'n Rustbane right paw.

For a second, he was certain he was going to miss it entirely, that he was going to sail straight past the pistol and into the turbulent waters below. Then, by one of those mad strokes of luck that only seemed to happen to other people, Rustbane tried to pull the gun out of Sylvester's way and his evasive movement, instead, gave the flying lemming the opportunity he was looking for.

He reached out a paw and yanked on the barrel of the pistol as hard as he possibly could.

Startled, Rustbane let go of the gun, and it went skittering away across the deck to rest up against . . .

Sylvester, deflected, caroming off at a wild angle, could hardly believe his eyes as he saw what the pistol rested up against. He barely had time for his disbelief to register, though, before he himself hit the deck and slid.

All the breath was punched out of him by the impact of landing. Darkness filled his vision. His ears still worked perfectly well, however, even though there seemed to be a rushing river very close at hand.

"Yoohoo," said a voice he'd thought he might never hear again.

"You devils!" yelled Rustbane in fury. "Give me that gun."

Slowly the pain began to ebb from Sylvester's midriff.

"Ask a bit more nicely," said Viola in her best "sweetness and light" tones.

Rustbane's intake of breath was like a garden rake being pulled through gravel.

"*Please* give me back that gun."

"No," said Viola.

"I have another one," said Cap'n Rustbane.

"Oh, no, you don't," said another voice and this time it took Sylvester a few moments to recognize it.

When he did, awareness flooded through him alongside his by now rapidly returning vision.

Jeopord! That treacherous ocelot has chosen this of all moments to strike against his skipper. The battle's won against the Specter of Justice, *but that doesn't mean the survivors won't be able to marshal the remains of their forces and launch some kind of ragged attack. This is the worst time for Rustbane to be confronted by a mutiny!*

In an instant of cold clarity, Sylvester recognized within himself the odd truth that his sympathies lay with the pirate who'd been preparing so brutally to slay the Spectrum officers and who was planning to take Sylvester's own life – that his sympathies lay with Rustbane rather than the mutineers.

But there was absolutely nothing he could do about it, one way or the other.

Drooling in fury, Cap'n Rustbane looked first at Viola, then at Jeopord then at Viola once more.

"You wouldn't be sending your old comrade to his doom, would you?" he said to Jeopord, even as his eyes were still on the smaller foe. Behind Viola stood a very determined looking Mrs. Pickleberry. In front of the two lemmings was a small black figure.

Rasco! How in the heck did you get here?

As if he'd heard Sylvester's thought, the little mouse turned and winked at him.

"We've spent a dozen years together at sea," the gray fox was saying, "ever watching each other's back. Haven't we, Jeopord? Now, just give me the gun."

"I think not, Cap'n."

"So ye still call me 'Cap'n,' do ye, ye varmint?"

"Just my little joke," replied Jeopord in an oily manner. "Just my little joke."

"A joke, is it? But I still am your cap'n, may the goddess darn it!"

"Not any longer, Rustbane."

Rustbane growled and Sylvester's spine froze. He'd never heard anything so frightening as that long, low sound. He glanced again across at Viola and the others, and saw it had petrified them, too.

Jeopord, by contrast, seemed hardly fazed by it. The purloined pistol dipped momentarily in the air, but then was pointing steadily at Rustbane's heart once more. That little dip was the only sign he'd heard the threat.

"Give me my gun. That's an *order*, Jeopord."

"We don't take our orders from you, Rustbane. Not any longer."

Rustbane sat down on the barrel from which Sylvester had launched his crazed leap. "So this is mutiny, is it?"

Jeopord leered. "I've heard it called that, yes."

"Stabbed in the back by me own best pal, me Jack o' Cups hisself." Rustbane had begun to wheeze, as if the shock of the betrayal had aged him by many years. Sylvester, watching him, didn't trust this impression any more than he trusted anything else about the gray fox. Cap'n Rustbane was putting on a performance, that was all. There were very few times when he wasn't putting on a performance.

"Oh, pass me an onion, someone," said Jeopord.

"Betrayed by my one true friend."

"And a clean handkerchief."

"Loved you like a brother, I did."

"That's not what you said when you had me flogged last year. Old Lumberbrains, handling the cat-o'-nine-tails, was prepared to stop when he'd got within an inch of my life, but you told him the *Shadeblaze* was going metric so he should carry on until he got within a *centimeter*, you scum!"

"It was for yer own good," Rustbane said, but even he didn't seem to believe his words.

"Just as this is for yours," countered Jeopord with a sarcastic chuckle. Behind him, out of the remaining wisps of smoke, a gaggle of other pirates materialized, as if they'd been standing there whole time but had only now decided to let themselves be seen.

"Bladderbulge," said Jeopord, gesturing behind him with an indolent paw. "Truss up the Cap'n here the way you'd truss up one o' those turkeys you burn."

"With pleasure, Jeopord," said the cook, moving forward. "Do I get to stick him in the oven afterwards?"

"I'm still thinkin' about that."

"You treacherous swine!" Cap'n Rustbane burst out. "You'll be sorry for this, mark my words."

"I'll mark 'em, all right," said Jeopord, visibly relaxing. Obviously, as Bladderbulge advanced upon the deposed skipper, the ocelot felt he was now in complete command of the situation. "About two out of ten, I'd say."

"Ha!" Cap'n Rustbane let rip with a string of nautical oaths. Mrs. Pickleberry blinked admiringly. "Without me – *me*, d'you hear? Without me, you're just a rabble of rabid street curs, waiting for death to come along and claim your miserable rotting hides. If it wasn't for me, you'd all have danced to the tune of Jack Ketch long ago, and be moldering in your unmarked graves. I made something out of you, I did! I made you into pirates. Pirates who could be proud to hold their heads up high, unafraid to look offal like the Queen of Spectram's pantalooned dandies in the eye." He waved a paw toward the floating planks that were the sole relics of the *Specter of Justice*, and to the lifeboats vanishing in the distance. "Without me you'd be nobodies, not the fearsomest crew there's ever been a-sailing on the seas of Sagaria!"

The gray fox paused for effect, wiping the back of his wrist across his lips. Bladderbulge was a statue beside him, the rope suspended between the fat pirate's paws.

"Without me," Cap'n Rustbane continued, his voice hardly above a whisper, "you'll never find Cap'n Adamite's treasure. You'll go to your graves still trying to hunt it down."

Murmurs spread through the thronged cutthroats. Rustbane's final remark had obviously struck home among some of them. Once more the direction of the pistol in Jeopord's paw wavered; once more the ocelot almost immediately brought it back under control.

"Don't listen to him," said the ocelot. "Pay him no mind. Do you think he'd share the treasure with the likes of us if he ever did find it? Do you? Do you really?"

Those words obviously hit their targets, too.

"Nah, he'd never let us have so much as a sight of it, not Rustbane, he wouldn't," said someone.

Another of the pirates began to laugh bitterly. "Our bones'd be bleached powder on the ocean bottom afore Terrigan Rustbane'd give us so much as a doubloon amongst us."

Jeopord's eyes twinkled triumphantly. He'd pulled the other pirates back on to his side again. A word from him and they'd have Rustbane swinging from the yardarm before the gray fox could so much as blink.

Rustbane saw that too. He snarled. "I'll have your head for this, you big motheaten pussycat."

"Perhaps," said Jeopord with an infuriating smile. "But it's not going to be today, is it? Today you're going to be taking a long walk off a short plank. Besides, it's the lemming who knows where the treasure is, isn't it? Not you. Finish tying him up, will you, Bladderbulge? Get a move on, man!"

With a show of enthusiasm the corpulent cook renewed his efforts trussing the fox. Sylvester could see, though, the reluctance in the badger's eyes. However much fealty the pirates might profess toward their new skipper, it was obvious at least some of them were still, at heart, loyal to Rustbane.

❖ ❖ ❖ ❖ ❖

The new skipper of the *Shadeblaze* proved to be one who saw no need to stand on ceremony. A mere fifteen or twenty minutes later, Sylvester stood with his arm around Viola on top of a bundle of provisions as Cap'n Rustbane was led by a posse of pirates, all with their swords pointing towards him and ready to pierce the thick cocoon of rope Bladderbulge had wound around him. In front of Sylvester and Viola sat Mrs. Pickleberry and Rasco, the two keeping a wary distance from each other. This was a moment Sylvester hadn't really wanted to watch, but Jeopord had insisted they did.

Sylvester was still trying to sort out his feelings about Cap'n Rustbane. On the one hand the gray fox had been intending to kill all three of the lemmings, and would have lost not a moment's sleep over doing so. On the other, well, the fox had the quality of inspiring loyalty in the unlikeliest places. Sylvester remembered the times they'd spent in the captain's cabin, and he couldn't help feeling that a kind of friendship had been brought into being then, and that, as with any friendship, it came with certain obligations. Of course, he wasn't going to grab a weapon from somewhere and rush to Rustbane's rescue, but he felt it was what he *ought* to be doing.

"When you knocked that pistol out of the old rogue's paw," Viola was murmuring in his ear, "and it came sliding across the deck to land right at my feet, I just couldn't believe it. Bookish Sylvester, suddenly turned into a lemming of action? So stirring! So wonderful! So dashing! So magnetic! So" – she nuzzled him a little more – "sexy!"

"Oh, get along with you, you little strumpet," Mrs. Pickleberry grated, glancing back over her shoulder.

One of the pirates had started beating a slow, solemn tattoo with his foot on the deck, and now others took it up. With each of those dread-laden beats, Cap'n Rustbane took another step forward, another step nearer to where the plank jutted out from the side of the ship, another step closer to his doom.

Jeopord watched from next to the plank. He was smiling.

"Do you have anything to say before you go?" he asked as the gray fox reached him. He reached out and took the mightily plumed tricorn hat from his erstwhile skipper's head.

"To you, nothing!" spat Rustbane.

Then he turned his eyes to run a fearsome green-eyed gaze over each of his erstwhile crew, one by one, finishing with the trio of lemmings and the little black mouse who'd contributed to his downfall.

"To the rest of you? Why, yes, I do have something to say."

As was his wont, he waited until the tension had screwed up to an intolerable pitch before continuing.

"Enjoy it while it lasts. That's my advice to you, to all of you. It won't last long, but enjoy it while it does. But there's a black spot on each and every one of you, and I've put it there, I have. There isn't a jack among you who isn't dead already. It's just that none of you knows it yet!"

Before anyone could move to stop him, Cap'n Terrigan Rustbane jumped up onto the plank. Apparently moving without difficulty despite his encumbering bonds, he scampered briskly along the plank until he reached its very end.

"Dead, every last one of you!" he cried.

Then, with a whoop of what sounded impossibly like triumph, he took a single step backward and plummeted into the gray waters of the unmindful ocean.

Jeopord stood motionless. The only sounds were the creaking of the *Shadeblaze's* timbers and the snapping of the Jolly Roger on the mast-top high overhead as the wind tore at the banner.

Only when Jeopord raised Rustbane's feathered hat into the air and slowly lowered it onto his own head did it seem the pirates could fully believe that the skipper, who for so long had held the power of life and death over them, had finally been vanquished.

Their cheers split the air. Jeopord bowed to them like a conjurer who has successfully pulled off the most mystifying trick of his career.

Late that night, as Sylvester lay sleepless, he thought he heard a splash that was somehow *different* from the splash of the ocean swells against the sides of the *Shadeblaze*. But he wasn't sure and it didn't seem to matter, so he turned over in his bunk and shut his eyes even tighter than before, and wished that sleep would finally come.

CANNIBAL STEW

o, Jeopord has the coordinates, does he?" said Viola.

"He has the coordinates," Sylvester confirmed. "He made me an offer I couldn't resist," he added ironically.

"And that was?"

"Being keelhauled then boiled alive and hung from the highest yard arm, and more in the same vein if I didn't tell him what he wanted to know. And to make matters worse, he also found Rustbane's two-thirds of the map in the fox's cabin."

"So, in other words, he has the entire map," Viola said and sighed.

"That about sums it up." Sylvester reflected that it was a miracle Jeopord hadn't sent the lemmings and the mouse along the plank in the wake of the gray fox.

Perhaps it was just a whim of the ocelot to keep them alive. Perhaps he was waiting until the inspiration came to him for some particularly imaginative way of executing them. It was impossible to tell.

For now, though, each breath they took was like a gift given to them by a merciful fate.

But! thought Sylvester, *I didn't tell him everything, especially the rather important fact that Cap'n Adamite put the "X" alongside the wrong island. That's a little secret I'm going to keep to myself until the time is right. It might be a way to delay our demise.*

The *Shadeblaze*'s new skipper had seen no need to keep them locked up. The *Shadeblaze* itself served as a perfectly good prison cell, did it not? All around it, the ocean stretched as far as the eye could see. They had the run of the ship, although dreadful things had been threatened should they go too near the longboats.

Viola and the rest were still alive. That was the good news, Sylvester mused. The bad news was the future. Every time his thoughts turned towards what the future held, he felt like curling up and dying on the spot.

What would Jeopord do with the single, all-encompassing wish the magical chest of the Zindars offered him?

It didn't bear thinking about.

What would the fate of Sagaria be?

Sylvester shuddered.

Viola, sensing his despair, held him closer. "It's all going to turn out all right. You'll see."

"She's right, you know." Rasco was sprawled on a pile of ropes nearby. The four captives were sunning themselves on deck near the stern of the ship – not that there *was* much sun. Mrs. Pickleberry had fallen asleep for a while. The big sunhat with which she'd covered her face had risen and fallen in a monotonous dance in time with her breathing. A couple of minutes ago she'd woken up with a snort and a snuffle and a few other noises that the rest had pointedly ignored. Now she was looking around for something to do – always her most dangerous mood.

"That's fine for *you* to say," grumbled Sylvester.

"It's not just me as says it," Rasco replied, shifting on top of the ropes in an attempt to make himself more comfortable. "It's Madame Zahnia."

"Madame Zahnia?" exclaimed Sylvester. The conversation between them had been going around and around in circles ever since yesterday, when Cap'n Rustbane had finally been consigned to the waves. Here, at last, was something new. "How come you never told us this before?"

Rasco shrugged. "I donno, mon."

"That damned woman betrayed us," grunted Mrs. Pickleberry.

"I'm not so sure Madame Zahnia's sole purpose was to throw us to the wolves," Sylvester said.

"It was important you find your way back aboard the *Shadeblaze*," agreed Rasco, "and she figured the best way of arranging that was to ensure the pirates found you and made you prisoners once more."

"Huh!" said Viola's mother.

Viola leaned forward, regarding Rasco intently. "Why did she figure we should be on the *Shadeblaze*?"

Rasco spread his hands. "I don't know. If Grandma Zahnia knew the reason, she didn't tell me. But what I think is that Madame Zahnia didn't know the reason either. It was like she said to you, Sylvester, if everything's going to come out well in the end, then it's important a pre-ordained pattern of events is followed, and you folks being on board the pirate ship is a part of that pattern."

"But what if Cap'n Rustbane had put us all to death?" said Sylvester. "What then?"

"That's why she sent me after you," Rasco replied. "To try to make sure it didn't happen. And if it did . . ." He smiled. "Well, maybe that would have just been part of the pattern of events it was so important must come to pass."

Sylvester gulped. The trouble with people who made or received prophecies, he'd concluded, was that the very act of seeing visions of the future made you insensitive to such seemingly trivial matters as people losing their lives.

Yet, Madame Zahnia had seen fit to send Rasco in the train of the pirates and their captives. And, it was indeed largely thanks to Rasco's intervention that they were still alive – Viola and Mrs. Pickleberry, anyway.

The lemmings hadn't long been reunited following Jeopord's takeover of the ship before Sylvester had managed to coax out of Viola what had happened.

"When I was standing there on the plank, trembling all over and thinking these were the last few breaths I'd take," Viola had explained, "I happened to glance downward and there, bobbing along in a little boat, was Rasco. I could hardly believe it! He was spreading out a fishing net over the surface of the water and signaling that it was safe to jump, that he'd catch me in the net. I'd hardly gotten myself aboard the rowing boat beside him when – *splash* – there was Mom landing in the water beside us. Then we waited for you, but . . ."

Remembering the way she'd paused after saying these words, looking at him as if he should complete her sentence for her, Sylvester was embarrassed all over again. He hadn't been able to bring himself to tell her that the reason he hadn't followed her and Mrs. Pickleberry wasn't gallantry or courage or anything praiseworthy along those lines, but sheer stupidity. Unlike Mrs. Pickleberry, who'd picked up on Viola's cue and realized the waters beneath the plank held safety, Sylvester had been completely undecided. He might well have paid with his life for that indecision.

"Which was why we came back aboard," Viola had told him, after the pause had stretched nearly to breaking point. "We had to rescue you."

With the result that Rasco and the Pickleberries had become captives alongside Sylvester – that was the truth of the matter. If they died, that'd be the cost of his stupidity. He couldn't even console himself with the thought that he'd carry the guilt to the grave, because he'd almost certainly be dead before they were.

Just before.

"Madame Zahnia knew all of this was going to happen," Sylvester said wonderingly. "She didn't tell me in so many words, but now I look back on some of the things she was saying, it seems clear."

"My grandma," said Rasco, rubbing the side of his nose, "she's a cunning old coot, that one. Before I left Ouwinju to come after you she told me that, unless one of us did something really insane, we'd all come out of this with our skins intact."

"Easy enough for her ter say," observed Mrs. Pickleberry.

"Did Madame Zahnia foresee Jeopord would get his hands on the map or the coordinates, which are basically the same thing?" asked Sylvester.

"How can I tell? I am not her confidant."

Sylvester didn't believe the denial, but decided not to pursue the matter. He was beginning to get a glimmer of an idea as to why the ocelot had so far spared their lives.

"No one else knows Jeopord has the map, do they?" he said.

Viola looked at him in perplexity. "What do you mean. *We* know, don't we?"

"But none of his crew do. He swore the four of us to secrecy, on pain of terrible death. See, here's the way I reckon it . . ."

The others bent toward him as he explained in a low voice the theory he'd developed. Jeopord wanted his captives to know he possessed the map, because that way, they'd be aware of just quite how unnecessary their survival was to him. That's what he wanted them to think, anyway. But the truth was he actually *did* need to keep them alive. If he threw them overboard to the sharks it'd be immediately evident to the rest of the *Shadeblaze*'s crew that either he'd extracted the treasure's coordinates from Sylvester or he owned another copy of Cap'n Adamite's chart. The crew of the *Shadeblaze* had recently mutinied against one captain: the thought of mutiny must be ripe in their minds. Jeopord couldn't run the slightest risk of tipping them into another mutiny. And, if word got out to the crew that he had the map, there'd be half a dozen pirates willing to chance their paws to wrest it from him.

"Makes sense." Mrs. Pickleberry spoke grudgingly, but she was nodding her head. Earlier, she'd told Sylvester she was beginning to dislike the cut of his jib somewhat less than he probably deserved. After untangling this declaration in his mind, he'd decided to accept it as a compliment.

"I think this whole business about the chest of the Zindars and the single incredible wish is just a myth," said Viola, changing the subject.

Rasco gave her a whimsical smile. "My grandma doesn't."

"Yes, well . . ." Viola twitched her ears as an indication of what she thought about Rasco's grandma.

"It doesn't really matter what we think," observed Sylvester. "It's what Jeopord thinks that counts. We're going to be dragged along with him until he's located the very spot where the treasure is supposed to lie. After that . . ."

He broke off. There was no sense in reminding the rest what was likely to happen as soon as Jeopord didn't need them anymore.

Viola shivered, wrapping her arms around herself. "To think, we'd managed to escape and get so far from the pirates it was as if we'd left them behind in a different world, and now we're back in the same boat as before."

Rasco and Sylvester groaned.

She looked puzzled briefly, then realized what she'd said. "Oops."

"Ye think Rustbane's dead?" she Mrs Pickleberry.

"How could he be anything else?" said Sylvester.

"He's survived tighter scrapes, from all he told us," she responded.

"Tighter than being thrown into the ocean many miles from shore, trussed up like a birthday present?"

Mrs. Pickleberry nodded. "Wou'n't surprise me to see him come climbing up over that taffrail any minute now."

All eyes turned toward the taffrail in question. What Mrs. Pickleberry described was an impossibility, Sylvester knew, yet he couldn't help half-expecting to see Cap'n Rustbane's snarling gray face above the brass of the rail.

"You're kidding," said Rasco at last.

"Mebbe."

"Having him back might be an improvement," Viola murmured gloomily.

"I know what you mean." Sylvester touched his head to hers. "Jeopord seems even worse than Rustbane ever was. And the worst thing about Jeopord is that we barely know him, so we've even less of a chance of guessing what he's thinking or what he might do, than we ever had with Rustbane." He paused a moment before he spoke the next few words, reluctant to utter them. "Besides, though it goes against the grain, I think I actually *miss* the old buzzard."

"Fox," corrected Mrs. Pickleberry.

All the correction did was remind Sylvester of how Cap'n Rustbane had made a joke out of calling the lemmings hamsters. He wished he could hear the insult again, if only the once.

When Mrs. Pickleberry had awoken she'd put her sun hat on the deck beside her. Now a sudden gust of wind blew across the area and picked the hat up off the boards, so that it tumbled away. Rasco sprinted in pursuit as the straw hat, possessed by a mind of its own, danced along the deck.

"There's a wind coming up." Viola shuddered as if suddenly pierced by shafts of cold.

Indeed there was. Without Sylvester and the others having noticed it, the sky had filled with heavy-looking dark clouds. Off in the distance, he could see the slanting gray lines of heavy rain.

The *Shadeblaze* lurched beneath them. The bat in the crow's nest started a berserk chatter of warning. Pirates ran to and fro along the length of the ship yelling instructions to batten down the hatches, fasten anything loose, take shelter.

Rasco gave up Mrs. Pickleberry's straw bonnet for lost. He watched it flutter away into the leaden sky like some enormous wayward moth.

"Come on!" Sylvester shouted at the mouse. "Come with us!"

"Sure thing, mon." Rasco scurried to join the rest.

Their arms around each other for protection against what had already turned into a full-scale gale, the lemmings and their smaller friend made their way below deck. Following their own footsteps, they soon found themselves back in those same dank cabins where Rustbane's crew had incarcerated them long ago as the *Shadeblaze* left Foxglove behind. The last time Sylvester saw the sky before going below, it was an angry gray turmoil. Several tall, thin columns of blacker darkness reached upward from the sea, their tops broadening to become lost in the ashen sky.

The next few hours were a misery of pitching floors and shrieking timbers as the *Shadeblaze* did her best to survive the tempest. Soon, Sylvester felt his whole body must be one single mass of bruises from being thrown so often and so hard against the cabin walls. Viola and Rasco were in no better shape. Only Mrs. Pickleberry, perhaps because her center of gravity was so low, seemed able to maintain any measure of stability as the ship bucked and heaved. The worst of it all was that they had to endure the commotion in near darkness, because little or no light crept in through the small portholes and the lemmings dared not keep a lamp lit for fear of scattering burning oil everywhere.

A long, grating shudder ran up the full length of the ship. Suddenly the heaving and tossing of the vessel lessened and it began a different movement, rocking slowly from side to side.

"What was that?" shrieked Viola, clinging to Sylvester.

"I don't know."

The whole ship seemed to be creaking in protest at whatever had just happened.

"We ran aground," pronounced Rasco from somewhere in the gloom.

"Ran aground?" said Sylvester and Viola at the same time.

"There's a reef or sandbank somewhere under the water," explained Rasco, "and the good old *Shadeblaze* done got itself stuck on it."

Sylvester could visualize what must have happened. As if in agreement, the ship pitched once more, sending himself and Viola staggering to crash hard against the end wall of the cabin.

"Surely," he said once he'd got his breath back, "that must mean we're close to land?"

"Not necessarily," replied Rasco, whose knowledge of matters maritime seemed profound (as might be expected of one who'd spent much of his life in the dockside taverns of Hangman's Haven). "Not necessarily," he repeated more slowly, as if the first time he'd said them the words hadn't been depressing enough for his taste. "You can find reefs many a long league from the nearest shore. There are whole mountain ranges under water, and their peaks come close enough to the surface to snag an unwary vessel such as ours has been, thanks to this storm."

"So we might be stranded here forever?" said Viola in a querulous voice. "Just waiting for the food and drink to run out, with no chance of being able to sail to land?"

"That's it in a nutshell."

Sylvester wished Rasco would stop sounding as if he relished their predicament quite so much.

Viola persisted. "Then what?"

"Well," said Rasco, "you can predict what'll happen when the food supplies start getting low, can't you?"

"Everyone gets very hungry?" said Sylvester hopefully, knowing it was the wrong answer.

"That too," said Rasco, "except pretty soon 'everyone' starts to be a smaller and smaller number."

The implication was obvious.

Sylvester gulped.

"Oh, how *exciting*." Viola's voice had regained a lot of its confidence. "You mean everyone starts eating each other?"

"You got it in one, mon. It's happened a thousand times before on the lawless oceans of Sagaria. First to end up on the dinner plates is the smaller and weaker creatures. Creatures like lemmings, in point of fact, 'cause they got a fair amount of good, succulent meat on 'em for an animal their size."

"Mice are even smaller," Mrs. Pickleberry pointed out.

"But we're faster," said Rasco amiably. "And, being as small as we are, we're better at hiding in places no one else can get to."

Still the *Shadeblaze* rocked from side to side. Although it was hard to be sure over the cacophony of protesting timbers, the storm seemed to have abated a little.

"We oughta go back up on deck," said Mrs. Pickleberry. "Find out the worst."

The idea made sense. Rasco, whose eyes were better adapted to the dark than the lemmings', found the cabin door and led the way.

Lumbering out into the open in the wake of Viola and Mrs. Pickleberry, Sylvester found he'd been right in his impression that the storm had calmed down a little. The sky was still gray, but it was a watery, pale gray rather than the menacing near-night of earlier. There was still a little rain falling, but it was just a gentle shower, the droplets gleaming and sparkling like diamonds as they drifted in what was left of the wind.

Jeopord was standing a little apart from his crew, who were clustered close to the stairs that led down to the captain's cabin. Sylvester hadn't been there since the mutiny, but he somehow doubted that it was still filled with all the books and papers that Cap'n Rustbane had so reveled in. It didn't strike Sylvester that Jeopord was the reading type.

The ocelot was at the base of the *Shadeblaze*'s mainmast, looking up it as if there was the answer to some profound riddle at its top. His lips were moving in what Sylvester did not have to hear to know was a long stream of curses. Sylvester turned toward Viola to say something that he forgot even before he began speaking because, past her shoulder, he could see something that set his heart singing.

"Land," he breathed.

Viola gazed at him blankly. "What?"

"Look." Sylvester pointed.

She turned her head and gave a little squeal of happiness.

Their experience of Blighter Island was enough to have taught Sylvester of the foolishness of judging an island by its appearance from the sea. Despite this, in any other circumstances, any self-respecting ship would have taken one look at this place and hauled hard on the rudder to turn toward open ocean. It couldn't have been more than a couple of miles away, yet Sylvester could make out hardly any details of its surface. It was just a gray, hunched mass, poised above the surface of the sea as if waiting to swallow anything or anyone that came too near. There was a sort of menacing, heavy silence surrounding it. Even the breakers crashing against its shore seemed to make no noise, as if the sound had been absorbed by a thick blanket.

Sylvester felt a cold draft run up his spine, warning him, but he ignored the premonition. Just the sight of land, *any* land – when minutes before they'd been trying to reconcile themselves to the idea of the *Shadeblaze* being stuck here for the rest of eternity – was like a drink of cool water after a long day under the desert sun.

"There's hope for us after all," he said quietly.

Strangely, Jeopord didn't seem at all interested in their proximity to salvation, and neither did the rest of the crew. Surely the lookout, perched high in the crow's nest, must have seen the island no matter how thick the sky had become with rain?

Then Sylvester realized what the captain was staring at so intently.

Even from this distance, it was obvious the bat who'd served as the *Shadeblaze*'s lookout was dead. The little creature was slumped backward over the side of the crow's nest, its head offset from its shoulders at an impossible angle. Even though Sylvester had never met the bat, had never even known its name or if it was a male or a female, he couldn't help feeling a twinge of grief for its passing. The little creature, known solely through its cries of alarm or exhortation high above, had been one of the *Shadeblaze*'s fixtures, as if it had been up there in the crow's nest from the day the ship was first launched. For all Sylvester knew, that might indeed be the case.

What was Jeopord going to do for a lookout now?

As if the weatherbeaten ocelot had heard Sylvester's thoughts, Jeopord slowly turned to look in the direction of the little huddle of captives.

Lemmings! though Sylvester, his panic rising. *We're small enough to fit into the crow's nest, but I've never had much of a head for heights.*

Jeopord pointed.

Oh, relief! He's not pointing at me, *he's pointing at—*

"Me," said Rasco. He chuckled. "It's the obvious solution."

"He can't be expecting *you* to—" started Viola.

Rasco held up a paw. "I don't mind. I'm looking forward to it. Being at the top of a mast ain't going to be much different from getting from one place to another in Ouwinju. I like it, being able to see a long way, and the air seems cleaner up there. 'Sides, it'll keep me out of the way. Down here, I never know from one moment to the next if one o' these cutthroats ain't going to take a fancy to using me as target practice for his cutlass."

By this time Jeopord was beside them.

"A fancy speech, little vermin guy, but it don't matter all your cogitatin' of why you're going to obey me orders because you'd be obeyin' them anyway, this being my ship an' all."

Rasco grinned up at him. "Don't you find it better when your crewmen are willing?"

Jeopord regarded him with a dismissive sneer. "Don't make much difference to me what they're thinkin' so long as they do what I tell 'em."

Rasco shrugged. "Well, you're the boss."

"I surely am, and don't any of you forget it."

"Not that it makes no great difference," interposed Mrs. Pickleberry.

Sylvester could see the ocelot's face flush with rage.

"What do you mean, you old baggage?"

"This ship ain't going nowhere, is it?"

"It's just a reef, is all," said Jeopord, his temper already beginning to subside. "This ain't the first time the good old *Shadeblaze*'s been stuck on a reef, not by a long road, and I'm sure as all get-out it ain't going to be the last. We pirates know how to deal with these things."

"Uh-huh?"

Her skeptical grunt brought Jeopord's anger back again. His paw strayed to the sword at his belt. Sylvester knew Mrs. Pickleberry was treading very close to the line between life and death.

"So, how you goin' to be gettin' us off this pretty little perch then?" she continued, as if oblivious to the danger.

"Well, first of all," began Jeopord, as if explaining something elementary to a very young, very stupid child, "what we do is we lighten the load."

Mrs. Pickleberry looked around her. "How'd you do that?"

"By getting rid of excess burden," said Jeopord.

"Meanin'?"

"Unnecessary personnel."

"Such as us?"

"Such as you and three-quarters of the crew, maybe more."

Sylvester was appalled. "A massacre, you mean?"

Jeopord started to laugh. "No, not that, my piggy little friend – although I'd not hesitate if it became necessary. Despatchin' you four to Davy Jones wouldn't matter a belch one way or the other, but I need my crew to sail the ship once we've floated her free, don't I? Stands to reason."

"Oh."

"So, I'm going to fill up the longboats with everyone except a skeleton crew to maneuver the *Shadeblaze* off this reef, and you're all going to go across to that there uninhabited island for a day or two" – he jerked a claw back over his shoulder toward the hulking gray mass behind him – "leavin' the rest of us here to do the work that has to be done."

"Um, Cap'n," said Viola quietly.

"Quiet, you little chit."

Sylvester knew he ought to punch the ocelot in the eye for addressing Viola so rudely. He also knew he wasn't going to.

"But, Cap'n—"

"I said—"

"Just *look*, will you, you great oaf!"

"I'll be . . ." said Jeopord, and this time his sword came a few inches out of its scabbard.

But he turned to look at where Viola stood by the rail, and past her, and he saw what she had seen.

"Sheesk!" said Sylvester.

Speeding toward them through the heavy seas from the island were a score or more of long, narrow boats, each of them manned by a dozen oarsmen. From this distance, it was impossible to tell what type of creatures were paddling the boats so industriously, but Sylvester could see the small dark dots of heads rising and falling as the oars swished through the water.

"I don't think that island is uninhabited after all," said Viola sweetly.

Jeopord stared at her for a long, poisonous moment, then turned on his heel and began barking orders.

φ φ φ φ

By the time the boats from the island were alongside the *Shadeblaze*, everyone aboard the pirate vessel, the captives excluded, was armed to the hilt and ready to repel boarders. Rasco was ensconced in the crow's nest and, for the past few minutes had been yelling reports on the islanders' progress to anyone on deck who was prepared to listen to him.

Sylvester and Viola were leaning against the rail, gazing down at the boats. What they saw was not very reassuring.

But you should never judge people by appearances, Sylvester chided himself. *First impressions are often woefully misleading.*

Even so . . .

The people of the island represented as many different species as the crew of the *Shadeblaze*, probably more, including several that Sylvester didn't recognize, even from illustrations in scrolls. Only a few of them were wearing any clothes, which Sylvester thought was not unreasonable bearing in mind the heat this close to the equator. It was the *other* things the people were wearing that offered cause for concern.

Skulls.

Big skulls and little skulls, short flattened skulls and long thin ones – there were more types of skulls festooned on ropes and cords around the islanders' waists and necks than there were kinds of islanders. Sylvester could see whenever a boatsman stood up that these people even wore ankle bracelets made out of the polished carapaces of insects. It seemed as if the islanders must be in the grip of some kind of death cult.

He gripped Viola's hand tightly.

"Just for once," she said, "it's reassuring to know there are a hundred fully armed cutthroats on board."

Sylvester nodded mutely.

"Welcome to our land," called one of the newcomers. He was a black-and-white terrier of ferocious appearance and he had only one ear, the other having been gnawed off at some indeterminate point in the past. "Do you come in peace?"

"Idiotic question," said the pirate nearest to Viola and Sylvester, a groundhog who didn't look too reputable himself. He turned to give them the benefit of a chisel-toothed grin. "What are we supposed to reply, eh?"

He had a point. The *Shadeblaze* was firmly aground on an invisible reef and wouldn't be going anywhere for hours yet, more likely days. Jeopord was hardly likely to tell the islanders he hadn't come in peace.

The ocelot didn't answer the question directly. Removing the dagger he'd been clutching between his teeth, he called back down to the terrier, "Cap'n Jeopord at your service, sir, and this is my fine vessel the *Shadeblaze* and her sterling complement."

The pirates gave a collective growl that Sylvester thought might, at a stretch, be described as friendly.

It didn't seem to faze the terrier in any way, though.

"My name is Kabalore and I am the chieftain of these, the people of Vendros!"

Sylvester racked his memory but couldn't recall having seen the name Vendros on Cap'n Adamite's map. The *Shadeblaze* must have strayed well off her intended course. Either that or, of course, the island had been charted all right but Barterley Smitt hadn't known a name to give it.

"Well met, Kabalore!" cried Jeopord.

"Will you come ashore to enjoy our hospitality?" called Kabalore.

"Nothing would give me greater pleasure."

"Excellent. Then let me arrange for your arrival."

"But," said Jeopord.

Sylvester saw the island chieftain's face fall in disappointment. "There is a difficulty?"

"I, myself, and some of my crew must stay here with the *Shadeblaze* in order to free it from the accursed clutches of this doubly accursed reef."

"But *then* we can welcome you to our feasting?"

"Then it would be our delight," replied Jeopord.

Sylvester looked at him through narrowed eyes. Clearly Kabalore hadn't noticed the tone of Jeopord's voice, but anyone who knew the ocelot pirate at all would have recognized the underlying message conveyed. Jeopord wasn't going to land on Vendros, not if it was the last thing he did.

Jeopord thinks we might all be going to our deaths, Sylvester realized, *but he's prepared to accept that as the lesser of two evils. The most important task ahead of him is to set the* Shadeblaze *free. He can worry later about how he's going to get her to port with only a handful of crew. He's planning, if worst comes to worst, to let us be distractions to keep the islanders occupied while he and his cronies work on the ship.*

"Them's cannibals, them is."

Sylvester jumped in startlement. He hadn't heard Cheesefang coming up behind them. Either the sea rat must have been moving with unusual quietness or Sylvester had been more lost in his thoughts than he'd realised.

Cheesefang grinned. Clearly, he was in one of his better moods.

"Cannibals," he repeated.

"How do you know?" said Viola, gripping Sylvester's arm so tightly he thought he heard a sinew pop.

"Seen 'em before," said the sea rat. If anything, he'd begun looking even scruffier and more disheveled since the departure of Cap'n Rustbane. "'Ere and there on the Seven Seas. Places where ol' Cheesefang's bin that few others 'ave – few others 'ave and *lived*." He nodded deeply once, then twice, as if he'd just said something of the utmost sagacity. "It's the skulls that give 'em away. Me, I can't understand why they keeps 'em. Sort of like hanging on ter the peach stone after yer've eaten the peach, if ye ask me, but it's their custom, like."

What a strange coincidence, thought Sylvester with one part of his mind – one very *small* part, because all the rest was panicking at the prospect of being cooked and eaten. At least, he *assumed* cannibals cooked the people they ate first. Maybe they ate them raw? Maybe they didn't even kill them first? *What a strange coincidence that we were talking about cannibalism less than an hour ago. Only then, of course, we were thinking of it as the last resort of desperate, starving people, not as a way of life.*

"So what are we going to do?" he asked Cheesefang. His voice hardly trembled at all, he was sure of it.

"Whatever the skipper tells us to do, o' course."

"Even if that means getting killed and eaten?"

Cheesefang leered. "Even if that means getting killed and eaten?" he said in a cruel lampoon of Sylvester's tones. Then his expression changed and he beckoned the two lemmings closer to him.

Sylvester noticed, not for the first time, that the sea rat smelled powerfully of grog, as if he took regular baths in the stuff. But that wasn't the only aroma that hung around Cheesefang. It was obvious the pirate didn't take regular baths in anything at all.

"See, this skipper of ours ain't as muttonbrained as you might be a thinkin' 'e is," said Cheesefang in a low voice. "I knowed Jeopord for many a long year, I 'ave, and he's a bright 'un and a bold 'un. He ain't a patch on the last skipper we 'ad, but then there ain't a pirate on the 'ole wide Seven Seas is ever goin' to be a patch on Cap'n Rustbane. 'E was somethin' special, 'e was, but Jeopord's somethin' special too in 'is own way. 'E might let us walk into the gaping jaws of death, 'e might, but 'e wouldn't let them jaws come closin' down on top of us. 'E'd be bound to find some way of rescuin' us before it's too late."

"Are you sure of that?" said Sylvester.

"Not very," said Cheesefang, "but what I think ain't all that important, is it? The cap'n's goin' to carry on and do exactly what 'e wants anyway. So we might as well look on the bright side, doncher think?"

This wasn't, Sylvester reflected, very reassuring, but he suspected it was the cheeriest news they were likely to get out of the old sea rat. Might as well grab ahold of it and hope for the best, the way they say drowning lemmings grasp at straws.

Cheesefang's attention had shifted. "Where's Three Pins?" he asked Viola.

"She went below for something," Viola told him. "I don't know what."

All this while, Jeopord and Kabalore had been carrying on negotiations about how the crew were going to get to the island of Vendros. Up and down the deck Sylvester could see burly pirates slowly relaxing, with swords being put back in scabbards and maces being hung once more from belts.

"To the longboats!" cried Jeopord at last. He'd already selected a dozen crew to stay behind with him. He gestured everyone else toward where the longboats hung. The pirates closest to them began stripping off the tarpaulins with a practiced dexterity. The atmosphere among them was becoming almost cheerful now, as if they'd been told they could have an unexpected vacation, starting now. If any of them recognized the islanders as cannibals, the way Cheesefang and presumably Jeopord had done, it wasn't obvious in their attitude.

Sylvester hung back a little and looked around for Mrs. Pickleberry.

"Where is she?" he said vexedly to Viola.

"Don't ask."

"But—"

"Hush. She's no fool, my mom. If she wants to stay behind she wants to stay behind, and there's no use you worrying about it. She'll have a plan of some kind in that hard little head of hers, you'll see."

Sylvester looked at her dubiously. "You're sure about that?"

"Sure as sure."

"Well, okay then."

☙ ☙ ☙ ☙

The night sky was dark and cloudless and filled with a million stars. Some of those weren't really stars, Sylvester knew, but red sparks floating upwards from the eagerly blazing fire that had been built by Kabalore's people on the beach. The crackling of the flames and the chanting and yelling of the islanders almost completely drowned the continual noise of the waves breaking against the shore, as if the ocean were breathing deeply as it slept through the ruckus of the celebrations.

So far nothing had happened to threaten the visitors, but Sylvester was fairly sure it was only a matter of time. Cheesefang obviously thought the same. The rat had circulated among the other pirates begging the loan of a cutlass here and a dagger there, which he'd passed to Sylvester and Viola with strict instructions they should use them if there was the slightest pretext. As an additional safeguard, he stuck close to the two lemmings, keeping an eye on them in an almost paternal way. If he was worried by the absence of Mrs. Pickleberry, he didn't show it; after asking Viola once or twice if she knew where her mother was, he abandoned the subject.

The odd thing was, Sylvester ruminated, that none of the pirates seemed to have gotten to know any of the islanders. In the ordinary way, if you mixed two groups of people like this for a feast, there'd have been temporary friendships forming, perhaps a few congenial arguments starting. At the very least, people would have been telling each other their names, but there was nothing like that going on. The pirates sat on the sands on one side of the giant bonfire, the islanders on the other. The only intermingling going on was when islander serving wenches went round among the pirates with great tubs of a fiery green liquor and heaped plates of steaming viands.

Sylvester and Viola, without consultation, stuck to the vegetables.

The green grog was a different matter. Having checked that the goblet he'd been given was made out of a coconut shell rather than what he'd at first thought, Sylvester was happy enough to watch it being replenished more than once. He was going to regret this in the morning, he suspected, but he barely cared. The hooch was building up his courage, readying him for the confrontation with the islanders he was certain would materialize sooner or later. Besides, Cheesefang was drinking at least three times as much as Sylvester was.

Viola took one sip of it, gagged, and refused to touch another drop.

Something had been puzzling Sylvester, and he wormed closer to Cheesefang to let himself be heard above the hubbub.

"Excuse me, Mr. Cheesefang."

"Huh?"

"I said, 'Excuse me.'"

"I knows. That's why I said, 'Huh.' Ain't no one said 'excuse me' to this ol' sea rat since 'e was an infant in 'is mother's arms. Not that I can remember being in me mother's arms, o' course. She kicked me out of the 'ouse before I could walk, before I could barely toddle."

"How dreadful."

"Not really. I'd discovered I could get a good price for the family silverware down the market and I'd been sellin' it off one piece at a—"

Sylvester coughed pointedly. "I'd like to ask you a question, Mr. Cheesefang."

"An' I'd go easy on the 'Mr.' as well, you young sprout. Makes me nervous, it does. Ain't no one called me 'Mr.' since—"

"Quite so," said Sylvester. "But I'd like to say—"

"What's stoppin' ye?"

"Well, *you* are."

"Sorry I spoke, I'm sure. Fancy another tankard o' this excellen' grog?"

"Well, I wouldn't mind."

"*Sylvester!*" hissed Viola. "You've had quite enough. You've had *more* than quite enough."

"Aw ..."

Cheesefang ended the discussion by grabbing a passing serving wench, this time a chipmunk, and directing her to fill Sylvester's goblet and his own.

"Now, what's this question of yers?" said the sea rat with a genteel hiccup.

Sylvester floundered around for his question.

"Oh, yes. You say these people are cannibals?"

"Sure as eggs is eggs."

"But cannibals are people who eat people of their own kind, aren't they? If you ate another sea rat you'd be a cannibal."

"I would?"

"But if you ate a" – it was *really* irritating, but the only animal that came to mind was a lemming – "if you ate a lemming, for example, just for example, I'm not really suggesting you should, heh heh, but if you ate a lemming you might be a vile murderer and very, very sick because the flesh of lemmings is poisonous to sea rats as I'm sure you know, but, er, where was I?"

"You were tellin' me I'd be better off not eatin' lemmings."

"Ah, yes. If you ate a lemming, it wouldn't be cannibalism, would it? So how can these people be cannibals when they're of every species under the sun and, to judge by the skulls they wear, the people they eat are of every species too?"

From where Sylvester was sitting, the sea rat was silhouetted by the leaping flames of the bonfire. He could see Cheesefang scratching his head as if amused, but he couldn't see if there was a grin on the old pirate's face.

He suspected there was.

"Sylvester, me old chum?"

"Cheesefang."

"You seen much of the world?"

"Not really."

"Wot? A womanizer like you? Perish the thought you is a innocent!"

Sylvester glanced sideways at Viola. She was lapping up every word. He was likely to regret this later. Womanizer, indeed!

Although he did rather like the *idea*.

He stared down into the depths of the grog in his goblet, suspecting it might have betrayed him.

Did I speak those words out loud?

"You didn't," Viola assured him.

That wasn't as reassuring as it might have been.

"Thing is," Cheesefang was saying, "what cannibalism is, it ain't the actual species that is important."

"It ain't—isn't?"

"It's the intellect."

Keeping the words "intellect" and "Cheesefang" in his mind at the same time was one of the more difficult tasks Sylvester had ever accomplished.

"The intellect?"

"Yes," said Cheesefang as he tried to assume a superior expression, then giving up he took another gulp from his goblet instead. "See, cannibals ain't really interested in what the meat o' their victims tastes like. What they want to do is eat the *brains*, so they can add the wisdom an' intellect an' courage an' all o' their fodder to themselves."

"They think they can make themselves cleverer and braver, you mean?"

"Xactly. And 'oo's to say they ain't right? Splendid good grog this is, ye 'ad some?"

"Er, yes."

"So," said Cheesefang as if the word were a treasure he'd discovered after a long search, "these Vendrosians, like any other cannibals, they don't care if yer lemmings or sea rats or raccoons or ground'ogs or badgers. All they care about is if ye can *think*."

"Oh."

"An' if yer a good fighter."

"Ah."

"Leastwise, that's what it's been like with all the other cannibals I tripped over."

"So when do you think they're likely to pounce?"

"Pounce?" The sea rat shrugged, looking at Sylvester through reddened eyes.

"Attack us. Try to make us their supper."

Cheesefang looked around the scene. The flames were illuminating everything on this side of the fire, but what might be going on on the other side was impossible to tell, now that the night had deepened. Every now and then the fire would give an especially bright eruption, and for a moment the pirates could catch a glimpse of the islanders further up the beach, but those moments were short and long between.

"Any second now, I should think," said the sea rat. He sniffed knowledgeably.

As if they'd heard him, the islanders suddenly raised the intensity of their chanting. Off to the left, behind the line where the trees met the sand, heavy drums began to beat.

"What're they singing?" said Viola.

"Who can tell?" Sylvester replied.

"They's singing an 'ymn," said Cheesefang. "An 'ymn to one o' the many gods they worships. They's askin' for divine blessin's on their, well, tell the truth, on their menu."

"On us, you mean?" said Sylvester.

"True 'nuff."

"Don't you think we ought to be doing something about it?"

"What makes you think we ain't?"

Despite Cheesefang's words, it didn't look as if any of the pirates were in any condition to fight off attackers. Some of them were definitely asleep. Others were very nearly so. The green grog had not been without its efficacy.

It had worked on Sylvester too, as he was discovering far too late. He managed to get to his feet, but only just. The borrowed cutlass he'd succeeded in pulling out from his belt looked alarmingly like rubber in the firelight. He supposed this might be useful. If the blade were made of cold steel he'd be likely to hesitate before plunging it into another sentient creature. A *rubber* blade, on the other paw . . .

He didn't have a chance to complete the thought. The islanders, who'd obviously spent the past few minutes organizing themselves, suddenly came charging in two troops around the sides of the blinding bonfire. Even if he hadn't been able to see them, Sylvester would have known their evil intent. Their scream was wordless, but it was understandable in any language.

Kiiillll!

Suddenly, the sea of drunken pirates changed entirely.

Sylvester could have sworn that most of the buccaneers were as near comatose. The cannibals should have been able to saunter among them slaughtering at will.

Nothing could have been further from the truth.

A wall sprang up between the advancing islanders and the nearest pirates. It was a wall of shining, finely honed steel.

Suddenly aware of what he should do, Sylvester stared at the cutlass Cheesefang had given him. Holding it in a grip that felt as if it had been formed before time began, he switched it from one side to the other, enjoying the way it felt so under his control. A moment ago it had seemed like a rubber blade. Now it was a *killing machine*. All the wooziness from the green grog had strangely vanished. He knew Cheesefang was standing on his one side, Viola on the other, each of them likewise brandishing a weapon. Somehow, he felt distanced from what they were doing.

He might never feel this way again, but at this moment, Sylvester Lemmington was a pirate.

And he gloried in that status.

He wanted to kill himself a few cannibals.

The cannibals obligingly charged.

THERE ARE WAYS AND THERE ARE WAYS

or a while, it seemed as if the pirates might prevail. They were outnumbered more than two to one by the islanders, but they were skilled and vicious fighters every one, even under the influence of the green grog. Sylvester, Viola and Cheesefang fought back to back, forming a triangle of whistling lethality as their swords flashed in the fitful red light from the bonfire. Sylvester learned not to shut his eyes in revulsion whenever his blade notched into the flesh of an islander; he was unable, though, to train himself to stop saying "oops, terribly sorry" each time.

The night was filled with the clash of metal upon metal, and with the screams of the dying.

The islanders were beaten back once, but then renewed the attack in a second wave.

Casualties on both sides were horrendous.

Cheesefang took an ax blow in his side and blood spurted. The rat screamed in agony, then resumed fighting with a terrible grin on his face. The islander who'd wielded the ax, another rat, was the first person Cheesefang slew after sustaining his wound.

Slowly, slowly the attackers were driven back a second time.

But then, from the thick jungle at the top of the sands, there poured another host of islanders, a reserve force that had remained in hiding so long as it looked as if the cannibals on the beach might conquer unaided. The newcomers were mainly older people, but they were armed as well as any and, while they might not have the same strength as the younger fighters, they more than made up for it in guile.

The pirates didn't stand a chance.

It was all over soon after that.

◆ ◆ ◆ ◆

Far out to sea, Sylvester could see the lights of the *Shadeblaze*. Surely the pirates aboard the ship must have been able to hear what was going on. If Jeopord had thought to turn his telescope toward the shore, he would have been able to watch the cannibals' treacherous attack on his comrades. Sylvester recalled Cheesefang's reassuring words to him before they'd come on this doomed trip ashore: *He might let us walk into the gaping jaws of death, he might, but he wouldn't let them jaws come closin' down on top of us. He be bound to find some way of rescuin' us before it's too late.* It was surely long past time for Jeopord to be coming to their rescue . . .

He said something of this over his shoulder to Viola, who was tied with him, back to back.

"It's hard to see how he *could* come to the rescue," she observed.

"What do you mean?"

"The *Shadeblaze's* presumably still firmly lodged on the reef. I didn't actually check, but I don't think he has any longboats left out there, so he and his men would have to swim to reach us, and true pirates don't swim, remember? Besides, even if he had the means to get here, he's got only a dozen pirates, not much of an army against a host of cannibals. I think we're done for, darling."

"There's no need to be fatalistic," he said grumpily.

"I'm not being fatalistic. Just facing the facts. We're both going to be lemming roasts by the time this night is over."

"Hmmf!"

If Jeopord had only about a dozen pirates on the *Shadeblaze*, there were only about a dozen of them still alive here on the island. The carnage as the islanders strove to subdue the buccaneers had been extreme. Many of the pirates had adhered to the principle that they'd rather be dead than surrender, and with reluctance the islanders had granted them their wish. But the Vendrosians had paid a very heavy penalty too. For every one pirate corpse lying in hideous stillness on the sands, there were at least three or four dead islanders. The *Shadeblaze's* complement had acquitted themselves impressively.

"Keep yer spirits up, mateys," said a familiar voice from a couple of yards away.

For some obscure reason, the Vendrosians had permitted Sylvester and Viola to bandage up the old sea rat before they were comprehensively tied up. It couldn't have been a matter of compassion; the islanders had emphatically demonstrated that compassion was a concept alien to them. Perhaps, with so much "food" already dead, they wanted to preserve, for as long as possible, those of their prey who still clung to life.

Sylvester gulped. It seemed Viola was wrong about being dead by the end of the night, but the prospect of being kept alive for weeks or months until a cannibal butcher decided it was their turn next to be a banquet was even less appealing than death.

The Vendrosian leader, Kabalore, and a handful of his biggest deputies now started moving among the captives, kicking and pulling the pirates to their feet. The air filled with nautical curses.

Sylvester and Viola, pushing backward against each other, were able to struggle upright before the little posse of islanders reached them, but Cheesefang, his movements still impaired by his wound, was less fortunate. The cannibals weren't gentle with him as they forced him to stand. The old sea rat had screamed just the once when he'd originally suffered the wound. He screamed a lot more than once now.

"You'll pay for this," said Sylvester grimly to the tormentor nearest him, a stoat who had more skulls draped over his body than even Kabalore himself. As soon as he'd spoken the words, Sylvester began berating himself inwardly for having been so stupid.

The stoat turned a terribly yellow-eyed stare upon him.

"I'll be picking my teeth with your jawbone, soon enough," he said. "If you don't hold your cack until then, I may not be too fussy about whether or not you're still alive at the time."

Sylvester swallowed hard.

"Coward!" snapped Viola.

For a moment, Sylvester thought she was speaking to him, but no, it was at the stoat she spat the word.

The stoat looked astonished. "Who the blazes do you think you are?"

"Viola Pickleberry, of course, and you?"

The question flummoxed the stoat still further.

"My name's—hey, I don't have to answer to scum like you!"

"What a very unusual name," sneered Viola.

"It's not my—"

Kabalore had noticed the exchange. "Leave her alone, Strimcrack. We've enough work to do without getting involved with the prisoners. Get those two apart," he said with a nod at Viola and Sylvester, "and then tie 'em up again separately like the others."

"Right y'are, sir!" cried Strimcrack with a display of good humor. Turning away from Kabalore, however, he added under his breath to Viola and Sylvester, "I'll see you two pay for this disrespect. Pay in agony and fear."

"Ooh-er," commented Viola loud enough for Kabalore to hear.

The remark earned her another murderous stare from Strimcrack as he bent to sever the bonds holding the two lemmings. He was not gentle in doing so and both of them suffered a welter of gashes and bruises. When he retied their wrists behind their backs the stoat made sure to tighten the cords so that they sank deep into the flesh.

"You'll be wishin' you 'adn't vexed ol' Strimcrack, you will."

"Oh, poot," said Viola, despite the fact that her face was pale with pain.

Once all the surviving pirates had been rounded up and herded to a place uncomfortably close to the pulsing red embers of the bonfire, Kabalore strutted in front of them, holding a couple of the skulls of his necklace out in front of his chest as if they were trophies he was especially proud of.

"Welcome to the island of Vendros!" he cried, just as he had when the longboats had first landed on the island's shore what seemed like many long hours ago.

His comrades set up a chorus of cackles and hoots into the dark skies. Clearly, they thought Kabalore's remark represented the height of wit. Sylvester could see them cavorting in a grotesque ritual dance behind Kabalore on the far side of the subsiding fire.

Kabalore waited until the din had died down a little before he spoke again.

"We regret we did not inform you beforehand that your stay here is destined to be a permanent one."

Once more, his cronies went into a fusillade of exaggerated laughter.

"Come again," murmured Cheesefang into Sylvester's ear. "Yer've been a luvverly audience. Thangyoo, thangyoo. I'm gonna be 'ere all next week, wiv a matinee on We'nsday."

"And," Kabalore was saying, holding up a black-and-white paw to his comrades to tell them to quieten down, that the really good bit was yet to come, "we're *especially* looking forward to the stay you're going to have *inside* us!"

This time Sylvester thought the noise was going to shake the stars loose from their positions in the heavens.

"I wonder if this guy is going to be still as funny when he grows up and hits puberty," said Viola caustically when she could make herself heard. She seemed unaware that Strimcrack was still fixing her with a lethal glare.

Sylvester wished he could find it within himself to joke like the other two. All he could see ahead was a long tunnel that got quickly darker and quickly narrower with, at the end of it, himself being slaughtered and butchered in the most revolting manner imaginable and then cooked and devoured by the kind of people he'd never even wanted to *meet*, let alone get eaten by. It wasn't the most cheering of anticipations and there was no use pretending otherwise. Jeopord had clearly written them off, so there was no chance of rescue from that quarter.

Aside from Jeopord, there was really only Mrs. Pickleberry and, doughty as she was, what could anybody honestly expect an elderly lemming to accomplish, even if she was armed with not one, but two, sturdy rolling pins?

If she was even still alive.

He and Viola had come a long way from Foxglove, and there'd been many times when Sylvester had thought they wouldn't survive to live another hour – or even another minute – but he'd never experienced such an abandonment of all hope before. This really was it.

Kabalore, his cohorts having finally fallen relatively still, now addressed himself to the dozen or so bedraggled captives who stood in front of him with their hands tied behind their backs. Clearly, he'd expected to see them with their heads hung low in despair and dejection, and he quailed when he saw the reality.

These were pirates and they met his gaze with glares of defiance and threat.

All except one, who wasn't a pirate at all: Sylvester Lemmington.

Kabalore recovered his composure swiftly.

"I owe it to you, to you *steaks* and *chops* and *roasts* and *hashes*" – he lingered over each word with greater lipsmacking relish than the last – "I owe it to you to tell you what's going to be happening to you next."

"It'd be quite all right if you just left us in ignorance," Sylvester piped up.

"Silence, squirt!" said Kabalore.

The pirates murmured and grumbled in an ominous way, but Kabalore obviously thought they were safely under control and he was in no danger.

"As you can see," continued Kabalore, gesturing around him at the numerous corpses of pirates and islanders, "we already have a plentiful supply of fresh meat. Indeed, we're going to have to feast for a week and a day and guzzle as hard as we can the whole of that time if we're going to get through it all before it begins to go" – he gave a dandified sniff – "off."

Sylvester's insides turned coldly acid.

The cannibal chieftain beckoned behind him, and several burly islanders unwound long, dark whips from their waists. The whips looked vicious and intimidating, even when idle. The captives hardly needed the demonstration one of the Vendrosians gave, making his lash crack like a lightning strike.

"My friends here," said Kabalore, "are going to escort you to comfortable accommodations in the cave we islanders call the *Larder*."

The whip-wielders pressed forward and, grumble and swear as they might, the pirates had little choice but to obey orders. Soon, they were being herded in single file up the beach to where, unnoticed by Sylvester earlier, there was a notch in the thick wall of jungle vegetation. They plodded along a beaten path between the trees and tangled bushes, trying to see what lay ahead in the unreliable light of the blazing torches their captors held aloft. The noise of the sea breakers died out behind them, only to be replaced by the eerie sounds of the island jungle at night. Sylvester could sense eyes everywhere in the darkness watching him, not with any malice or intent to harm, but with a sort of cold, dispassionate curiosity. In a way, he found it almost comforting. This seemed far less frightening than his first experience of a jungle, back on Blighter Island. Or maybe it was just that there was no room left for any more fear in his mind. The whips, the cries of coarse mirth from the sweat-streaked islanders, the name of the place they were going to – all of these were enough to cram a small lemming brain with so much terror that it blanked out. It was almost as if there were no terror there at all.

"Don't worry," said Viola suddenly. She was walking directly behind him.

"Don't worry?" he said incredulously. Their talking attracted a glare from the nearest islander, but the weasel did nothing to stop them. "Don't you think that there's really rather a lot to be worried about?"

"We'll pull through, somehow or other. Something will turn up, you'll see. Something always has before."

She was right in that last remark, of course. Otherwise they wouldn't be here to have the conversation, but Sylvester couldn't help feeling the logic was like that of someone who jumps off a high cliff and, for most of the fall, can't understand why people said it was dangerous.

Sylvester decided not to point this out. Let Viola cling to her hopefulness, however misplaced. It was obviously her lifeline.

He wished, for some reason he couldn't understand, that Mrs. Pickleberry were here. He'd never have thought the day, or night, would come when he might yearn for the presence of the curmudgeonly old lemming as reassurance, but he did now.

I wonder what she's up to, he said to himself. *I wonder if Jeopord's discovered she's aboard the ship?*

And Rasco. I miss the little nutcase so much. I hope he's safe.

Nearby, a whip struck skin and a pirate yelped in pain or outrage or both.

Sylvester put his head down and kept walking.

◈ ◈ ◈ ◈ ◈

When they reached it, perhaps half an hour later, the Larder proved to be far more spacious than Sylvester had expected. When Kabalore had talked about "comfortable accommodations," Sylvester had assumed the worst: somewhere dark, cramped and cold, its walls dripping with foul water, its shadows filled with small creatures with large, venomous bites. Instead, the captives were ushered into a wide cavern with a sandy floor. There were niches in the walls where the guards could lodge their torches, lighting up the space warmly. The walls were also fitted out with metal rings and ropes, and briskly, with the ease of long practice, the Vendrosians secured their captives. Sylvester found he could walk perhaps three paces to one side or the other, but not much farther. Certainly the rope, tied from a ring about a yard above his head to the binding that fastened his forepaws behind his back, didn't have enough slack in it for him to be able to turn himself right around. He and the others were going to have to learn to sleep standing up. What they were going to do about other bodily functions he didn't know; he hoped he wasn't going to be the first of the captives to find out.

It was some consolation that Viola was the next prisoner along the wall. At least they hadn't been separated. On his other side was Cheesefang and that was heartening as well. Sylvester didn't know that he *liked* the disreputable, temperamental sea rat, but at least he'd grown accustomed to him. The other pirates Sylvester knew only from having seen them on occasion around the deck of the *Shadeblaze*. He had no idea what any of them were called.

Once the Vendrosian guards were satisfied none of the prisoners could escape their bonds, Kabalore ambled into the Larder carrying a bulging wineskin and bearing a broad complacent grin.

He bowed sarcastically to the tethered pirates, then raised the wineskin to his lips. A long stream of the potent green grog jetted into his mouth, and he drank with loud satisfaction.

"That's better," he said at last, lowering the skin and wiping the back of his paw appreciatively across his mouth. He laughed. "I do hope you folks won't regard us as terribly ill-mannered if we leave our guests on their own for a while, will you? As you know, my friends and I have some concentrated feasting to get done, and there's no time like the present to get started on that sort of job."

He and the guards cackled loud and long at this display of humor.

To make sure the prisoners knew their place, a couple of the guards lashed out with their whips, the savage blows drawing blood wherever they fell. Sylvester cringed, certain he or Viola was going to be next, but fortunately they were spared. At last, with Kabalore in the lead, the islanders left the pirates to their own devices.

"Now, there's a stroke o' luck," said Cheesefang as soon as the cannibals were gone.

"What is?" said Sylvester.

"Them bastards done left us with their torches."

"So?"

"Flame burns through rope, dunnit?"

"It also burns through flesh," Sylvester pointed out. "Besides, the cannibals have obviously thought of that. Our ropes aren't long enough for any of us to get anywhere *near* one of the torches."

"See these?" said Cheesefang, opening his mouth wide.

Sylvester turned his head and found himself staring in sick fascination at what looked like a stone wall a moment after a herd of buffalo has stampeded through it.

"Them's teeth," said Cheesefang, making the wall wobble nauseatingly.

"Er, yes," replied Sylvester. "I'd guessed that bit."

"And we was given toothypegs," the sea rat continued, "for a purpose, which purpose is *chewing*. And ropes is made for getting chewed through, see?"

Sylvester doubted Cheesefang's teeth were good for chewing through anything tougher than porridge – and only porridge that hadn't been cooked by Bladderbulge, at that. He mumbled something tactful to this effect.

"I know that," countered Cheesefang, his voice full of exasperation. "Them's good *pirate* toothypegs, which is to say there's a lot o' them missin' and the ones has survived is a bit on the bluntish side. Same for me as it is for me mates 'ere, see?" He rotated his head to indicate the other pirates. All were listening intently to the conversation. "That's prob'ly wot them cannibal bumheads was counting on when they thought it was safe to leave us alone. But wot they didn't notice is that *you*, Sylvester," Cheesefang continued, "you an' Little Miss Droppydrawers there—"

"How *dare* you call her Little Miss—"

Cheesefang ignored the protest. "You two ain't got pirate teeth yet. Yer toothypegs ain't matured into the well developed pirate standard. An' yer rodents. Yer whole lives is built aroun' chewin' stuff. You gettin' me?"

"I think so," said Sylvester, hackles still ruffled, "but however sharp our teeth are, they're not going to help us. The rope's behind me and Kabalore and his crew didn't leave me enough leeway to turn myself round to get at it."

"Don't have to." Cheesefang looked and sounded incredulous. "You tryin' to tell me that you an' Little Miss Droppydrawers 'aven't ever 'ad to escape from a prison cell?"

"Um, no. We haven't. We're law-abiding citizens."

Cheesefang spat. "*Lemmings!* Clueless. I *tol'* Cap'n Rustbane, the triple-breasted goddess bless his soul, I *told*'im gettin' involved with lemmings was a big mistake, but did 'e listen?"

"No," said one of the other pirates, a beaver with two hooks in place of forepaws.

"I want your help I'll ask for it, Pimplebrains," snarled Cheesefang.

Pimplebrains? thought Sylvester in bewilderment. *Is that a name or an insult?*

Cheesefang was taking deep breaths, as if trying to get his sanity under control. "Then I s'pose," he said heavily to Sylvester, "yer ol' Uncle Cheesefang's goin' to 'ave to talk you through this one."

"How to, er, turn ourselves around when the rope's too tight to let us?" said Viola, sounding as puzzled as Sylvester felt.

"Yes. No. Sort of. Good to find ye've not fallen asleep, Miss Droppydrawers. See, wot ye've—"

"Cheesefang?"

"—got to . . . Yes?"

"You call me 'Miss Droppydrawers' one more time and you're going to find your ugly head jammed firmly up the aperture your drawers would ordinarily cover. Got that?"

Cheesefang looked suddenly nervous. A gleam came into his eye that Sylvester had seen before. It was that gleam of mingled awe and admiration that tended to be in the sea rat's eyes when Daphne Pickleberry was around. Now, clearly, Cheesefang had discovered that her daughter deserved something of the same.

"What ye have to do," continued the rat, a tone of unaccustomed politeness entering his voice, "is back yerselves up against the wall as hard and as far as ye can possibly manage, see? Watch me."

Cheesefang shuffled back and back on the sands until, standing upright, he was nearly flat against the wall almost directly under the metal ring to which he was tethered.

Sylvester saw at once the point of the maneuver. The rope from the metal ring dangled right alongside Cheesefang's face. All the old pirate had to do was turn his head and, with a certain amount of juggling, manipulate the rope with his mouth until it was between his teeth.

"Gotcha!" said Sylvester in admiration.

Lemmings aren't the same shape as rats, they're somewhat, well, *pudgier*, to be forthright about it, and it proved a lot more difficult for Sylvester and Viola to accomplish what Cheesefang had demonstrated, but at last, they succeeded.

"Ye ready?" said Cheesefang.

"Uh-huh," grunted the two lemmings.

"Then get chewin' as quick as yers can! No knowin' when those cannibal swine be gettin' back."

Sylvester didn't need the urging.

The rope was made from some type of local vines, twisted tightly together, and it tasted like a bar of old soap that had been left on the side of the bath to dry and crack for a year. Or, at least, that's what Sylvester thought. He tried eating soap exactly once when he was very young and going through what his mother had euphemized as his "experimental stage" (his father had used franker terms for it, the only repeatable one being "nuisance"), and strangely enough, he could remember how it tasted, despite the span of years.

Disgusting.

And here he was on a cannibal island facing the same prospect but this time with reluctance. Not only did the rope taste disgusting, it was tough. Out of the corner of his eye, Sylvester could see the back of Viola's head and could tell she was finding the rope as resistant to her teeth as he was. Both of them began to gasp from the effort and the pain.

At last, Sylvester found that only one strand of the rope in his mouth was left intact. He chomped down hard on it and felt the fibers beginning to disintegrate. Unwilling to have the rope on his tongue anymore, he danced away from the wall, jerking with his wrists as hard as he could.

The rope resisted for a moment, then snapped.

Sylvester went sprawling flat on his face in the cool sand.

A few moments later, Viola did exactly the same. They lay there, their heads a few yards apart, grinning at each other with the satisfaction of a difficult task achieved, the sound of their breath echoing all around the cave.

There was a curious muffled drumming noise. Lazily, Sylvester turned to see the pirates, unable to clap the hands that were tied behind their backs, were stamping their feet to applaud the two lemmings.

"Thanks, folks," said Sylvester smugly.

"Ahem," Cheesefang said a minute or two later, once the pirates had quietened again. "Yer still not done, you two."

"What?" said Viola.

"One o' yer's got to gnash through the rope at the other one's wrists, ain't yer?"

"I don't suppose the islanders left any swords or daggers lying around, did they?" said Sylvester with implausible optimism. "Even a pair of scissors would do."

The cave filled with the pirates' derisive laughter.

"Kabalore may be stupid, but 'e's not stupid," said Cheesefang.

Sylvester sniffed. "Just wondering." He glanced across the floor to where Viola was wriggling to her feet. "I'll do it," he told her. "Once your arms are free, you can untie me."

She looked as if she might be about to object, then he saw her change her mind.

Gnawing through the ropes at Viola's wrists was somehow not as bad. Sylvester guessed it must be that this was fresher rope than the one that was hanging from the wall. Or maybe it was the proximity of Viola, her familiar warmth, that made him feel more cheerful. Whatever, it didn't seem long at all until she was rubbing her forepaws together to get the blood circulating in them once more, and a minute or two later she was picking with her sharp, nimble claws at the knots that bound him.

In less than half an hour everyone was free. The two lemmings were the heroes of the day. No one even *thought* of calling them hamsters.

Cheesefang sidled over to the cave entrance and peered outside.

"Garn," he pronounced, his face twisting into a scowl as he turned back to face the others. "Now, there's a rotten stroke of Lady Fate if ever I did see one. Them 'orrible cannonballs 'as posting a posse of guards not an 'undred yards from 'ere. They's feastin' and boozin' away like they got a grudge against their guts, but they's armed up to the eyeballs with spears and cudgels and longbows and swords. Most o' the blades they're carrying be *ourn*, by jingo! Ain't no way to escape this direction, there ain't."

Viola looked downcast. "This calls for a curse," she said.

The pirates gasped.

"*Bottom!*" she exclaimed, putting a lot of feeling into the word.

There was a moment's silence, then the pirates started sniggering.

Sylvester put his arm around Viola's waist comfortingly. "I don't think they regard that as much of a curse," he said.

"When you've all finished being idiots," said the beaver called Pimplebrains coldly from the rear of the cave, "there's something important I'd like to show yers."

All eyes turned toward him.

"There's another way out of this cave," he said, pointing with one of his metal hooks. "Look."

Now that the beaver had drawn their attention to it, it was obvious. Sylvester couldn't understand why none of them except Pimplebrains had noticed before. Maybe the flickering of the wall-mounted brands had deceived their eyes into thinking it was just another shadow. Or maybe it was because they were all focusing so intently on ridding themselves of their hated bonds.

Partly concealed by a vertical fold in the rocky wall of the cave there was a pitch-black cleft.

"Could be just 'arf a yard deep," observed Cheesefang cynically.

"It ain't," Pimplebrains retorted. "While you lot was putting on yer variety show about bottoms" – the sneer almost dripped – "I was exploratizing back 'ere. I reckon this crevice goes a long, long way into the hill. I couldn't go too far, because I was running out of light and, unlike Jeopord and his kind, I can't see in the dark. But I got far enough to smell the breath of the sea and the open sky, somewhere way in the distance."

"Blimey," said one of the pirates, a one-armed weasel. "I'm game for this." He leaped to the wall and snatched down the torch from the niche. "The rest of you comin' with me and Pimplebrains?"

The beaver held up a hook in caution. "Could be it's a dead end. We could get stuck in there an' not be able ter find a way back."

"It's worth the risk," cried the weasel.

The rest of pirates raised a motley cheer – a very quiet cheer, because of the guards outside the cave entrance. Soon, everyone except Pimplebrains was equipped with a torch, and some carried two. By silent agreement, Cheesefang was the person to lead the way into the dark, narrow passageway, with Pimplebrains following right behind him. Sylvester and Viola came next, then the remainder of the party.

The ceiling in there wasn't much higher than some of the larger pirates' heads, and when a stalactite hung down, which was frequently, it was even lower. There was a fair amount of bumping and thumping as unwary creatures collided with the stone pendants, not to mention the astringent smell of burned fur from accidents with the torches. The stalagmites too were a menace, often rendering an already narrow passage almost impossibly so. Once or twice Sylvester, as he struggled to clamber around a particularly large stalagmite, was certain he wasn't going to be able to squeeze himself through. Each time he managed it, of course, but he winced at the thought of how much of themselves the bigger animals must be scraping off on the sharp flints of the walls.

It took him a time to realize, what with all the exertion, but the air in the crevice was a whole lot colder than in the big cave the cannibals called the Larder.

He shuddered. How long could it be before their escape was discovered? Surely the islanders would instantly guess where the pirates had gone. They'd lived here since time immemorial. They must be fully aware of the back exit to the Larder.

Sylvester cursed himself. He should have thought to persuade Cheesefang and the others to leave a false trail outside the cave mouth, so the Vendrosians might be deceived into thinking the fugitives had fled into the deep jungle. Too late for that now. Half his life he seemed to be thinking of good ideas long after they'd have been useful.

He gritted his teeth and told himself crossly to get a grip. The only good option at the moment was to get as far from the Larder as possible. If Pimplebrains was right, they'd eventually come out into the open air. Then, if they were very lucky, they could lose themselves in the night before the cannibals even realized they'd gone.

"Strike me timbers and lash me thighs!" said Cheesefang suddenly in astonishment, up ahead.

"Gawd luvaduck!" agreed Pimplebrains. The awe in his voice was obvious.

Sylvester pressed forward with renewed vigor, holding his torch out in front of him.

When he saw what the other two had seen, his jaw dropped. "Blimey," he breathed.

"What is it?" said Viola, close behind him. Then: "Oh!"

For Sylvester, it was like the first time that, as a very small lemming, he'd been taken by his parents to the temple back in Foxglove. The interior of the building had seemed larger, somehow, than the open sky outside. He felt as if there might be clouds and thunderstorms up near the temple's painted ceiling. The sheer scale of the place gave it an ambience of the most profound mysticism. He'd gaped in awe. It had been a long time before Hortensia and Jasper had been able to persuade him to come with them to the family pew.

In the years since, his mind had grown a little more sophisticated, of course, and he tended now when entering the temple to have to control his lips from moving into a mocking curl. But that reduced not at all the sense of unadulterated wonder that flooded through him as he gazed into what was a far vaster chamber than the Foxglove temple.

The rest of the pirates now stumbled out of the constricted passageway and were gathered together in a huddle. No one spoke very loudly. It would have seemed somehow disrespectful.

The torchlight could penetrate only a small distance into the cavern. Its far walls could be detected only as occasional glimmers, occasional impressions of things that might or might not have been actually seen. Sand covered the cavern's floor. The walls were a conglomeration of steep, misshapen rocks that were so black they might have been coal; the dancing of the torchlight made them seem like the claws of some enormous creature – at rest now but ready at any moment to pounce upon its prey. Overhead in the ceiling, the torches' flames made crystals twinkle like the red embers that had floated in the air above the cannibals' bonfire.

But none of these were what caught Sylvester's eye.

In the middle of the cavern, lying three-quarters of the way over to one side, was a ship that dwarfed the *Shadeblaze*. Somehow, Sylvester knew it was a ship, even though it looked nothing like the pirate vessel. Its hull didn't just cover the lower half of this ship but extended all the way round. It was made not of wooden planks, like the *Shadeblaze*'s, but of some dull gray metal that seemed to swallow light and give nothing back in return. There were some angular markings engraved into the hull near the bluntly pointed tip that made no sense in any of the languages Sylvester could read, living or dead. But far more obvious was the huge, circular, splinter-rimmed hole in the hull about one-third of the way back from the ship's prow. It was high up near where the water line would usually be, but as the ship sat askew on the sandy floor, it was close enough to the ground for them to walk through. In the hole one could see nothing but the menace of dark shadows. Even those were enough to convey that this ship was damaged beyond all hope of repair.

"What in Sagaria is that thing?" said Cheesefang.

"I can tell you what it is," chipped in Sylvester.

"Ye can?"

"Yes. Sometimes it's valuable having an archivist along with you."

Cheesefang snorted. "I'll believe ye. Thousands'd rather tear orf their own 'eads. So, go on then. What is that thing?"

The rat was trying to keep his voice nonchalant. The big giveaway was that he couldn't bear to turn his gaze away from the huge edifice that filled the center of the cavern.

Sylvester's own voice became humble. "It's one of the ships of the Zindars."

"Of the wot?"

"The Zindars." Sylvester explained as concisely as he could. The pirates gathered around him, listening eagerly to his narrative. For once they were silent. That is, until there was mention of the Zindars' treasure chest, and the fact that Jeopord possessed the map old Cap'n Adamite had created. The map that showed the location where the treasure chest was buried. Sylvester felt it was time, way past time, that the pirates should know all this. There had been far too many secrets kept back from this crew, first by Throatsplitter Adamite, then by Terrigan Rustbane and, most recently by their latest captain, Jeopord.

At the same time, something made him hold back from telling them that the map Jeopord owned showed its "X" alongside the wrong island.

Think of it as my insurance, he decided. He glanced at Viola and she nodded back, clearly understanding his thoughts.

"Ye mean," said Cheesefang, stroking his jaw with the paw that wasn't holding a guttering torch, "the treasure chest of the Zindars could be right 'ere in front of us?"

"Unlikely," said Sylvester promptly. "Vendros isn't the island marked on Cap'n Adamite's map."

"I remember Cap'n Adamite," struck in Pimplebrains. "He was all right, he was."

"Thank ye for that," said Cheesefang sardonically. At last, he turned to look Sylvester in the eye.

"But ye think this . . . *object* belonged to the Zindars?"

Sylvester gulped. "Yes, I do. I think this must have been one of the sites of the great last battle between the Zindars and their persecutors from the stars. I think a bolt from one of the foe's great energy weapons punched the hole in the side of the Zindar vessel that we can see in front of us. They must have had other ships, obviously, because they were able to escape from Sagaria back to the starways, but—"

"So 'ow come yer thinks their treasure chest ain't buried 'ere?" Cheesefang interrupted.

Sylvester gave his very best imitation of a carefree laugh. "It *could* be buried here. I'm not saying for definite it isn't, but it also could be buried in any one of a thousand *other* places. And, like I said, Vendros isn't the island indicated on Adamite's map."

Cheesefang glowered. "I served under Josiah Adamite for many a long year and, lemme tell you, years were very much longer back then. 'Specially if ye was serving on the *Shadeblaze* when Cap'n Adamite was the skip. And I can tell ye this, safe in the knowledge that there's none here can countersay me, ol' Throatsplitter was a devious bugger and there's no way he would tell the truth if there was the chance to tell something different. Most particerlarly when he was concoctin' hisself a treasure map."

Sylvester tried not to let his astonishment show. It was as if the sea rat could somehow read the dead captain's mind.

"So," Cheesefang continued, once more scratching his jaw, "wot I'm sayin' is this could just as likely be the island where the treasure's buried as anywhere else in this part of the ocean. My guess is ol' Josiah'd have made sure 'is treasure map was of the right *region*, 'cause he'd need that information hisself if he was goin' to navigate here. But I think 'e prob'ly put a mark on the chart indicating the wrong island, just to get up people's noses, like."

Sylvester said nothing. Apparently, that was enough for Cheesefang to know that he'd penetrated the lemming's, and Cap'n Adamite's, secret.

"Wot I'm thinking," Cheesefang concluded, "is that we should mebbe start diggin', jus' on the offchance. The dead ship's here. There's no better clue than that, that these Zindthings stuffed their chest inter the ground somewhere near it?"

Sylvester could think of a thousand reasons why this line of reasoning was flawed, but all he did was stand there with his mouth opening and closing like a goldfish's.

"This place is colossal," said Viola. "You could be searching here forever and *still* not know if the treasure chest lay just one more spadeful away."

"It's a chance I is willin' to take, Miss Droppydrawers," said Cheesefang with what probably seemed like civility if you were a sea rat.

"Cheesefang?" said Viola in a deceptively light tone.

"Ah, yerss?" The sea rat looked anxious. He'd obviously remembered their last conversation on the subject of drawers.

"Are you *fond* of your head?"

"Er, yerss."

"Then just be careful, you hear?"

"Um, yerss." The relief in the sea rat's voice was manifest.

Despite the objections of Viola and Sylvester, the sea rat was determined the pirates should give the cavern floor at least a perfunctory search for the Zindar's chest. He ignored their warnings that it surely couldn't be too much longer before the cannibals discovered they were missing and came in hot pursuit.

All this time, the group of pirates had, without any particular volition, been moving slowly toward the enormous gray vessel. As they grew closer, Sylvester began to appreciate how truly gargantuan it was. And there was more, it was heavy. He had the sense it had so much mass it was drawing them toward it by gravity. Just the hole in its side was bigger than the Library in Foxglove, the place where he'd spent so much of his life. He wished he could see farther into that hole, but the light from their torches seemed incapable of penetrating its blackness.

He shivered.

Who knew what secrets there might be hidden in the Zindars' ship?

"Besides," Viola added, "we don't have any spades."

"Yes, we do," said Pimplebrains.

They'd just reached the prow of the mighty ship, and now the feeble light of their torches probed into an area of cavern that had been invisible to the pirates before. It seemed to have been the scene of a battle, or at least a skirmish, because on the sand lay enormous, unrecognizable bones and skulls, rusted weapons so huge a whole troop of rats and lemmings might find too heavy to raise, and, scattered hither and thither with no apparent reason, curved plates of what Sylvester guessed must once have been metal armor.

"That stuff's too big for us to dig with," he said.

"Nah," said Cheesefang. "There are some smaller bits as well, see?"

He was right. Between the monstrous swords and the mammoth breastplates were plenty of pieces of metal more in proportion to lemming paws. Pimplebrains didn't have to, of course, because he could scrabble at the ground with his metal hooks, but the rest of the party went scavenging amongst the detritus on the cave floor to find suitable digging implements. The item Sylvester eventually settled on looked as if it might once have been a muzzle-guard. He could barely lift it. He deliberately chose not to imagine the scale of the creature whose muzzle must once have needed guarding.

Once everyone was equipped, Cheesefang called for order.

"You, I mean *you*, Sylv and Droppydr—ahem, Viola, you go with Pimplebrains and dig on the side of the ship we just come away from."

"The side the cannibals is likely to come out into first, you mean?" said Pimplebrains dourly.

"Ye's got it in one," Cheesefang confirmed. "Ye's pretty bright for someone with pimples for brains." He waited for the others to laugh. No one did. "Next you's'll work out how to pick your nose with them 'ooks."

"They've feasted on many a pirate's gizzard," observed Pimplebrains with frightening quietness, eyeing Cheesefang's throat. "Tearing flesh, they're good at that."

But the beaver clearly had no inclination to take the argument any further, because with a nod to the two lemmings he led them back round the bow of the Zindar ship.

"This is dimwitted," said Viola, gazing around at the great tract of vacant sand, which was featureless except for the trail of shuffling footprints the pirates had left as they advanced toward the ship. "Like Sylvester said, we could dig here for the rest of our lives and still have hardly started."

"You're right," said Pimplebrains with a chuckle. "But Cheesefang? He's too stupid to think that through, even though Sylvester here told him so in so many words. Cheesefang's going ta set everyone to digging as fast and furious as they can dig, hoping to get the treasure out of the ground and into his pockets without Jeopord knowing. 'Cause, my little friends, if the cannibals ain't the first to come and find us, it's going to be Jeopord. An' I'm not sure which of them as I'd prefer it to be."

Sylvester screwed up his eyes in confusion. "I don't think I follow that. Anyway, how will Jeopord know where we are?"

"He's got *instincts*, that mangy old cat has. I've seen him track someone he's never even clapped eyes on halfway across the open ocean and find him as easy as can be. He's like Rustbane was, that way." Pimplebrains took a deep breath. "And he's like Cap'n Rustbane in lots of other ways too, one of which is not sharing booty if he can possibly get away with it."

Sylvester thought back to Cap'n Rustbane's condemnation of Threefingers Bogsprinkler for pilfering goodies from the treasure room. He recalled the fox's grand speech about how the human had been stealing not just from him, but from the whole crew and blinked at the fox's hypocrisy.

"So what you're saying," Sylvester pursued, "is that Jeopord wouldn't mind losing a few more of the *Shadeblaze*'s complement so as not to let them have any of the riches that might be their due?"

"Bingo," said Pimplebrains. "At least them cannibals would likely keep us alive a while, so we might get another chance of escape. Jeopord, though? He'd as soon see us cut down where we stood."

"So what are we doing here?" Letting his muzzle-guard drop to the sand, Sylvester gestured around them.

"We're staying out of Cheesefang's sight, is what we're doing. We might even see if there's a good place to hide inside this." Pimplebrains jerked a hook toward the vessel looming overhead.

Viola wrapped her forepaws around her chest. "Spooky."

"Sure is," Pimplebrains replied. "Which makes it a good place to hide. Pirates is a superstitious lot for the most part. Like anyone else, the stupider they is the more superstitious they is, and Cheesefang's as stupid as they come."

Pimplebrains grinned broadly and Sylvester found himself beginning to like the old beaver.

"Tell you one more thing," said Pimplebrains. "Whichever way Jeopord and the crew come hunting for us, it ain't going to be through the Larder. There ain't enough of them to fight a battle with a couple hundred Vendrosians. They're going to find the *other* way into this place, the one you can smell if you smells real hard. And the first folks they's going to trip over are—"

"—Cheesefang and the others," said Viola softly. "You've really got this worked out, haven't you, Pimplebrains."

The beaver grinned again. "And, as a matter of fac', I 'ave learned 'ow to pick me nose with me hooks, only it's not something I do in front of ladies, see?"

The three of them laughed briefly, then Sylvester looked warily at that gaping wound in the vessel.

"You really think it'd be safe for us to go in there?"

"I didn't say as it'd be *safe*," said Pimplebrains. "Wot I said was it might be the best thing for us to do."

Viola bent forward and put her head slightly to one side, as if that might let her see farther into the darkness. "What do think might be in there?"

"Haven't a clue, young miss. No way to find out without going in there to look, I reckon." Pimplebrains hefted his torch. "You two game?"

"As game as we'll ever be," said Sylvester, hefting his own torch high.

"Then let's be getting at it," said Viola, surprising the other two by flouncing ahead of them across the short stretch of sand to reach the side of the ship. When she reached the tortured metal rimming the great chasm, she didn't hesitate or look right or left, she just jumped straight into the blackness.

Sylvester and Pimplebrains hurried to follow.

⚜ ⚜ ⚜ ⚜

"The Zindars must have been enormous," said Viola an hour or so later. Her whisper seemed to echo away into infinite emptiness.

They'd lost count of the number of chambers they'd come through, the number of corridors they'd traversed. The rooms in here – cabins, Sylvester supposed – were built on a scale that surpassed anything any denizen of Sagaria might have been able to use. He'd read the old bestiaries in the Foxglove Library and he knew that some of the lemmings of old who'd explored inland had come across creatures that made even human beings seem tiny, but none of those had been remotely as big as the Zindars must have been.

A thought troubled Sylvester. Well, *many* thoughts troubled him at the moment, but one of them was uppermost.

If the treasure chest was built on the same scale as the Zindars themselves, how would the pirates, even if they found it, get it away to the *Shadeblaze* from wherever it was buried? How would they even be able to open its lid?

The air in here smelled not so much musty as dead, as if it had been breathed too many times and was now, after all this time, reluctantly being breathed again. The floors and walls were remarkably clean, although Sylvester confessed to himself he wasn't certain exactly which were floors and which were walls – or which were ceilings for that matter. It depended on which way up the Zindar vessel was supposed to be. Was it lying on its side in the cavern's sand, or was it the right way up? There were monumental protrusions jutting out from surfaces that Sylvester would ordinarily have guessed were furniture, but they didn't help him orient himself at all, since some stuck up from the "floors," some hung from the "ceilings," and some were halfway up the "walls."

For the most part, the surfaces beneath their feet were empty of clutter, but every now and then the explorers would find themselves having to step gingerly through a field of twisted metal and broken glass. It was as if a mighty fist had systematically pulverized a hardware store, including its windows and display cases.

Most impressive of all was the silence.

It made them whisper.

It made the three of them walk on tiptoe.

It was a silence that had a distinct presence all its own.

It was, Sylvester decided, the silence of time.

"You were surely right, this is a good place to hide," he said to Pimplebrains. "You could conceal an army in here and no one'd ever find it."

"That's the good news," the beaver responded. Just over the past few minutes he seemed, unaccountably, to have become glummer and glummer.

"There's bad news?"

"You seen any food anywhere?"

Sylvester contemplated. "Now you mention it, no. That is, er, a bit of a drawback for a hiding place."

"And," added Pimplebrains, curling his lip, "can you remember the way we came?"

"Well, we came into the ship, of course," said Viola, rolling her eyes, "and then we . . . Oh, I see what you mean."

"I blame meself," said Pimplebrains gloomily. "You two, you don't know any better. But me? I'm a pirate and a warrior bold, the veteran of many a doughty campaign and hazardous expedition. I know better'n to come in here without memorizing the way we took, but . . ."

"You were as awestruck as we were, weren't you?" said Viola.

"'Awestruck' is a 'ceedingly hifalutin' word. 'Gobsmacked' is more my style o' thing to be. But, yes, I've been gobsmacked, and it's made me careless. Which ain't no excuse."

Sylvester laughed lightly. "There's dust on the floor," he said. "We can easily find our way back out again. We just follow our footsteps."

Pimplebrains looked down and his face crumpled in consternation and horror. "I am stupider than I ever thought possible," he breathed. "Oh, may the triple-breasted goddess forgive my imbecility."

"What are you talking about?" said Sylvester. He'd believed he'd just solved their problem, but now he was just confused.

"And you're no better," the beaver growled.

"What?"

"If we can see our footsteps in the dust, so can anyone who comes following us!"

As if in answer, there came a tiny, furtive sound from the corridor they'd not long ago left.

Somebody was in here with them!

MANY RIDDLES SOLVED, MANY OTHERS REMAIN

Pimplebrains and Viola heard the sound too. Without saying a word, the three did their best to melt into the wall. Sylvester could hear Viola fighting to get her breathing under control. He did the same himself.

"What about these?" he whispered to the pirate, nodding toward his torch.

Pimplebrains glanced at him, then returned his gaze toward the gloom at the far end of the chamber they were in. "We hang on to 'em," he pronounced. "They're the only weapons we got, 'ceptin' my hooks and your trotters."

"They are *not* trotters!"

"Don't matter. Now shaddap."

"But whoever it is'll see us."

"Unless they're deaf they already know 'xactly where we are, so that don't matter. Now shaddap or I'll do the shadding for yer."

Sylvester drew breath to protest again, then thought better of it.

Was it his imagination or was there another of those stealthy little noises from the corridor? No, not his imagination. He'd definitely heard something. It was a soft sweeping noise, as if someone were pulling an empty sack across the metal floor. There was nothing hostile about it; nothing like the hiss a sword might make when drawn from its scabbard, or the clank of a morning star's chain or the zing of a bowstring being tensed. But the very ordinariness of the little noise sent a shiver down Sylvester's spine in a way none of those other sounds could have done.

There it was again.

"What do you think it is?" said Viola, her voice so soft as to be almost silent.

"How the hell should I know?" answered Pimplebrains rudely. "How the hell should any of us know?"

Her eyes sparked.

Sylvester put his paw on her shoulder. "Hush."

Viola froze for an instant, then bobbed her head in acquiescence. She took his hand in hers and interlaced her claws with his. No words were needed. They were both terrified but it could have been worse. They might have been terrified alone.

There was a different sound, the rattle of claws on a hard surface, and this time it came from directly outside the chamber door.

"I can see you," came a voice. "Who are you? What are you doing here?"

Sylvester started to reply, but Pimplebrains put a hook on his forepaw to restrain him.

"Let me handle this," the grizzled beaver hissed. Louder, Pimplebrains called, "We're honest adventurers. We intend to bring you no harm."

A small shape, barely larger than Sylvester himself, came into view around the jamb of the doorway. The light was too poor for them to make out any details, but Sylvester felt Pimplebrains relax. The person they could see seemed to be on his own, or her own, perhaps.

"I've heard people say that before," said the stranger coldly, "and the next thing I've known they've been trying to make a casserole out of me."

Pimplebrains laughed mirthlessly. "We're not cannibals, if that's what you're thinking."

"That's what *they* said too." Very slowly, the stranger was moving toward them, paws moving silently now on the metal floor. "Or a fricassée," it added.

Pimplebrains looked perplexed. "Eh?"

"A fricassée. If they didn't fancy a casserole, they usually decided on a fricassée instead. Terribly predictable, don't you think?"

Pimplebrains rolled his eyes at Viola and Sylvester. "We've got ourselves a nutter here."

"You say you're not cannibals?" the stranger continued, drawing inexorably closer.

"Not us," confirmed Sylvester, peering at the oncomer. "You're ... you're a lemming, aren't you? Just like us."

Pimplebrains coughed. "Not me."

The stranger ignored the hook-handed beaver. "Yes, I can see you two are lemmings like me, only many years younger, but that doesn't mean anything. That buffoon of a cannibal chieftain, Kabalore, has several lemmings in his flock. They're just as bloodthirsty as any of the rest of that mob, just as keen on casserole."

"Or fricassée," Viola put in.

The stranger was close enough now that they could see him nod. "Or fricassée," he concurred. "Although, usually, I haven't hung around to find out the culinary particulars."

Sylvester shuddered. "How did you escape them?"

"I haven't, always," replied the stranger in a frighteningly mild manner. He settled back on his haunches and regarded them dispassionately. "Sometimes, I've run them through with my sword or split their skulls open with my ax." He smiled coldly. "No matter of conscience for me that I've killed a whole host of cannibals since I got here. It's been me or them."

"Understandable," said Pimplebrains.

"You know something?" said the lemming. "If it turns out you've been lying to me, and you're cannibals yourselves, or if you try to harm me in any fashion, I'll kill you with just as little concern. Though" – his gaze wandered – "it's hard to see how you could have got here if you were part of Kabalore's tribe."

"They had us imprisoned in the big cave they call the Larder," said Sylvester, the words coming in a rush. "They were going to kill us and have us for supper, but they already had too many other dead bodies to eat so they were saving us for another day. Only Pimplebrains here" – he gestured toward the beaver, who was regarding Sylvester as if he wished he weren't doing so – "spotted there was a back way out of the cave, a narrow cleft that led us here. That was when we—"

The older lemming held up a paw. "Please, I don't need your complete autobiography." The smile he gave this time was far warmer, taking any sting out of his words. "You've just told me as much as I need to know."

"I have?"

"You've proved you're not cannibals."

"Really?"

"Yes, really. You see, none of Kabalore's people can see that cleft."

Sylvester furrowed his brow. "I don't understand. It's not the biggest of crevices, I'll admit, but at the same time it's pretty obvious it's there, if you look at it. It runs all the way from the ceiling of the Larder to the—"

"You just said it yourself," interrupted the other lemming. "'If you look at it.' The thing is, none of the cannibals are capable of looking at it. Even if they knew it was there and went in search of it, they'd still not be able to look straight at it or even catch a glimpse of it out of the corner of their eye."

"That's—" Sylvester began.

"Not impossible," said Viola. "Never say impossible. It's impossible, Sylvester Lemmington, that you left Foxglove and came halfway around the world to find yourself hiding from cannibals inside an ancient vessel left behind by an almost forgotten people – yet it's happened. So, don't say it's impossible for people to be incapable of seeing something that's directly in front of their noses." She wrinkled her own nose prettily, as if she'd found a secondary meaning in what she'd just said and added something in a mumble.

"Eh?" said Sylvester.

"Nothing," she said.

Pimplebrains gave a heavy sigh, as if to express to the world at large that it wasn't his fault he'd been lumbered with a couple of morons. "So, this trick of yours," he said to the old lemming, "'ow d'you do it then?"

"I'm not so sure I should tell you. Not until I'm a bit more certain of who you are. Just because I know you're not going to make me into a casserole—"

"Or a fricassee," said Pimplebrains.

"Quite right. Or a fricassée. Just because I know you're not of a cannibal inclination doesn't mean I know you're my friends. So, are you?"

"Like I said," Pimplebrains rumbled, "we mean you no harm."

"But anyone can say that."

Sylvester put his hands on his waist. "We're lemmings," he expostulated. "We're lemmings like you are. Doesn't that tell you enough about us? Lemmings don't harm each other, everyone knows that."

The stranger raised an eyebrow. "Oh, really? Where I came from there was a lemming who—"

"Where *did* you come from?" said Sylvester, a certain suspicion suddenly popping into his mind.

"Why, from Foxglove, of course." The stranger continued speaking despite gasps from Viola and Sylvester. "That's the only place you're likely to find any lemmings these days, apart from solitary stragglers like me, of course. Even those poor Lhaeminguas-forsaken wretches out there in Kabalore's tribe" – he jerked his head in the general direction of the Larder – "even they're originally from Foxglove."

"How long ago did you leave Foxglove?" said Sylvester, fixing the stranger with a stare.

The older lemming spread his paws. "I don't know. I've no way of telling. I've spent what seems like a hundred years living inside this Zindar ship, where there's neither day nor night to be seen, so I can hardly count the time. There are strange gardens in here where vegetables grow, so I'm never short of food. It's not the worst of prisons, I can tell you, but it's a prison all the same. Whenever I leave it I have to be cautious because even though the cannibals can't reach this cavern from the Larder, they know the way in from the beach entrance, and sometimes they stray in to have a look around. I try to stay out of their sight. I fight them only if I really have to, because one of these days, Kabalore or one of his lieutenants is going to wonder why every now and then one of their number disappears."

Sylvester was impatient with all these details. "What's your name?" he said, trying a different tack.

"What's yours?" the older lemming countered.

Sylvester paused before answering. Did he *really* want to give away his name to a complete stranger, to someone who might prove to be his enemy? But there was a growing certainty within him that he knew who this other lemming was, that he'd reached the end of the personal quest that had taken him out of his settled existence in Foxglove and brought him all the way here. His heart was ready to explode with his joy.

In the end he didn't say his name. He just said, "Hello, Dad."

The other lemming blinked once, twice. "I was beginning to wonder if it might, might just possibly, against all the multifarious odds be you, Sylvester. But I didn't dare hope it could be. Welcome, my son."

They flew into each other's arms and for a long while everything else, even Viola, was completely forgotten.

$$\phi \;\; \phi \;\; \phi \;\; \phi \;\; \phi$$

Much later, the four friends were in a different part of the ship, sharing a meal of cabbages, carrots and various unrecognizable vegetables whose colors Sylvester would never before have associated with vegetables. Jasper – Dad – had taken them to one of the Zindar gardens he'd mentioned. It was really more like a large cultivated field than a garden, with vegetables growing in long neat rows under a strangely alien light, the source of which seemed to be the empty air overhead. It was as if the sun were shining on them through a thin green haze.

As they ate, Jasper told them a story that Sylvester had long suspected was the truth.

"Once upon a time," he said, "a very long time ago, before lemmings settled down and learned to behave like civilized beings, our ancestors were foragers who lived in herds." He grinned. "We were ferocious fighters too, if all the legends are true, but we usually didn't fight – except amongst ourselves over, ahem, mates. Most of the time the herds lived peaceably enough, settling down in one place and eating whatever fruits, vegetables and berries we could find there. So long as the weather was favorable and the plants flourished we stayed where we were but, of course, it couldn't always be like that. If there were a harsh winter or poor summer, the food supplies would run low and the herd would migrate in search of better living conditions.

"The trouble was – no one ever said our ancestors were terribly *clever* – the herd would migrate in a straight line, swarming over fields and through forests until it found a better home. Even when it came to a river or lake, our ancestors would keep on going, swimming through the water in search of the land beyond. Which was perfectly doable, of course, assuming the river wasn't too wide and didn't have too strong a current, or the lake wasn't too big. The real trouble came when it wasn't a river or a lake at all, but the sea. Our ancestors didn't know this when they came to the edge of the water, how could they? So they just struck out into the waves expecting to reach the other side, same as they'd done a hundred times before. Only for them, there wouldn't *be* another side, because they'd be drowned long before they got there.

"It was a tragic occasion any time a lemming herd was wiped out this way, but there were always other herds so our people didn't die out. As ruthless as it might sound, there were enough lemmings in the world that losing a herd here or a herd there didn't matter very much."

Sylvester felt Viola, sitting alongside him, cringe as she thought of those long-ago mass drownings, the shrieks in the air of the exhausted, struggling lemmings growing weaker as they succumbed to the surge of the waters.

"But as time went on," Jasper continued, "we learned better. There are some that say it was the Zindars that taught us, but I think it was more likely that we *had* to learn. You see, the lemming species was almost wiped out entirely by the wars that raged the length and breadth of Sagaria when the enemies of the Zindars came. There weren't enough lemmings left after the Zindars and their foes had fled back into space to be able to risk losing a herd – there were hardly even enough left to *form* a herd. It was change their ways or die out altogether, so far as our ancestors were concerned, and luckily for us, they chose to change their ways.

"They settled down in Foxglove, where they learned how to plant the vegetables they wanted, and how to store food in the good times so they wouldn't be starving in the bad times.

"And they all lived happily ever . . . except they didn't.

"They *would* have lived happily ever after, if it hadn't been for the fact that we lemmings, well, we're not nearly as stupid these days as our ancestors were – in fact, we've become one of the more intelligent species of Sagaria – but—"

Jasper caught sight of Pimplebrains's wrathful glower and gulped noisily. "Along with beavers," he said hastily. "Mighty intelligent animals beavers are too. Certainly more intelligent than lemmings. Especially the ones that have hooks for hands."

Pimplebrains' glower subsided and Jasper resumed his account.

"Our big problem, as lemmings, is that we're *gullible*. When we settled down, leaving behind our existence as wild foragers, we discovered the great advantages of sharing information with each other. In a way, it was a part of our learning to discover that the best way toward a new source of food isn't necessarily in a dead straight line. Today, if ever we *did* need to move to richer pastures, we'd send out scouts in all directions, and when they got back and told us what they'd found we'd believe their accounts. That's the sensible way to do it. That's the *intelligent* way to do it, as I'm sure our beaver friend would agree."

"Harrumph," conceded Pimplebrains.

"But," Jasper went on smoothly, "our natural acceptance of what other people tell us is also a great vulnerability. We're instinctively truthful and, while we know we ought to scrutinize every statement for possible falsity, in practice we tend to believe whatever we're told."

Sylvester groaned. He remembered how, half a world away, he'd been hoodwinked thoroughly by a gray fox who called himself Robin Fourfeathers, even though it'd have been obvious to the most simple-minded of lemming newborns that the fox was lying through his teeth – and he had far too many teeth to lie through. Sylvester had believed Cap'n Terrigan Rustbane because lemmings *did* believe what they were told.

His father was grinning at him. "It's been far too many years since last we were together, young fellow, but I can bet I'm reading the thoughts that're going through your mind."

Somehow, Sylvester felt, it didn't seem as bad confessing to your father what a fathead you'd been as it was confessing to anyone else, or maybe it felt worse – he couldn't decide which, but he confessed anyway. He was still in the midst of the warm glow that had begun to envelop him when he'd figured out that the strange, shabbily clad lemming was his long-lost father.

And he was still swathed in the wonder he'd felt when Jasper had explained how he, Jasper, was still alive.

Wonder, yes, but fury also.

There were treacheries so deep they could never be forgiven, and not all of them were piratical ones. Indeed, the villainies of rogues and murderers like Cap'n Josiah Adamite and Cap'n Terrigan Rustbane, may Lhaeminguas in an especially forgiving moment rest their souls, seemed almost negligible alongside what had been done to the citizens of Foxglove by the successive generations of—

"The Hairbell family," said his father. "They were the first to realize how we lemmings could be exploited, and they didn't wait so much as an indrawn breath before they started doing just that."

"The Hairbell family?" asked Viola, perplexed.

"What makes you think your present Mayor Hairbell's the first of his lineage?" said Jasper.

"He may be the last," snarled Pimplebrains, who was clearly moved by Jasper's account. Sylvester had a fleeting notion that Pimplebrains might be a lemming in exceptionally ambitious disguise, but dismissed it. It was easy to see, though, that the big beaver was infuriated by Hairbell's actions and rooting on behalf of the lemmings of Foxglove.

"There've been others?" Viola said.

"Right back to the very first days," said Jasper. "Some of them have been called Hairbell, most have given themselves other names, but they've all had this thing in common. They all seem to spring up out of nowhere. What they *say* is that they're long and loyal citizens of Foxglove. The truth is that they hide in Mugwort Forest behind Foxglove and raise families there, and whenever one of the old mayors looks like he's just about to die there's someone new that comes along and starts jockeying for that office."

Sylvester blinked rapidly. This was all becoming too much to take in in a single sitting.

"You mean we've been subjected to a long conspiracy by the Hairbell family?" he said.

"Exactly," said Jasper.

"Why would they exploit us?"

"Because they were greedy."

Pimplebrains looked confused. "They was?"

Jasper started tapping deliberately on the floor with the claws of his right forepaw, as if he were trying not just to say his words but write them down.

"Just because lemmings are small, and just because they're gullible, doesn't mean they're without resources."

"I bin learning that." Pimplebrains looked at Sylvester, then at Viola.

"Foxglove is perhaps the richest community in the whole of Sagaria," said Jasper, leaning forward.

Pimplebrains's jaw dropped. So did Sylvester's.

"It's not something the lemmings advertise a lot," said Jasper.

"I imagine not," Sylvester said, once he'd cleared the dryness from his mouth. He imagined the scrolls at the Library might be worth a little, but surely not so very much?

"It's Mugwort Forest that holds the secret," said Jasper.

"It has a secret?" Every now and then Sylvester thought he should venture into Mugwort Forest but, as he approached it, the ominous darkness between the tall trees and the creaking of the trunks as the wind blew them against each other would make the stiff hair stand up all over his body and he'd turn around and pretend he'd never really intended to go there in the first place. "What's in Mugwort Forest?" he said.

"What's in Mugwort Forest," said Jasper, "is the treasure chest of the Zindars."

"But that's *impossible!*" cried Viola.

Jasper smiled at her. "Why do you think so?"

"Because the treasure chest of the Zindars is here!"

"What makes you believe that?"

"The diary of Throatsplitter Adamite," she said, looking to Sylvester for support. "What we were told by Cap'n Rustbane. The reason we're here." She waved her forepaws. "Jeopord's obsession."

Jasper's eyes narrowed. "Jeopord?"

"We've not quite told you *everything*," interposed Pimplebrains ponderously.

There was another long explanation.

"You mean they're out there?" said Jasper at last.

"Yes," Sylvester replied, "but we can deal with them later. You were telling us about Mugwort Forest, Dad."

And, he thought, *a very long time ago you were supposed to be watching me in my swing and you forgot about it. I love you very much, Dad, I could hardly help but do so, yet you're not the best father there's ever been.*

Of course, he said nothing of this.

He just smiled.

The way lemmings do.

"After the last battle between the Zindars and their interstellar foes," said Jasper wearily, as if this were a tale he might have told too many times before, "the only thing the Zindars wanted to do was flee – flee as far and as fast as they possibly could if it'd preserve their leathery hides. We think of them as gallant heroes, but it wasn't quite like that. They weren't the bravest of folk, the Zindars. They came to Sagaria because they thought it'd offer them a safe refuge. They didn't much care about the fates of the people who were already here. They must have been running since long before the first lemming took its first steps under the gaze of Sagaria's sun, and they weren't going to stop running any time soon. In a way, they were like lemmings, only their flights were on a vastly huger scale.

"They fled across interstellar space. Our ancestors fled across land and water. There's no real difference." Jasper waved his paw at the unnaturally greenish light, the tidy rows of plants and the metal walls of the Zindar vessel. "Just technology, which is only a matter of convenience."

"Mugwort Forest?" said Pimplebrains. "You were goin' to tell us about it."

"The Zindars recognized their spiritual kin," said Jasper.

Sylvester stared at him. "Lemmings?"

"But of course."

"So they gave their treasure chest to the lemmings?"

"You're almost as bright as I was, back in the day," said Jasper.

"And the lemmings hid it in Mugwort Forest?"

"Not immediately."

"When?"

"After a few centuries had passed. After our ancestors had realized the funny-looking box they'd been given might hold something of value. After they'd broken about a million teeth trying to bite through the pretty brass lock on the outside of the chest. It was then that it dawned on them that this was an object that would probably be more valuable preserved than violated."

"So they hid it in Mugwort Forest to keep it safe?" said Viola.

"That's about the long and the short of it," Jasper said.

"And it's been lying there ever since?" While the two younger lemmings marveled over ancient mysteries and their spiritual implications, Pimplebrains was of a more pragmatic bent. "So we could just go there and dig it up if we knew where to look?"

"But you wouldn't know where to look," said Jasper. He smiled at Sylvester, then at Viola and finally at Pimplebrains. "It's like the cleft at the back of the cave the cannibals call their Larder. You could think you were looking right at it when, in actual fact, you'd be looking right past it."

"I don't understand," Pimplebrains said.

"Nor me," added Sylvester.

Jasper sighed. "It's something the Zindars learned how to do," he began. "Why do you think they were able to live on Sagaria for so long before their enemies found them?"

An idea was beginning to form in Sylvester's mind. "Was it because this world of Sagaria is like a tiny island in an enormous ocean where there are countless thousands of other tiny islands, and all of them are a very long way apart?" His mouth went dry as he thought of the immensity of an ocean in which Sagaria was just a minute speck of land. "Going from one island to the next searching for the one that sheltered the Zindars could take thousands of years, maybe longer even than that."

Jasper shot him a respectful grin. "You're beginning to comprehend something of where the Zindars and their enemies came from, my boy, and you're right. It would have taken a long time to find the Zindars' hiding place even at the best of times, but the Zindars made the search even more difficult using this . . . this concealment trick of theirs."

He paused, staring at the ceiling far overhead.

"I don't know," he continued more slowly, "if it was a mental ability of theirs or if it was some kind of a machine they constructed that deflected people's perceptions, that blinded them to the light, you could say. The machines the

Zindars made, a lot of them weren't like anything anyone on Sagaria would recognize as being a machine." He gestured around him. "Some of them are obviously machines, even if we haven't the slightest glimmering of an idea of how they work or even what they do. But there are others . . ."

Jasper stopped again, seemed to conduct a brief inner dialogue with himself, then shrugged.

"It's hard to explain," he said. "It's even hard to think about and that's coming from someone who's done the next best thing to dwelling among living, breathing Zindars for all these years. That's what it's been like, holed up here in their vessel. I lose count of the number of times each day I expect to turn my head and see a Zindar looking right back at me. Never happened yet, but I'd not like to bet my life on the fact that it never will."

Viola shuffled slightly where she sat and Jasper obviously realized he'd strayed off the point. Since he and Sylvester had pulled themselves free of that first, wonder-filled embrace, there'd been a lot of straying off the point. Father and son had so much they wanted to tell each other that again and again they found themselves trying to say it all at once.

"Whatever the truth," said Jasper, "I'd been living here a few months – at least, I *think* it was a few months, although it's impossible to be sure of the passage of time in here – when I discovered that a few of the Zindar . . . talents were beginning to rub off on me. One of them was this trick of hiding things in plain view, like the cleft at the back of the Larder or the chest in Mugwort Forest."

Pimplebrains was regarding Jasper with a coldly speculative gaze. "You say there are others of these tricks you've discovered how to do?"

"Not discovered exactly," said Jasper, leaning forward a little in the direction of the weatherbeaten old pirate. "That'd imply I set out in search of the Zindar abilities. No, this was just something that *happened* to me. That's how I know the whole story of the Zindars without anybody telling me it. I just simply know. The only discovery involved was discovering that these abilities had somehow seeped into me, from the air the Zindars breathed all those aeons ago, perhaps, or the walls they brushed against, or—"

"Or," said Sylvester in another unexpected leap of the imagination, "from the plants you ate." He gazed at the growing crops. It seemed odd they were perfectly motionless. Always you expected crops to move, if only slightly, in the breeze. "Those are Zindar fruits and vegetables, you know, Dad."

Again, Jasper shot him that respectful glance. "I can see there's something Zindar rubbing off on you too, son. Haven't you noticed?"

"I have," said Viola. She smiled at Sylvester. "Your eyes are brighter and you seem to be thinking a whole lot better and more quickly. At first I thought it was just the joy of being reunited with your dad, but then I realized the same sort of changes were going on in me as well."

Viola turned toward Pimplebrains.

She didn't even need to speak the question. "No change here," said the beaver hoarsely. "I'm the same as I've always been, sad's the tale to tell, but you two youngsters . . . yes, like Jasper here, I can see somethin's been happenin' to you. An' I'm pleased for you."

No one spoke for a moment or two. When Jasper broke the silence, his voice was dreamy. "So perhaps it's only lemmings who're affected by the air in here, or by the Zindar food or the whatever it is that might be responsible. I've often wondered why the cannibals, who used to come here quite often before I took it over as my own territory, never seemed influenced at all. We know that the time when the lemmings began to settle down and stop their periodic death rushes roughly coincided with the time the Zindars left this world. Could it be that—?"

"That there's some affinity between Zindars and lemmings?" Sylvester finished for him.

"Those were roughly the lines along which I was thinking, yes. Maybe the Zindars changed our ancestors in some fashion, as a way of leaving something Zindar behind on this world. Maybe they tinkered with the way we're made, made us cleverer. That could be why we're more in tune with Zindar ideas than most others seem to be."

"What about the cannibals who are lemmings?" said Viola. "You mentioned there were some."

"Perhaps they were just never among the ones who came here," said Jasper with another shrug, "or perhaps the vessel deliberately repels rogue lemmings like them. Lemmings who've turned so far from the principles the Zindars inculcated into our ancestors. I really don't know, my dear. These are all new ideas to me. It's as if the arrival of you two has rekindled my own imagination."

"I don't think I like it," said Pimplebrains, looking around as if he expected, at any moment, a ghost to leap out from behind a stand of corn. "I don't think I like the notion of other people bein' inside my head and meddlin' with what they find there."

Nobody could think of any answer to that.

"What does it feel like when you're making things . . . disappear?" said Viola.

"It doesn't feel like anything," Jasper replied. "I just do it, as if I've always known how to, as if it comes as easily as breathing or walking."

"And the other tricks you talked about?" said Pimplebrains. "What're they?"

Jasper looked suddenly reluctant. "I'm not sure I should go into details."

"Because you've just met me and why should you trust me?" said Pimplebrains.

"I c'n understand that. Makes sense to me." He smiled. Where Cap'n Rustbane's or Jeopord's smile might alarm the viewer because of the number of teeth they held, Pimplebrains' did the opposite; it alarmed the viewer because of the number of gaps. You had the immediate conviction that, if suitably enraged, the old beaver might leap at your throat and *gum* you to death. "Maybe later, when we's all got ter know each other a bit better."

He let the sentence trail away. There was no guarantee they'd still be alive beyond the next morning. Some of the pirates outside might be happy enough to let them live, although it'd be stretching the truth a bit to believe that pirates like Cheesefang were actually their friends. But it was all too obvious that Jeopord would kill them the moment he thought they were no longer of any use to him. Even if they managed to escape Jeopord and his henchmen, there remained Kabalore and hundreds of Vendrosians, who'd kill them as soon as look at them for the sake of feasting on their corpses. There was only the tiniest of chances they could get to the shore without being seized or slaughtered by someone and once there, if they wanted to escape the island, they still had to think of some means of getting out to the *Shadeblaze*. It was a long way to swim.

It wasn't difficult to work out what the three lemmings were thinking. Pimplebrains carried on speaking as if they'd spoken their thoughts out loud.

"See, I think we're gonna get away from here just fine. Leastways, you three are because of your Zindar magic, so if I sticks right close to you there's a good chance I'll be okay too."

"I wish I could be so confident," said Jasper drily.

"You should be," countered Pimplebrains, "because I can tell you've gained them Zindar abilities real strongly."

Jasper's eyebrows rose, not for the first time since they'd met him. "What makes you say that?"

"Remember, back when you first found us, little Miss Droppy—um, really can't think where that came from. When Viola here was sayin' how impossible it was that she and young Sylvester had survived a voyage halfway aroun' the world, yet they'd somehow gorn and done it?"

"Yes."

"Well, think how *doubly* impossible it is they should travel halfway aroun' the world and just *happened* to run into the one person in the whole of creation Sylvester's been lookin' for! Doubly? Not even that. A hundred times, a thousand times, a *million* times more impossible. Yet they done that too, and you know why I think they was able to?"

Jasper's eyes were glinting. "Tell me."

"Because you *brung* them here."

"I bru—er, brought them here?"

"That's what I said, brung. You din't even know you was doing it, most like, but you reached out with some strange Zindar power wot you din't realize you had, and you tugged your darlin' baby son to you as sure as he was a fish and you had him on the hook."

Sylvester looked at the pirate with something like disgust. The idea of having a hook lodged at the back of his throat, why, he could almost taste the cruel metal already.

"Ugh!" he said, then added, "How could you say such a thing?"

"'Cause that's what I believe happened, is why."

"Me too," breathed Jasper. He turned toward Sylvester. "I'm so terribly sorry, son. If I'd known, I'd never have brought you through such peril, never wanted you to risk your life. Whenever I've thought of you and your mother, which has been many, many times each and every day, it's been of the happiness I hoped the pair of you found living in peace and tranquility in Foxglove. Not fighting battles and risking death."

"Don't worry, Dad," said Sylvester, beginning to grin.

"Eh?"

"You did me the biggest favor you could ever have dreamed of doing. You brought me out of a prison, a prison I didn't even know existed. All these harum-scarum adventures? I'd not have missed them for the world."

"Me neither," said Viola.

◆ ◆ ◆ ◆

It seemed impossible as well for Jasper to have survived to come halfway round the world to find a precarious safety on Vendros. After Sylvester had swiftly recounted all that had happened to Viola and himself since they'd rescued a weasel called Levantes from the Foxglove River, Jasper related his own story.

At first, he told them, when he'd heard he was one of those whose turn it was to go on the Exodus in quest of the Land of Destiny, his heart had been full of exhilaration and eagerness, though the thought of leaving behind his beloved Hortensia and their infant son, Sylvester, hurt like a dagger being thrust into his side.

"I won't be away for long," he'd kept telling Hortensia, "and when I get back here, everything's going to be so much better for the three of us. Once I know the way to the Land of Destiny, we can swim there and start building ourselves a new life, somewhere far from Foxglove and its villainous mayors."

Each time he'd said this his wife had replied, quietly but with a stony determination, "No one ever *has* come back, Jasper. What makes you think it'll be any different for you?"

At last she'd stopped saying that. He'd thought it was because she'd begun to see his point of view. Now he knew it hadn't been that at all.

The great day came.

Jasper kissed his son goodbye, and he kissed the cheek Hortensia offered to him. Then, with a couple score of other lemmings, almost all of them male, almost all of them roughly his own age, he set off for the Mighty Enormous Cliff. They found Mayor Hairbell waiting for them there and, of course, High Priest Spurge, ready to pour upon them the blessings of Lhaeminguas for their quest. Jasper had been uneasy about accepting those blessings. He trusted Spurge no more than he trusted Hairbell, which was a lot less far than he could have thrown either of them, but the morning was bright and sunny and he didn't want to shatter the excited anticipation he saw on the faces of the other lemmings who were setting off with him on the Exodus.

Mayor Hairbell and the priest were flanked by a squad of drummers. Everyone else from Foxglove was blanketing the hillside that overlooked the Mighty Enormous Cliff a couple hundred yards back from the edge. Jasper imagined he could see Hortensia watching from there, Sylvester in her arms, but he knew this was likely self-deception; lemming eyesight is not the best.

The drummers began an insistent, slow, sharp beat.

Rat-a-*tat*! Rat-a-*tat*! Rat-a-*tat*! Rat-a-*tat*!

Jasper and his comrades gave the crowd and their dear ones a last solemn wave, then turned toward the Mighty Enormous Cliff and the misty gray expanse they could stretching out far beyond it.

The beat of the drums became faster, more dramatic.

Rat-a-*tat*-tat! Rat-a-*tat*-tat! Rat-a-*tat*-tat! Rat-a-*tat*-tat!

Jasper felt his breath trying to clamp itself down somewhere deep inside his chest. With a huge effort he released a gasp, then sucked in air as if he might never be able to do so again.

Rat-a-*tat*-tat! Rat-a-*tat*-tat! Rat-a-*tat*-tat! Rat-a-*tat*-tat!

Then the rhythm of the drums became a steady roar and Jasper knew the time had come.

Jostled by his friends, he ran as fast as he could toward the lip of the Mighty Enormous Cliff. Before, when he'd come to the cliff, he'd stopped just before he reached the edge.

Today, he didn't.

Today, he just kept on running, ever faster, even though there was no longer any ground beneath his feet.

"I think I blacked out when I splashed into the water. One moment I was falling, falling, falling. The next, I was fighting for my life against the crashing waves. The cold of the water seemed to want to freeze my blood in my veins. Through the spray, I could make out that a dozen or more of my fellows were already dead, smashed on the sharp rocks at the bottom of the Mighty Enormous Cliff. And the cliff itself, I could see that too. Its dark brown, nearly black face towered above us, stretching so high it seemed it must touch the sun. I knew there was no way back. I knew how savagely I and all my friends had been deceived. My suspicions had been correct. We'd been sent to our deaths by people who wanted us out of the way because we were troublesome to them.

"What could I do?

"All I could do was *live*. I couldn't give up and drown, like some of the others were doing. If I could only survive, then one day I might be able to get back to Foxglove and see these murderers brought to justice.

"It was the least I could do. Not just for myself, but for the wife I adored and the son I treasured. The rocks and waves hammering the others were dangerous. The rocks and the waves hammering them were death. Even though it seemed insane, I had to put distance between me and them by striking out toward the open ocean.

"It was desperately difficult pushing against the current, but I managed somehow. Soon it became easier, soon the waves were only great lazy swells that, though they tried to pull me back toward the Mighty Enormous Cliff, weren't too insistent about it. By now, the calls and shrieks of my onetime companions were faint and distant. Very soon, I could hear nothing of them at all.

"I could have drowned then too. Earlier, the water had seemed searingly cold. Now, I didn't notice the cold at all. The slow rise and fall of the waves had almost lulled me into a fatal sleep when something bumped me.

"At first I was angry. How dare something disturb my relaxation? It was a piece of driftwood, a log that must have been brought down to the sea by the Foxglove River not long earlier, which had selected me to save. Some last scintilla of common sense told me to grip it as tightly as I could, to climb right onto it if possible. Hours later, as the sun sank inexorably into the horizon, the darkness of the night was matched by my own inner darkness as consciousness left me."

Jasper had no idea how long he drifted out to sea on the log. It could have been one day or ten. Had this been the height of summer he'd have been baked alive. Luckily, the weather was cooler and presumably cloudy, because somehow he lived long enough to be picked up by a slave ship, the *Bugbear*, out of the Ganshambling Islands.

This wasn't the best of all possible news, for obvious reasons, but it was fractionally better than being baked until he was lemming jerky or sinking to the bottom of the sea to be picked clean by carnivorous fish – or so Jasper thought later. At the time he was consumed by his own misery, as first he went through the rigors of recovery from near-death, then he had to acclimatize himself to rowing all day long under the lash of the slavemaster.

A year later, he and the other slaves managed to free themselves. The slavemaster who'd delighted in whipping them through rain and shine was strung by the neck from the highest yardarm, along with his skipper and the rest of the crew.

The slaves soon taught themselves (those that didn't already know) enough seamanship to sail the *Bugbear* wherever they wanted to. Then they ran into a difficulty they hadn't foreseen.

In the Ganshambling Islands, slaving is legal, and not just legal but the major contributor to the economy. Though the rebel slaves had done exactly what anyone else in their position might have done and liberated themselves, according to Ganshambling Islands law, they had committed a whole stack of heinous crimes and many other nations, despite the revulsion they felt toward slaving, recognized the legitimacy of Ganshambling Islands law and were prepared to send back there any fugitives they caught.

"They wouldn't," said Jasper, "try very hard to catch us and, if we just lived quietly somewhere and made lives for ourselves, they'd turn a blind eye. But if we sailed the *Bugbear* into port they'd have to take action, action of *some* kind."

So the slaves had steered the ship in an erratic course round the ocean, avoiding the major inhabited nations for fear of being arrested or re-enslaved, or being slaughtered by pirates. Wherever they found a fertile but uninhabited coast or island where they could safely stock the ship with provisions, they did so. For the most part, though, they were caged by the shores of Sagaria's seas. Some were content with this fate. Some resented it but learned to live with it. A few, sooner or later, found they could bear it no longer and took their own lives.

"I can't tell you how often I came close to that myself," said Jasper, "but each time I drew back from that dreadful final precipice. I had a wife and child whom I wanted one day to be with again, and there were villains I wanted to see pay for their crimes."

When, after years at sea, they came by chance close to a new island they had no reason to think it would be different from the others.

Some of the inhabitants rowed out to greet the *Bugbear* as if they were long-lost friends. Only later that night did the folk who'd risen against the tyranny of the slavers' lash discover they'd been the victims of treachery.

Pimplebrains gulped. "You all ended up in the pot."

"All except me, obviously. I managed to escape; I sneaked into a big cave that

I later discovered was called the Larder. To me, it was just a cave, although I was made sick to my stomach by the bones littering its sandy floor. At the back of the cave was a narrow passage through which I fled, thinking it might lead me only to the bowels of the world. But even that I would prefer to being slaughtered for someone's banquet. As you know, instead I found my way into this ship and it's been my home ever since. In a place this big, it was easy enough to hide any time a posse of cannibals ventured in here in search of me. Then, as I . . . changed, I was able to take more effective measures to conceal myself, such as close off the route that led from the back of the Larder to here."

"You're a brave fellow," said Pimplebrains. "I'd like to shake your paw."

The grizzled old beaver held out a hook and Jasper took it.

Sylvester just stared at his father, his heart filled with awe.

I knew you'd turn out to be a hero, but I never guessed how much of a hero you'd be.

COMBAT UNBECOMING

At some point they slept, even though Sylvester could have sworn he'd be too excited ever to sleep again after having discovered his father. Pimplebrains was the first to light out, as it were, leaning slowly over sideways at a greater and greater angle until finally, he was asleep on the metal deck. Viola soon followed. Sylvester and Jasper remained awake quite a while longer, talking about this and that, mainly about Hortensia. Jasper was amused to discover her cooking hadn't improved any over the years. Sylvester would never know which of the two Lemmingtons succumbed to sleep first. There seemed to be a smooth transition between drowsily conversing with his dad and being woken up by Viola putting her foot in his ear.

"Clumsy oaf," she said, and not to herself.

Ablutions completed and a breakfast partaken of some curious fruits that looked like blackcurrants and tasted a bit like the smell of roses, the three lemmings and the old hook-handed beaver looked at each other with what Sylvester soon recognized as a sense of anticlimax. Conversation was desultory and forced. Yesterday had been a day unlike any other, one of those days to be remembered for a lifetime. Now, Sylvester and Jasper were beginning to realize that there was so much they didn't know about each other, so many shared years they'd lost, and that now was the wrong time to start repairing that gaping emotional wound.

"We'd better see what Cheesefang and the gang are up to, I suppose," said Pimplebrains at last.

The other three pounced upon the idea as if it were the product of genius. Anything to be *doing* rather than just hanging around searching for threads of conversation that seemed always just out of reach.

With Jasper in the lead, the little party headed for the massive hole in the vessel's hull. Unlike yesterday, they had no need of torches. As they entered each massive room, Jasper clapped and that strange, cloudy light came on. Sylvester suspected there was no need for Jasper to clap his paws, that his dad was just doing this to make the switching-on of the illumination less unsettling for the others.

Sometimes their course followed the path the three newcomers had scuffed up in the dust; more often it didn't. Sylvester realized Jasper knew his way around and was following the most direct route. Yesterday, Sylvester and the others must have wandered considerably as they explored the unknown territory.

Eventually, their trek brought them to the dark gash. This time, Jasper smacked his paws together to switch the light off.

"No sense in alerting anyone out there to the fact we're on our way," he murmured tensely.

Even Jasper stumbled on occasion as they made their way through the last fifty yards or so of darkness to reach the tear in the hull.

As they did so, Sylvester slowly became aware that there was a commotion outside.

"What's that?" he hissed to no one in particular.

"How should I know?" three voices replied as one.

When they reached the mouth of the perforation it was all too obvious what was going on. The colossal cavern surrounding the vessel was not entirely dark. More than one bonfire had been built while the lemmings and the beaver slept, and the flicker of their flames lit the distant cavern walls fitfully with a vexed dark redness. There was no one in sight as Sylvester and the others peered at this ominous scene, but it was clear that somewhere very close there was an all-out battle in progress. The air was filled with the clash of steel on steel, with the yells of angry creatures, with screams of pain that were all too often abruptly stifled or worse, that continued endlessly in an almost pleading fashion.

To the friends in the opening, it was as if two armies were fighting on the cavern floor in front of them, but armies made up of invisible warriors.

"They're round the far side of the ship," murmured Jasper after a few moments. He repeated the sentence more loudly, obviously realizing there was no point in keeping his voice low. Whoever was in the fray wouldn't hear him even if he shouted at the top of his voice.

Pimplebrains stood with one ear cocked to the air. "I recognizes a few of them voices," he said slowly. "Them's men from the fine ship *Shadeblaze*." He felt at his waist for a sword that wasn't there, a sword that had never been there since he'd lost his paws. "I need to go and join 'em, fight alongside of 'em. Them's my shipmates. I owe me hearties that much."

Jasper put a paw on the larger animal's shoulder. "Don't be a fool."

"It's honor." Pimplebrains's voice indicated that was explanation enough.

"I thought there was no honor among pirates."

"Then you thought wrong."

Sylvester shifted uneasily from one foot to the other. In a way, those were his and Viola's shipmates too, even though by force. He felt a certain obligation.

Jasper was eyeing him. "I know what's going through your head, son, and I also know it's damnfool stupid, but you wouldn't be a son of mine if you weren't thinking it."

"Really?" said Viola sweetly. "You mean you're *both* idiots?"

The older lemming turned his gaze to her. "Sometimes you remind me of his mother when she was your age."

Pimplebrains was jumping down to the sandy floor of the cavern. He held up his hooks to them.

"I'm sure you understand."

Then he was gone, running toward the prow of the Zindar ship, his feet kicking up little puffs of sand.

"I hope we see him again," said Viola somberly.

"Me too." Sylvester squeezed her paw.

"We better go find out what's happening, I suppose," said Jasper. He sniffed. "When you've been in here as long as I have, you learn that the best thing intruders from the outside world could do is kill each other and save you the bother, but it sounds like some of these are friends of yours?"

Cheesefang, a friend? thought Sylvester. *All those other cutthroats and vagabonds, my friends? Well, I suppose some of them are. Maybe. In a way.*

"I think so," he told his father.

"Before we go, then . . ."

Jasper vanished as suddenly as Pimplebrains had, but into the shadows of the ship. He returned within moments, clanking as he moved. In his arms were three not very rusty swords and an ax that looked blunt enough that the greatest threat it offered to victims was probably blood poisoning.

Jasper saw Viola looking skeptically at the ax.

"Just for show," he assured her. "It impresses people."

He gave each of them a sword, then jumped down onto the sand. "I'd offer to help you down," he said to Viola, "but as you can see, I've got my hands full."

"If you offered to help me down," Viola replied so quietly only Sylvester could hear her, "I'd bury your own ax in your skull. Even if it took me all day," she added.

Sylvester laughed. Jasper looked at them in puzzlement.

"Nothing," Sylvester told him, jumping down beside his father. In a flurry of ragged skirts, Viola joined them.

The three lemmings moved cautiously along close to the sheltering bulk of the great ship. The light of the bonfires didn't reach here. The darkness seemed even deeper than inside the ship. Sylvester could see Viola ahead of him as just an impression of presence in the gloom. Beyond her, leading the trio, Jasper couldn't be seen at all. Sylvester reassured himself that even if a group of combatants did spill around to this side of the ship, they'd be unable to see the lemmings in the stygian shadows. He clutched his sword very tightly, enjoying the way it balanced itself in his grasp.

Yesterday, all I knew to do was wave a sword around in the air vacantly and hope its sharp edge hit somebody else before theirs hit me. Now, I'm appreciating the weapon's heft, knowing that if I have to use it I'll be able to give a good account of myself. Dad was right. There's something in the air of the ship, or maybe in the Zindar crops, that changes the way we think, that makes us sharper, more alert, more clever.

Suddenly Viola stopped. With difficulty, Sylvester kept himself from running into the rear of her. He shook his head. He'd been so lost in his thoughts he hadn't realized they'd reached the front of the ship. There was a little more light here, just enough for him to be able to see the faces of his companions.

Jasper was looking worried. "I don't want either of you trying to be heroes."

"We won't," said Viola.

"Good."

Inching forward, they peered around to the far side of the cavern.

At first, Sylvester couldn't understand what was going on. That there was a savage battle underway was obvious, but it just seemed to be a chaotic sea of barbarity without any rhyme or reason. Who was fighting whom? Was everyone just trying to kill everyone else? Then, as bloodied blades rose and fell in the darting red light from the great pyres, and as the screams of mortal agony and snarls of wrath rose to an impossibly high crescendo and then rose farther still, he began to distinguish the different parties involved in the fierce and feral fray.

Over there was Cheesefang, surrounded by the dead bodies of his comrades. Sylvester couldn't be sure, but it seemed to him that Cheesefang must be the only one left of the party of pirates that had escaped from the rear of the Larder – except, of course, for Pimplebrains, who was hacking his way to Cheesefang's side.

Cheesefang's sword arm was a vicious blur in the air, the sword itself almost invisible except when it chopped into the neck of an adversary, or paused briefly in the act of running one through. Sylvester had always thought the sea rat's boasts about his fighting prowess were just arrant braggartry. Now, he could see they weren't. The rat was a formidable warrior. The dead and dying all around him were proof enough of that.

As was Pimplebrains. The hooks, where once the beaver's paws had been, were moving as swiftly and lethally as Cheesefang's sword. Sylvester watched, not knowing if he should turn away, not knowing if he wanted to carry on watching or if he just wanted to throw up. The beaver sank a hook deep into a swarthy raccoon's throat and pulled back with a mighty yank, ripping out flesh and esophagus amid an explosion of blood. Even as the raccoon sank to his knees, the life already fleeing from him, Pimplebrains was moving on, working his way toward where Cheesefang was battling grimly.

Battling grimly against cannibals.

Last night, Jasper had told Sylvester and the others that, while the cannibals had lost all awareness of the narrow rocky passage that led out of the back of the Larder, they still knew of the shore entrance to what Sylvester had begun to call, in his own mind, the Cavern of the Zindars. A party of them – a *large* party, to judge by the body count – must have strayed in here within the past hour or two, perhaps just by chance, perhaps searching for the "food animals" that had miraculously escaped from the Larder despite the guards placed at the cave's mouth. Whatever the reason, the cannibals had arrived and found Cheesefang and his cronies engaged in the futile task of trying to dig up a treasure chest that was buried not here, but half a world away.

They'd been led by the one-eared black and white terrier Kabalore. The dog, his flanks bloodied by a score of shallow wounds and by the gore of the pirates who'd put them there, was fighting as ferociously as Cheesefang. Where the sea rat was wielding a sword and dagger, Kabalore was armed only with a cudgel, but so skilled was he in its use that Sylvester wouldn't have liked to judge which was the more effective weapon. The pirates seemed to think the same because, while they were making short and ruthless work of most of the cannibals, they seemed leery of Kabalore. The terrier was having to take the fight to them rather than beat off their attacks.

And the pirates the terrier was attacking? To go by the disposition of the various battling parties, Jeopord must have come ashore with the skeleton crew he'd retained, then followed the cannibals in through the shore entrance to the Cavern of the Zindars. Seeing Cheesefang and the rest under attack, Jeopord and his henchmen must have weighed in to go to the rescue.

Sylvester felt his grip on his sword tighten even more.

"I can't just stand by and watch this," he told his father.

"Don't be such a fool."

"Stop acting like a father. I grew up while you were gone. I have friends there."

Sylvester pointed with his sword. A small part of him was surprised the blade was hardly trembling at all.

"They're all rapscallions and rogues."

"True, but—"

"They're *our* rapscallions and rogues."

Sylvester started. The voice that had interrupted was Viola's. She too was holding her sword out in front of her.

"You're a good person, Jasper," she said, speaking in quick stuttery phrases, "but the years you've lived in hiding have turned you into someone who thinks the only important thing is self-preservation. There's more to life than that, more to *living*. Join us, don't join us, it's up to you but your son and I aren't going to watch Cheesefang die because we were too cowardly to go to his aid."

Back in Hangman's Haven, Sylvester had discovered the knack of running faster than the eye could see. He still didn't know how he did it. Maybe it was a Zindar talent he'd somehow inherited from ancestors who'd been alive when the Zindars were still here on Sagaria. Who could ever know? It had always been a case of running *from* something, something that terrified him.

Now he discovered he could do it while running *toward* danger too.

And so could Viola.

They ran shoulder by shoulder into the throng of fighting creatures.

Sylvester found he was yelling, although the words he was yelling weren't words at all.

Almost without volition on his part, his sword stabbed forward to jab into the flesh between a cannibal rat's ear and jaw. The rat let out a great scream and dropped his own sword, putting up his paw as if there might be some possibility of staunching the spurt of blood.

Sylvester stepped aside nimbly as the rat fell.

"Sorry," he said.

But that was the last of the old Sylvester, the Sylvester who was only too happy to kowtow to power, to do whatever had to be done to fit in with Foxglove society, to *pretend he was someone else*.

The Sylvester he was now was the *real* Sylvester!

He discovered this as he kicked out wildly at the chin of one of the cannibals, a raccoon that must have weighed four times as much as Sylvester but was already beginning to understand it shouldn't have picked a fight with the lemming.

Yes, Sylvester loved his role as Junior Archivist and Translator of Ancient Tongues, and that was a love he'd never lose. Unraveling the webs of knowledge and reasoning was perhaps the best and most deliriously enjoyable pleasure any intelligent being could experience. Yet, that was no reason for archivists to retreat from the real world and refuse to take any part in what it had to offer. He guessed he'd understood this ever since Cap'n Terrigan Rustbane and the crew of the

Shadeblaze had abducted Viola, Mrs. Pickleberry and him from Foxglove. Ever since the three of them had been forced either to accept adventure or die fighting against it, but it was only now, as he ducked a malevolent thrust from a cannibal's spear, that he really knew it.

Again, he realized he'd become something more than he used to be. Either he'd been given something by the ghosts of the Zindars, or it had been something that'd always been inside him, something he'd only now learned to release.

A weasel with a hideous gash across his forehead, the flaps of flesh spread wide to reveal the yellow-white of the skull beneath, staggered towards Sylvester. A mace held high above his head and eyes red with hatred, he half-tripped on the outstretched paw of an eviscerated wood rat, then watched his guts spill out as Sylvester chopped viciously with his sword across the weasel's midriff.

Sylvester glanced sideways at Viola.

She was covered in blood.

He'd thought Cheesefang was an efficient killing machine.

Viola was something else.

In the corner of his eye there was a blur. Operating on pure instinct, Sylvester swiveled away from the direction of the blow, deliberately falling to one side at the same time as he brought his sword – the perfectly balanced, wonderful sword his father had given him – round in a whistling arc to slice directly across the muzzle of a black and white terrier.

Not just *any* black and white terrier.

Kabalore was silent for a split second, then let out a shriek of anguish. The cannibal chieftain stared at Sylvester as if staring alone might strike the lemming dead in his tracks.

Sylvester refused to be intimidated.

"Behind you!" yelled Viola. "Look out behind you!"

He half-turned and saw a blue mongoose charging toward him, skulls on a belt around its waist and a horrific open wound where its scalp should have been. He then realized he should never have taken his eyes for one moment off Kabalore.

Forget the mongoose! The terrier's the one'll kill you.

Sylvester slid once more to his side, kicking out with his rear legs.

One of the blows struck home. Kabalore gave a *yippp* of dismay and keeled momentarily off balance.

Sylvester took advantage of that moment, squirming forward and probing in front of him with a sword that now seemed less a weapon than a part of himself.

A swipe of his sword took Kabalore across the back of one of the terrier's forelegs, ripping into the tendon.

The dog screamed.

The pain must have been almost beyond enduring, yet somehow Kabalore stayed upright. He swung his cudgel with almost supernatural speed toward Sylvester's head.

This is it, thought Sylvester. *I've done my best. I've fought like no other lemming has probably ever fought, and it's all been for nothing. I hope the end's as quick for Viola as it is for me. Maybe, if I'm lucky, I can deliver one last blow against this cannibal murderer.*

He rolled away from the descending cudgel, knowing his maneuver was too little, too late.

He raised his sword blindly.

There was a crushing kick in his flank.

The mongoose! He'd forgotten the blue mongoose.

He'd turned his gaze away from it in order to focus on the more immediate threat, Kabalore, but the mongoose kept on charging through the red haze of its fury and the even redder haze of the blood seeping from its terrible head wound, and it stumbled straight into Sylvester's sprawled body.

He looked upward and saw, silhouetted against the dim flicker of the reflected flames on the cavern's faraway ceiling, the mongoose trip over him. The mongoose was wielding an ax far bigger and obviously far sharper than the one Jasper had unearthed from the shadows of the Zindar ship. As the mongoose stumbled over Sylvester, the ax came swinging uncontrollably downward to lodge itself in the middle of Kabalore's face.

More blood pouring.

A weariness of soul crept into Sylvester as he shoved himself upright, trying not to slip on the accumulated gore that covered the cavern floor with a slick coating. He launched a furious blow with his sword at the blue mongoose, realized even as he did so that the creature was dead already, that it had been fighting on beyond all limits of endurance, that his killer strike had been a wasted effort.

Kabalore was dead too. That much was obvious.

Viola was alive.

She shoved her face right up against his and bellowed in his ear to be heard over the din of battle.

"I think we're winning!"

"How can we be?"

"What?"

"How can we be winning?"

"The cannibals! Those we haven't killed are running for the exit!"

It was true, Sylvester saw. A posse of cannibals was heading as fast as it could for the far side of the cavern, presumably for the gap in the wall through which there was escape to the island's shore.

"Let them go!" he cried. "Let them go! They're not the real enemy!"

Viola had found a dagger somewhere. A gopher wished she hadn't as it fell to the ground trying to push its innards back where they came from.

"They're not?" shouted Viola.

"No! The ones who want to kill us are Jeopord's crew."

"Oh, by the lacy smalls of the triple-breasted goddess," she said, beginning to laugh.

"As Cap'n Rustbane might have described it," responded Sylvester.

It was the wrong time for laughter. It was the wrong time for anything except fighting as viciously as you could and shutting your mind to the horrors you were inflicting upon your foes. Even so, Sylvester found himself laughing along with Viola. He had no idea what he was laughing about. All he knew was there was something very funny in the blood-drenched air.

Jeopord quenched the fires of his mirth.

The big ocelot had been fighting like a mad dog on the far side of the battle area, and Sylvester had been entirely unaware that Jeopord was no longer there.

Now, the ocelot was advancing toward him, a grin on his toothy face. Farther back, Cheesefang was turning an anguished gaze in the direction of the two young lemmings. The sea rat had taken a blow somewhere that Sylvester couldn't see.

"Hello, traitor," said Sylvester to the ocelot.

"Fine words," replied Jeopord, as if they'd bumped into each other in the Foxglove marketplace and were hunting around for a few social niceties to exchange before they could mercifully escape from each other. Sylvester had seen his mother do this a thousand times. He'd never before realized it might be such a sophisticated art.

"But you *are* a traitor, aren't you?" said Sylvester. "You betrayed Throatsplitter Adamite because you thought Rustbane might be your better bet, and then you betrayed Rustbane the very first moment it suited you to do so. Now, you're betraying Cheesefang, who'd have served out the rest of his life as your crony if you'd let him, such was the loyalty he had for you. All these folk you've betrayed, Jeopord, and likely a thousand times more and you think it's odd I should call you a traitor?"

The ocelot's eyes opened wider than Sylvester had seen them do before, wider than he'd believed it possible any ocelot's eyes could open. For a moment, he thought that maybe, just maybe, his moral castigation had gotten through to some scintilla of honor buried deep within Jeopord's psyche.

He should have known better.

"Honor? Treason? They're all born out of yesterday! Anyway, why the hell am I listenin' to a hamster?"

"Not a hamster, a lem—"

"Lay off my boy!" said a different voice.

"Dad!"

Jasper shot Sylvester a sloppy sideways grin. "You didn't think I was going to watch you two get yourselves killed, did you?"

"Oh, great," said Jeopord with heavy sarcasm. He turned away from them briefly to despatch two heavily weaponed mink with a single blow. "Now we got folksy stuff."

"You have a sword?" said Jasper.

"As if I didn't," replied Jeopord.

"Then *fight*, you scum!"

Jasper sprang straight toward Jeopord's throat.

For a moment, the perplexed ocelot looked as if he'd leave it too late to step aside. At the very last second, as the older lemming whistled through the air toward him, he thought to flinch away just enough that Jasper landed in the blood and gore beyond, slithering and windmilling as he tried to keep his balance on the treacherous surface.

Jeopord grinned a hideously evil grin.

It was obvious Jasper was going to be easy prey.

The ocelot took a pace forward.

"Leave my dad alone!"

"And my future father-in-law!"

"Your what?" said Sylvester.

"Shut up, dimwit. Skewer the blasted tom!"

The other combatants were, for the most part, keeping their distance. Whatever was brewing among this little group was evidently something it was best for outsiders to stay out of.

Sylvester was almost dancing as he moved forward. The sword sang in his grip. He thought he'd probably just had marriage proposed to him. He wasn't sure. He'd not hold it against Viola if later she told him it had all been a dreadful mistake, a few words misunderstood in the heat of battle. That was it. That was surely all it could ever have been. A babe like Viola Pickleberry might *dally* with a goofball like Sylvester Lemmington, but surely she'd never think of actually *hitching* herself to him.

The old Sylvester would be tripping over his two front feet around now, thought Sylvester. *The new one's using the moment to carry the battle to a murderous carnivore ten times his own size. The new one's either extraordinarily stupid or he's become a Zindar spawn.*

Jeopord glanced back over his shoulder at Sylvester, then glanced at him again. The ocelot chuckled. "I'm keeping you for later."

"For you," puffed Sylvester, "there isn't going to *be* any later."

"Tough talk from a hamster."

For once, Sylvester didn't even bother to contradict the slur. It was beneath his contempt.

"You frightened of a lemming?"

Jeopord looked as if he couldn't believe his ears. "Me? Frightened? Of a *lemming*? You got to be jokin'."

"Then put up or shut up!"

Jasper spoke again. "Which lemming is it you're frightened of? Me?"

"Or me?" said Sylvester, beginning to smile bleakly.

"Or me?" said Viola.

Everyone turned to stare at her.

"Well, why not? He's just a mangy old tom cat with breath you could use to fill a sandwich. No match for a lemming."

"Exactly, m'dear," said Jasper. "So, cesspit face, on guard with you!"

With exaggerated courtesy Jeopord bowed toward Jasper. "Could I do you all three at once? Make myself a lemming kebab?"

"No!" Even Sylvester was startled by the vehemence of his own voice. "This scum is mine and mine alone."

"Suicide by pirate, is it, hm?" said the ocelot, regarding him mockingly.

"Don't be a fool!" yelled Jasper.

"I've told you before, Dad. Stop calling me a fool. You were away too many years to have the right to order me around as if I were still a child."

Jasper fell back. Anger chased another emotion across his face.

A fine time to start an argument with my father, thought Sylvester bitterly.

He didn't have time for any further thoughts, because Jeopord was upon him.

The ocelot's sword was larger than Sylvester's, which meant that by all the ordinary standards of combat, Sylvester was hopelessly outclassed. Sylvester's sword was about the size the ocelot would have used as a dagger, only flimsier. He knew what he had to do was use his diminutive size as a strength rather than a weakness, and to substitute speed and guile and quickness of thought in place of weight of weaponry.

The trouble was, he'd never learned how to do any of these things.

He was going to have to improvise.

Well, I guess that's what the very first warriors had to do, back when Sagaria was young. The thought wasn't as reassuring as it should have been, because hot on its heels came another. *And very few of them lived to a ripe old age, if the legends are anything to go by.*

"Lhaeminguas be with you," cried Viola, surprising him.

Well, any myth in a storm.

All of these notions were flashing through his mind, even as he found himself slithering to one side in a sort of graceful form of sustained collapse. He hadn't a clue how he'd ever repeat the maneuver if he had to, but it seemed surprisingly effective. Jeopord's sword came swishing down and missed Sylvester altogether, instead chunking firmly into the packed, blood-soaked sand.

For a moment, the ocelot had to wrestle with the weapon to dislodge it, and in that split second Sylvester darted forward and slashed his own sword across the inside of the bigger creature's forepaw, just above where Jeopord gripped the sword's pommel.

The ocelot let out a high shriek of pain as blood spurted from the wound, almost blinding his foe.

Sylvester put up a paw to wipe the sticky hot liquid out of his eyes.

Although Jeopord was clearly in agony, that didn't seem to hamper him much. He pulled his blade out of the ground and tossed it to his other forepaw, catching it neatly and beginning to twitch it threateningly. The ocelot put his injured paw up to his mouth and clamped his teeth over the wound to stanch the flow of blood. His eyes flared yellow in insane fury.

Viola and Jasper got themselves out of reach of that feverishly scything, bloodied but razor-sharp blade and scrambled for cover. The rest of the fracas had fallen into a lull as the combatants stopped to watch the fight between Jeopord and Sylvester. Out of the corner of his eye, Sylvester could see Pimplebrains looking at him with an expression that could almost be pride. The old beaver had managed to get himself alongside Cheesefang, and the pair of them had dealt out death to cannibals until the survivors had turned and fled.

So that's what Pimplebrains thinks of his skipper, thought Sylvester, darting to one side and then the other, as Jeopord's sword sought him. Evading the slashes would have been hard enough had the footing been just the cavern floor, but Sylvester was having constantly to readjust himself as the scattered bodies of pirates and cannibals got in the way. What made it even more difficult was that most of the dead and mortally wounded animals were larger than Sylvester, some of them considerably larger. Large or small, the dead and wounded had blood that was slippery and Sylvester was wading through far too much of it.

He balanced on the outthrust leg of a dead dog, and realized it was Kabalore's.

Kabalore was a lot bigger than me. He didn't fare too well, did he?

Jeopord's sword was a river of silver exploding toward him.

Sylvester sprang away to his left, somersaulting through the air and continuing to roll after he hit the ground. He hammered into the side of a dead stoat and lay there for a second, winded, the world performing crazy dances in front of his eyes.

When things came back into focus, he saw Jeopord advancing toward him once more, his face fixed in a crazy grin. The ocelot had let his wounded paw fall to his side, and seemed not to care that his lifeblood was still pouring copiously from it.

Uh-oh, this is it.

Sylvester didn't know where he got the strength, but it came from somewhere and allowed him to twist away, kicking up a cloud of sticky wet sand into Jeopord's face.

The pirate screamed a terrible oath.

"I'll get you, you—"

"Not in front of the fairer sex," said a voice that Sylvester had never expected to hear again.

"Rustbane!" Jeopord gasped.

The gray fox bowed with a flourish of his cape. "At your service."

Whatever the fox's attempts at suaveness, he was looking the worse for wear. His costume was faded, wrinkled and a little shrunken and the same could be said for his face, but there could be no doubting the assurance with which he held himself.

"So sorry," said Rustbane with a nod to Viola. "I meant to say 'fairer gender.'"

"You're dead!" cried Jeopord.

"Not so you'd notice." The fox pinched himself as if to check. "Still here."

"But I—"

"Killed me yourself? Yes, I thought you'd think that. But you were wrong. Wrong, as you've been about so many things, Jeopord, my old Jack o' Cups."

"You were dead!"

"I was. But then I wasn't. Confusing, isn't it?"

"And now you're—"

"Exactly. Now I'm here, and I find you about to impale my very good friend Sylvester Lemmington, one of the finest – perhaps *the* finest – hamsters Sagaria has ever been lucky enough to know."

"Lemmings," said Sylvester hoarsely. Still winded, he felt as if his throat had been used as a cheese grater.

"Pardon?" said Cap'n Rustbane, turning to look at him.

"Lemmings. I'm a *lemming*, not a hamster. I've told you before."

This is crazy, thought Sylvester. *I want to laugh. I'm just about to be skewered six ways to yesterday, and the main thing I want to do is roar with laughter. I think my throat would burst if I tried it.*

"Quite so," said Rustbane gravely. "I'll try to remember that in future. I don't mind so much if it's hamsters getting impaled, but lemmings – that's different."

He faced Jeopord.

"You and I, we have a score to settle, my Jack o' Cups. If it were merely a matter of a lemming or two I could possibly find it in my heart to forgive you, but it's me you tried to kill and I really do take the most profound exception to that."

Jeopord's eyes moved shiftily. "I don't suppose it's any use tellin' you it was only a joke?"

Rustbane answered with deceptive mildness. "No, I'm afraid that won't wash."

"That I was jus' doin' it for your own good?"

"That neither."

"That I was doin' it out of loyalty? That I knew you'd escape the jaws of death somehow, you bein' Cap'n Terrigan Rustbane, after all. I thought it might be doin' you a good turn to let you lie low while me an' the lads" – Jeopord gestured around him at the scene of carnage – "tackled these here cannibals? A special *nasty* breed of cannibals they was too. I thought to myself, I thought, 'Jeopord, me old cully, your ol' drinking bud and lofty skipper, to wot you owes the greatest love an' respect a man could 'ave – well, an ocelot, but same thing – the greatest love an' respect an *ocelot* could 'ave, you've got to—"

"Nope," said Rustbane. "Good try, but nope."

"Then defend yourself, scumbag!"

With a roar the ocelot leaped at Rustbane, his sword singing in a lethal arc.

Sylvester didn't know where Rustbane's sword came from. One moment the gray fox was seemingly unarmed, the next his blade was clashing against Jeopord's, forcing the ocelot back on the defensive.

Jeopord gave a howl of frustration as he was thwarted by the savage resistance the gray fox offered.

"Why can't you just go ahead and simply *die?*" he said with exasperation.

"Actually, I'm not really the 'dying' type," Rustbane said calmly. "To put it another way, it's not my style."

"Kill that bloody vulpine!" Jeopord shouted to the nearest pirates. Only two were within earshot, a toothless skunk and a one-eyed wolverine, but they seemed very reluctant to carry out the order.

"Or by the devil's grandmother's underwear, I'll kill you two meself." This threat seemed to spark little enthusiasm to obey the new skipper. Nevertheless, they slowly advanced toward the gray fox, their cutlasses drawn.

Two silvery flashes appeared abruptly in Rustbane's paws. He fired the flintlocks at the same time, making it sound like a loud single bang. The two pirates crashed against the cavern wall and fell to the sandy floor, where they lay motionless.

"Two black spots mended," said Rustbane. He stuck his smoking pistols back into his belt, then drew his sword again. "Now, we can continue undisturbed me, ol' Jack o' Cups." Rustbane gave Sylvester a cocky little grin. "Maybe I'm just a ghost, not a flesh-and-blood fox after all. Wouldn't that be a fine and fancy turn up for the books, eh? Take *that*, you cur!"

This last was to Jeopord, who'd renewed his attack. Fending off his foe's sword with his own, the gray fox kicked out unexpectedly. Jeopord had just been sneakily drawing a dagger from the folds of his trousers. Rustbane's foot caught the ocelot's paw in the act, driving the blade back into Jeopord's flesh.

The ocelot howled again, this time in agony as the sharp serrated blade tore into him.

The fight was actually over in that moment, although it took a couple more minutes for Jeopord to realize it. His face twisted in pain and with his injured leg uncertain beneath him, the ocelot didn't stand a chance. Sylvester could see temptation crossing Rustbane's face, the temptation to toy with the ocelot's anguish and misery, to protract the process of finishing Jeopord off, but the emotion was only a fleeting one. The two pirates went back a long way. They'd been friends much more than they'd been foes. The gray fox owed it to his Jack o' Cups to make this as rapid as possible.

Sylvester, frozen where he lay, watched in fascination and with a certain amount of grudging respect as the ocelot, despite everything, fought back viciously against his old skipper. His curses filled the air. His sword seemed almost liquid, so swiftly did it change direction as he sought each new angle of attack against the gray fox. For his part, Rustbane was doing the minimum possible, just defending himself when he needed to, attacking whenever he judged that Jeopord's guard had dropped. The fox was barely breaking breath.

"I can't bear to watch," Viola whispered in Sylvester's ear. At some point, she must have wormed her way unnoticed across the gory terrain to snuggle up against him.

"Me neither," said Sylvester, but he carried on watching anyway as Viola buried her face in his shoulder.

Finally, Jeopord's resolve was breaking down. The movement of his sword arm lost its fluidity, becoming a series of jerks. The power with which his weapon clashed against Rustbane's audibly decreased. Those moments when Rustbane could stab through Jeopord's guard became more and more frequent.

"Throw down your weapon, my old comrade," cried Rustbane at last. "Let me make this quick."

"I'm not done with ye yet, y'old bastard," grunted Jeopord.

But it was clear that he was. His chest was heaving like the waves of stormy sea. Blood was streaming from the deep wound in his hip. He could scarcely limp. That his damaged leg hadn't already collapsed beneath him was a miracle. Even the effort of keeping his sword held out in front of him seemed to have become too much because suddenly, in spite of the defiance of his words, the weapon turned groundward, slowly falling from his grasp as Jeopord toppled to his knees.

"I never thought it would come to this," said Rustbane, seeing his adversary helpless before him.

Jeopord just cursed him.

"And I wish it hadn't, old friend, but you betrayed me, you cast me to the sharks and there's no way Cap'n Terrigan Rustbane could let such a heinous crime go unpunished. No choice about the punishment either. It has to be death, don't you agree, eh, me old Jack o' Cups?"

Jeopord cursed again.

Rustbane's voice was almost tender. "Fare thee well, my friend."

Moving faster than sight, the tip of his word slashed across Jeopord's throat.

Blood sprayed.

The ocelot crumpled in a ghastly silence, not even lifting his paws to the wreckage of his neck.

His face now empty of all sentiment, the gray fox looked down at his dying comrade-in-arms and slowly sheathed his sword.

"So die all those who would attempt to see the back of Cap'n Terrigan Rustbane," he remarked to no one in particular. "It's a terrible thing to contemplate how many have died because of the lack of learning that lesson."

The gray fox turned his head and stared straight at Sylvester. "Hamsters included."

"I'm not a—"

"My little joke."

"Okay."

None of the other combatants showed any inclination for fighting after witnessing the demise of the ocelot. The few surviving cannibals who hadn't yet fled did so now. Cheesefang and Pimplebrains began clambering toward their skipper with big goofy grins of welcome on their battered faces. The other pirates were pretending as best they could that, despite their having pledged allegiance to Jeopord after the mutiny, their loyalties had *really* lain with Rustbane all along.

Sylvester heaved himself to his feet, pulling Viola beside him.

The only person who seemed still to be eyeing the gray fox warily was Jasper.

"You're probably the only one who's ever bested me and lived to tell the tale," Rustbane said conversationally to Sylvester.

Sylvester's mouth dropped open. "Me?"

"You. Don't act the innocent to me. At every turn, you've done almost exactly the opposite of what I wanted you to do. You've annoyed me to the point where I didn't know whether to nail your head to the wall or just drown myself. Somehow, I restrained myself, with that admirable self-control upon which, over the years, so many gentlemen and scholars have favorably commented. I've come, despite myself, to *like* you. Like you quite a lot. What d'you think of that, eh?"

Sylvester looked at the sprawled, bloodied corpse of Jeopord, whom Cap'n Rustbane had also liked quite a lot, and couldn't think of anything to say.

"Too embarrassed to answer?" said Rustbane, misconstruing. "Well, I can't say that I blame you. Who can tell how many folks are wandering the Seven Seas and wishing that Cap'n Terrigan Rustbane could like 'em, or even just say a kind word about 'em? You must be the fortunatest hamster – lemming – in the whole of Sagaria to have been blessed by—"

"'E does go on a bit, doesn't 'e?" said Jasper in a histrionic whisper that echoed all the way around the walls of the cavern. "Big-headed too, this friend of yours, Syl."

The echoes soon reached Rustbane's ears. The gray fox paused and his eyes flickered red with fury, then focused again in a gimlet gaze that would doubtless have pinned Jasper to the spot, had Sylvester's dad been looking.

"And who," said the gray fox in a menacing whisper, "is this?"

"My dad."

"I thought he'd fled the Lemmington nest long ago."

"He did, but now I've found him again."

"Like something you've scraped off your shoe and promptly stood on again?"

Sylvester bristled, but kept himself in check. "Like, for example, you," he said.

Rustbane looked as if he were about to snap an angry retort, then he seemed to swallow the unspoken words and nodded. "Point taken, and well spoken. He's your beloved pater and I shouldn't have talked of him that way." The fox stepped toward Sylvester and Jasper, holding out a paw. "Any friend of young Sylvester is a . . . well, put it this way, I'll not slit your gizzard without so much as a by-your-leave. The name's Rustbane, Cap'n Terrigan Rustbane. You may have heard of me as Doomslayer, or Deathflash. Warhammer, perhaps?"

"Nope," said Jasper, not taking the proffered paw. "Can't say as I have."

"This place smells of blood," said Sylvester interrupting an exchange that seemed destined to become nothing but pricklier. "Let's get out of here."

"You forget something, my small friend," said Rustbane, drawing his attention away from Jasper as if out of treacle. "A small matter of the treasure chest of the Zindars. It's what we all came here for through stormy oceans and tempestuous climes, you may remember." He looked down at one of the silver pistols nestling in his belt, as if debating with himself whether to put a bullet through someone's brain now or later, then squinted at Sylvester with a brightly glinting eye.

"It's not here," said Sylvester, spreading his paws.

Viola, beside him, gave a little murmur of confirmation.

Cap'n Rustbane put his paws to his sides, tilted back his head and gave a mighty guffaw. His peals of laughter seemed to go on for an unconscionably long time, yet Sylvester couldn't detect any humor in them whatsoever.

Finally, Rustbane sobered himself, rubbing his eyes to wipe the mirth from them.

"Oh, dearie me," he said. "I could have sworn you just said that—"

"It's true," interposed Jasper. "The Zindars didn't leave their treasure here. They buried it . . . elsewhere."

Another peal of laughter from Rustbane, this one even more artificial than the last. Standing behind him, Cheesefang joined in. The sea rat's attempt at laughter sounded like someone trying to swallow a bag of forks. Next to Cheesefang, Sylvester noticed, Pimplebrains stood silent.

"But what of old Throatsplitter's map?" Rustbane said at last.

Jasper looked blank.

Sylvester hurriedly explained to his father about Cap'n Josiah "Throatsplitter" Adamite and his treasure map. As he did so, he saw Jasper's face relax.

"Oh, that," said the older lemming at last. "Yes," he added to Rustbane, "there's treasure of a sort here. Perhaps that's what the map's referring to."

"Treasure?" said Rustbane eagerly. "It's good to know at least one generation of Lemmingtons can talk about the stuff that's important. Treasure, you say? So just tell me, old hamst—fellow, where is it?"

Jasper bowed mockingly, imitating Rustbane's own grandiloquence of gesture. "Right here alongside us."

"It is? Where? Show me or I'll—show me, please."

Again Jasper bowed, this time extending a paw out to one side and pointing.

Rustbane gazed in the direction of Jasper's extended claw. "I can't see nothing."

Sylvester began to laugh. "Yes, you can."

The gray fox shot him an angry glance, eyes narrowing.

"It's the biggest thing you can see," Sylvester explained.

Realization dawned slowly on the fox's face.

Surrounded by its aura of inconceivable antiquity, the hulk of the Zindar vessel loomed toward the distant cavern ceiling.

Everyone fell silent as the implications sank in. Here, indeed, was a treasure of inestimable worth. The lemmings and Pimplebrains already knew that somewhere within it was an element capable of improving the way people could think, of making them cleverer than they could naturally be. There were also those cunning machines, like the ones that invisibly tended the crops of fruit and vegetables. Jasper had mentioned in passing a couple of others he'd discovered during his years dwelling within the Zindar ship, but Sylvester hadn't had the time to quiz him further. Who knew how many other machines there might be, still silently running after all these centuries, and what they might be capable of doing?

Miracles, perhaps.

They would certainly seem like miracles to the people of Sagaria.

The person who owned the Zindar ship could be monarch of the world.

There was one problem.

"How," breathed Rustbane, "are we going to take it with us?"

THE LONGEST VOYAGE OF THEM ALL

They couldn't, of course, take it with them. Sylvester, Cheesefang, Pimplebrains, Viola and Jasper all took turns trying to explain this as sympathetically as possible to Rustbane. It wasn't so much that the pirate skipper was inconsolable (although he was that too) as that he was incapable of conceiving that *any* treasure, and most particularly a treasure of this unique magnitude, couldn't be hauled away and spent.

"Perhaps we could just live here?" said the fox hopefully. Before he had been gray, now he was positively ashen.

"We've driven off the cannibals for now," Sylvester pointed out, "but how long do you think their fear's going to last? A week? A day? An hour?"

"Between us we could—"

"No," said everyone.

"Not even if—"

"No!"

"It's not as if," said Jasper eventually, "the Zindar vessel's going to go away, is it? I can trick it so the Vendrosians can't see it any longer. They'll not interfere with it. You'll be able to come back any time you want with a whole army of pirates and—"

"But I want the treasure *now!*" howled Rustbane.

Through all of this, Sylvester was relieved that his companions had better sense than to mention the location of the chest of the Zindars, the trove after which Rustbane had been searching. The idea of another horde of pirates descending upon Foxglove, this time with no reason to curb their savagery, was one that Sylvester dared not countenance.

On the subject of companions . . .

"Here's a question for you," he said to Rustbane, changing the subject so abruptly that the gray fox didn't have time to notice it was happening. "Where's Mrs. Pickleberry? You know, Three Pins. And where's Rasco?"

The gray fox brushed what looked suspiciously like a large, globular tear from the corner of his eye. "On the *Shadeblaze*."

With many a stop and start, Cap'n Rustbane related how he'd been saved from a watery grave by Viola's mother and the chirpy little mouse acting in tandem.

"They was braver than any of my cullies aboard the old *Shadeblaze*," confessed Rustbane, his voice becoming hoarse with emotion. "I can tell ye that. Braver by far. My Jack o' Cups, he was a vicious brute when his temper was aroused, for all he was a darling boy." Rustbane looked at the heap of dirty yellowish fur that had once been Jeopord. "If he'd known what they were up to, they'd have been kebabed, cooked and eaten before they were given a chance to die."

Viola's forehead furrowed. "How did they manage it?"

"What? Being keb—"

"No, rescuing you. Saving your life."

Rustbane grunted, annoyed that the center of attention was shifting away from himself. "Let them tell you themselves."

◊ ◊ ◊ ◊ ◊

It took a few more hours before they were able to persuade the gray fox to leave the Cavern of the Zindars, but finally the little party half-escorted, half-dragged him down to the shore where Jeopord and his men had left the longboats. Through fear or prudence, the cannibals didn't trouble them, although Sylvester thought once or twice he could hear the sounds of distant drumming and chanting. The sun was low in the sky, painting the tips of the waves with blood, as they maneuvered three of the boats down over the sand and into the water. Of course, Rustbane refused to row, such menial tasks being beneath him, but Cheesefang and Pimplebrains took an oar apiece and soon the leading craft bearing the gray fox, his new lieutenants and the three lemmings, was slicing through the choppy water of the bay. In the dusk, the *Shadeblaze* was a hulk of darkness lit only by yellow lamps hung at bow and stern. As the longboat came closer, a few further lamps were lit. It seemed that Rasco and Mrs. Pickleberry were preparing the ship to welcome the weary travelers.

Soon, Sylvester could hear the two aboard the ship, their voices drifting across the darkling waters of the bay.

"I must most humbly beseech you—"

"Wotcher bleating about now, yer daft oaf?"

"Please, oh treble-pinned one, you're—"

"Out with it!"

"Ma'am, it is a matter of circumstance that—"

"You got my rolling pin?"

"I fear not. However, *ma chérie*, although I hesitate to trouble you—"

"I got a itch."

"Mrs. Pickleberry."

"Yes?"

"You are standing on my—"

"Why's that daughter o' mine takin' so long gettin' here? I bet she's canoodlin' with that scoundrel Syl—"

"You're standing on my tail!"

"I am? Why didn't yer say so in the first place?"

Sylvester smiled. All seemed well aboard the good ship *Shadeblaze*.

A few minutes later, the longboat was heaving to under the wall of the *Shadeblaze*'s side. A rope ladder dropped from somewhere invisible above and Pimplebrains scampered agilely up it. Watching, Sylvester couldn't make out how the old beaver manipulated his hooks in order to climb so nimbly. Next up was Rustbane, still morose, and then Viola, Jasper, Sylvester and, finally, Cheesefang. Just before he clambered onto the ladder, the sea rat fastened lines to metal rings at the two ends of the longboat, so that the boat itself could be hauled up behind them. Then it was the turn of the next longboat.

Soon, everyone was back aboard the ship.

There seemed to be miserably few of them. Only a couple of days ago the *Shadeblaze* had been crowded and bustling. Now, the creaking of her timbers as she rocked gently in the swell seemed to inhibit people from talking louder than a murmur.

Rustbane, without saying a word to anyone, made his way to the captain's quarters, those quarters that, of course, Jeopord had inhabited during the fox's absence. The hushed crew could hear Rustbane swearing sturdily, then there was a crash as the first of the usurper's possessions was hurled up the wooden steps and onto the deck. It was followed by more. Wordlessly, Cheesefang and Pimplebrains moved over and began pitching the articles over the side into the blackness where the ocean hid.

Nobody said very much. Viola engaged her mother in a long hug. Sylvester realized that, during the past few days, Viola must have become resigned to never seeing her mother again much as Sylvester had long ago had to face the fact that he'd probably never see his father again. Now Sylvester was reunited with his father and Viola was reunited with her mother. It should have felt more like a happy ending.

The company remained mute while Bladderbulge, who to, Sylvester's unreasonable joy, was among the survivors, waddled off to the galley and began throwing together some vittles for their belated supper. Rasco, who'd earlier been calling high-pitched greetings from the crow's nest, scrambled down the rigging to rejoin his friends.

"So, tell me," said Sylvester a long while later as the four lemmings and the mouse gathered around a brazier on the poop deck, "just how was it you managed to save our vulpine friend?"

What never occurred to Sylvester was that of course his father and Daphne Pickleberry had known each other as adults, way back in the long ago. The two had recognized each other at once, and were soon laughing and joshing the way that old, albeit not particularly close, family friends are wont to do.

The subject of Mrs. Pickleberry thinking that Mayor Hairbell might be a suitable spouse for her young daughter had come up and she hotly denied ever favoring the notion. "It was all me 'usband's idea, the daft old bat."

Nothing would suit her better, Three Pins insisted, than that Viola should marry a swashbuckling hero of the seas like Sylvester Lemmington had proven himself to be. Indeed, she spoke so unexpectedly fondly of him that Sylvester was concerned Viola's sentiments might turn against him, but luckily this seemed not to be the case. Mrs. Pickleberry also spoke very fondly of Hortensia, Sylvester's mother. He'd never known the two were particularly close friends, but perhaps Mrs. Pickleberry's admiration was born of the fact that the lemmings were half a world away from home, and from Hortensia.

Sylvester wasn't sure if he liked the new, mellower Mrs. Pickleberry. After a while, he decided he didn't, but he could tolerate her as a mother-in-law if that was the price he had to pay for having Viola by his side for the rest of his life.

Probably.

"Wot I did was—" began Mrs. Pickleberry.

"What we did," Rasco corrected politely.

Mrs. Pickleberry drew an impossibly deep sigh. "What we did was, well, we felt we 'ad to save the life of that scoundrelly skipper o' yourn."

"Rustbane?"

"Ye catch on fast. See, spratling, I had a fair ol' hunch the mangy fox'd make sure we got home, one way or the other, just so long's we didn't get too far up his nose. After all, 'e'd harf a dozen times told us he was going to kill us or have us flogged, and none o' the times had he actually done so. Seemed as obvious as the 'air on an old man's bottom to me that Rustbane had reasons of his own for keepin' us alive. Jeopord, on the other paw, he was somethin' different. There was a mean streak down his back that was 'arf a yard wide. Obvious he'd kill us jus' as soon as he could think up a nasty enough way."

Sylvester was pretty sure he followed her reasoning.

"So, you and Rasco?" he prompted.

"Rasco and me," said Mrs. Pickleberry firmly, "we decided that we had to save the skipper, which involved givin' him a life raft o' sorts."

"Unfortunately, we could find only a cork," Rascoe said.

"A cork?"

"Yes." The mouse shrugged. "It was the only thing close at paw."

"So, when you said the cork could be used as a life raft," he continued, groping his way forward, "you didn't actually mean it was used as a raft."

"Not in so many words, no. It was wodjer might call a metaphoricule life raft."

"Something he could hang on to in a spiritual way?"

"Yes."

"Something that would give him faith in the future when the dark curtains of pessimism sank down all around barring him from the sunbeams of hope?"

"You do go on a bit, doncher, Sylvester?"

For a second, Sylvester couldn't think of an appropriate response. Mrs. Pickleberry was accusing him of going on a bit?

"Tell it your own way," he said at last, yielding the point.

Mrs. Pickleberry drew a whistling breath. She might have mellowed toward her prospective son-in-law, but that didn't mean she couldn't enjoy her moments of triumph over him. Sylvester made a mental note to make sure he and Viola enjoyed their marital life together as far from his in-laws as he could manage.

"It was lucky for us and our plans," she said, "that the pirate wot the mutinous ocelot deputed to tie up Rustbane was a pal of yers, Bladderbulge, none uvver."

Aha! thought Sylvester, comprehension dawning. *That explains a lot.* The portly badger had been one of the gray fox's closest allies. Sylvester recalled that odd moment when Bladderbulge had been tying Rustbane up after the mutiny, and the reluctance he had seen in Bladderbulge's eyes.

"There was so much rope wrapped around that scurrilous fox," Mrs. Pickleberry was saying, "you couldn't hardly see where rope ended and fox began. 'E looked like someone had been making a sausage and forgotten to cover the two ends. No one could tell there was more underneath them bonds than just fox."

"More underneath?" Sylvester asked.

Mrs. Pickleberry rolled her eyes. "Sylvester?"

"Yes?"

"What is Bladderbulge's job?"

"Er, he is the cook."

"Very good. What kitchen utensils do cooks usually have at their disposal?"

"Well, er, pots, frying pans, that sort of thing."

"My, ye're the fast guesser ain't ye?" She turned to Viola. "Are ye sure ye want to spend yer life with this dumbskull for a lemming?"

"Mom!"

"Anyways, with the speed of Sylvester's mind 'ere, we would'a played this guessing game for a week. What Bladderbulge used was a . . . knife!"

"Yes, well, that would've been my third guess," Sylvester said, silently cursing himself for not thinking of the most logical tool to cut a rope with.

"Sure ye would," said Mrs. Pickleberry heavy with sarcasm. "Now that we got that cleared up . . . The badger laid the knife against the fox's spine, sharp side outermost, runnin' from the base of Rustbane's tail up the middle of his back. Then he – Bladderbulge, that is – began winding around fox and knife alike with his ropes. By the time he'd done you couldn' tell there was the means of Rustbane's releasing built into the very bonds that held him, like."

Sylvester was still having a hard time figuring out the details.

"But what good would that be to Rustbane?" he said. "He couldn't reach the knife to do anything with it ."

"Yes, Mom," Viola chipped in. "How would the knife being there help the cap'n?"

Mrs. Pickleberry raised an eyebrow. "Them that say pirates can't swim – that it's part of the job description, like – that ain't strictly true. Not when ye're Cap'n Terrigan Rustbane, it ain't. Cap'n Terrigan Rustbane ain't come across a rule in his life that he ain't broken as a matter of principle, and this one ain't no exception. He can swim like a fish, like two fishes."

"Even when he's trussed from neck to toe?" said Viola.

"Sure. 'E can still wiggle, can't 'e?"

"I suppose so," murmured Sylvester thoughtfully. "That's how eels get around in the water. And sea snakes. And otters too, I think. And leeches. And—"

"Soooo." With a glare, Mrs. Pickleberry overrode him. "So, as I was sayin', Cap'n Rustbane can swim like an eel when he has to, and this was one o' the times he was goin' to be 'avin' to, if you gets me drift."

"Even when he's trussed up like a birthday gift?" said Viola, drawing some of her mother's irritation away from Sylvester.

"Even then. He's a talented feller, that Rustbane. 'S a pity he ain't a lemming, might make a better son-in-law than some I could mentions."

Oh well, decided Sylvester. So much for the mellow Mrs. Pickleberry. That didn't last long.

"Where was I?" said Mrs. Pickleberry.

Viola reminded her.

"Well, as I was sayin' afore I was so rudely interrupted, off his plank Rustbane jumps, and into the water he goes – *kerrsplosh* – and he sort o' thrashes around a while to make it look good. Then—"

"But I saw him drifting away from the Shadeblaze," said Sylvester.

"So you did." Mrs. Pickleberry reached out and patted him on the side as if to tell him that even numbskulls could get a few things right, like stopped clocks. "There was one more thing Bladderbulge did when 'e was knottin' up the fox, an' that was ter leave a loose end o' rope free. As soon as Rustbane landed in the water, right after him went our little friend here."

She gestured at Rasco. The little mouse grinned and bowed.

"I landed in the water," he said, taking up the story, "and, oh, the waves were so high and the water so cold for a diminutive mouse like *moi*. But I plucked all my courage into a single pluck, and I swam to where the great big fox was splooshing in the sea, and I seized the end of cord Bladderbulge had left and put it between my teeth. With a cry of '*bon voyage!*' (my little joke, you see) I began to swim—"

"Very little," said Mrs. Pickleberry firmly.

"—back to the . . . What?"

"'Very little,' I said."

"Pardon?"

"Your joke."

"I'm sorry, I don't understand."

"Ye said yer joke was little."

"I did. I know that."

"I was just saying it was very little."

"It was. Is that not what I said?"

"No. You just said it was little. Not very little."

Rasco shrugged and put his paws up as if pleading to the heavens. "Little, very little, what difference does it make?"

"All the difference in the—look, just get on with it."

"That is what I was trying to do, Three Pins."

"Din' look like it to me." She sniffed.

Rasco looked as if he might be tempted at a moment's notice to strangle someone, but carried on where he'd left off.

"I swam back to the *Shadeblaze* with the loose end of rope. As planned, Daphne was hanging a much longer piece of rope from a porthole of her cabin near the water level, and it was the work of a moment to tie the two ends together. Then, once she had pulled me into the cabin alongside her, all we had to do was watch Rustbane fall away behind the stern of the *Shadeblaze* until everyone else had got bored with the spectacle. As soon as that happened, we began pulling him in, like he was a mighty fish and we were the fisherfolk who'd caught him. It was a hard haul for two creatures so inconsequentially sized as ourselves, but luckily our two friends, Bladderbulge and Cheesefang, soon came to aid us, and before too long the good cap'n was bobbing in the wake below our porthole.

"Then came the part most *difficile.*"

Rasco looked around him as if, even now, there might be hostile spies listening. Sylvester idly wondered if anyone else had ever called Cap'n Terrigan Rustbane "good" before.

"You see," said Rasco, "Cap'n Rustbane had to wiggle until—"

"Like a eel," interposed Mrs. Pickleberry.

"Like an eel," Rasco conceded. "He had to wriggle like an eel until he was directly against the hull of the *Shadeblaze*, his back to its timbers, and rub up and down against them, worrying at them so the sharp blade of the knife could cut through the rope."

"Ahhhhh," said Jasper. "So that's how you did it. The edge would never have cut through all the layers of rope but it didn't have to. Just one piece of rope, so long as it was the right piece of rope."

"Then," agreed Rasco, "all the rest would unravel. That was our plan, you see. And the loose coils of rope would drift away in the ocean current under the cover of darkness, so that by morning they'd be long gone and none aboard would be any the wiser."

"While Rustbane would have crawled in through the porthole and be safely sleeping it off in Daphne's cabin, so that—"

"Not exactly," said Rasco with a sidelong glance at Mrs. Pickleberry.

Jasper did a double-take then smiled. "Of course. The porthole might be big enough for you to crawl in and out of, but foxes are much larger animals than mice, and lemmings for that matter, so Rustbane wouldn't have been able to get through."

"It wasn't just that," said Rasco in a very low, embarrassed voice.

Jasper narrowed his eyes. "Then what was it?"

"My good friend Three Pins here, she—"

"Out with it!"

"There's the matter of whether it would be *seemly* to share her cabin with a—"

"With a fox? She's a lemming, for goodness' sake!"

Mrs. Pickleberry's expression was wrought of stone. It was clear she wasn't going to say nuffink, not nohow.

"She is," said Rasco, in the tones of one venturing into a maze that might prove to have no exit, "a *female* lemming."

"Pshaw!" exclaimed Jasper.

Viola bridled in defense of her mother. "It's easy enough for you to say 'pshaw!'"

Looks like there might be stormy times ahead between Viola and her father-in-law too, mused Sylvester. *Perhaps it might be best if my darling and I found a desert island somewhere to settle down.*

"You're right," said Jasper. "Shall I say it again?"

"My mother was rightly concerned about the . . . proprieties."

Rasco cleared his throat, a sound like someone scraping claws along a nail file. A very small nail file.

"It was not Three Pins who was concerned about the, ah, proprieties of sharing a cabin with Cap'n Rustbane. It was, ahem—"

He stopped speaking. Everyone else except Mrs. Pickleberry stopped breathing as the implications sank in.

"Mom?" said Viola at last.

This is nuts, Sylvester decided. *A moment ago we were all ready to ridicule Daphne for declining to share her cabin with a fox. Now we're ready to criticize her because it was the fox who got himself tied up in ridiculous knots.*

It is at moments like these that imminent sons-in-law lay the foundations for years of future happy coexistence.

"Well," he said. "What a stupid damn fox."

After a long, reflective silence, Rasco somewhat tentatively continued.

"That Cap'n Rustbane, he is the athletic one, no? Even though he'd been in the icy waters for more hours than there are claws on a mouse's paw, once he'd shed the ropes that bound him, Rustbane wasted no time about scaling the side of the *Shadeblaze*. He climbed over the taffrail under cover of night, and found his way to the galley, where Bladderbulge hid him until—"

"Until we ran aground near the cannibal island," concluded Sylvester.

Rasco nodded.

"Even after that, once Jeopord sent us ashore to what the ocelot thought would almost certainly be our gruesome deaths."

"Gruesome," said the mouse, nodding again. "Yes. I like that. Gruesome. Deaths? Not so good."

"It was only once Jeopord and his landing party had got the *Shadeblaze* afloat and set off for the island themselves, hoping to find that the cannibals had killed us or we'd killed the cannibals – preferably both – that Rustbane came out of hiding."

"You have hit the nail right on the thumb." It was an expression Rasco had used before.

"So, Rustbane cared no more than Jeopord did what happened to us?"

A new voice spoke from somewhere in the darkness behind Sylvester.

"Of course I cared. Aren't you all, all of you, the very jewels of my heart?"

"You've been 'ittin' the grog," said Mrs. Pickleberry breaking what was, for her, a very long silence. "You's smashed, Terry, isn't yer?"

The gray fox, teetering as he ventured into the glow cast by the brazier, thought about this for some while longer than he should have.

"I am," he concluded, "stone-cold drunk."

No one spoke.

"It's rather like being stone-cold sober," Rustbane said, "only with one very significant difference."

He looked from face to face, as if expecting somebody to start a guessing game as to what the difference might be.

"Good," he said, when no one spoke. "I suppose you've been wondering what I'm planning to do next?"

"No, in fact," said Sylvester.

"Then you should have been," said Rustbane airily. "Always important to be thinking about your skipper's intentions."

"Well, we weren't."

"I'll tell you anyway."

"Please do."

"Not that I *need* to, you understand."

"We understand."

"You'll be aware that my crew of this joyous bark has been severely depleted by events of late?"

"Of course."

"The *Shadeblaze* requires a full complement if she's to return to her former ways of buccaneering and ocean roving." Rustbane seemed to be getting into his narrative swing, despite or perhaps because of the grog. "Accordingly, it is my plan to sail with this skeletal crew only as far as Hangman's Haven, then pick up, by bribery, coercion or just plain brute force, another forty or fifty cully boys of suitable skills and criminal temperament."

"That may be your *intention*," said Sylvester very carefully, "but it's not in fact what's going to happen."

Rustbane sighed histrionically and struck a pose with his fist on his waist. "Oh no, not another mutiny, so soon after the last. I don't think my nerves could take it, dearie."

"Not a mutiny," said Sylvester.

The gray fox clapped. "Oh, good. So, what makes you think I'm going to obey your . . . requests? Come on, Sylvester. Do tell."

"You're going to do what I say because I know where the *real* treasure of the Zindars is hidden."

Jasper and Viola stared at Sylvester as if he'd gone crazy, or betrayed them or both. Despite all previous evidence to the contrary, he knew what he was doing. This was the new, Zindar-influenced Sylvester. He'd never thought as clearly as this in his life before. It was like bathing in cool spring water.

Rustbane froze, instantly sober. "But what about that huge edifice in the cave?"

"That was just the second prize, the runner-up award."

"Then it's back to the island we go, and this time we're not leaving it 'til – by jingo! – Cap'n Terrigan Rustbane has the treasure of the Zindars trickling between his clammy little paws. Only" – there was a long silence, broken only by the slapping of wavelets against the *Shadeblaze*'s timbers – "how do I know I can trust you?"

"What makes you think that you can't?"

"Let me see now," said Rustbane, beginning to pace up and down on the deck, his chin in his paw. "There's the fact that you been long enough among pirates not to know truth if it came up and bit you in the leg. That's just for starters. Then there's the fact you might be thinking if you hoodwink ol' Terrigan Rustbane, genial son o' a gun as he is, you might be able to leave him in the lurch somehow. I didn't get to where I am in the world by not suspecting each and everyone, you know. It's the pirate way, see?"

"I believes Sylvester." It was Daphne who'd spoken. "Even though he is a bit of an ar—"

"Mo–*om!*"

Rustbane nodded. Clearly, he was more inclined to take Mrs. Pickleberry's word for it than he was just about anyone else's. Put that another way: He was less *dis*inclined to take Mrs. Pickleberry's word for it. She had, after all, masterminded the scheme that had saved his life. And she'd sacrificed Elvira for his sake.

"So, you think I should trust him?"

"I feels it in me waters, yes."

The gray fox returned his gaze to Sylvester. "And where might the treasure be?"

Sylvester inclined his head with a smile. "We've been through all this before."

"Threats of torture?"

"Yes."

"Threats to kill your girlfriend? What was it dear Jeopord used to call her? Little Miss Droppydrawers?"

Sylvester refused to rise to the insult. "Yes, you tried those too."

"Threats to hold my breath and scream?"

"No."

"Should I try it now?"

"Not unless you actually want to hold your breath and scream, I wouldn't."

Rustbane twisted his mouth vexedly. "We seem to be at an impasse."

"We do indeed."

"Supposing, just supposing, I was to entertain for one minute the conceivability of concurring with your wishes by way of bargaining for the location of Throatsplitter Adamite's treasure. Just supposing this – and it ain't no more than a fairy tale we're entertaining here, you understand – what exactly is it you'd be a-wanting me to do rather than head for Hangman's Haven as fast as the *Shadeblaze's* somewhat decrepit sails would permit?"

"Take us home to Foxglove."

The fox appeared baffled. "Foxglove?"

"The home of the lemmings. Where you seized us."

"Oh, *that* Foxglove! When you're as experienced a traveler as me too many of the places you've been tend to blur into one, as you'll understand. Daffy little place. Has a big library. An even bigger temple. A mayor and a high priest you'd rather flush down the jakes than say a how-d'ye-do to. I remember it. A nice spot to settle down if you want to watch your brain cells atrophy, I'd say."

Again, Sylvester kept his temper in check. This was his home town the fox was slandering. *He's just trying to needle you. Don't let him get away with it.* He could see Mrs. Pickleberry was coming to the boil and he gestured to Jasper that he should try to calm Three Pins down.

"That's it," said Sylvester. "Foxglove."

"What in tarnation's name d'ye think would induce me ever to go back to such a tedious little hole?"

"You want the treasure, the chest of the Zindars."

"There's that." The fox let out his breath in a long gust. "There surely is that."

"Once we're all safely in Foxglove, I'll tell you where it is."

"You're sure you *want* to go back to Foxglove, lad?"

Startled by the sudden new tack the skipper had taken, Sylvester didn't reply immediately. "Whyever shouldn't I? Why do you ask the question?"

"Because it's going home. Going *back*. It's the longest voyage of them all, you know, the one that takes you back to where you started."

For a moment, Sylvester could have believed the gray fox was speaking out of genuine concern for him. Did he want to go back to the placid tranquility of Foxglove? Sylvester had discovered what roistering life on the high seas was like. He'd come within a hairsbreadth of his death more times than he could rightly remember and, though each hair-raisingly close brush with death had terrified him to his very core, he had to admit that each time it had also been fun. Perhaps not *right then*, but afterwards, looking back on the thrill of survival against the odds. Could he really give up the zest of adventure, the spice of not knowing each morning if you'd live to see the sunset, for the sake of the measured serenity, the small enclosed world, of Foxglove?

Could *Viola?*

Sylvester glanced at her. He could see the same questions racing through her head, the same indecision.

He raised an eyebrow to her. *What d'you think?*

She opened her paws. *No one can ever take away from us the adventures we've had, but the escapades have to stop sometime. Better while we're still alive than . . . later. Now it's time, maybe, that we were looking forward to a different sort of adventure.*

He pursed his lips, agreeing with her. They'd still have a few weeks of voyaging on the *Shadeblaze* before they got home, after all, and who knew what might happen during that time. After all, there was work to be done at home in Foxglove, not least exposing the truth about Mayor Hairbell and High Priest Spurge, and about the Great Exodus. And Lhaeminguas. That last was going to be the most difficult of all. The folk of Foxglove, staid and traditional as they were, weren't going to be too keen on the notion of giving up Lhaeminguas.

As he turned back to Rustbane, Sylvester felt this might be one of the hardest things he would ever had to say.

"Yes. We want to go back to Foxglove."

"And you want me to take you?"

"Yes."

"With the barest of skeleton crews?"

"Yes. You can manage. You have four lemming volunteers to supplement your pirates, after all."

"And a mouse," Rasco pointed out.

"And a mouse," Sylvester said.

"You're all five of you lubbers," objected Rustbane.

"Ahem," said Mrs. Pickleberry.

"Except one," said Rustbane hastily.

Rustbane pretended to be considering the proposition, although Sylvester could see by the gleam in those greenish-yellow eyes that the wily buccaneer had already made up his mind.

"Once I've landed you there safe and sound you promise you'll tell me where I might find the chest of the Zindars, do you?"

"I've already told you as much."

"Your word on it."

"You know you have my word on it."

"Or I'll put a black spot on you."

"Tremble, tremble. You already have. Don't you remember?"

"I wasn't counting you rotten lot. Or any man-jack among my crew who'd remain secretly loyal to me. Though there are some among the people aboard the ship right now that I'd reckon are just bending with the way the wind's blowing, and'd stab me in the back again as soon as look at me. Them – *them* – them'll discover the full horrific meaning of the black spot when it's applied by Cap'n Terrigan Rustbane, you can take my word they will."

Viola shuddered. "Why always with the cruelty, Rustbane? It's easy to make people fear you. It's harder, but worth it, to earn their respect instead."

Rustbane ignored her. Abruptly, he stuck out his paw to Sylvester. "Cap'n Terrigan Rustbane must be going soft in his dotage but, all right, you got yourself a deal, young Sylvester. Shake on it."

Slightly warily, Sylvester shook.

With a final squeeze of Sylvester's paw, Rustbane turned away.

"Turn her prow toward daybreak," he bellowed to any of the crew who might still be awake. "Until then, me hearties, catch yerselves some sleep if you can. Your skipper's Terrigan Rustbane again, and stab me if each new day's not going to be the best you ever had in your lives!"

A Sound like a Thundercrack

The voyage home was far less eventful than the outward journey had been, which was lucky because everyone aboard the *Shadeblaze* had to work from dawn until dusk, and then straight on through until dawn again, just to keep the big old ship sailing on her course. Sylvester and Viola learned the old pirate trick of catching sleep a few moments at a time while engaged in the task to hand. Several times a day, Bladderbulge would appear bearing food, and Sylvester and Viola ate it where they stood. The only break they ever got from the relentless toil was when nature forced them to visit the jakes.

One advantage of the jakes aboard the *Shadeblaze*.

You visited them as rarely as you possibly could.

This is the life! thought Sylvester less and less frequently as the voyage wore on. A thousand times or more he cursed himself for refusing to let Cap'n Rustbane do what he wanted and stop off at Hangman's Haven to pick up more crew. But Sylvester knew in his heart of hearts what would have happened then. With his ship full of pirates, Rustbane would have felt less compelled to take the lemmings home. The hunt for Cap'n Adamite's treasure would have been put off for another day, and that other day might be a long time in coming, what with all the excitement of buccaneering with a full complement again.

Sylvester was beginning to think Rustbane might have been right, that the voyage home really *was* always the longest of them all.

Every few days there'd be that cry from Rasco in the crow's nest, "land ahoy!"

Eventually, Sylvester could barely be bothered to raise his head to look. They never actually put in to shore, anyway. There was no need. With so few people aboard, the *Shadeblaze*'s supplies were more than enough for the while. And Rustbane was keen to get the journey over with, keen not just to get his paws on the treasure of the Zindars but also to get back to what he regarded as his proper business, pirating.

"Land ahoy!" yelled Rasco as Sylvester was stooping to wind some rope on a capstan.

Thrills 'n' spills, thought Sylvester wearily. The rope seemed to be getting heavier and rougher with each new minute that passed.

There was a touch on his shoulder.

He looked up.

Cap'n Terrigan Rustbane was beaming at him as cordially as a pirate could beam.

"Here, take this."

Rustbane was holding out the ship's brass telescope.

"Wha—" blurted Sylvester.

"I think you'll want to have a look. Here, *take* it, I say."

His paws numb from the rope, Sylvester had to concentrate hard not to fumble as he accepted the instrument. Raising it to his eye was an even tougher task.

He couldn't see anything but gray. Maybe a little bit of blue as well but, if so, it was a blue-gray.

"Not that way," said Rustbane gently. "You're looking straight out to sea."

He took Sylvester by the shoulders and turned him around.

"*Now* do you see?"

And Sylvester did.

The first thing he saw was the Mighty Enormous Cliff. His pulse beating faster and faster, he slowly raised the telescope, watching the rocks and fissures of the Mighty Enormous Cliff swim past his gaze. Past the top of the cliff he could see the darkness of Mugwort Forest spreading out like a stain across the low hills in which Foxglove nestled. And there, just to the right, he could see some of the rooftops of his home town. There was the library where he'd spent so much of his life reading about exploits that now seemed positively dreary beside the adventures he'd had. And there, Sylvester's mouth puckered, was the temple, the seat of his enemies' power.

"Home," he said, at once realizing the stupidity of what he'd just said.

"Of course it's your home!" cried Rustbane, clapping him on the back. "Did you doubt for one instant the navigatory skills of Cap'n Terrigan Rustbane?"

"Er, no, but—"

"Did you doubt the *word* of Cap'n Terrigan Rustbane? Hm?"

"Of course not, but—"

"But *what*, Sylvester, my old boyo?"

"I think I need to sleep."

Sylvester crumpled at the knees.

And slept. Right there on the deck.

Rustbane let him.

⚓ ⚓ ⚓ ⚓

"Wake up, Sylvester!"

His eyelids seemed to have a coating of glue inside them, but somehow he managed to force them open. He saw a gray sky, out of focus.

"Wha—"

"Wake *up*!"

"Viola?"

"Who else?"

For a split second he'd thought it was her mother shaking him into unwelcome consciousness. He didn't say so.

"What time is it?"

"Morning. Cap'n Rustbane set the *Shadeblaze* to anchor when dusk fell. You've been sleeping here on deck all night."

He could believe it. One side of Sylvester felt fine and well rested. The other side felt . . . flattened. He must have been so exhausted he hadn't moved at all on the hard wood beneath him.

Sylvester sat up, shivering in the early-morning chill.

"We're home," he said stupidly.

"Not yet." Viola pointed. "We still have to climb the Mighty Enormous Cliff."

Sylvester felt his blood run cold. "Why aren't we just rowing over to the beach? That's how we got on the *Shadeblaze* when we left Foxglove."

"Apparently the wind is blowing from the east today and the surf is too rough for us to land on the beach. The only area calm enough to approach is at the base of the cliff," replied Viola.

Sylvester gaped at the sheer stony wall. It seemed somehow even more intimidating than it had last night. Different seams of rock in different colors of gray and brown wove in and around each other. The stones jutting out from the face were angular and lethal-looking. Some appeared ready to go crashing down into the waves at the cliff's foot if disturbed by even so much as a fly landing on them.

"*Climb* it?" repeated Sylvester after a while.

"Can you think of any other way up?"

"Lemmings aren't very good at climbing, you know," he began, then realized what he was saying. "Oh, of course, you *do* know."

"I used to," she said with a little laugh. "Nowadays, I'm not so sure. I've seen what adventure can do to a lemming. We're all of us – you, me, Mom, your father – much *more* than any of the lemmings we were when we'd never left Foxglove."

"Still—"

"Still what, Sylvester Lemmington? You getting an attack of cold feet before you've even given it a try?"

"Well, yes, as it happens."

She frowned, folding her forepaws in front of her. The watery sunlight seemed to give her an aura. "You remember what you discovered when we were escaping from The Monkey's Curse back in Hangman's Haven, Sylvester?"

How could he ever forget?

"I was able to run faster than any lemming has ever run before."

"Well, possibly," she allowed. "Certainly it was far faster than any of us had ever known a lemming could run. Whatever the case, that ability has always been inside you, Sylvester, and probably inside all of us, if only we knew it. You found out about it because you were suddenly scareder than you'd ever been before."

"So?"

"So, what the Zindar ... influence, I suppose we have to call it. What the Zindar influence did to us was open us up to the potential that had been living inside lemmings all this time. The part we notice the most is how much better we're thinking than we used to. But hasn't it dawned on you, Sylvester, that you've just been working about three weeks without a break? You didn't use to have that sort of stamina before, none of us did."

"I suppose so." Sylvester wondered if maybe he'd lost the power of clear thinking again. Or maybe it was that he'd just woken up. He'd never been at his best first thing in the morning. That was *one* part of him the Zindar magic hadn't changed for the better.

She laughed again and punched him on the shoulder. "I've got faith in you, even if you don't."

"What about your mom?"

Viola wrinkled her nose. "What about my mom?"

"She wasn't in the Zindar ship with us. She hasn't got whatever it is we got when we were there."

Viola didn't let this faze her. "Mom's a tough old boot. She'll cope somehow."

"You think so?"

"I do, and if she can't we'll come down and fetch her later. 'Sides, I think Cheesefang and Rasco between them will be able to think of some way of getting her up the Mighty Enormous Cliff, don't you? I mean, it's only a measly old rock face, after all."

Sylvester gulped, not too audibly, he hoped. He wasn't entirely convinced his unnatural turn-of-speed ability was still going to function when rotated through ninety degrees, from horizontal to vertical.

"Where's your mom?" he said, stalling for time.

"She's waiting by the longboats with your dad," said Viola brightly. "I do think your mom ought to look to her laurels, you know. Mom and Jasper are getting on awfully well."

Sylvester contemplated this scenario as he got groggily to his feet. He was pretty sure there must be some hereditary component to the male lemming reaction toward females. If so, his own taste would reflect, or at least bear similarities to, his father's. If that were so, Hortensia's marriage was safe enough.

On the other hand, and the thought momentarily paralysed him, *I think Daphne's* daughter *is the cutest thing since bees' knees were invented, so isn't it possible that . . . ?*

No, he told himself firmly. *That way lies madness.*

He allowed Viola to lead him to the longboats. Mrs. Pickleberry and Jasper weren't the only ones standing there looking impatient. With them were Cheesefang, Pimplebrains and, inevitably, Rustbane. The gray fox had a smug look on his face as if Sylvester and the other had been expecting to skip off and leave him behind but he, Rustbane, had outwitted them through sheer cunning. In fact, Sylvester was glad to see him there. Once upon a time he'd regarded Rustbane as the most insane individual he'd ever met. Now, Sylvester thought of him as a stabilizing influence, one who might allay the hotheadedness of people like Mrs. Pickleberry.

"In yers gets, yer poxy landlubbers," said Cheesefang, launching a gob of spittle over the side into the water as if he'd like to do the same to the lemmings.

"You're not coming with us?" said Viola.

"Nope."

She looked crestfallen. "Oh, I'm sorry about that."

"Well, *'im*" – Cheesefang gave a derisive jerk of his head toward his skipper – "'e says I has ter stay back 'ere on the *Shadeblaze* and look after the old bucket like she was my own. It's a 'onor really, I s'pose."

Viola darted forward and gave the old sea rat a peck on the cheek. "Well, I'm sure all of us will feel much safer with you here guarding our backs."

"You is?"

"I is."

"Hmmf," said Mrs. Pickleberry, "you lay a digit on my daughter and you'll find yerself strangled with yer own tail."

It was difficult to tell if Cheesefang paled under his customary layer of gray filth, but Sylvester suspected that he did.

"Right y'are, ma'am," said the rat.

Mrs. Pickleberry was first into the longboat Cheesefang indicated, with the other lemmings following her. Then Rasco, who'd insisted that he'd rather die, oh yes, than be left out of what he called the exploratory party. Then Pimplebrains and, finally, with a crash that made the longboat threaten to collapse into a heap of splinters, Rustbane.

"You can row," said Mrs. Pickleberry to the gray fox.

Rustbane looked as if he might object, then he saw the way Mrs. Pickleberry was staring at him and humbly reached for the oars.

Getting to the base of the Mighty Enormous Cliff took less time than Sylvester would have expected, Rustbane being a far more efficient and powerful rower than most of his crew. The fox pulled the longboat to an unsteady halt about ten yards from where the waves smashed against the jagged rocks under the vertical face.

"I suppose you'll be wanting to go first, Sylvester?" he said sardonically, raising his voice to be heard above the shriek of the breaking waves.

Sylvester felt his heart at the back of his throat and swallowed hard to get it to sink back down into his chest again.

He was saved from having to say anything by Pimplebrains.

"Reckon it's me who'll lead the way," said the old beaver heavily, flexing his hook-bearing wrists in front of him. "Seeing as how you did the rowin' an' all, Skip."

He winked at Rustbane.

Rustbane didn't wink back. This sort of familiarity was not encouraged among the crew of the *Shadeblaze*.

"Glad to hear you's in agreement," said Pimplebrains, oblivious to the glare Rustbane was giving him. "Now, if you'll be excusing me."

Before Sylvester could blink properly, the beaver had grabbed a coil of rope from the bottom of the longboat and was over the side and swimming strongly to where the spray of the waves was throwing up a tall, wrathfully white curtain.

"He'll drown," said Jasper anxiously.

"Not him," said Rustbane. Sylvester, sitting next to the fox, could have sworn he added, "and more's the pity," in an undertone.

As they watched, Pimplebrains climbed up onto one of the larger rocks with a nimbleness that seemed incongruous with the portliness of his body. An especially large breaker tried to blast him from his perch, but the beaver clung on easily enough. As the spray subsided, he raised a hook to wave at the party in the longboat.

"That's *two* pirates who can swim," observed Viola.

"You're talking in apropos of exactly what, young lady?" inquired Rustbane.

"You once said pirates couldn't swim. Except it turns out you can, and now we discover Pimplebrains can as well. I'd be reassured right now if you could tell me pirates can't climb rock faces too. Nothing like an obsessive liar to let you know what the truth is."

Rustbane harrumphed. "You wouldn't like to be the next to swim to shore, would you, m'dear?"

"I'll be doin' that," said Mrs. Pickleberry.

Before anyone could stop her, she dove over the side.

"I never knew your mom could swim that well," said Sylvester a few momenta later as Mrs. Pickleberry clambered up on to the rock alongside Pimplebrains.

"Neither did I."

Somehow or other, it turned out Sylvester was the last one to swim. By then, the longboat was beginning to feel a very cold and lonely place and he was glad to leave it. He'd have been even gladder if leaving it didn't mean having to plunge into roiling waters that looked as if they'd enjoy nothing more than ripping a young lemming limb from limb.

He stood at the bow of the longboat, giving the little craft one last farewell.

The sea surged.

The stern of the longboat went down under the impact of a house-sized volume of water.

The bow went up, making a noise like the cracking of a whip or an elastic band suddenly released from tension.

Making a noise that *wasn't* like the cracking of a whip, or of an elastic band suddenly released from tension, but more like the air erupting from a punctured balloon, Sylvester shot skyward.

The next thing he knew he was clinging onto a small thorny twig that stuck out from the face of the Mighty Enormous Cliff about twenty yards above water level. Looking down at the waves hammering against the craggy rocks, Sylvester couldn't decide whether this was twenty yards too high or not nearly high enough.

"Ah, hel*lo*!" he called down to his friends.

Viola shouted something back up at him, but he couldn't make out what it was. The thunder of the waves was louder than he'd ever thought a sound could be.

He could hear Pimplebrains, though, or maybe he was just reading lips, when the beaver called up to him, "Catch the rope!"

A moment later there was a lasso of rope around Sylvester's neck.

"Thanks for the warning!" he cried. Looking down, he realized Pimplebrains hadn't been able to hear him.

A good thing too, he thought, just as he realized the root of the plant he was gripping was beginning to think of tearing itself loose from the rocky crevice in which it had grown.

He looked despairingly around for a pawhold.

There!

Just above him there was another crack in the surface of the rock. If he could only *stre-e-e-e-tch* an arm far enough, but that meant removing one clutching paw from his only support, the plant to which he clung. And once he'd released that grip he was committed to ...

Sylvester's mind reached a point of panic so intense that suddenly he burst through it into an area of total calm.

He could reach that fissure in the rock face, no problem.

Easy.

See, he'd done it already!

It was easy to jam a claw down into it, mooring himself securely.

As if on cue, the little branch he'd been holding on to broke, tumbling away toward the anxious, upward-looking faces of his friends.

Sylvester dangled by a solitary claw.

Let's not panic, he told himself.

He dangled a little longer, swaying gently from side to side with the wind. There was no other pawhold in sight.

On second thought, let's!

◈ ◈ ◈ ◈ ◈

"It was the most astonishing thing I've ever seen," said Pimplebrains as the party rested on the grass at the top of Mighty Enormous Cliff. "Quite astonishing."

Sylvester smiled modestly. "It was nothing. We lemmings do that sort of stuff all the time."

"Mrs. Pickleberry didn't."

"Well, she's, er, she's built differently and she's, ah, less callow."

"You were *marvelous*," Viola told him.

I was just terrified, he thought. *That was all. And because I was terrified I was able to ...*

What his friends had seen was Sylvester dangling by a precarious grip, staring back down at them with a look that could have been painted on stone and still given small children nightmares. Then, even as they watched disbelievingly, he'd blurred.

While they were still blinking their eyes at this, they'd noticed that, somehow, Sylvester was already at the top of the Mighty Enormous Cliff despite appearing not to have touched any intermediate point between there and his immediately previous perch. Viola and Mrs. Pickleberry and Rasco had seen the effect before, of course, but even they had marveled at its repetition here.

Once at the top, Sylvester, as baffled as anyone else by his prowess, had cast the rope down so the others could climb up. For Pimplebrains and Rustbane, the smaller animals had had to tie the rope to the base of a convenient birch tree.

Jasper put a paw on Sylvester's shoulder. "Whatever you say, son, I'm proud of you. You did good."

Sylvester wished they'd all just shut up about it. He was getting more embarrassed by the moment.

Rescue came from perhaps the most unexpected direction of all.

"What's that?" said Rustbane suddenly, sitting up and scenting the air, his nose and whiskers twitching.

"I don't hear nuffink," Mrs. Pickleberry replied testily.

Sylvester wondered why she sounded so worried, then realized she must be apprehensive about the welcome the returning adventurers might receive from the likes of, say, Mayor Hairbell.

"Hush," insisted Rustbane. "It's the sound of people – lemmings – chanting, I think, and drums."

Jasper obviously heard it too. He'd gone completely still. Under the gray fur, his face paled.

"What is it, Dad?"

"Something I remember all too well, my lad. Things haven't changed at all since my day, have they?"

"Stop talking in riddles, Dad! What hasn't changed?"

But Sylvester already knew the answer.

By good fortune or bad, they'd returned on the day of the Exodus that Mayor Hairbell had been planning all those weeks ago before Sylvester and the Pickleberries had been abducted by the rioting pirates. The devastation the pirates had inflicted on Foxglove, not to mention on Hairbell himself, must have caused the mayor and High Priest Spurge to postpone the event until order could be restored.

But not indefinitely.

Today a new generation of "troublesome" lemmings was heading toward a watery death at the base of the Mighty Enormous Cliff.

Unless . . .

"Come on!" cried Sylvester, leaping to his feet. "We can stop this!"

"Whyever would we wish to?" said the gray fox languorously, lounging on the grass, sniffing a daisy he'd just picked, twirling its stem. Yet Sylvester could see a gleam of anticipation in the pirate's eye. There was the prospect of action here and Cap'n Terrigan Rustbane never turned his face away from fighting if he could help it.

Jasper looked dubious. "There's barely a pawful of us and who knows how many hundreds the mayor can call upon if his authority's challenged?"

Mrs. Pickleberry had set her jaw like rock. "Are you man or are you mouse, Jasper Lemmington? Don't answer that question."

Jasper's shoulders slumped. "You're right, of course. It's our duty to stop it if we can."

"Then what are we waiting for?" cried Rasco, jumping up to stand by Sylvester. From somewhere he produced a diminutive cutlass and slashed experimentally with it at the air in front of him.

"Terrifying," remarked Rustbane, looking down his nose at the mouse. "Such ferocity in one so small."

Over the brow of the plateau that led to the Mighty Enormous Cliff came the first few lemmings. They halted abruptly on seeing the ragamuffin party that stood between them and the precipice. Others backed up behind them. The chanting that had been growing ever louder trailed off in unharmonious disarray.

"Keep going! Keep going! You'll be proud of yourself when you venture forth. It's your good fortune to seek out the Land of Destiny. The great spirit Lhaeminguas calls upon you to take the leap of faith."

His heart sinking, Sylvester recognized the voice as that of Hairbell, and a few moments later the portly mayor himself came into view. Sylvester had been looking forward to his final showdown with the tyrant, but now that it was actually imminent he wished the moment could be delayed a little. This was all happening too quickly, too soon.

Immediately behind Mayor Hairbell came High Priest Spurge, clad in his ceremonial robes and an aura of acute piety.

"Rat-a-*tat*-tat! Rat-a-*tat*-tat! Rat-a-*tat*-tat! Rat-a-*tat*-tat!" went the drums, but then they lost their rhythm. "Rat-a-*tatter*-tatterta! Rat-rat-a!"

Hairbell saw Sylvester and he gave a contemptuous laugh. "The spratling's returned, has he?"

Then Rustbane nonchalantly got to his feet and Hairbell lost a whole lot of confidence in a whole lot of a hurry.

"The p-p-pirate!"

The word went through the ranks of lemmings as a wave of whispers. "The pirate. The pirate. The pirate. The pirate." Sylvester couldn't tell if the marchers were terrified or excited at the prospect of seeing their mayor discomfited. Although the people of Foxglove bent to Hairbell's will because lemmings tend to be law-abiding folk, the mayor was far from popular. The last time Rustbane had confronted him, Hairbell had been comprehensively humiliated. It was surprising, really, that the mayor had been able to regain any authority at all.

Rustbane pulled one of the flintlock pistols from his belt and blew across the top of its barrel suggestively. With his other hand, he drew his sword from its scabbard and tossed it to Sylvester, who caught the weapon deftly enough but staggered a little under the weight.

"I've a feeling you might need this, young hamster."

"Lemming."

Sylvester gave the gray fox a grin. Once upon a time, the pirate had treated him as vermin. Now, it was as if they were equal partners.

"Watch my back then."

Rustbane laughed. "But of course."

"We're all in this together," said Jasper sternly, "and me more than most of you. That swine lied to me to make me go on the Exodus. Really he wanted to kill me. And you tell me he's been pestering my wife."

Before anyone could move to stop him, Jasper was striding across the grass of the plateau toward where Hairbell and Spurge stood open-mouthed. The drummers had by now stopped all attempts at sounding their tattoo. In other circumstances, Sylvester might have laughed to see them with their sticks, forgotten in the drama of the unfolding scene, still raised as if held in the air by invisible threads.

It was only when Jasper had come within a few yards of Hairbell that the major recognized him.

"*You!*" Hairbell spat.

"Thought you'd never see me again, didn't you?"

"I—"

"Thought I was dead and gone? Drowned. A victim of your vile plottings, like so many others before and since."

"No, no, of course not." Hairbell was doing his best to recover both his composure and the ascendancy. "I'm delighted by your return, Jasper. It is Jasper, isn't it? Tell me, what is the Land of Destiny like? Did you meet the great spirit Lhaeminguas himself? Was he as mighty and imposing as all the sacred texts say he is? How many of our people have made it to the Land of—"

"There *is* no Land of Destiny!" cried Jasper.

"Surely that can't be true!"

"There's no Land of Destiny like the one this holy fool" – Jasper turned a withering glare on High Priest Spurge, who cringed away as if from boiling acid – "prates about in his temple. Or, rather, there are lots of lands of destiny. The whole world is full of lands where lemmings like us could follow their fortunes. But the way to find them isn't by leaping over the Mighty Enormous Cliff into the Great Wet Without End. The only place that route takes you is to drowning. The way to all those lands of destiny is by ship across the seas, sailing under the scudding clouds with the slap of canvas and the creaking of timbers. Or it's inland, trekking over the mountains to find those countries whose people sometimes come to visit us but which we're too pusillanimous to venture to ourselves.

"But it's suited you well, hasn't it, Hairbell? You and all the Hairbells before you, whatever their names. It's suited the preachers like your pathetic crony, Spurge, to keep the lemmings imprisoned in Foxglove as your near-slaves as surely as if there were iron bars around the town stretching from the ground to the sky. Then, every few years you've culled every lemming who's shown the slightest signs of initiative by sending them on the Great Exodus. Not content with having got rid of me, you were planning to send my only son to the same watery grave. Great Exodus, huh?" Jasper spat on to the grass between them. "Great Suicide Leap, more like!"

Hairbell fluttered his paws. When the Mayor spoke, Sylvester could tell the words were addressed less to Jasper than to the crowd of lemmings behind, some of whom were beginning to rumble angrily.

"This is all delusion, Jasper, delusion, conspiracy and slander. Or maybe just a misunderstanding." The Mayor chuckled a ghastly, artificial chuckle. "Yes, that's it. Just a misunderstanding. Come, come, Jasper" – he moved as if to put an arm around the other lemming's shoulders – "surely we can talk this over, two old troupers like us."

Jasper dodged away. "And you've been making up to my wife!"

"Your widow, dear fellow, your widow. At least, that what everyone thought she was. *She* thought she was your widow too, which makes it all the more remarkable that she's consistently rejected my adv—dear me, what was I talking about. I can hardly get my words in order on this happy, happy day, when one, two, three, *four* of our citizens have returned to us. That's Daphne Pickleberry back there and young Viola. I'm so charmed to see—"

"Another who's suffered your unwelcome *advances*," said Sylvester darkly. "What is it about the Lemmington clan's women, Hairbell. It seems you can hardly keep your paws off them and you don't even try."

Hairbell glanced at Viola and the expression on her face told him not to try to lie his way out of Sylvester's accusation.

Jasper turned to Sylvester with a mirthless laugh. "So we both have our arguments with this slimeball, don't we? But I'm older than you are, son, so I claim precedence. Give me that sword of yours."

Wordlessly, Sylvester passed the cutlass to his father.

"Listen, all of you!" shouted Jasper to the mob of lemmings beyond Hairbell, Spurge and the silent drummers. "You've been duped! Generations of Foxglove's lemmings have been duped. Betrayed! Tricked! Fooled! Lied to! Slaughtered by this power-crazed tyrant and his father and grandfather before him, and by *their* fathers and grandfathers."

The sporadic rumbling among the lemmings increased in volume.

"Many years ago, someone invented a lie in order to terrify the lemmings of Foxglove into obeying his orders. Then a willing collaborator set up a temple where he told your ancestors there was a great spirit called Lhaeminguas who would visit his wrath on Foxglove unless everyone did what the spirits – which meant the high priest, because there *were* no spirits and never have been – unless everyone did what the high priest told them to do, which by the strangest of coincidences was what the mayor was *also* telling them to do.

"The mayors and high priests of Foxglove have been playing that same trick on the good folk of Foxglove ever since, living on the fat of the land because everyone believes the spirits want the world to be that way.

"But it's *not* that way.

"The world's full of adventure and discovery and excitement, things that have been lost from Foxglove for far too long. Just like I said, the whole world's a land of destiny, if we want it to be."

"Blasphemy!" roared High Priest Spurge, finding his voice at last. He held out a straight arm, a long claw extended from it to point at Jasper. "Blasphemy, I say! The great spirit Lhaeminguas has heard your blasphemous thoughts, Jasper Lemmington, and punished you by driving you insane, for surely, only a madman would utter the lies and calumnies you have just uttered."

Jasper laughed in the High Priest's face. "That's the genius of your hoax, isn't it? If anyone penetrates the lie, you tell the rest he's insane or treasonous or working to undermine the good of Foxglove. Or if someone just has doubts you tell him the great spirit Lhaeminguas will visit devastation upon him for the crime of not believing strongly enough."

Hairbell clearly didn't like the way the argument with Spurge was going. He decided to try a different tack.

"Good citizens of Foxglove! None of us could ever forget the day, not so long ago, when a vicious pack of monsters, led by that cutthroat scoundrel of a fox over there, did their best to destroy the center of our town entirely."

Sylvester could see the mayor had succeeded in snatching back the initiative from Jasper. Quite a few of the lemmings were regarding Hairbell with something like respect on their faces.

"It was a Lemmington who brought the pirates into our midst the first time, and now look what's happened. Lemmingtons have brought the filthy monsters *back* again, intent on wreaking yet more havoc!"

It was a difficult charge to deflect.

Jasper didn't even try.

"More smoke and mirrors from this puffed-up jackanapes! The next thing he'll be telling you is that Lhaeminguas brought the pirates down upon Foxglove as punishment for everybody's laziness and moral laxity."

"I was just *getting to* that part!" said Hairbell crossly.

"Well, it's all baloney. I've seen more of the world than perhaps any lemming before me, and I can tell you there's no such thing as the great spirit Lhaeminguas. He doesn't exist. He never has and he never will. Spirits are just inventions by people, people who want to use the threat of the invisible to make others obey their will."

"Ahem," said Rustbane, who'd sauntered up while Jasper was speaking. He towered over the assembled lemmings. Many fell back from the touch of his shadow. Pimplebrains was still reclining some distance away by the edge of the cliff.

"Yes," said Jasper, looking up, clearly quite unintimidated by the much larger creature.

"Not *all* spirits."

"You know of a real one?"

"Yes."

"Who?"

"The triple-breasted goddess. There ain't a pirate in the world doesn't offer worship to the triple-breasted goddess."

"And why's that, do you think?" Jasper's voice was like a polished needle.

Rustbane rubbed his chin. "I should think probably," he said, "it's because we want to."

"So do you actually *believe* in her?"

"Well, yes and no."

"Mostly yes or mostly no?"

"Both, really."

Despite himself, Sylvester was beginning to snicker. "Don't follow the line, Dad. Rustbane'll have you jawing here all day and getting precisely nowhere, if you let him."

Hairbell jumped at what he thought was an opening.

"So, you pirates believe in the spirit world too, do you?" he said, rubbing his forepaws and gazing at Rustbane with an awful parody of admiration.

"Like I said to my good friend Jasper, it's a matter of yes and no."

"This, er, this supernumerarily privileged goddess of yours, though, she—you definitely think she's a—"

"There's only one way to find out, Mayor Hairbell," said the gray fox with deceptive gentleness.

"There is?"

"By going to the spirit world and finding out for yourself." To clarify his meaning, the fox tapped his pistol to his nose. "I could help you with that, if you'd like."

Jasper held up his paw. "That's my task," he said. "My pleasure," he amended.

"Don't, Dad!"

"What?"

"He's unarmed. If you cut down someone who's defenseless it'll be the same as murder. You'll be no better than the slimeball."

"Then give him a sword, someone!"

"No! Killing him's not the way!"

"Then what would you suggest?"

"Exile?"

Hairbell, his gaze darting back and forth between father and son, began to snigger. "Exile? And how do a pawful of you propose to send me into exile when the whole population of Foxglove, loyal as they are to their mayor and respectful of the great spirit Lhaeminguas" – he waved an imperious paw behind him at the now-silent ranks of lemmings – "wish exactly the contrary?"

"What makes you think they're so loyal?" said Jasper.

"I know my people," said Hairbell with a complacent smile.

"Why not ask them?"

"Huh?"

"We'll ask them."

"We will?"

"Yes."

"Ask them," said Hairbell heavily, "if they'd rather take the word of a renegade and blasphemer over that of the mayor who's served their interests faithfully and well for all these years?"

"That's about the sum of it, yes."

"If you really think that—"

"I do."

Jasper raised his arms over his head, appealing to the crowd of lemmings. "How many people here think we deserve to decide our lives ourselves? How many of you are tired of being told what to do and what to believe in? How many of you are tired of being afraid, of living a life dominated by fear of what Lhaeminguas might do to you if you don't obey the every last whim of Hairbell and Spurge here?"

There was an appalled silence. Sylvester was convinced his father had alienated all the Foxglove lemmings. Glancing over his shoulder, Sylvester told himself the cliff edge wasn't really so very far away, and the chances of surviving a leap over it were really quite good, all things considered. And the longboat was still down there, wasn't it?

"Step forward," cried Jasper, "step forward anyone who'd like to lift the yoke of tyranny from their shoulders."

Most of the Foxglovians stared at the ground, clearly ashamed to meet Jasper's gaze. A few stared at the sky instead. A hushed silence hung over the gathering. The only sound was the distant splashing of the breakers at the foot of the Mighty Enormous Cliff, the honking of a high-flying gull and the shuffling of countless uneasy paws on the grass.

Hairbell grinned triumphantly at Jasper.

"So much for your little uprising, eh, Lemmington? The spirit Lhaeminguas must be weeping over your treachery and betrayal. It's in obedience to the will of the spirit that, far from being exiled myself, I must shoulder the unpleasant duty of expelling you and all your equally disgusting companions from the happy home of Foxglove, where—"

There was a small, barely audible stir among the crowd.

"Bullrich!" said Sylvester.

Viola's little brother looked up at him. "Yeah?"

"What're you doing?"

"I'm sayin' we should get rid of Fatty Hairbell, is what I'm doin'."

"Get back in line, you noxious little brat!" shouted Hairbell.

"Nope," said Bullrich. He shut his eyes. Despite the defiance of his tone, he was trembling. Clearly, it had taken him all of his courage and more to push to the front of the crowd and defy the Mayor. Now he was expecting to die.

"You'd send a child like this over the cliff, would you?" said Sylvester, his anger rising.

"He's young to go seeking the Land of Destiny," replied Hairbell, obviously fighting hard to keep any note of desperation out of his voice, "but he's a plucky little fellow and I thought he deserved the chance to—"

There was a *smaaaccck* that seemed to make the clouds shudder in their course across the sky.

Mayor Hairbell flew in one direction. His teeth flew on independent trajectories in most of the others. The Mayor landed on his back several yards from where he'd been standing.

"So you'd send my baby son off on your suicide trip wouldjer, Hairbell?"

shouted Mrs. Pickleberry dusting off her hands.

"Mom!" cried Bullrich, throwing himself at her. She wrapped her free arm around him, pulling him close to her ample belly.

Surprisingly, the Mayor was still alive. Hairbell raised a hideously bloodied face from the grass and stared venomously at Mrs. Pickleberry and the others.

"Seize these criminals!" shouted High Priest Spurge. "Seize these ruffians who'd assault our beloved Mayor."

No one moved to obey the priest.

But people did begin to move.

First one lemming stepped deliberately forward, then another.

"We're tired of you, Spurge," said someone. It was Mr. Snowbanks the innkeeper, Sylvester noticed with surprise. He'd never thought of Mr. Snowbanks as a rebel of any sort. "Tired of you and your spirit buddy, Lhaeminguas. Most of all we're tired of Hairbell over there. Get out of here. Get out of Foxglove and never come back."

"Don't you realize the great spirit Lhaeminguas will curse you all for this?"

"I don't believe in the great spirit Lhaeminguas. I haven't for years." The innkeeper wrapped his paws across his stomach and stared at Spurge. "But I was too polite to say, like."

"Heretic!"

"We're tired of being afraid," said Mr. Snowbanks. "Tired of being frightened by your bogeyman. Life's too short as it is without having to live it in constant fear and trembling of what the darkness holds. Jasper Lemmington's right. The Land of Destiny's wherever we choose to find it, not where you tell us it is. You may think I'm just a fat, stupid lemming, and who knows you may be right, but I'm not so stupid that I can't realize my own ideas are *mine*, and precious beyond measure for just that reason. You've tried to turn us lemmings into a mindless herd and you've damned near succeeded, but inside us all there's a unique individual. I can't speak for any of those other unique individuals, but I do know what I believe myself. I don't care if there is a great spirit Lhaeminguas, and I don't care if he curses me right down dead here where I stand for wanting my freedom, because I can't think of any worse curse than not having my freedom."

"Listen to this blasphemy," hissed High Priest Spurge to the crowd. "Are you going to let Snowbanks utter these words and live?"

"Snowbanks is right!" yelled someone at the back.

"We've had enough of that rotten priest!"

"And the mayor!"

"String 'em up!"

Spurge sneered. "Have you all lost your minds?"

"Yes," said Doctor Nettletree, stepping toward him, "and it's wonderful."

"Even *you*?"

"Me most of all," replied the doctor. "I see people at their most vulnerable and sometimes the most I can do is make it as easy as possible for them as their lives ebb away. I've never noticed the slightest sign of any of your spirits. All there are is life and death and, with luck, the minimum of suffering in between."

"Traitor!"

"No, Spurge, you're the traitor. You're the one who's been trying to enslave the good people of Foxglove. Now we've called you on it, you and Hairbell, and it's time for you both to go."

Jasper began to giggle. "I've had the most splendid idea," he said. "Why don't we give Spurge and Hairbell the opportunity to test the strength of their *own* faith?"

"You mean—" began Rustbane, also chuckling.

"Yes," said Jasper. "A Great Exodus just for two."

Sylvester was horrified for a moment, then realized his father's proposal wasn't nearly as heartless as it seemed. The longboat must surely still be somewhere close to the bottom of the Mighty Enormous Cliff, so if Hairbell and Spurge survived the fall they should be able to reach it and row away. Row away to *where* wasn't a matter Sylvester wished to contemplate at the moment.

"I'm sure they'll be only too glad to, Dad," he said loudly. "Shall we give them a bit of help?"

"No!" shrieked Spurge, trying to find an escape route through the throng of angry lemmings. "Don't do that."

"Your faith too weak?" said Rustbane in an ugly voice.

"Have mercy!" the priest wailed.

"How many hundreds of lemmings did you send to their deaths over the years?" said Mr. Snowbanks, prodding Spurge in the chest with his clenched paw. "Did you have mercy on any of them, you old fraud?"

"I, I—"

Already half a dozen younger and fitter lemmings had picked up Mayor Hairbell from the turf and were bearing him toward the cliff edge. The mayor seemed too groggy from Mrs. Pickleberry's cruel blow to protest, let alone put up a fight.

"I can't swim," wept Spurge.

"Did that ever stop you from sending anyone else over the cliff?" demanded Doctor Nettletree. The physician held the priest's gaze for a long moment before speaking again. "No, I thought not. I think you've just booked yourself a passage to your very own Land of Destiny, Spurge."

"Let me," said Rustbane, reaching forward.

The gray fox picked up the high priest as if Spurge were hardly more than a feather. Almost at once, the lemming began to struggle, but the fox was easily able to wrap his claws around Spurge, imprisoning the priest as if in a cage.

"It's been a long time," said Rustbane urbanely out of the side of his mouth to Sylvester as they strode toward the precipice, "since I've thrown someone over a cliff. I wonder if I can remember how to do it right."

"I should think you will," said Sylvester, grinning. "I don't imagine it's one of those skills people forget too readily."

"I do hope you're right. I'd feel such a nincompoop if I got it wrong and Spurge here just landed *kersplatt* on the rocks."

"That is," Sylvester assured him with ponderous sobriety, "one of those eventualities it's horrible to even muse on."

High Priest Spurge just whimpered.

At the edge of the cliff, Rustbane paused. "Nice day for a swim," he observed.

Spurge said nothing. The priest appeared to have lost consciousness.

Secure in the grip of a bunch of Foxglovians, Mayor Hairbell just groaned.

"Would you like me to attend to this one as well?" Rustbane politely asked Hairbell's captors.

They muttered something which Rustbane clearly took to be assent.

Standing on the lip of the cliff with a lemming in each paw, Rustbane looked out over the sun-drenched ocean and guffawed.

At last his laughter died down.

"You'll never know," he said in a low voice to the two captive lemmings, "the kindness I'm about to perform for you."

With that he pulled his right arm back over his shoulder and, with a grunt of exertion, hurled the High Priest Spurge as far out to sea as he could. The priest's scream was lost in the distance. There was a noiseless splash as he hit the water.

Rustbane swapped Hairbell from his left paw to his right and again hurled his victim powerfully out into the waves.

"That was indeed kind of you," said Sylvester to the gray fox. "If we lemmings had chucked them over the side, chances were the two rogues would have landed on the rocks."

"*Kersplatt*," agreed the fox.

"As you say, *kersplatt*. As it is, though, they might very well be able to make it to the longboat and survive, mightn't they?"

"Not if they row out to the *Shadeblaze* they won't," said the fox. "I can't imagine Cheesefang would give our friends a hospitable welcome, can you?"

"No," said Sylvester.

"Now, I think, we have the other half of the bargain to attend to, no?"

"You want me to tell you where the treasure of the Zindars is hidden, do you?"

Rustbane clapped his paws. "Being aboard the Zindar ship really did hone your intellect, didn't it? You got the correct answer straight away, without having to use up your second and third guesses."

"It's here."

"Here?" Rustbane looked around him as if expecting to see the corner of a buried chest sticking up out of the turf.

"Not precisely here," said Sylvester, "but close by."

"Just *how* close?"

"Very."

"*How* very?"

Sylvester gestured toward the dark line of trees a few tens of yards away.

"Just over there," he said, "in Mugwort Forest."

"Oh," said the gray fox, gaping. "That's rather a lot of forest, don't you think?"

Sylvester hadn't given too much thought to what was going to happen after they'd returned to Foxglove and Rustbane demanded guidance to the hidden treasure. It was a problem he'd all too willingly pushed to one side of his mind, focusing instead on all the more immediate problems that came his way. Now, he wished he'd paid it more attention.

He'd often noticed before that the gray fox's smile seemed to contain far too many teeth.

Now there seemed to be more teeth than ever.

"I'm sure I'll think of something," he mumbled.

"Good, good," said the pirate. "Only don't be too long about it, will you, there's a good chap?"

Jasper, overhearing, pushed through a knot of lemmings who were trying yo congratulate him on his return and on his pluck in standing up to Mayor Hairbell and High Priest Spurge.

"Oh, we'll find your treasure for you," he said airily to Rustbane. "No problem."

"Really?" said the pirate, raising an eyebrow. "As I've been telling your scion, it's a very big forest to go looking in."

"It is," Jasper conceded, "but I learned a thing or three during my time in the Zindar ship, and one those talents is a sense for stuff that was made by the Zindars, or that they were closely associated with."

"The great spirit Lhaeminguas wouldn't play a part in this, would he?" said the fox skeptically.

Jasper curled his lip. "That he wouldn't. This isn't magic we're talking about, or maybe it is. Who's to know any longer where the borderline should be drawn? But it's something I can do and I don't need any help from spirits in the sky to do it."

Rustbane gestured with a loose-wristed paw toward the forest. "Shall we go there now?"

"No, not tonight," Jasper replied.

"But I might choose to insist."

"You might choose to do whatever you want, but tonight you'll be doing it without me. This evening I have a reunion I want to go to."

"A reunion?"

"With my wife."

"Ah." Rustbane paused. "Yes," he said after what seemed a very long time, "I can understand that. I must keep my patience in check until the morning then."

"Do that."

ϕ ϕ ϕ ϕ ϕ

When Hortensia Lemmington opened the door of her cottage and saw Jasper standing there on the doorstep, the first thing she did was slap his face.

Hard.

The sound was like a thundercrack.

Sylvester, who'd hung back to allow Mom and Dad a little privacy, was appalled. He expected Jasper to turn on his heel and go straight back to the Mighty Enormous Cliff and take the leap that'd release him back into the wide, adventure-laden world of Sagaria.

The second thing Hortensia Lemmington did was throw her arms around Jasper's neck and burst into loud, racking tears.

Sylvester was pretty appalled by this too.

Parents weren't supposed to show this kind of emotion towards each other, especially in front of their offspring.

When the two began kissing each other passionately, he felt his stomach roil. He also felt a mite resentful. After all, even though he hadn't been missing, presumed dead, for nearly as long as his father had, he still reckoned his mother might show him *some* sign she was glad he too was back, that he'd survived.

The kissing went on and on and, what was worse, it was getting *noisier*.

"I can tell what you're thinking," said a voice.

Sylvester looked up, startled. He'd thought he was alone, standing there by the garden gate. "Celadon!"

The elderly archivist smiled, stroking his whiskers. "None other, my boy."

Before he really knew what was happening, Sylvester found himself embracing his mentor.

"Careful there, young fellow-me-lad," cried Celadon, laughing. "These old bones are liable to break if you crush them too hard."

Sylvester was laughing too. "I didn't know whether you were alive or dead. The last time I saw you—"

"I could say exactly the same about *you*, Sylvester. I didn't know – none of us here in Foxglove knew – if we'd ever see you and the Pickleberries alive again. Once Doctor Nettletree had seen me back to my health again and I felt well enough to do a bit of work, I read every text in the library relating to pirates and freebooters and various criminals of the high seas, and what I read did nothing to reassure me, I can tell you. Pirates seem to be universally a bad lot."

"Of course they're a bad lot," exclaimed Sylvester, standing back to get a better look at this old scholar whom he loved so much. "That's the whole principle."

"I suppose you're perfectly right, dear boy. If they didn't have hearts blacker than the deepest night they wouldn't be pirates, would they? But even so" – Celadon shuddered as if a chilly draft had blown from one end of his spine to the other – "what I read of their cruelties and bloodthirstiness made me wake up screaming from my dreams more times than I like to remember. Let me tell you, there was one of them I encountered in my reading called Cap'n Josiah 'Throatsplitter' Adamite and, of all the bottom-feeding knaves who ever plagued the oceans, he was the one who—"

"But I know all about Cap'n Adamite!" cried Sylvester. "Why, to Viola and me and Mrs. Pickleberry, he's practically a friend of the family."

Sylvester proceeded to tell the tale of Cap'n Adamite's manuscript, the search for the treasure chest of the Zindars and much more than he'd ever intended to tell Celadon. For his part, the old librarian listened patiently, a twinkle in his eye.

When Sylvester finally ran out of words he realized his parents had gone inside, leaving Celadon and himself out in the deepening twilight.

"I'd leave them be for a while," said Celadon, putting a friendly arm across Sylvester's shoulders. The two began to amble along the lane. "They'll have a lot of talking to do. Time enough for them to celebrate their only son later, I'd say."

"Do you think they're—"

"Quite probably that too."

"Well," said Sylvester dubiously, "I suppose I could go round to the Pickleberries' place and spend the evening with Viola."

"Um, I wouldn't do that either."

"Oh?"

"I passed the Pickleberry establishment on the way here and I think, ahem, I think Daphne Pickleberry is having something of an argument with her husband. There was a considerable sound of crockery being smashed. A *quite* considerable sound. It almost masked the sound of their voices. But not quite."

"Oh." Sylvester and Celadon took a few more steps in silence before Sylvester spoke again. "What about Viola?"

"She and her brother seem to have decided that they should take a little excursion. There was every chance a frying pan or other kitchen utensil might hit them by mistake if they stayed at home where Mr. and Mrs. Pickleberry are, ah, having their discussion. I saw them out walking in the general direction of the Snowbanks Inn."

"You did?"

The old archivist smiled genially. "I should say that's where they were heading. Viola was talking about how she hadn't had a decent sit-down six-course meal for longer than she could rightly recall, and her brother was saying the same even though the little horror—er, cute little fellow, I mean, is renowned for packing away his tucker like he'd never be allowed to eat again. Interesting thing, though, my boy. Viola and Bullrich seemed to be getting on quite well, for once."

Celadon dug around in his jacket for his pipe. Once he'd managed to free it from a pocket that seemed reluctant to give it up, he discovered Sylvester was no longer by his side but was instead trotting up the dusty lane ahead of him.

Ah, well, thought Celadon with a wistful sigh. *When you're that age I suppose the vigor of spring flows in your veins all the year round. I'll warrant the young fellow hasn't even thought to leave his parents a note telling them where he's gone. I'd better do it for him. Now, where in tarnation did I put that pencil?*

❖ ❖ ❖ ❖ ❖

For once, the Snowbanks Inn was fairly empty. The first person Sylvester saw when he burst in through the door was Mr. Snowbanks himself, who was wiping off the surface of a table with an apron that had seen not just better days but better weeks and maybe months. About a year ago, Mrs. Snowbanks had decided that her true purpose in life was not innkeeping but poetry. This meant Mr. Snowbanks had twice as much work to do, while his wife swanned around the countryside in the company of unsuitable male lemmings half her age declaiming sonnets in loud voices to various resentful flowering plants. Clouds came in for a bit of imposed declamation too. The joke around town was that this explained why the skies above Foxglove were so often a clear and untrammeled blue.

It also explained why the Snowbanks Inn, and Mr. Snowbanks, looked so down-at-heel these days. Although, Sylvester reminded himself, by comparison with some of the places he'd been in during his travels, like The Monkey's Curse, the Snowbanks Inn was a model of pristine hygiene.

The second and third people Sylvester saw as he entered the inn were Viola and Bullrich, who were sitting on either side of a long oak bench in the Snowbanks Inn's dining room and looking as if it was only by mutual negotiation and colossal effort of will that they weren't having an argument.

Both of them looked pleased to see him.

"We thought you'd want to be with your parents," said Viola, rising from the table to give him a peck on the cheek.

"So did I," he admitted, "but, well, you know how it is."

Her brow wrinkled. "Ours are having the most tremendous fight."

"So I heard."

"So the whole of Foxglove's heard, I should imagine. Mom isn't the most restrained of lemmings when she loses her temper, and she's really lost it with Dad tonight."

"What did the poor fellow do?" said Sylvester, settling down on his haunches next to her. She and Bullrich had already devastated a soup course, he could see.

"Told her he thought you were an unsuitable suitor for his daughter."

Sylvester's mouth went dry. "And she—"

Viola nodded, her lips pursed in a grin. There was a crumb of bread caught in the fold at the corner of her mouth. Sylvester thought it was the most beautiful crumb of bread he'd ever seen in his life. "Mom seems to have taken a real liking to you."

Sylvester recalled how, back aboard the *Shadeblaze*, she'd mellowed toward him a bit. It hadn't lasted.

"But that's only," Viola said when he mentioned this, "because Mom'd never, ever let someone know if she'd begun to like and respect him a lot."

"She *respects* me? I find that hard to believe!"

"Me too, but she does."

Bullrich chortled.

"Shut up," Viola said to him across the table, then resumed what she was telling Sylvester.

"Anyway, Dad started off with this rant about how we'd all been instrumental in expelling Hairbell from Foxglove, and how Hairbell was the best husband I was likely to get, and *now* look at the second-rater I'd got my heart set on, and—"

"You've got your heart set on me?"

She rolled her eyes. "Really, Sylvester Lemmington, how dense can one lemming possibly be? I must have told you a thousand—no," she added, fending him off. "Not in front of Bullrich."

"Bullrich could be persuaded to go and, oh, I don't know, jump off the Mighty Enormous Cliff or something."

"A very good idea, but no. Not in front of Mr. Snowbanks then."

Unnoticed by Sylvester, Mr. Snowbanks had approached the little party and was standing over them, notebook in hand. They exchanged a few words about the scene out on the plateau and the expulsion of Hairbell and Spurge. Finally, Mr. Snowbanks cast a significant glance at his open notebook and said, "What would you like, Sylvester?"

Despite his mother's cooking, Sylvester had never eaten here before.

"Is there a menu?"

"No."

"Ah, then what would you suggest?"

"Well, you can either have *all* the dinner or just some of it."

"Not a huge amount of choice then?"

"As you might say, no."

Sylvester thought for barely a moment. "I'd like the complete dinner, please."

"With beer, mead or wine?"

Sylvester quickly checked what the other two were drinking. "Mead, please."

"Your meal will be with you in a moment."

Mr. Snowbanks shuffled off toward the kitchens.

Sylvester looked around him. Aside from themselves, the dining room was empty. There were a few more customers in the bar, where Flossie Grapedangle (whom the gossips whispered might soon be the second Mrs. Snowbanks if the first didn't abjure her poetic inclinations a bit sharpish) was serving up drinks with a will.

"Where *is* everybody?" he said quietly.

"At home, I suspect." If Viola was miffed that the conversation had switched from matters of romance, she didn't show it. Bullrich looked disappointed. "Like your parents, like my parents, Foxglove has taken a heck of a jolt to its system today, you know."

"I'd expected them to be throwing a party in the town square."

"Not everyone's pleased to see the back of Hairbell and Spurge. It's asking a lot to expect people to abandon their beliefs just like that. Those are the things they've thought were true the whole of their lives, and so did their parents and grandparents before them. They might not have *liked* the world being the way they were told it was, but at least they were comfortable with that explanation. They knew where they were."

"I suppose so."

At that moment, Mr. Snowbanks arrived with Sylvester's soup. "Acorn and squash, with a bit of basil," said the innkeeper, dumping the big wooden bowl in front of Sylvester.

He dug in.

"That big gray fox," said Bullrich, "is he a friend of yours?"

Viola giggled. "I suppose he is. We've spent weeks thinking exactly the opposite, though."

"He could have killed us if he'd wanted to," observed Sylvester mid-slurp.

"But he didn't."

"No, he didn't."

"You finished that soup yet?" said Mr. Snowbanks, materializing at Sylvester's side again.

"Why, yes, thank you, I have," said Sylvester, staring down in surprise at his bowl.

"Next you got the nut loaf with gravy."

"I do? That sounds good."

"Better believe it."

"You don't happen to know where, ah—"

"An' here's yer mead."

Snowbanks thumped a large wooden goblet down on the bench in front of Sylvester. The goblet was full of a liquid that seemed to be wondering if it were alive or dead.

"Thanks," said Sylvester weakly.

"Me," said Viola, "I think our friend Rustbane is right here in the Snowbanks Inn."

"You say?"

"Listen."

From upstairs, now that he cocked his ear toward the inn ceiling, Sylvester heard the sound of snoring.

"Our friend."

"Mr. Snowbanks accepts anyone who can pay his bill."

"And Rustbane is . . ."

"Sleeping."

"So if we had any sense we'd—"

"But we're not going to do that, are we, Sylvester? Tomorrow we're going to head off to Mugwort Forest with your dad in the lead and Cap'n Rustbane in the rear. Do you think Cap'n Rustbane is the ideal person to discover the Zindar chest?"

"No. Of course I don't."

"Here's yer nut loaf with gravy," said Mr. Snowbanks. "It'll make yer very regular, this will."

"Thanks," said Sylvester. He peered at what the innkeeper had put in front of him. Some of the nuts in his nut loaf looked as if they might sprout at any moment. The gravy was, well, gravid. Unfortunately, Mrs. Snowbanks had been the culinary half of the Snowbanks partnership. Still, the meal looked edible, especially to someone in Sylvester's state of starvation.

"Them friends of yours, *they* liked it well enough," said Mr. Snowbanks, seeing the doubtful expression on Sylvester's face.

"Friends of mine?"

Snowbanks jerked his head toward the ceiling, which, on cue, creaked. "That fox. 'Eaven knows how we got him into his room and it's the Honeymoon Suite, the biggest we 'ave. Even so, he's got one paw stuck out the window and his tail up the chimney. Pity he didn't have the good sense of that nice beaver, the one with the hooks. *He's* sleeping in the back yard. Got all the room he needs to spread out and be comfy. And we got the mouse in the attic room, the one with the sm—the one conveniently close to the lavs, I mean."

"And they all liked the nut loaf, did they?"

"That they did, young Sylvester."

Mr. Snowbanks slouched off, whistling tunelessly.

Sylvester, fork in paw, returned to an earlier theme. "What I can't get over is how *normally* everyone's taking things. A couple of hours ago, Mr. Snowbanks there was facing down the two most powerful people in Foxglove. Now he's just the same as he always was, as if nothing out of the ordinary had happened."

"It's because it's just too big," said Viola. "Bullrich, stop picking your nose with the mustard spoon."

"Too big?" said Sylvester.

"Too much to react to right away. Their whole world's been turned over. Same as my dad and your mom, really. If we'd stayed out three hours late without telling them where we were, we'd have been the focus of attention for quite a while, more's the pity. But we've been away for weeks and your dad, even longer than that, and they probably thought we were all dead, whatever the brave face they put on it. Everyone's just taking a little while to get over the shock, is all," said Viola.

"I suppose everyone's in shock, us included," agreed Sylvester. "Oh look, my nut loaf's disappeared. I'm sure I've had only a couple of mouthfuls. I must have been more ravenous than I thought."

"Wasn't me," said Bullrich in what Sylvester didn't until later realize was probably not a *non sequitur.*

MUGWORT FOREST

here wasn't frost on the ground the following morning, but the air was crisp enough that Sylvester felt there ought to be. He and Viola had left the Snowbanks Inn later than he liked to think about, herding between them Bullrich, who'd been barely awake. Sylvester had fallen over twice on the way upstairs to his bedroom, but that had been all right. He lay awake a while listening to the reassuring sound of his father snoring in his parents' room. It was a sound that reminded him of his childhood, when everything had seemed so much easier somehow. His mother had left him a pie on the kitchen table for when he got home. He was almost tempted to eat it, just to quieten the rumblings of his stomach. Strange he should still be hungry after all that nut loaf, but wisdom had conquered mead at the last moment and he'd put the pie under his bed with the others.

His final thought last night had been, *I must work out a way of getting rid of . . .*

After that, darkness, until Mom had woken him in the morning, bustling cheerfully around his room. "I was going to bring you breakfast in bed, but your father said the two of you had urgent business to conduct with the fox this morning. He's already out in the garden talking away to himself about how his flowers have been neglected."

Once she'd gone, he hauled himself out of bed and looked at his face in the mirror. Not a pretty sight. *How can the Snowbanks Inn's mead taste so innocuous when it's going down, yet do this to a poor lemming in the morning?*

Turning back toward his bed, he discovered he'd picked up a scarecrow on his way home. He wondered where.

He also wondered why Mom hadn't noticed or, perhaps, why she hadn't liked to say anything.

He found Jasper in the garden, as Hortensia had indicated.

"Before I left on the Great Exodus, son, I had the best radish patch in the whole of Foxglove," said Jasper as Sylvester approached, "and now?" He gestured. "You can't even tell that part of the garden was ever cultivated. Looks like an untamed jungle, it does."

"No, it doesn't," said Sylvester.

"You'd think that—what?"

"It doesn't look like an untamed jungle. I've been in an untamed jungle, Dad. I almost didn't come back out of it again. I know what I'm talking about."

Jasper absorbed this in silence.

Eventually he harrumphed. "Well, it's still a pity about my radishes, that's all I can say."

"Um, Dad?"

"Yes, son?"

"Not so much of a pity as you might think. I don't know if you remember, it was so long ago, but Mom really hates radishes."

"She does?"

"And I was just little. Every time you made me eat one of your radishes, I upchucked."

"You did?"

Sylvester nodded. "I've never been able to look a radish in the eye since."

"You haven't?"

"No."

"Son, you're trying to tell me about something more than just radishes, aren't you?"

"Yes, Dad."

Jasper thought this over, scuffing his feet on the lawn.

"I've got a lot to learn, haven't I?" he said. "A lot to learn about what's happened since I've been gone. I can't just expect to walk back into the house and think everything's going to be the same as it was with you and your mother. The two of you, you've both changed over the years. I don't mean just in the obvious ways, like you've gotten bigger and your mom's gotten prettier, but in ways that aren't so visible but are maybe more important. You're different people, really, not the same folks I left behind when I went over the Mighty Enormous Cliff, thinking I was on my way to the Land of Destiny. And if I don't accept that fact and work along with it rather than against it, then this might not turn out to be the happy family I dreamed about those lonely nights in the Zindar ship, is it?"

"Something like that, Dad. Mom and I love you. You should have heard all the times she'd talk on and on about you as if you were the finest lemming the world ever knew, or the times she wept herself to sleep at night. We love you and it's fantastic we've got you back again, but there's a lot of adapting to be done."

"You're right." Jasper sounded almost sad as he said it. He cleared his throat. "These are weighty subjects to be talking about so early in the morning. Especially since we'd better not tarry too long here before picking up Rustbane and Pimplebrains from the inn."

"And Rasco. He'll be wanting to come with us."

"He's got a mighty big heart for a mouse so small, hasn't he, that one?"

"He has indeed."

"You've had breakfast?"

"I grabbed some berries Mom gave me."

"Same here. Her cooking hasn't improved by any chance, has it?"

"No."

"I thought it might not have. Still, there's not too much damage she can do to fresh berries, is there?"

"Don't say things you might regret, Dad."

"I see you're wearing that cutlass the pirate gave you."

"Yes. I see you've got a sword too."

"Never hurts to take precautions."

"That's what I thought as well, Dad."

By tacit agreement, father and son talked about inconsequentialities as they strolled to the Snowbanks Inn. There, they found the two pirates and Rasco were up and about.

"We was just getting ready to come and fetch you," said Pimplebrains, who looked not at all the worse for having slept the night in the open. "We done finished our breakfasts a time ago, wonderful nut loaf, by the way, and Mr. Snowbanks has a lot of it."

"I've no doubt," said Sylvester, pleased despite himself to see the gruff old beaver again.

"Now," said Rustbane, appearing around the side of the inn rubbing his paws together, "it's time to go off on our treasure hunt, isn't it?"

Sylvester grinned back at the fox. "Yes."

"Well, what are we waiting for?"

Pimplebrains had managed to get hold of a spade from somewhere. Presumably it was a gift, either voluntary or involuntary, from Mr. Snowbanks. Having been made with lemmings in mind, it looked almost like a child's toy as he held it with surprising adroitness in the hook where his right forepaw should have been.

The three smaller animals had to almost run to keep up with Rustbane and Pimplebrains.

"Slow down a bit, you two," called Sylvester for the dozenth time as the gap between the leaders and the stragglers began opening up yet again. They were just passing Doctor Nettletree's cottage at the time, and the doctor was leaning on his gate watching the morning sunlight.

"Where are you off to?"

"Mugwort Forest."

"Mind if I come along?" Doc Nettletree addressed the question to Jasper, but it was Sylvester who answered.

"If you'd like."

"Good. I'll do that. Oh, I seem to be carrying my poker. I'll just bring it with me rather than leave it here in the garden where it might get rained on."

"That seems a good idea."

Sylvester and Nettletree grinned conspiratorially at each other.

"And along the way," said the physician, "I can catch up on news with your father. There's really a lot of news for him and me to catch up on, after all this time, isn't there, Jasper?"

Sylvester let out a piercing whistle. Pimplebrains and Rustbane had almost rounded the next bend. They paused, looking back.

"You're going the wrong way," Sylvester shouted.

Once he and the rest had caught up with the two pirates, he added, puffing, "In fact, you're not, but if you'd carried on going the way you were, you soon would have been. Getting into Mugwort Forest isn't as easy as you think. There are some places the trees just won't let you in, where they'll raise thorns and tangles to keep you out. You have to use one of the gates."

"Fighting trees, eh?" said Rustbane, giving the beaver a sidelong glance. "Not sure that I ever came across such a thing before."

"They don't fight," said Sylvester, suddenly close to losing his patience. The sun wasn't yet fully clear of the horizon and already it felt like it had been a long day. "They just obstruct. Willfully."

"Hmmf," said Rustbane.

"It's true," Doctor Nettletree chipped in. "If you don't believe us, just go ahead and try barging into the forest on your own."

"Better listen to what they tell you, Skip," said Pimplebrains. "Them's locals, after all. We could get ourselves killed if we don't heed their telling."

Cap'n Rustbane's yellow eyes narrowed. "All right," he said after a second or two. "But if this is some trick . . ."

Sylvester snorted. "After all this time you think I'd try to trick you? I just want you to find the blasted treasure and clear off out of Foxglove and leave us all in peace just as quick as it can possibly be managed. Got that?"

The gray fox splayed out a paw on his heart and assumed a grieving tone. "Oh, my dear, aching soul. And to think I'd begun to look on you as a friend."

"You don't have friends. You're a pirate, remember? Now, about fifty yards round the next bend you'll find a stile on the left. If you two have to keep charging ahead of us, wait there and I'll tell you where next to go."

Moments later, the pirates were once more in the lead.

"What was all that about?" said Doctor Nettletree.

"Yes," Jasper said. "What was this stuff about intelligent trees?"

"It seemed a good idea to start getting them unsettled. They're far bigger than we are and far stronger. I don't think Pimplebrains has a mean bone in his body, but at the same time, he's likely to do whatever Rustbane tells him to. And Rustbane ... well, let's just say I wouldn't put it past him to decide we're surplus to requirements, as soon as he's got his treasure,. So I also wanted to suggest subtly to them who's boss. If they're going to find the Zindar chest, it's going to be because of Dad here. They know that much. But let 'em keep thinking they'd be lost without the help of folk with local knowledge and we'll be the safer for it, and so will Foxglove."

"You've got a wise head on your shoulders, son," said Jasper with a chuckle. "I wonder where you got it from? Must've been from your mother, I reckon."

A while later, Sylvester made a great palaver of deciding that one of the gaps in the forest edge was a gateway through which it'd be safe for the treasure-seekers to venture, and in under the cool shadow of the trees they trooped. He couldn't help remembering, as they tramped forward on a mulchy path, what it had been like in the jungle on Blighter Island. The two places could hardly have been more different. There, every step he'd taken had seemed full of menace, as if he were stepping closer and closer to some hideous, amorphous peril. The shrieks and cries of the jungle animals had been like claws and beaks tearing at his soft flesh. Here, the sounds of the wild creatures were oddly reassuring, even though he was certain some of them could present danger to someone so small as a lemming. The shade of the forest was calming and tranquil. This was home to him, or could very easily become so.

He imagined Rasco, riding on Pimplebrains's shoulder ahead of him, must feel exactly the opposite.

The pirates came to a halt in a clearing where the morning sunshine formed curtains of watery gold. It was still too early in the day and cool for there to be many insects around, but the few that were buzzed petulantly at the intrusion.

"Time for you to start doing your mystic stuff, Mr. Lemmington," said the gray fox with a mocking nod to Jasper. He reached his arms out to either side and fluttered them. "Ooo-eee-ooo-eee-ooo."

Jasper gave an angry little grunt. "Want a demonstration of the spooky stuff?"

Rustbane cackled. "Go ahead."

As Sylvester watched, Jasper walked coolly across to the gray fox, grabbed a couple of pawfuls of the long, soft white fur on Rustbane's chest, and pulled himself up until he could deliver the pirate a mighty smack on the nose.

Then he climbed down again. Only as Jasper returned to where he'd been standing did Rustbane react.

"Yarr*owwwww!*"

Sylvester couldn't understand why no one, especially Rustbane, had done anything to stop his father, and then understanding flowed into him.

No one else here spent long on the Zindar vessel except Pimplebrains, and maybe this sort of stuff doesn't work on beavers. Maybe the reason the Zindars gave such a boost to lemming civilization was that there was some kind of psychic similarity between Zindars and lemmings. Who knows? But Dad was using one of the Zindar talents he's gained, and I was the only one who saw him do it because I'm lucky enough to have been similarly endowed.

I reckon that Dad really might *be able to lead us directly to the treasure chest.*

"What happened?" bellowed Rustbane. Both he and Pimplebrains had their swords drawn and were glancing around the clearing in taut little jerks of the head as if expecting a hostile horde to leap from the pools of forest gloom at any moment.

"I haven't the slightest idea," said Jasper airily.

Doctor Nettletree just looked befuddled.

"That was *you!*" shouted Rustbane to Jasper, his cry causing birds to start up squawking from the treetops around.

"Was it? But that'd have involved spooky stuff, wouldn't it?"

Rustbane growled, and took a step toward Jasper, sword hissing in the air as he pulled it back over his shoulder. His eyes had gone from yellow-green to the ominous dark red of molten lava.

He was stopped only by Pimplebrains's hook on his shoulder.

"Don't do it, Skip, you'll regret it if you do. That threadbare little fart's the only one that'll allow us to find the treasure. Without him we might as well just pack up and go home."

Rustbane gave one snarl of frustration then another before he gave up fighting against Pimplebrains's restraint.

"Later," was all he said to Jasper. Then he went back to nursing his nose with his paw.

Pimplebrains, astonishingly, gave Jasper a wink when he was sure his skipper wasn't looking. "I reckon you'd better hurry up and find this 'ere treasure."

"I will," said Jasper coldly, "do my best. Kindly, though, keep that *barbarian* in check."

Pimplebrains's eyes widened. "Living dangerously, are we?"

"Is there any other way to live?"

The beaver gave a bark of laughter. "Touché."

"Now, shall we stand here wasting any more time or shall we begin our search?" said Jasper.

"Begin the search," said Rustbane.

The gray fox had managed to staunch the flow of blood from his nose. He would have a swollen bruise there for quite some while, it was obvious. It was also obvious that Rustbane knew this and was not best pleased by it. His movements seemed to be those of a machine, over-precise in their attempt to imitate casualness.

Jasper threw back his head. His whiskers twitched. He licked a claw and held it up to test the air.

"That way, I think," he said very firmly, pointing.

The day wore on. Sylvester was glad Viola wasn't with them, and especially glad Mrs. Pickleberry wasn't. As it was, Rustbane's patience was sufficiently volatile that it wasn't so much a question of if he might explode in a rage as when. Jasper had warned them that discovery of the treasure, even with the benefit of his Zindar senses, might not be easy or quick but even Sylvester hadn't anticipated quite the amount of toing and froing through the forest that would be involved. The first time he fell headlong into the brambles it was agony. By the fourth or fifth time he no longer noticed the gouges and pain. He did, though, as the sun reached its zenith overhead, begin to notice with increasing acuity the fact that he was hungry.

How could it be that the nut loaf last night didn't fill me up?

The next deduction might or might not have been powered by Zindar-enhanced mental facilities. Sylvester was never afterwards able to decide the truth.

That little swine! I'll—

"I think we're close!" cried Jasper.

He'd said this two or three times before, so no one got overwhelmingly excited. Nothing like a few false alarms to water down enthusiasm. Even so, the others gathered around him.

"I hope this is going to be a bit more impressive than the last time," said Rustbane with a pained sniff.

"I do too," said Jasper pointedly.

"Where do you want me to start digging?" said Pimplebrains.

"I said we were close. I don't yet know *how* close. If you'd all just shut up your chattering for a moment I might be able to figure it out."

Again he threw his head back.

Rasco began to squeak something, but Sylvester stood on his foot to shut him up. Doctor Nettletree still looked as if he was wondering why he'd come along on this expedition. Sylvester was glad the doctor had retained his poker. He was becoming more and more convinced Pimplebrains would do them no harm, and less and less convinced Rustbane's intentions were equally benign.

"Oh, we are close," said Jasper, "so very, *very* close I can almost taste the Zindar chest."

For the first time in some hours, the gray fox looked as if he didn't want to kill someone.

"Where, me hearty, where?"

Jasper took four paces forward, followed by another. He paused as if scenting for prey, then took two exaggerated paces sideways.

"Here," he said, mainly to himself. Raising his head, he turned to look at Pimplebrains and spoke more loudly, "Here's where you should start digging."

He pointed to the ground directly beneath his feet.

Rustbane shouldered Jasper aside in his eagerness to get to the spot. The lemming picked himself up from the undergrowth with a rueful smile and walked over to join Sylvester and Doctor Nettletree. The three Foxglovians watched as Pimplebrains dug and Rustbane issued unnecessary and usually contradictory commands. Rasco darted around dangerously beneath the two big animals, yipping excitedly.

It took no more than a couple of minutes before Pimplebrains paused in his digging and threw the spade to one side.

"What've you found?" panted Rustbane.

"Don't know yet, Skip, but there's something tough here, something that made the spade blade spit off it."

Rustbane turned away with a show of disappointment. "Just a rock, I'll have no doubt."

"Didn't feel like no rock to me, Skip." Pimplebrains was on his belly on the ground, attacking the exposed earth with his hooks.

"We've been through this before."

"Not like this we ain't, Skip."

Abruptly, Pimplebrains sat up on his haunches. Both of his hooks were still invisible in the hole he dug. The muscles on his red-furred forelegs bulged as he hauled on whatever it was he'd dug those hooks into.

There was the sound a boot makes when it's being pulled out of sticky mud, only a hundred times louder.

What Pimplebrains pulled up was a fountain of wet black earth and, firmly grasped between his hooks, a brass-strapped wooden box that seemed almost laughably small. It couldn't have been much bigger than Sylvester's head.

"Is that all?" said Rustbane with an expression of unspeakable contempt.

"What're you complaining about?" said Jasper with unexpected aggressiveness. "Back on Vendros Island you were heartbroken the Zindar ship was too big for you to drag away with you. Now you're already bitching that the real treasure of the Zindars is too small. Are you actually stupid or do you just think it's chic to act that way?"

How big, Sylvester was thinking, *does a wooden chest have to be to hold a wish, even if it's the biggest wish in the world?*

"You're calling me stupid?" said Rustbane icily.

"If the cap fits," replied Jasper.

Rustbane gave him a long, venomous stare, then turned away as if Jasper were something unpleasant he'd discovered on a sidewalk. "Hurry up and open the damnable thing!" he told Pimplebrains.

Pimplebrains was examining the chest, turning it over this way and that between his rusty hooks. "Could be more difficult than you think, boss."

"What do you mean? Just hit it with that blasted shovel of yours, can't you?"

"You're welcome to try."

Rustbane looked startled. He wasn't accustomed to his crew, even close cronies like Cheesefang and Pimplebrains, addressing him with such frank dismissiveness.

"Let me have a look."

"You're welcome." Pimplebrains passed him the chest, which was about the same size as Rustbane's paw. The fox was right. It was ridiculous that something so small and seemingly flimsy could be of any value; the slats of wood from which it was made were softened by the soil in which it had lain for so many decades, if not centuries, the three brass straps wrapped around it corroded by the acid waters of the earth.

"It has a keyhole," observed Rustbane, turning it over and over in his paws much as Pimplebrains had been doing, "but we have no key."

The gray fox looked over sharply at Jasper. "I don't suppose, Mr. Mystic Man, you have the first idea where the key might be?"

Jasper spread his paws. "I think you either have the key within you or you don't."

"Meaning?"

"Meaning what you want it to mean. Meaning what you know in your heart of hearts it means."

Sylvester suddenly heard something Madame Zahnia had told them in her treetop mansion.

What the old myths say is that the boundaries of the mortal world are marked by a wall of . . . a wall of something that's called the Ninth Wave. On this side of the Ninth Wave, there's the world we know, and not just this world, but all the stars of the firmament too. On the far side of the Ninth Wave, though, ah, things are different there. That's the Otherworld, that is, on the far side of the Ninth Wave. It's where magic happens, and it's where the soul journeys in dreams, or after it's left behind this mortal realm.

What was it Cap'n Adamite had written in his journal?

The true location of the treasure?

Let me commit to writing no more than that it can be seen only through the fall of the Ninth Wave.

"Stop!" Sylvester shrilled.

"I do *beg* your pardon?" said Rustbane.

"Don't try to open it!"

"And why in the world would you say such a thing?"

"It'll mean your death."

Rustbane held the chest up in front of his face, scrutinizing it as a judge might scrutinize a prizewinning melon. "Oh, surely you exaggerate."

"Don't be a fool!"

"In the times of his dying, the one thing that kept Josiah Adamite cheerful was the notion that eventually you'd track down the chest of the Zindars and that it'd cause your death. I, ah, found his diary."

There was a calculating light in Rustbane's eyes now as he gazed at Sylvester.

"So, you know about Cap'n Adamite, do you? Old Throatsplitter? And you say he left a journal? You're a much smarter little hamster than I'd ever have credited. Not very difficult, of course but still, well, I've underestimated you."

"There's a key to the chest's lock all right," said Sylvester hotly, "but it's not made of brass or iron or gold. The key the Zindars demand – demanded – of anyone seeking to open their treasure chest is something far more valuable than that."

"It is?" There could have been no one else in the forest now but Rustbane and Sylvester, so intent were the two on each other.

Sylvester dropped his voice to a whisper.

"It's your soul. That's the only key you can offer that'll open it."

"Then I'm in no danger, am I?"

Sylvester's jaw dropped. "Huh?"

"I'm a pirate. I have no soul." Rustbane gave a light laugh. "There's nothing the ghosts of the Zindars can do to harm me. Here" – he tossed the little box to Pimplebrains – "see if you can smash this open with that shovel of yours."

Pimplebrains caught the thrown chest reluctantly, then let it fall to the ground.

"I'd rather not."

"You forget, Pimplebrains, you have no choice in the matter. I'm your skipper and you're my crewman. You do what I say or you—"

"Die?"

"I see you're catching on."

"But if the little guy's right, and he's been right about most things lately, anyone who forces this chest open is doomed anyway."

"You pay attention to such superstitions?"

"Like I said before, you be the one to open it, Skip."

"This is insubordination."

"It's survival."

Rustbane rolled his eyes. "Oh, very well, if I'm surrounded by nothing but turncoats and cowards . . ."

"Have this back." Pimplebrains stooped and picked up the box gingerly, then passed it to his skipper.

Now that he had it in his paws once more, Rustbane seemed much more chary of the Zindar relic.

"Such a little thing," he mused aloud.

"We should put it back in the ground," said Sylvester with certainty. "It's not meant for us."

"Because we're not noble enough or fine enough?" challenged Rustbane.

"That's about it," Sylvester replied. "The person who ventures to turn the lock on that chest, they have to be certain the soul they're using as their key is honorable, that it'll survive the ordeal."

"What if I could force it open without having to use a soul?"

"You'd not be able to, but if you did you'd die."

"You're so sure of that?"

"Yes."

"Then *you* open it."

Rustbane cast the battered, waterlogged little wooden box so that it landed on the grass at Sylvester's feet.

"Me?"

"Yes, you."

"What makes you think my soul is pure enough?"

"Call it instinct. Call it sheer sadism on my part. Call it whatever the hell you like, but if the person who opens that chest is likely to meet a ghastly fate, I'd much rather that person were you than me. I'm sure you understand."

"I won't do it."

"Are you so sure of that?"

In a cascade of silver the two flintlocks were in Rustbane's paws and they were both pointing at Sylvester. The dark tunnels of the twin muzzles looked to Sylvester like the swiftest road to his own personal doomsday.

Sylvester began to laugh.

He could have done nothing more effective to disconcert the gray fox.

"You're staring at your own death, you shrimp of an individual, yet you think you can laugh at me? At me – Cap'n Terrigan Rustbane, Doomslayer, Deathflash, Warhammer? The scourge of every ocean passage across the broad world of Sagaria?"

"You're so . . . so *pathetic*."

Rustbane's claws tightened on the triggers of the pistols.

"I'd shoot you now if that weren't too quick a death for you."

"My dad's not the only one to have learned a thing or two from having lived in the Zindar ship, you know."

Very deliberately, Sylvester put the little chest down on the grass in front of him. When he straightened up again he locked Rustbane's gaze with his own.

The effect was as if he'd stabbed the gray fox's eyes with needles.

Rustbane reeled away, pressing his wrist against his eyes, trying to bat away the pain.

"You can't be doing this!"

"Watch me."

As Rustbane watched, Sylvester advanced on him slowly, deliberately, then leaped up on the fox's arm. He dislodged the flintlock pistol in that paw so it fell to land with a *ploomph* on the soft ground, then jumped across to the other arm and did the same to the other pistol. Finally, Sylvester hopped back down to the ground and returned to stand by the chest.

Rustbane stared at his empty hands, then at the two silver pistols lying at his feet. His mouth opened and closed like a goldfish's but no words came out. Sylvester could understand why not. What Rustbane had just witnessed was an impossibility, an impossibility if you were Rustbane, that is. He had seen everything Sylvester had just done, and yet had been completely powerless to move a muscle to stop him. The same had been true for the others. Even the birds and insects had frozen in the air for those few moments while Sylvester was disarming the fox.

The most confusing thing of all was something Sylvester wasn't going to admit to anyone right now, and only to a select few later. *He* didn't know how he'd done it either. It was as if the Zindar spirit, or whatever it was inside, had suddenly decided to take over.

Now that spirit, while he could sense it was still curled up somewhere inside him, was quiescent once more.

He wondered when it'd next choose to make its presence felt.

Rustbane stooped to pick up his pistols.

As he touched the first he gave a sudden yelp and a loud oath, and leaped backward, clutching his paw as if it had been scalded.

"I think those pistols have just become neutral," said Pimplebrains.

The big old beaver waddled forward and picked up the two guns, putting a hook through each trigger guard. Whatever it was that had stung Rustbane into retreat seemed not to affect Pimplebrains.

"Whose side are you on?" hissed Rustbane at his crewman.

Pimplebrains considered before replying. "I'll give it to you straight, Skip. I'm like the guns. I'm neutral. I'm not on either side any longer. I been loyal to you for many years through thick and thin and I'd like to stay loyal to you, but I got other loyalties as well now. What the little feller – what Sylvester's been saying makes a whole lot o' sense. If we start meddling with Zindar stuff, we ain't got no idea what's likely to happen. Opening up that box could destroy the world with us in it, for all we can tell. So I'm just going to watch what happens. If you and Sylvester fight, which I reckon can't be helped now, the high horses you both gotten up on, then I'll not take sides. At least, I don't think I will but I won't stand by and watch either of you kill the other in cold blood. I owes you each that much."

"Traitor!" thundered Rustbane.

"You could put it like that, yes."

The gray fox's sword was in his hand now and before anyone could move – even Sylvester, with his recently enhanced reflexes – Rustbane had vaulted forward and plunged his blade right up to the hilt in Pimplebrains's chest.

The beaver said nothing and made no move to defend himself. He just stared at his erstwhile skipper and friend through eyes from which the life slowly ebbed, before slumping to the ground.

As Rustbane tugged his blade clear there was a fountain of the beaver's blood.

Sylvester was too shocked to move. Ever since their experiences in the cavern on Vendros, he'd grown fond of the genial beaver.

"Murderer," said someone quite calmly beside him.

Sylvester turned.

The speaker had been Doctor Nettletree.

Rustbane sneered. "The village sawbones has something to contribute to the conversation?"

"I can tell a murder when I see it," said the doctor, raising his poker in defiance. It looked pitifully small by comparison with the cutlass in Rustbane's mitt. "And that *was* a murder. You've killed someone who was a far better person than you, just because you didn't like what he was telling you. So what's next, you scoundrel? Kill us all so there aren't any witnesses to your shame? Well, let's just see you try."

Rustbane laughed sarcastically. "Shame? Me? A pirate? Pirates don't have shame, you backwoods ninny, and, most especially of all the pirates sailing the seas of Sagaria, *Cap'n Terrigan Rustbane* doesn't ever feel shame. If I want to kill you, I'll do exactly that but mostly I don't – you and Jasper and Rasco, anyway. I want you to be alive so you can tell the world about my cruelty and murderousness, because the more people hear about it the more they'll fear me, and the more people fear me, the happier I am. Got that?"

"But me?" said Sylvester.

"What about you?"

"You said you wanted to let the others live, but you didn't say that about me."

"You and me have bad blood between us now, Sylvester, too much bad blood in the past few minutes for there to be any outcome but that one of us die at the hands of the other."

"Excuse me," squeaked Rasco.

"*What?*" snapped Rustbane, looking at the mouse as if at a lump of gristle left on the plate.

"Could you kill me too?"

"Have you lost your senses?"

"See, Rustbane, I'm on Sylvester's side. He's my buddy. So if you gonna kill him I think you gotta kill me too. Savvy?"

"It'll be easier than blowing my nose, I can assure you," snarled the fox, making a lunge at Rasco which the mouse easily evaded.

"How do you blow your nose if you can't catch it?" cried Rasco with a laugh that belied the seriousness of the situation. Before Rustbane could pull back his sword for another slash at him he'd darted between the fox's legs and scampered up the moss-covered bole of an old sagging birch tree.

All this time, Jasper had been standing quietly, simply observing. If the slaying of Pimplebrains had had an effect on him, he'd shown nothing of it. If anything, he seemed slightly bored. There was a wry twist to his mouth as if this sort of barbarism was only to be expected if you were so foolish as to consort with pirates and suchlike lowlifes.

Now he raised his head and fixed Rustbane with a stare so terrible that, even though the fox was many times larger than Jasper, he cowered.

"So you think you're going to kill my son and leave me alive, do you?"

Rustbane tried to rally his bravado. "How do you plan to stop me?"

"There are a hundred dead cannibals on Vendros Island who thought they could mock the humble lemming when they found him, but each of them died in the shadows of the cavern behind the Larder. They got a surprise when the lemming fought back, I can tell you. For some, the end came so quick they still had the expression of surprise on their faces as they died and it's going to be the same for you, you mangy specimen of the vulpine species."

"No, Dad," said Sylvester thickly. "This is my business and I'll finish it."

"Don't be a fool, son."

"It's something I have to do, Dad. You've got to let me. I'm not a child anymore."

"I don't want to lose you a second time, Sylvester, not after we've found each other again."

"Same here, but this is my fight. I was the one who brought the pirate back to Foxglove. I have to deal with the consequences of my decision."

The sword in Sylvester's paw seemed very heavy, then suddenly it seemed as light as a feather. To a Zindar, it would be.

"Stand back, Dad. You too, Doctor Nettletree and you, Rasco." The last was directed somewhere above Rustbane's head, where the mouse had scuttled along to the tip of a birch branch and seemed to be readying himself to jump down on to the fox.

Then, directly to Rustbane, Sylvester said, doing his best to growl, "Cap'n Terrigan Rustbane, I challenge you to combat."

To Sylvester's surprise, Rustbane bowed his head, and not in one of his usual sarcastically mocking bows but as a sign of genuine respect.

"Whatever hex you put on my flintlocks," said the pirate, "can you take it off again?"

"It's off already. The only place it was ever on was in your mind."

"Then let's each take a pistol." The gray fox looked at Doctor Nettletree. "You're a medical fellow. You're accustomed to seeing death close up. Unhook them from that *corpse*" – he jerked his head toward the ungainly sprawled body of Pimplebrains, which Rustbane clearly now regarded as just a heap of dead meat rather than the remains of a friend – "and bring them to us."

Sylvester was horrified at the prospect. The pistols were the right size for a fox, not for a lemming. Even using both paws he'd barely be able to lift one of them.

Then he smiled. His sword had begun feeling airily light in his paw. He knew, although he couldn't have identified the source of this knowledge, that it was going to be the same with the flintlock.

Doctor Nettletree didn't have the advantage of Zindar abilities and made heavy weather of disentangling the weapons from the dead Pimplebrains's hooks and dragging them across to a place roughly midway between Sylvester and Rustbane.

"They're both loaded, I trust?" said Sylvester. The world was, he knew, full of dead people who'd failed to be sufficiently suspicious of the gray fox.

Rustbane nodded. "I keep them that way, but you're welcome to have them checked. Doctor Nettletree, I wonder if you'd oblige us again?"

The doctor bent over and examined the two pistols in turn.

"Both fully charged," he reported.

He backed away from the silvery weapons as if he didn't want to be near them any longer than was strictly necessary. Sylvester could sympathize with the doctor. He'd felt the same way about the pistols ever since the first time he'd seen them, a lifetime ago. For now, however, they'd lost the terror they'd always held for him.

The fox stepped forward and scooped up the guns.

Sylvester tightened his grip on the handle of his sword, expecting trickery.

The fox, reading his mind, merely chuckled and tossed one of the pistols so that it landed at Sylvester's feet.

"There's your weapon, hamst—lemming."

"I thank you."

Rustbane looked his own pistol over, one side and then the other, as if seeing it for the first time. "The traditional thing in these circumstances," he said chattily to Sylvester, "is for each of us to retreat twenty paces, backs to each other, then turn and fire at a signal. But I don't think there's room here for us to go twenty paces without walking face-first into a tree trunk, so let's make it just ten, shall we?"

Sylvester inclined his head. "Ten seems perfectly sufficient to me," he said as if he knew what he was talking about.

He threw aside his sword and then bent down to pick up the pistol Rustbane had given him. As he'd anticipated, it felt perfectly comfortable in his paw. It was something of a stretch for his claw to reach the trigger, but he coped with that by adopting a two-fisted grip, one paw on the gun's butt, the other wrapped around the trigger guard.

"How will I know you'll go the full ten paces?" he said to the pirate. "How can I be sure you won't wait until my back is turned and put a bullet through me?"

"You have my word as Cap'n Terrigan Rustbane."

"Joking aside," said Sylvester shortly.

Rustbane put on an expression of mock outrage, then his eyes lost their humorous glint. "Well, you have your father and your friends to watch over me. I'm sure Doctor Nettletree would biff me with his sturdy poker if I so much as hiccuped when I shouldn't."

Sylvester was dubious. Doctor Nettletree's poker seemed a puny weapon to use against someone the size of the gray fox but there was no sense in arguing. Besides, the one whom Rustbane should be worried about wasn't Doctor Nettletree – it was Jasper, or even Rasco.

"Really, you know," said Rustbane with an affected yawn, "it's me who should be worried about cheating."

"How so?"

"Your father, here. If the ancient Zindar talents you've absorbed make you able to freeze time the way you did, how much can your father do, who was in the Zindar vessel for years, not just a single night?"

"Dad wouldn't cheat."

"Even when he sees his only son about to die? It's hard to believe that someone *wouldn't* do everything they could, fair or foul, to save the life of their child."

"That," said Jasper, "is just something you're going to have to worry about, isn't it, Rustbane?"

"I suppose so. Besides, I don't think even you could move faster than a speeding bullet, and the bullet that'll be traveling toward your son's heart will be speeding as fast as I can speed it."

"Stow the chatter," said Sylvester, wondering momentarily where his courage was coming from. "Ten paces. Doctor Nettletree here will count them out for us. Then we turn and fire. May the best lemming win."

Deliberately, he turned his back on Cap'n Rustbane.

This could be the end of it all, despite Rustbane's assurances, despite the other three being there. He could shoot me now and I'd be dead before there was time for anyone to do anything to stop it.

But the bullet in the spine he expected didn't come.

Instead, he heard a shuffling sound that he interpreted as Rustbane turning around likewise.

"You're okay so far, son," said Jasper. "You still sure you want to go through with this?"

"Oh, what larks," commented Rustbane. "I haven't fought a duel like this for, oh, months at least. It was my two hundred forty-seventh duel, and the two hundred forty-seventh that I won. What's your own record at dueling, Sylvester?"

"Like yours, it's a hundred per cent," Sylvester replied. "Stop babbling, Rustbane. If you're too frightened to face me, say so now."

"Me? Frightened? The possibility of being frightened isn't in the heart of a pirate, and most especially isn't in the heart of Cap'n Terrigan Rustbane. Prepare to die, Lemmington. Such a pity when we might have been friends."

"*One!*" shouted Doctor Nettletree, cutting off Rustbane's flow of words.

Sylvester took a pace.

Behind him he heard Rustbane do the same.

"*Two!*"

Each number felt like a hammer blow to Sylvester's head. If he were wrong about the extra speed and strength the Zindar vessel had given him, each step was a step along a very short path to where the end of his life lay waiting for him.

"*Three!*"

Doctor Nettletree's shout seemed to be coming from a different world, a world infinitely far away. Sylvester felt as if his soul were floating through the mists that lie in the space between worlds.

"*Four!*"

It would be so easy, wouldn't it, for him just to let go of his existence here on Sagaria and wander in those mists forever? Oh, to be sure, Viola would weep for him a little, but she'd find someone else, someone more reliable, someone who wouldn't go traipsing off for escapades on the distant oceans.

"*Five!*"

Maybe Jasper and Hortensia would shed a tear for him as well, but of course they had each other, and that would dilute their grief until it was just a tiny sting.

"*Six!*"

He could almost welcome death. He just hoped that the physical pain of the bullet's impact wouldn't be too great.

"*Seven!*"

Better to die than to go back to living the way he had been, spending each and every day translating lies that smelled of ancient dust.

"*Eight!*"

Except there was no reason he had to do that, if he were living with Viola. There'd be nothing to stop him going back to sea, with her by his side, so they could find new adventures on islands and continents where no lemming had ever trod before.

"*Nine!*"

There was quite a lot to live for perhaps. What had made him so foolhardy as to challenge a wily old campaigner like the gray fox to a duel? How could he, Sylvester Lemmington, hope to survive against the famous Cap'n Terrigan

Rustbane, renowned in every corner of the world for his skill in fighting and his cruelty? This was truly the—

"*Ten!*"

He heard the click as Rustbane cocked his flintlock.

Sylvester spun around, raising his own pistol, tugging back the hammer as he did so.

In some ways it's been a good life. In some ways, not so much. This is a rotten time to be leaving it, though, just when everything seems to be opening up in front of me. But when is there ever a good time for one's life to finish?

Suddenly everything seemed to slow down, as if he'd entered a dream.

Rustbane, twenty paces away, looked enormous, bigger than the sky.

The gray fox was slowly, slowly raising his pistol.

Sylvester had never fired a gun in his life, he suddenly realized. He didn't know how to aim this thing.

He aimed it anyway, closing his eyes so he wouldn't be able to see all the things he was doing wrong.

BANG!

That was Rustbane firing. Already the pirate's bullet was dashing relentlessly through the air. Rustbane had virtually been born with a gun in his paw. There was no way his aim could miss. The best Sylvester could hope for was to get off a shot of his own before death took him.

Eyes still tightly shut, he squeezed the trigger.

And that was what saved him.

No one had ever told Sylvester that pistols pack a recoil when you fire them.

The recoil threw him backward more than a yard to land in a tangle of limbs on the mossy forest floor. Something that buzzed like a wasp flew angrily past him to bury itself noisily in the undergrowth. The gun jolted itself free of his grip and rocketed somewhere further behind him. He was defenseless for when Rustbane came to finish him off, as surely the gray fox would now do.

But why was Rustbane taking so long about it?

Certain that he was about to stare directly at his own doom, Sylvester raised his head.

No one was looking at him. Instead, Jasper, Doctor Nettletree and Rasco were all gazing at an untidy pile of gray fur on the far side of the glade.

"What's happening?" Sylvester croaked.

"You've shot him," Jasper said without turning his head.

As if reminded by Jasper's words that he was a physician, Doctor Nettletree strode to where Rustbane lay.

"He's still alive!"

"Too foul for even Hell to take him, I expect," said Jasper.

"No," said Doctor Nettletree in a cold fashion. "Wherever he's going to go, he's going there soon. It's a miracle he's clinging on to life at all and he won't be able to keep it up for long."

Sylvester felt every muscle in his back protesting as he groped his way to his feet.

"Let me speak to him. I need to speak to him before he goes. I owe him that much. He was right when he said that, if only things had turned out a little bit differently, we could have remained friends for the rest of our lives."

"Yes," said the voice of the gray fox, sounding like a breeze turning over autumn leaves. "Yes, let Sylvester come to me. I never thought he'd be the one to usher me into the darkness, but I'm glad it's him."

Sylvester rested on his haunches by Rustbane's side.

"You sure this isn't a trick?" he said.

"No tricks this time," whispered the fox. "I've run out of all my tricks."

"You didn't give me much choice but to kill you, you know."

"I know, and you're a grand marksman, young Sylvester. For a hamster, anyhow."

"A lemming. Not a hamster. A lemming."

"Have it your own way."

For a few moments, Rustbane said nothing and Sylvester thought life had departed him, but then, "Jeopord nearly did for me, back on Vendros, you know."

"What're you talking about."

"I hid it well but he managed to wound me. No one's been able to do that to Cap'n Terrigan Rustbane for many a long year. The wound wasn't serious, just a tickling of the ribs, but it told me the time had come that I should start thinking of letting my life run down. For a while, I thought that maybe the prospect of the treasure would get my old juices flowing again, but even that wasn't enough. The show I put on about forcing you to open the casket? It was just a show. All of my life has been, in a way, just a show. I've been very skilled at making sure no one but me can see behind the scenery I've erected on my life's stage. That no one discovered that the props are made of paper and string. But *I've* known."

"Stop talking so much. You don't need to." Sylvester tried to take Rustbane's paw. Even using both his own, the paw was too large for him to hold comfortably, but he held it as best as he could.

"Oh, but I do," said Rustbane, rallying yet again. "I've let my greed, my avarice, rule me all my life. Each new day I've let the tides of avarice pull my ship away from shore and out into the seas of adventure but the tides aren't flowing anymore, at least, not for me. The tides are tired, like I am. I'm an old pirate who's lived years longer than any pirate could expect to. I should've had my gizzard slit a thousand times or more, yet each time I've been able to sidestep the blade. Not now, though. It's fitting it should have been one of my own bullets that killed me. Fitting that the bullet should have been fired by someone I so sorrowfully underestimated. If there's really another life after this one, like some folk say, I'll know not to make that mistake again."

The fox made a curious half-coughing noise that Sylvester realized was laughter.

"You saved my life," Sylvester said. "More than once."

"I didn't have any choice. I thought the only surviving copy of old Throatsplitter's map was the one inside your head. I *had* to keep you alive. It was pure selfishness, I assure you."

"I think it was more than that."

"Then you think wrong."

Neither of them said anything for a few heavy seconds. Sylvester could almost feel the gray fox's life tugging at the cords Rustbane desperately held on to.

But the cords were already stretched to the limits of their endurance. They couldn't last much longer.

"I didn't do all of the things you think I did," said the fox at last. His voice was now so hoarse Sylvester could barely make out the words. "Some of them, yes, but not all."

"I think it'd have been impossible for a single person to commit all the crimes you're supposed to have done," said Sylvester, trying to soothe him.

Again that horrible half-coughing noise. "I tried, though, believe me, I surely did try. There wasn't an evil I didn't think about doing. It was just that there were some I didn't have the time or ability to put into practice. Even so, I took my pleasure more times than could be counted in making pipsqueaks squeak.

"I wish it hadn't been like that, now I look back on it, but it was too late. Word of mouth had made me into a legendary, almost mythical pirate captain who was unkillable. Who would've thought it could happen to an abandoned fox cub, found on the doorstep of an orphanage a long, long time ago. Violence and abuses were common practice back then for someone weak and left alone in this vast world. A slap instead of a pat. A kick instead of a hug. Abuse instead of a kind word. I remember once, that in a silly, naive way to gain affection, I plucked some flowers and gave it to the matron of the orphanage. She trampled them underfoot, slapped me in the face and told me that bribery didn't work with her. I should've known better. That day I made a promise to take revenge on the world that had put me there. The *world* was the enemy. I trained my mind and my sword arm and designed the most fearsome weapons ever made. It paid off, didn't it? I've left a mark, haven't I? Even though it's a mark of death and fright." The fox coughed slightly. Sylvester could feel grip of his paw grow weaker. "Well, we've all got to play our roles and choose our path in this world, don't we? Now, I wish I'd played the other role. I should've held out and chosen the other path. The one you took, Sylvester. I toyed with the idea of leaving it all behind and starting anew but the legend had grown out of all proportion and my enemies would've sought me out for revenge wherever I went. I would've never been safe. I decided to ride it out until the end. But at night, it was in my dreams. Dreams of another life. That's why I set out for the treasure, I wanted a new life. That would've been my wish. But I understand now. The wounds I had caused this world would never heal just because I became someone else. As I said before, the monster inside of me would never have been truly expelled. It would always remind me of the bricks upon which I had built my new life. A perhaps likeable exterior but a rotten foundation, which was bound to collapse. I would never have gotten that beautiful and simple life I longed for. Not until I had paid for my deeds. What was that name I told you when we first met?"

"Robin Fourfeathers. You said you were called Robin Fourfeathers."

The gray fox settled himself more comfortably for death. "That's it. Robin Fourfeathers. I think I'd have liked to have been Robin Fourfeathers in real life, not Cap'n Terrigan Rustbane. I wish I'd been liked by many, loved by some, always sought out in the tavern by people who wanted an evening of good company, jokes and song. It would have been a better way to live than being feared by half o' Sagaria, and that half the better half.

"One more thing, Sylvester."

"Yes?"

"That black spot I put on the crew of the *Shadeblaze* when Jeopord was making me walk the plank and everyone else except Three Pins and Rasco was just letting him do it, you remember?"

"I remember only too well," said Sylvester quietly.

"Well, I rescind it. Let it never be said that Cap'n Terrigan Rustbane went to his grave leaving people alive he'd intended to kill. I forgive 'em all, present company included.

"Oh, and I abandon my claim to the Zindar treasure, even though it's mine by rights according to the pirate code. Whatever's in that chest is yours, young Sylvester. Yours and your sweetheart's, to do with as the pair of you see fit. Just, when you're enjoying it as you go down the years, spare a thought from time to time for old Terrigan Rustbane, who wished it to you on his deathbed out of the goodness of his heart."

Sylvester smiled wryly. The gray fox had perhaps seconds to live but he still wanted to believe it was out of his grace and charity that he was allowing others to have his treasure.

"And the *Shadeblaze*," said Rustbane, scrabbling at Sylvester's arm. "See it goes to a good home, will you?"

Suddenly Rustbane stiffened, and his eyes opened wide with amazement. To Sylvester it looked as if the gray fox were staring into another world, somewhere as far from and as near to Sagaria as could possibly be. The fox's grip on Sylvester's arm tightened, painfully so.

"It's *you*, isn't it?" said the pirate in an unearthly hiss. "Come to welcome me, have you, Throatsplitter?"

Cap'n Adamite promised he'd be here at the end to give Rustbane a surprise he wouldn't like receiving, thought Sylvester, feeling ice travel down his spine.

"Two old pals together, are we, Josiah? Aye, the two of us'll make merry wreaking a swathe of destruction across the face of the next world together, won't we?"

This may not prove to be as much fun as you think, Rustbane. But Sylvester said nothing out loud. Why make the gray fox's last moments of life any more miserable than they already were? Time enough for Rustbane to discover the truth. Besides, the old buccaneer might have relented, although Sylvester, remembering the Cap'n Adamite he'd come to know through the journal, somehow doubted it.

"I'll be with you as soon as I can, me ... old ... hearty ..." The last two or three words came out of Rustbane's mouth as a series of spitting noises and were followed by a rush of dark red blood. Those unique yellow-green eyes slowly lost their focus and then closed for the final time. With a sigh that seemed to have been brought up from the deepmost pits of the world, Cap'n Terrigan Rustbane fell back against the forest floor and expired.

"Took his time about doing it, didn't he?" said Jasper heartlessly.

Sylvester looked up at his father's face through a blur of incipient tears. "How can you say that?"

"Easily. He's not worth your pity, son. He caused misery and suffering all his life long, and the world's a better place without him in it. Any good you saw in him, Sylvester, was *your* good being reflected back at you by someone too wicked to absorb any of it himself."

"He meant a lot to me!"

"Then I'll not take that away from you, Sylvester."

And, he was the one who closed the circle, thought Sylvester, wiping his eyes. *The circle Madame Zhania was talking about. Was I really saved by that recoil when I fired that gun or did he miss me on purpose? If the latter is the case, then it would explain another of Zhania's mysterious foretellings. That there would come a time when one of us would have to give the greatest gift of all to close the circle. Did Rustbane give that gift? By sacrificing himself?* He realized that he would never know the answer to these questions for as long as he lived.

Jasper pulled his son to his feet. There were birds singing among the upper parts of the trees as if nothing at all had happened.

"Come on now, lad. You've got a treasure chest to open."

THE TREASURE CHEST OF THE ZINDARS

here's a small clearing in the middle of Mugwort Forest where stands a single gray stone. On it are the crudely chipped words:

HERE LIES CAP'N TERRIGAN RUSTBANE
THE MOST FEARED PIRATE THAT'S EVER BEEN

*

HERE LIES ALSO THE FOX ROBIN FOURFEATHERS
WHOM I WOULD HAVE LIKED TO HAVE KNOWN

No one visits that glade very often, except a librarian and his wife. They place fresh flowers at the foot of the stone and tidy up the leaves and twigs the forest has dropped since last they visited.

Sometimes, when there's no one there to hear it, there's a great moaning sound from underground, as if someone were begging for release from torment.

More often, though, there's just silence.

The birds rarely fly overhead.

❖ ❖ ❖ ❖

The prow of the ship that's been renamed the *Lightblaze* slaps down onto the surface of the water and sends up a great plume of spray. Sylvester, standing on deck and peering ahead, takes the brunt of the soaking, freezing surge.

"Bleurrggh!" he says.

His wife, standing nearby, doubles up with laughter as he shakes himself like a terrier. The baby she clasps in her arms wakes up and begins to wail. Their two older children scamper around on the deck, creating a whirlwind of high-pitched giggles as they imitate their father's contortions.

"Less o' that frivolitizin'!" cries a well-known voice. "Or I'll be takin' me cutlass to yers, d'yer hear, you 'orrible little landlubbers?"

"Eek!" says little Nimbus, stopping in his tracks and pretending to tremble with fear.

"Aargh!" agrees his elder sister, Molly. "It's Grandma."

"And she's armed."

"Armed and dangerous."

Clutching each other to save themselves from falling over, they go off into another peal of giggling.

"Waaaah!" says the baby, who's called Anemone.

Down the deck toward Viola and the dripping Sylvester comes a doughty-looking figure clad in a black leather jerkin, black leather pants, black leather boots with silver buckles, and a black leather hat, bearing a brightly colored parrot feather that's almost as tall as the pirate herself.

"Welcome, Three Pins," says Sylvester, grinning.

"That's *Cap'n* Three Pins ter you, Sylv."

"I was just watching us get closer to home," Sylvester says, gesturing to where, in the distance beyond the *Lightblaze*'s voluminous figurehead of a triple-breasted goddess, a familiar landmass is crouching over the sea.

"Foxglove," says Viola. "It'll be good to see it again after all this time."

"It's been only a couple of weeks."

"Long enough when you've got these little horrors to look after." She gestures at her brood.

"True enough, my darling. True enough."

"Be good ter get you lousy lubbers off of my ship," remarks Mrs. Pickleberry, tapping the pommel of one of the cutlasses she bears in her belt. The belt itself is of interest, having been woven of a profusion of different bright colors of vine and with a golden buckle in the form of a skull and crossbones.

"Mo–*om*, you don't mean that."

"An' wot makes yer think I don't, Little Miss Droppydrawers. Amn't I Cap'n Daphne 'Three Pins' Pickleberry, Scourge of the Seven Seas, the vilest, most defiantest pirate there ever was or ever will be?"

Oh, well, thinks Sylvester. Rustbane told me to be sure his ship was in good hands, and what better hands than Daphne's? When we got back from Mugwort Forest on that fateful day, we found there'd been some changes made at the Pickleberry household. Viola's dad had taken himself a room at the Snowbanks Inn, citing "irreconcilable differences" to anyone in the bar who'd listen to him about why he wasn't planning to live at home anymore. He found a real soulmate in Mr. Snowbanks, he did. Mr. Snowbanks who'd discovered only that morning his wife wanted to leave him for one of her long-haired poetastic friends. Back at home, Daphne had told Viola and Bullrich she'd decided she liked the pirate life, and was determined to go back to it as soon as she no longer had kids to look after, so Viola told her she wasn't a kid anymore and . . . well, there wasn't much crockery left to break in the Pickleberry household by that time, but what there was, the pair of them broke anyway, and then Viola came straight round to my place to discover I wasn't there, but Mom told her she could stay, her and Bu—

"Hi, Sylvester," says a voice at Sylvester's elbow. "Did you know you're soaked from head to toe?"

Bullrich.

Well, there are drawbacks to every arrangement, aren't there? Besides, it won't be long now before Bullrich will be of an age when he'll be wanting to leave their home to start a family of his own. Already Viola and Sylvester have been dropping heavy hints about him getting a job of some sort, rather than lying around in bed all day reading unsuitable magazines.

"Can't think why," growls Mrs. Pickleberry, completely ignoring her son, "the pair o' you don't leave the sprogs at 'ome and sign up on the good ship *Lightblaze* as crew. Think of it. You ain't known freedom 'til you been up to yer gunnels in the tang o' the salty brine."

"Brine's always salty," murmurs Sylvester, ever the pedant. "If it's not salty it isn't brine."

Mrs. Pickleberry stares at him as if there ain't no plank that's long enough. "Ree-erly?"

"Yerss."

She takes a swat at him and misses. "Impertinence aboard me very own ship!"

The kids have never properly stopped giggling since their grandmother appeared, but now they reach a crescendo. Sylvester doubted the wisdom of bringing them along for this vacation, but Cap'n Pickleberry was insistent. "A nice sea cruise'll bring some color to their cheeks and some grit in their backbones, yer mark my words," she said, and she's a difficult woman to contradict when she's got a cutlass in one hand and your throat in the other.

Seeing so little of her grandchildren is probably the one thing Daphne regrets about her life on the ocean waves, thinks Sylvester. *She loves them so much and they know it too. Little perishers wrap the old baggage round their little claws, they do.*

Cap'n Pickleberry, as skipper of this sturdy vessel, unlike her predecessors, is not a true pirate – not in the strictest sense of the word. She has an agreement with the Spectram Royal Navy, whereby she undergoes missions that the officers of that corps consider too dangerous, or which the powers-that-be in Spectram regard as politically inadvisable to be seen doing. That way, she finds all the excitement and danger she could wish for without having to burden her conscience by committing crimes against innocents. Although Cap'n Pickleberry would never admit this is a factor, her legal status makes it unlikely she'll end her days like so many pirates do dangling by a rope from a yardarm.

Still, sometimes she lets her thoughts stray to buccaneerly obsessions, not least of those being treasure.

"Is it true you once found treasure, Dad?" asks Nimbus with that uncanny timing children have.

"Yes, you little terror, it's true," replies Sylvester, putting a paw on his son's head. "And one of these days I'll tell you about it, but not now. Now it's time for you and your sister to have supper, and then it's off to bed for the pair of you. Tomorrow, when you wake up, we'll be rocking at anchor off Foxglove and you'll be almost home."

"Aw, Da–*ad*!" protests Nimbus, sounding in this moment quite astonishingly like his mother.

A long while later, there's only Viola and Sylvester and the moonlight left out on deck. The *Lightblaze* reached her mooring just as summer's late twilight finally fell, and she's resting easy there now, moving back and forward on the light swell just enough to make the anchor chains creak.

"Is it true you once found treasure, Dad?" Viola's imitation of her son's voice is unsettlingly accurate.

"Yes, it's true," responds Sylvester as if he were indeed replying to Nimbus. "The greatest treasure in the world, it was. More than that, the greatest treasure there's ever been in the world. It belonged, way back when Sagaria was young, to some people called the Zindars who were visiting here from their home somewhere beyond the stars. When they went away again, they left a chest of treasure for when the time came the world was ready to receive it."

"How did you find it, Dad?" If it weren't for the pressure of Viola's arm on his, Sylvester would swear it was his son doing the asking.

"A combination of luck and guidance," says Sylvester modestly. Grandpa Lemmington was there."

"I love my grandpa."

"I know you do. He was there and so were your uncles, Rasco and Nettletree."

"Was Grandma Lemmington there? Or Grandma Pickleberry?" This is an old and oft-told tale and the questions hold no surprises any longer.

"No, they weren't."

"Uncle Cheesefang?"

"Nope."

"Or Mom?"

"No. I left her at home because she was being a total pain in the—"

"Da–ad!" Her grip on his arm becomes like a vise.

"It was just your two uncles and Grandpa and me," Sylvester hurries on. "And, oh, a couple of other people you don't know. It was up in Mugwort Forest. Your Grandpa Lemmington was really the one who found the spot where the Zindar treasure was buried."

"Then why wasn't it *his* treasure?"

"Because someone else, one of those other two people I mentioned, thought it was theirs, you see. And that person was someone who couldn't be trusted to have the treasure. So I ended up having a fight with them, and by the time I'd won the fight the treasure had become mine."

"Yet you just gave it away, without even looking in the chest?"

"That's right."

"Why'd you do that, Dad?"

"Because it was the right thing to do."

"But the treasure of the Zindars was yours by now, wasn't it, Dad?"

"Yes, it was, but I discovered the thing about having treasure is to make sure you're the one who owns it, that it's not the treasure that owns you. And if it doesn't own you, then it's easy enough for you to decide not to keep it, if you don't want it."

"Why would *anyone* ever not want treasure? Were there lots of gold rings and ruby bracelets, Dad? Were there perfumes fit for a princess and paintings so fine it hurt your eyes to look at them? Were there pieces of eight so many they flowed through your hands like a waterfall? Were there cloths spun from sunlight and butterflies with wings of dreams?"

"None of those, my boy, none of those. What there was inside the treasure chest of the Zindar was a *wish*."

The childish voice is filled with a practiced disappointment. "Only a wish, Dad? Did you open up the chest and take a look at this *wish*?"

"No. I left it where it was."

"Why?"

"Because if I'd have taken that wish into me, I would have been the most powerful person in the world, and it isn't right for any one person to have so much power. So, I didn't unlock the treasure chest, even though I knew how to. I just left that wish where it was."

"Is that all you did with it, Dad?"

"No. I put a wish of my own inside the casket alongside the Zindar one. My own wish was very little, you see, so I was able to slip it in through the keyhole without any difficulties. And my wish is still there so that, someday when the time's right for the Zindar chest to be opened, they'll find my wish too.

"When I'd done that, me and your Grandpa Lemmington left your uncles Rasco and Nettletree to ... to clear up things where we'd been digging up the treasure, and we took the Zindar chest back out of Mugwort Forest and all the way to the edge of the Mighty Enormous Cliff."

"Why?"

"Because it was the right thing to do."

"Why?"

"Because it *was*, that's all. With your Grandpa Lemmington beside me, I threw the casket as far as I could away from me toward the ocean, and we both watched it twisting and turning as it flew through the air, down, down and ever down, past the sharp and murderous rocks at the foot of the Mighty Enormous Cliff to land in the place beyond them where the waves muster themselves for their final attack on the shore.

"We thought the chest would float, but it didn't. When it landed in the water it made not the slightest splash, just went from air into water as if the two were really just the same. For a moment the seething waters stilled, so we could see as the chest sank straight to the bed of the sea, where it lay on the sand as if it had been there always."

"Is it still there, Dad?"

"Yes. And sometimes – hardly ever, but sometimes – you can catch a glimpse of it if you're good enough and wise enough and clever enough. Maybe when you're older, Nimbus, you'll be one of those people who can see it. It depends, I'd say, on whether or not you eat up all your oatmeal for breakfast, and whether you're nice to your little sister."

"But Da–*ad*, sometimes she's a pain in the—"

"It's only because she takes after your moth—*ouch!*"

The full moon looks down on them benignly. It's the only one, aside from Viola, who can hear Sylvester's tale.

"But if you do see it," Sylvester continues, rubbing his shin, "no matter how good and clever and wise you are, you'll also have to be very, very lucky. You see, the treasure chest of the Zindars is hiding behind what some people call the Ninth Wave."

"Surely the ocean's just *full* of waves, Dad? Isn't nine kind of a small number for a wave to have?"

"What's meant is *every* ninth wave, son. Sailors say that every ninth wave that comes to shore is a bit bigger than the rest. Then there are other people who say this mortal world of ours is surrounded by the Ninth Wave, and that only by going *through* the Ninth Wave (which is to say, unless you're very special, by dying) can you see into the world beyond."

"Is it that kind of Ninth Wave the treasure chest's hiding behind, Dad?"

"No, son." Sylvester looks over and sees, limned in silver by the light of the moon, the face of his beloved wife.

"No, Viola," he adds in a voice so quiet it isn't even a whisper. "The Ninth Wave is the wish I gave to the treasure chest of the Zindars. Ever since I slipped it through the lock, my wish has been in the process of coming true. My wish that we lemmings assume our rightful place in Sagaria, so that we can walk proudly beside the other peaceable creatures of the world and call them our friends, just as they call us their friends. That's enough of a wish for me. Even though my wish is so very small by comparison with the Zindar one, it's helping the Zindar wish come true too.

"By the time, long in the future, when someone knows it's right to unlock the chest, it'll be because their wish is the same as the one the Zindars gave to Sagaria.

"The power to wish the same wishes they can."

EPILOGUE

I n his later years, Sylvester retired from being chief librarian and, together with Viola, started one of the most renowned orphanages in Sagaria. Although they were grandparents by that stage and most of the education and practical issues were managed by their daughter, Anemone, and her brother and sister, Viola and Sylvester still took part as often as they could.

One summer evening, when the sun had begun to set, Viola was reading aloud to a group of children. It was a fantasy story about pirates, treasures and adventure on the high seas. She could see her students' eyes wide with excitement. Sylvester sat in a corner, also eagerly listening. Viola was looking for a place in the tale that'd make a natural stop and also would serve as a cliffhanger for tomorrow's reading session. She found one a few paragraphs down the page, and was dropping her voice a notch or two to increase the atmosphere when a weak knock was heard coming from the open door of the orphanage.

She glanced up from the book and all the children turned as one to look at the door. A little fox cub stood on the doorstep, looking shy. He had holes in his pants and his vest was in tatters. He was holding a small bouquet of wildflowers in his grimy paws. The cub shifted his feet nervously as if wanting to hide his mucky shoes and kept staring down at the floor.

"I–I wonder if you'll accept someone l–like me," he stammered, still not looking up. "If you don't, I–I fully understand, madam, and . . ."

A hug silenced the flow of words. He was unable to speak anymore as he was being embraced with the greatest affection he had ever felt. For a moment, he froze at the enormity of it all, but then a warm feeling spread through his thin and undernourished *body. His whole being relaxed in that embrace and all his fears and worries were immediately cleansed from his mind. A hesitant smile crept across his face, which soon turned into an affectionate grin. He closed his eyes and tenderly put his short arms around Viola and deeply inhaled the scent of his new life.*

At that precise moment, the lid of a small chest resting on the ocean floor opened. A pillar of light brighter than a thousand suns rose from the ocean. It was later said that its blinding illumination reached the farthest fringes of Sagaria. It lasted for only a second or two, but it was enough to bathe the world in a golden radiance. People who saw it thought that all the stars in the universe had fallen. The children and Viola ran to the window to watch. Sylvester grabbed his walking stick and stumbled after them as fast as he could.

The little chest started to ascend and shot right through the sap-green waves and up toward the evening sky. Higher and higher it went, leaving a sparkling tail of multi-colored light after it as it left the world. It headed into the velveteen, infinite space and soon vanished among the bright and twinkling stars.

THE END

ABOUT THE AUTHOR ·

ohn Dahlgren, a psychologist and a member of the Swiss Psychologist Federation, has been working as a marketing director for a pharmaceutical company in Switzerland since 1998. Born in Stockholm, Sweden, he grew up close to the vast and untamed landscapes of Scandinavia, and was influenced from an early age by Nordic sagas, fairy tales and mythologies. This environment fired his imagination and later inspired him to become a fiction writer. He has studied creative and fiction writing at Oxford University, where he earned high praise for his work. Currently engaged in several book projects for both younger readers and adults, he lives in Neuchâtel, Switzerland, with his wife and two children.